THREE CITIES

THREE CITIES

A NOVEL BY

Sholem Asch

CARROLL & GRAF PUBLISHERS, INC.
New York

First Carroll & Graf edition 1983

Published by arrangement with the estate of the author.

ISBN: 0-88184-009-2
Cover art by Harold Seroy

Carroll & Graf Publishers, Inc.
260 Fifth Avenue
New York, N.Y. 10001

Manufactured in the United States of America

CONTENTS

VOLUME I: PETERSBURG

Book One

CHAPTER PAGE

I. THE CAPITAL 3
II. MADAME'S BOUDOIR 17
III. THE DINNER 27
IV. NINA'S EVENING TOILET 38
V. THE MIRKIN FAMILY 45
VI. GABRIEL HAIMOVITCH MIRKIN 50
VII. ZACHARY'S BOYHOOD 56
VIII. HOW ZACHARY LEARNED THAT HE WAS A JEW 62
IX. THE MOTHER'S DEATH 68
X. THE FATHER'S MISTRESS 73
XI. THE MOTHER'S SHADOW VANISHES 80
XII. A STRANGE WOOING 86
XIII. ZACHARY'S BETROTHAL 92
XIV. A DROP IN THE OCEAN 97
XV. MADAME KVASNIECOVA 105
XVI. FLOODS OF TEARS 112
XVII. A MIDNIGHT PRAYER 118
XVIII. THE RESTAURANT DANAN 122
XIX. CHERRIES IN SNOW 127
XX. A PETERSBURG NIGHT 133
XXI. AN ENCOUNTER 147
XXII. FATHER AND SON 153

Book Two

XXIII. MISHA 159
XXIV. OSSIP MARKOVITCH 165
XXV. NAUM GRIGOROVITCH ROSAMIN 171
XXVI. HELENA STEPANOVNA 178
XXVII. A VOICE FROM THE GRAVE 184

CHAPTER PAGE
XXVIII. WRESTLING WITH FATE.......... 190
XXIX. THE AWAKENING OF THE BLOOD.......... 196
XXX. CAUGHT IN HIS OWN SNARE.......... 202
XXXI. WHITE ROSES.......... 211
XXXII. AN EXCHANGE OF ROLES.......... 216
XXXIII. AT MADAME KVASNIECOVA'S AGAIN.......... 222
XXXIV. POLISH SOUP.......... 226
XXXV. PATERNAL WORDS.......... 230
XXXVI. A MOTHER'S HAND.......... 235
XXXVII. BE COMFORTED.......... 242
XXXVIII. A BOX AT THE THEATER.......... 246
XXXIX. MOTHER AND DAUGHTER.......... 251
XL. THE ORDEAL.......... 255
XLI. THE OLD LION.......... 261
XLII. WORDS 268

VOLUME II: WARSAW

Book One

I. DAWN 277
II. RACHEL-LEAH'S DAY BEGINS.......... 286
III. NEIGHBORS 293
IV. PAN KVIATKOVSKI.......... 301
V. FRAU HURVITZ COOKS PAMPHLETS.......... 309
VI. A SABBATH HOUR ON A WEEK-DAY.......... 318
VII. MIRKIN RECEIVES INSTRUCTION.......... 325
VIII. FEAR OF ONESELF.......... 336
IX. MATERNAL COMPASSION.......... 342
X. SABBATH MUSIC.......... 347
XI. KITCHEN SONGS.......... 360
XII. A THIRSTY SOUL AT THE SPRING.......... 366
XIII. THE FIRST DOUCHE OF COLD WATER.......... 372
XIV. THE LAST BRANCH IS SAWED OFF.......... 377
XV. A HUNGRY GUEST.......... 384
XVI. CONQUERED PRIDE.......... 389
XVII. THE CLUB AT THE DAIRY.......... 393
XVIII. IN THE SCHOOL.......... 398
XIX. BOY AND GIRL LOVE.......... 407
XX. HOURS OF TORMENT.......... 414
XXI. A WARSAW MANUFACTURER.......... 418

CHAPTER PAGE

XXII. IN THE ARMS OF HUNGER AND COLD............ 426
XXIII. THE ATTACK ON THE COMMUNITY HOUSE..... 435
XXIV. FRAU HURVITZ "PUTS SOMETHING IN THE SOUP" 443

Book Two

XXV. EARLY SPRING.............................. 452
XXVI. THE CAFE IN DZIKA STREET..................... 458
XXVII. COMRADE ANATOL.............................. 466
XXVIII. LODZ 473
XXIX. BACK COURTS................................ 480
XXX. "THE POOR MAN'S GOD"......................... 486
XXXI. A JEWISH MAGNATE............................ 492
XXXII. THE CITY OF STEEL........................... 499
XXXIII. SON TO FATHER.............................. 504
XXXIV. A MEETING.................................. 509
XXXV. FATHER TO SON............................... 516
XXXVI. UNDER THE TREE.............................. 523
XXXVII. THE FATHERLAND............................ 528
XXXVIII. THE FIRST OF MAY......................... 534
XXXIX. IN THE RAT TRAP............................ 541
XL. A MOTHER'S CRY................................ 546
XLI. IN THE CAGE.................................. 551
XLII. AT DAWN...................................... 557
XLIII. NEW PATHS.................................. 561
XLIV. A RAY OF LIGHT IN THE DARK WOOD......... 567

VOLUME III: MOSCOW

Book One

I. WHO ARE THESE BOLSHEVIKS?................... 575
II. THE HÔTEL MÉTROPOLE......................... 584
III. NOAH'S ARK.................................... 593
IV. THE BOLSHEVIKS ARE SUMMONED FOR TRIAL 601
V. IN THE GOVERNOR'S PALACE..................... 610
VI. NIGHT SHADOWS................................ 625
VII. ON THE ROOF OF THE THEATER................. 639
VIII. APOCALYPTIC DAYS........................... 649

CHAPTER PAGE
IX. BEFORE THE FINAL VICTORY.................. 657
X. THE NEW DISCIPLINE.................. 668
XI. COMRADE RYSHKOV AND COMRADE ISMAILOVA 676
XII. CAVIAR AND CHAMPAGNE.................. 687
XIII. THE SERVANTS.................. 695
XIV. THE KREMLIN CALLING.................. 707

Book Two

XV. THE COMMISSAR IS HERE!.................. 718
XVI. PORCELAIN.................. 727
XVII. MISHA "MOLODYETZ" ON TOP AGAIN.................. 737
XVIII. THE CONSTITUENT ASSEMBLY.................. 745
XIX. ZACHARY'S MEETING WITH HIS FATHER....... 758
XX. THE GREAT ILLUSION.................. 770
XXI. FLIGHT.................. 778
XXII. THE HUNTED QUARRY.................. 787
XXIII. DIALOGUES IN THE NIGHT.................. 798
XXIV. REVENGE FOR PAST GENERATIONS.................. 808
XXV. GNAWING DOUBT.................. 819
XXVI. FALLEN BY THE WAYSIDE.................. 830
XXVII. MOSCOW.................. 835
XXVIII. LINEN-HUNGER.................. 842
XXIX. THE GRACE OF PATERNAL LOVE.................. 851
XXX. ON THE STEPPE.................. 857
XXXI. TWO SWALLOWS.................. 865
XXXII. COMRADE MAREK'S KINGDOM.................. 873
XXXIII. PETERSBURG LADIES.................. 886
XXXIV. ACROSS THE BORDER.................. 892

VOLUME I

PETERSBURG

BOOK ONE

CHAPTER I

THE CAPITAL

From the Warsaw Station a long trail of little one-horse sledges lined with straw was slowly making its way through the soft, watery slush of the Vosnessensky Prospect towards Issakievsky Square. The sledges straggled in several long, apparently endless processions. The sheepskin coats of the drivers, some of whom had clouts tied round their feet with pieces of string, while others wore felt boots, were steaming like the flanks of their spirited black horses. Men and beasts breathed heavily as they struggled through the dirty gray gutters flowing along the ice-covered bridges in the dark thick fog which, rising from the canals, was gradually enveloping the whole of Petersburg.

Now and then a light troika flew through the slow-moving lines of sledges. The swift horses splashed the drivers from head to foot with the mud that flew from their hoofs, and gave them something to swear at. The drivers took liberal advantage of the opportunity; when they were not pelting each other with free samples from their stores of abuse, they addressed their horses, bestowing on them at one moment the tenderest terms of endearment and the next cursing them to the tenth generation with the most fluent oaths.

These little one-horse sledges were conveying the riches of the south into the capital of the Czar. The plains of Champagne sent their choicest vintages, of which Petersburg consumed more than all the rest of the world. Closed wagons bearing roses, carnations and violets were brought from the Riviera to the metropolis of Nicholas the Second; crates of the earliest fruits from the forcing houses; exquisite perfumes, soaps and other cosmetic accessories from France's best factories; rare jewels; cooling mineral waters: in short, the finest and most expensive luxuries that Europe possessed came in prodigious abundance to the Warsaw Station and thence to the capital. From the Warsaw Station the riches of the whole world streamed into Petersburg; the other railway stations of the city received and distributed the wealth of Russia itself.

In a narrow side-street off the Vosnessensky Prospect, through which the one-horse sledges were now lugging their crates and baskets of wine, fruits and flowers, stood an old and spacious building. It dated from the time of Alexander I and was built in the typical Petersburg Empire style. The yellow-washed façade had two entrances which were guarded day and night by liveried doorkeepers. The front of the gigantic building, which was so long as to be almost uncanny, stretched nearly to the end of the street. The side, which faced on another cross-street, was almost as long. Yet there were only three families lodged in this huge structure. The whole of the ground floor was reserved for a general's widow, to whom the house belonged. The first floor was rented by a rich land-proprietor, and the top floor—that was occupied by the advocate, Solomon Ossipovitch Halperin.

The corridor that led to the reception-rooms of the celebrated advocate had been packed with clients ever since three in the afternoon. It was a corridor such as was often to be seen in Petersburg, well lighted and heated, with long rows of sofas covered with red plush, and large Empire mirrors on the walls. It was pleasant to wait in that corridor, and clients who had secured admittance by bribing the attendants waited there until four o'clock, so that, when the advocate's reception-rooms in front were thrown open, they might be among the first to enter.

And when the tall doors opened, the great rooms soon swarmed with human beings—peasants, land-proprietors, Jews. From every province of the Russian Empire came a stream of litigants; people who had been wronged, who were oppressed by the Czar's officials, goaded by the pitiless laws, persecuted by judges and attorneys, tortured by the petty ill-will of local authorities—they all sought refuge in the capital and there appealed for justice to the supreme court or the highest State officials. Petersburg, the seat of the Czars and their officers, mistress of a hundred million human beings inhabiting a sixth of the globe, absorbed daily thousands and tens of thousands of people drawn from the remotest corners in the whole breadth of Russia, pilgrims to this European Mecca in search of justice, safety and protection, concessions and privileges; for all affairs concerning the boundlessly great and rich empire of Russia were decided in Petersburg alone. And quite a respectable proportion of the pilgrims filled the corridors and the official and private reception-rooms of the advocate Halperin. For, though a Jew, Halperin was celebrated far and wide in Russia for his acuteness, his eloquence (he was counted one of Russia's best orators) and his influential connections.

In the suite of spacious and lofty reception-rooms, whose perspective confused the eye, stood huge, solid Empire presses filled with law books, senate decisions, high court verdicts, and other juristic works. Between them, on mahogany benches and chairs, sat the poorer clients, mainly Jews from the provinces. They were first handed over to the advocate's assistants, for they were mostly people who had been officially expelled from their homes. The lawyer's second in command selected the more important and interesting cases, and ushered his chosen clients into a private room. Complicated and sensational cases which might be expected to rouse public attention and get into the papers, such as, for instance, actions brought for revolutionary propaganda, ritual murder and so forth, were reserved for the celebrated advocate himself. In the smaller side-rooms waited the rich and esteemed clients, most of them being timber, petroleum or sugar kings, and other commercial magnates of the first rank who had come to consult the advocate about some concession or the taking of their sons into the business so as to secure them a right to reside in Petersburg or Moscow.

In the drawing-room, however—and the window-recesses of the drawing-room, hung with heavy silk curtains, contained massive French armchairs, while on the walls could be seen original paintings by Levitan, Eivasofsky and Rerich, who was just then becoming famous: the tables and corners were decked with massive and costly bronzes and Petersburg vases—in the drawing-room the lady of the house was entertaining an unusual guest who, like all the others, was waiting to be received by the lawyer: it was no less than the Privy-Councillor and Senator Akimov.

All the other clients had simply been informed that the advocate could not see them until later, as a very important case had detained him in the Senate House, but Senator Akimov had received a private message conveying the lawyer's regrets and explaining that he was busy with important documents on which the life of a human being depended; he begged the senator to content himself with the company of his, Halperin's, wife for a quarter of an hour.

The quarter of an hour was long since over. The privy-councillor, a thick-set little gentleman with a short beard and a gleaming high forehead ending in a wide bald skull, kept rubbing his knees nervously with his soft, almost effeminate hands. His light blue eyes strayed restlessly over the room. Akimov's nervousness was due far more to his annoyance that a Jew should dare to keep him waiting, than to the actual reason which had brought him here to consult that Jew. Yet he tried as far as possible to hide his agitation, and carried on with the lady of the house the usual polite conversation on trivial matters, such as the recent *première* at the Opera House, the bad weather and the latest railway catastrophe in the Caucasus. The lady of the house, a voluptuous middle-aged beauty with gleaming black silky hair and bold black eyebrows, a pair of charming dimples and one or two piquant beauty patches on her carefully tended cheeks, revealed two rows of glittering, sharp white teeth, and in her close-fitting black silk dress from one of the best shops in Paris, which was relieved only by one string of pearls, looked extremely elegant and attractive. The somewhat long shape of her eyes made her face look Mongolian rather than Jewish. And if the unusual situation in which the senator found himself had not kept hammering almost painfully at his brain—ever since he had been in the Jewish lawyer's drawing-room he had felt far more strongly than before, without knowing very clearly why, the seriousness of his situation—the society of Madame Halperin might have given him great pleasure. She was quite free and unrestrained and guided the conversation so skilfully and naturally that the senator was at first filled with surprise that a Jewess could be so unembarrassed before him, and at last actually impressed.

Meanwhile the celebrated advocate was sitting at his solid mahogany office desk in a richly carved armchair, a remarkable piece of furniture belonging to the period of the Spanish Renaissance and reminding one of a throne. Along the walls of the big room ran huge carved bookcases. The floor was covered with a thick carpet, on which heavy leather armchairs were disposed. A subdued light was shed from several lamps with green shades. Halperin's long, thick, black hair, which had a few strands of gray, was somewhat disordered; the short graying beard which framed his rather long face emphasized strongly its Jewish character. The lawyer looked more like a young rabbi, and the soft regular line of his upper lip, which was covered by a little mustache, lent his face a certain youthfulness akin to that of a student.

The advocate ran his slender bony fingers through his beard and knitted his lofty brow. But there was no sign of any document on which a human being's life depended, nor was there any sign of a client. The lawyer was alone and his thoughts were occupied with the unexpected visitor who was sitting with his wife in the drawing-room. Halperin was anxiously pondering what attitude he should take up in this Akimov case. He had already learned in what a disagreeable situation the all-powerful senator found himself; a few things had been hinted at in the papers, discreetly and in veiled terms, and others he had himself heard in the corridors of the Senate House. There was a signature which the senator was said to have forged, involving misappropriation of State moneys on a gigantic scale. "And he, the bitterest of Antisemites, the most deadly reactionary, comes to me. He's certainly been elsewhere already. And been turned down, of course," the advocate meditated, "and there must naturally have been good reasons for that. Apparently the mighty Akimov has fallen into disgrace and they want to smash him. Otherwise they would have hushed up the business before it could become public. So the Minister, for some reason or other, wants to get rid of Akimov. But for what reason? Probably the Court has dropped him. But why has he come to a Jew? Of course his friends have advised it, they've sent him here—nobody would suspect a Jew of collusion with Akimov! Oh, I know them! The whole business is hopeless in any case, and they expect to prove that a Jew is prepared to defend anything, even forgery and misappropriation of State money, let the accused be his very worst enemy, so long as he can make money out of it. . . ."

Halperin's brain worked rapidly. And he accompanied his thoughts with words uttered in the sing-song rhythm of the Talmud school from which, all his life, he had been unable to wean himself.

"And yet perhaps for that very reason . . ." he spun out the thread of his thoughts, murmuring to himself, "Akimov is President of the Supreme Court, and just because he is such a bitter Antisemite it might, perhaps, be the best plan to take up his case. The newspapers will star the case, it will grow into a sensation, all Russia will be talking about it . . . and if I defend him it will make a big noise: 'The vocation of an advocate is above all political considerations, above all passion, and here is a shining example of superiority to party.' And I'll decline the fee! 'Yesterday I defended a revolutionist, today I defend a privy-councillor, a reactionary and Antisemite: justice ignores all distinctions of party. . . .'

"Yet the case is unpromising; more—it's disreputable. Forgery—no trace of an ideal motive there! And if the others have refused the case it's certainly because they've been given a hint. Akimov, you're done for. You've come up against the Jewish God in a hopeless cause. . . ."

Halperin's first thoughts had prevailed. Now he felt vexed that his thirst for fame and popularity should have made him waver for an instant and tempt him into "compromises"; he, whose principle it had been never to defend any dishonest case.

"Yet how do I know that his case is dishonest? I should find that out from himself, and then act in accordance with the real state of the matter. Whether it's Akimov or an obscure droshky driver—if he's innocent, then he must be defended against the whole world; if he's guilty, then the case must be declined as I've always done."

The advocate was proud of his decision. Deep in his heart a feeling of petty revenge threatened to flare up: "Great Akimov, now you'll wriggle in my grip just like some little Jew in the net of one of your paid creatures!" But he quickly repressed this emotion of hatred and revenge by means of a far stronger and more intimate one, by his vanity, which now expanded within him: he, Halperin, an unknown Jew from the provinces, had reached a height where senators waited for him in his drawing-room and sued to him for protection! This movement of vanity was the weapon with which he fought his racial emotion of hatred and revenge and kept the scales of justice even, as in his opinion a lawyer must always do in considering every case.

"Any one who comes to me for protection shall receive it, no matter who he may be—but only if he has a right to it!" These words he uttered not merely in his thoughts, but aloud and with emphasis, as if he were addressing a jury. And deliberately to accentuate his Jewish appearance he ran his fingers through his long, unkempt hair and his short beard to give them a still more disheveled look; then with his thin hands behind his back he proceeded to the drawing-room to receive his visitor.

The greeting on both sides was correct, but cool. Neither of the two men could do anything to help that. The advocate knew the senator well by sight, and the sly, light blue little eyes which so often had rested upon him when he was conducting some defense before the Supreme Court were firmly imprinted on his memory. Yet now that the lawyer saw actually before him the familiar face of the president, who had never looked at him but with ironical contempt, he could not control himself; the human passion of revenge flamed up, making him forget the impartiality demanded by justice. His wife, however, an astute reader of men, grasped at once what was happening within him and skilfully helped him over the painful situation.

"It's a good thing you've come at last, Solomon Ossipovitch. I'm afraid the president"—for so Akimov was generally addressed—"is beginning to weary of my society."

"Excuse me, Konstantin Ivanovitch, but I could not come sooner; my professional duties prevented it. I had to look over urgent papers that must be in Court tomorrow early; a human life depends on them!"

"I quite understand; your duties must come first. But I've really passed the time very pleasantly, thanks to the company of . . . Excuse me, I've forgotten your paternal name."

"I haven't mentioned it to you yet," replied the lady of the house with a smile. "Olga Michailovna."

"Yes, of course, Olga Michailovna. The time passed very quickly in the company of Olga Michailovna." The senator repeated the name, as if he wished to learn it by heart.

The conversation came to a stop, for neither of the men knew how to lead up to the theme that concerned them. Once more the lady saved the situation.

"As far as I understand, the president came to see *you,* Solomon Ossipovitch, and it was for your sake that he has been putting up with me all this time."

"Yes, Olga Michailovna is right; I really came to see you, Solomon, Sol . . . excuse me . . ."

"Solomon Ossipovitch." The advocate gave his full name.

"Excuse me, yes, I came to see you, Solomon Ossipovitch."

"Will you be so good as to come to my room? I'm sure you'll excuse us, Olga Michailovna."

"Yes, yes, I hope you'll excuse us, Olga Michailovna." The senator re-echoed the lawyer's words. "You'll understand, a business transaction . . ."

When they were seated in their capacious leather armchairs in the lawyer's private office under the light of the green shaded lamps the two men found it much easier to speak.

"Aren't you surprised to see me here, Solomon Ossipovitch?" began the senator.

"A doctor and a lawyer have no right to be surprised at anything that may happen in the course of their profession. But won't you be so good as to tell me what I have to thank for the honor of this visit? That would appease my curiosity at the same time."

"But haven't you seen anything in the papers?"

"What the papers say does not interest me. We have read nothing here and know nothing."

"Solomon Ossipovitch, it's a very serious business that has brought me to you. You know my views and my position in society. If in spite of that I seek your help, it is because I want to show the world that I have no wish to shelter myself behind the minister of justice, or seek refuge at Court or among my relatives and friends. The fact that I choose you as my advocate, a man who, so to speak—you must excuse the expression—is outside influential circles, who is perhaps indeed in a certain sense—you really must excuse the expression—hostile to them, will show the whole world that I am fighting with the gloves off, as it were. Your words, the words of a man—you must excuse me—

who so to speak belongs to a different sphere, a different class, will be more readily credited; they'll make a far better impression and be more effectual in demonstrating my innocence, my complete innocence, in a matter into which, as I can soon convince you, I was drawn entirely against my will and without my knowledge."

Solomon Ossipovitch deliberately refrained from helping the stammering senator by a single word or gesture. His face remained hard as steel. From the senator's words, particularly from the phrase "a different sphere," he deduced the correctness of his assumption that Akimov had been passed on to him by other advocates who had been unwilling to undertake the case. In the words "a different sphere" he recognized the voice of the celebrated defender of the Black Hundred, the deputy Sologub, whose favorite phrase it was.

"But what do you really want me to do? Perhaps you would be so good, Konstantin Ivanovitch, as to inform me of the full facts?" said the advocate dryly.

"It's a matter involving the signature of the head clerk of my department, the department of forestry, of which I am chief. On the strength of that signature 100,000 roubles were lifted from the State bank. The radical papers and the revolutionaries are now spreading the slander that I forged the signature of my head clerk, Michail Krasnikov. But that's a brazen lie. For as you know I am the head of the department, and without my signature the money could not be paid out."

"Was the money actually lifted?"

"Yes. Of course the money was lifted!"

"Who lifted it?"

"Who? The devil only knows! My secretary, or the head clerk's next in command, or the head clerk himself: who can say?"

"And you, Konstantin Ivanovitch, you appended your signature to the paper?"

"I fancy I must have. I am the departmental head. But how am I to know whether the papers I sign are in order or not? The paper was laid before me along with several others and I signed it."

"Did the paper bear at that time the signature of the head clerk, Michail Krasnikov?"

The senator sat up very straight: "Of course that's the crux of the whole question. As far as I can remember his signature was on the paper. Now he says it wasn't and that his signature is a forgery. Honestly, how can one remember such details after such a long time? And that is why I have come here to ask your advice."

"Konstantin Ivanovitch, before we go further please allow me to make a very important statement. First I must explain to you that everything we say here will never go beyond these walls. Nobody can overhear us. See, I open all the doors to show you that there is not a soul in the ante-chambers and the other rooms. The walls are thick and nobody can hear us. And as an advocate it is my duty to inform you . . . I fancy you know it as well as I do, for if I'm not wrong you are yourself a doctor of law . . ."

"No, I was only two years at the cadet-school."

"I beg your pardon. This is what I want to explain. We advocates are in exactly the same position as doctors. If a doctor is to apply the proper remedy he must know all about the disease; only after knowing that can he make his diagnosis. In such matters we aren't men with human passions, but merely scientists objectively examining a case. This room, these walls, must know the full truth. The law also has so arranged things that no admission which the client may make to his advocate in his advocate's office can be used as evidence in court; nor can it be employed against the accused in any circumstances, either by the public prosecutor or by anybody else. It is also entirely against the ethics of my profession for an advocate to divulge, even to his most intimate friends, what his client has told him in his office. So in that direction you can be completely reassured."

The senator sat down again and raised his head. His blue eyes were glittering now; his nostrils and his upper lip were quivering with rage.

"I would remind you, Solomon Ossipovitch"—he brought out the name sharply between his clenched teeth—"that in spite of whatever may have happened you are addressing a privy-councillor, the head of the department for forestry, Count Konstantin Ivanovitch Akimov."

"And I would remind you," retorted the advocate, blinking his eyes, a faint smile on his pale lips, "that you are addressing the defending counsel of the same Konstantin Ivanovitch Akimov."

With these words the lawyer pushed his silver cigarette-case across to the Count.

"I've quite forgotten to offer you a cigarette. Please excuse me."

For a whole minute there was silence.

"If we go on like this we shan't get very far, we'll only waste our valuable time," the advocate began at last. "I thought when you came here and intrusted me with your confidence, which—you may be assured of that—I know how to prize and honor, that you were prepared to trust me fully. For we must have trust in each other and forget everything that may divide us when we leave this room—the different classes and spheres to which we belong, and the different views that we profess. We must consider only one thing: that we are both interested in the same cause. And just as a sick man trusts his doctor completely and tells him everything, even the most intimate things, so you must trust me. For only in that way will it be possible for me to help you out of a position which, as a man experienced in such matters, I regard as a very grave danger to your honor and freedom."

The senator sat without saying a word. He seemed to have grown smaller, and his feeble back appeared to be bowed under the impact of the words which the lawyer's metallic voice had shot at him. His face grew pale, his eyes took on a glazed and rigid look, and his small teeth glistened between his open lips. He rubbed his frail white hands together: hard as he tried to maintain his composure he could not conceal from the advocate the conflict that was going on within him between his pride and his wish to defend himself.

"What do you want to know?" he asked at last.

"I want to know whether, when the bill for the sum of 100,000 roubles was laid before you, the signature of the head clerk was already upon it or not."

"I can't remember," said the senator, avoiding the lawyer's eyes.

"You can't remember? That is not an answer. I would remind you that if I ask you this question it is only because I wish to spare you the unpleasantness of being asked it by the public prosecutor.

Surely I don't need to tell you that when the public prosecutor asks it your answer will have to be perfectly clear!"

The senator grew still smaller. Under the lawyer's powerful voice and piercing glance he seemed completely to break down.

"I chanced to be in a state at the time that makes it really impossible for me to remember. A lady of my acquaintance was celebrating her birthday and we had been drinking a little; you can surely understand, Solomon Ossipovitch!"

"I understand. Where did you sign the bill? In your house?"

"No, Solomon Ossipovitch"—the senator completely capitulated, "it was neither in my own office, nor in my office in the department. It was in a place that I don't find it easy to mention . . . the house of the Polish opera singer Petrovna, Maria Petrovna. . . ."

"Was the paper brought there for your signature?"

"Yes, yes."

"Who brought it? Your secretary, or a messenger from the department?"

"No, no. The junior clerk Shulgin—he's a good friend of the Polish lady—gave it me."

"And at that time the paper did not yet bear the head clerk's signature?"

"No. But the clerk Shulgin said that he had brought it from the department and that the head clerk would sign it next day. It was then too late to get his signature, for he had left the office rather early. That often happens in our department."

"The head clerk, then, hadn't signed it. Shulgin put the head clerk's signature to it himself, isn't that so? And you knew about it?"

"No, no, I didn't know about it. By the holy name of God, I knew nothing. How could I have known when the thing only happened next day?"

"And who got the money? Shulgin or the Polish lady?"

"Shulgin kept half, the Polish singer the other half."

"And you received none of it at all?"

Once more the senator tried to raise his head and his eyes, but they sank immediately before the steely glance of the lawyer.

"Only 50,000 to pay a debt of honor—but the whole sum can

be replaced. My wife is going to sell her estate at Salomonka along with the timber to three Jews and repay the whole sum. And if things come to the worst I'll go to Court, I'll fall at the Czar's feet and confess everything. I was drunk—that was all. . . . He is kind, our Little Father, he has a kind heart, he will forgive me. . . . And if I can't secure admittance to him I'll send Ekaterina Sacharovna, my dear wife. She'll certainly be able to move the Czarina. The Czarina loves her and will speak for me to the Czar. . . . They can't execute me, at any rate; at the worst they'll transfer me for a time to the provinces, isn't that so, Solomon Ossipovitch? . . . What can they do to me, after all? They can't execute me! . . . Certainly it will damage one's good name a bit. . . . To come such a cropper, and through boozing! . . . We were drinking some kind of spirits that night—gin, they call it; it comes from Holland or England. Oh, these damned English are to blame for everything!"—so the privy-councillor kept muttering to himself without a pause.

Solomon Ossipovitch rose from his high-backed armchair and, without paying any attention to the senator, began to walk up and down the room. In passing he said: "Does the public prosecutor know all this already?"

"He has asked me to call on him tomorrow morning at ten. But you'll help me, of course, won't you, Solomon Ossipovitch? You Jews know how to get yourselves out of all sorts of fixes. You've got the best brains in Russia, after all. Everybody told me to go to you, to you and to nobody else—you're the only one that can help me! If you, Solomon Ossipovitch, take up the case, then it's won, that's what everybody says. You with your good Jewish head will soon find some loophole in the law that will get me off. And we'll have strings pulled in high quarters, too; we'll manage to get an audience of the Czar. Nobody will dare to put up any opposition. It's merely a question of evading the law, that's all. And that will be your business, Solomon Ossipovitch. . . ."

The senator had become sanguine and confident again with extraordinary rapidity; like a child who has done something wrong, he seemed to think that he had absolved all his guilt by his confession.

Solomon Ossipovitch came to a stop, remained standing in the middle of the room, and gazed at the senator in silence. There followed one of those pauses which he loved to introduce into his addresses to the jury before he brought out some melodramatic surprise. He raised his thin white hand, threw back his wild mane of hair over his "lion head" (he liked to hear this phrase applied to it by admirers) and began, using all the compass of his metallic voice:

"Most esteemed Konstantin Ivanovitch Akimov, for twenty-eight years I have remained at my post like a true soldier in order to defend the downcast and the persecuted. I have always had *one* principle: to it I have remained faithful during all my career, and it has won recognition from friend and foe alike. All the courts know of it, all the judges, all the advocates: never have I raised my voice"—the lawyer's voice now swelled to its full resonance—"never have I employed my clever Jewish brain, which you, senator—and I fully appreciate the compliment—have had the kindness to praise, never have I used my Jewish abilities, which you have also praised, except in cases where I have been entirely convinced that my client was innocent and that I was defending a just cause. But I am sorry to confess that I cannot say that in the present case, my dear privy-councillor! So unfortunately I cannot undertake your defense; it would be against my unshakable principles."

"And the things I've told you, all that I've . . ."

"I can reassure you again on that score and give you my word that everything you have said in this room shall remain between its thick walls and never be heard of."

"So you've simply extorted an admission from me? That's it, is it? And for what purpose? Simply out of pleasure in your cunning, your Jewish cunning?"

"No, senator, you may rest assured; I have extorted no admission from you. I simply wished to make certain whether I could undertake your defense or not. That's what I do with all my clients, and that's what I've done in your case."

"I shall go to the Czar and accuse you. He will understand and forgive me, but as for you!" The senator forgot himself so far as to raise his fist.

The advocate replied coolly: "I am sincerely sorry you're so upset about it. Go to the Czar then! The Czar can do everything, I—nothing!"

With these words he opened the door for the senator and shouted to his servant: "Ossip, help His Excellency the Count on with his overcoat."

CHAPTER II

MADAME'S BOUDOIR

When the advocate had somewhat recovered from his agitation he continued his consultations with his other clients.

All Russia passed through the office doors of the famous lawyer. A delegation of peasant dissenters, led by their pastor, presented a petition asking him to bring their case before the department for dealing with nonconformist religions, as they were being hindered by all sorts of persecution from worshiping their God in their own fashion. There arrived also a Jewish delegation from a small town which had suddenly been declared a village; because of this the Jews had lost their right to live in it and must within a few days leave their native place along with their children and their belongings. Then he received a Jewish woman whose only son was charged with having conducted revolutionary propaganda during the notorious revolt of workmen in the silver mines of Transbaikalia. This youth was one among a few dozen others who were charged; the case was a sensational one and Halperin, along with several other well-known advocates, appeared for the defense. There were announced, too, rich Jewish magnates from Moscow who wished to turn their businesses into limited liability companies so as to purchase real estate—a large zone of forest land in Siberia was in question. And so on in an unending stream. Halperin's two assistants flitted in and out perpetually, bringing the chief the documents for each case, on which he noted down the necessary instructions, as well as thick tomes of senate decisions, law books and the like. Halperin handled these juristic problems with the same dexterity as a rabbi dealing with the various codicils of the Talmud.

The younger of his assistants was Zachary Gavrilovitch Mirkin, the son of a rich Jewish timber dealer in Siberia. He had abandoned the mercantile career which was traditional in his family and had studied law. He was still young, having just left the university. Yet it had been quite easy for him to secure a post in the famous Halperin's office, not so much, however, because of his legal abilities as for personal reasons: while he was still a student he had been a frequent visitor at the lawyer's house and was regarded there more or less as one of the family. The great wealth of his father made the only son a welcome suitor for the hand of Halperin's only daughter, who showed that she was not indifferent to the young man. Yet in his conduct in the office he gave no sign that he stood on such a familiar footing with the family. He did his work seriously and humbly. Indeed the clothes he wore were more than humble, they might actually be called shabby, although he was the son of one of the richest men in Russia and had at his disposition large sums of money which always lay ready to be drawn upon in his father's counting-house in Petersburg.

The other and more important assistant of the famous lawyer was Jacob Shmulevitch Weinstein. He came from a Jewish colony in the neighborhood of Minsk, was the child of poor parents, and had worked his way up by his own efforts. Pushing and industrious, he had starved his way through college. He had succeeded in becoming the celebrated advocate's assistant by virtue of his extraordinary, almost phenomenal memory. Weinstein was the type of old-fashioned Jewish scholar with an all-inclusive and never-failing memory. He knew by heart every high court verdict that might be required. In addition he had an indefatigable diligence and sat up night after night studying all the material that might be necessary for any lawsuit; whereupon he surprised every one by his positively incredible grasp of detail. Besides his knowledge he had all the acuteness of a Talmudist. True, his acuteness found less appreciation from his chief than his knowledge; for it was not always applied in a strictly righteous fashion. . . .

Unlike Zachary Gavrilovitch, Jacob Shmulevitch expended a great deal of care on his appearance. He was always faultlessly dressed. He devoted his most particular solicitude to his cuffs; they always descended with a dazzling glossiness to his very knuckles, allowing the gold cuff-links to be seen. He also gave the most scrupulous attention to his somewhat long two-pointed beard, an appendage strongly in favor at the time in certain Jewish circles. He seemed to set great value on his Assyrian appearance, and did everything he could to emphasize it. Evil tongues declared—unjustly, however—that he dyed his mustache and his eyebrows a little so as to look more Assyrian. That was actually unnecessary, for almost all his face was covered with a vigorous growth of black hair. Every morning the young lawyer had to expend much labor on allocating various hairy islands on his face to their proper stations, the hair on his cheeks to his side-whiskers, that on his upper lip to his mustache, where it belonged, and that on his chin to his beard. But his hair refused to obey the strict commands of its master. Hardly did he take his eye off it when it obliterated his neat scheme, running together like water. Then Jacob Shmulevitch had constantly to be severely putting it in its place again. For this punitive purpose he employed a little brush whose bristles were almost as sharp as needles, which he kept in action all day whenever his hands were free for a moment.

Weinstein was ruled by a great sense of his own importance. In his bearing, his words and all his gestures, his self-consciousness was strongly in evidence. He spoke in an almost alarmingly soft and circumspect voice. He employed the utmost caution and solicitude in his pronunciation of Russian, particularly as regarded accent and grammatical construction. This caused him to make wearisome pauses in his conversation. He was very proud of the fact that he lived in Petersburg and possessed the right to live there, and although he usually avoided in his speech all slang expressions, he nevertheless called Petersburg by the local popular term "Peter" and always referred to the islands as "Ostrova." On the other hand he carried an idiosyncrasy of his, that of substituting the Russian H for the consonant G, to arbitrary and almost ridiculous lengths. He employed the H for the G not only in using genuine Russian words, but also for Jewish names; so he invariably pronounced the name "Goldstein" as "Holdstein." By such means he wished to make people believe that his ancestors came from the interior of the Ukraine, a region which he regarded as particularly distinguished. Nevertheless all his pains were of no avail, for every one acquainted with him knew that he came from Minsk, where people were quite able to pronounce a G.

It cannot be asserted that Solomon Ossipovitch, the celebrated advocate, was very fond of his chief assistant. The reason for this was probably that he saw in his lieutenant an image of himself, reminding him of the time when he was climbing the first few rungs of the ladder. The very ambition of his assistant reflected his own traits. Yet he prized Weinstein's ability and knowledge, especially as they were very useful to him. That was sufficient to make the attitude of the two men to each other correct and respectful; yet they were very far from being friendly, and both of them felt this quite clearly.... Naturally the assistant regarded himself as far more talented than his chief and considered that he should be in the celebrated lawyer's position and had far more right to it than its occupant. He regarded as a personal misfortune the fact that he had been born in Russia at an unlucky time when Jews were no longer permitted to become attested advocates, so that he had to be taken on as the mere assistant of an older man, who in a more auspicious age had secured the right to practice his profession.

As usual, the advocate today invited his two assistants to dinner. Jacob Shmulevitch almost always declined this invitation, giving as excuse work urgently waiting to be done. But this time the advocate had prepared a special bait for him:

"Tonight we're having Aaron Jacovlevitch of the big Moscow tea firm dining with us, as well as the rich Goldsteins from Baku, who themselves expressed the hope that my head assistant might be present."

Weinstein had a weakness for rich people. And he made a great point of being in rich people's society. Nor did he ever miss the opportunity.

"But, Solomon Ossipovitch, I'm not dressed for dinner at all!" the head assistant said somewhat mincingly.

"That's all right, I'll take the responsibility for that."

But before leaving his office Halperin first sent for the law student, Asher Silberstein, his son's private tutor, to receive from him his weekly report. As ever the report was most unfavorable when it came to mathematics. The lawyer could not understand why his son showed such little interest in his studies. He himself came of a family which produced good brains. Consequently he blamed his son's backwardness on his wife's family, a frequent custom of his. "Aha, the Grünbergs!"—the thought passed through his mind while he listened to the adverse report on mathematics.

"But on the other hand Misha shows good progress in Russian history, and particularly in Russian composition. His abilities come out distinctly in all subjects where it's a question not so much of acuteness as of feeling," the student went on.

The advocate expressed his surprise.

"It's this rage for sport that's to blame for everything," the student added, "this latest silly craze. The boy's thoughts are always turning on football matches, outside lefts, goals and such like things. He dropped his lessons the day when the Russians played the English team in the Circus. We knew nothing of such things in our time," he concluded virtuously.

The advocate could not help smiling at the "we"; he reassured the tutor: "Sport isn't so bad as all that. But measure must be observed in everything. Too much of it is bad. I shall talk to Misha. But they're keeping dinner waiting for us. Olga Michailovna must be getting impatient." With these words the advocate took the young student's arm and led him through the long corridors into his commodious private dwelling.

The dining-room lay in the opposite wing of the building, where the lawyer's private quarters were. The house had its own stair leading from a separate outside door, and was completely cut off from the offices. Intimate friends of the Halperin's used the private stair. The house consisted of various bedrooms, the boudoirs of the mother and the daughter, a study for the son, the servants' quarters, and the great dining-room, which opened out of the drawing-room already described. It lay at the very end of the second wing and had four windows facing the street.

In his wife's boudoir, a replica in size and shape of his private office, Halperin found the friends of the family already assembled. The dinner had been kept waiting, as usual, for the master of the house. One of the results of his immense practice and his late office hours was that the dinner-hour could never be exactly prophesied. It was always late, and this caused much vexation to the servants and any member of the family who was going to the theater. Yet no alteration in this arrangement was possible, for the advocate insisted even with passion that all the members of his family should assemble at the chief meal of the day, as was "the custom with all respectable people." (Halperin always used this phrase to justify his claim.) He was a foe to solitary meals, and both he and Olga Michailovna liked to have the better-class people of their circle present with them at dinner. Consequently the evening meals in Solomon Ossipovitch's house always resembled small gatherings.

This evening, too, the advocate found a fairly large company in his wife's boudoir, which was furnished in a mixture of the Louis Seize style, with its feminine grace, and the bad Russian Empire style, and displayed all sorts of ingenious lighting effects (which were a great rage in Petersburg drawing-rooms at the time and were directly influenced by Meyerbold's stage effects). In addition to the standing guests of the family certain others had been invited this evening, who, after dinner was over, were to hold a conference with the advocate in one of the other rooms. Among the constant guests must be mentioned first of all Naum Grigorovitch Rosamin, called "The Englishman" by the family for short. Naum Grigorovitch loved to flirt with the English language and everything else that came from England. He was always dressed in the English fashion in wide trousers and smartly cut morning-coats and had a particular partiality for striking and elegant ties. His ties and his fingers were adorned with bizarre jewelry belonging to his grandmother's time. On his fingers glittered curiously worked rings, almost resembling brooches, and round the knot of his tie writhed three serpents with topaz eyes. "The Englishman" had been one of the first men in Petersburg to appear in public clean-shaved. He was no longer young, but his bearing was very youthful. He was a distant relative of Olga Michailovna, but nobody could establish the exact degree of relationship. It was beyond dispute, however, that he nursed the deepest respect for Olga Michailovna. Among his circle of acquaintances he was called "Olga Michailovna's shadow." As he had a great deal of time at his disposal (he was the son of one of the best-known tea magnates in Moscow), while Solomon Ossipovitch was always occupied, "The Englishman" was far oftener in Olga Michailovna's society than her husband was. She went to art exhibitions, races, theaters and night-clubs with him. Generally, however, he escorted her to shops where antiques could be had. Her boudoir and Solomon Ossipovitch's whole house bore signs of his taste and his partiality for antiques. He was a passionate lover of everything old and regarded himself as a great connoisseur in that sphere. Almost every day he discovered another masterpiece in the antique shops of Petersburg. And every time he visited Olga Michailovna—and that happened daily—he brought news of some newly discovered Rembrandt, Van Dyck or Rubens. This time he had rooted out a genuine Boucher and was just in the course of describing volubly how he had run that precious treasure to earth in a little shop in the Vosnessensky Prospect.

In rich Jewish circles it is almost a rule that any social gathering must include one Christian, either masculine or feminine, and generally some one with a good-sounding name but little money. In the present case this species was represented by an impoverished Countess Sapaha, or to give her her full name, Maria Nikolaievna. She was a lady of mixed Polish and Russian ancestry, an old and intimate friend of Olga Michailovna. The beginnings of this friendship were wrapped in obscurity. According to one version Countess Maria Nikolaievna was a school friend of Olga Michailovna, and had attended with her a girls' seminary in Olga Michailovna's native town, Charkov. A few years after her marriage the Countess had gone to live in Petersburg; there the two women had met again and renewed their friendship. About the fate of the Countess's husband there were conflicting reports, from which the inquiries of the celebrated advocate himself had been unable to extract the kernel. Some of the Countess's acquaintances said that the Count had gone to America, or more exactly Alaska, and perished there; others maintained that he had died in lower Russia; the Countess herself declared that he had met his death in an unfortunate accident while hunting. However, the lawyer had far too little leisure to devote any intensive interest to the life-story of his wife's friend. He only knew that the Countess was poor and was being supported by Olga Michailovna. The Countess accepted these contributions as a loan which would be repaid when she had won her action for the restitution of her husband's property, consisting of great estates in Volhynia. Although she was the only non-Jewish member of the party she had far more Jewish feeling than Olga Michailovna and the other ladies of her circle. She was interested in everything Jewish and knew all the phases of the Jewish problem in Russia. About such matters she spoke with as much fire and passion and with as lively an interest as if she herself were of Jewish ancestry. Even certain Jewish customs and usages she made her own, and she also knew a few phrases of Yiddish. When any one expressed surprise at this, Maria Nikolaievna would explain that she had acquired this knowledge during her frequent dealings with Jews on her husband's estates, which were situated in the heart of Volhynia, a province colonized mainly by Jews.

The Countess and "The Englishman" represented the constant guests in Olga Michailovna's boudoir. Among the guests who had been especially invited for that evening were Boris Haimovitch Goldstein, one of the brothers Goldstein who were known all over Russia and who owned the oil wells in Baku, and a cousin of "The Englishman," a member of the rich Moscow tea family of Rosamin. And, as at most evening parties, there was to be found also the always welcome and adored David Moiseievitch Landau.

When the celebrated advocate entered arm in arm with the student and followed by his two assistants the gentlemen rose to their feet. Olga Michailovna greeted her husband with a smile: it was one of those amiable dreamy smiles which affected her eyes rather than her lips.

"Tired, dearest?" she asked.

"No, but we've kept you waiting a long time this evening; you must all be dying of hunger."

"I've explained everything to our guests already. Akimov, Senator Akimov has taken up a great deal of your time today," replied Olga Michailovna.

"You would have been better employed in taking up my case, Solomon Ossipovitch; it would be better for you to advise me in my lifficulties than to help a forger," the Countess threw in. (Everybody vas acquainted with the Akimov affair through the evening papers.)

"I must impress upon you very emphatically that Akimov's visit o me had no relation with his case," said the advocate, putting on a evere expression.

Everybody knew that the opposite was the fact, and everybody vas proud of the advocate because Akimov had sought his help and ecause he categorically denied it.

To give the conversation a different turn the advocate addressed The Englishman."

"Well, what have you discovered today, Naum Grigorovitch? A Rembrandt or a Van Dyck?"

A supercilious smile accompanied this question, and without waiting for a reply the lawyer turned to the "ever-welcome" David Moiseievitch.

"I'm delighted to see you. Whenever you appear there's sure to be news. For without news to tell you would never grant your friends the leasure of your precious company. Have I hit it?"

"It's a mere trifle this time," replied David Moiseievitch, smiling. He was a tireless busybody, and in Jewish circles in Petersburg nothing could be done without his having his fingers in it. "We'll talk of ny trifling business after dinner; we can settle it later along with Boris Haimovitch and our respected friend Aaron Jacovlevitch." With these vords the "ever welcome" David Moiseievitch glanced at the petroleum nd the tea magnates: both nodded their heads in agreement.

At the pained look in their faces the advocate could not repress a mile. He guessed that David Moiseievitch wanted money from them or some of his important projects and had brought them here for that urpose. And both gentlemen looked the part: they had the dejected ir of two hens about to be slaughtered. The tea magnate Aaron acovlevitch looked the more despondent of the two.

Boris Haimovitch, the petroleum king, a hard, bony, tall figure xpressing iron will and firm character, simply smiled. But his smile nnounced that he had withdrawn himself into a steel fortress whose key was safe in his own pocket. "I'll give you something if I choose to, but if I don't choose to nothing will move me," his smile seemed to say. Aaron Jacovlevitch, on the other hand, coughed. This cough, however, was not caused by annoyance, but by self-complacence. It had something caressing, coaxing in it. By this cough the millionaire assured himself of his own excellence. Nor did it seem to come from his throat, but rather from his belly. His mighty belly actually shook while he coughed. And as if he wished to keep it from being disturbed by the cough, he stroked his silk waistcoat down with his soft, white, fleshy hands.

But Halperin's attention was soon diverted from these observations; at the other side of the door the voice of his daughter Nina could be heard: "Are you going to let us literally starve tonight?"

Thereupon appeared a black tangled mop which consisted of innumerable curls. Nina hurriedly entered her mother's boudoir, but stopped at the door when she saw such a large company. Yet the pause lasted only for a moment until she recognized that it was made up of people she knew. Then with both hands she distributed greetings right and left, calling everybody by his or her full name. Suddenly she stopped, ran up to her father and pressed her slim young body against him. Laying her slender young arms, as graceful as the necks of two swans, round his shoulders, she buried her little face, which seemed to consist of nothing but two eyes and a forehead, in his beard and kissed him passionately:

"You're a bad papa. You leave us all to starve. Couldn't you send your Jews and their 'rights' packing before this?"

"I can get on with all the other Antisemites, except this one here!" The advocate stroked his daughter's curly head. "Well, how have things gone with you today, my little Antisemite?"

"I had Sophia Arkadievna with her Count Savarov to tea today," Nina whispered in her father's ear; but then without waiting for an answer she left him and turned to her mother:

"If you think I'm going to wait till your servants make up their minds to serve dinner you're mistaken. I'm going out this evening. I'm going to begin." With these words she ran up, not to Zachary Gavrilovitch, as might have been expected, but to the head assistant

Jacob Shmulevitch, who the whole time had been standing in a corner like a mute, filled through and through with reverence for these great men whose acquaintanceship meant so much to him.

Nina took the assistant's arm. He blushed.

"Mamma, we're going to begin. All those who are hungry follow me!" And she dragged out the embarrassed Jacob Shmulevitch, who strove with all his might to maintain his dignity. But the impetuous girl had demolished the carefully built self-importance of her table partner in a moment.

CHAPTER III

THE DINNER

AT TABLE the advocate met his son Misha, a high-school boy of eighteen. Halperin had just time to throw his son a significant glance. That glance was not noticed by the guests, but the son interpreted it rightly: "So that damned tutor has been to see father and told him about my last report." Yet Halperin was forced to lower his eyes with curious abruptness when they encountered those of his son. The youth's clear blue eyes possessed a peculiar power. Their glance had a brilliance which may have been caused simply by their weakness. There was something magnetic in the gaze of those strange blue eyes, a quality which nobody else in the family possessed. They must have been a legacy from some distant and unknown member of the family who had lived in some other age and some other land, and from whom the youth had inherited his eyes.

The dinner was in the true Petersburg style. The long ample table which occupied almost the whole length of the great room was covered with porcelain and silver. Course succeeded course, supplemented by all sorts of tit-bits, smoked fish, sauces, mayonnaise and vegetables of all kinds. And substantial joints and roasts followed one after the other endlessly. The table talk, as invariably in every class of society in Russia, turned on the Jewish question, Russia and the revolution.

A stranger who knew nothing of the circumstances might have

concluded from hearing the conversation that he was not among persecuted Jews, but in a company of Russian patriots.

Someone spoke of the enmity between Russia and Austria and referred to the aspirations that Austria was always encouraging among the smaller nations, particularly Poland and Ruthenia; these efforts for national independence must of necessity lead to revolts against Russia's power.

"As for the Poles," replied another, "I would be very glad to see the last of them. Russia derives no benefit from the Poles; on the contrary, they cause us nothing but embarrassment. And besides, Poland enriches itself at the expense of the great Russian markets, which it exploits. Without us it couldn't exist for a single day."

"We won't give up a single yard of our territory; we'll shoo our enemies before us with our caps." Aaron Jacovlevitch, the tea magnate, repeated the catchword which had achieved such a melancholy notoriety during the war with Japan. He obviously could not bother to say anything more original, for he was at that moment occupied in devouring a mayonnaise sandwich that tasted excellently.

"Why shouldn't Poland have its freedom? I can't see why a nation shouldn't have the right to free itself from foreign domination if it wishes to; we Jews in particular should sympathize with that." As was customary among the young in Russia at that time the student Asher Jefimovitch Silberstein put in his oar so as to represent his generation.

But the celebrated advocate cut him short in an authoritative voice; it sounded like that of a judge giving sentence:

"From the Carpathians all the way to the Pacific Ocean which separates us from America—that is our goal! The Carpathians and the Pacific are our natural frontiers. God has given us them. All that is the sacred soil of our little mother Russia, and woe to them who dare to touch it."

"Quite right," murmured the tea magnate, pushing another mayonnaise sandwich into his mouth.

"Pardon me, Solomon Ossipovitch, but your views seem to imply that all the nations which belong to the Russian Empire must remain united to it for eternity, simply because this Czar or that has subdued them. The very same thing—don't think I mean any offense, Solomon

Ossipovitch—is said by all our reactionaries and Chauvinists," Jacob Shmulevitch Weinstein interrupted.

"The fact that the Chauvinists and reactionaries say the same thing doesn't affect my position, my dear Jacob Shmulevitch. In the first place even the Chauvinists and reactionaries may say something true for once, and in the second, the important thing is not what they say, but their use of it to justify an imperialistic standpoint and a policy of the mailed fist. But my views express a quite different standpoint. To my way of thinking Russia is not an empire, not a State or a nation; Russia is something more, something greater. Russia is a philosophical conception, a form of life. One can be a Russian even though one does not live in Russia, though one has never seen Russia with one's eyes. But the opposite case may also happen. There are Russians born of Russian parents who have attended Russian schools and served in the Czar's armies, and yet are not Russians. They are Frenchmen, Englishmen, whatever you will, but not Russians. For to be Russian means to have a perpetually vigilant conscience that never ceases demanding from us an account for our actions. No nation in the world but us possesses that wakeful conscience. To be a Russian means to be prepared at any time to sacrifice our personal happiness for the good of our brothers. To be a Russian means to live in a perpetual fever. Originally, of course, we were conquered by actual violence; during the various reigns of the Czars, Turks, Rumanians, Caucasians, Siberians, Poles, White and Little Russians and the various Kirghiz tribes have been incorporated with us. The Czars, if you prefer the expression, have conquered us by force, but since then we have gone through a refining crucible: its name is the Russian soul. We have all grown up in *one* spirit, which works in us omnipotently and has created a common ideal, love of humanity. And the very fact that we have all lived together for such a long time under an unjust, dreadful system of oppression has itself created in us a common ideal of freedom and an intense longing, a thirst for justice, a bond that is stronger than religion. This common bond that unites us gives us also hope for a great future. All these things have matured in us a certain method of life, one might also call it a philosophical conception, to which all of us, all the nations of Russia, have voluntarily agreed, that we might live under one ruling system. And any nation that desires to detach itself and break us into helpless fragments is merely helping to clear the way for military conquests and egoistic aims, and is committing the blackest treachery against the great ideal of a spiritual and high-souled Russia, the Russia of the future."

"Bravo! Bravo!" The tea magnate was so excited that he no longer could hold his nose in check and sneezed violently.

Even the oil king, the dry, reserved and cautious Boris Haimovitch, joined in the universal applause. His eyes were staring with admiration, and with a fixed smile he kept on nodding his head emphatically.

The "ever-welcome" David Moiseievitch wiped his mouth with his napkin, got up, went over to Solomon Ossipovitch, threw his arms around him, and kissed him: "You have expressed my very soul!"

His example proved infectious. The tea magnate, too, even the oil king followed it; only "The Englishman" remained calmly where he was sitting. The ladies blew kisses to the orator.

"So in your opinion, Solomon Ossipovitch, the conquest of such great tracts of land and the subjugation of so many peoples by the Czars was a good thing—please do not be offended with me for drawing the conclusion!" By these words Jacob Shmulevitch sought to restore his prestige, which seemed in a bad way before all these rich people.

"At first it was not a good thing; on the contrary, at first it was probably a wrong. But it led to something great, for out of it came—Russia."

"Many examples of such things can be found in history." The tutor thought it was his duty to come to the lawyer's assistance.

"The best Russians we have are the Jews. That's really the only conclusion, especially after listening to the way you spoke about the idea of Russia. I've never heard such things said about Russia in a company of Russians. These people are always talking against Russia, *n'est ce pas, ma chérie?*" said the Countess, offering her aid to the conversation.

Her tribute heightened still further the general admiration for the speaker; and so it was Jacob Shmulevitch's fate that he, who had actually taken pains to shine in the eyes of the wealthy magnates, should not be able to show a balance in his favor at the end of the evening. The "ever-welcome" David Moiseievitch was once more thrown into a perfect rapture of delight; once more he passed his napkin across his mouth, got up, and went over to Solomon Ossipovitch: "Forgive me, Olga Michailovna, for disturbing the order of your table; but your husband has spoken tonight like a prophet. The real pity is that we are the only ones to hear his divine words. All Russia should hear what Solomon Ossipovitch has said tonight, all Russia, as God is my witness!" Thereupon he went up to Solomon Ossipovitch yet once more and warmly wrung his hand. He controlled himself and refrained from a kiss this time, however, so as not to disturb the table too much. Consequently the effect was not so powerful as he had hoped for; this time the magnates did not follow his example. The tea dealer contented himself with repeating David Moiseievitch's phrases, coughing meanwhile: "Prophetic words! Prophetic words! All Russia should hear them," at the same time devouring rapidly a third mayonnaise sandwich.

"Dearest, you're talking all the time and eating nothing. Everything has grown cold. And you're keeping our guests from eating too. They're too interested in listening to you."

"Oh, how can you say such a thing, my dear Olga Michailovna? I could sit the whole night and listen to Solomon Ossipovitch's conversation. Golden words come from his mouth, far more precious than the most exquisite food!" exclaimed David Moiseievitch.

"The whole night . . ." echoed the tea magnate.

Solomon Ossipovitch did not like to be interrupted even by his own wife. Speaking was for him the stuff of life, its creative form. And when he had guests for dinner he always felt an irresistible compulsion to harangue them, just as his forbears had been wont to elucidate the Torah at table to their Chassidic followers. Consequently his wife's interruption completely put him off. Olga Michailovna quickly perceived this by the offended glance he cast at her and at once set about repairing her mistake by an adroit turn: "He's so tired! He's had to speak from morning to night. First a long session in the supreme court, and after that a very long and exhausting afternoon consulting with his clients. He sleeps badly at night. He needs a little rest and quiet at dinner-time at least!"

"Olga Michailovna is right! Take care of yourself, Solomon Ossipovitch; your health is very precious, very precious," said David Moiseievitch anxiously.

"Take care of yourself, take care of yourself, Solomon Ossipovitch," echoed the tea magnate.

These words were balsam to Solomon Ossipovitch's vanity, and so he quickly regained the excellent spirits out of which his wife's remarks had shaken him: "No cause for worry. We'll rest later in the other room. This isn't the time for that."

The conversation turned to lighter themes, greatly to the relief of the younger members of the party, above all the advocate's two children.

"Papa, Karsavina is dancing tomorrow evening. We're all going to see her. Won't you come too?" his daughter cried across to him.

"That isn't a bad idea," said Olga Michailovna approvingly; "it would be a rest for you."

"I can't afford the time, unfortunately, my child. Get one of your admirers to take you."

Conversation turned to the stage and the ballet. Now "The Englishman," who was thoroughly at home in this sphere, took the uncontested lead.

Nina, who was sitting at the other end of the table, formed the center of the younger generation, just as her mother formed that of the older. She spun around her fine webs of glances and gestures, words and smiles. But she seemed to take particular pleasure in humbling Jacob Shmulevitch's dignified self-importance; she treated his pride with less ceremony than if it had been an old rag.

"Jacob Shmulevitch," she said, turning to the assistant, who was sitting opposite her, "you've never yet invited me to go with you anywhere, either to a theater or a night-club. Oh, yes, one receives invitations from all sorts of possible and impossible people, but never, of course, from those one wants them from. I know that you're always busy, but that itself would make an invitation from you a very special honor."

"You really think so? Really, I have never thought of it before." Jacob Shmulevitch tugged in embarrassment at his white cuffs.

"Why have you never thought of it? Well, it's no wonder that Jewish girls have to fall back on Christians! Our own young gentlemen, of course, are always busy working for the revolution and other lofty objects! And if you find for once someone who isn't concerned with the revolution and has time to devote to a girl he's so proud that you can't get within speaking range of him."

"How do you know that I mayn't be working for something, Nina Solomonovna?"

"What? You're working for the revolution, too? Then you're done for as far as I'm concerned! For in that case you're just as wearisome as all the others. Your whole charm in my eyes is that you represent the ideal type of the man who knows how to employ his time well and lead an individual life."

"Oh, Nina Solomonovna, you're very hard on me!"

"Only because you persist in ignoring me. Why this very day—for two hours I sat quite alone in my boudoir! There were two or three young gentlemen in the house, and none of them even thought of coming to see me for a little while. Don't you think that is a reason for being hard?"

"But surely not for such a young and beautiful lady!" retorted Jacob Shmulevitch with a mincing bow, which, as he hoped, showed his fine figure to advantage.

"You've got your answer now!" Zachary Gavrilovitch shouted mockingly to Nina.

Nina flushed and ceased from her pin-pricks. Jacob Shmulevitch triumphantly stroked his beard and congratulated himself on having so adroitly and gallantly reduced the silly girl to silence.

Shortly after dinner the advocate asked his wife and the other guests to excuse him and withdrew with the tea merchant and the oil magnate to the drawing-room. Several gentlemen were already there in answer to David Moiseievitch's invitation. Among them was a colleague of the famous advocate whose presence he regarded as a great personal triumph, also a young man whom nobody knew or wished to know. He sat quite apart from the other guests. In Russia at that time a revolutionist or two often appeared inconspicuously at such gatherings as these. The young man was not even presented to the company, but every one knew who and what he was . . .

The advocate invited the gentlemen into his private office and carefully shut the door.

David Moiseievitch Landau had all his life occupied himself with public affairs. He was now in a sense the intermediary between the revolutionary elements and the "sympathizing" rich bourgeoisie. In a few brief words he explained the object of the conference. It was a question of important papers that had to be secretly smuggled out of Russia. They contained explicit information concerning the secret Black Hand, who ruled everything at the court of the Czar, also concerning the organization of pogroms, the cruel torture of political prisoners, and the oppression of various peoples. The Czardom would be gravely compromised in the eyes of Europe by those documents. For the cost of their publication in foreign countries, the establishment of a foreign news journal and other necessary work (such as the purloining of important papers from various State departments and their dispatch across the frontier) a large sum of money was required. This gathering of rich Jews in the advocate's house was intended to provide it.

As at every assembly in Russia, whether legal or illegal, whether concerned with revolutionary or business affairs, there was a vast amount of talk. The two advocates talked out of pure pleasure in talking. David Moiseievitch described in detail the perils involved in the purloining of such papers, and thus justified his demand for pecuniary sacrifices from the Jews. The only one who did not speak was the unknown young man with the little black beard and the glasses. He looked like a pupil out of a Talmud school who had just finished his course of study. No word came from his lips, but his sly busy eyes regarded attentively behind their glasses this assembly of capitalists. A contemptuous smile played round his thin lips.

One of the last to claim his right of speech was Boris Haimovitch. Usually he was a silent man, but when money was in question he always became eloquent. With his glance firmly directed at the strange young man he began: "We must be clear and above board about this. We are capitalists. Why do they come to us for money? We are against the revolution."

"It isn't a question of the revolution, but of compromising the present régime who organize the pogroms"—David Moiseievitch tried to avoid the dangerous rock.

The advocate came to his assistance:

"How can you say such things, Boris Haimovitch? We know you, and we know you're no opponent of the revolution. No decent man in Russia is against the revolution, and least of all a Jew."

Here the strange young man, who had remained silent until now, got to his feet: "Would you like to know, gentlemen, why we have come to you? We have done so because the capital of Russia is concentrated in your hands. Russia's oil has just spoken," at these words he glanced at Boris Haimovitch, "and here beside me sits Russia's tea: farther along sits Russia's sugar, and Russia's forests is opposite me." The young man pointed to the various gentlemen with an almost cynical smile on his lips. "It's only the poor Jews in Russia who are deprived of their rights, not Jewish capital. That is why we come to you."

"I see! That's why you come to us!" retorted Boris Haimovitch, smiling dryly. "But if we suffer from no restrictions or persecutions, what interest can we have in supporting a movement against the régime that has put the wealth of the country into our hands? Let us be frank: If you were in a position to do it, say by seizing power (which won't happen very soon, however, let us hope), you certainly wouldn't impose restrictions on the poor Jews, but on the Jewish capitalists. Isn't that so?"

"I trust and hope so," the young man confessed.

"Let me go farther: you would not only restrict the further accumulation of Jewish capital, but you would also see to it, I fancy, that the total capital in our possession would come into the right hands, as you put it, and be shared out to everybody; in other words you would take from us all that belongs to us."

"I hope we should see to it that there was a radical leveling of private capital."

"And yet you turn to us, the representatives of that same Jewish capital which you want to destroy, for support for your movement?"

"We do not turn to you as representatives of Jewish capital. We recognize no distinction between Jewish and non-Jewish capital. Capital has nothing to do with nationality; it is international."

"Yet you don't turn to the other capitalists, but directly to us, the Jewish capitalists."

"We do that because we wish to exploit for our ends the discontent with the present régime among certain sections of the population. We know that you are fettered, too, and that the injustice you have to suffer makes you ripe for us. The indignation against the present order that burns in your hearts is a motive power driving you into our arms as with a whip, whether you will or no. We use your discontent for our own ends. Later, when we have achieved our aims, we shall see what we have to do about you." While the young man was saying this the smile never faded from his lips.

"Thanks very much for your frankness. For my part I won't raise a finger to help you. I refuse to give you money to undermine my own existence."

It is impossible to tell how the discussion would have ended had not Solomon Ossipovitch risen to make a powerful speech.

"If we Jews," he began with an emphatic gesture, "are ever to achieve equal rights in Russia, you may take it that they will not be voluntarily granted; they must be extorted. As a section of the oppressed people of Russia we help the revolution, and we say, just like you, my friend from the opposition: we shall use your revolutionary temperament, your youth, your readiness to sacrifice yourself, in order to reach the goal for which we are all striving. Then we shall see what we have to do about you. But until then our road goes the same way and we are prepared to travel it together; you with your temperament, we others with our money. Am I not right, David Moiseievitch?"

Once more Solomon Ossipovitch was the object of general admiration.

After that the tea magnate Aaron Jacovlevitch was able to have the last word.

"And I tell you, gentlemen, that we, the rich Jews, have to pay dearly for our riches. We must pay the reactionaries and we must also pay *you,*" he pointed to the young man. "We must pay out money for the Church and for *these* objects as well. In that respect we are far worse off than the poor Jews, believe me, gentlemen." Having said this he coughed his gentle solicitous cough, meanwhile caressing his waistcoat comfortingly.

Before the advocate ended his hard day's work and retired to his bedroom, the guests having left, he knocked at his son's door: "Misha!"

Half-undressed, Misha apprehensively opened the door. He seemed very surprised at seeing his father.

"Misha, show me your school report. If I remember rightly the marks were given out today."

The youth of eighteen gazed at his father with his great blue eyes, which shone like two marvelous and rare precious stones between the fingers of their long black lashes.

"Papa, I can't help it. Sarmatyn, the mathematics teacher, is a beast; he's given me bad reports twice already."

"Misha, you know that I, in my position, daren't let down the standards of the circle I move in."

"I know it, father, but what can I do . . . ?" stammered the tall youth. His face grew sad and took on a childishly piteous look that his father was never able to resist; the blue eyes were half-hidden behind their lids. "I can't stand mathematics . . ."

The father glared at him angrily. But his anger quickly melted like ice in the sun before the helpless and yet marvelous and powerful glance of those curious blue eyes. Proudly the son gazed at his father. And the father could not endure that gaze, and instead of uttering the eloquent rebuke that he had intended he stroked the young man's hair and said: "I hope, Misha, you'll try to keep in mind what I've mentioned: remember my position."

CHAPTER IV

NINA'S EVENING TOILET

WHEN DINNER was over Nina took Mirkin's arm and said: "Zachary Gavrilovitch, if you have nothing better to do I would like you to help me to change my dress. The Savarovs were here today and they insisted that I must come to a masque at their place tonight. And my Sophie has gone off with her sergeant. I promised to let her off long ago. Now I've nobody to give me a hand. Mother's busy with her guests—besides I prefer some one without any particular preferences in dress, otherwise you run the danger of having something you don't like pushed on to you, as mother is so fond of doing. I fancy you will do admirably."

The red Bokhara rug on the sofa made a vivid background for the girl in the red light of a lamp standing in the corner. Her black curly hair was pressed against another rug, a richer one with countless pale-yellow checks. It gave her face a hue as of old ivory.

"Zachary Gavrilovitch, you have a strange way of looking at one. Things that nobody else dares to say with their lips you say with your eyes. I want to make you a confession: I'm more afraid of your eyes than of other people's tongues."

Mirkin smiled and stroked his little black beard with his hand.

"So you've discovered a sixth sense in me, Nina Solomonovna? I hadn't any idea that I had a sixth sense."

"I mean it seriously—you really have a sixth sense. It seems to me that you know everything I think and everything I want to do before I know it myself. All this evening I felt that you knew everything about me, sitting there in your corner. You notice everything I do and think, nothing is hidden from you. I must tell you frankly, Zachary Gavrilovitch—I don't like this sixth sense of yours."

Zachary Gavrilovitch smiled again:

"So without my knowledge you're making me your conscience. It isn't very pleasant, this rôle that you've imposed on me."

"If it isn't so why am I afraid of you? Yes, really, I'm afraid of you; and I'm afraid of nobody else, only of you."

"That question isn't very easy to answer, Nina Solomonovna. Perhaps you're afraid of yourself. Everybody is afraid of something, one of God, another of some human being. If there's no god handy, then one gets hold of some human being that one can be afraid of. But to hear such things from you surprises me: I felt quite assured from your own words that you were entirely free from such weaknesses."

"I thought so myself, and I really am too. Yet I'm afraid of you. And I can't say that the feeling is an unpleasant one either—on the contrary, it gives me pleasure and I am resolved to be afraid of you; it's a good thing, it's much the same as knowing one has a father confessor at hand. Yes, Zachary Gavrilovitch, it's really a good thing, for one can do anything one likes if one only has a father confessor at hand."

"I doubt very much whether it's a suitable rôle for me; for I don't like to judge anybody, if only because I don't want to be judged myself. Yes, I hate being judged!"

"Then why are you so 'pure,' yes, so scandalously pure and respectable? I must say I think it's mean to be so honorable, so pure and respectable as you, Zachary Gavrilovitch."

Mirkin was still smiling: "It seems that it's you who have the sixth sense, not me; for you seem to know everything about me."

"You look very pure, at least, or—perhaps it's only a good disguise? Do you know why I asked you to come here? Because I want your help in a vulgar, scandalous business. You know, of course, that I'm going to the Savarov's this evening. They're going to give a private performance. *Leda,* the piece is called, *Leda and the Swan.* Kierenov has written it specially for this performance. You know the subject, of course? I am to take part in the performance, too, it seems, and I want you to help me to dress. Then you must escort me to the place. You must know everything, so that you may bear part of the guilt, too. That's why I asked you to come. I want you to share in a 'sin'; perhaps that will make you a little more human."

"Perhaps your idea is a little different: to get my permission so that it may be easier for you to go. You didn't ask my help so as to shock my respectability, but so as to save your own, so that you might be able to do certain things with an easier conscience," retorted Zachary, still smiling.

"Yes, for that, too . . . If you know about these things I can do them with an easier conscience. It's enough for me that you know about them. Why should that be so, Zachary?"

"It's because, in spite of everything, you're a timid little girl—don't be offended!—Yes, little Nina (don't be offended at my calling you that either!) you want a free pardon for all your peccadilloes; you're afraid of accepting responsibility even for them."

Nina let her great eyes rest reflectively upon him: her eyebrows formed a symmetrical double bow above the straight pure line of her nose. She did not know whether to take his words as an insult or to turn them into a joke.

When Nina broke off the conversation Zachary, too, was thrown into confusion. He became conscious of the unnaturalness of his position.

"What on earth made me preach at her like a moralist?" he wondered for a moment. A faint feeling of annoyance rose up in him, yet beneath that he remained cool and unshaken.

Nina quickly collected herself. She laughed frankly and with that was rid of her embarrassment. Then she began in her accustomed half-girlish, half-womanly vein of coquetry: "You must really forgive me, Zachary Gavrilovitch, for having chosen you for this part without your knowledge or consent: but you know us women; we're all so spoilt that we think the whole world belongs to us and we can take anything in it that we like."

"If I can serve you in anything, please don't stand on ceremony; I'm always at your disposal," replied Zachary, entering into her ironical tone.

"But now, Zachary Gavrilovitch, you must really help me and in quite a different way, not as my 'conscience,' but as the opposite: you must help me to look as sophisticated and corrupt as possible, that is, supposing you give your consent. I'm going to a party crammed with esthetes: Boris Abramovitch Levinstein, the famous critic of dancing, is to be there, as well as several other great connoisseurs. It is a dance for a select company, the kind of company that Sophia Arkadievna receives: for people with the highest social cachet. And as far as I can make out from Sophia Arkadievna's mysterious hints it isn't impossible that her salon will be graced tonight by the presence of one of the Grand Dukes, by esthetes belonging to the royal family.—Do you understand now how weighty and grave my rôle is tonight?"

While saying this Nina rose from the sofa as lightly and easily as a bird flits from one branch to another and vanished behind the dark Japanese screen which shut off her toilet table and her wardrobe. Behind the screen shone the white radiance of a lamp.

"What is there so extraordinary that's going to come off at Sophia Arkadievna's tonight?"

"Why, don't you know yet? *Leda,* 'Leda in a state of nature.' A dramatic-poetic dance tragedy, specially composed for tonight. Gardianov from the Imperial Theater is to produce it; but the actors are all amateurs belonging to the highest society. Professional actors and dancers are debarred."

"And what part are you to take in the performance? Are you a spectator or . . . ? May I know?"

"You are really naive, Zachary Gavrilovitch! This is a Greek night—and do you think I could be a mere spectator when that's so? Besides, the ballet is planned so that all the spectators will take part in it, as Bacchantes, nymphs, fauns, loves and other mythological figures, flute-players, cup-bearers and God knows what else. The essential idea of a private performance like this is to help to abolish the barrier between actor and spectator, art and life. Everything, as Levinstein puts it, must be transformed into 'action'; art must pass into life. So who can remain a mere spectator? The spectator is always a disturbing factor: he makes one conscious of the mask, reminds one that it is merely a play. But in this case it isn't a matter of mere play, but of life; art—so Levinstein says—must be resurrected again in life."

"And what rôle are you to play in this 'life'? Forgive the question, but seeing that you've already imposed on me the part of your conscience, I should like to fulfill my duty thoroughly. You haven't taken on, for instance, the part of Leda?"

"No, they find that my figure is still too girlish, too undeveloped for that part. The jury of experts have chosen Sophia Arkadievna.

You must surely see it—statuesque, blonde, a Helen: All I've been given is a humble part as a love in Leda's train. You see, Zachary Gavrilovitch, I confess everything and hide nothing from Your Reverence."

Thereupon Nina emerged from behind the Japanese screen: "You'll have to help me to fasten my dress, Zachary Gavrilovitch, but I warn you beforehand it won't be a very easy business. For the subtle point of my costume is this: that it can't be properly fastened."

She stood before him like a slender vase. Behind the screen she seemed, by some magic art, to have transformed her hair. Her locks had become, as it were, alive and active, and curled round her head like serpents: they seemed animate strands of hair, things that led a life of their own and could shine out and fade away again . . .

Her costume consisted simply of a short tunic. Between her naked body and it there was nothing. . . . The tunic was of bright red velvet and was so tight that Zachary found it almost impossible to fasten hook after hook upon her naked back. . . .

"Fasten every fourth one and leave three open—that's the proper way," Nina instructed him over her shoulder.

Through the slit of the garment he could see gleaming, firm flesh. Down the middle, like a living eel, ran the nobly slender spine. Nina's flesh also seemed to have a life of its own; it quivered and shrank at each involuntary touch of his fingers. Her skin was naturally bronze colored; it still retained, too, the sun rays it had absorbed all summer at the seaside (there are bodies which can retain their tan from one summer to another), and was like a fruit ripened in the warmth of the sun.

"There! I can't do any more!" cried Zachary, flushed deep red with his labors, his forehead covered with sweat. "But what's this? Half of the costume is missing!"

"There isn't any more," replied Nina. "This is how it should be."

She turned round and showed herself off. Her firm young body, tightly encased in the sheath of the short tunic, appeared far more mature than it was in reality. The garment outlined the gracious lines of her form down to the smallest and most delicious details.

"And you really intend to go like that?"

"Like what?" asked Nina with naive surprise.

"Like that——" Zachary pointed at her costume.

"Oh, I'll be very relieved if I pass the expert examination at the gate of Sophia Arkadievna's paradise. 'Severely Greek' is the password. That means: wear nothing at all. To get past the critical angels at the entrance I'm going to put vine leaves in my hair and a garland of red roses round my brow: that will make me look like a real Bacchante for the triumphal car of the great god, don't you think, Zachary Gavrilovitch?" she asked, while she bound the roses round her forehead.

Zachary smiled in his beard: "As your father confessor I'll put up a prayer that they may refuse you admission into paradise."

"I always knew you were a good young man; whether you want to be or not—you can't help yourself."

Zachary felt uncomfortable. He felt that he was in danger of forgetting his rôle and did his utmost to stick to it, so as not to play another and more perilous one....

"And now bring me my fur coat, Zachary Gavrilovitch; it's getting late."

Zachary Gavrilovitch wrapped her in her sable fur coat, which was as warm, soft, and alive to the touch as her young girlish body. ... He helped to pull on her high snow shoes. Floating in a delicate cloud of gardenia perfume, the waving flames of her hair uncovered, she stepped out into the street with Zachary. There the broad-shouldered Petersburg coachman Ivan was already waiting for her, restraining with a tight curb the splendid stallion that was yoked to the low elegant sledge.

They sat closely together, wrapped tightly in their fur rugs. To a merry tinkling of bells the black stallion flew like an arrow through the yellow fog that lay on the streets of Petersburg. The snow on the bridges was soft and yielding, and the runners of the sledge cut deep furrows in it as in some pure and delicate substance. A cloud of whirling snow beat in their faces. The lights from the street lamps and the shop windows covered with rime-flowers illumined the black shapes of the houses, which in the darkness fell away into one indeterminate mass. Everything gleamed and sparkled in the yellow fog, even the glistening ice-crusted marble house fronts on either side of them. Sledges drawn by gleaming black horses flew past. Each tried to outrace the other. Only the soft hiss of the sledge runners cutting through the snow and the dancing hoof-steps of the horses could be heard.

Nina and Zachary drove on wrapped in innumerable rugs, pressed close together as under a blanket. Zachary's hands could feel the softness of Nina's fur coat, soft as her body. The snow whipped their faces pleasantly, but Zachary felt it as little as he felt the cold and the wind. Here in the gleaming yellow cloud he felt, enhanced a thousand times, the warmth of her breath and her cheek and drank in deep draughts the warm perfume of her body which came to him even through her furs. . . .

During the whole journey they did not speak. Pleading phrases and prayers flew through his mind: they crystallized and urgently begged for utterance: "Nina Solomonovna, why are you going to this place? Please don't go to Sophia Arkadievna's; company of that kind isn't for a girl like you."

And Nina Solomonovna's only desire was to hear these very words. The sledge stopped before Sophia Arkadievna's house in the Morskaia, but Zachary did not give the thirsty girl the refreshing draught she longed for. . . .

She coolly reached him her perfumed hand and followed the Swiss attendant, who held the door open. Through a lighted window Zachary saw her quickly disappearing between the pillars and lights of the warm vestibule into Sophia Arkadievna's house.

Now that he was left alone Zachary Mirkin did not know what to do with himself. He sent the sledge back and wandered through the streets. They were just coming to life. Over the bridge flew countless sledges with a merry ringing of bells, drawn by dancing black horses. The pavement was packed with a crowd coming out of a cinema. The gleaming yellow fog that hung low over Petersburg seemed to be entangled in the shine of the innumerable electric lights, which made the falling snow sparkle like diamond crystals, glitter and then die away. From the streams of human beings, the warm light of the electric lamps, the flying horses, the soft ringing of the sledge bells poured warmth, comfort, happiness and a kindly radiance that made every heart beat faster, every foot step out more quickly, and filled everybody with joy to be alive. Zachary felt as though he had been flung into the street by Nina. Amid all the gayety and noise he was seized by intense loneliness. He hastily looked behind him and turned back. When he reached Sophia Arkadievna's he cast one more glance into the festively illuminated vestibule with the great pillars behind which Nina had disappeared, as if he wished to impress quite distinctly on his mind the traces of her little feet which only a few moments before had flitted up the marble stairs.

And he felt a longing to be alone in a warm room instead of being abandoned to the cold windy street. He waved for a droshky and told the coachman to drive him home. He wrapped himself up tightly in the rug as though afraid that the wind might blow away the warmth of his body and destroy something in his heart. Once home, he went straight to his bedroom, took off his clothes and stretched himself out on his bed. Against his usual habit he did not pick up a book to read himself to sleep. He switched off the electric light, drew the blankets close round him and tried, as he had often done as a child, to conjure an image out of the darkness. A figure floated before his eyes; it had Nina's face but the body of another woman. . . . In his nostrils, on his lips, he seemed to feel a faint whiff of perfume; but it, too, seemed to be a mixture of various perfumes. . . .

CHAPTER V

THE MIRKIN FAMILY

ZACHARY GAVRILOVITCH came of a remarkable family. It may be said that he educated himself, or more correctly that he grew up without any education, although he had passed through the high school and won his law degree at the university, and now, while still young, was already the assistant of a celebrated advocate.

The only son of one of the richest men in all Russia, he was quite alone in the world, without a family, without a fatherland, without a home. He had grown up without either a religious or a family tradition, although he belonged to one of the most distinguished families in Russia and was the descendant of wealthy people and famous rabbis. But he did not feel that any of the feasts and holidays, either the Jewish or the Christian ones, were his, though he always took part in them all.

Moses Chaim Mirkin, the founder of the Mirkin dynasty, who lifted the family name out of the general flood of obscurity and insignificance and raised it to esteem, came from a big city in Lithuania. He was a supporter of the Jewish "enlightenment," which was at that time coming to the front, took great pleasure in perusing profane writings in the Hebrew language and studied German and Russian all his life. He was one of the first Jews in his city to dress in the "German" fashion, and he trimmed his beard. He was also a great mathematician. On Sabbath evenings his house was a center of intellect. There all the enlightened elements in the neighborhood met. At these gatherings there was much debate over Isaak Baer Levensohn, the father of enlightenment among the eastern European Jews, serious problems were disclosed, forbidden writings and pasquinades against the rabbis, which were passed in manuscript from hand to hand, were read out. In the intervals the company set each other conundrums or had a short game of cards.

The happy days of Alexander the Second's reign arrived. A new spirit appeared among the Russian Jews, a longing for culture, a desire to take their part in the greater world. The future glowed for them in the rosiest hues, and they prepared themselves for the new and happy life which they thought was at hand. The province of Lithuania seized the lead; it was the first to cast off the romantic spell exercised by the name of Poland as well as the movement for national independence which was being supported both publicly and in secret at that time, and began to hail every Russian gendarme and official as a herald of the new life from the East. The Russian language became the key admitting one to the great family of "Russia."

The Jews, who were still cut off from the outer world and inclosed within the sevenfold wall of their peculiar ways of life, prepared themselves, with that eager zeal for adaptation which is characteristic of their race, for the coming new life. Once more it was

Lithuania that made the first start, thus becoming the vanguard of Russian Jewry.

Moses Chaim Mirkin was a typical child of his age. He had suddenly discovered the way the Jews must go, but he was not content to take it himself; he also saw that others should follow his example. He busily carried on his propaganda and, although more than avaricious, actually provided money to give Jewish children an opportunity to learn Russian. He himself spoke nothing but Russian in public, though with a very bad accent. He was the first to inaugurate the new habit of taking off one's hat in one's house, installed a samovar, and initiated "at homes." He also combated fanaticism, the traditional Jewish dress, the Yiddish "jargon" and various Jewish customs that had been handed down. His favorite saying was: "It's high time to begin a new life and become like other people."

Nevertheless this did not prevent him from following a vocation which was very little in keeping with his free-thinking sentiments. He lent out money at interest. In the course of his business he naturally began to accept pledges. So that he became a pawnbroker like many another, except for this difference, that he kept his pledges not in a shop, but in an iron safe secured with many locks and chains. Every pledge was furnished with a ticket inscribed with a number and the name of the owner in Russian and German. A great many wedding presents, also much family jewelry, found their way into Moses Chaim Mirkin's safe. Later, when public opinion in Russia became more liberal, Mirkin extended his business by negotiating loans for the land-proprietors of the district and the higher State officials in his native city. With that began his rise to power. Land-proprietors were not so frugal then as now. When in the mood for it they gambled away at the card table whole villages, forests and towns, and sometimes stretches of land that were as big as small states. These land-proprietors were always in need of ready cash. Instead of brooches, necklaces, golden pendants, marriage rings and Sabbath candlesticks—bills of exchange, I.O.U.s and mortgages on estates, fields and forests now flowed into Moses Chaim Mirkin's iron safe, until at last he secured the great forest lands of Pustyna.

Lolling in his roomy carriage drawn by three white horses, Moses

Chaim Mirkin, still wearing his warm traveling fur coat, although it was May, drove through mud and mire by unfamiliar paths into a strange and unknown world. He saw immense stretches covered with dense groves of oaks whose crowns were so close together that they did not let through the sunshine or the light of day. These trees with their interwoven branches and roots blocked the path of this man who for the first time strove to invade their hidden mysteries. With his forester on the driver's seat, his clerk Sorach by his side and a musket in his hand, Moses Chaim Mirkin penetrated into the darkest depths of the forest lands of Pustyna, which he had secured by an adroit stroke: that is, by paying their owner, a Polish prince, a certain sum over and above the bills of exchange already reposing in his safe. But he himself had had no idea that the forest lands of Pustyna were so huge, so widespreading, so enormous as they turned out to be; that they covered such a gigantic stretch of land.

Moses Chaim Mirkin had been on the road since six o'clock in the morning, and yet the forester declared that they had not yet completed a quarter of their way. This was only the beginning.... No man's foot had ever touched these forests; the first who ventured to penetrate them was their new proprietor. He sat in his carriage and turned over in his head plan after plan for making use of them: he would fell the trees, clear the ground, set up saw-mills, build houses. Projects raced through his mind. The trees must have read the man's thoughts, for they blocked his way.... They produced a hundred obstacles to keep the carriage from piercing farther into their depths. At one point the horses stumbled and fell over huge roots, at another the great solemn oaks stretched their branches straight across the path, forming a thick, dense wall. A rustling and whispering came from the trees and rose to an uncanny sobbing, so that the horses stopped in terror and pricked their ears and listened: What was this coming towards them?—But Moses Chaim Mirkin was not a man to be easily daunted: Drive on! Forward! The food that his wife had packed for the journey was finished. So the little flask of spirits that lay in the carriage had to serve as food; they went on. But then the carriage came to a bog which there was no crossing. Beneath the withered trees white patches of snow were still gleaming. At the other side of the bog stretched a green carpet of moss. No human footstep had ever penetrated here, no human eye had ever seen this place. Moses Chaim Mirkin ordered the driver to drive on: "If there's nothing else for it, we'll sleep in the carriage for the night. We have two guns and there's still some drink left!" But the horses simply refused to go on. They pricked their ears and listened, expanding their nostrils and sniffing. Suddenly they spurned the swampy ground with their hoofs, tore away with the light carriage, and paying no heed to the coachman's whip and his hand tugging at the reins, turned back and flew from the place, madly plunging over roots and branches. Part of the carriage was left behind in the path. Moses Chaim Mirkin was flung out on one side, the clerk Sorach on the other. The galloping horses dragged the rest of the splintered carriage after them. So Moses Chaim Mirkin was driven out of his own property and the forest of Pustyna remained unsurveyed.

When the rumor began to spread in the town that Mirkin had bought the forest lands of Pustyna, everybody laughed and said: "What will he do with them? There's no water in all that stretch. There'll be nothing left for him but to eat his oaks. . . ." When he heard such sayings Moses Chaim Mirkin would nod his head: "Right enough, what can I do with them? There'll be nothing left for me but to eat my oaks."

For thirty years Moses Chaim Mirkin left the forest lands of Pustyna untouched. Meanwhile he occupied himself in rebuilding his town and inaugurated a tremendous activity unknown in it till then. He did not let a minute go past unused. Hitherto the town had consisted of several government buildings and the scattered wooden houses of the inhabitants: the rest was mire and bog. Moses Chaim Mirkin undertook to build on the bog. He drained large stretches and bit by bit set up real streets. They consisted at first of wooden houses. The planks were tarred with a brush made of swine's bristles. "A house like that will stand for four hundred years. I build for four centuries!" was his favorite saying.

When presently brick houses came into fashion he built brick houses. On the border of his forest estate his brickworks smoked day and night. Day and night long rows of heavy wagons creaked townwards, loaded with bricks from his brickworks. That went on until he had transformed the great Lithuanian town from a wooden into a brick one. . . .

During the few years before his death Mirkin lived in solitude, forsaken by his children, in the smallest room of his great house, and calculated perpetually how many square meters his untouched forest lands of Pustyna came to. This reckoning was a sort of specific against asthma, by which he was tormented in his last years. As he concocted new plans or counted up his riches, it had such a beneficent effect on him that he could fight down the dreadful fits of coughing that otherwise would have mastered him. Just about that time the government decided to lay down a new railway line which was to connect the southern province of Lithuania with West Russia. This line was to run straight through the forest of Pustyna. And before one could turn, a whole little town had sprung up at one edge of the forest, colonized by railway laborers, officials and Jews prepared to draw their living from the forest, which was to be felled. Several stations were to be erected in the middle of the forest. This news reached Moses Chaim Mirkin on his deathbed. His brain immediately began to draw up plans, and he calculated how many towns he would be able to build in the forest. This occupation eased his sickness and even lengthened his life for a little, until the asthma took full charge and began to throttle him. Then Moses Chaim Mirkin lamented in his heart: "The forest of Pustyna is beginning to live, and I must die. . . ."

Nobody heard his dumb complaint, for a fit of coughing strangled it for ever.

CHAPTER VI

GABRIEL HAIMOVITCH MIRKIN

Moses Chaim Mirkin left behind him two sons and two daughters. His daughters he had married off to rich suitors in Lithuania, and, being a shrewd business man, he had paid off their husbands' share of the estate during his life-time, so that after his death his own sons might have it all. His elder son Joseph Mirkin had followed his father's occupation and consequently was chosen to run the paternal business. So he remained in his native town. The younger son Gabriel was, according to his father's views, to become an advocate. Just as every old-fashioned Jewish father wished one of his sons to become a Talmudist, so that the world might be enlightened even after his death, old Mirkin was firmly resolved to have a "learned" son. By this means also he wished to expiate his sins against the "enlightenment," above all the sin of usury. When his two sons had passed through the high school—they were the first Jewish high school boys in the city—the elder entered his father's business, and the younger was sent to study law in Petersburg, the Imperial residence. At that time there was no difficulty raised if a Jew wished to study law, for there were still very few Jewish lawyers.

But soon it appeared that the younger son possessed surprising business capacities, while from the first the elder showed none, and only wasted the paternal inheritance. (It is true, such immense wealth could not be altogether exhausted even by his constant "unlucky" transactions.) Gabriel, the younger son, plagued his head with Roman Law simply to please his father. He did not plague his head too gravely, however. In recompense he made the acquaintance of a large circle of Christian students to whom he felt attracted. (From his childhood he had had a dislike of Jews.) His extravagance and the ample supplies that his father freely allowed him made his Christian friends wink at his Jewish ancestry. They belonged to the *jeunesse dorée* of the time, and spent their nights with soubrettes and can-can dancers in the pleasure resorts of Petersburg. Gabriel Mirkin kept pace in these matters with his friends and learned from them smooth manners and an easy way with women: but, most important of all, he established connections with the future high officials of the State. This circumstance Gabriel Haimovitch was wise enough to exploit later for his business interests.

It was in his student days, too, that he came to know his future wife Natalia Ossipovna Saruchin. The name was not hereditary, but went no further back than the girl's father. Father Saruchin, a well-known doctor in Petersburg, was of Jewish ancestry. Whether or not he had been baptized was not certain. His household observed, like all the other households in Petersburg, the orthodox Russian way of life. Ikons with little red lamps burning before them hung in the corners of his consulting-room, his dining-room, his drawing-room. Natalia's mother looked like a Christian—her father, it must be confessed, less so. His nose was emphatically hooked, his forehead high, his eyes deep-set and veiled, and a network of little wrinkles lost themselves in his side-whiskers.

The Saruchins' house was regarded as aristocratic. Young Gabriel Haimovitch was impressed by the white-gloved Petersburg lackeys who served at table; he was impressed by the abundance of empire furniture in the style of Alexander I that he found in the doctor's house, the massive bulging cupboards, the solid sideboards with their heavy bronze ornamentation, and the immensely long table. Most of all young Gabriel Haimovitch was impressed by the fact that the members of the family always used the ceremonious form of address in speaking to each other. Even the mother and the daughter did so. But a really deep impression was made upon him by the blue-veined alabaster-white throat that rose from Natasha's low dress. From it hung on a slender velvet band a little locket containing a strand of hair and a miniature showing a face that he did not know. All this seemed so marvelously simple and sweet in Gabriel's eyes that he never forgot it afterwards.

Gabriel had been introduced to the household by a nephew of the doctor's who was a fellow student and an intimate friend of his. Doctor Saruchin had a family of five daughters, of whom Natasha was the third, and so he received Gabriel, as he received all young men, with the greatest affability.

Gabriel was not clear in his mind whether he might not have to submit to baptism as the price of winning Natasha's hand. This possibility, indeed, was very attractive to him. He was in a sense disappointed when it appeared that he need not change his religion. On the contrary the fact that he was a Jew and came from a populous center of Jewish life where the traditional customs and usages of his race were still maintained made him peculiarly eligible in the eyes of his future father-in-law. For although Doctor Saruchin was already quite assimilated and had no longer any connection with the Jewish community, he shrank, for reasons perhaps unknown to himself, from taking the ultimate step.

After the death of his father, Gabriel returned to his Lithuanian home (by that time he had entirely given up his law studies). His two years in Petersburg had changed him so much that nobody knew him. Even at that early date he had parted his young blond beard into two points, the mode in Petersburg then. After the English fashion he wore a gold watch chain dangling on his velvet waistcoat, wide trousers, a black "Prince Albert" frock coat with a rose in the buttonhole, and a little hard Derby hat. So, as a genuine Petersburg dandy, he attracted much attention in the town. His correct urban Russian and his fine manners made him a welcome visitor not merely in rich Jewish houses (which it must be confessed he avoided) but also in those of the Russian state officials staying in the town.

He was suddenly seized with the idea of approaching the Ministry of Railways and offering a quotation for the delivery of railway sleepers for the new line. The forest of Pustyna, which lay in the direct route, could provide sleepers at a much lower rate than any of his competitors could offer. Gabriel's connections in official circles in Petersburg, his open-handed ways, his nightly appearance at card parties and in the boudoirs of ladies of questionable virtue, did not a little for him, and his offer was accepted. This was his first big deal with the Ministry of Railways, and at one stroke the firm of Mirkin Brothers became known in Government circles.

Soon, however, Gabriel saw that he would never go very far if he remained tied to his brother. He was weary to death of living in the midst of a Jewish colony, and disgust rose in him at the filth of the town and the countless Jews with whom he wished to have nothing to do. He felt impelled towards the greater world. So—with that boldness of spirit that characterized him—he abruptly forsook the paternal business, left to his brother all the properties, pledges and notes of demand on land-proprietors and noblemen, retained for himself only the forest lands of Pustyna and the contracts with the Government, and returned to Petersburg. There Natasha, with her alabaster neck and her mysterious locket hanging from the black velvet band, awaited him.

Just about that time the Government set about their enormous project of building the Siberian railway. The work was begun simultaneously at several points in the tremendous stretch of land lying between Moscow and Vladivostok. As a lion sniffs his prey in the jungle, so Gabriel scented the colossal profits which the existence of the new railway would enable him to realize. He began by forming a huge syndicate in Petersburg. In it great Jewish capitalists were associated with high state officials, and the names of several grand dukes were also secured for the sake of impressiveness. And then began in central Russia and Siberia the buying up of enormous stretches of forest land adjoining the future railway line. The task of the high officials and the grand dukes was to see that the Ministry of Railways purchased the sleepers for the endless leagues of the new railway from the syndicate at a price which could only be dictated in Russia.

After Gabriel's marriage to Natalia his business kept him perpetually shifting from one Russian town to another. As his presence at the scene of action was absolutely essential, he decided to transfer his home from Petersburg to the very interior of Russia.

Natalia was a delicate woman inclining to lassitude. The damp exhalations of the Petersburg canals among which she had grown up seemed to have got into her bones. She could not keep pace with her husband. So she was soon tired out by the strain of coping with his indefatigable energy. Hardly was everything settled comfortably in one town before they had to leave it for another. And then the children began to come.

The first three were girls. Not one of them survived. Then Zachary was born. All four children saw the light somewhere between Moscow and Ekaterinburg, each one in a different town.

Up to the time that Zachary was born Gabriel Haimovitch had seriously considered going over to the religion whose usages he had always kept.

At bottom nothing in his life distinguished him from all his friends. Not only were all the Orthodox Russian feast days celebrated in his household: from time to time he also went to church, simply so as to fulfill what he considered a social obligation. All his friends and business acquaintances as well as the members of staff belonged to the Orthodox Church. Whenever a special national festival such as the Czar's birthday was celebrated he had to be present. Of course everybody knew that Mirkin actually belonged to another faith, but this was winked at in his case. For in the provinces of central Russia where he lived there was scarcely any Antisemitism and no opposition that could not be bridged; besides, his way of life was so completely that of his neighbors that no difference could be remarked. Some of his acquaintances did not even know that Gabriel Haimovitch belonged to another faith. It was only his Jewish papers and his Jewish name that now and then created difficulties for him in his dealings with the Government. So he saw no reason why he should not take the ultimate step and go over completely to the religion according to whose forms and customs he lived.

But meanwhile the party of reaction had climbed to power once more—the régime of Pobiedonosev and Alexander III began. Nor, after Alexander's death, were the hopes centered in the new Czar fulfilled. Pobiedonosev ruled over Nicholas II as he had ruled over Alexander. During that period there awakened in Mirkin, as in so many of his compatriots, a dumb protest which expressed itself in his case in a firm resolve to stick to his religion. It seemed to him a piece of cowardice to go over just then, and without cause, to the Russian religion. So he postponed the step until the time when a son should be born to him, for he did not wish his heir to suffer unnecessarily by being a Jew. But when the hour came the hatred of the Jews in Government circles had become so violent that it roused Gabriel Haimovitch to defiance. He did not want to give the appearance of acting under a tyrannical compulsion. He postponed his intention once more until the reaction should slacken and he could take his step with a clear conscience.

So he could only bring up his son in the life, the usages and festivals which he himself refused to adopt officially "in the letter," but which he yet followed illegitimately, as it were . . .

Consequently the son grew up in a completely Russian atmosphere just like the children round him. He was different from them in no way. Just like the boy in the next house Zachary crossed himself in front of the ikon in his nursery before going to sleep, looked forward with excitement to his Christmas tree and his gayly-colored Easter eggs, and impatiently waited for the feast day when the ice was broken so that the image of the Savior might be dipped in the water. . . . Up to his twelfth year Zachary had no idea that he belonged to a different race, a different people, a different religion. His comrades in the school and the recreation park treated him just as they treated one another, and did not know that anything distinguished him from them.

When Zachary was about to enter the high school his mother suddenly left the house and went abroad.

The boy was told that his mother was ill and had to go away for a cure. So little Zachary was left alone in the great house in the middle of Central Russia. He never saw his mother again.

CHAPTER VII

ZACHARY'S BOYHOOD

His father was continually traveling to and fro between Petersburg and Ekaterinburg. So Zachary, his tutor Stepan Ivanovitch (an elderly high-school teacher who had lost his post because of some transgression or other), the housekeeper Maria Ivanovna and the domestic staff, consisting of a cook, a housemaid and a manservant, were the sole inmates of the great house in Ekaterinburg. His mother's room on the first floor was locked up: on the other hand the great drawing-room with the massive furniture and the numerous bronze statues which had been transported from Petersburg was open, though it was never used. The spacious dining-room with its four windows, its twenty-four leather-covered chairs and its enormously long table, was also open, as well as Gabriel Haimovitch's study with the huge writing-table, the heavy bronze ink stand, the two toy locomotives which served as paper-weights, and the photographs of high officials and generals in gold frames. Daily the housemaid and the manservant cleaned the rooms, beat the heavy Persian carpets and dusted everything, although a visitor rarely came.

During the first weeks of his solitude little Zachary grieved eeply for his mother. Nevertheless he was ashamed to show it, for e knew that it was absurd for a high school boy to be sentimental. Yet when Stepan Ivanovitch was asleep (and Stepan Ivanovitch, who vas very fond of spirits, seized every opportunity he could find to fall sleep), Zachary would steal unobserved to the drawing-room on the irst floor, where on a little table near the stove a big photograph of is mother stood in a gold frame, and stroked her pointed face and slim heeks; and he would talk to the photograph as to a living creature: "Dear Mamma, I love you, I love you."

Then he would press his nose to the cold glass and kiss his nother's snow-white neck. For a long time he would stay in the huge oom, in which it was always cold, for the fire was seldom put on, nurmuring to himself: "Dear Mamma, I love you, I love you."

In the photograph in the gold frame Mamma wore, just as she ad done on her reception days, her blue silk dress which fell away ehind into broad folds suggesting a crinoline and was buttoned up o the neck. A white lace shawl lay lightly over her shoulders and rms; in one hand she held a fan. Her hair was piled up on the top f her head and fixed with combs. A single curl fell over her smooth row, and it looked as though it were pasted there. For hours Zachary vould stand before the photograph and study his mother's face. He ooked deep into Mamma's blue eyes, though they did not answer his ut always gazed away towards the window. They were so lovely nd exerted such a charm upon him that the boy would bow over the lass and cover Mamma's eyes, Mamma's straight long nose, Mamma's ips with kisses. And sometimes, too, he would bury his face in Mamma's soft white throat.

He loved everything in his mother's portrait: the white roses hat she wore on her bosom, the fan, the white lace shawl. Through he glass covering the photograph he imagined he could still feel the nique, warm, scented fragrance of his mother's clothes, together vith the smell of naphthalene which she had always kept in her ward-obes to preserve her dresses from moths. . . . A longing seized him o fling himself on the photograph and kiss every inch of his mother's ress. But he never dared actually to do this.

His mother had always repulsed him when he tried to indulg his childish longing to caress her: "You're a big boy now, you'll b going to the high school soon and wearing a uniform. A big boy lik you shouldn't be such a baby."

Sometimes, too, Mamma had threatened to tell his father of him "What would happen, Zachary, if your father noticed how childisl you are?"

And Zachary was more afraid of his father than of the red haired mathematics teacher or the black angel with the drawn swor on the holy ikon.

Yet he could not resist his longing to fondle Mamma's hands an fingers, to stand close to her knees and breathe in the warm fragranc of her perfume, to play now and then with her fan or the fringes o her shawl.

So he did secretly what his mother forbade him to do wheneve he came across one of her dresses lying about. Even if he found on of her shoes he would press it to his heart and kiss it, saying: "Dea Mamma, I love you, I love you so much."

When he was left alone in the house after his mother's departur he fell ill: he suffered for a long time from a nervous fever. Week passed before he could get used to his solitude. He suffered as a chil does when it is weaned from its mother's breast. When at last, by supreme effort of the will, he resolved to submit, he poured out hi love for her on the photographs and dresses she had left behind.

His love for his mother left a deep and lasting mark on Zachary it influenced his whole attitude toward woman. For a long time afterwards, and even sometimes during his years of adolescence, he coul not go to sleep, especially if he was in a state of dejection, withou picturing in his imagination that he was pressing his face against hi mother's soft white throat. He still did this occasionally, now that h was a young man: he could feel while doing so the perfume of he body, and a chaste and tender emotion would fill him, a divination o a goodness that is not of this world, for it can proceed only from pur mother-love. He became once more a helpless child and resigned himself wholly to the protection and security of his mother's arms.

This attitude of his to his mother had such a deep effect upon hir that it influenced his opinion of every woman he met. Even now that he was a man he could not regard any woman except with the purest and noblest feelings. For in every woman, even the demi-mondaines and prostitutes with whom his later years as a student inevitably brought him into contact, he saw a symbol of his mother and his boyish love for her.... So his mother's white lace shawl made every woman pure for him; every woman gave out the soft tender fragrance of his mother, which he had breathed as a child; every woman stood for him on a pedestal wrapped in a cloud of glory and of motherhood.

As he grew older his obsession with his mother decreased a little. His impatient longing for a letter from her also left him. He sat no longer, as formerly, for whole evenings at the piano, setting to music his love poems to his mother, poems he had never posted, for he was ashamed of divulging his feelings to her. His mother's place was taken by young girls, sisters of his friends, whom he met at the bandstand in the park or at dances, and at whom he occasionally made eyes when he saw them sitting in their boxes in the theater.... But his mother's position was also superseded for him in great measure by his nurse Maria Ivanovna.

In the house in Ekaterinburg Maria Ivanovna was called by her paternal name; such an honor is usually accorded in Russia only to people of better class, never to domestics (as though common people were unworthy of receiving any public acknowledgment that they, too, had fathers). Maria Ivanovna was a simple woman of the people. She could hardly read and the little that she knew she had learned in the Mirkins' house. Nevertheless, since she knew the Russian alphabet, she was accorded the distinction of being called by her paternal name: besides, she was the housekeeper. In spite of her simple and primitive ways this woman possessed an admirable natural intelligence. She understood the slightest nod of her mistress and guessed her wishes by pure instinct before Natalia Ossipovna was herself aware of them. Maria Ivanovna had entered the Mirkins' house after Zachary was born; she had been recommended by a neighboring family as a healthy wet-nurse. After the child was weaned she still remained in the house, at first as a mere housemaid. But soon, through her intelligence, her interest in everything that happened in the house, her fidelity and above all her disinterestedness, she won the hearts of her employers: more, without any one knowing or marking how it came about, she became an important member of the family. This position she won entirely by her own efforts. The mistress of the house was always ill, and was occupied one half the day with her house duties, the other half with her social obligations. So Maria Ivanovna assumed of herself, without any one having intrusted her with it, the conduct of the household.

To little Zachary she was more than a nurse, more even than a mother. For a long time after she had weaned him he could only go to sleep if she knelt down by his bed and lulled him in her arms. Even when he grew into a big boy and went to the high school Maria Ivanovna still exercised a great influence over him. She alone could make him eat some distasteful dish prescribed by the family doctor for the sake of his health. She could even make him take cod liver oil. It was her influence that got him to bed at the proper time and persuaded him to do his home exercises thoroughly and obey his tutor Stepan Ivanovitch. It was above all by virtue of her physical strength that Maria Ivanovna exerted this influence on the boy. She was tall and powerful; the short sleeves of her blouse displayed two white round arms; her tightly-fitting blouse outlined a superb bosom. She was in fact a voluptuously beautiful woman. She was always particular, too, about her clothes, and invariably wore a black skirt, a white blouse, a white apron and a gay-colored peasant wrap round her shoulders. When it was necessary she did not hesitate to lay the high-school boy over her knee and thoroughly belabor him on the seat of his school uniform.

The whole house stood in fear of her, the servants no less than the perpetually sleepy Stepan Ivanovitch and the children; probably, too, the feeble sickly mistress of the house in her white warmly-carpeted bedroom on the top floor had trembled at her housekeeper's imperious voice and firm step and inexhaustible energy.

Maria Ivanovna was the first to rise and the last to go to bed in the Mirkins' house, only retiring after she had made an inspection of the whole place and seen that everything was in order. She drew up the menus for all the meals and kept the keys of the cellar and the pantry.

She deified her foster child, little Zachary. He was her god, her life, and she guarded him like the apple of her eye. Often she would stand for hours outside his door and listen to see that he was sleeping soundly and that nothing ailed him. When he was ill or a little out of sorts she would not leave his bed even for a moment, and he always fell asleep in her arms. In her he found a safe protection from those dark and terrible dreams of fear which every child brings with it from the unknown world whence it comes.

Maria Ivanovna wielded undisputed power over the boy from the moment when he was left alone with her in the great house after his mother's departure.

She decided what clothes he should wear, and without her permission he never dared to cast off his warm underclothing, no matter how heavy and burdensome it might feel. She prescribed what he was to eat. From fear of her he never dared to stay an hour longer than usual at the skating rink with his companions, or listening to the military band in the park. He had to be back punctually for his specified meals and his lessons with his tutor. If he did not arrive in time she greeted him with strong words, and, if these had no effect, she had recourse to her hands.

Yet it was not merely her physical strength that made him so obedient to his father's paid housekeeper. Her complete mastery over him sprang from the intense maternal love which she lavished on her foster child. Zachary could not escape from her motherliness, for motherliness exuded from every pore of her emphatic vigorous body, her strong round arms, her eyes, her mouth. In every word she spoke he could feel the trembling maternal solicitude that she nursed for him. In every glance he could see the maternal glow that burned within her. Through the uncannily long and cold winter nights of central Russia, when the white snow covered everything, making a new earth for mankind, when the frost swept in from the forests of Siberia and beleaguered the city like a troop of wolves: through these long nights the boy would toss sleeplessly on his bed. His thin body would seek warmth beneath the pile of blankets and rugs, but in vain. With shut eyes he would try to conjure up the face and form of his distant mother, but he could not. On such nights Maria Ivanovna, after standing for hours like a faithful dog outside the door of her Zachary and listening to his restless turnings, was filled with a sense of his loneliness and helplessness. On her tiptoes she would steal into the boy's room, go over to his bed, take his thin wretched body in her strong arms and lay his face on her full warm bosom, which seemed almost about to burst her tightly fitting bodice. She warmed his body in this way, his face, his lips, and in a tender maternal voice she whispered in his ear over and over again: "My little pigeon, my poor, unhappy orphaned child, why aren't you asleep? Sleep now, sleep, sleep!"

The boy felt himself enveloped in maternal love; a new home, an inner home preserved and shielded him from all evil. His fear vanished and he fell asleep.

For a long time still Maria Ivanovna held the beloved little body in her arms. Only when she heard the boy's deep quiet breathing did she leave the room on tiptoe.

CHAPTER VIII

HOW ZACHARY LEARNED THAT HE WAS A JEW

It was through Maria Ivanovna, too, that the boy learned what he was, who his forefathers were and what religion he belonged to. It happened as follows.

When Zachary was about twelve—it was the second winter after his mother left the house—a letter arrived from his father saying that this year he could not be home for Christmas Eve; his business compelled him to spend the Christmas holidays in Petersburg. Maria Ivanovna should herself make arrangements for the festival and give the servants their usual presents. Zachary's present he, Gabriel Haimovitch, would himself send from Petersburg. Maria Ivanovna commanded that, in place of the great pine tree with the countless candles which had been annually set up while her master was at home, a small tree should be bought; nor should it stand as before in the drawing-room, but in the dining-room, and to it were to be tied only the presents for the domestic staff, but not those for the young master.

Like every child (and he was a very sensitive one) Zachary awaited the Christmas festival with glowing cheeks and beating heart. When he heard of Maria Ivanovna's instructions, he turned to her in despairing astonishment for some explanation of her incomprehensible conduct.

"It isn't really your feast day, my little pigeon, nor that of the gracious master, but only of the servants. That's why I have ordered the tree to be set up only for them."

"Not my feast day? But it's for us all. Christ was born on Christmas Day so that the world might be saved."

"No, little pigeon, it isn't your feast day; you belong to a different people and have another religion. Your religion doesn't keep this feast day; it has other feast days of its own."

"I belong to another people? How can you say such things, nurse? Have you lost your wits? What can you mean—I have another religion?"

"Yes, little pigeon, your father, your grandparents, your mother—they all believed in another religion, they had other feast days. I'll find out when your feast days are; then we'll prepare your own holy days for you according to your own religion; then you won't need to keep other people's feast days any longer."

Zachary stood and looked at his nurse with wide-open eyes and gaping mouth and quivering nostrils. He could not understand her words.

"It is time you knew: you're a big boy now and it's high time you acknowledged your own religion. A child can go to all manner of schools, it seems, and yet grow up as ignorant as a silly calf."

The boy became silent and bit his lips with anger. Then came a burst of fury; he flung himself on the nurse and beat and kicked her. She quietly let him go on striking her, took his head between her hands and kissed him.

When he got over his rage he rushed up to the first floor, went into the great cold drawing-room, and closed the door behind him. His first impulse was to run to the photograph of his mother, kiss her face and tell the portrait of the nurse's evil doings. But he did not do so; he cast only one glance at his mother's photograph and rushed over to the great broad silk-covered sofa. There he flung himself down, buried his face in the cushions and burst into tears.

Maria Ivanovna was standing outside the door and she said imploringly: "Open to me, my little pigeon, you'll get your death of cold; it's so cold in the drawing-room!"

Zachary made no answer.

"I'll go into the town and find if there's a rabbi to be found. I'll find out what your own feast days are. Don't be troubled, my child, oh don't be troubled, I implore you!"

When young Zachary had got over the first shock of having a new religion his longing increased more and more to learn what this religion really could be that he belonged to, what its feast days were, and how one celebrated them. Why had all this been concealed from him? Why were there other religions, different from the one that every one round him confessed? And why did people believe in those other religions? His curiosity burned him like a consuming thirst, and there was nobody who could still it. The instinct of self-preservation which he had inherited from his forbears warned him to conceal the news from his companions for the time being. He was not ashamed of what he had learned; on the contrary it gave him inward elation, as though a treasure of great price had fallen unexpectedly into his lap; but he regarded the news as a great mystery belonging only to himself, which he was not yet prepared to divulge to others.

Maria Ivanovna did what she had promised: she actually discovered the one little synagogue in Ekaterinburg. Although it was sanctioned by the authorities, the synagogue was hidden away in a huge courtyard. On the Sabbath, on the feast days, on New Year's Day and the Day of Reconciliation not much more than a dozen people ever attended it, most of them former Jewish soldiers of Nicholas I who after the expiry of their service had been given permission to settle in central Russia. The worshipers in the synagogue were distinguished in no way either by their speech or their clothes and general appearance from the other inhabitants of the town; and none of their Russian neighbors would have thought of looking askance at them.

One Saturday—it happened to be a Russian feast day and the children had got a holiday from school—Maria Ivanovna ordered Zachary to put on his warm fur coat, wrapped herself in her thick cloak and her head cloth, and led the boy to the little synagogue. When she reached the door she gently pushed him in. With his heart pounding and his knees trembling the boy entered the room. Maria Ivanovna remained outside and waited patiently in the frost and wind for Zachary to come out again.

Inside the boy's eyes were arrested by such strange and novel things that he did not know whether to be afraid or glad. The place had no resemblance to a church. Not a single holy picture hung on the walls; not a single cross was to be seen. Men were standing there, Russians in short fur coats; but over their coats they had put curious white clothes such as Zachary had never seen before. It made them look like women. Farther away, close by the wall where candles were burning (what else was there the boy could not make out, for he was afraid to venture nearer), another man was standing also veiled in a white cloth and intoning or singing something. If it was a song it had no likeness to the hymns the priests sang in the church, and besides the words were quite incomprehensible. All the other men repeated the first man's words after him. But, strangest of all, they were all wearing their fur caps just as if they were not in a church at all, but outside in the street. One of them stepped up to the boy (Zachary could only see his white beard emerging from his fur coat and the white cloth, which now seemed quite uncanny), stuck a book in his hand and invited him to step forward. Zachary started back and ran out. Maria Ivanovna, her face red with cold, was waiting. She led him home again.

The nurse never asked him what had happened in the synagogue, nor did Zachary tell her anything about it. But curiosity consumed him more and more: his imagination was captured more and more by the picture he had seen, the Jews in their white cloths, and the quite subterranean look of the synagogue. He was convinced that he had seen something mysterious of which he must tell no one.

Actually he felt elated that he, too, belonged to this mystical and secret religion in which none of his friends had part, and that none of them had ever seen the things his eyes had seen.

"Why does Papa never go there?" he asked the nurse when they were nearly home.

"It's not for us to question what Papa does; you may be sure he knows why he does anything or doesn't do it. Perhaps he does go when he's in Petersburg; there's certainly a bigger church of your religion there."

At first Zachary thought of writing to his mother about his experience and begging her to explain everything to him. But he could not bring himself to intrust to his mother the "secret" that the nurse had divulged to him. A certain feeling of shyness kept him from laying bare his heart to his mother. (This shamefaced shyness before women Zachary was unable to overcome even as a young man.) So he wrote to his mother as usual of his progress in his studies, of his friends, of sledging expeditions, skating and such like things; but he said nothing about his "secret."

Nevertheless when a few weeks later his father returned the boy found enough courage (although he was less intimate with his father than with his mother and was far less fond of him) to divulge his "secret" and ask for an explanation. It was his overwhelming desire to learn what he really was that gave him courage.

Gabriel Haimovitch was sitting in his study before his gigantic writing-table with the two locomotive models, which always teased the boy's imagination. A greenish reflection from the great desk lamp fell on him. Zachary, wearing his high-school uniform, sat awkwardly opposite him, almost lost in one of the huge chairs. He contemplated his father's broad reddish-fair side whiskers, which were already heavily streaked with gray; contemplated his shaven chin and his full pendulous lower lip. Zachary began by giving his father a report of his school progress, his marks in arithmetic and Russian grammar, and his other dealings with his teachers and class-mates. He did this in a businesslike, almost military tone, as Gabriel Haimovitch had trained him to do.

When the report was finished and his father seemed pleased—the boy could tell this from the gentle smile which he threw across at him—Zachary began at once without any trace of fear: "Is it true, Papa, that we belong to a different religion?"

Gabriel Haimovitch became rigid in his chair. An unnatural flush swept over his great white cheeks. (It afflicted him whenever he had to carry out disagreeable tasks or grew excited, and was the sign of an incipient disease.) The points of his beard trembled. He asked in a severe tone: "Who told you that?"

"Maria Ivanovna."

Gabriel Haimovitch got up angrily and shouted into the next room in a strange, hoarse, almost discordant voice, such as Zachary had never heard him use before: "Maria Ivanovna, come here! At once!"

He passed his hand gently over his son's hair—Zachary was not accustomed to such marks of tenderness from his father—and said: "Go to your room; if I need you I'll send for you."

Zachary met his nurse in the doorway. She, too, had a red face; but she entered the room with a firm and assured step.

Through the door the boy could hear his father's loud voice. Its hoarseness agitated him most of all.

"How could you dare?" Then followed a coarse word that made the boy equally ashamed for his father and the nurse.

But Maria Ivanovna's voice outshouted his father's. Zachary could hear it even in his room.

How long the dispute lasted Zachary did not know. It might have been ten minutes or it might have been two hours. But when he was summoned to the study his father greeted him quite calmly, although his cheeks and eyes were still red and his ears seemed to be burning. His father told him to come nearer, drew him close against his knee —a thing he had never used to do—and said: "When you're older you'll understand everything, understand it for yourself. Until that time comes you have no need to understand. At present you mustn't trouble about anything but your studies; all you must strive for is to become a good man, to love all men, do evil to nobody, keep straight and help others wherever you can. That is our religion, the religion of all men whether they are Christians or Jews. Do you promise faithfully?"

"Yes," replied the boy loudly and firmly in a tone quite unlike his usual one, a confident tone such as he hardly ever used, at least to his father.

The father took Zachary's head in his hot hands and said: "Now give me a kiss and go to bed, my child."

CHAPTER IX

THE MOTHER'S DEATH

A SHY, RESERVED boy, Zachary found it difficult to make friends; but once he was devoted to any one it was with the whole ardor of his exalted soul; then he was as jealous of his chosen friend as of a beloved woman. During his years at the high school he had one or two friendships of this kind which had a deep influence upon him. But in spite of his violent and jealous love for his friends the boy felt lonely and passed his youth without knowing real happiness.

Shortly before the end of his term at the high school he learned that his mother had died abroad. Death had come upon her before he could see her again. It had been settled that in summer after his final examination he was to travel to Geneva to see his mother: but before the winter was over she was dead.

The sad news was brought to him by his father. One winter day Gabriel Haimovitch arrived unannounced at Ekaterinburg. Zachary noticed at once a black crêpe band on his sleeve, and his heart contracted. Strangely enough Maria Ivanovna, too, immediately noticed the black crêpe on her master's sleeve and the black band on his hat; she grew pale and bit her lip. The servants also had come to their conclusions; they did not dare to raise their voices and went about the house on tiptoe. Gabriel Haimovitch washed, went to his room, and sent for Zachary.

Before Zachary had time to sit down his father began in a strange voice, an affected voice—or so at least it seemed to Zachary: "My dear boy, I must prepare you for very sad news. I have personally taken on the task of breaking it to you, and I have come to Ekaterinburg for that purpose alone. It is solely for that that I've made this long journey . . ." his father's teeth chattered; he sought for words to finish his sentence but could find none. Zachary—he was now a youth of eighteen with a dark downy growth on his upper lip and chin—stood as stiffly before his father as he did when the rector questioned him. His feet seemed wooden, his whole body felt stiff, and the blood faded from his round young face. Pale as death he stood before his father gazing straight into his face with twitching lips, and remained silent.

"I know you will need a father's love and kindness now; for that reason, solely for that reason, I have come personally," again his father struggled to find words and avoided Zachary's eyes. His gaze strayed over his glasses to the darkness outside the window.

Once more Zachary felt something dishonest in his father's voice. It hurt him more than the dreadful news that he was about to hear.

He still maintained a stubborn silence; but his underlip quivered.

"Your mother is dead," at last his father brought out the dreadful words. "She died on the 19th of February at eight o'clock in the morning in a sanatorium for lung diseases at Davos."

Once more Zachary felt there was something insincere in his father's voice. It turned him to stone: he stood without moving and said nothing.

"As you know your mother was ill, always ill; she suffered from enlargement of the liver, and her lungs, too, were affected. The disease was an old one, it dated from her girlhood; it was caused, no doubt, by the Petersburg air, the damp, the canals. That is why she has lived for such a long time abroad. She needed the sun and had to go into a sanatorium. Unfortunately I could not be with her always, as I would gladly have been. My business constantly prevented me."

Zachary still remained silent; his lips were trembling. He did not cry, he kept his composure. Serious and deathly pale, he looked his father straight in the face. And still his father avoided his glance and gazed out through the window.

"The only offense against your mother that I can charge myself with," his father began again hesitatingly, after a pause, "the only serious offense, is that I was not beside her deathbed at the hour when she needed me most. I can account for that by the fact that I did not know how serious the position was. Nobody knew. The end came unexpectedly, suddenly, and my grave responsibilities to my firm, with whose existence the happiness of thousands of families is bound up, kept me chained to my desk. So I can justify myself before you, my son, and before God and my fellow-men. All the same it is an unforgivable sin, yes, I know it, I feel it, an unforgivable sin that I, her husband, was not beside her when she was dying. The only one there was Aunt Annie; but I, her husband, was not there. I shall never be able to forgive myself. . . ." At these words he drew out a white handkerchief and held it to his eyes.

"Why is he doing that? Why? Why?" Zachary asked himself the question, and it cut him like a knife. He meant the handkerchief that his father had put to his eyes.

"But you have nothing to say? You stand there dumb? Why are you silent; why do you say nothing?" His father had suddenly noticed Zachary's motionless rigidity.

Zachary was awakened out of his stupefaction as by a knock on the head: "Yes, yes, forgive me, father, forgive me—I would like to be alone for a little now." And he turned to leave.

"I understand, my dear boy, I understand," replied his father, and a stream of genuine tears burst from his eyes.

"Stop that! Do stop that!" Zachary suddenly shouted at his father so violently, in such a furious voice, that Gabriel Haimovitch was startled. He could not understand such an outburst. When he saw that Zachary's fists were clenched he sought to calm him: "Restrain yourself, my dear lad, restrain yourself. Everything in measure! We must submit to God's will." But Gabriel Haimovitch's words were wasted on the empty air: Zachary had rushed out and shut himself in his room.

"It was too great a blow for him; I should have thought out some way of breaking the news gradually. He shouldn't have been told straight away. It's been too much for him, too much. . . ." The father went on muttering to himself. Then he rang for Maria Ivanovna.

"Look after him, look after him as if you were his mother; I'm anxious about him; it was too great a blow for him, too great a blow."

"Calm yourself, Gabriel Haimovitch, calm yourself: the child will have a good cry and everything will be all right again. After all she was his own mother who bore him." While saying this she lifted her white apron and dried with it the cold sweat on Gabriel's lofty brow, cheeks and beard. The old man did not notice that it was him instead of his son that the nurse was comforting.

"Why, you're bathed in sweat, Gabriel Haimovitch," she added.

In his helplessness Gabriel Haimovitch let Maria Ivanovna wipe his face as if he were an infant having his tears dried by his mother. Meanwhile he went on muttering to himself without stopping: "Why did he shout at me? . . . And why wouldn't he let me cry? Why?"

Suddenly he noticed that Maria Ivanovna was wiping his face and trying to comfort him. Ashamed, he pushed her away, drew out his white handkerchief, and himself dried his face with it.

"Go to him: I'm anxious about the boy."

Zachary had shut himself up in his room. He could not cry, nor did he wish to. He sat down at the table, put his head on his hands and tried, as so often before, to summon up his mother's image. But this time he could not; he could no longer remember how his mother looked, could recall neither her face, nor her figure, nor her hands. He was forced to get up and gaze at the little photograph of his mother that hung on the wall above his bed.

The photograph awoke no sad thoughts in him. The face no longer reminded him of a living human being very near to him, who had just died. The photograph seemed to him like a reproduction of some picture that one sees every day without actually knowing whether the figure shown in it ever really existed or was merely an imagination of the painter. Hard as he tried to summon up the memory of a living being once near to him, the memory of her physical presence, so that he might become fully conscious of his grief, he could not. He knew that he should do what every one did in such cases: he should weep, should tear his hair in grief, should in some way evince his agony, his sorrow. But he was aware of nothing, could do nothing: for by no means could he summon to his mind any picture of his mother's death. The huge photograph upstairs in the drawing-room, the white neck, the eyes, the face—all these had ceased really to live for a long time and yet they were still alive. He had only to shut his eyes to see her and smell the perfume mingled with the odor of naphthalene that clung to her clothes. Was that being dead?

Zachary was ashamed to leave his room, since he could neither weep, nor scream, nor do any of the things that must be expected of him. He could hear Maria Ivanovna walking up and down outside his door. Like a dumb animal she walked up and down there, tried to spy through the keyhole or a crack at what he was doing and how he felt, yet did not dare to address even a single word to him. . . . And yet he longed so intensely that she might call him; for then he would have an excuse for leaving his room. . . .

He was ashamed of himself for having shouted at his father and for not letting him cry.

"How could I do such a thing? How could I? What right had I? What a nasty creature I must be! A degraded creature! I wouldn't let him cry when his tears came of themselves, his tears for the death of his wife and my mother."

Zachary saw theoretically how unjustly he had acted, yet he could not feel that he had done wrong. His feelings told him that he had been right in acting as he did, even though he could not understand the reason and object of such conduct.

He left his room sooner than everybody had expected—and without being summoned. Before his door he found Maria Ivanovna; she was wiping her eyes in her apron. When nobody was looking she cried quietly to herself; but she would have given anything rather than let others see her tears.

"Why are you crying like a fool?" he shouted angrily at her. His face showed no sign of tears. He knew that and it seemed to him that now everybody must see how heartless he was.

He softly entered his father's study. Gabriel Haimovitch was sitting just as he had done before and staring out through the window at the darkness. A deep pity for his father rose up in Zachary as he watched him unobserved and saw how helpless and unhappy he was. "And I, brute that I am," Zachary thought, "cut short his tears without pity. I did that, I, who have a stony unfeeling heart myself. What a miserable creature I am!" Softly and shyly he went over to his father. "Can you forgive me, father? Please, please, forgive me!" he cried, and at these words he could no longer restrain the tears that now came of themselves to his eyes. It was not his mother's death that summoned them, but his remorse at the way he had used his father.

"Is it you, Zachary, my boy?" His father awoke out of his brooding. "Well, have you got over it now, my child?"

"Forgive me, father, I was so rude, so insensitive! Forgive me!"

"I've nothing to forgive you, my dear boy. I understand. I understand. We must try to comfort each other now. Come here to me, Zachary."

Zachary went up to his father, but instead of flinging himself into the arms opened for him he seized his father's hand and pressed his moist quivering lips to it.

CHAPTER X

THE FATHER'S MISTRESS

AFTER passing through the high school Zachary went up to Petersburg University. The great house in Ekaterinburg was kept open so that the family "tradition" might be maintained: but Zachary, Maria Ivanovna and Mamma's photograph migrated to the capital, where the father ran the head office of his great business. Zachary was accommodated in a modest little flat. His father stayed on in the palatial Hotel Europe.

As, after his arrival in Petersburg, Zachary came to know his father's way of life more intimately, he soon discovered the true reason why his mother had gone abroad. His father and mother had separated. The cause of their separation had been his father's relations with another woman, a Petersburg opera singer.

These relations still continued. Gabriel Haimovitch had set up his mistress in a luxurious establishment in the most modern quarter of the city; it was in the Kameno-Ostrovsky Prospect. She had her own carriage. The lady in question, once a celebrated beauty, was well known in Petersburg by her professional name Helena. Officially Gabriel Haimovitch resided at the hotel; in reality he only entered his name in the hotel register and lived with his lady. Irresponsible rumor would have it that she had borne him several illegitimate children.

When Zachary learned all this he was about twenty and in his first year as a law student at the university. The relations between his father and the opera singer came to his knowledge without his having to be told very explicitly about them. In the circles where his father introduced him the fact was so universally known that nobody thought it necessary to conceal it from the son. Now that he knew of Helena's existence Zachary understood for the first time the pain and sorrow that looked out of his mother's beautiful eyes. He felt all the bitter resignation in the smile on her thin lips, her look of humbled pride. She was one of the "rejected"—she with her proud alabaster neck had been cast off for a cheap opera singer! Oh God, how she must have suffered! How much bitterness she must have had to swallow! One could see that still in a thickening that showed on her long throat; all the bitterness seemed to have gathered there. . . .

Zachary felt within himself the sadness that enveloped his mother's image; the secret that he had discovered was in a way a commentary on his mother's portrait. Now he looked upon it with quite different eyes and could read everything in that face which for many months had moldered in the ground. . . .

"Oh God, how much the poor creature must have had to suffer! Why, he murdered her, murdered her with his own hands!" Zachary groaned to himself.

Yet he nursed no anger against his father. When he was not with him he felt something like anger at him, it is true; perhaps it was really anger, perhaps something else: a feeling of pity for an unhappy human being. "He did not understand mother, he never saw her as she was, the unhappy man!"

But when Zachary was with his father and looked in his great watery blue eyes with the bulging bags beneath them, when he saw his father's familiar nose and reddish-fair side-whiskers—then every angry thought vanished and all that remained was filial love and respect.

"I have no right to judge him. Who can say what brought him to do what he did? Who can say how much he has suffered because of it?" the young man told himself.

When a human being who is near to us does something that is wrong it binds us to him just as closely as his good actions, perhaps indeed still more closely. Could it have been the cruelty of his father to his mother that now drew Zachary so powerfully to him? In any case Zachary felt a deep respect for him which was quite unaffected by his deep sense of his father's injustice. He did not dare to criticize his father even in secret, and as a matter of course he always silenced Maria Ivanovna whenever she uttered any reproach against his father or tried to enlist him against "that woman," with whom—so she said—his father's alliance was "a scandal and shame in the face of God and man."

"She's to blame for everything; she put him up to everything. You don't know women, my little pigeon. You're still a young innocent, although you've got a mustache sprouting under your nose! She put him up to treating your mother so badly, the trollop! Be on your guard against her!"

"Be silent! Be silent at once! It isn't for you to talk about my father; every word against him is an insult to me—do you understand? Be silent at once! How dare you talk like that?" he shouted at his nurse.

He himself thought no evil of "that woman who was to blame for everything," nor would he allow any one else to speak evil of her, and particularly after he came to know her. Incredible as it may sound, he himself made the first advance; more, he himself actually hinted to his father that he would like to make Helena Stepanovna's acquaintance. Gabriel Haimovitch had always taken care not to mention that name before his son, and the two of them never referred to "that woman"; yet the father knew that his affair was known to Zachary. Nevertheless he reddened when he heard Zachary uttering the lady's name, and his ears burned as they had done when his twelve-year-old son asked him about his religion. He became as awkward as a child that has been caught doing something wrong. Zachary was disagreeably struck by his father's embarrassment; he reproached himself with lack of tact, although he had brought out his request frankly, without any afterthought and as delicately as he could. Yet now that the ice was broken the father seemed to be very pleased that his son had mentioned Helena's name, and replied in a natural, almost indifferent tone:

"If you're really eager to make Helena Stepanovna's acquaintance we'll pay her a visit together some time. She, too, will be very glad to see you."

The "woman" was not at all so dreadful as Zachary had pictured her; on the contrary she comported herself very modestly and her attitude to Gabriel Haimovitch was entirely respectful. She did not *tutoyer* him, nor did she treat him with tell-tale obsequiousness. They talked together like good friends and did not once display embarrassing signs of intimacy. . . . Nor were any children to be seen to greet his father familiarly as "Papa." Helena Stepanovna was a stately blonde. Her complexion and the shoulders that emerged from her filmy dress were snowy white misted with rose. Her head was framed in numberless downy curls which made it seem bigger than it was. She smoked very thin cigarettes one after the other in a long mouthpiece. Her face was covered somewhat too thickly with powder, which occasionally fell in light showers. She used a strong perfume which could be perceived far and wide. . . .

It was not his mother's refined discreet perfume, but a different one, and that very fact pleased Zachary without his knowing it. Helena Stepanovna was a happy, frank creature with warm and natural manners. When father and son entered the father kissed her hand, but Zachary could not bring himself to the point of doing that. She stretched out both hands to the young man and commanded him to sit down beside her on the sofa. In the soft light of the shaded lamp she went on talking to him as naturally as if she had known him for years. So all the fears, the heart-poundings, the youthful embarrassment that Zachary had felt on entering her boudoir vanished at once.

"I've known your father for a long, long time, for many, many years, ever since we were both young. That makes me all the more glad to know his son. I've heard a great deal about you, about your school days, even about you when you were quite a little boy. I lived through your childhood with you, in a sense," she said with a frank friendly smile, handing him a cup of tea. Her voice had a pleasantly warm and musical ring.

It turned out that Helena Stepanovna was acquainted with all the details of his boyhood. She inquired after Maria Ivanovna and asked whether the nurse still watched as strictly as ever over his health and his meals.

"You must free yourself a little from her influence, my young friend; it's high time you did. You're not a child now with a nurse who can dictate your comings and goings to you."

Thus she tried to encourage him.

"And you've left Stepan Ivanovitch behind there in the house? Is he still as sleepy as ever? Do you still feel your left arm painful sometimes, the one you sprained on the ice when you were fourteen? I can see the pneumonia you had after that chill when you were seven has left no bad consequences. Do you still get your catarrh every autumn? Well, you don't need to take cod liver oil now, I should think, for one can see that you've grown up into a fine fellow."

Zachary glanced at his father in astonishment. How did this woman come to know all about his childhood? But before he had time to express his surprise Helena Stepanovna gave him the reassuring explanation: "We have grown up with you, my young friend, without seeing you, without knowing you. Here in this distant place we have lived through all your illnesses: we were kept informed of everything."

Zachary felt both pleased and displeased. Actually all this was an insult to his mother: for after all Helena Stepanovna was a stranger. How could she be so interested in a strange child whom she had robbed of his father? Nevertheless Zachary could not resist feeling a pleasant sensation of warmth: there had been some one unknown to him and far away from him who had followed every event in his life.

This feeling quickly created a cordial, almost intimate atmosphere. Helena Stepanovna produced several photographs of him, all taken after his second year in the high school. They were mounted in a big frame and stood beside her mirror. Among them he recognized a snapshot taken on the ice, a group photograph of the fourth class in the school, and several others that he had sent to his mother. Apparently his father had pocketed a copy of each during his short visits to Ekaterinburg.

The feeling that these things were an insult to his mother grew stronger within Zachary; he felt that he must take her side, feel for her now that she herself could no longer do so, be jealous for her: "How could they take and keep my photographs?" Yet the knowledge that he, though quite unknown to Helena Stepanovna, had always stood there beside her mirror, brought him closer to her.

Helena Stepanovna did not urge him to stay for dinner, and that pleased him. His father did not stay either and that also pleased him. Father and son left the boudoir together with the promise that Zachary would soon return again. "Whenever you feel you want to visit me, any time you like, with or without your father—just come—without ceremony—as you would to some one you've known for a long time."

On leaving, Zachary kissed Helena Stepanovna's hand, and her penetrating scent no longer seemed so common to him as it had done at his arrival.

On their way back in the sledge father and son were silent for long periods; the few words they exchanged were about trivial matters. Yet in the middle of one of those conversations the father let fall a few words, more it seemed to himself than to his son; it was as if he were thinking aloud: "I'll never marry again—I've had enough of marriage . . ."

And the son replied, also as if to himself: "Why not?"

Nothing more was said on the subject.

Maria Ivanovna immediately discovered that Zachary had paid a visit to "the woman who was to blame for everything." How she discovered it remained a riddle, for nobody had said anything to her. But Maria Ivanovna had a fine nose for things that were in the air. Her displeasure did not find expression in words, but it could be distinctly felt.

She went about with an offended expression: at such times she was always disagreeably polite and formal. But this time she was absolutely insufferable. She stood about in corners, her eyes swimming with tears, and morosely prowled about the house. One day Zachary found his mother's photograph draped in voluminous folds of crêpe and garlanded with white roses as if she had died only the day before.

"What do you really want? She's a good friend to father and has been for years, and she's not in the least as dreadful as you think.

Helena Stepanovna is a very good woman, and I'm certain that it's lies what people say about her. She's a good woman, and you should be ashamed of thinking evil of a good and pure woman."

To this rebuke Maria Ivanovna replied not a word. But when Zachary had finished she growled into her headcloth: "They've forgotten the dead, both father and son. How is it that she gets round you, the trollop?"

"Don't interfere in these matters, do you hear?"

"Why, certainly! Who am I, after all? I'm only a servant: what say can I have in such matters? But when your heart is bleeding surely you can be allowed to speak. As soon as you're under the ground you're forgotten by your own flesh and blood."

"Now look here, nurse, listen to me. It isn't as you think," said Zachary in his defense.

It was of no use. Whenever he visited Helena Stepanovna he was made to feel Maria Ivanovna's cold jealousy, and something in her affection for him seemed to be killed.

But he could not help himself; he had to visit Helena Stepanovna. He seemed actually to be attracted by her. His original aversion to her had turned to affection; out of enmity had come friendship. For after all Helena Stepanovna was the only human being in the great, strange city except his father whom he knew and with whom he was closely bound. She knew all about his life, and she also knew so well how to treat him that the hours he spent in her boudoir were the only ones when he really did feel at home. Besides, Helena Stepanovna was an intelligent woman, in that resembling his mother, and quite different from Maria Ivanovna, who hitherto had represented womanhood and motherhood to him.

Zachary often arrived at Helena Stepanovna's without his father. He always found in her what he needed most: the guiding hand of an experienced and intelligent woman, who had the purest maternal feelings for him. She could talk so frankly, naturally and calmly about the things that troubled him, even the most intimate of them, that he felt no embarrassment or shame before her and told her all his secrets.

And it can be claimed that through her father and son were brought closer together. In Zachary's first few months in Petersburg the two of them, who hitherto had seen each other very seldom and did not know much about each other, had already become intimate. Gabriel Haimovitch found a need to be much in his son's company. It was the first time that he had ever felt it. He grew proud of his son. Often he came for supper to Zachary's flat, ate with enjoyment Maria Ivanovna's simple messes, and spent the evening with his son. He talked about business matters, about his friends, and sometimes also about politics. Zachary, who was not used to such treatment, felt more warmly drawn to his father every day and nursed a profound, grateful respect for him.

CHAPTER XI

THE MOTHER'S SHADOW VANISHES

Gabriel Haimovitch was growing old. Dark rings shadowed his eyes, and the bags beneath them grew heavier and heavier. He was always tired when he visited his son in the evening, and had to rest on the sofa for a little until he recovered. And the older he grew the more marked became his sentimentality and his dependence on his son. During his last years at the university Zachary was visited daily by his father.

Gabriel Haimovitch spoke more and more frequently to him of his forbears and his race. He often expressed regret that he had neglected his traditional religion so much and passed his whole life in a foreign environment. In this way he came to speak of the theme that he had always avoided mentioning to Zachary during his childhood.

"The more they hate us, the more strongly I feel our worth and above all our superiority to them; just try to picture them living for half a year in our shoes—what would become of them?"

By "us" Gabriel Haimovitch meant the Jews, by "them" the Christians. His son looked at him in astonishment: what had put such thoughts all of a sudden into his father's head? What had happened to the old man?

The universal reactionary atmosphere in the country, and more specifically the Antisemitism and the oppression of the Jews, had driven the aloof and detached Gabriel Haimovitch into the ranks of his compatriots.

"I'm very sorry I didn't give you a Jewish education and that I concealed everything about your race from you so carefully while you were young. But that doesn't matter now; the mistake can be repaired. The one thing essential now is to stick to our own people," he began one evening when he arrived in a very tired state.

"What has happened, father?"

"Nothing has happened, but I'm sick to death of it all—their speeches in the Duma, their special laws directed against us, their whole attitude to us!"

Zachary remained silent.

"I'm sorry I didn't settle abroad long ago and bring you up there in quite a different atmosphere; it would probably have been better for the whole family."

Zachary flushed: it was the first time his father had mentioned the "family." From these words Zachary divined all his father's loneliness and disappointment.

"And here have I spent all my life in a kind of dream, thinking that I was working for others and that I was somebody, that I was sharing in the development of the country, that I had taken root in the life around me, and was a citizen of a great nation. God knows I'm a Russian by my very nature and have never been anything else—for I ignored my original nature, I've never really known it! And then suddenly you have the feeling that you've spent your whole life out in the street, as it were, and have never known the true happiness of having a home."

One day Gabriel Haimovitch took Zachary to his counting-house and handed him a large sum of money with instructions to bear it to a well-known Jew in Petersburg for an important object involving the honor and name of the whole Jewish people.

"I want to show them that I am with them in these sad times, and I want my son himself to give them the money; they must be made to see that my son and I are with them."

Zachary performed his task. When it was known from whom the money came he was greeted with astonished looks, and at first there was some hesitation in accepting the donation: "Hm, Gabriel Haimovitch Mirkin—we thought that he belonged to the other side for good...."

Only at Helena Stepanovna's, where he now spent all his leisure along with his son, did Gabriel Haimovitch feel happy. Her house was the only one in Petersburg that the two men visited. In consequence of his deliberate separation from the Jews the father had hardly any connection with Jewish society. He obviously had not felt at home recently in the Russian circles composed of high State officials and generals whom he did business with and had often visited at one time, and he cut adrift from them more and more. Only at Helena Stepanovna's did he really feel happy, and he did not conceal the fact from his son. Under her influence he regained once more his assurance and his confident bearing; with her his hopes revived and his courage and good-humor returned.

She always knew what tone to assume to put him in the right humor. At the first glance she could see where the shoe pinched him, and would set herself to soothe him down. When she saw that his eyes were dull she knew that he had had worries during the day. And she would lightly waft away his gloomy thoughts as by a wave of her fan: "Good God, there's no reason for getting annoyed and making life sadder than it is.... They're all poor sticks, you could buy them all with a three-rouble note, from the office boys to the grand dukes. Just let them smell your money, and you'll see they'll fawn on you like poodles.

"And after all," she would continue, if the desired effect was still wanting, "who are these people? What have they done for Russia? What are they doing for it? You've always had to put through your plans in the teeth of their opposition. Do you think people don't know that? Just today Michail Georgevitch of the *Financial Times* was here and we talked about your great plan for the Transbaikalian Railway ... And have you read what the Moscow *Morning Herald* has been saying about the twentieth anniversary of the Siberian Railway? They devote a whole column to you. Three whole pages, I'm told, are given to you in the new Russian Encyclopedia. I have it here too; Michail Georgevitch sent it to me. Believe me, Russia knows quite well who is building it up and who is pulling it down; and one day it will pay its debt to the full."

All the articles that Helena Stepanovna mentioned had been inspired by her and paid for out of Gabriel Haimovitch's money; a collection of them always lay in readiness in her boudoir to comfort the old man when necessary....

The son saw what a great influence this woman had on his father, and one evening as they were driving home from her house he began: "Father, why don't you marry her? I think it would be good for your..."

His father did not let him finish. A warning glance made Zachary pause. Then Gabriel Haimovitch stared up at the dark sky.

"I've already told you that I had enough the first time..."

After a pause he went on: "Helena Stepanovna doesn't belong to our religion; that's one obstacle among several others. I wouldn't advise you either, my son, to marry a woman of another religion. I was always a liberal and I still am today. I recognize no difference between Jew and Christian—still I wouldn't like to see it, as long..." Gabriel Haimovitch did not finish his sentence.

A few days later he went to the headquarters of the Jewish community and had himself and his son officially registered as members. He explained that this had not been done before because he and his son were strangers in Petersburg and had for many years lived in Ekaterinburg, where there was no Jewish community.

After that Gabriel Haimovitch began to concern himself publicly with Jewish affairs and devoted considerable sums to Jewish objects.

In this new work he came to know the celebrated Jewish advocate, Solomon Ossipovitch, and after completing his studies Zachary entered the advocate's office as his assistant.

Actually Gabriel Haimovitch was against Zachary's going into the legal profession. He had counted upon his son's entering the Petersburg office after finishing his studies, and finally taking over the business which he himself had built up into one of the wealthiest and most publicly respected in Russia. So that, when his son mentioned his own plans, Gabriel Haimovitch's disappointment was great. A quarrel might have resulted if the adroit and ever vigilant Helena

Stepanovna had not come to the rescue. Thanks solely to her intercession the father agreed that Zachary should serve for a few years in the famous advocate's office, so that for every eventuality he might have a profession to fall back upon. Zachary did not absolutely reject the idea of entering his father's business later, and thus the decision was postponed for a time.

For more than a year now he had been working in the advocate's office. He still maintained his own little flat; his father lived officially at his hotel and unofficially with Helena Stepanovna. Recently, however, Gabriel Haimovitch had frequently talked of taking a big house where he and Zachary could live together.

Zachary kept on postponing his decision on that head....

Since the conclusion of his studies nothing of great note had happened in Zachary's life, except that soon after his entrance into the lawyer's office he had fallen in love with Nina. In spite of her youth Nina was famed for her beauty in all Petersburg, and that she should make a deep impression on Zachary was only to be expected. After all she was the first woman to enter his life, the first truly feminine being since his mother, whose lovely image he had carried in his heart ever since his childhood.

Both Gabriel Haimovitch and Helena Stepanovna knew of Zachary's secret love; and although he had not spoken a word about it, Nina's parents knew it too; but the one who knew it best was Nina herself. Everybody regarded the affair with approval and hoped that it would lead as soon as possible to the happy end which they all desired.

Before we conclude our description of Zachary's childhood and student years, one more episode must be related which, though it has no direct connection with the events in our story, is yet of some importance and worth mentioning.

When one evening shortly after he had got his doctor's degree Zachary arrived at his flat, he found to his astonishment that Maria Ivanovna was not there. This happened very rarely, at most twice in the year when Maria Ivanovna attended the great church festivals; at other times she hardly ever left the house, for she felt herself a stranger in the huge city and had no acquaintances. Zachary went into Maria Ivanovna's room and saw that her trunks were packed and that even her bedclothes were tied up in a bundle. He could not make out what all this meant and waited in high impatience for her return. When at last she arrived, weary and downcast, he gazed at her in surprise and asked, pointing to the trunks: "What does this mean, Maria Ivanovna? Are you going on a journey?"

"The moment has come for me, too, Zachary Gavrilovitch," for the first time she called him by his father's name, "the moment has come for me, too, to leave you. I promised your poor mother before she left the house for ever to guard her only son and stay with him until he finished his studies. Now, thanks be to God, you are grown up and need me no longer. I have faithfully kept my vow to your dead mother; now I can go my own way."

Zachary let her finish. He could not make out what she meant at first. Finally he came to the conclusion that something had offended her.

"What's gone wrong with you? Have you gone out of your senses? It's the only explanation I can find for your words."

"You don't need me any longer; what use have you for me now? When you were little it was different; you're grown up now, and there are other people you can depend on to interest themselves in you."

Zachary laughed heartily.

"Oh, that's what you're getting at! You can't keep me tied to your apron strings any longer, eh, for now I'm really grown up?"

"That isn't what I meant. . . . I mean something . . . something different."

"What do you mean?"

"You know quite well what I mean. . . . That woman you all pour out your secrets to—she's bewitched you, or something . . ."

Zachary put his arms round her and kissed her: "Are you jealous?"

"I'm not jealous, but your mother in her grave is jealous; it's a great sorrow to her that her own son should turn against her."

Zachary grew pale and his arms fell from the nurse's shoulders.

Nothing he could say was of any use. Maria Ivanovna refused to stay. With difficulty he succeeded by calling in his father's assistance (Gabriel Haimovitch as her master still possessed a certain authority over Maria Ivanovna) in persuading her to return to the house in Ekaterinburg. She was allotted an ample allowance for the remainder of her life.

Maria Ivanovna took the big photograph of Zachary's mother back with her to Ekaterinburg and set it up again in the cold, unused drawing-room.

With that the last shadow of his mother vanished....

CHAPTER XII

A STRANGE WOOING

WHEN ZACHARY rose from his bed on the morning after the party at Sophia Arkadievna's to which he had escorted Nina, he had come to a decision. Ever since his childhood he had been unaccustomed to do anything on his own responsibility, but always to obtain first somebody's sanction for it. So he decided, before he asked Nina the decisive question, to confide it first to her mother. It seemed to him that he would achieve his designs on Nina most easily in that way. With Olga Michailovna he had felt on almost intimate terms for a long time; for he had divined the mother in her long before he had discovered the woman in Nina. This made her far more accessible to him than Nina was. All the same the feelings he had for Olga Michailovna were not merely the feelings one has for one's mother; his respect for her, however, kept those other feelings from rising....

Zachary dressed more carefully than usual and with a pounding heart entered Olga Michailovna's boudoir.

Women often summon their maternal instincts to their aid when they fancy they can no longer impress sufficiently by their feminine charm. There are women also who take a special pleasure in pouring out their maternal feelings on certain men, in scolding them, punishing them and simultaneously flattering them. This attitude is not the product of calculation, but of natural causes.

Olga Michailovna was one of those women. Although she had not by any means resigned in favor of her grown-up daughter, and indeed was quite aware that her ripe experience gave her an advantage over the immature Nina, she was not loath, nevertheless, to enhance her charms by employing the particular gift with which nature and time had dowered her—her warm maternal sympathy.

When Zachary entered her boudoir he found her sitting in an easy chair in her favorite place by the stove. To him she seemed wrapped as in a cloud in the unique mystery that emanated from her presence and her being. She was busily embroidering.

Olga Michailovna's boudoir was warm, bright and comfortable. She was wearing as usual a black silk dress with a lace collar. Black was her favorite color, since it best set off her fine complexion, emphasized her black hair and eyebrows and gave stateliness to her figure. The warm reflection of a transparent white china vase lay on her glistening black hair, which, smoothly parted in the middle, fell on either side of her bent head. She knew that it was Zachary by his knock, and she called to him through the door in her deep, full voice, that always made his heart beat faster: "Is it you? Just come in, my dear."

Yet when Mirkin entered she did not seem to notice him, but kept her face bent over her embroidery. Then, after a while, she lifted her head in surprise and gazed at him affectionately.

"Oh, it's you, Zachary Gavrilovitch? Just come over here. Manka (the housemaid) told me a little while ago that you were asking for me. But do come nearer, my young friend: I had a feeling that you were wanting to see me. I've sent poor Naum Grigorovitch away, all for your sake"—she smiled at him and held out her beautifully shaped hand to be kissed.

"Yes, I wanted to see you. Please forgive the liberty."

"It's a good thing you've come, for in the first place I want to give you a good scolding—you must allow that privilege in a woman far older than you. Now, tel me, Zachary Gavrilovitch, why did you let Nina go to that fancy dress ball last night? I thought you were both sitting in Nina's room, but this morning I learn that you not only gave her permission to go, but helped her to go!"

Mirkin was silent. He was always more embarrassed with older women than with those of his own age.

"What's really wrong with you, Zachary Gavrilovitch?" she asked, staring at him with her fine black eyes.

"How do you mean, Olga Michailovna?" Mirkin glanced at her apprehensively, like a boy looking up at his mother.

"Forgive my frankness. You know that we in this house all love you. So I'll take the liberty of being quite open with you. If I had any right to preach at you I would say: 'it's high time for you to become a man, a free independent man conscious of his responsibilities. It's high time for you to leave your nursery behind you, Zachary Gavrilovitch.' Don't be offended with me; I'm saying this out of pure affection. You really aren't angry with me . . . ?"

"Of course not, Olga Michailovna, quite the contrary; I'm very grateful to you, thankful to you," replied Zachary, flushing.

"First of all then, why are you so uneasy? A man has no right to be uneasy. Only we women have that right. Why have you no assurance? In other words why are you still such a child?" cried Olga Michailovna impatiently. "It's high time you were a man—do you hear, Zachary Gavrilovitch?—a free, firm, resolute man!" So she upbraided him with motherly severity.

"Yes, yes, Olga Michailovna, it's quite true; just go on! Please go on, say everything you want to say! I'm grateful for every word."

"I know that your upbringing is responsible for it all; I know it. You've always been on old women's leading strings. You've always been shielded by old women. First it was Maria Ivanovna, and now the rôle has been taken up by 'the lovely Helena.' It really doesn't suit her. And the one thing that I could wish for you is: free yourself once and for all from old women! Be yourself for a change, yourself, yourself! Will you promise me that?"

Mirkin listened patiently to her lecture. His face was burning. But her words did him good; a feeling he had never known before flooded all his body; it was somewhat like the feeling he had had as a child when his mother put him to bed and carefully tucked him in the warm blankets. . . .

"And what ought I to do, do you think?" he asked. "Tell me, Olga Michailovna."

"Oh, that's just what's wrong with you, if you don't mind my aying so; you always ask others: 'What ought I to do?' Do you think I've taken over the rôle of Maria Ivanovna and 'the lovely Helena'? No, that's not why I'm talking to you like this. You shouldn't ask other people: you should ask yourself! You must cease depending once and for all on outside influences. You must stop asking other people. You must put an end to your hesitation, your shilly-shallying, your lependence on other people's authority, and take responsibility for ourself. It may be very comforting to leave all the responsibility to others, but it isn't very manly, Zachary Gavrilovitch; it's more what one would expect of a boy than of a man."

"You're quite right, you're quite right," said Mirkin, more to himself than to Olga Michailovna.

"I know you won't misunderstand me, and that's why I've taken he liberty of talking like this. All that I'm thinking of is your good. Do you believe that?"

"Thank you, thank you, Olga Michailovna," said Mirkin, seizing her hand and covering it with kisses. She did not withdraw her little white hand. With the other she stroked his hair. He leant his head gainst her knee and was filled with infinite comfort.

"Why are you such a child? And you're twenty-seven! Really, t's high time you were a man, Zachary!"

A few moments followed in silence. A tender feeling had sud-enly awakened in Olga Michailovna, and she felt slightly faint. She ecame aware that Zachary was holding her hand and caressing it with his lips. She let him continue and went on: "There. Now I've colded you enough. You came to me for advice and kindness. And efore you could speak I began to scold you. Forgive me."

"Thank you! Thank you!" Mirkin kept on murmuring.

"Well, what was it you wanted to speak to me about, Zachary, when you came in?"

"It was nothing, nothing, I just came to be given a scolding, hat was all. I know that I deserve it, and particularly from you. Oh, es, I did want to speak to you about something, though." Mirkin emembered now why he had come, and began stammeringly to search or words, his heart pounding. "I wanted to ask you for your daugh-er's, for Nina's hand . . . will you let me have it?"

In spite of all the maternal assurance that she displayed for the irresolute young man's benefit this question cast Olga Michailovna into some confusion. But it lasted only for an instant. A soft, almost girlish blush swept over her beautiful face and then vanished, leaving her delicate creamy complexion unchanged.

"Have you spoken to Nina about it?" she asked. He could distinctly hear the beating of her heart.

"No."

"Why have you told me first?" She smiled, showing her teeth which were as white as the necklace of pearls round her neck.

"I thought that perhaps it might be better to discuss it with you first. Why, I don't know; but I find it far easier to speak to you. You understand me, you know all about me . . . and I wanted to beg you, too, Olga Michailovna, to see it through."

"To see what through?" asked Olga Michailovna.

"What I've been speaking about . . . I mean Nina's consent, i I'm not too distasteful to her . . . that is, Olga Michailovna, if you'r agreeable . . . so I would like you to . . ."

"And why are you so unwilling to do it yourself?"

"But I will do it. I've wanted to for a long time. Every da I've come here with the firm intention of doing it, and yet I've neve done it."

"But that's just what I'm always demanding from you—decision How can I do this for you when you aren't prepared to do it yourself?"

"But I am prepared, I really am. I think of nothing else, an I will do it, Olga Michailovna."

"Then why don't you? Are you afraid that Nina might say no?"

"Yes, there's that, too, but it isn't only that. What could happen after all, even if she did say no? Everything would be clear then, a least," said Zachary, once more as if to himself.

"And yet you don't do it. Why?"

"That's just it, Olga Michailovna. I haven't the courage."

"Zachary Gavrilovitch," said Olga Michailovna with sudden vic lence, "do you realize what you're asking of me? Do you know wha you're saying? You want to propose to Nina, and yet you don't, be cause you haven't got the courage. And you expect me to speak fo you? You know that I am Nina's mother. My life is bound up with hers. How can I speak to her about this, even if I wished to? I would like very much to have you as one of the family, I frankly confess it; more, I think it would be highly desirable." Again she blushed like a young girl. "But how can I approach Nina in the name of a man who hasn't the courage to approach her himself? Do you realize what you ask of me in wanting me to assume such a part?"

"No, Olga Michailovna, it isn't a question of courage after all. Yes, now I see it quite clearly, there's something else too. If it was merely a question of courage I could manage it somehow or other. But there's something else. To you I can say quite sincerely and with all my heart and soul: Olga Michailovna, I beg you for the hand of your daughter, but I can't say it to Nina . . ." Zachary's voice died away.

Olga Michailovna remained in horrified silence. She breathed with difficulty, and once more her heart beat loudly, she did not know why. While Mirkin had said those last words he had gazed steadfastly in her eyes, more openly and boldly than she had ever known him do before. She was completely taken by surprise. His eyes glowed, his lips trembled. His hurried breathing, his looks, all his bearing expressed a hidden passion that she could not understand, did not want to understand.

Once more Olga Michailovna blushed, but the blood gradually faded again from her face, which resumed its delicate pallor. Once more she lost her composure for a moment, bowed her head and evaded his passionate, burning glance that astonished her by its boldness. But soon she collected herself and managed to regain her usual equanimity. In a dry, almost matter-of-fact tone she asked: "Tell me, Zachary Gavrilovitch, do you love Nina Solomonovna?"

"I don't know," replied Zachary, his burning glance still firmly fixed upon her.

"You don't know?" she asked with an astonished smile which showed her fine teeth. "You don't know, and yet you ask me for her hand?"

"Because I want you . . . I would like you . . . to be my mother."

A quiver ran through Olga Michailovna's body. She swayed

slightly, closed her eyes, clenched her little hands and said, her eyes still shut: "Be silent! Don't talk such nonsense . . ."

Nevertheless she drew him to her with convulsively trembling hands and with shut eyes kissed him on the brow.

Mirkin tried to catch her hands.

"Compose yourself now, my child," she said in a calm voice, smiling her usual smile. "We'll talk about it later. I think that's Nina coming."

CHAPTER XIII

ZACHARY'S BETROTHAL

ACTUALLY hurried footsteps could be heard outside. Before she reached the door Nina cried: "Are you alone, Mamma?"

Before Olga Michailovna had time to collect herself Nina knocked and, without waiting for a reply, entered. She was in deshabille. A fur-trimmed silk dressing-gown was loosely flung over her Japanese pyjamas. Her loosened hair clung in disordered curls round her bare throat. She was not in the least surprised to find Zachary in her mother's room. As though she had expected it, she said:

"Of course! With Mamma as usual! I'm so sorry to have interrupted you. But it's a good thing I've caught you, Zachary Gavrilovitch. I wanted to tell you that things can't go on like this; you'll either have to accompany me to my friends' houses, or I'll have to go with you to yours. It isn't much of a pleasure to be driven by one's cavalier to the door and then have to face the company alone, when all the other ladies come with their own protectors. If you refuse, there will be nothing left for me but to find some one who'll go with me a step or two past the outside door. Just imagine, Mamma, Zachary Gavrilovitch saw me safely last night to Sophia Arkadievna's door and wouldn't go a step further. And he should be feeling sorry now, too for in some ways it was interesting, very interesting."

"Nina, what are you thinking of? Why, you haven't dressed yet!"

"What does it matter? There's nobody here." She looked at Mirkin.

Neither Mirkin nor her mother paid much attention to her words. Both sat motionlessly in their chairs and did not seem to listen to what she said: they could not rouse themselves at once from their trance.

"Oh, I see that I'm interrupting you. No doubt you've been talking of very important matters. I ask a thousand pardons. I wouldn't disturb you for worlds," said Nina, turning to go.

But Mirkin suddenly got to his feet. Fixing his eyes on the corner of the room he began: "Nina Solomonovna! I beg you to do me the honor, the undeserved honor," he clung to the word like a drowning man, "I beg you . . . I know that I don't deserve the honor . . . I know, I know . . ." he stammered, but then collected himself and said rapidly and clearly: "Will you give me your hand? Will you marry me? Yes, that's what I wanted to ask you."

Nina gazed at him in astonishment.

"Have you gone mad? What's come over you? This is so sudden! Why, I'm not even properly dressed for such an occasion!"

"Please don't laugh at me. I know I don't deserve it, but my whole happiness depends on your answer." Then he fixed his eyes on Olga Michailovna and nodded: "My happiness and my life."

"No, I'm not laughing; but I don't understand. Ah! now I see!" Nina exclaimed, as if she had beheld a dreadful vision. "*That's* what was being discussed! Now I see why the atmosphere was so solemn!" she cried, becoming seriously angry.

"Yes," Olga Michailovna suddenly said from her armchair, "Zachary Gavrilovitch has been asking me for your hand, Nina."

"And he went to Mamma first as usual, before informing me!"

For a moment Mirkin lost his composure, but quickly regained it again. More to the mother than the daughter he said: "I did that, Nina Solomonovna, because I didn't know how you might look on my offer, because I didn't dare to . . ."

"But you *dared* to my mother?"

"Yes, I dared to your mother," replied Mirkin firmly.

"Since that is so, you can get your answer from my mother!" Thereupon she turned to go.

"Nina, what are you doing? Haven't you a heart?" cried Olga

Michailovna from her easy chair. "Zachary merely confided his hopes to me."

"This is my business, Mamma. Isn't that so?" Nina exclaimed. Her face was twisted in a grimace of pain and rage such as her mother had never seen upon it before.

"Yes, Nina, you are right," said Olga Michailovna, lowering her beautiful eyes before her daughter's.

Then an unexpected thing happened. Instead of marching out through the door as she had intended, Nina rushed to her mother, flung her arms round her neck, and wept like a child; she covered her mother's face and hands with kisses and said in a voice choked with sobs: "Forgive me, Mamma, oh, do forgive me! I didn't mean to hurt you, I didn't mean it. You forgive me too," she said, turning at last to Zachary.

"Why should I forgive you, my child? There's nothing to forgive," said Olga Michailovna, lovingly embracing her daughter.

During this whole scene between mother and daughter Mirkin stood on burning coals. His only wish was that the floor might open and swallow him; yet he had not the strength to go, to leave the room, as his sense of propriety told him he should. His feet would not obey him. They seemed rooted to the floor. To excuse himself he kept on muttering without a stop: "It's all my fault, all this is my fault. I'm a fool, an awful fool; forget what I said. Forgive me." At last he found the strength to walk towards the door.

"No, Zachary Gavrilovitch, don't go! I beg you not to go. You've asked me a question and you shall have an answer. Don't go! Don't let him go, Mamma! Please, Mamma, keep him here, just for a moment, I won't be long. And you mustn't go either, Mamma. For God's sake, don't go, I'll be back in a moment." And she ran hastily from the room.

As if turned to stone Olga Michailovna and Mirkin remained rigidly as Nina had left them. Olga Michailovna was sitting in her comfortable armchair. Mirkin stood motionlessly in the middle of the room. Neither spoke a word, neither ventured to look at the other. Olga Michailovna seemed to have completely lost the maternal pride and self-complacence which a few minutes ago she had drawn upon so freely. She was now like a raw schoolgirl caught telling a clumsy lie. The blush that rose to her cheeks burned there steadily. She covered her eyes with her beautiful white hand; her breast rose and fell, and the pearls that gleamed like living drops on her full round bosom were troubled by her breathing. She knew that she must say something, do something. She must extricate herself from this impossible, this scandalous situation in which she found herself; she must save herself. But she could 'hink of nothing. It was as if she were standing before a judge. Mirkin found himself in a similar situation, except that his was somewhat ludicrous as well. Several times he tried to raise his eyes and say something, but he remained silent when he saw Olga Michailovna's shut face.

This painful situation had already lasted for five minutes or even longer, and Nina had not yet returned. The tension grew. But neither of them could summon the courage or energy to move. Nina's command seemed to have rooted them to their places, where they awaited what was to come.

At last Nina appeared fully dressed. She was not wearing one of her usual bizarre costumes, but a black velvet dress of the utmost propriety falling to her ankles. She had flung over it a shawl of Venetian lace, which enhanced the softness and feminine grace of her neck. Her hair had been methodically brushed for the occasion and confined by hairpins, so that it did not curl round her face in its usual picturesque confusion. In this guise she looked much more elegant, dignified and sedate.

"Now, Zachary Gavrilovitch, you can say what you have to say to me," she said, turning to the embarrassed Mirkin.

At that moment Olga Michailovna's energy returned to her. She rose and softly made to leave the room.

"No, Mamma, it's too late now. As he's already said it in your presence you might as well listen." And Nina tried to hold her mother back.

Silently Olga Michailovna kissed her daughter on the brow and tried to release herself.

"No, Mamma, you simply must stay, or else I'll go as well, for this proposal concerns you too. . . ."

"Nina, what's gone wrong with you?" cried her mother, turning pale.

"Nothing, Mamma. But you must stay. Please sit down again in your chair." She took her mother's arm and led her over to the armchair. As if hypnotized Olga Michailovna obeyed.

When she was seated once more Nina turned to the pale-faced Mirkin: "Well, what have you to say to me? I'm prepared to listen."

"Nina Solomonovna, I beg you to honor me with your hand." Mirkin repeated, as if at the word of command, the sentence he had now learned by heart.

"And you, Mamma, have you given your consent?" asked Nina, once more turning to her mother.

"Nina, what's the matter with you? What have I to do with it? You have to decide this, not I." Olga Michailovna had found her tongue again.

"No, Mamma, it shall be as *you* wish it. Have you given your consent: yes or no?"

"Yes," replied the mother in a low voice, as if she were ashamed.

"Then I give my consent too. Here, Zachary Gavrilovitch, here you have 'our' hand!"

Olga Michailovna tried to rise. She bit her lower lip and remained silent.

Mirkin did not dare to take Nina's hand. But she seized his and pressed it firmly; then she bent towards him and kissed him.

"And now, my dear, come over to Mamma. She must give you a kiss too." She led Mirkin to her mother, whose heart was throbbing so loudly that they could hear it.

"Mamma, give him a kiss!"

Olga Michailovna blushed as shyly as a bride and at her daughter's command touched Mirkin's brow with her lips.

"And now we must tell father the news!" cried Nina. She rang for one of the servants and sent him to the office with the request that her father should come at once.

During the few minutes before Solomon Ossipovitch arrived they all three sat in silence without knowing what to do or say. Zachary's proposal seemed to have made the atmosphere still more tense. But when the famous advocate appeared in the doorway with his hair on end as usual, Olga Michailovna at once regained her old assurance, her feminine pride and matronly importance. Her voice trembling with emotion and happiness, she said to her husband: "Solomon Ossipovitch, a great happiness has been granted us; Zachary Gavrilovitch has just asked for Nina's hand and Nina has accepted him." She pronounced the second half of the sentence with particular emphasis.

The advocate, who had been expecting the event for a long time, exclaimed joyously: "Thank God! This makes me very happy." Then he embraced and kissed Mirkin.

"And now, my dear, tell the butler to put some champagne in ice. Zachary Gavrilovitch, you will stay with us for dinner?" asked Olga Michailovna.

"Mamma, I think Zachary Gavrilovitch should first go to his father and tell him the news," said Nina.

Once more Olga Michailovna blushed at the thought that she, the mother, should have overlooked such an obvious demand of propriety; she replied in confusion: "Yes, my child, you're quite right. Zachary Gavrilovitch must go and tell his father. I had quite forgotten. It was my joy that made me . . ." She drew out her embroidered silk handkerchief and wiped a tear from her eye.

"But you'll be certain to come later on in the evening with Gabriel Haimovitch; that's understood, isn't it?" With this command she dismissed her future son-in-law, who bowed deeply over her white hand.

At table, however, in spite of the good spirits into which the news had put Solomon Ossipovitch and Misha, mother and daughter avoided each other's eyes.

CHAPTER XIV

A DROP IN THE OCEAN

A few days after the foregoing incident Mirkin was walking towards the advocate's office a little before the consulting hour when he noticed a crowd in front of the door. He went up to it. But it was some time before he could find out what was the matter. In the middle of the crowd a Jewish woman was standing, and a more remarkable specimen of the genus Mirkin had never seen in his life. Her very clothes were strange; she wore a felt hood with black ribbons, and over it a head cloth. She stood there half-frozen, her nose red with cold and her eyes red with crying, in the middle of the crowd. She twittered like a bird in a language which nobody could make out. In her right hand she clutched convulsively a crumpled and tattered letter. She refused to release it, and showed only the address to the people round her, holding the letter at a safe distance from them, and giving them to know that she wished to see the famous advocate, Halperin. "He must speak for my son, Moses Ben Chaim," she muttered repeatedly to herself.

Later Mirkin discovered that a kind-hearted porter, who had read the address on the letter, had brought her here from the Warsaw Station, where she had arrived with a crowd of other passengers by the morning train. But the doorkeeper had refused her admittance, pointing out that his master's consulting hour was four o'clock. The old woman did not know a word of Russian and could not understand what the man said. She insisted that she must see the lawyer, and the doorkeeper drove her away repeatedly. So she had stood for hours before the house in the freezing cold, hoping that she might find some Jew to whom she might make herself understood. But there was no Jew to be seen far and wide. A great number of men with beards passed, it was true, and assuming that they were Jews she addressed them in her language; but none of them could understand her. So since early morning the Jewish woman had stood shivering in her cloak before the advocate's house, with her Polish hood that she had donned on top of her wig in honor of "Pietersburg," muttering continually to herself: "He must speak for my son, Moses Ben Chaim." But the doorkeeper would not even let her stand in the doorway, for with a torrent of words she assailed every man who entered or left the house, seized him by the arm and kissed his hand, taking him for the famous advocate; and upon all of them, with streaming eyes, she thrust her letter. She was not to be moved from the door, however, and several passers-by became curious and stopped to examine the strange figure more closely. A Turkish fruitseller, thinking she was of his nationality, addressed her in Turkish. But the Jewish woman could not understand him. The little scene would probably have ended in the old woman's being taken to prison, if Mirkin had not appeared at the right moment.

As soon as the doorkeeper saw him he left the old Jewess standing and explained the matter.

"She's been here ever since early this morning; she came straight from the station with her bundle in her hand. She's been told that the consulting hour is four o'clock, but she won't go away. She pesters everybody that passes the door."

Mirkin cut the doorkeeper short and ushered the old woman in.

As she took him for the great advocate she overwhelmed him with a torrent of words. They poured gutturally from her old lips: "Kind sir, you can save my boy, you alone, the holy rabbi said so. Oh, *Panie,* kind sir!"

Mirkin could not make out a word that she was saying, and yet he seemed somehow to understand. A new feeling awoke in him. The more strange the old Jewish woman seemed to him, the more incomprehensible her words, the more deeply he was teased by the desire to discover who and what she was. He found a chair for her in the waiting-room and by signs and dumb show signified that she was to remain sitting. Then he proceeded to the advocate's private apartments.

Olga Michailovna was out. The house-maid informed him that she had gone for a drive with Naum Grigorovitch; the master was still at the courts; Nina Solomonovna was in her room, but in low spirits, for she had a headache.

Mirkin went to his office, which he shared with Weinstein. There he began to put in order documents that would be required during Halperin's consultations.

But his thoughts refused to concentrate on what he was doing. From the corridor he could hear the faint moans of the Jewish woman, which sounded like the clucking of a dying hen, and it would not give him peace. He was tormented by the thought: "Who are these people in their far distant settlement? How do they live? What language can this be that they speak? How strange and remote they all seem, like people in a far distant land, in a land that one will never reach!

Like the Eskimos or some other unexplored tribe of the great Russian Empire."

During his service with the advocate, which had lasted now for over a year, he had had more than one opportunity of talking to Jews from the Jewish settlements, and he had become superficially acquainted with their life and the specifically Jewish problems created by the special laws against them and the curtailment of their rights. But what he had seen today was something quite new. It was a mystery risen from the depths of an unknown and secret world. For the first time he felt how profoundly that world touched him.

He himself could not understand why he should take such a keen interest in this new case.

When at last the Jewish woman was admitted to the lawyer's office, it was a laborious business to discover what had brought her to Petersburg. Nobody understood her language. The hopes that had been set on Jacob Shmulevitch, who himself had come from a Jewish settlement, proved to be illusory. Jacob Shmulevitch was offended that any one could dare to think that he understood such "jargon." He insisted with emphasis that in his paternal home nothing but Russian had been spoken for three generations. More violently even than the others he refused to have anything to do with this case. Meanwhile he held his pet hair-brush daintily between his thumb and little finger, surreptitiously passed it over his beard and mustache, and rolled his Russian "r's" as only he could roll them: "I simply can't understand how any one can come to Petersburg to get legal advice without knowing the language of ourr countrry."

It was the celebrated advocate himself who saved the situation. He could still remember the language of his childhood and was delighted to have the opportunity of speaking his mother tongue again. Although the old woman's pronunciation was strange and difficult to understand (she spoke with a strong Polish accent, drawing out her words in a sort of sing-song, and employed many phrases from the Talmud besides, for she belonged to a Chassidic household), yet Halperin was able with a little effort to follow her.

It was a dreadful story that the old woman told in her characteristic speech: "I have a son, before God, the only son of his mother.

He's a Talmudist, there isn't such another in the whole world. He has his certificate as a rabbi. He's married, too, and has two children. And then, because they forgot to score out the name of his younger brother—who is dead, God preserve us all!—from the register, they called him up for service, although as an only son he should have been exempted. But he's very pious and would rather—God save us!—suffer death a thousand times than depart from God's true way. Not to speak of eating pork and other filthy things. Well, he got through one year of it, a bad and terrible year; you wouldn't believe it! They did everything to him they could think of. They tore the very flesh from his bones. But he didn't budge from the Lord's way by a hair's breadth, God be thanked. Even under the tyranny of the Goyim he led a strict Jewish life. He did his duty and said his prayers to himself all the time. Whenever he could manage it he put on his prayer mantle and his phylacteries, or cast a glance at a good book that he always carried in his haversack. But the Goyim couldn't bear the sight of him sticking so faithfully to his religion, and they set themselves to make him break —God forbid!—the holy commandments. Perhaps it was God's will. Perhaps the Lord wanted to try him to see whether he would withstand temptation and hold fast to his religion as in duty bound. Well, one day they had their joke with him. The man over him—he's called a sergeant—and some of his comrades, fell on him, took a piece of *trefe* meat—well, it was pork—and stuck it in his mouth. Of course he struggled. Why shouldn't he? It's written that a Jew must even—God preserve us!—give up his life rather than leave the right way. Well and good, they flung him on the ground. Of course they were drunk. For if they hadn't been drunk they must have known that it was wrong to do such things. Even their own religion forbids it. Well, then they tried to shove the pork into his mouth. Oh, that my ears should ever have to hear such things! That Reb Chaim Jidel's only son, that a grandson of the famous author of *The Light of Life* should have such a thing done to him!" at these words the old woman sobbed bitterly. "So when they tried to push the unclean flesh into his mouth of course he struggled. And as he was struggling he tore the tunic of one sergeant and bit the hand of another sergeant. After all, does one know what one is doing in a state like that? Well, after that they brought him up before the higher officers for attacking his superiors. There's a heavy penalty for that. Well, he could find nobody to take his side. For who knew what really happened? He never even wrote to me. So they condemned him to twenty years' penal servitude; that meant Siberia. And now he's on his way there, in chains and fetters. I didn't know what to do, so I went to the rabbi—long may he live!—and kept on knocking at his door until they had to let me in. And I shouted and screamed and asked him how he could allow a grandson of the man who wrote *The Light of Life* to rot his young life away in prison. Then the rabbi said that the best thing I could do would be to go to Petersburg. 'There's a great advocate there,' he said, 'a friend of Israel, and, if he will, he can save your son.' What won't a mother do for her child? So I took my life in my hands and I've come to the great gentleman in Petersburg. Kind sir," again a flood of tears poured from the old woman's eyes, and she fell at the lawyer's feet, seized his hand and kissed it, "save my child, my only, my learned son!"

For a long time the advocate sat in silence, his face pale. With nervous fingers he stroked his great mane and tugged at his unkempt beard. The old woman handed him the letter which she had been clutching: "Here, read, kind sir, read what the holy rabbi says about him. The holy rabbi wrote this letter with his own hand, sir. You will be sure of Paradise, and every sin will be forgiven you for the good work of saving a Jewish soul from the cruel hands of the Goyim."

These last words moved the advocate more deeply than the story itself, not so much because of the rewards they prophesied, as of the strong racial faith that rang through them.

The lawyer got up and began to walk up and down the room. He had not said a single word till now. His two assistants stood beside the table regarding curiously their strange client.

"I can see nothing, nothing at all that I can do!" the lawyer kept muttering to himself in a language that the Jewish woman could not understand. "He was sentenced by court martial."

"And for a trifle like that, for the sake of a bit of pork, is it right for a man to risk his life?" Suddenly Jacob Shmulevitch found his tongue in the "jargon" of the old woman. "What harm could it have done him if he had eaten it?"

"Oh, kind sir, what a thing for the gentleman to say! Better death a thousand times than do a thing like that, God forbid!" cried the Jewish woman.

"My dear woman, only one man can help you in this business, the Czar himself!" suddenly exclaimed the lawyer. "There's no appeal against a sentence by court martial, and no other human being can help you."

"But the Lord of all the earth can help me!" The old woman pointed upwards with her hand.

Shamed by her reply, the lawyer went on more to himself than to her: "Certainly, certainly, the Lord of all the earth. But the Lord of all the earth can only do it through the Czar, for your son was sentenced by court martial. But who is to go to the Czar? Who can lay the case before him? Do you know what kind of an age we're living in?"

"The rabbi told me what I must do to move the Czar's heart to pity." The woman now spoke with confidence. "Even the Czar is in God's hand."

A smile flitted over the lawyer's lips: "But meantime you may be seized at any moment, seeing you haven't a permit to stay in Petersburg, and ruthlessly sent home again."

"Then is there no help for me?" asked the woman, turning deathly pale.

"I can't see what we can do in this case. I see no possibility, no way out. . . . We haven't access to the Czar."

"I won't go away. The rabbi sent me to you, sir, and he certainly knew what he was doing. My boy is in danger of his life. Where can I go? I'll kneel on the ground in front of the Czar's palace. Yes, even if they trample on me with their feet! I'm afraid of nothing now. My boy is in the power of the Goyim." Once more the old woman cast herself at the lawyer's feet.

Halperin looked around him in embarrassment, as if seeking for help from his assistants. Jacob Shmulevitch made an angry grimace. The lawyer consulted with his lieutenants in a low voice.

"Solomon Ossipovitch, surely something can be done; this . . . this is a dreadful business . . ." stammered Mirkin.

"What can we do with her? She hasn't a permit to stay here. She may be sent home at any moment. Jacob Shmulevitch, can't you find out from some of our other clients from the settlements if there's a way out of the difficulty? They must know of some way or other of staying secretly in Petersburg for a little. Make a few inquiries, will you? Ask Frau Hurvitz, for instance. She belongs to Warsaw, too, I think. You know the woman I mean, our revolutionist's mother."

"I don't want to have anything to do with the business. It'll only have disagreeable consequences for us."

"I'll see to it. I'll attend to the matter," Mirkin put in.

"But what do you know about permits? You've never had any experience of such things!" cried the lawyer, himself walking towards the apartment where the poorer clients sat. His piercing eye rapidly ran over the row of people waiting for him; at his appearance they all rose to their feet. He caught sight of a Polish Jew among them and signed to him to step forward. The Jew smoothed his beard, cleared his throat and followed him.

"Weinstein, from Vilna, father of the student Lev Ossipovitch Weinstein?" questioned the advocate, who knew by heart all the names and circumstances of his clients.

"Yes, I've received a letter," began the man, referring to his own case.

"I don't want to discuss that at present. I have a request to make of you. Of course you're staying here in Petersburg without a permit—don't be alarmed!—I won't report you. Can you take a Jewish woman with you and find lodgings for her?"

"I'm staying with the Kvasniecova," replied the Jew, looking down in embarrassment.

"I haven't asked you for any details," said the lawyer sharply, raising his voice, "we all live in Russia as we must, not as we would like to. Take this woman with you."

"There are—er—women there. . . ."

"I tell you again that I know nothing and wish to know nothing about the place. Be so kind as to take the woman with you. Go with this man," he turned to the old woman. "We'll see what we can do."

"Jacob Shmulevitch, please take a note of the name of this woman's son and the regiment he served in."

"Now go, go!" the lawyer helped the woman to get to her feet. "You said yourself that everything is in God's hand, remember."

"And now for the others, in turn. Who is the first?"

A deputation of Unitarian peasants, led by their pastor, followed the lawyer into his consulting office. . . .

CHAPTER XV

MADAME KVASNIECOVA

IN THE same street as Halperin's office and dwelling-house stood the "Pension Kvasniecova," famous over all Petersburg. It was situated at the rear of an old house. The courtyard through which one had to pass to reach the "Pension" was uncannily huge and always filled with lumber. A junk dealer used it as a store for his old furniture, another hawker flung his old iron and tin there, and a fish business with premises in the front of the building used it for storing hundreds of empty herring barrels. . . . So the courtyard was like a labyrinth and any one who ventured into it ran the danger of getting lost. Through this labyrinth, then, one penetrated to Madame Kvasniecova's establishment, which was known to a great part of the population of Petersburg and particularly to the higher State officials, as the "Pension Kvasniecova." Nor had it earned that title undeservedly.

In the basement Madame Kvasniecova ran a "tea-room," with the help of her manager, Vassily Alexandrovitch. Over the entrance hung two blue sign-boards, upon which was portrayed with primitive vigor a crowd of Russians in white smocks sweating round a huge samovar. Their living counterparts, with their white smocks thrown open to expose their huge hairy chests, sat reeking in their own sweat in the back rooms of the place, and through the door poured a steam as dense as that from a Turkish bath. The "Pension" was on the first floor above the tea-room. This floor was traversed by a long corridor, on one side of which the huge, lofty rooms had been divided into little cubicles by flimsy partitions and—obviously in haste—hung with flowered wall-paper which was always peeling off. The "Salon" alone, with its four windows looking out on the street, had remained untouched. Its furnishings consisted mostly of red, plush-covered sofas and armchairs, and black tables with carved tops. It was a waiting-room for the guests who frequented the ladies of the establishment. On the other side of the corridor, opposite the "Pension," there was a huge door with a brass plate on which was inscribed "Madame Kvasniecova. Private."

Yet behind that door there flowed an endless stream of tears, like a stream of blood flowing from the wound that was called "Russia." . . .

Madame Kvasniecova made use of her high-sounding name only in the part of the building known as the "Pension." In her private flat on the other side of the corridor she bore the name which she brought with her from her home in the neighborhood of Odessa; there she was known as Deborah Leah Braunstein.

In the little cubicles of the "Pension" glittered the ikons of her adopted religion, lit by tiny red lamps. But in her private dwelling hung a tablet with three commemorative inscriptions: it bore in Hebrew and Russian script the names of her father, her mother, and her husband, and beneath them the dates of their deaths were noted according to both the Jewish and the Russian calendar. On all the tables lay prayer-books and Bibles, which looked as if they were much used. Beneath the tablet was a little chest on which stood two small brass Sabbath candlesticks with half burnt candles in them.

Madame Kvasniecova was a powerful elderly woman with a full red face and a long, extraordinarily thick neck, which might have been the wide funnel of a boiler, and her thick round figure, which seemed to be cast in one piece, was indeed not unlike a boiler. Over her gray hair Madame wore a brown wig, not so much for pious reasons, as because of her "profession." She was an adherent of the Orthodox Russian Church, which she had joined in her husband's lifetime, together with him, for purely material reasons, so that they might live in Petersburg unmolested and go about their business. But later she had become passionately devoted to her new faith, celebrated all the church festivals, attended church regularly, and on every opportunity offered a consecrated candle for the good of her defunct husband's soul. Yet this did not prevent her in the least from remaining constant to her tribal religion. The practical old saw which says that two stitches are better than one was enough for her. . . . As well as the Orthodox festivals she observed all the traditional Jewish feasts, keeping herself well informed of their precise dates. Deborah Leah was so clever in combining the festivals of the two "Gods" that no incongruity or opposition between them could be marked. Thus in her own fashion she settled a religious quarrel in which mankind had been involved for a thousand years. She never omitted to lay on the Easter table, beside the colored eggs, the garlanded swine's head and the cakes which the priest would later sprinkle with holy water, the Matzoth, or Jewish Easter loaf, as well. In the evening she celebrated the "Seder"; next morning she went to church and exchanged the Easter kiss with the other worshipers, saying: "Christ is risen." And side by side with her Christmas tree gleamed the eight candles of the old Jewish Menorah.

This reconciliation of the Gods behind the backs of the ruling religions had actually been first thought out by her husband, Anshel Kulak, who had transferred his business from Odessa to the capital after his marriage to her. And, in pious tribute to the memory of the deceased, Deborah refused to countenance the slightest alteration either in her business or her religious arrangements.

All the festivals, the Jewish as well as the Orthodox, Deborah held quite privately in her bedroom which lay by itself at the extreme corner of her large flat. In it hung a large ikon, beside which, beneath a picture of the holy sepulcher, stood a Palestine money-box of a traditional pattern, a Rabbi-Meir-Baalness money-box, which had been sent to her from Jerusalem. And so that no bone of contention should exist between the two deities, whenever Deborah Leah poured fresh oil into the ikon lamp she took care to put an equivalent sum of money in the box. When the box was full she herself bore it to the synagogue and had it emptied by one of the elders. She lived and had all her meals in her bedroom, rested there after her labors, and there at night, after closing the shutters, counted her savings, which she kept hidden in a secret place. . . . The other rooms of her flat she gave up to poor Jews who were staying in Petersburg without a permit.

Deborah Leah ran her "Pension" on the most strict, sanitary and respectable lines. Under her firm supervision nothing of a scandalous nature was tolerated. Her "clients" were not numerous; they consisted almost exclusively of respectable married men who wished now and then to have a quiet and inconspicuous holiday. Clients were not admitted without a recommendation (this was most scrupulously seen to by the manager, Vassily Alexandrovitch, of whom we shall have more to say presently). Deborah Leah's relations with the police were irreproachable; she was always punctual in paying them the agreed weekly honorarium, and so the local inspector, whenever he met her in the street, saluted her most respectfully. In spite of her profession Deborah Leah was much esteemed in her neighborhood, if only for her kindliness and her generosity in contributing to charities; moreover, her "ladies" had strict instructions not to offend the neighbors in any way. Among the higher officials, too, Madame Kvasniecova was known and esteemed. Consequently her house was the safest refuge possible for any one who wished to stay in Petersburg without a permit.

Of course it was not for filthy lucre that Deborah Leah extended her hospitality to these unfortunates—she did not accept a farthing from them—but for the spiritual welfare of her deceased husband, to whom, to her great sorrow, she had borne no children.

In passing the door of the famous advocate during his consulting hours she had frequently noticed anxious Jews and Jewesses, whose appearance, clothes and submissive bearing proclaimed that they came from one of the Jewish "settlements." Once or twice she had stopped and talked to the poor, worried creatures. Over and above the worries that had brought them from their distant provinces to the capital they almost all had another: that of not knowing how they were to remain in Petersburg without falling into the hands of the police. Deborah Leah began by taking one or two of them into her house out of pity; but gradually her house was transformed into a regular hotel for people who were in Petersburg without a permit. At intervals she herself would go to the advocate's to inquire whether any one required lodgings for the night. At first she was greeted by looks of alarm, but soon she won the confidence of those frightened people, and gradually her house became known as a secret refuge and her address was passed from hand to hand among them.

Deborah Leah laid down only one condition for her lodgers: they had to perform their devotions within her walls. Through her half open door she used to listen to the melancholy cadences of the prayers which had lived on in her heart, long unheard, but yet not forgotten; and, a thick prayer-book on her knees, she softly murmured them along with the others. . . .

Most of her lodgers did not even know what kind of a house they were living in. The "ladies" of the "Pension" were strictly forbidden to cross the threshold of Madame's private quarters. Deborah Leah herself very seldom made her appearance in the "business" part of the house; this happened only when a high official visited the "Pension" and Madame, as its representative, felt she had to pay her personal respects to the distinguished guest. The business management of the place was entirely in the hands of the faithful and reliable Vassily Alexandrovitch. He was also the liaison officer between the "Pension" and Madame's bedroom.

So Deborah Leah's private quarters opposite the "Pension" became little by little the meeting point of most of the unhappy creatures whom the arbitrary administration of the law and the barbarity of officials drove to seek redress in the Capital. Gradually it came to be an asylum for Jewish misery. The rooms were stained with tears; sighs from broken hearts beat against their walls, and lugubrious laments from the Jewish psalms. And the landlady took the most lively interest in the fates of her lodgers.

To these night quarters fate also brought the old Jewish woman Esther Hodel Kloppeisen, who had come from the utmost end of the great Russian Empire to secure justice for her son. The strict piety and traditional costume of the old woman had at the first glance awakened esteem in the heart of Deborah Leah. But when she learned what had brought the old woman to Petersburg she was so overwhelmed with emotion that she at once summoned her manager, so as to impart to him the deep impression made on her by what she had heard.

From Vassily Alexandrovitch's appearance one might have thought that he ran a business for the sale of sacred relics and crosses, and not a place of public entertainment. Like his mistress, he, too, was past his first youth. He evoked a feeling of respect at sight, chiefly because of the gray hair, scrupulously oiled and brushed, which fell smoothly over his ears, because of his well-groomed beard and his dignified attire. During "official hours" in the "Pension," Vassily Alexandrovitch always wore a black frock-coat and a velvet waistcoat over which was stretched a heavy gold chain.

Like his mistress, he was strictly pious. It may be said without exaggeration that the pious atmosphere prevailing both in Madame Kvasniecova's private dwelling and in the "Pension" was due in no small measure to the deep religious susceptibilities of the manager. The piety of the establishment was a proverb in Petersburg. People said jocularly of God-fearing women: "She's as pious as one of Kvasniecova's 'ladies.'" The *bon mot* was a little exaggerated, of course, as far as the "ladies" of the "Pension" were concerned. Yet it had a kernel of truth; for as Vassily Alexandrovitch was an honest and responsible man he insisted not merely on a high standard of behavior for his "ladies" (for instance, they had to greet with proper respect the highly-placed officials who were his regular clients), not only on a strict observance of the laws of hygiene (in the interest of the aforesaid clients' health); he also saw to their religious and moral welfare. Accordingly he made the "ladies" attend church punctually every Saturday evening for vespers and personally escorted them there to see that they showed proper reverence for the priests and the other representatives of the Church. Vassily Alexandrovitch did this because he considered that if one followed the precepts of religion one's whole conduct must necessarily be on the right lines and one could not go wrong....

It must be added, however, that Vassily Alexandrovitch did not insist on obedience to the precepts of his own Church exclusively. On that point he was quite tolerant. Every religion was equally good in his eyes, and every human being who remained constant to his religion earned his respect and trust.

Evil tongues maintained that Madame Kvasniecova's double faith was due to Vassily Alexandrovitch's influence, and some even added that the relations between Madame and her manager had been more than merely business ones ever since her husband's death. But that was merely vulgar gossip. In reality her kindness to pious strangers without a legal permit had the manager's enthusiastic approval; indeed, without his consent, it would have been impossible for Madame Kvasniecova to commit safely a "crime" of such a serious nature. Vassily Alexandrovitch was such a true friend to all religious people that he could look on calmly even while Madame's guests said their prayers for the soul's good of his "rival" Anshel Kulak, Madame's deceased husband, of whom, so slanderous tongues said, he had been boundlessly jealous even during his lifetime, and against whom he was still supposed to nurse a grudge for the devotion with which the widow honored his memory. . . .

Considering all this, one can imagine what a deep impression the story of Esther Hodel, retold in her own language by Deborah Leah, made upon Vassily Alexandrovitch. He drew his huge checked handkerchief from the tail pocket of his fine frock-coat, blew his red nose vigorously into it, then wiped his eyes several times and said with tears in his voice: "And such things happen in our holy Russia when a human being tries to obey the commands of his religion! No,— I must tell this to His Excellency Akim Maximovitch Zapuchin, the next time he honors us with a visit. I'm convinced that His Excellency Akim Maximovitch will find a way of coming to the rescue; he's on intimate terms in the very highest quarters."

Then he turned to old Esther Hodel and said respectfully: "Just be patient and stay here with us! We'll see what we can do for you. Thanks be to God, we have a large circle of friends, and what other people can't do we can."

Old Esther Hodel jumped up as if stung by a tarantula; for during his speech the "goy" had lightly patted her with his hand. The old woman's behavior delighted the reverential Vassily Alexandrovitch beyond bounds.

Now Madame Kvasniecova also drew out her handkerchief, passed it over her nose and her tearful eyes, and said: "You're in good hands here, mother. This Christian," she pointed at Vassily Alexandrovitch, "is a pious man and has influential friends among the officials. The best people come here—the highest-placed and most respectable people. We'll rouse all Petersburg. Just stay here quietly as long as you like. You'll have kosher food from the Jewish restaurant. You'll want for nothing: you'll have the best there is to have: just stay here and pray to God as the rabbi told you."

Esther Hodel turned up her eyes piously and began to rock her body as though praying: "The power of the rabbi . . . I see it now . . . the holy man has wrought a miracle. . . ."

And the Jew who had brought her said with a sigh, a little enviously: "God grant I may find help as quickly as you've done!"

Then Esther Hodel devoutly fell on her knees in a corner and seriously began in a lugubrious voice the first psalm: "Blessed is the man . . ."

Madame Kvasniecova and Vassily Alexandrovitch stood with a benevolent and dreamy expression and gazed for a long time at the Jewess piously rocking as she recited her prayer, full of intense joy that such a pious being should have found a lodging with them. Then Vassily Alexandrovitch returned to the "Pension" again, where his services were urgently required. . . .

CHAPTER XVI

FLOODS OF TEARS

Mirkin had not expected that his encounter with the old Jewish woman would make such a deep impression upon him. Most remarkable of all: he had understood all that she said. How could that be explained? A hidden nerve seemed to have set to work, taking up her incomprehensible words and conducting them to his brain. Soon he had quite mastered the idiom.

Hitherto he had brought to the daily examples of injustice which came the lawyer's way a purely professional interest of a somewhat lukewarm kind. But after seeing the old woman and listening to her laments that afternoon all this injustice had come home to him. It was something that concerned himself. Was it perhaps the elemental cry of the blind faith rooted in his people that moved him so deeply? During his year's service with the lawyer he had been shocked more than once by the appalling accidents of daily life. But this time it was a far greater thing that moved him; he stood trembling and amazed before a thousand-year-old mystery, before an inaccessible and secret mystery which nevertheless still had a strong and deep life in all the members of his race: shaken, he stood before a faith which he himself had never possessed.

He was firmly resolved to espouse the old woman's cause and do what he could to help her. As for several days she did not appear, he decided to seek her out in her quarters. Perhaps she might need money or other help; perhaps she hadn't been able to remain there; perhaps she was already in prison and in danger of being packed off to Warsaw again.

Mirkin knew that the old woman's lodging was not altogether respectable. But he did not know its real character. Many things connected with the lawyer's profession were kept secret from him. These mysteries were known only to his colleague, Jacob Weinstein, with whom the lawyer often consulted in his private office without asking Mirkin to be present. Madame Kvasniecova's house was one of those mysteries, for it was never mentioned. Mirkin quietly made a note of the address.

One evening after leaving the office he went to call on the old Jewish woman. While he was mounting the steps before the brilliantly lit entrance, he heard a few gay bars of piano music coming through the freshly painted door of Kvasniecova's "Pension." It was the tune of a popular cabaret song, yet it sounded so sad that Mirkin was overcome by an incomprehensible feeling of melancholy.

As he approached Kvasniecova's private door a quite different melody met his ears; he could hear broken voices lugubriously intoning psalms. He stopped and listened to these two violently contrasting sounds coming from rooms so closely adjoining. Both rooms bore the same name, the only difference being that on the door of the one was the inscription "Café Kvasniecova," while the other had a plate with the legend: "Madame Kvasniecova. Private." For a moment it seemed to Mirkin as though the two melodies melted into a single harmony, the one completing the other. . . .

It was not an easy matter for him to gain admittance; and he only succeeded at last by introducing himself to Madame Kvasniecova herself, who had to be summoned from her bedroom. In the room which he entered he found a few women and several dejected Jews. Some sat in a corner by themselves, a few gathered around a table, others were sitting on a bench beside a little chest on which two candles were burning. They were all rocking over psalm-books and reciting the ancient songs with broken voices. For ever since old Esther Hodel had taken up her abode with Madame Kvasniecova the place had become a regular prayer-house. The old woman had been commanded by her rabbi to recite certain chapters from the Psalms thirty-seven times daily as long as she remained in Petersburg: if she did that she would be certain to find help. The psalm recitals of the old woman proved contagious and the others followed her example. So in Madame Kvasniecova's a regular competition in psalm recitation began. It could no longer be computed in yards, but only in versts; each of the lodgers religiously daily reeled off whole versts of psalms as if for a wager. . . .

Just as hospital patients are jealous when the doctor devotes particular attention to one of them, so the lodgers in Kvasniecova's had for a long time been jealous of the old woman from the provinces, in whom so many people were interested. And now that the celebrated lawyer's assistant himself came to ask after her, a discontented muttering arose and a loud feminine voice made itself heard in a corner of the room. It belonged to a woman in a black dress who did not wear a wig but her own hair. Her hair was somewhat untidy, giving an added touch of animation to her energetic and attractive face which, in spite of the countless furrows in her low forehead, was made remarkable by a pair of beautiful eyes and the firm and gracious lines of nose, mouth and chin. She exclaimed: "Just look how they all fawn on that old woman, from the lawyer down to Kvasniecova's lodgers! As if she were the only mother here with a son in trouble! I must put on a hood, too; perhaps then the whole world will begin to take an interest in my son as well."

"That's different. She has a learned son and he's sitting in prison because he remained true to his religion," said another woman, trying to appease her neighbor.

"My son is a great scholar, too. Do you think he hasn't studied? He was in his third year at the university when he was twenty-one, and he knows languages that only two or three other men in the whole world know. All the professors praise him. I've a letter from one of them. Can one only be a scholar if one preaches in a synagogue? Is that all that counts with you? Don't you care if a young tree full of hope has its branches lopped off?"

"How can she compare herself with the old woman? The old woman's son is a rabbi, and he's sitting in prison for our sake."

"My son is a rabbi, too. Yes, a rabbi, and he's sitting in prison, too, for our sake. Has he ever robbed or killed any one?"

"Who asked him to meddle with 'those things'?"

" 'Those things' are of just as much value as refusing to eat pork, perhaps even of more value, let me tell you! They're of more service to the world. I'm not in the least ashamed of my boy's 'crime.' If every mother's son was a 'criminal' like mine we should all be better off today." With these words she left her companions and went up to Mirkin, who was standing beside the old Polish woman and questioning her.

"Will you be so kind as to tell me, Mr. Assistant, how long I must sit in this brothel and listen to these people mouthing psalms? I've left a whole houseful of children at home and I've come here to save my son. Are you going to do something for me, or aren't you? Tell me frankly. One can get no satisfaction out of the people in your office," she said desperately.

"Be quiet! Be quiet! Don't shout! She'll hear!" One of the women pointed towards Kvasniecova's bedroom door.

"What do I care? I'm past being afraid of anybody. What use is it to me, all this psalm-snuffling? It doesn't get any farther than the beds across there in that brothel. . . ." The woman pointed in the direction of the "Pension."

Mirkin knew the woman. She was called Hurvitz and came from Warsaw. She had been for two months in Petersburg trying to fight a charge against her son, a student of philology, who was accused of belonging to a secret society of Polish socialists "for the overthrow of the existing order." The police had found in his room a whole mass of papers supposed to belong to his party; these papers, however, were written in a quite incomprehensible language.

"Your son's papers are still in the hands of a professor. They are written in Coptic. In all Russia there are only one or two people who understand that language. Until the professor sends in his translation of the papers nothing can be done," replied Mirkin.

Although his reply did not sound very hopeful the woman drew herself up proudly. Her beautiful animated eyes sparkled, and an involuntary gleam of satisfaction played round her finely-cut lips.

"And these people think there is only one mother in the world who has a learned son. . . ."

But before she had finished the sentence her joy had changed into a grimace of pain. Her eyes filled with tears and she said more to herself than to Mirkin: "The hardships we had to suffer to get him through the high school! We had to work ourselves to skin and bone to earn the fees for every quarter. For every book, every uniform . . . my husband is a poor teacher, he runs a school for poor children . . . for whole nights we lay awake until we knew he had passed. . . . We couldn't eat or drink until we managed to get him into the university. We felt we had the weight of the whole world on our shoulders. . . . And then suddenly he's taken away, and we don't even know where he is!"

"He shouldn't have meddled with 'those things.' Who asked him to?" interrupted a Jew who had been absorbed in his psalms. He turned down a corner of a page to keep the place, rose to his feet and began in a surly voice:

"The rich people can afford 'those things.' But what business is it of poor people? A poor man must hold his tongue, listen and hold his tongue. . . . Your son got through the high school and was sent to the university—lots of people would give anything to be as lucky! What more do you want? It's 'those things' that cause all the trouble. What business was it of his?"

"Shame! Shame! To rise against the authorities!" The wrinkles in the cheeks of old Esther Hodel deepened when she grasped what it was that was being talked about.

Then Frau Hurvitz, the student's mother, leaped to her feet. Her hair rose on her head. Even the two natural ringlets on her forehead stood on end. Her eyes darted flames. The other lodgers turned aside in fear and withdrew to their former places. Frau Hurvitz thrust out her lower jaw and her chin looked still more formidable. Her full breasts heaved as she began: "Whose business is it to concern themselves with 'those things'? Is it the business of the rich? They're quite content with things as they are. They benefit enough from them, God knows! What have they to complain of? They can live in Petersburg as long as they like; they can carry on their businesses as they please; they have no difficulties to face. No, the poor people are the only ones who have any reason to concern themselves with 'those things.' And I'm proud that my son concerned himself with 'those things.' If he had asked my permission I would have told him to carry on; for it's better for the world to be destroyed altogether than remain as it is. I'm not afraid! As far as I'm concerned they can fling me in prison, too."

"Well, you've said your say now!"

"Yes, I've said my say!" repeated Frau Hurvitz in a firm voice, and she angrily turned away.

It is impossible to tell how this scene might have ended had not Madame Kvasniecova suddenly appeared in the doorway of her bedroom. Her clothes and voluminous apron stuck out from her as stiffly as if they had been made of leather. From her belt hung a huge collection of keys, which rattled at every step she took. She stopped on the threshold of the room where her lodgers were sitting and with a kindly expression on her ravaged face, while her little eyes darted rapidly over the company, she began with a good-humored smile. "I thought that unhappy people like you did nothing but pray. But apparently you spend your time quarreling."

The lodgers calmed down; everybody withdrew into his own corner. Only the Jew who had argued with Frau Hurvitz retorted smilingly:

"But who's quarreling? The lawyer's assistant has come, and we're all pouring out our hearts to him."

Without replying Madame Kvasniecova shut the door of her bedroom, and presently peace reigned in her house.

CHAPTER XVII

A MIDNIGHT PRAYER

DURING all the foregoing scene a man had sat motionless at the window, apparently taking no notice whatever of what was happening in the big room. He did not join in the recitation of the psalms, nor did any book lie open before him. Resting his great head with its long beard on his huge hand, he stared in silent meditation out into the darkness.

The extraordinary stature and strange silence of the man had attracted Mirkin's attention from the start. The man was so sunk in himself that he hardly seemed to be present. His little Lithuanian cap was pushed back from his enormous forehead; his face was hidden by his long beard; and now he had closed his eyes and seemed to be gazing into himself.

Mirkin convinced himself that the old woman was being well looked after for the time being, listened for a while to the lodgers' discussions, and turned to go. The unknown man rose and followed him. At the entrance, still brilliantly lit, the stranger stopped him; the strains of the cabaret song were still being given out by Madame Kvasniecova's tuneless piano. Mirkin started on seeing the extraordinary size of the man, his huge head, his huge beard, and his disproportionately long arms. Beside the stranger Mirkin looked like a boy. In a powerful, metallically resonant voice the stranger introduced himself: "I'm Moses Baruch Chomsky, an elder of the Jewish Community in Tolestyn."

Mirkin stood staring speechlessly.

The man proceeded to explain his case. He had come to Petersburg at the orders of his community, a small town in the province of Vilna. The Government had suddenly declared the town a village and decreed that all Jews—who were forbidden by law to live in villages—should leave the place. Chomsky had knocked at all the doors of the great Petersburg for redress, and now the matter was in the hands of the advocate Halperin. Mirkin could give the man only vague answers, as he himself did not know much about the case; so he fobbed him off with generalities, such as "We'll do everything we can." The Jew listened thoughtfully and seriously and said nothing.

When Mirkin stepped into the street the Jew walked on silently beside him. Surprised, Mirkin asked him if he, too, was going to Issakievsky Square.

"I may as well go to Issakievsky Square; it makes no difference," said the stranger half to himself, walking on beside Mirkin.

Mirkin had intended to hire a sledge, but as the Jew interested him he decided to walk on foot.

"Where can one go?" said the Jew, once more as if to himself. "This is no place for me. For almost a month now I've been here and haven't once put on my praying robe and my phylacteries."

"Why is that?" asked Mirkin.

"Surely you don't expect me to worship in an unclean place!" replied the Jew in Russian.

Mirkin was silent.

"For two weeks I wandered about the streets, for I didn't want to take the lodgings I have now. I am the superintendent of our community; I have grown-up children, married daughters; never had I crossed the doorstep of such a house before. And now in my old days I, an elder of the Jewish Community of Tolestyn, must live in a house of sin. . . ."

After a long pause he began again: "For two weeks I never changed my clothes or lay in a proper bed. I wandered from one café to another and spent my nights in the railway station. Once I was actually arrested; but I managed to get off by bribing the policeman. How long could that go on? I couldn't stand it any longer. If it had been my own business that was at stake I wouldn't have stayed another minute in this iniquitous town, even if it meant losing all my wealth or—God forbid!—my life. But it was a matter concerning a whole community. The commune sent me here as their representative." Once more the Jew fell silent; it was as though he had swallowed something difficult and was waiting until it was down. Then he went on: "But as for praying to God in such a house—how can one? And these stupid people actually recite psalms there! Why, it's the most outrageous blasphemy! It only provides amusement for those harlots across the passage.... Yes, Frau Hurvitz was right in what she said!"

Once more the man was silent.

"But why should one complain about human injustice? What do we matter when they dare to sit in judgment on God Himself? Twelve peasants in Kiev are going to pass sentence shortly on the God of the Jews!"—This was an indirect reference to the approaching trial of Mendel Beilis for ritual murder. After that the man remained silent for a long time. This time he seemed to be chewing on a very hard mouthful, and it took him a long time to swallow it down. The two men walked on in silence.

The night was pitch black. No star could be seen. A dense darkness pressed down from above. In the darkness the street lamps and the lighted shop windows seemed doubly brilliant, radiating circles of light outside of which everything sank back into obscurity again. Only the dim outlines of the huge buildings could be distinguished rising defiantly into waves of darkness. They did not look like actual buildings, but like shadows of gigantic invisible shapes floating somewhere in the air.

Mirkin and the Jew reached the uncannily huge Issakievsky Square. Like two drops in the ocean they were lost in the darkness that lay over the great empty place. A gigantic palace of granite and steel took up the whole breadth of the square. No glimmer of light was to be seen in the square itself; but from the high brilliantly lit windows of a massive building in a side street a festive radiance was flung across it.

"The cabinet is sitting tonight," said Mirkin, pointing to the illuminated windows in the huge building.

"The cabinet is sitting tonight," replied the Jew mechanically.

All at once the stranger seemed uncanny to Mirkin. To get rid of him, he said: "I go over the Troitsky Bridge. Which way are you going?"

"I'm going the same way, to the Winter Palace."

"What takes you to the Winter Palace?"

"Nothing. I go there. . . . Every evening before going to sleep I walk to the Winter Palace."

"To the Winter Palace? But why?"

"You ask why? I go there to say my prayers," replied the Jew.

Mirkin was too astonished to reply. His companion also remained silent. They walked the whole way to the Winter Palace without saying a word.

The square in front of the Czar's palace lay in still deeper darkness than Issakievsky Square.

No light showed in the offices of the various ministries that lined the square. But in the middle of the square the lights of the four lamps round the Alexander Column flickered, fighting the darkness that was waiting to engulf them. The night stretched out its claws against the imperial palace itself, which stood like a house of the dead in the blackness of space. Only from a window in one of the top floors did a single beam fall down on the square. It seemed to waver in the air as it fell.

A violent wind sprang up from the direction of the Neva, tugging at the hats and coats of the two wanderers. The Jew stopped in the middle of the square; Mirkin thought he was trying to keep his hat from being blown away, and stopped too. Suddenly he saw that the Jew had upraised his unnaturally long arms, which seemed still longer in the darkness. Mirkin had a feeling that the man was reaching up into invisible worlds with his long arms. And all at once, stretching his great hands towards the flickering beam in the Winter Palace, the Jew began to pray in a loud resolute voice; the words did not seem to come from his throat, but from an enormous depth: "Pour out Thy wrath on the peoples that do not know Thee, on the tribes that blaspheme Thy name. Destroy this house, so that not one stone remains upon another, as Thou didst with Assur and Babylon!" He continued standing with outstretched hands and gazing heavenward.

"What are you saying?" asked Mirkin in terror, seizing the Jew by the arm.

"My prayers to God," replied the Jew, disappearing into the darkness.

Mirkin found himself alone.

CHAPTER XVIII

THE RESTAURANT DANAN

In the Restaurant Danan on the Morskaia, Gabriel Haimovitch Mirkin was giving a dinner for Nina, his son's fiancée, and her parents. Only the immediate parties were present: the famous advocate and his wife, Nina, Zachary, and Gabriel Haimovitch himself. But stop: there was another: Olga Michailovna's cousin and "inseparable shadow," Naum Grigorovitch, who was regarded as one of the family. Helena Stepanovna, Gabriel's wife at one remove, was naturally absent. So as to avoid all awkwardness she had herself made arrangements to spend a few days with one of her friends in Gatchina until the family celebrations of Zachary's engagement were over. The dinner took place after the opera, where the company had listened to Chaliapin as Mephistopheles and admired a new star in the heaven of the Russian ballet, Madame Karsavina. Misha had been included in the theater party, but his father peremptorily refused to allow him to go on to the restaurant. Already concerned about Misha's bad marks and his forthcoming examination, he did not want the boy's high-school uniform to attract unwelcome attention and thus make matters still more difficult for him than they were.

The men were wearing their university badges pinned to the breasts of their evening coats. As always, Gabriel Haimovitch wore his Order of Anna of the third class, which he had been given for his services in constructing the Siberian Railway.

The dinner for the small party was served in a private room, partly because of the intimate nature of the occasion, partly because of the anti-Jewish feeling which at that time, on account of the Beilis trial, had reached its highest point of virulence in the Capital. Quite apart from this the Beilis trial could not be mentioned in the presence of the lawyer; for, as he had been unable to come to terms with the committee of defense, one of his rivals had been given the brief instead of him. The high-roofed but cozy room where the party sat round the festively decked oval table was brightly lit by electric lamps fixed to the four corners of the roof and on the walls. Their light was reflected from the tall marble pillars and broken into a thousand iridescent hues on the crystal chandelier, and gave a warm glow to the golden bronze fittings of the room. Behind each guest's chair stood a man in snow-white livery, who served the courses on the flower-decked table with light, almost imperceptible movements.

Like all Russian social banquets the meal was imposing, superabundant and extravagant. There were Portuguese oysters which had been brought to Petersburg in their own wagons, Russian caviar and French champagne. The waiters eagerly flitted about, offering the guests the best that was to be had; they displayed smooth, living trout in nets, whose azure-glazed scales still seemed to keep something of the mystery of the mountain streams from which they were taken; wretchedly cheeping, marvelous-hued game-birds in cages; fresh vegetables that pleased the eye by their bright colors. All these were shown in their natural state to stimulate the appetites of the guests.

The conversation was slow in starting and somewhat stiff. The two families were only distantly acquainted. Gabriel Haimovitch liked Nina and her mother from the start; Olga Michailovna conquered him by her reserve and her dignified bearing, Nina by her curious charm, which made a deep impression upon him. On the other hand Halperin's coldness and aloofness repelled him. Solomon Ossipovitch never forgot for a moment the respect that was due to him from others and from himself. Like so many men who live in the glare of public fame he always expected outbursts of admiration from every new acquaintance, no matter who he might be. But Gabriel Haimovitch, too, had no mean opinion of himself. The coolness between the two fathers weighed somewhat on the party's spirits. But there was no need to talk very much; the excellent champagne and the excellent music provided by a Rumanian orchestra made up for that.

Besides, the coolness between the two fathers gave Nina an opportunity of displaying her lively temperament by maneuvering and coaxing them into a better mood and creating a more friendly atmosphere. From her ears hung two brilliants, like the purest blue water and as big as nuts, which Gabriel Haimovitch had bought for her a few days before from the famous Petersburg jeweler, Parshe; they had been destined for the mistress of a Grand Duke, but old Mirkin had outbid him, and shortly before the party started for the theater had sent the stones to Nina in a huge bouquet of violets from Nice. (Gabriel Haimovitch knew how to make presents charming and acceptable to ladies.) Round her slim girlish neck Nina wore the necklace of oriental pearls that Zachary's mother had bequeathed to him as a gift to his future bride. But still more brilliantly than her pearls and diamonds gleamed her jet-black curly hair and her olive-skinned body. It shone out, like a precious stone in its setting, from her dress of black Spanish lace worn over a slip of amber-hued satin.

Nina was sitting between her father and her future father-in-law. She had resigned Zachary to her mother, in whose silent elegance he seemed to be quite absorbed; Nina had one bare arm round her father's neck and the other round her father-in-law's, and kept whispering compliments into the ear of each in turn, so that more than once both of them were smiling at the same time. So by her grace and adroitness she put them both in a good humor.

The conversation turned to the subject of houses, and particularly that of finding a suitable house for the young couple. Here "The Englishman" seized the lead, and showed the liveliest interest in the question. Where should the young couple live? In a house with all the modern comforts in the new and elegant quarter near the Kameno-Ostrovsky Prospect, which was the last note in modernity at that time? Or—and "The Englishman" supported the idea with vigor—in some old palace in the aristocratic Nabereshnaia which had been built in the time of Alexander I by the celebrated architect Quarenghi? Or in some other street in the neighborhood of the Admiralty Palace? Of course the old building would have to be modernized and furnished with central heating and a lift; the work of reconditioning must be executed by a capable architect, so that the style of the building would be retained; the furnishings must be antique, either Empire in the Russian style or Louis Quinze. On the ground of his wide knowledge of antiquities and his acquaintance with all the antique dealers in Petersburg, even the most obscure of them, "The Englishman" offered to find ways and means of procuring furniture that in style would be beyond reproach.

"Oh, yes, a house where dead aunts and other ancestral ladies walk at night, or sit in the old armchairs in their favorite corners, or look for forgotten love letters and other records of their sins in the drawers of the old wardrobes!" Nina mocked in the best of spirits.

"Sometimes you're really horrid, Nina," said Olga Michailovna, suppressing a smile that gleamed for a moment in her beautiful eyes. "I often ask myself whom you can inherit that quality from."

"No, Mamma, I'm quite serious; it may be romantic to live in the true Petersburg spirit of the Middle Ages, as if one were the Queen of Spades, but we have enough spirit and life of our own and don't need to raise the past out of its grave. What do you say, Papa?" she asked, stretching out her right hand to her father; at the same time she turned an appealing glance towards Gabriel Haimovitch on her other side: "God knows I'm frightened enough of the spirits within me, so why should I need a house full of spirits as well . . . ?"

"Never fear, Nina Solomonovna. We'll help you to drive the spirits out of the house and out of yourself." Old Mirkin kissed the hand which she had held out to him.

To appease the offended "Englishman" the lawyer shouted to him across the table: "We can do nothing, Naum Grigorovitch. The present generation are quite different from us. They have no trace of romance, everything is dry realism to them. We can't agree with them there."

"It's the truth," replied old Naum Grigorovitch with a smile and a sigh, glancing into Olga Michailovna's beautiful eyes.

Olga Michailovna, who was sitting on Gabriel Haimovitch's right, pushed back with a graceful gesture a curl that had strayed on to her brow and said: "All the same, I don't envy the new generation." Then with a smile she turned to Naum Grigorovitch: "We, Naum, will remain true to our generation, won't we?"

The white-uniformed waiters were now serving with noiseless movements the trout which a few minutes before had been wriggling and jumping in their net. Gabriel Haimovitch spitted a portion of trout on his fork and with his left hand pointed at his son: "That chap there is one of the old generation."

"Say that again. Gabriel Haimovitch!" exclaimed Nina delightedly. "I've told my new lord that already. I really don't know how I'll get on with him: either he'll have to get used to my generation or I to his—and I can hardly picture that."

"Well, we'll be very glad to take him into our generation, Naum. What do you say?" said Olga Michailovna, and, without noticing what she was doing, she put her round bare arm round Zachary's shoulder; he was sitting on her right.

Zachary and Olga Michailovna both blushed, but nobody noticed it.

Zachary sat bent over his plate and did not dare to lift his eyes and look across the table, where his fiancée was sitting beside his father. His whole being was filled with Olga Michailovna. He was happy simply to be sitting beside her and to feel her arm near him. He breathed in deeply the fine perfume of her shawl, her dress, her bosom; breathed in the fragrance of her body, her hair, her very soul. Her soft and involuntarily coquettish glance which seemed to promise so much did not disturb him, did not excite or attract him, but only created within him a sense of complete peace and absolute security. He did not feel any guilt because of the passion for her that filled his whole being. On the contrary, that passion made him feel ennobled and purified. And quite strange, almost ludicrous thoughts rose in him, thoughts which though vague and remote insisted on being heard, thoughts still unripe which he himself could not explain. . . .

His official engagement to Nina woke in Zachary something resembling a sense of guilt. For a moment he had the feeling, sitting in that room with his father and his fiancée, that something quite wrong, something dishonorable was happening. But he had only to cast a brief side-glance at the serene figure of Olga Michailovna and breathe in her fragrant perfume to recapture again the certainty that everything was as it should be.

The childlike feelings that he nursed for Olga Michailovna seemed to strengthen and purify the more vague ones that he felt for his fiancée.

CHAPTER XIX

CHERRIES IN SNOW

AFTER they had finished their dinner Gabriel Haimovitch suggested an excursion to the islands to listen to a gypsy band. Halperin categorically declined the invitation for himself and his wife: "That isn't the kind of thing for us, Gabriel Haimovitch; it's more in the line of young people like you." But Nina was enchanted by the proposal and insisted on going. The lawyer and his wife drove home; the rest of the party hired two sledges and drove at a gallop across the Neva towards "Ostrova" (as the islands are called in the Petersburg dialect).

Nina and Gabriel Haimovitch sat in the first sledge. His huge body and great voluminous fur coat quite filled the sledge and seemed to envelop the girl as well. The driver knew whom he was driving and where he was going. At a gallop that was permissible after midnight in no town but Petersburg and to none but diners in the Restaurant Danan, the sledge dashed across the broad Neva. So Zachary and Naum, who were in the second sledge, soon lost sight of their companions.

The wind raised by the racing sledge scattered the crystalline snow blanket of the Neva into the air and pelted the passengers' faces with flakes, though the night was windless and the moon and stars rode clear in the sky. The champagne had reawakened all the old life in Gabriel Haimovitch and literally rejuvenated him. The desires of vanished years awoke. He drank in the perfume that breathed from the warm furs of the girl sitting beside him, as his son had done a few days before; and he whispered ardently in her ear: "I'm very glad, very glad, Nina Solomonovna, that you've consented to become Zachary's wife. It's made me very happy and I thank you from my heart."

"I'm glad, too, Papa . . . please let me call you papa, Gabriel Haimovitch, I beg you to . . ." Nina put her hot face to his and rubbed it against his cold fat cheek.

"We'll be friends, won't we, Nina?"

"Certainly we shall, Papa!" She put her arm round his broad shoulders and stroked his side-whiskers. "I simply love side-whiskers! Why doesn't Zachary wear side-whiskers? I love to see a man looking manly, strong, tall, broad. I must persuade him to wear side-whiskers like his father."

"Yes, he's still a boy, my Zachary. He has still to be awakened. He's a dear good boy, but a boy. I don't know what to do about him."

"Yes, Papa, that's what I'm always saying, too. I don't know why I fell in love with Zachary. It must have been something in his blood . . . I must have guessed his father in him . . ." With a laugh Nina snuggled nearer. Gabriel Haimovitch suddenly became grave.

"I'm so happy! You don't know, child, how happy you've made a forlorn old man."

"But, Papa, you aren't an old man! I only wish Zachary was as old as you."

"Oh, yes, girl, believe me, a forlorn old man . . . I've always been lonely. We never had a family life, but now you'll create one for us. You don't know how much I've longed for it!"

"Don't talk like that, Papa! It isn't right of you to talk like that. You're a strong resolute man, Papa; you should talk in quite a different way!"

"It's happiness that makes me talk like that, my daughter, happiness," the old man pressed Nina's head to his breast, "happiness and joy."

"I must say you have a way with you when you send a lady a present, Papa! Diamonds in a bouquet of violets! The young men should take lessons from you, not from their contemporaries. That shows how much experience you must have had!"

Gabriel concealed a smile in his beard.

"Yes, Papa, there must have been more than one lady you've robbed of her heart and her wits! It's a good thing for us girls that you're past your young days." She playfully threatened him with a finger.

"All over, girl, all over," murmured the old man.

"You must tell me everything about yourself, Papa, everything. You mustn't conceal anything from me."

The sledge stopped in a little snow-bound grove in front of the famous gypsy cabaret, the "Fontanka."

"Where are the others?" asked Nina. "I thought they were just behind us."

"Every horse can tell who's sitting behind it," replied the old man. Now the bells of the second sledge could be heard.

Gabriel Haimovitch was well known at the Fontanka. Hardly had he appeared when the whole staff, from the youngest waiter to the pock-marked Tartar proprietor, rushed out of the dance-hall, from which came sounds of revelry.

"Ah, it's Gabriel Haimovitch, our little father! Oh, how long it is since we had the honor of seeing you here! Help the ladies and gentlemen off with their furs! What a pleasure, what a day of rejoicing! The red room is occupied for the moment, but it will be cleared for you at once. Go, Kolka, my compliments and clear the other guests out! Have patience just for a moment—not in the hall, no, please take a seat here in my office until the room is put in order."

Fifteen pairs of hands were eager to take the furs and serve the guests. But the Tartar proprietor would not hear of it; he refused to be deprived of the privilege.

"Is Natalia still with you? She hasn't left you yet?" asked Gabriel Haimovitch.

"She's still here, little father, still here, of course! How delighted she will be! Will you graciously permit me to send her to your room along with the orchestra?"

"No, only she herself is to come, and the acrobatic dancer. I must have the acrobatic dancer."

"Certainly, little father, certainly. You should have seen her last turn, the one she finished a little while ago in the dance-hall. The whole audience went mad. Serviettes were flying in the air, by God! Oh, she was great, the acrobatic dancer. And tonight we have a particularly distinguished company, crowds of high officials, not the measly kind that never pay. The Court is represented, too. Grand Duke Boris has arrived and Prince Arbasoff with a party. And lots of gentlemen from the Ministry of Trade are here, too, and crowds of rich people. They almost came to blows over the brilliants that our

Kokotchka has for sale—as presents for the acrobatic dancer. He's done good business tonight, our Kokotchka. . . ." The garrulous Tartar kept on babbling away at Gabriel Haimovitch.

"Don't deafen me with your Kokotchka and your acrobatic dancer! See instead that the champagne is put on ice," old Mirkin interrupted him, "and go and see whether the room is free yet."

"Which brand would you like? Monopol?"

"The usual."

Several waiters started off at the same time to execute the order. In a few minutes the small party was led into the red room, which was still filled with the smoke of strange cigars and the smell of strange perfumes. The Tartar tried to waft the smoke away with a serviette.

"Ah, Gabriel Haimovitch, do you still remember that day when you came here with the officials of the Ministry of Railways? That was a banquet! Oh, what a night that was when you had Natalia brought in in a bath filled with warm champagne. . . . Nothing else would do, it must be a bath of champagne!" The Tartar luxuriated in memories while he set the table afresh.

"Who asked you to speak, son of a dog?" Gabriel shouted at him. "Keep your words until you're paid for them!"

But the Tartar knew his customers. The more they shouted at him to shut his mouth and stop babbling, the more they wanted him to glorify their heroic deeds.

"And that other time, Gabriel Haimovitch, when you gave the dinner to Count Karvin, the chairman of the Banking Commission—do you remember? That night you had little naked French girls to wait on your guests . . ."

"I've already ordered you to be silent, do you hear?" shouted Gabriel Haimovitch in the voice that he used to his clerks and that brooked no contradiction. His reddish-gray side-whiskers and his eyebrows curled with rage, and the hair that fell smoothly on either side of his head quivered in sympathy.

"At your service!" said the Tartar in a soldierly voice and went on with his work in silence.

"In Russia you can do nothing with sober people, you must make them drunk first if you want to get anything done, otherwise they keep on blocking your way." With these half apologetic words old Mirkin turned to his companions. "Of course one has to drink with them. And now the fellow's dishing up all these old stories!"

"Oh, Papa, don't be angry!" said Nina, stroking the old man's cheeks with her hand, from which she had stripped her glove. He was astonished at her daring to do so.

Smilingly he begged the Tartar's pardon for the "son of a dog"; but the Tartar took the expression as a compliment and respectfully thanked him.

Meanwhile the waiters had brought in champagne and fruit. The fruits were bedded with cotton wool in little baskets like tender infants. There were fresh green pears and red plums and foreign peaches. Nina, who was sitting beside Gabriel Haimovitch on the sofa, fastidiously felt the fruits with her slender fingers. She picked up a pear and laid it back again, took up a fig, smelt it and with a bored air pushed it away.

"What would you like, Nina?" asked old Mirkin.

"Nothing, a silly whim, nothing . . ."

"But what is it? Tell me, child. In God's name tell me!"

"I should like some cherries. I don't know why—but as we were rushing across the Neva in the wind and snow I suddenly thought of cherries."

Gabriel Haimovitch made a sign to the waiter and ordered him to bring the proprietor.

When the pock-marked Tartar appeared, obsequiously old Mirkin asked him: "Tell me, old friend, wouldn't it be possible to hunt up a few cherries? Just see what you can do!"

"Impossible, little father, so help me God, impossible! I've telegraphed thrice already to Nice: 'Send cherries.' 'Not ripe yet in the hot-houses' was the answer." The Tartar gave emphasis to his words by beating his chest.

"Are you lying, you blackguard?" Gabriel Haimovitch glared at him with raised brows.

"Papa, how can you say such things? There's no need for it," Nina sought to appease him.

"No, no, young lady, Gabriel Haimovitch can say what he likes to me!" The Tartar smote his chest. "He knew me when I was only a kitchen-boy with the former owner. He is my benefactor. He lent me the money to buy the business when the owner died. I simply went to his office. 'How much do you need?'—'So and so much.'—'Go to my cashier.'—He didn't know me and yet he trusted me. And I paid back all the money out of drinks and tips, nothing else. That is Gabriel Haimovitch!"

"You're to hold your tongue about that, too, do you hear?"

"Certainly, Gabriel Haimovitch."

"And yet you're lying. You have cherries!"

"A single basket, a dozen cherries, a score at most. For the Grand Duke Boris. A week ago he told me: 'Telegraph to Monte Carlo and tell them to have cherries here by the twenty-second. If they aren't here I'll flay you alive.' That's what his highness had the condescension to tell me through his secretary. I thought at least a box would arrive, but all they sent was a lot of paper and cotton wool and there inside it, wrapped up as if they were children to be kept warm, not more than twenty cherries. There were no more ripe in the hot-houses, they wrote. But I will let you have them. I know the Grand Duke will thrash me, he'll flog me soundly—but what does that matter? It's you my thanks are due to, my benefactor. Everybody shall know it—the gracious gentleman lent me thirty thousand roubles to buy the business, and he didn't even know me. I was still a lad at the time. I've to thank him for everything. Permit me, Gabriel Haimovitch, to kiss your noble hand!"

"That's enough, I tell you. Go now and fetch the cherries; this young lady feels a desire for 'cherries in winter.'"

While Gabriel Haimovitch was giving these instructions to the Tartar he drew a little diary out of his breast pocket: without paying any attention to the company he jotted a few words in it with a gold-sheathed pencil hanging from his watch chain.

"Zachary, don't forget to come to me tomorrow at the office before you go to the law courts. I have something to discuss with you," old Mirkin suddenly shouted across at his son to everybody's surprise.

Meanwhile the Tartar had vanished and the company silently drank champagne. After some ten minutes the Tartar reappeared carrying a huge porcelain platter. It was filled with pure white snow, and, as if in defiance and mockery of nature, in the snow were embedded ripe red cherries. The springlike red of each single cherry laughed out of wintry whiteness.

"My compliments, Gabriel Haimovitch!" said the Tartar, setting the platter in front of Nina.

Nina picked up a cherry, wiped it in the fresh snow, dipped it in her champagne and stuck it in Gabriel Haimovitch's mouth: "Taste it, Papa!"

Then she lifted the platter and handed it back to the astonished Tartar.

"Take this back and keep it for the Grand Duke. I don't want you to be whipped."

"What's wrong with you, Nina?" asked old Mirkin.

"Nothing, Papa. I wanted the cherries because I thought they couldn't be got. Now that I see they can be got I've no further desire for them." Her black eyes laughed mockingly at him.

"Take the platter away!" old Mirkin said in an annoyed voice.

"Papa, don't be cross!" Nina put her finger to her mouth and her eyes still rested laughingly on old Mirkin's face.

Old Mirkin could not help smiling. The Tartar seized the opportunity: "Gabriel Haimovitch, will you graciously permit Natasha to enter now? She is longing to see you."

"Good," replied old Mirkin graciously.

CHAPTER XX

A PETERSBURG NIGHT

Zachary Mirkin was sitting at the other end of the table beside "The Englishman"; he remained obstinately silent. "The Englishman" brought out a word now and then, but Zachary stubbornly kept his mouth shut.

He glanced across at his father; the feeling of estrangement from his father that he had felt as a child returned again:

"Who is he really, that stout broad-shouldered man sitting opposite me beside my fiancée, my future wife, the future mother of my children? Who is that man with the great fat cheeks, the great reddish-gray side-whiskers and the watery blue eyes . . .?" The bags with the innumerable creases that hung beneath old Mirkin's eyes were familiar to Zachary and awoke in him a memory of some bond that connected him with this man; but the rest of his huge body—it was the first time that Zachary had felt this—seemed to belong to a stranger.

"What has he been up to all these years, alone in Petersburg, without his family? Who were his friends? Who is he? Who knows him?"

Nina soon guessed what was going on behind Zachary's high gleaming forehead. Suddenly she stretched out her arm, bare, brown and slender, to him across the table. With her slim nervous fingers she made a few magical passes in his direction: "Come here, Zachary, here, beside me; I haven't seen you all evening." For the first time in their acquaintance she "thou'd" him quite without warning, but then, as though she were herself shocked at her conduct, went on more ceremoniously: "I'm very concerned about you. Do come here beside me, please, here on the sofa. Forgive me, Naum Grigorovitch, for stealing your companion."

Mirkin blushed shyly and crossed to the other side of the table, where he sat down beside Nina and his father.

After her few glasses of champagne Nina was in high spirits. She held her glass to Zachary's mouth. He took a sip. Then she reached the glass to his father; then she herself drank it off.

"There! Now I know both your thoughts," she cried laughingly, putting her arm round Mirkin's shoulder and ruffling his hair with her fingers.

"Do you know, Gabriel Haimovitch, that Zachary is very thick with my mother, Olga Michailovna? They're such good friends that I'm often jealous of Mamma. Yes—I tell you quite frankly—I'm afraid that Zachary fell in love with Mamma first and with me only after that. Isn't it so, Zachary? Admit it!"

"Yes, I'm very fond of Olga Michailovna and respect her deeply," replied Mirkin with a smile.

"Olga Michailovna is a lady that one can still be jealous of," added his father gallantly.

"But I'm not in the least jealous," Nina laughed. "On the contrary I'm very glad, Zachary, that you are so fond of her; that brings me nearer to you, makes me more closely related to you, in a way. . . . It's just the same as with Naum Grigorovitch. Naum Grigorovitch pays court to Mamma, too, and so I'm fond of him as well." She stretched out her hand to "The Englishman." "I don't know why, but I have a weakness for every man that has a weakness for Mamma. In reality *that* was the real cause of our whole relationship. Do you know that, Zachary?"

Nina's words had a constraining effect on the others. For a moment the conversation halted. But the painful silence vanished at once when a little sharp-featured face peeped in through the door curtains and in an affected Russian enunciation asked: "Nina Solomonovna, may one be allowed to come in for a moment?"

"Oh, it's you, Boris Abramovitch! Do come in!"

There are various species of mice: church mice, theater mice and even cabaret mice. They are as different from one another as the places where they have their holes. In spite of its consequence the cabaret mouse lives a solitary life, wanders as if in a dream through the world of reality, and is distinguished from all the other species of the mouse world by its unquenchable thirst for the æsthetic. Everything in our poor little world is stupid, vulgar and commonplace to it: and, while it regards its manicured nails, it seeks salvation for its tragic ego in some great new thesis that will raise the whole world out of its degradation. By the world one means, of course, the mouse world—by the great thesis, some new medium for art, some new expression for its spirit, some new criterion for its content. And as the cabaret mouse can find comfort for its thirsty soul only in abstract forms, it looks forward to world redemption through the ballet—in its opinion the most appropriate vehicle for the rhythm of modern life (it must be noted, however, that this particular cabaret mouse derived its scanty livelihood from the ballet, which it helped to popularize in the drawing-rooms of Petersburg by means of elegant essays). Yet as the great thesis that was to redeem the ballet, expressing the "cry of the modern soul," was not yet found, our cabaret mouse was forced to sink deeper and deeper into degradation. His degradation consisted in lying all day in bed gloating over a Greek Bible and pornographic pictures which his intimate friends had sketched from life, and spending his nights in drawing-rooms of the type of Sophia Arkadievna's, where private performances were given. The worst moment of degradation, however, was when our æsthetic mouse spent the whole night in the Fontanka Cabaret, seeking refreshment for his panting soul in the perfumes of beautiful women and gratuitous champagne, varied by an occasional evanescent flirtation with some disengaged soubrette or gypsy girl. . . . Such a cabaret mouse was none other than the celebrated critic of the ballet, Boris Abramovitch Levinstein, whose sharp-featured face was now peering with a Mephistophelean grimace through the curtains at the door of the red room.

He introduced himself in a manner that showed he was aware of his own consequence. He was tall, thin and anæmic and looked as if he had been carved out of a block of wood. This impression was heightened by his tightly-fitting black frock coat and a black waistcoat buttoned up to his neck like that of a Protestant parson. (Thus he emphasized his "individual note.") He bowed with elaborate and affected politeness, waited quietly until somebody should ask him to be seated, and then bent over Nina Solomonovna's white hand, which she held out to be kissed.

"I've been longing all evening to find a human being in this Sahara that people call Petersburg. So you must forgive me for taking refuge with you. I heard from Sophia Arkadievna that you were here. These gentlemen will forgive me the liberty . . ."

"But, Boris Abramovitch, we've been absolutely longing for you! Do sit down. We're all friends here: this is my Papa, Gabriel Haimovitch. That is my fiancé. Naum you know, of course. You're very welcome and you've come just at the right moment. We've been discussing a subject that you could throw a lot of light on. We thirst for your words of wisdom, master."

Old Mirkin raised his great eyebrows when he heard those words of Nina's. He was obviously displeased with her for drawing a complete stranger into an intimate family circle. But Nina knew how to manage him; with her cool slender fingers she smoothed out the wrinkles on his brow.

"Boris Abramovitch is really one of my friends. We can be quite frank before him. And he's such a clever man. You'll soon see for yourself, Papa——" She deliberately gave the conversation a lighter tone as her instinct counseled her, and loosened it as if it were, so to speak, a belt that had been drawn too tightly.

"We're all eager to hear what you have to say on the subject," she turned to Boris Abramovitch. "We have just been talking of family sentiment. What is the family, actually? Explain it to us, Boris Abramovitch."

"The family, the family. . . ." Boris held up two fingers of his left hand. "The family is matter, a member of the family is form molded out of that matter."

"And when one falls in love, for instance, what is it that one really falls in love with, Boris Abramovitch: the matter or the form?" Nina inquired.

"Form is mutable, matter constant. Love is elemental, sexual. The elemental in human beings seeks the constant, not the transient. One doesn't fall in love with externals, but with the blood, the race, with matter. At first women married the tribe, then the family, and only as a last resort, in our decadent age, the individual. Do you know how hunters capture wild animals? They lure them into their snares by the sexual effluvium of their females. The human being is captured in the same way. Every family has its peculiar family effluvium; and if I may be permitted to use the expression, I should like to designate that the sexual effluvium."

"Do you hear that, Papa? That's the real Boris Abramovitch! Your health! Have a drink, Boris Abramovitch! Then it follows from what you say that, seeing I've fallen in love with Zachary Gavrilovitch, I must fall in love with his father at the same time," Nina went on laughingly. "And I must admit I'm very fond of him, this Papa of mine," and she laid her head on old Mirkin's breast.

The old man quitted her declaration by kissing her on the brow: "And I return the compliment with interest."

At this point the door softly opened and the Tartar admitted Natalia the dancer and her Jewish partner.

Natalia was not a gypsy, but an Armenian. In her great Semitic eyes lay all the suffering of her oppressed and enslaved people. She was no longer in her first bloom, but already over forty. Her firm body inclined to fullness. Her pitch-black hair was combed smoothly back and fastened in a great knot at her neck. A huge comb was stuck in it, after the style of the Spanish gypsies, and one or two red carnations. When she saw her old friend Gabriel Haimovitch she rushed at once towards him; she stretched out her full arms, tossing aside the long fringes of the cream-colored Spanish shawl wound round her vigorous body, which was well-preserved in spite of her night life. But a serious glance from beneath old Mirkin's raised brows sufficed to check her first impulse and remind her of her position.

With an embarrassed smile on her lips she remained standing by the door and curtseyed slightly behind the back of her partner, the Jewish "gypsy" who played the mandoline for her.

The player ran his fingers over the strings and then Natalia began with a decorous, almost businesslike air to sing her gypsy ballads.

Although her voice had suffered from alcohol there still remained something touchingly elegiac in it. She sang with feeling and seemed herself to live through the sorrows of the long-forgotten gypsy heroes, the Cossacks and their sweethearts burning with love, rage and jealousy, with whom the romantic gypsy ballads are filled. The gypsy songs moved the little company, as they never failed to move Russians. The champagne, the gypsy songs, and Boris Abramovitch's brilliant talk, transported Nina into an artificial state of melancholy rapture.

She leaned her head on Zachary's breast, played with his fingers, and hummed softly after the singer: "Yet once more... Yet many, many times more ..."

Suddenly she whispered to old Mirkin: "Gabriel Haimovitch, send the singer away, please, I beg you! Let's be private."

Gabriel Haimovitch handed the singer an ample bank note and said with a smile: "The lady doesn't wish to hear any more. She has her moods. So go now, Natasha. We'll send for you some other time."

"I, too, had my moods once; now I must put up with the moods of others." Natalia left the room, obviously offended.

Nina grew sad.

"I don't know why it is—but I can't restrain myself when I hear gypsy songs. They stir me too much. It's as if they reminded me of something."

Then she added, half to herself: "It's as if I were afraid of something when I hear them."

She snatched her champagne glass, put it to her lips, and said half-jokingly, half-seriously, at the same time turning with one of her charming smiles to both father and son: "You'll have to keep a close eye on me!"

"Why, Nina Solomonovna?" asked old Mirkin.

"I really don't know why, but sometimes I'm afraid of myself. I don't know what I may do tomorrow; it's quite true! For instance I went a little time ago to that performance at Sophia Arkadievna's. You should be really sorry that you took me there, Zachary. Yet it was an interesting evening, highly interesting! Only I hope you won't let me go to such entertainments in future," she smilingly threatened Zachary with her finger. "I met some one there, one of 'these' women. There were lots of interesting people there, weren't there, Boris Abramovitch? And so I happened to meet that woman there, and she told me lots of things. About the yokel that's so popular in Petersburg drawing-rooms at present, of course, you know whom I mean: Rasputin. At first I simply couldn't understand how intelligent aristocratic women, women of culture, could associate with ordinary peasant women; and there's no jealousy either, they actually love one another, and the fashionable ladies learn from these ordinary women how to be passably common and primitive, just to please the little yokel. It's as if he had fused them together in *one* sacred flame. But then this woman explained the matter to me, so to speak. She gave me hints too, of what really went on behind the scenes. And I must confess—that these things didn't leave me quite cold. For in spite of everything we're—well,—the devil knows what we are!"

The others remained silent; not even Boris Abramovitch opened his mouth. Nina flung a glance at Zachary. She seemed suddenly to remember something, or to be trying to excuse herself for something and she grew cross. Turning to old Mirkin she said in a complaining voice: "Gabriel Haimovitch, I've already told your little Zachary, and I tell him again, that it's a scandal to be so respectable as he is. He's always putting me to shame and reminding me how degraded I am. No, no, Zachary," she suddenly turned on her fiancé, "I haven't taken a fancy for the yokel; but one thing surprises me," she now turned to the others too, "I'm surprised that I wasn't indignant, that I wasn't overcome with disgust at these doings. After all, I'm a moral woman, even though Zachary may think me degraded. What do you think about such things, Boris Abramovitch? Won't you be good enough to utter a few illuminating words on the question?"

"In Russia, my dear,"—Boris Abramovitch moistened his dry lips with champagne—"among Russians there exists a quite different kind of morality from anywhere else in the world, I might even go the length of saying a higher kind of morality, not the egoistic kind that guards private property like a policeman, but what I may take the liberty of calling collectivist morality. It is a morality of the family, not of the private individual. It is, so to speak, the morality of 'all-togetherness.' We still live in a younger society, or it may be an older one, a collectivist society such as prevailed, let us say, in ages when tribal authority or the rule of the matriarchy still existed. For that reason there is no privacy among us, nothing purely personal. Haven't you ever noticed that we have no secrets? All Russia gives me the impression of a huge public bathing place. In Europe people are ashamed of their neighbors' nakedness, but we take a special pleasure in showing our nakedness to one another. . . . And inwardly it is just the same. A Russian is not only incapable of keeping a secret; it's actually a keen pleasure to him to confess his sins and beg some one's forgiveness. And if he hasn't anything on his conscience at the moment, then he promptly invents some sin or other, just to have something to confess. What does that prove? It proves that the Russian can't live alone with his ego, in his own world. Unlike all other people, he needs some form of collectivism as his natural order of life—and not only in social matters, as among our peasants; he needs collectivism still more profoundly in his intimate personal life; he's afraid of being alone with himself; he must have his fellow men round him and in his heart. All Russia is one fraternity. And even if in our country the social demarcations are far sharper and cut far deeper furrows than in any other country, after all they are only furrows, cleaving the mere surface of earthly possessions. The rich have vodka three times as often as the poor. But inwardly, in its being's being, in its soul, Russia is a collective mass. Hence its need to confess its sins as well as its good deeds and its most intimate experiences. With other peoples their social life probably arose out of necessity or compulsion; but to the Russian it has always been as natural a need as food, drink and air."

This harangue came with spasmodic violence from Boris Abramovitch's lips; nevertheless he behaved as if he were bored with everything, even his own eloquence.

"That's the real Boris Abramovitch!" cried Nina a second time. "Papa, have you ever heard anything as good before? Your health, Boris Abramovitch! Have a drink with me."

"Every race that is proud of its own unique originality thinks that about itself. I had a Jewish colleague at the university; he was a Zionist. Everything you've just said, Boris Abramovitch, about the Russians, he put forward as the true character of the Jewish people whenever he argued with me and tried to win me over to his ideas," young Mirkin threw in.

"That may be so, for there is in one respect an actual and great similarity between the Russian and the Jewish peoples, I mean in their communal life and their desire to stick together. Every people that has a history filled with suffering possesses that sentiment of fraternity. The difference between the Russians and the Jews consists rather in this: that the Russian loves to confess the evil that he does to his fellow-men, while the Jew prefers to confess only his good deeds. He conceals the evil within him, or forces himself to suppress it. The reason at the back of this is that the Russian likes to have something on his conscience; without a few pecks of sin, as it were, he doesn't like to show himself in the street, and if he shouldn't happen to have committed any he thinks up a few sins simply that he may be able to promenade with the mark of Cain on his brow. The

Jew, on the other hand, likes always to have a clean conscience so as to be on the sure side. The slyness for which Jews are so famed consists in keeping their 'account' in the spiritual ledger perpetually balanced, as if an inspector might come along at any minute. A Jew may commit the meanest offenses, but he will always find some way of putting them in such a pure light in his own mind that they are changed into little virtues. If nothing else will serve, then he will make the good Lord his accomplice, as Jacob did. If a Christian had tricked Laban like Jacob—even if only in a small fraud like the peeled wands—he certainly would have felt guilty; but Jacob actually made a good deed out of it, on the excuse that it was necessary for his wife and children. The Jew is always prepared to transform his dirty, brutally egoistic interests into holy virtues. That's the kernel, if you'll excuse my saying so, of Jewish cunning."

"You've expressed my inmost soul, Boris Abramovitch!" Nina stretched her hand to him across the table. "I've often puzzled over that—that some people can do the meanest things, and yet their crimes turn into good deeds with a sort of halo round them; while there are others whose actions always turn out wrong, no matter how good their intentions may have been. And I'm one of the last kind. I may want to do some action that's entirely good and honorable, but always something comes out of it that pricks my conscience. And I tell you this: that's just why I can't stand Jews. It's mean and shabby always to be in the right. I'd much rather be a sinner, like the Christians. Papa isn't a Jew in that sense either. He always likes to have some trifle, at least, on his conscience. Isn't that so, Papa?" she turned to old Mirkin. "And Naum Grigorovitch has something on his conscience, too, oh, I know! But that man there," she pointed at Zachary, "is a Jew through and through. Always pure as a dove! I simply can't imagine how I'm to live all my life with him. But things like that change in later life, thank God! Eh, Zachary? Come here: we'll drink to your sinful thoughts. That brings him much nearer to me. Drink, Zachary!" She held her glass to his mouth. "To your sins!"

"We'll do our best to multiply them for your sake, but you mustn't complain of it afterwards, my girl!" old Mirkin exclaimed.

There was a knock. Another interruption. Between the parted

folds of the curtain appeared a tall, slender blonde with a bouquet of white roses in her arms. Her golden hair seemed to have been loosened by the prolonged dissipation of the evening, and was tumbling down as if blown by a wind. While she was still a good distance away she stretched her long, snow-white arm out towards Nina from beneath her short fox-skin cloak, and exclaimed in a musical voice: "Excuse the liberty, Nina! But I heard you were here with your fiancé, and I couldn't leave without kissing you and congratulating you."

"Oh, Sophia Arkadievna, you're actually here!" Nina sprang up and ran over to her. The women kissed each other ardently and long.

"Let me introduce you! Gabriel Haimovitch Mirkin, my papa; my fiancé, Zachary Gavrilovitch Mirkin; Naum Grigorovitch Rosamin: Sophia Arkadievna, Countess Arkasoff."

The gentlemen bowed in silence.

"I don't want to disturb you. May you always be well and happy! I only wanted to kiss you, Nina, that was all. Excuse me," said the Countess, casting a glance at the men. Her great sad eyes rested a little longer on Zachary, as if with that one glance she wanted to read him.

Count Arkasoff, who was standing in the doorway in his fur coat ready to go, was forced to fetch his wife. He was still a young man; his movements were quiet and he had weary Mongolian eyes.

"Please excuse me for appearing here in my overcoat," said the Count with an ironical smile. He shook hands coldly with the gentlemen and led the Countess from the room on his arm.

"And that is Sophia Arkadievna, Countess Arkasoff?" said young Mirkin in surprise.

"Yes, what is surprising in that? That's she so young and beautiful? No doubt you thought she was an old hag?" said Nina, somewhat spitefully.

"No, I'm just surprised... I'm surprised," said Mirkin half to himself, "that she's so sad; her eyes have such a melancholy look. And I thought she was always cheerful and gay."

"How do you know that she's sad?" asked Nina.

"By her words 'May you always be well and happy.' Happy people don't say such things."

"That is true," agreed the wise Boris Abramovitch.

"I don't know what makes me think so, but I have the feeling that she's of Jewish ancestry. Of course that's out of the question," said Zachary.

"You've guessed the truth. She was really a Jewess, but had herself baptized so as to marry the Count. But how did you hit on the idea that she was a Jewess? She doesn't look in the least like one."

"I really don't know, it just occurred to me. I fancy it was partly her eyes, and her words too. 'May you always be well and happy.' " Mirkin repeated the Countess's words again as if he wished to impress them on his mind.

"Ha, ha, little Zachary, the Countess seems to have made a deep impression on you! I'm not jealous of Mamma, but I'll be jealous of the Countess."

"Well, then everything is perfect now. You said yourself, girl, that you wanted Zachary to have something chalked up against him," said old Mirkin, laughing.

But before they had time to finish discussing the impression the Countess had left they received another visit. There was a knock and two attendants bore in a huge basket of red roses, so heavy that they could scarcely carry it. They were followed by a young man, tall and lean, and of a strongly Semitic aspect which was still more saliently emphasized by his bony, sharply-cut nose and hanging underlip. When the procession reached the table the attendants deposited the basket before Nina and vanished. The young man stepped forward. He made a low bow to Nina and Gabriel Haimovitch which made the tails of his long frock coat swing out behind him. Thereupon he began in a solemn tone: "Gabriel Haimovitch, permit me to offer my congratulations on the occasion of this joyful event in your family."

Old Mirkin ignored the young man's hand, seized the bell, and rang violently. When the Tartar proprietor anxiously hurried in the old man said in a calm, businesslike voice: "Tell your servants that they are to remove this basket, along with that gentleman there." Thereupon he turned back to his companions and continued the conversation.

"Oh well, we'll meet again sometime, Gabriel Haimovitch!" said the young man, and shaking his head he left the room, trying to smile amiably with constrained lips.

"That is Misha Molodyetz, the biggest rogue in Petersburg," said old Mirkin to the others in justification of his rudeness. "He's been worth millions at various times, lost them and won them back again. For years he's been seeking an opportunity to get into business relations with us. He isn't allowed to darken the door of my office.... Well, it's about time to be going. The people in the dance-hall seem to have found out that we're here."

Old Mirkin rang for the bill. He paid, tipped the waiters lavishly, and amid their and the proprietor's profound bows and blessings helped Nina on with her fur coat.

As they were about to leave the room their way was blocked by a group of young men who tried to stop them. Two of the men were very young, wore civilian dress, and displayed the ribbons of their orders on their evening coats; behind them stood several officers in uniform.

"Say what you like, they belong to the 'Beilis crowd' ... They all belong to the 'Beilis crowd,' even though they do themselves up in evening dress," shouted one of the youths; the others greeted his words with drunken laughter.

Old Mirkin acted as if he did not hear them. He took Nina's arm firmly and tried to pass the drunken group and reach the door. But Zachary stopped; white as paper he stepped right up to the speaker and said: "What do you want, you ... ?"

But before he had time to say more he felt a powerful hand seizing his arm and vigorously dragging him away.

"Good night, gentlemen! Will you be so kind as to make way for the lady?" old Mirkin cried to the drunken group, with a friendly smile. Instinctively they opened a path for Nina, bowing at the same time. Their laughter stopped at once.

"Do you want to stop a bullet, my lad? If I had paid attention to the insults of every drunk I met I would certainly never have built the Siberian Railway!" old Mirkin whispered to his son as they stepped out through the door.

Outside the keen icy wind invigorated them; after their long sojourn in the smoke-filled room it was doubly refreshing. The sky was quite dark and the night seemed just to have begun, although it was already quite late. There was no moon, and the stars were very faint. The pauper population of the Petersburg Islands were gathered round the sledges standing before the cabaret. They were waiting for the guests to leave, so that they might get alms. Mothers were there nursing infants under their cloaks, and with older children clinging to their skirts. There were also ragged gray-beards standing barefoot in the snow. They blew on their hands and shivered with cold although they were gathered round a fire which the cabaret proprietor had lit for them.

Still pale and shaken by the scene he had just passed through, young Mirkin had not yet had time to assemble his thoughts. His father was waiting for an attendant to fetch the two sledges, and now, looking at the shivering beggars, he muttered furiously through his teeth: "Sodom!"

"Gabriel Haimovitch, for God's sake tell me what has happened? Has some one dared to insult you in my house?" With these words the Tartar proprietor came rushing out.

"Son of a dog, nothing has happened! Who told you that anything had happened? Here's a hundred roubles! Distribute them among these people in the name of Nina Solomonovna Halperin." Old Mirkin drew a hundred rouble note from his breast coat pocket and handed it to the Tartar, pointing towards the beggars.

An oppressive silence reigned during the return journey. Although the painfulness of the incident had been considerably softened by old Mirkin's presence of mind, everybody remained sunk in silent reflection. But while Nina was waiting at her father's door for the footman to open it, she pressed, for the first time, a quick kiss on Zachary's mouth and said with a smile: "And yet I like your father best!"

CHAPTER XXI

AN ENCOUNTER

NEXT MORNING Mirkin got up very late. He remembered that his father had made an appointment with him at the office and hastily dressed. Then he hired a sledge and drove to the great building in the Nevsky Prospect where his father's office was situated.

Although it was already the end of March, it had begun to freeze again after a comparatively mild spell. The snow on the bridges was dry, hard and brittle. Pedestrians hurried through the streets with flaps over their ears and shoulders drawn up, blowing on their hands. A chilly mist wrapped all Petersburg in a tender milk-white haze. The sky looked like a great rime-covered window-pane through which angels were trying in vain to catch sight of the earth. Even the sun, which broke now and then through the fog, seemed to be firmly frozen to its station and unable to stir from it.

The Mirkin counting-house was in a new building. The black marble façade glistened with icicles. As soon as Mirkin entered the lofty office he was met by such a wave of warmth, coming apparently from all the human beings engaged there in such ceaseless activity, that it seemed they must all be exuding hot steam.

It was a considerable time before he was admitted to his father. The waiting-room outside old Mirkin's private office was crammed with an interesting looking collection of people, some in uniform, others in civilian clothes, most of them wearing stiff and wary expressions and high stiff collars. But there were also men who looked like workmen, with black Russian shirts and top-boots; women in solemn black with head shawls; beautiful young ladies and worn old scarecrows; officials with morose looks and thick portfolios under their arms, who grumbled to each other about having their valuable time wasted.

The two office attendants in their uniforms and shining top-boots energetically, and yet with that light and smiling courtesy of which only Russian attendants are capable, established order among the waiting crowd, asked each visitor the nature of his business, and conducted him to the appropriate department: though it must be confessed that this caused dissatisfaction to the majority of the clients, who were denied any chance of seeing the head himself.

"The chief must not be disturbed . . . an important conference . . . it will not be over for a long time yet . . . perhaps you would be good enough to see his secretary?"

Mirkin was a rare visitor at his father's office; yet the attendants knew him.

"The gracious master gave instructions, Herr Zachary Gavrilovitch, that you were to be good enough to wait for a little while. The gracious master will come presently."

The heavy door of old Mirkin's office opened. The pleasant aroma of cigar smoke mingled with a waft of warm air floated from the room. Then the little fair-haired Senator Akimov appeared; Zachary had seen him on the afternoon he had visited Halperin, and so recognized him. Behind him loomed the tall broad figure of old Mirkin. While old Mirkin was escorting his visitor to the door he shouted in his powerful deep voice: "Vassily, show Zachary Gavrilovitch to my room. I'll return in a moment," he added, turning to his son, after he had said good-by to the senator. Thereupon he mustered his waiting clients, who had risen at his appearance, and addressed them in an imperious voice, yet very courteously: "You must forgive me, gentlemen; it is impossible for me to receive you today; you must be content to see my departmental managers. They have instructions to meet you in every possible way. Vassily, show the pensioners into my secretary's room: he knows what to do."

"Gabriel Haimovitch, I have most important business to discuss with you." With these words a tall, thin gentleman with a high stiff collar stepped up to old Mirkin.

"You must address your business to the proper department. I'm very sorry, I haven't time to listen to it," retorted old Mirkin, smiling politely, and he shut the door behind him.

"Father, wasn't the gentleman that left you just now Akimov, the Privy Councillor?"

"Yes," the father replied to his astonished son, and he delved his freckled hands into the side pockets of his ample velvet waistcoat, across which hung his heavy watch chain.

"What has that forger come to ask you for?" asked Zachary.

"Forger!" Old Mirkin made a grimace. "Call him what you like; but after all he's Akimov the Senator, chairman of the commission for the State forests, and a privy councillor."

"He came to Solomon Ossipovitch about his case, but he was shown the door."

"That was hasty and gratuitous. One shouldn't be in such a hurry to judge. In Russia all things are possible. You lawyers understand nothing but the law. Whatever is written in the law books is law, whatever isn't written there isn't. No, my boy, Russia has another idea of justice. What was it that Boris Abramovitch said last night? 'In Russia people have a different idea of ethics and morality.' He's a clever fellow, that dance critic! You wouldn't think it to look at him. And it's just the same with justice as with morality. Things that are called crimes in other nations are no criterion for Russia. Our sympathies are with the human being, not with the law. What did that dance fellow say again? 'A morality not of the separate individual, but of the whole tribe.' And it's the same with justice: 'Justice not for the individual, but for the whole family, the tribe.' "

"For the caste, for the class—isn't that what you mean, father?"

"Oh, now you're talking exactly like a socialist. I don't like to hear you doing that—it's not because these people are socialists that I object to them, but because they want to apply their German or English doctrines quite mechanically to Russia. But a German shirt doesn't fit a Russian in the least. If ever another sense of justice, a social sense as you call it, arises among us, it won't be imported from abroad; it will grow out of the profoundest depths of the Russian soul and be in harmony with the Russian character, with Russia's own conception and own criterion of justice, an authentic Russian product. I've told you before that Russia hasn't crystallized yet. The Russian is only beginning to be himself. He's still shaky. He may be a millionaire today, an absolute ruler over huge tracts of the earth, a great merchant or a great estate owner, and tomorrow he may be, without any visible reason, a drunkard or a vagabond; the Russian is still young and so he must be treated like a child, like an innocent child that doesn't know that it's doing wrong. . . . Only last night you wanted to quarrel with a drunken youth because he insulted you, deeply insulted you. What would have happened if I hadn't dragged you away? His comrade would have drawn a revolver and shot you down. Perhaps he would have been sentenced to a month's imprisonment for it; perhaps not even that. But I'm certain of this: my good-night greeting made that youth red with shame at his conduct. And if that same youth were informed today that he had insulted a young man in the presence of his fiancée, his conscience would torment him, and he would run to beg your pardon at once, Jew or no Jew. And do you know who it was that insulted us last night? Akimov's son. I know him quite well; he has borrowed money from me more than once."

"Akimov's son!" cried Zachary. "And you told the father all about it?"

"That was why his father came to me, to beg my pardon. I don't know who told him that we had a disagreeable scene with his son last night. The son—so the old man said—was ashamed to face me, and so he sent his father to beg my pardon. Perhaps you fancy he did that out of cold calculation, because he needs me? I'm convinced that isn't the case. His conscience drove him to do it; and maybe his companions told him later what he had done. All the same I've snatched the opportunity and lent the father the hundred thousand roubles that he needs to balance his books. I know that I've acted in a very Jewish way in doing that, but I couldn't help myself, it was my race at work in me."

"To balance his books!" young Mirkin laughed. "A very mild term for embezzlement!"

"I've told you once already: in Russia there are no crimes, in Russia there are only errors and mistakes, and I'm convinced that even at Court the whole matter will be looked upon as one of balancing the books and not of embezzlement."

"And he took the money?"

"At first he raised objections. 'What does this mean?' he asked. 'I've come to you to apologize for my son's rudeness, and you repay me by an act of kindness. I can't accept it. It shames me too deeply; frankly, to tell the truth I really don't know where I'm to get the money; at the ministry they want to settle the matter quietly, and the public prosecutor has instructions to postpone the charge for the time being; Ekaterina Sacharovna has cast herself on the Czar's mercy and the "peasant" has helped too: 'One must help a good friend out of the mud,' he said. 'That is God's will.' But they insist that the money must be replaced so as to balance the books, and I don't know where I'm to lay my hands on it; and now you freely offer it to me. That is too Christian,' he cried. 'But you know,' I told him, 'the Jews are the best Christians'—and I wrote out the check. Besides it isn't a bad stroke of business by any means. This Akimov will rise to power again sometime: Ekaterina Sacharovna and the 'peasant' will see to that. And a man remembers a kindness shown him when he is down and out far longer than a benefit received when he is in power—particularly if he is a Russian."

"You must allow me to doubt whether that was the real motive of your action, father," said young Mirkin.

His father passed his hand over his mustache, as if he wanted to swallow something without being noticed. Then he smoothed the long tips of his side-whiskers and leaned back in his capacious leather armchair.

"I'm a business man, and I have my business principles and business methods. I'm not ashamed of them; they've successfully set me where I am today. But this time I haven't thought of myself, for I imagine that what we have already will be amply sufficient for you and your children, if you have any. But tell me: didn't you say something recently of a Jewish woman that had come here from Warsaw about her fool of a son? If I remember rightly he was sentenced to twenty years' penal servitude in Siberia. You're quite at a loss over the case, for it was a court martial that sentenced the man, and the only one who can give him a free pardon is the Czar himself. . . . You know of nobody, do you, who can bring the matter before the Czar?" old Mirkin leaned over his broad mahogany writing-table and pointed his bronze paper knife at his son.

"Forgive me, father, forgive me! I didn't mean what I said just now."

"You may be sure I know that," old Mirkin smiled. "Well, I've told Akimov the whole story; I've told him about the Jewish soldier, or rather about the pious Jew in a soldier's uniform whose only possession is his religion, for which he's prepared to sacrifice his life. Oh, it's good to have a religion!" the old man said with a sigh.

"And what did Akimov say?" asked Zachary impatiently.

"Say? He cried. Cried like a child. He shed sincere tears, beat his breast and swore that, at the first audience granted him by the Czar, he would fall at his feet and beg for mercy for the Jewish soldier instead of himself. 'I'll tell the Little Father everything,' he cried. And I believe he will; more, I'm convinced that this Jewish soldier will help Akimov's case. The Czar will burst into tears when he hears the soldier's story and pardon Akimov along with him. None of you know what Russians are really like. They're children; they strike and don't know why, they do good and don't know why. Only your office must send me at once the name and regiment of this soldier and his place of birth, so that I may hand on these particulars to Akimov. He expects to be admitted to the Czar any day now, as soon as he has squared his books. I'll let you know when it happens."

"Father!" cried Zachary as he had once done in Ekaterinburg when his father made that surprise visit. And he made to fling himself into his father's arms.

"And you wanted to fight last night because of a drunk youth's insulting words, and you were furious when I dragged you away. All you could think of was a duel! Just consider what excellent results that insult has had: a man has said he's sorry, another will be freed from prison, and your old Jewish woman will be able to return happy to her home. But if things—God forbid!—had turned out differently, I would have had to mourn over a death today." The father smiled.

"You're quite right, father," said Mirkin in the voice of a schoolboy being given a lesson.

"But this is not what I wanted to talk to you about. I asked you to come here for a special purpose. What was it again? Just have patience for a minute. Don't get up, don't get up!" Old Mirkin drew out his diary, put on his glasses, and rapidly turned the pages. "Oh, yes, I wanted to talk to you about Nina. Shall we do it here? Or wouldn't it be better to do it somewhere else? I've finished here for today. It's been the best day, thank God, that I've had for a long long time: I've saved the old Jewish woman's son. Wait! I have an idea! You haven't lunched yet, have you? Ring up your office and say that you won't be back today. I want you to change your way of life radically. That's really what I want to talk to you about. We'll go to the Hotel Europe; we won't be disturbed there. After that we may go along to Olga Michailovna's, perhaps; I would like to find out how Nina feels after that unpleasant business last night."

CHAPTER XXII

FATHER AND SON

After father and son had sat down at a corner table in the great dining-room of the Hotel Europe, which at that early hour was still almost empty, Old Mirkin began as if he were talking to himself: "She's by no means a simple little person, your Nina, but a very interesting woman, and a pretty complicated character, too. Not at all an easy morsel to digest—you must forgive the expression! I fear, my boy, that you'll have to be prepared to lead quite a different life from the one you've led till now, if you want to live happily with her."

Zachary listened in silence.

"I know women. I tell you again: Nina isn't a simple woman . . . but on the other hand she's an extraordinarily interesting and warm-hearted human being, a real Russian in her feelings. Don't be alarmed by the things she says! I know how to estimate them. They're girlish gaucheries mingled with a little feminine coquetry—but at the real bottom of her soul she is a dear, good, pure creature. No, no, I wouldn't be shocked by her words, but she needs guidance. Every woman needs guidance. One never marries a completely formed human being, and that is why I want to speak to you: you won't be offended?"

"Speak quite frankly, father."

"First of all I'm very glad that you've chosen Nina. I believe she's the wife you need; she'll awaken you. Yes, my boy, you need to be shaken up. You give me the impression of walking through life in a dream. You must forgive my saying so, but in spite of your time at the high school and the university and the fact that you're twenty-seven, you've never emerged from your boyish dreams yet. I know, certainly, that it's my fault: your upbringing, your perpetual loneliness, your lack of family life—that is my fault. All the same it's high time now, Zachary, that you left the dreamland of childhood and became a man, a man knowing his own will and prepared to act for himself without waiting for others to tell him. You aren't offended with me for speaking so frankly?"

"No, not at all! Olga Michailovna said the same thing, exactly the same thing."

"I'm really very glad to hear that; I'm delighted. You must take yourself in hand a little. I want my son to be a bold, self-reliant man. And I believe that Nina Solomonovna will help you a great deal there; she'll carry you on with her, and that seems to me just what's needed."

"And what should I do, father, in your opinion?" said Zachary, abruptly interrupting his father.

"The first thing, in my opinion, that you should do is to give up the occupation you have chosen. You aren't really very fitted for the legal profession. Don't be offended if I say that it won't fit in the least little bit with the life that I fancy you'll have to lead if you marry Nina. You must come into my firm! We'll make you vice-chairman with a yearly income that will allow you to lead the life that Nina expects. Your duties won't be heavy; we have capable clerks to look after that. Now and then you'll have to assist at legal conferences and work in collaboration with our legal advisers. A position like that will make you independent and give you the status in society that every one will be glad to accord a son of mine. You'll have the power, too, for there will be people dependent on you.... You'll have to have a house, a stylish, fashionable, first-class establishment in Petersburg, either an old palace such as 'The Englishman' wants you to get, or a modern house. Your 'Englishman' has nothing to do, and so he'll have ample time to hunt out antique furniture for you. You'll have your own car and you must keep horses. Do you fancy Nina would settle down in your bachelor quarters?... She expects you to provide a house where she can receive guests without feeling ashamed, and she has a right to expect that; and you have just as much a right, my boy. Your grandfather didn't labor in vain in trying to pile up a good income, and your father has done the same to the best of his powers; and with God's help he's managed to put something by that his son can enjoy and live on happily."

"Do you think that's happiness, father—a fashionable house, and evening receptions and balls, like those at Sophia Arkadievna's?"

This question put old Mirkin somewhat out of countenance. He remained sunk in silent reflection. Then, taking off his glasses and holding them in his hand, he made a sign to the waiter, who was just bringing the wine, not to disturb him. When the waiter had noiselessly set down the white Bordeaux and the glasses and was disappearing, the old man shouted after him: "Don't serve the fish until we tell you; we don't want to be disturbed."

"Very well, sir," replied the waiter, going.

"Here's to your happiness!" old Mirkin lingered on the word, his eyes grew red and protruded over the heavy bags below them. "Here's to your happiness! . . . Who knows what happiness is? I've seen many, many people, and nobody has ever been able to tell me what happiness is. But I want my son to have a home, a home, a thing his father never had." The old man stopped.

"Father!" said Mirkin.

"I don't deny it; I know it was my fault. Or perhaps it may not have been actually my fault, but a curse or something like that. However that may be, I've never had a home. I wish something else for you. And there's a longing growing in me, too, my boy, to warm my old bones, if you'll let me, at your fireside at least, seeing I've none of my own. . . . Life becomes wearisome and one longs for something or other. Yes, I would like to see you happy. . . ."

Zachary remained silent. His father's fate made his heart sore and filled him with deep pity, as once before in his boyhood.

"Why do you talk like that?"

To change the subject the old man went on: "And yet in spite of everything I believe that Nina will be a good wife. She'll make the house comfortable for you. Her moods don't matter. That will change. After the marriage she'll be a grand lady—just like Olga Michailovna."

"Do you think so, father?"

"I'm convinced of it. I know of many instances of that happening. But you must change a bit, too, you must become more of a man. But tell me, are you deeply enough in love with Nina to be prepared to do that? You seem to me to be pretty cool in your attitude to her; but perhaps that is just your usual way?"

"To tell the truth, father, I don't know."

"What's that?—Oh, you young men of today! It's hard to understand you. You don't know? And yet you are taking such an important step!"

"Yes, certainly. I really couldn't have acted otherwise. But I haven't got used to the idea yet and it seems a little strange to me."

"Oh, that's what you think? That must be changed, and after your marriage it's sure to be changed. All that's needed to change it is a comfortable home, a really pleasant home. It's time you had it, my boy, high time! Perhaps I'll come and stay with you, too, if you don't mind. To tell the truth I'm sick of hotel life."

"But how could we do that?" asked Zachary in astonishment.

"Oh, that's quite simple: we'll rent a big place or buy a house. Yes, it would be best to buy a house; we'll call it 'Mirkin House.' I'll have my own separate apartments in it. Nina will be the lady of the house. We'll receive guests all together and give suppers for our friends. In a word we'll make Petersburg our home in 'Mirkin House.' We needn't ever return to Ekaterinburg again; there's nothing there to take us back—now."

Zachary hesitated for a while before he was able to ask the question: "And what will happen to Helena Stepanovna?"

"To Helena Stepanovna? What will happen to Helena Stepanovna? Why, she has a home of her own!"

"I meant . . . would Helena Stepanovna like it . . . forgive me, but would she like your staying with us?"

"Why should she either like it or dislike it? She has her own life to live."

"Father, forgive me for asking you the question, but . . . what will happen to her?"

"I've told you already what will happen to her! Helena Stepanovna has enough money to keep her, and if she needs more I'll let her have it. The affair must end some time." The old man smiled.

"Father, you're surely not thinking of breaking with Helena Stepanovna?" Zachary almost shouted these words.

"I've intended it for a long time and now I'll do it too. I fancy she herself is prepared for it."

"Father, how can you do it? That woman has devoted her whole life to you!" Zachary cried indignantly.

"What do you know about it, whether she's devoted her life to me or not? It isn't for you to judge that. You yourself can't surely wish your father to go on leading an irregular life. No, it's time for your father to become like other men."

"But, father, father, how can you do a thing like that? Aren't you the least bit sorry for the woman who has done so much for you?"

"Sorry or not, it must be done! With things that must happen you can't stop to think, no matter how high the stake may be. Besides, my relations with Helena Stepanovna are my affair, and you must allow me to settle my affairs myself."

Zachary remained silent.

"Waiter, you may bring the fish now," said old Mirkin, making a sign to the man, who had remained standing at a respectful distance.

The meal proceeded mainly in silence; when the two men spoke it was about trivial things.

After they had finished, they drove together to the Halperins'. As they entered Olga Michailovna's boudoir, Nina came running towards them with a letter in her hand.

"Just think, that insolent man who insulted us last night was young Akimov, the son of the famous forger!"

"What? How do you know that, child?" asked old Mirkin in astonishment, taking out his gold pince-nez and carefully wiping them.

"I've just had a letter from him begging me to forgive him; he says he was drunk. He's actually sent me flowers."

"This is interesting, very interesting." Old Mirkin took the letter from Nina and looked at it carefully from every side.

During this scene the son attentively watched his father. A monstrous suspicion rose in him, from which he shrank as weak natures do when they are seized by anger. Zachary shrank from it—and from his father.

"He bought this letter for her, as he buys everything."

These words were on the tip of young Mirkin's tongue; but he pressed his lips to Nina's hand and remained silent.

BOOK TWO

CHAPTER XXIII

MISHA

OLGA MICHAILOVNA was a most convincing mother to other people's children and in all circumstances where her attraction as a woman derived added charm from an assumed maternal rôle. But she was much less convincing as a mother to her own children, for that involved her in serious obligations, demanding the sacrifice of her freedom.

Nina had developed very quickly; she had forcibly broken down the barriers of her upbringing and—to the great annoyance, to the actual despair of her mother—had announced that she was grown up. But the mother imagined that it was still her duty to keep Misha in a state of tutelage because of his effeminate nature, although he was in his last year at the high school; or, more exactly, the famous lawyer and his wife thought that their son was still a child and still content to pass his life in the school-room. . . .

But neither of them knew what went on in Misha's heart and head behind the walls of his room. . . .

The father was too overloaded with work to know his children properly, and the mother was too occupied with herself.

As Nina grew up, a sort of amicable understanding established itself between mother and daughter. Olga Michailovna resigned herself to think that Nina was an adult human being, a woman like herself. So a kind of friendship grew up between them as from equal to equal; the "mystery" that all women hold in common had a great share in bringing this about. But the relations between mother and son were of quite a different nature.

It cannot be said that Olga Michailovna had any very great affection for her only son. Even while Misha was still small enough to have his fair hair stroked, his mother's feelings for him had never been very cordial; she liked the girl much better. But ever since Misha had begun to pass for grown up, this youth with the beautiful blue eyes and the innocent childish bearing had become alien, indeed actually distasteful to her. And strangely enough her antipathy to her son had the most excellent grounds: in his beauty.... While Misha was a child her women friends had often set him on the table and had never tired of contemplating his lovely little face, his curls, and his elegant little limbs; they loved to kiss him and fondle him and admire the truly marvelous and noble lines of his body; in short, they treated him exactly like a beautiful prize puppy. At that time Olga Michailovna had already felt a sort of antipathy for her doll-like son. A disguised jealousy was mingled with it, for the child diverted the visitors' attention from the mother to himself, and so she was actually annoyed by their admiration.

"A doll, that's all he is!" she would say.

So long as Misha was little she could endure his beauty; but when he grew up without losing his girlish good looks she began to have an actual antipathy to him.

Olga Michailovna had dreamed of having a tall, strong, manly son with broad shoulders and muscular arms and a virile young growth on his face; but what she saw when she contemplated Misha was a boy with a soft, yielding, girlish body, a smooth, oval girlish face, an innocent expression which seemed to invite kisses and caresses, and great blue eyes which never met one's own, but diffidently glanced aside; yet if they did for once venture to glance at her there always seemed to be some hidden intention in them, some evil thought. Yet they were not brazen or challenging, but languid and almost beseeching—they begged for compassion, for tenderness.... Where could the boy have got his disposition? His resemblance to herself made the mother distant and cold towards him, and more than once she confessed confidentially to her inseparable shadow, "The Englishman": "It's strange: my daughter has a boy's strength of character; but my son, I really can't understand it—Misha might be a young miss."

Misha divined instinctively his mother's feelings towards him and repaid them in kind. For his father, however, he felt a certain respect, chiefly because of his fame (which awakened a feeling akin to envy in the boy), but also because of his capacity for hard and unremitting work. For his mother, on the other hand, he had nothing but tolerant pity, even a sort of contempt. He was the only one in the house who completely saw through his mother. Occasionally he compared her mentally with the mother of his friend Markovitch, who had devoted her whole life to her son; he thought of what his friend's parents had done for him, and then of the perfunctory attention his mother gave to himself, and he came to the conclusion that she was an egotist and a pleasure-seeker who still clung to her girlish fantasies and was jealous of her daughter's youth. Mother and son were quite aware of the feelings they nursed for each other.

In his parents' house Misha lived almost alone. His father was too busy to have leisure for anything more than a sort of official interest in Misha's studies, his marks and school reports, which he regarded as important for his son's future. Olga Michailovna was very clearly aware of her son's feelings for her and too proud to pretend to be anything but what she was before him or to show him more affection than she felt. To spare herself unpleasantness and domestic scenes, which she hated, she avoided him. So Misha was left to himself and his own circle of friends, above all to his friend and school-mate Ossip Markovitch.

Dinner was over. Misha's parents and Nina had gone to the opera with Gabriel Haimovitch. Misha was alone; he was waiting for his friend Ossip. To pass the time until Ossip came he glanced over the financial page of the evening paper; he wanted in particular to see how Siberian silver shares stood in which he was "interested."

Misha's interest in stocks and shares was more or less theoretical, it must be confessed, and was due to the influence of his friend Markovitch.

Misha longed for a sudden success. His father's fame oppressed him. He was ambitious to become something himself and to achieve quickly as brilliant a name as his father. That he could never achieve this through one of the usual professions he was perfectly aware; even if he were to study law and enter his father's office he would always remain the son of his father; besides, Misha had very little wish to study. He dreamed of becoming a flier (flying was new at the time and the names of the pilots were in everybody's mouth), or of gaining wealth at one blow by speculation.

In the State flying school, which he longed to attend, Misha knew that as a Jew and the son of a "radical" lawyer he could not hope to be taken on. He very seriously considered getting baptized so as to follow this career, and only his irresolute character and his fear of the material disadvantages, if his father stopped his allowance, held him back. As for speculation on the exchange, there another difficulty confronted him; no matter how hard he tried to understand the nature of finance, he could never do so with the complete success of his friend Markovitch. Besides, finance did not really interest him at bottom; his interest in it was purely superficial, and assumed to please his friend. So he did not know what he would be at. He refused to think of his studies; instead he longed for some event that would cut them short. Nor had he any particular enthusiasm for any other profession, and his interest in speculation and flying never went further than reading what the newspapers had to say about them.

Meanwhile he had made a discovery which first surprised, then amused, and finally interested him; he had become aware of the effect his good looks produced. And indeed he could not help arousing people's admiration by his extraordinary boyish grace. Both sexes were struck by him, men no less than women. . . . There was such languorous charm in his pliant body that everybody longed to go up to him and caress him as if he were a beautiful Siberian hound pacing by with lazily harmonious movements and noble carriage. His smooth, girlish face, but above all his deep blue eyes, expressed such aloof sadness, such ambiguous innocence, that he won the hearts of young and old alike. His eyes resembled his mother's; large and somewhat Mongolian, they were veiled by long, thick, marvelously regular dark lashes. Like his mother's the lids were delicately arched. Strangely blue, deep and brilliant, his eyes shone like two stars beneath his girlishly low forehead. Their glance could be so innocently corrupt that one could not tell whether he knew it or did not know it. It was as if the handsome boy went about with an open knife in his hand without being in the least aware of whom he stabbed.

At first Misha had no idea that his eyes, his graceful body, his languid almost beseeching movements possessed such power. But later he was told of it—by his school companions and by girls in the dancing-class. As he grew taller and his beauty grew more striking women began to notice him, all sorts of women, young and old, society ladies, friends of his mother and his sister, women of all classes down to his mother's housemaids. There were men, too, who flattered him. This general admiration was expressed in various ways, jokingly and seriously, by word of mouth, by ardent glances and secret caresses. Thus the youth became conscious of his power.

By the time of which we are writing he was perfectly aware of it, and his looks no longer embarrassed him as they had done in his childhood, when women were always kissing him. He knew that he was handsome and that his beauty was a power to be used. So he was resolved to set it off to the best advantage, and was impatiently waiting for the time when he could lay aside his high-school uniform and get his suits made by the best tailor in Petersburg. Already he devoted great care to his shirts and collars and made a point of always having socks and handkerchiefs of the same shade. In his waistcoat pocket he always carried a hand mirror; he pulled it out whenever he had a chance, contemplated himself for hours in it, tried which parting suited his curly hair best, and took pains to make his smooth pure face and the glance of his blue eyes as expressive as possible. He was at present occupied in doing this, the columns of the financial page having grown wearisome.

Steps could be heard in the passage. But it was not his friend Markovitch as he had expected: Anushka; his mother's maid, opened the door and stopped humbly on the threshold.

She did not enter, but remained where she was. She kept her head with its white cap and its thick black hair bowed on her breast, like a heron hiding its head between its wings.

"What do you want?" asked Misha in a voice that was half petulant and half coaxing.

Anushka bowed her head still lower and hid her face in her thin arms, behind which only her eyes and mouth peeped out.

"Dearest, dearest, dearest!" she stammered, and her eyes and mouth widened with longing for him.

"How often have I told you that you aren't to enter my room unless I call you?"

"Forgive me, dearest, I couldn't endure it any longer."

"Go now, go! I'm expecting a visitor."

"Just one minute, let me look at you just one minute—there's nobody in the house."

"No! Go at once, or else I'll kick you out!"

"Just one second! I'm just going, I'm happy now I've seen you." She fixed her black eyes greedily upon him.

Misha got up and hastily went over to her. The nearer he came, the more violently her body trembled and quivered beneath her black dress. Her hands convulsively clutched at her breast. Her pale face peering at him in burning desire from behind her arms became still paler, the features seemed to sharpen and quicken; her heart beat so madly that she panted; a hot breath came from her nostrils and her open quivering lips; her mouth twisted as if she had swallowed a bitter draught.

"Go now, at once!" He seized her by the back of the neck and brutally made to push her out. But the girl sank at his feet and twined her soft pliant arms round him. Then she pressed her round pale face between his knees and kissed his hands with hysterical passion, panting in a voice hoarse with desire: "You beauty, you beauty! Oh, you're as lovely as an angel!"

She lifted her pale face to his as to a sacred image and went on imploringly with wide eyes and burning lips: "There's nobody in, they're all away: let me love you!"

"You'd better get out at once!"

"All right, dearest, I'm going, I'm going!" Her slender body trembled as in a fever.

She tried to rise so as to obey his command, but she could not; for when she lifted her burning face towards him her long thick plaits had loosened and fallen about her. Without knowing it Misha was standing on her hair. She said nothing, but merely gazed up smilingly at him.

"Why don't you go as I've told you?"

She smiled up at him without answering.

"What's gone wrong with you? Have you lost your senses? Don't you hear the bell? Must I go to the door myself, you damned fool?"

She still dumbly smiled at him with her face upraised. She seemed to take pleasure in the pain he was causing her.

"Oh, go to the devil!" He flung her away and himself made to answer the bell. Not till then, when he moved, did he notice that his feet were entangled in her hair, that he had been standing on it all the time. More out of good-nature than pity he stopped and asked: "Have I hurt you? I couldn't help it, I never noticed—forgive me."

"Oh, it's nothing, nothing!" Her eyes shone and there was a blissful smile on her lips.

CHAPTER XXIV

OSSIP MARKOVITCH

A YOUNG man stepped into the lobby. Anushka helped him to take off his overcoat. An elegant dandy was now revealed; the shade of his necktie and handkerchief, of his socks and his stylish brownish-gray waistcoat were all in exquisite agreement. He stood for a moment looking about him. His long nose sniffed delicately, as if intent on absorbing the smell of all the objects round him, even those that his eyes could not see. There are people who see with their eyes, and others who see with their lips. The new arrival saw with his nose. His nostrils were as sensitive as the lenses of a good camera. With them he seemed to take in the whole house before having really seen it.

Before going farther he stopped beside the mirror in the lobby, took out a pocket comb, and groomed his smoothly parted and elegantly shorn hair, employing his hands also for that purpose. Then he threw a final appraising glance at his tie to assure himself that it was exactly in place. Yet he did not seem quite to trust the big glass in the lobby, for he quickly drew a little mirror out of his waistcoat pocket and once more examined himself to see that everything was in order. He was interrupted in this occupation by Misha's voice shouting from the door of his room: "Is that you, Ossip?"

"Yes, it's me," replied the young man; his voice betrayed secret fear and uncertainty.

"You aren't wearing your school uniform?" exclaimed Misha, stepping out of his room.

"No." Ossip started nervously. "Your father and mother aren't at home, are they?"

"No, there's nobody in. They've all gone out with our new relations, the Mirkins."

"I like to dress properly, I don't want to go about forever like a clown in that school uniform." Markovitch at last replied to Misha's question.

"Well, how are you?" asked Misha.

"Have you seen today's paper? Siberian silver shares have risen fifteen points. My father has won fifty thousand roubles today, perhaps sixty thousand even. You should have taken my advice and bought a few shares."

"Yes, I read about it in the paper, but I hadn't the money," replied Misha. "Come to my room."

"I would rather sit in the drawing-room."

"Why the drawing-room? I don't like sitting there; come along to my room instead. Anushka will bring us something to drink."

"Let's sit in the drawing-room just for a little while! I love your drawing-room."

Without much enthusiasm Misha led his guest to the drawing-room, switching on the lights only at one end of it.

"Do put on the other lights! I like so much to see a drawing-room fully lighted up."

Misha switched on all the lights; Ossip seated himself in one of the cushioned chairs and with an elegant air crossed his legs. He was very distraught while he talked to Misha; his animated black eyes kept flitting from one object to another; they ravenously drank in the pictures, the beautiful furniture and the luxurious carpets.

"Where have your people gone to?" he asked, casting a stolen glance at the silver cabinet; his upper lip quivered so violently with envy that he had to bite it with his teeth.

"To the theater or to some restaurant, the devil only knows where! Since Nina got engaged to Mirkin they've done nothing but rush from one restaurant to another; old Mirkin gives them no peace."

"A great card, your old Mirkin; he has the biggest timber business in all Russia."

"I don't care much for our new connections. The old man isn't so bad, but the son—he's a curious, funny customer! One never knows what he's thinking. Besides, he seems to be more in love with mother than Nina. All day long he sits with mother. No doubt she fished him for Nina, but he's caught pretty fast in her net. I steer clear of them all."

Ossip smiled more with his sharp, thin, twitching nose than his lips. His black eyes gleamed while they devoured the pictures in their heavy gold frames: "It's stupid of you to avoid them. Do you know who the Mirkins are? The old man rules the stock exchange; he could fill your pockets with gold at one wave of his hand. If I only had connections like that I would know what to do with them!"

"They don't interest me. Well, we've sat long enough in the drawing-room now. I hate this drawing-room. Come, let's go to my room. Anushka will bring us something to drink."

"No, let's go to the dining-room instead. You really *must* take me there! Please! I'm so in love with your side-board," Ossip coaxed.

As he passed through the apartments that lay between the drawing-room and the dining-room no article of furniture escaped his eyes. He could not gaze his fill of them. Without himself knowing why, he felt a wave of bitter envy rising in his heart. He compared himself with Misha, whom he always regarded as half an idiot, and he was tormented by the thought that Misha, and not he, should have the luck to be the son of rich and famous parents.

For although Ossip Markovitch had said so casually that his father had just made a coup of from fifty to sixty thousand roubles (Misha naively wondered why the family lived so wretchedly in that case), that very day his mother had had to sell her last half-dozen silver knives and forks to a small antique shop in the Sadova so as to be able to buy the elegant gray waistcoat and silk handkerchief for her son. Ossip had secretly confided to her that he had been invited to the Halperins and that it was not impossible that he might meet the Mirkins there. For this visit he had to be suitably dressed, cost what it may. For in spite of their bitter poverty the Markovitch family had only one desire—that their son should make friends with boys belonging to rich houses, and to secure his entry to these houses they were prepared to undergo any hardship and make any sacrifice. The Markovitches, too, had been rich once in Poland, their native country. But as far back as Ossip could remember his parents had always lived in Petersburg in the greatest poverty. His father was a stock-jobber in a small way and his income was never sufficient to keep the family in food. Poverty was a constant guest in the dark, three-roomed dwelling. The father and mother had not been able to afford new clothes for years; their garments were darned and their shoes down at heel; they went without food; but Ossip, their only son, had to have the best of everything, so that he might not feel ashamed before the wealthy companions with whom, at his parents' wish, he associated.

The Markovitches dreamt of riches and deified wealth. The life of Russian millionaires was an open book to them. Every event in Baron Ginsburg's family, in the houses of Polyakoff and the other great magnates, was known to them and ardently discussed long before it happened. And for their son they had only one wish: that he might grow rich. How that was to happen the Markovitches had no definite idea, it was true. Their most frequent dream was of a rich marriage. Their son, they were agreed, must get into the upper classes. With this idea he was brought up, and for this end he was instructed to make friends with his wealthy school companions. So while the Markovitch family starved their son went to a fashionable school which was attended exclusively by the children of rich Petersburg Jews. They had chosen it for that very reason; and to conceal Ossip's poverty they dressed him with exaggerated elegance and provided him with the best uniform that could be got and patent leather shoes. And when Ossip succeeded in making friends with some new wealthy companion there was more pride and joy in the Markovitches' hearts than if they themselves had come into money. Whenever he returned from a visit to a rich friend's house he was questioned exhaustively about everything he had seen there. His sorely tried and worried mother, on whose shoulders rested the task of satisfying all her son's needs, asked him indefatigably what the drawing-room and the dining-room were like, what he had had to eat, whom he had met and talked to.

The youth himself seemed also resolved to acquire all the qualities necessary for his future rôle as millionaire. He would post himself in front of the big restaurants and muster the dresses of the ladies; he knew the names of the most recondite dishes on the menus although he had never tasted them, was well up in all the makes of motor-cars, had at his finger tips the names of all the well-known singers, dancers and courtesans who moved in the fashionable world, as well as the addresses of all the better class brothels. He was just as well informed in the latest rises in shares; in that sphere he had already overhauled his father.

Whenever he visited a rich school-friend he always liked to be received in the drawing-room, the dining-room or some luxuriously furnished boudoir, so as afterwards to tell his parents how millionaires lived and what their houses were like. Yet that was not the sole reason; for it gave Ossip a very genuine pleasure to sit in these beautiful rooms, so unlike those at home. But along with his reverence for the rich and his longing to be accepted by them, he felt such a devouring envy of their comfortable existence that it turned his reverence into burning hatred. When he saw the luxury of some rich magnate's house, he grew pale to the very lips and involuntarily clenched his fists, and a curse at all this comfort enjoyed by others burst from his heart. He had the feeling of an outsider looking through the window into the bright and luxurious homes of the rich. . . .

So that as Misha led him through these rooms and showed him his mother's boudoir and—at the visitor's urgent request—his sister's room as well, Ossip was consumed with jealousy. He compared his wretched, cramped, dark home, where day and night the electric light had to be kept burning, with the splendid apartments in the lawyer's house. And while he contrasted his own position in the wretched flat with the opportunities Misha enjoyed because his father was famous and his sister was going to marry into the all-powerful Mirkin family, there came into Ossip's head the thought that occurs to all poor people some time or other: "Why should one man have everything and another nothing?" He hated his friend for his wealth and cursed him in his thoughts, wishing him all manner of evil. For a moment he put himself in Misha's place: "God, how far I could go if I had his chances!"

This thought would not leave him: his imagination kindled when he considered the great things he might achieve if he were in Misha's position. And when he sank into a comfortable, deep, cushioned armchair in the brightly lit dining-room he felt as if he were completely in Misha's skin; he saw himself as the son of the house, the son-in-law of the famous advocate, and felt so comfortable in that part that he had not the slightest desire to return again to sober reality. But then Misha woke him out of his dreams: "Are we just going to sprawl about in these chairs like all these women on mother's reception day? Let's go somewhere!" Misha exclaimed.

"Where could we go? We haven't any money. I have fifty copeks, it's all that mother has left. . . ." He was so completely under the spell of his fantasies that he had blurted out the truth, but at the last moment he had sufficient presence of mind to qualify his words: "All that mother has given me; but we would need a ten-rouble note at least, and where are you to get it? Far better just to stay here."

"Wait a minute, I'll see what I can do," cried Misha, leaving his friend and returning to his room. He rang twice. It was a signal he had agreed upon with Anushka.

Anushka appeared in the doorway. She did not hide her face in her arms this time; her joy at being summoned by him gave her such courage that she entered with laughing eyes, her pale face shining with bliss, her lips open with longing.

"Anushka, I need ten roubles. Do you happen to have any money?"

Full of joy at being asked for something by him, and yet a little dismayed, she looked at him in mingled gratitude and desperation: "All I have is five roubles, a gold piece that the old Mirkin gentleman gave me the last time he was here. I'll fetch it at once," she replied with trembling haste, and she cast a rapid glance at him, imploring him to accept her offer.

"I need ten roubles, not five. Five won't be enough," replied Misha with a tearful grimace, closing his eyes and knitting his brow, and making an immediate impression on the tender-hearted Anushka.

"Just a minute. I'll run down to the doorkeeper; he'll lend me the money. I don't like to ask the other servants," said Anushka faintly.

"Then hurry. I'll wait."

"Just a minute!"

Anushka disappeared and Misha returned to his friend in the drawing-room. A few moments later Anushka stuck her head in and said breathlessly: "Misha Solomonovitch, just a minute, please. There's some one wants to speak to you."

Misha got up, went into the passage, and carefully shut the door behind him. Anushka was waiting for him. In her eyes was a curiously triumphant gleam which he did not notice, and she said joyfully: "I have the money, Misha. The doorkeeper lent it to me." With that she gave him the coins, which were warm from her hand.

"Good," said Misha. "I'll pay it back when I get my pocket allowance from father."

"You needn't do that, you needn't, you angel!" With her hands convulsively clenched Anushka gazed up at him as at a god.

"As you like," replied Misha, going into the drawing-room again, and he shouted to his friend: "I've got the money, ten roubles. We can go now."

A sneering smile appeared on Ossip's bloodless lips. His black eyes gleamed and his thin nostrils quivered: "You needn't ever be at a loss, Misha. Your beautiful eyes will get you whatever you want!"

On Misha's delicate cheeks a faint flush appeared, tinging them pink. It was the same girlish flush that sometimes appeared on his mother's face. And, as on hers, the faint red in his cheeks presently faded into the delicate creamy white of his complexion, through which it gleamed for quite a long time as through a transparent film.

CHAPTER XXV

NAUM GRIGOROVITCH ROSAMIN

"Mirkin House" was bought. It was not an ancient palace dating from the time of Alexander I as Naum Grigorovitch had wished, but a modern erection furnished in the American style with every comfort. An engineer had built it for himself, but had been compelled by shortage of money to get rid of it. It was not actually in the Nabereshnaia, but in the neighborhood of the Finland Railway Station, a modern and healthy quarter. The purchase had been carried through by old Mirkin, and he now threw all the verve and ardor which he usually brought to the realization of his plans, all the Mirkin energy, into the creation of "Mirkin House." Latterly, greatly to his enemies' delight, his energy had visibly relaxed. But since his son's engagement it had returned, and new founts of joy and vigor, hidden until now, seemed to have been unsealed in him. His agents received orders to find a suitable house at once; as soon as Nina gave her consent, it was bought. Dozens of workmen—masons, carpenters, locksmiths and painters—were at once set to work to remodel the house in accordance with the requirements of the Mirkin family. . . .

In old Mirkin's car, "The Englishman," Olga Michailovna, Nina and sometimes Zachary, too, made excursions to all sorts of antique shops for furniture that suited the ideas of "The Englishman" and the interior decorator. For old Mirkin hounded them on and absolutely insisted that the marriage must take place as soon as the house was ready for the young couple. "Why put it off?" was his invariable phrase.

Incited by Olga Michailovna, Zachary himself was actually induced to accompany his fiancée occasionally on those excursions. Since being brought into intimate relations with Nina's mother, he had felt more and more drawn to her, and he bowed to all her wishes. So, along with "The Englishman," he wandered through antique shops, galleries and art exhibitions, helping to buy the furnishings for the house. Frequently he was asked to express his opinion of this or that article of furniture for the house; after all it was to be *his* house. The furniture, the pictures, all the other things were being bought for *him,* for his daily use; he would have to spend his whole life with them. So how could he remain indifferent?

Yet Zachary simply could not feel that all those things that he looked at were being bought for him; simply could not feel that the house that was being set up was for him, was his house. Now and then, it is true, he expressed his views on the furnishing of certain of the rooms, sometimes on his own initiative, sometimes in answer to a question from his fiancée or his future mother-in-law. But he always did so with indifference, as if his own home were not in question at all, as if he were casually considering the matter on purely impersonal grounds.

This attitude was put down by the others to his phlegmatic temperament, and they did not trouble their heads too much over it. He himself showed by his detached and smilingly cool bearing that they must not count upon him in such matters; he put himself entirely in the hands of his future mother-in-law with her expert knowledge of artistic matters.

Once, however, Zachary lost his cool indifference; it was when he was summoned to view an old French carved bedroom suite which "The Englishman" urgently advised him to secure. Zachary regarded for a long time the huge bed with the pillars and the baldachin, which seemed to him to be made not so much for human beings as for the amorous play of angels. An uncomprehending smile suddenly twisted his lips. He simply could not grasp that he had any connection with that bed, and he turned to the artistic Naum Grigorovitch, "I simply can't understand. How can one take to a strange bed? After all a bed is the only piece of furniture that any one can call his own. It's his real home, in a way, almost like his skin."

"But you don't think, surely, of bringing your old single bed with you into the new house?" "The Englishman" smiled equivocally.

"Why not?" asked Zachary in surprise. "Why should I change my bed?"

"That'll be a fine state of things! You'll bring your single bed and Nina, I suppose, will bring hers? But in that case where is the new Mirkin generation going to be born that everybody is so impatiently waiting for, your father most impatiently of all, as I have noticed?"

This was said casually and jestingly; but it showed Zachary his real position and made him realize for the first time the meaning of the moral lectures given him by his father and Olga Michailovna. At last he saw clearly the step he was about to take and all the responsibility it involved.

"So all this really concerns me?" he thought to himself. But to "The Englishman" he replied jokingly: "Don't you think, Naum

Grigorovitch, that the bed's too old a one for bringing a new generation into the world?"

He said it without any afterthought, but its effect was very different from what he had expected. Mirkin's tone astonished Naum Grigorovitch, but as a good European (as he considered himself to be, alone among his friends) he always refrained from commenting on other people's private affairs, and changed the subject: "It seems to me you look upon the furnishing of your house as far too trifling a matter to give any attention to. Strange! For me the things that I have to spend all my life among are very important. Every piece of furniture that I buy for my house, every picture that my eyes will have to see daily, is for me a living thing. Don't tell me that these things are merely dead objects. When you get used to it you can distinguish the voice of every separate piece of furniture; every chair tells you the period it belongs to, tells you of the soul of the master who conceived it, the artistic mood that determined its lines. If you know how to look you can divine the artistic imagination of a master in the lines of a chair just as clearly as in the lines of a poem. One must be able to see poetry in furniture—in an old cupboard, an old chest, a table—just as one must know how to listen to music, to feel poetry or to respond to color. It surprises me very much, Zachary Gavrilovitch, that you're so indifferent to all these things, as if you were ashamed to show your artistic feelings openly. But your father understands perfectly and he's showing as keen an interest in every piece of furniture for the new house as he would in the qualifications and character of a new employee he intended to take into his office. He expressly wishes us to furnish the house with genuine antiques, no matter what the cost may be. Every day he rings me up to ask how the furnishing is getting on. I had no idea he would show so much interest in such things."

"Is my father as interested in the house as all that?" asked Zachary in surprise, and added half jocularly: "Then you should really show my father the bed, Naum Grigorovitch; he may be able to decide whether it's suitable for bearing the new Mirkin generation or not. For in the last resort I fancy that my father has the greatest interest in the new Mirkin generation, a much greater one than Nina Solomonovna or myself."

"Zachary Gavrilovitch, why are you so bitter today? It's a good thing that the ladies aren't here with us! I never knew—don't be offended—that you could talk so cynically about such things."

"Surely I haven't offended your sense of propriety, Naum Grigorovitch? After all, we're both men of the world."

"No. But the tone you assume, Zachary Gavrilovitch, is quite new to me. In any one else it wouldn't surprise me, the times being what they are, but I expected you—forgive me for being frank—to speak of your future domestic life in a different tone, or not at all. You know, of course, that we all look on you as a romantic, even Olga Michailovna."

At Olga Michailovna's name Mirkin flushed.

"I never thought you would take it so seriously, Naum Grigorovitch—it was just a passing mood."

"I know, I know," replied Naum Grigorovitch. "But forgive me for saying quite frankly that I'm always shocked when I hear the young people of today speaking so disrespectfully of their most sacred and intimate feelings. I simply can't get used to it."

Mirkin was surprised that such things should pain "The Englishman" so much. After all he, Mirkin, had jested at himself, at his own lot—whose affair was that but his own?

Like everybody else in Halperin's circle, Zachary had a slight contempt for "The Englishman." Perhaps without any afterthought, perhaps moved by an unconscious feeling of jealousy, the advocate did his best to put all his friends against Naum Grigorovitch. Whenever he met him he seized the opportunity of saying something biting or even contemptuous to make him ridiculous. Yet slightly as Zachary thought of this Petersburg dandy, he felt a certain affinity with him. It had its source in "The Englishman's" secret devotion to Olga Michailovna, of which Zachary, like everybody else in the house, was quite aware. Jealousy divided the rivals, yet their devotion to the self-same object united them just as strongly as it estranged them; it was as though their love for Olga Michailovna put them in the position of secret brothers. . . .

Zachary knew that "The Englishman" had renounced his own career for Olga Michailovna's sake. For her he had remained a bachelor and lived in his fancy only with her. He let no opportunity pass of showing his feelings openly to her; every time he called he surprised her with some little attention, an old china cup, a miniature or the like, although in doing this he made himself ridiculous in the eyes of all his friends. But he seemed to be indifferent to the opinion of his friends; he followed his feelings wherever they led him, without troubling what the others thought about it.

"Naum Grigorovitch, what is your real object in life?" Zachary put this question quite suddenly while they were getting into the car to drive back.

Naum Grigorovitch gazed at him for a long time. His blue eyes had a moist look. He wiped his hot brow with his silk handkerchief, meanwhile never taking his eyes from Zachary. At first he suspected that young Mirkin was making game of him and hinting at the emptiness of his life. But Zachary's grave expression and the gentle voice in which he asked the question soon convinced "The Englishman" of his sincerity and also explained Zachary's strange behavior. He saw that the young man's heart and head must be in a turmoil.

"I'll be as frank as you've been. Let's strip off for a moment the romantic fog that I've wrapped my life in for the sake of my own comfort and ease, and try to get to the bottom of things. I wasn't asked if I wanted to be born, and I was given no chance to consider its desirability. My father had certain sexual needs and so I was born —you see, *I'm* the cynic now. If my parents had known of the devices that we employ today to avoid unpleasant surprises I would certainly never have come into the world; for I'm the fifth child of my parents.... So, seeing that I'm an 'accident' in a way, I'm resolved to live my life in the manner that best suits my disposition and my feelings. I regard myself as a gnat or a leaf cast into the world. Instinctively the gnat and the leaf turn to the light, the bee to the flower. In the same way my instincts propel me towards the light, or the honey that pleases my palate. My father's wealth gave me the opportunity to refine my needs until they assumed a thousand shapes and forms. My father's wealth also allowed me to satisfy these refined needs. So I enjoy all the beauty offered me in the shape, lines and colors of old pieces of furniture, old porcelain, old pictures. If my tastes weren't so morbidly developed probably I could be content with the forms that actual life and my surroundings offer me—I would take pleasure in the sunlight, in the snow on the bridges, in a radiant blue sky, or in music. If I had grown up in a village amid different circumstances, no doubt I would have enjoyed the woods and fields, summer and winter, the primitive landscape. With my disposition I could certainly find happiness and enjoyment, the food I need, in any situation; for I go through life like a butterfly, like a sunbeam that can pierce even through a crack. I drink in everything that gives my sophisticated sensibility nourishment, that quenches my thirst. I extract from everything, as it were, the patterns that best suit myself. For instance, take my sexual needs; others try to find relief from them in satiety, but I seek it in perpetual abstention, in an intensification of desire. You all know what my feelings are for Olga Michailovna; I've never concealed them. My love for this woman who can never belong to me—for I would never dare, even in my thoughts, to demand from her the satisfaction of my desires—is the appropriate expression of my—let us put it bluntly—sexual needs. Nobody cast the romantic cloak over my shoulders that everybody laughs at me for; I assumed it myself because it best expressed my essential nature. I don't regard the wretched span of life as an end in itself, but simply as a short and narrow stream that issues in death, a stream that we happen to have fallen into and that flows into an infinite and eternal sea of nothingness."

"And that satisfies you?" asked Zachary. "That's enough for you?"

"What would satisfy us? That's perhaps the only divine thing in us, the one trace of immortality. Don't talk to me about 'satisfaction'!"

"If that's so, why are we alive at all?"

"Oh yes, if we could only avoid that!"

Zachary reflected for a little, then he said softly, more to himself than to "The Englishman": "But we can avoid *life.*"

"The Englishman" was silent for a little, as if he had to consider Zachary's idea very carefully: then he, too, said softly, half to himself: "Yes, we can do that."

After that nothing more was said.

CHAPTER XXVI

HELENA STEPANOVNA

"WELL, everything is settled about Helena Stepanovna, thank God!" old Mirkin exclaimed, when Zachary once more found himself in his father's private office.

"What do you mean?" asked Zachary in astonishment.

"What do *you* mean by your 'What do you mean?'? We've parted on the best of terms and without any unpleasantness, thank God! After all Helena Stepanovna's a clever woman," cried the old man, drawing out his handkerchief and wiping the sweat from his thick, red neck. Zachary remained silent.

"So now there's no obstacle left, thank God! Tell your 'Englishman' to hurry up with the furnishing of the house! I haven't so many years to live now."

Zachary still remained silent.

"And one hears some queer things about your behavior, too, my boy! Nina has been complaining that she's never seen you these last days. I can't understand you. Do you fancy, perhaps, that she'll run after you? These stupidities must stop!"

"What stupidities?" asked Zachary as in a dream.

"I mean your silly fooleries—you must excuse the expression, but I really can find no other one for them. A young fellow wins the loveliest girl in Petersburg and then before he's had a good look at her, in the middle of his courtship, before the wedding, he begins to neglect her! What kind of married life do you think you're going to have? What's wrong with you? What's on your mind? Tell me, are you dissatisfied with the engagement? Do you think it won't suit you? In that case there's only one thing to be done: break it off at once! What way is this to behave? We're setting up a house for you and you don't show the slightest interest. There's one thing more I'd like to say to you: I'm beginning to be sorry for *her,* your Nina. What is it you really want? Every man must surely know what he wants!"

Zachary let his father talk on and seemed to be attentively listening to him. But in reality his mind was occupied with quite different thoughts, and he suddenly responded to his father's reproaches with a burst of rage quite unusual in him.

"But this is impossible! This is unheard-of! This is . . ."

"What do you mean? What is unheard-of?"

"Your treatment of Helena Stepanovna. How can you do such a thing?"

The blood rose into old Mirkin's face. His ears burned. He was so angry that he could not bring out a word. But that did not last long. He leaned back in his swivel chair and said quietly and coolly, with an ironical undertone: "Of course, it's very modern and in accordance with the latest ideas for children to prescribe to their parents how they should behave, instead of the other way about. But I'll allow nobody —nobody, do you hear?—to meddle with my private affairs, not even my son."

"How is this your private affair? It's an affair that concerns us all."

Old Mirkin was once more completely in command of the situation: "Just because it's an affair that concerns us all I must put an end to it as quickly as possible. How do you know that it was so easy for me? It's possible that your father has just as much human feeling as you! Perhaps he, too, has to struggle against other factors, sentimental factors, egotistic factors, let us say. If I've made this sacrifice, it certainly wasn't for the sake of my own comfort, but for the good of us all. Who knows what effect it might have on Nina and her parents if one day some reporter concocted a sensational article on my relations with Helena Stepanovna? For—deny it a thousand times if you like— I remain your father. And it's my custom to clear all obstacles out of the way before I take any step."

His father's calm and natural tone disarmed young Mirkin. He felt now like a child confronted by a huge ball that it tries to grasp in its hands again and again without success. Every man of weak character loses his head when he is made to feel his impotence. So Zachary imagined he was dealing a deadly blow to his father when he said: I'm going to her, I'm going to Helena Stepanovna. I'll beg her pardon, comfort her, beg her to . . ." he searched for the right word.

"Yes, go to her; she's expecting you. She can't understand any more than the rest of us why you've been avoiding her lately. I promised I would send you to her; but you've no occasion to 'beg her pardon,' or 'comfort her' or 'reassure her.' You'll convince yourself of that presently. When you see her inform her that everything has been arranged as she wished. I'll write and tell her so too."

"Forgive me, father, but I must decline to give her your message."

"Perhaps you're right, Zachary; forgive me for being so tactless," replied his father coolly.

Zachary got up and feeling like a schoolboy after a lecture left his father's room with an awkward "Good-by." He hired a droshky (on the bridges the snow was already melting) and drove out to Helena Stepanovna's cheerful apartment in the Kameno-Ostrovsky Prospect.

He found her as his father had foretold; there was no trace of the tragic despair he had imagined for her after the break with his father. She greeted him with her usual smile and with that sincere welcome which she knew so well how to convey with cordial words and frank pleasure.

As always she was over-powdered; her fair hair rioted in a thousand ringlets. From the wide transparent sleeves of her dress she stretched out her pink, powdered hand, smelling of skin cream, led him to her boudoir and made him sit down beside her in her favorite corner of the embroidered sofa. As usual photographs of his father and himself as a child stood on every table, cabinet and other receptacle in the room. She spoke frankly and with great animation, questioning Zachary about Nina Solomonovna and the forthcoming marriage: "I understand it will come off very shortly now. You're only waiting, I suppose, until your house is ready?"

"Yes, that is so."—Then after a short pause Zachary burst out: "Helena Stepanovna, I've come to beg your pardon for my father's unheard-of treatment of you. We too, Nina Solomonovna and I, disapprove of this incomprehensible conduct of my father's. I want to assure you that all our sympathies are on your side."

"Oh, that's what you feel?" Helena Stepanovna's smile displayed the dimple in her cheek. "I've been expecting this for a long time and was prepared for it."

"After all these years you've lived together!" cried Zachary in astonishment.

"I know your father too well not to reckon on surprises. One mustn't be surprised at anything where your father's concerned, my young friend. He isn't an ordinary being like the rest of us. When we've reached a certain age we all know our places. But your father perpetually renews himself, there's no growing older with him. He can simply cast off his winter coat like an animal. And to be quite frank—I'm very glad it has ended as it has. Your father was too much for me to live up to. I'm an elderly woman and I know I have nothing more to expect from life. But your father still hopes for miracles. He refuses to resign himself, and he's right. He keeps on renewing himself. As soon as Gabriel Haimovitch's ship seems to have reached harbor, he suddenly hoists anchor again and sets out for new shores. Who can tell what your father may still do in the future?"

"I refuse to excuse him or defend him. His treatment of you gives you the right to have the worst opinion of him, Helena Stepanovna, and I want to assure you again that you have our entire sympathy."

"My young friend, you're very much mistaken. Gabriel Haimovitch and I are on the best of terms. I have the highest opinion of him. I myself advised him to take this step. I've said to him again and again: 'With you, Gabriel Haimovitch, one must always have one's trunks packed and be ready to go.' In our years together I've learned two things about your father: first, one mustn't cross him, for he'll brook no restraint; secondly, all objection is useless, for he will do what he wants to do in any case. There are secret founts of energy asleep in him, and there's no knowing when one of those reserves of power may fill his veins again and refresh his blood. I've always told him: 'I'll be sure to know when an explosion is approaching, and then I myself will tell you to leave me.' And actually I felt it far sooner than he did. It was the day that you got engaged to Nina Solomonovna. That day I said to him: 'The time has come.'—Perhaps I actually helped to awaken this new fount of life in him. And why shouldn't I? It would be a sin against God and man, it would be a shame to let that precious energy of your father's be lost. He's capable of marvelous activity at such times; his powers revive, his ideas get new life and it's at such moments that he hits upon his grandest plans. No, Gabriel Haimovitch's day isn't finished yet! And why put obstacles in his way? I believe too much in him, I value and love him too much, to put any obstacles in his way. And to cut things short—I myself did this, I myself broke off our affair. You need reproach your father for nothing, absolutely nothing."

"My father thought he had to do it for the sake of others, and that his connection with you, which I can't understand why you haven't legalized, might perhaps prejudice public opinion against us and damage the social consequence he hopes I will have after my marriage with Nina. All the same I simply can't make out what your connection with him has to do with us."

"Your father is right and I absolutely agree with him. Nina must occupy the position in society that she has a right to, and you as well. Your father's connection with a former opera singer is clearly an obstacle. There's only one thing that you can reproach your father with; if Gabriel Haimovitch loves anybody at all in the world, if he is capable of the slightest sacrifice, if he can deny the least demand of his egoism, it is for one human being alone—his son. Everybody else exists for him only to be exploited. I'm certain that his love and devotion to his son is the sole motive for this decision. And you must judge it accordingly. This last act of his had pure idealistic grounds. I assure you I feel for him. I, too, would probably have acted in the same way if life had been kinder to me; for my child I would have been prepared to sacrifice everything, even my love for Gabriel Haimovitch."

"Oh, you're too good, Helena Stepanovna," said Zachary, deeply affected, kissing her hand.

"I suppose, by the way, that your father intends to live with you in your new house?" asked Helena Stepanovna quite suddenly.

"Yes, he's no longer amused by hotel life. What do you think of the idea?"

"Your family life will certainly be a source of new happiness to Gabriel Haimovitch; I can see that and I feel for him. Of course, as a general thing, people used to life in a hotel find it difficult to settle down in a family. The old life draws them back again. In the present case, it's true, a counter-magic will be at work to bind your father to his 'home.' I mean your lovely Nina Solomonovna, to whom your father, I've noticed, is very attached. I'm convinced of that—she'll employ all her charms to bind Gabriel Haimovitch Mirkin to his 'home.'"

Without knowing why Zachary was conscious of a disagreeable sensation on hearing this last remark of Helena Stepanovna's. As was usual with him when he felt like this he smiled awkwardly and nodded without saying a word. At length he got up to go and, turning to Helena Stepanovna, gave her a profound bow.

"Oh, before you go," she said, seeming to remember something "there's a small packet I must give your father. Will you be so kind as to give it to him? Your father left it here by mistake, or he's forgotten that it's here, and it would be a pity if its contents were lost."

"I beg your pardon, Helena Stepanovna, but you must excuse me this one time. My father asked me to give you a message for him, and I refused him too; for I don't want to have any part in a matter so unpleasant to us all."

"My dear young friend, there's absolutely no need to take things so tragically that aren't tragic at all. Your father and I are old people—even if he isn't of that opinion. The little casket that I ask you to give your father contains something that is probably of greater and more profound interest to you than to him. It contains, in other words, the letters of your dead mother. At one time your father was in the habit of leaving important documents and letters with me, because he was perpetually traveling about. He has taken back all the other papers—they were mostly business documents—but he must evidently have forgotten this packet. I had thought of handing it to you in any case one day; for I know that these letters will interest you very much."

She handed him a silver casket of Russian work, which she took from a drawer. There was a pink ribbon tied round it, evidently by a woman's hand. Helena Stepanovna wrapped it in paper and said while doing so: "Believe me—I have preserved these letters as if they were holy, for in spite of all that has passed between your father and me I have always reverenced your dead mother."

Zachary took the package. For no particular reason he bowed coldly to Helena Stepanovna and scarcely touched her hand. Then he hastily left the house.

CHAPTER XXVII

A VOICE FROM THE GRAVE

ZACHARY flew rather than walked down the stairs, muttering curses through his teeth and calling his late hostess by unsavory names. The family instinct that lay in his blood rose up in arms: "Father did quite rightly. She's a lying whore. And how she tried to inflame me against my father with her smooth cunning words! She fancied I didn't understand her hints, her brazen insinuations against Nina. . . . How beastly! I should have answered her at once as she deserved!"

Zachary held the silver casket wrapped in its paper in his hand. He cast a glance at it: "I must give it to father as I received it. Why waken old memories again? Mother herself wouldn't wish me to know her secrets."

He took a droshky, but instead of driving to his father's office in the Nevsky Prospect he gave his own address. During the whole drive he held the silver casket on his knees, and he had a feeling as though he were clasping a dead hand that should be in the grave. "I must give it to father just as I received it," he told himself again. "It is mother's and father's common secret."

Nevertheless he took the casket home with him, and without knowing what he was doing, shut himself in his room with it and gave instructions that he was not to be disturbed.

He set the casket on the table and sat down on the old sofa that had accompanied him since his years as a student. His glance kept wandering to the casket; he had the feeling that it was an urn with the ashes of the dead, that it was a kind of dream and did not concern him. Once more he firmly resolved not to open the casket: "I don't want to know what's inside it. It has nothing to do with me."

But strange to relate—curiosity suddenly began to waken in him. It was mere curiosity, nothing more; he was not conscious of any deeper interest.

This strange mood soon took complete possession of him. He got up, seized the casket, tore off the paper covering and opened the lid. Annoyed at his own weakness in not sticking to his first resolve, he turned the casket upside down so that its contents fell out on the table.

There were old letters in a fine and delicate hand. The sight of the handwriting gave Zachary a delicious pang at the heart; the same thrill ran through his body which he had felt as a child whenever he managed to touch something belonging to his mother without being noticed.

At first his eyes were held by the beautifully executed crests and monograms on the envelopes which he deciphered as the names of various hotels and pensions. He seized a letter and was about to begin reading it; then he suddenly noticed a photograph of his mother peeping out from among the other letters.

He took up the photograph and looked at it. It was quite a small photograph taken while his mother had been abroad, and already very faded. His mother's face looked sad and ill. Her eyes beneath the finely curved eyebrows looked apathetic and dull. She wore a hat set high on her head, a traveling costume of English cut and a broad lace collar round her neck; in her hand she held a parasol.

"How lovely she is, how lovely! How could father have been quite cold to her beauty and so indifferent to her?"

From old boyish habit he put the photograph to his lips; but he was ashamed to press a kiss upon it.

Then he picked up a letter and read the beginning of one page at random:

"When I bore the grief of parting from my son, the sole joy of my life, I did so not because of my own guilt, but because my destiny ordained it. But now I see that I have paid too dear a price. I should have fought my destiny, no matter how feeble I may have been and how little prospect I had of gaining the victory. It would have been better to fall fighting my destiny than to flee from it like a coward, as I have done. . . ."

"Enough! Enough! What's the good?" Zachary told himself,

flinging down the letter. But his curiosity would not let him go. He took up another letter, inscribed with the name of a celebrated sanatorium for consumptives, and read:

"You must forgive me if, after all that has happened between us, I still go on pestering you with my letters. I have long since overcome my silly pride, which has robbed me of all my friends and sentenced me to live apart from my child, and it no longer matters to me what you may think of me. Yet you are the only one I can write to; for I have no interest in anybody else. And today, because the sun is shining in the sky for the first time after the long winter, and I can see the reddish tops of the trees, today a wish has come to me to write to somebody. Forgive me. . . ."

"Oh, God, how much she must have suffered, poor creature! She must have loved him to her last hour, in spite of all the misery he caused her."

This letter, too, Zachary flung away from him, seized the whole bundle of letters and put them back in the casket. A single letter remained lying on the table as if an invisible hand had intentionally left it there for him.

He unfolded it and glanced over the last page:

"I know that Zachary will never forgive me for forsaking him in his childhood and robbing him of a mother's love. It must have an effect, too, on his character. From my child I can demand and expect nothing, seeing that I sacrificed him so thoughtlessly to my egoism, my wounded pride and tarnished honor. I see now my unforgivable sin. What are pride and honor, that one should sacrifice everything for them? A true mother knows only one thing: mother love. My place was at home, even if I were shamed, sick, forsaken, outcast; my place was there with my child. It is just that fate should have punished me so; it is just that you should judge me so harshly; it is just that my child should have no feeling for me. Now at the end of my life I see clearly at last, and nothing remains for me but to beg your forgiveness, yours above all, whom I love, whom I must love even against my will, whether you are kind or cruel to me. Perhaps I love you all the more because you hurt me. See how completely I have overcome my pride! I confess openly that I love the hand that strikes me, that I am capable of anything, even of making peace with my worst enemies, if you ask it of me; for with God's help I have conquered my stupid pride. . . ."

Mirkin could not read any more. As if he were stopping a mouth that was screaming at him he flung the letter in among the others and snapped the lid shut.

"Poor, poor mother! He tortured you to death and you loved him up to the last moment!"

And yet he noticed with astonishment that he was not angry with his father. Those heartrending letters of his mother actually awoke in him a feeling of deeper intimacy with his father, as if he, too, like his mother, had conquered all pride.

"What can one do? Perhaps he, too, couldn't help himself. One thing is certain: he can't live with us!" This thought suddenly confronted him quite clearly. "Helena Stepanovna was quite right. I'll point that out to him quite frankly, this very day. I'll tell him frankly that he has no need to change his way of life. He's lived all his life in hotels; he must go on doing so. Why should he change? He chose that kind of life himself."

Zachary once more wrapped the silver casket in paper, tied the pink ribbon round it, and decided to hand over the letters at once to his father.

"Not another minute must they stay here; they belong to him, and he must digest them if he can!"

When he stepped out into the street it was still bright daylight; the sun was shining, spring had come. A soft fresh wind was blowing. The workmen clearing away the last of the snow were dripping with sweat as they shoveled it into huge wagons. The cobbles were at last visible, and the black soil round the trees. Mirkin was surprised to find that Petersburg, too, like every other city, stood on ordinary soil, not on snow.

It was a beautiful sunny day, and everybody seemed happy and talked and laughed more loudly and stepped out more quickly. Here and there a man was to be seen without his overcoat—after a long winter one notices such things.

Mirkin, too, felt the refreshing influence of spring. The spring wind blew away his disagreeable memories of the visit to Helena

Stepanovna and intensified the elegiac mood evoked by his mother's letters. He hired a droshky and drove to his father's office in the Nevsky Prospect. As he held the casket now it no longer reminded him dreamily of a dead hand; he carried something living, intimate and holy. "They must be preserved, they are family relics!" he thought suddenly. "I must tell father to lock them in the safe."

"And he almost forgot about them! How could he? They're mother's letters!" He was more surprised than angry at his father. But he did not find his father at the office, although it was still long before closing time. He was told that Gabriel Haimovitch had gone out of town.

Zachary hesitated whether he should leave the casket on his father's desk or take it with him. He decided to take it with him and ask Nina to keep it for the time being.

"Should I tell her about those letters or not?" Once more he hesitated and then decided to tell her. "She will be interested, and after all she should know."

He took a droshky and drove to the advocate's. It was the consulting hour.

As he entered he definitely decided to tell Nina. But Nina was out too. "Gabriel Haimovitch has been here; he arrived in his car and Nina Solomonovna went away with him for a drive," Anushka, the maid, told him.

Although his father often called for Nina with his car and took her for a drive, this time the news affected Zachary very strangely; he felt as if something quite extraordinary had happened. And the sun was shining so clearly and strongly through the great windows! The sunshine, the lack of snow in the streets that he had seen on his way, this unexpected excursion of his father and his fiancée—all these things struck him as so strange and alarming that suspicion woke within him and grew stronger and stronger. The spring seemed to be a confederate of his father and his future wife in some plot directed against himself.

"What can it mean?" he exclaimed, as if something quite out of the common had occurred.

Suddenly the thought came to him that the friendship which in the short time since his engagement had grown up between his father and his fiancée was not due to pure family sentiment. This desire for family life had awakened too quickly in his father—and he, Zachary, had been explaining it to himself by his father's age and his longing for a home! The various attentions that his father had shown Nina now assumed an alarming, inexplicable character; they were prompted, no doubt about it, by his filthy hidden lusts!

A hot wave flooded Zachary's veins. His shirt stuck to his back; his whole body was covered with sweat.

"What can it be? Have I gone mad?" he tried to reassure himself. "One mustn't think such things! I'm quite out of my senses, that's the only possible explanation! What can it mean? I'll kill him like a dog!" These dreadful words sent a thrill through his whole body, shot through his blood; his limbs trembled as if a naked nerve had been touched.

All at once he saw everything clearly, as if a veil had been torn from his eyes: "Mother and I, our fate is the same. I'm suffering what she had to suffer!"

He tried to fight against the thought. He seemed to be bound in a strait-jacket and he struggled to rid himself of it. But the fearful words grew stronger and louder within him: "Kill him, kill him like a dog! That's the first thing to be done."

In his heart he knew that all this was empty mouthing; in vain he fought, in vain he tried to shake off the fate that lay upon him—he could not. And yet his lips repeated ceaselessly: "Kill him, kill him like a dog!"

He was standing in the corridor between the offices and the lawyer's private flat while he talked to himself like this. He knew that at any moment some member of the family might appear and see him. It seemed to him that every one must be able to read his thoughts from his brow. Olga Michailovna herself might come out of her room and see him! Shame at the thought of her finding him roused him out of his trance. He went into the office and walked through the waiting-room where clients were sitting. For the sake of doing something, of devoting his mind to something and so getting rid of his thoughts, he went into the room that he shared with Jacob Shmulevitch

Weinstein. He found his colleague with a pile of documents in front of him.

"Oh, you're there, Jacob Shmulevitch!" Mirkin exclaimed in astonishment, as if he had met him for the first time after a long separation. "I'm glad I've found you! You'll have to get on without me today. I've something very important to see to."

"Don't mention it!" replied Jacob Shmulevitch without raising his head from his documents. "We're prepared for your going away soon in any case."

"Prepared for my going away?" asked Mirkin in surprise.

"Well, they say that you intend to change your profession and alter your whole way of life."

"Oh, that's what you mean? Yes, yes. I intend to change my profession and my whole way of life, yes, that's so," muttered Mirkin absently, leaving the room. Weinstein gazed after him and shook his head.

CHAPTER XXVIII

WRESTLING WITH FATE

MIRKIN strolled aimlessly through the streets. All his thoughts now circled round the remark that Jacob Shmulevitch had let fall, and again and again he repeated to himself: "Prepared for my going away."

The day, it seemed to him, refused to end as if out of spite. The clear young sun burned in full splendor. The sun smiled down on men and they smiled up at the sun. The carriages rolled faster across the bridges, the pedestrians walked faster, and everybody seemed to be hurrying to a great festival to which he had not been invited.

When he reached Issakievsky Square he noticed with surprise how broad and spacious it had suddenly become. And with astonishment he saw, too, that the statue of Peter the Great in front of St. Isaac's Cathedral was standing in the midst of a grove of trees. How had the trees come there? During the winter he had crossed the square twice daily and never noticed any trees in it—and now he saw quite tall trees there; they looked as if they had been washed and combed. Their twigs cast a fine network of shadows on the ground, now cleared of snow. The naked shoots were covered with a reddish bloom. The world was free, great and beautiful. "Prepared for my going away—everybody prepared for my going away. And just as the consulting hours will go on over there in the office when I'm away, so everything here will go on, too, go on existing when I'm away," Mirkin thought pensively.

"But where shall I be then?" he asked himself. And to scare away the thought that threatened him he plunged into the moving crowd. Everybody was hurrying towards the Nabereshnaia, the Neva.

The banks of the Neva, the whole width of the Troitsky Bridge, the whole length of the Nabereshnaia from the square in front of the Winter Palace as far as one could see was packed with crowds of people watching the play of the ice-blocks floating down the Neva. It was like the play of giants. Huge icebergs came down the river knocking sideways against each other; but in front of them the outlet to the Finnish estuary was blocked, so that one ice-mass had to grind on top of the other and a mighty battle ensued. The stronger and heavier blocks forced their weaker companions under the surface and battered and broke them until they floated off again.

The crowds, men and women, old and young, were fascinated by the spectacle. With childish gayety people who were quite unknown to each other were loudly exchanging appreciative comments.

Mirkin, too, paused and was at once swallowed up in the crowd. Here, in the midst of all these people, he could escape from himself, could flee from his own world, and in a moment he was held just like the others by this game of give-and-take between winter and spring.

Yet soon his thoughts began to hammer away in his head again, as they do in the brain of a man who is sick of a secret, deadly disease which he reveals to nobody, but with which his thoughts are always occupied. . . . He still held the silver casket with his mother's letters in his hand. It seemed to him that the casket had become a part of him and would stick to him all his life. And actually he no longer felt that he was holding anything in his hand. Somewhere, in his head or his heart, an invisible agency cast pale, indistinct pictures on a screen, pictures such as one sees in dreams, pictures beheld by his inner eye; it showed him the world as it would be after him. And as if a book had opened before him he suddenly saw with intense clarity the significance of the words: "Prepared for my going away."

"And why not? After all everything is as it should be and must be. The Mirkins' new house will soon be ready. Father and Nina will move into it; father will be happy to find a home at last. Nina will be happy, Olga Michailovna will be happy, everybody will be happy and content. Everything will be as it should. Only I am not content, so I must go. I'll vanish like the wind. Everything else will remain. The streets will be the same, the crowds will be the same. At Olga Michailovna's everything will be just as before. The furniture in my flat and the big cabinets in the office will still stand in the same places. The clients from the provinces will sit in the waiting-room and the passage. Jacob Shmulevitch will attend to them. The famous advocate will sit alone in his work-room, and everybody will wait impatiently for his door to open. Olga Michailovna, snow-white beneath her black dress, will sit in her favorite corner, her head drooping modestly, and examine a cup, a miniature, or some other trifling present that Naum Grigorovitch has brought her. Perhaps she will smile gratefully at him and 'The Englishman' will be in the seventh heaven. Nina with her tousled mop will loll half-naked on the sofa of her boudoir reading an indecent book that the ballet critic has lent her; or she'll exchange secret kisses and confidences with her friend, the fair Countess, in some more private room.... Every morning my father will be busy in his office and refuse to be disturbed. When he has replied to his correspondence he'll fetch Nina in his car and take her for a drive. They'll sit before some inn outside the town and drink vodka." Why, really, before an inn, and why vodka? But Zachary could not tear himself from the grotesque pictures that his moody fancy painted for him. "And perhaps they'll live together, too, in the new house, the two of them together—why not? I wonder how the new house will really look, with all the furnishings that Naum Grigorovitch has scraped together? What will father's life with Nina really be like?" Zachary simply could not picture it.

"And I, where shall I be? I won't be at all. These hands, these feet, these hips that I can touch now, my whole body won't exist any longer.... Yes, it will exist somewhere. Somewhere? No, it will have become something else." Mirkin simply could not picture, or more exactly, his sound instinct hid from him what his body, his self, would look like when he was no more. This reluctance he tried to overcome by rehearsing "The Englishman's" philosophical speculations, which he now almost shouted aloud: "If I'm a gnat what does it matter if I stop buzzing? If I'm a blade of grass I'll only be the sooner cleared from the face of the earth. In a hundred years, twenty years, one day after my death, one hour, one minute—what will it matter to me then whether I've lived my full span of seventy years or only a quarter of that? And for these people here, these people standing round me, for them I simply don't exist. Millions of human creatures live on the earth and none of them knows that I am alive. Then what can it matter whether I'm really alive or not?"

He cast a glance at the river and saw a gigantic towering mass of ice floating down. It still bore upon it the traces of some village or other human settlement; pieces of wood and other signs of human activity were frozen fast to it. This ice-block attracted everybody's attention simply because it told of some far-off human community. The thought shot through Zachary's mind: "If I flung myself into the river just now that block of ice would crush me to pieces. Perhaps it would carry some bit of me with it. If I want it to catch me I must throw myself in at once, otherwise I'll be too late and it will have passed me!"

He looked again at the great ice-block which, because of its size and its jagged edges, was dragging the others with it. Its sides were under water, but the flat surface on the top clearly showed traces of human habitation. One could see the places where sledges had scored it, and pieces of wood, chips of crockery, an old pot and several wisps of straw were scattered about on it. . . . And suddenly the thought of the people whc had lived upon it re-awoke in Zachary, too, the desire to live. He saw a village in his mind's eye; sledges raced through it. . . . Perhaps on that ice-block human beings had made love. . . .

And the block of ice which might have crushed his bones called him back to life again. . . . He gazed round him and he saw with astonishment how radiant and free, how great and spacious the world was. Beyond the Neva the sky stretched endlessly. Green roofs, golden church towers glittered in the cheerful beams of the sun. The golden flag-staff on the Admiralty Palace sparkled like a flame and threw off glittering rays that broke and melted in the air. The houses beyond the Neva, the Peter and Paul Fortress with its cathedral towers —everything looked like a child's toy. Really, the whole world looked like an absurd child's toy! The only thing that looked really great, austere and real was the endless sky. It seemed to arch higher over the earth; it was like an infinite ocean. Clouds floated in it, but the clouds were not so substantial, angular, palpable and absolutely circumscribed as the ice-blocks. The whole web of the sky seemed to be imperceptibly agitated by a fluctuant wind; it was like a tent softly quivering under a breeze. In the light transparent spring atmosphere nothing stood out concretely, the houses and trees were not palpable shapes. They were, so to speak, submerged in the transparent, soft, living air. All was a changing play of color. Above the earth hung the sky, where floating clouds, dark and bright, swam in the deep blue. Sometimes the clouds had an ambiguous and equivocal look; they were like the gleaming bodies of giants half seen through a flowing, transparent veil. Then they would assume palpable shape again; now a giant female form would emerge from the depths of the sea of light and spread out her mighty wings to dry them. Then again the clouds changed into a herd of snow-white sheep grazing in the skyey fields, their fleecy wool irradiated by the light. A lilac red glow transfused the air. It was the bare twigs, the liberated earth, that breathed it out, and it bathed every living thing. It bathed Zachary, too, sunk in his sick thoughts; his blood beat anew in his veins, desire braced his muscles. On his lips he could feel the savor of his blood, of his desirous blood.

"No, a day and a year are not the same. Eternity renews itself every second, the whole creation is renewed by every emotion we feel, by every beat of the heart. Eternity—that is life."

"A gnat? An eagle with tameless, unfettered will—that is man. He was fashioned for life. All else is sickly fancy, over-subtlety, cowardice. I, Zachary, cast by chance into life by a tiny atom of matter, am myself cause and end. I am the world, the universe, the creation. The world breathes in every breath I take; waves of pleasure run through the world and the air every time I feel pleasure. Now I know my true desire. I will give free way to it, all my veins shall break open, my blood shall drink desire until I am drunk with it—no, until I am quite sober."

His pores opened to receive that draft, to drink in freely the desire that until now he had repressed. He cast away his chains, tore the seal from a flask too long kept in darkness: the wine foamed up.

Now Olga Michailovna was imprisoned in Mirkin's mind. . . . Yes, Olga Michailovna herself, outstretched and naked, with her great full maternal breasts. She clasped him in her firm arms. He felt the coolness, the softness of her smooth body, her rounded belly. He saw her like Rembrandt's "Danaë," lying naked on her soft couch and waiting. . . . For hours he had stood before that picture, weaving secret pictures in his mind. Now he gave free license to his thoughts. His blood, that had been prisoned and sealed within him, awoke, flung off his fetters and broke forth.

"No, not death. For whose sake should I die? I shall demand my life from all of you and force from every one the tribute he owes me. No silly scruples, no weakness! Father is right; I am a Mirkin! I've been weak, shy and sentimental long enough. It's time for me to cease being a child, a weak, sentimental child. It's time for me to demand my tribute from life."

Suddenly he felt the full weight of the casket and what it contained. A thought burned in his mind: that that casket was to blame for the fact that he was so weak and childish, that he dared do nothing, could never come to a decision. A longing seized him to rid himself of the casket. It seemed to him that he held in his hands his whole life from the day of his birth till now. This casket had always stood in his way. It was high time to get rid of it. And as if with one stroke he wished to strip off the invisible fetters his mother had forged for him, he raised it and all it contained in the air and flung it in a wide arc into the river among the ice-blocks.

In actual fact it hit several of the blocks before disappearing; but before the letters had time to fall out it had vanished between the ice.

"Oh God, what have I done?" he cried out in terror. But at once he felt an inner relief and freedom—with that act something seemed to have ended and something new begun.

The crowd's attention was attracted by the falling casket, and they stared at the man who had flung it. To escape their glances he hurried away and mingled with the crowds that were making for the Nevsky Prospect.

The Nevsky Prospect was still more animated than the Nabereshnaia and the Troitsky Bridge. All Petersburg seemed to be out walking on this first day of spring. All along the Nevsky Prospect, in every free patch of ground, street vendors stood before their booths selling painted Easter eggs, sausages and meat of all kinds, cakes, pastries and other confections. Peasants and land workers, male and female, displayed all sorts of toys they had carved themselves: dolls, soldiers, wooden eggs. The children gazed longingly at the toys, the women bargained, the men looked at them with desire awakened by the first breath of spring.

Easter week had begun.

CHAPTER XXIX

THE AWAKENING OF THE BLOOD

When Mirkin returned to his flat feeling tired and empty he found a letter from Nina and his father awaiting him: they had celebrated the first spring day by driving out to Novaya Derevnya, intending to dine there; they had called for him, but to their great regret hadn't found him in; he must follow them with Olga Michailovna in a taxi; they would wait for him. Nina had added: "Dear Zachary, please don't let us down, or I'll be really angry. Mamma will be certain to come with you; you know you can do anything with her."

The maid informed him that the Halperins had rung him up several times, and Olga Michailovna had left word that he was to call or telephone as soon as he returned.

The news left Mirkin somewhat at a loss. For a moment he hesitated what to do. And once more, as always when he came in contact with his father, he had the feeling of a child who is presented with a big ball and does not know how to take hold of it. But soon he came to his decision: "I'll certainly go. And during our drive to Novaya

Derevnya I'll consider the matter again; perhaps we'll go there, perhaps somewhere else."

He went across to the telephone and called up Olga Michailovna. His heart began to hammer. It seemed to have a life of its own. He inwardly swore at himself for losing his self-control, but it was of no use: his heart led an independent life of its own and he had no power over it.

"Where on earth did you vanish to, Zachary? We've sent scouts all over the town to look for you," he could hear Olga Michailovna's soft, pleasant voice saying over the telephone.

"It's the spring that got hold of me; forgive me! I've been wandering through the streets like a drunk man; I've seen the ice floating down the Neva," replied Mirkin teasingly, surprised at his own hardihood in speaking in such a tone to Olga Michailovna.

"Come here at once! The 'young people' "—Olga Michailovna's nickname for old Mirkin and Nina—"have driven out to Novaya Derevnya and are waiting for us. But I'm afraid we will be too late now."

"I'll come at once," said Mirkin.

He had a good wash, put on a clean shirt and a dark suit, and while doing so felt that he had partly overcome his sick fancies. Yet while he finished dressing he could not rid himself of another feeling which made him bitterly angry with himself; he saw himself as a man sentenced to death and preparing for his last meal. "Why should I have such thoughts?" he asked himself. "What forces me to be different from my real self, from father, from Nina, from everybody else? Why must I accept life differently from everybody else?"

Yet he could not help himself. With that feeling he took a droshky to drive to Olga Michailovna's, and with the same feeling he stopped in front of a flower shop to buy flowers for her.

Having no experience in such matters, he bought a huge armful of blossoming twigs whose size could not help attracting people's attention. Then he got into the droshky again and drove up to the lawyer's private entrance in the Kasanskaya.

With his heart hammering uncontrollably and with the same gnawing sense of being a condemned man going to his last meal, he climbed the stairs behind the footman, to whom he had handed the huge bouquet, and entered Olga Michailovna's room.

"What is this?" asked Olga Michailovna almost apprehensively, when she saw Mirkin enter looking very pale, festively clad, the gigantic bouquet in his hands that he had taken from the footman.

"Forgive me, Olga Michailovna. This is the first spring day and I simply had to bring you a few flowers. Don't be angry with me for the liberty," said Mirkin hardily, but pale as death.

"Flowers for me? Why do you bring them to me?"

"Yes, they're for you, just for you," replied Mirkin.

"Well, I've no objection—thanks very much. Why, this is a whole tree; how did you manage to get it here? Come, sit down here beside me, Zachary Gavrilovitch." She made him sit down in her corner. "I've been waiting for you since five o'clock. Your father has been here to fetch Nina; they've driven out to Novaya Derevnya. We were to follow, but I waited for you in vain. Now, I'm afraid, it's too late. Where have you been hiding? Have you had anything to eat?"

"Forgive me, Olga Michailovna; I didn't know you were waiting for me. The spring simply made me drunk. I wandered about the streets and watched the ice floating down the Neva. I never saw such a crowd before on the Troitsky Bridge! Then I strolled across to the Nevsky Prospect and had a look at the booths of Easter eggs. I don't know myself what's gone wrong with me today."

"Really, what a child you are, Zachary! You let yourself be led away by the spring, and meanwhile an old woman has to wait for you, all by herself! Solomon Ossipovitch has gone to a conference at Landau's, the banker's. Misha is at his friend Markovitch's to do his home exercises with him, and I've been quite alone here waiting for you. Naum Grigorovitch himself hasn't shown his face today. The whole lot of you have deserted me on the first day of spring. You see how much I can depend on you!"

Mirkin kept staring at her while she was speaking. Satan himself might have chosen the setting to inflame further his roused feelings, thoughts and senses. Olga Michailovna was not wearing a black silk as usual; she had donned, obviously for the planned excursion, a low-cut dress of red silk: it was the toilet of a great lady; it set off the vigorous curves of her firm ripe body, outlined her rounded arms, her full neck and bosom, and here and there revealed her smooth skin with the downy pure bloom that lay upon it like a breath, a body netted with blue veins and breathing a maternal fragrance. . . . Zachary's passion stripped that body, which so long had slumbered in his longing and deeply hidden thoughts; every desire buried in him went exploring under the silk dress, in the folds of her body, under her breasts, between her white shoulders, her strong hips. These thoughts scattered his last remnant of common sense; his last trace of prudery vanished.

"Why do you look at me so strangely, Zachary Gavrilovitch?" she asked a little anxiously, blushing like a girl; her blood seemed to give the answer that his burning lips were asking for.

"Oh nothing!" he replied with a smile that was really strange. "You're wearing a new dress today, I see."

"You've actually noticed that! Since when have you begun to pay attention to ladies' clothes, Zachary? What's taken you today?"

"You must really forgive me . . . I don't know whether it's the sudden arrival of spring that's to blame. . . . Today I'm not quite . . . I feel as if I were drunk."

"I'm glad to see you like this. I didn't know that a spring day could have such an effect on you. That's a sign of life."

"Really, Olga Michailovna, I do feel like a child today. . . ." He broke off.

"Well, now, tell me what you've been doing with yourself all day."

"What can I tell? I've thought all sorts of stupid things; no doubt that's spring sickness. Olga Michailovna, would you like to go to Novaya Derevnya, or shall we go somewhere else? It's a lovely night, there's a strange stir in the air, all sorts of scents floating in it, and a quite eerie light on everything, as if the radiance of the white nights had come before its time."

"Where could we go now? You should have come sooner; your father and Nina will be back soon, that's certain. But what's taken you this evening? Why, you're actually poetic all at once. . . . I've never seen you like this before."

"I don't know, I don't really know myself," replied Zachary, putting his hands in front of his eyes.

"There's something brewing inside you, something I can't understand. What has happened? Do tell me, dear Zachary." She laid her hand maternally on his shoulder.

Zachary flinched. A trembling ran through him; he seized her hand, pressed it to his throat, and buried his lips and eyes in it.

A red wave rose over Olga Michailovna and swept over her bosom and face. She snatched her hand away. "To be quite frank, if I didn't know you I would be afraid of you. You're so strange tonight. . . ."

These words gave him courage.

"Olga Michailovna, I love you, you . . . you only, I love you. I don't care what you may think of me, that can't be helped now. I long for you madly . . . I thirst for you, for your body, for your soul, for all of you, all. . . . Have pity on me, take me, take me wholly, wholly to your heart, let me lose myself in you! I can't live without you, I shall die . . . I shall . . ." The words came in a torrent, and his mouth, his eyes, his whole body seemed to go out to her, while he sat as if rooted in his place.

Olga Michailovna sprang up. Her first thought was to leave the room, as her conscience, her honor as a wife and mother commanded her. But simultaneously another feeling awoke: her old familiarity with him and her honest anxiety for this orphan boy who had never known a mother's love. Women are never indifferent to motherless children; a mysterious law of nature seems to compel them to step into the missing place. There was also the thought that Zachary was her future son-in-law, that he had always shown a liking for her and confided more in her than in Nina. These things recalled to Olga Michailovna her maternal obligations to the young man who had found a home with her.

Besides, Zachary's state awoke her pity. And her pity softened her heart towards him. She was prepared to do anything for him, as if he were her own child. She regarded herself as his mother, she must take the place of a mother to him, if only in return for the trust and affection that this young man had shown towards her. To forsake him now would be to push him into the abyss with her own hands. She must be firm with him, must now provide him with the firm maternal guidance he had lacked all his life.

Olga Michailovna paused beside the stove, leaned her arm against the marble mantelpiece and covered her eyes with her hand. Her body trembled, and its agitation could be clearly seen beneath the flimsy folds of her silk dress.

There was silence for a moment.

"Have you gone out of your senses? How could you dare say such a thing? How could . . ."

"I'm out of my senses. . . . Perhaps even worse. I know that my life is ruined. . . ."

Olga Michailovna gazed at him, her hand still shading her eyes. In them challenge and surprise were strangely mingled. The childish tears in his eyes, the impotent childish longing and suffering in the hand he stretched out to her, rooted her to the spot and filled her heart with pity.

"I know that every moment I stay here with you is sinful, now that you've shown me your strange, your incomprehensible feelings. . . . I mustn't stay here another instant."

"Olga Michailovna, don't go, don't leave me! You surely can't leave me . . ."

He suddenly turned his face full towards her; there were tears in his eyes.

Her heart contracted; her hands trembled. There were tears in her eyes too. She took a step nearer, seized his head with her hands and looked into his face.

"Zachary Gavrilovitch, what is wrong with you? What has happened to you? Tell me!"

"I don't know, Olga Michailovna. . . . I long for you and I shall die if you refuse me." He raised his face towards her, while she still held it, and looked with childish supplication into her eyes.

"I love you, like a mother. . . . You yourself pleaded with me to do so. Is that not enough for you?"

Mirkin remained silent, gazing straight at her with a burning glance.

"What has taken you? Tell me! I love you as I love Misha, perhaps even more. How can you have such thoughts of a woman that you look upon as a mother?"

At her last words Zachary quite lost his control; he buried his face deep in her throat; in his nostrils, on his open lips, he felt the fragrance of the mother and the woman; his racing blood swelled his arteries with energy and his muscles with manly strength. He clasped her in his arms and his long tormenting desire for her burst out uncontrollably at last. He felt the softness, the coolness of her smooth body, and became a hungry child that after long deprivation flings itself between its mother's breasts.

"What are you doing? This is a great sin . . . almost incest. . . . But I'm . . . I'm almost your mother . . ."

She was panting. Pliantly, flexibly, her body yielded to his arms, in which the muscles were corded. Her whole body seemed to fill with milk, to become all a mother's breast. . . . In an exquisite agony she surrendered herself to his arms.

"What are you doing with me? What are you doing?" she whispered, her head resting on his shoulder.

"Mother, mother . . ." he panted with delight.

Their hearts beat against each other, the blood seemed to flow out of their bodies and mingle. . . .

"Mother, mother!" he kept on murmuring.

"What do you say? What?" she stammered.

"Give me all! All, all . . ."

"Yes, all . . . all . . ." she replied in a scarcely audible voice.

The hot breath from her open lips fanned Zachary's neck. . . .

CHAPTER XXX

CAUGHT IN HIS OWN SNARE

As a wounded animal drags its suffering carcass to some cave, there to die in peace, so now Zachary with bitter loathing conveyed his suffering body to his flat. But he was hardly aware of it. His thoughts were wrapped in a black mist; he seemed already enveloped in endless, infinite night, a night shot through by glancing rainbow lights. He had seen these lights before, when burning with ardor he had flung himself into the bosom of the eternal mother. . . . Their hues had not yet faded from his eyes. On his lips still burned a sweet and blasphemous glow, and it reminded him of something. That tingling on his lips he wanted to retain to his last moment, his last breath. He was not surprised that he felt it still, for he was not aware of his actual feelings. His drive home in the droshky had passed like a dream. Everything whirled before his eyes like a merry-go-round, the night, the stars, the street lamps, the lighted houses, the carriages and pedestrians gliding past him. But he himself floated in a black cloud and his eyes stared into an abyss of rainbow-colored light. . . .

He only came to himself when he reached his flat and found himself within the four walls of his room. He recognized his familiar study with the furniture he knew so well, the sofa where he rested whenever he was tired, the photographs on the wall, the chair standing beside his desk, the pile of papers on the table; and at last he began to comprehend what had happened. The black darkness with its changing lights vanished. Only on his lips he could still feel the last evanescent breath of that blasphemous glow. He was surprised that he was still alive: why did not death come of itself when one was ripe for it? Why did it wait until it was summoned? With amazement Zachary discovered that he could still walk, still move his arms. Was he not then already one of those who would never move again? . . .

He flung himself on the sofa and closed his eyes. Once more he would call back the dream that only a little while before had been so clear and distinct a reality. A happy smile appeared on his white face. What he was thinking of beatified him, and against his will, though in accord with all his thoughts, that beatific memory filled him with pure joy and with pride.

"My God, it can't be true, it simply can't be true! It can't be!"

But the memory of it became quite definite, the entry was unmistakably recorded: yes, it had been so.

He thought of the price that he would have to pay.

"Why doesn't the end come of itself when one wants it? What is it waiting for?" he asked himself, and then added aloud: "When death doesn't come of itself, then it must be summoned!"

He looked round his room. Now it seemed to him like a sealed tomb; he would never leave it again. Everybody expected *that* of him;

those who were near to him, those who hardly knew him, and above all —himself.

He saw his whole life. He had still a short stretch of the way to traverse; then he would come to a gap. He must leap across that gap. Sooner or later, what did it matter? There was no other way out. He must in any case reach that gap sooner or later; it was better to leap across it quickly. Yes, death must be summoned, the sooner the better!

And to gain a few minutes more of self-delusion he busied himself thinking of the final preparations. Letters would have to be written —but to whom? To Nina, asking her forgiveness; nothing more than that, only a few words: "Nina Solomonovna, forgive me!" But what was the use? Suddenly Nina seemed to him a being unattainably pure, a saint, a suffering saint: "Dare I write to her? No, I daren't. There's only one thing she can expect of me: to vanish from her path as quickly and as silently as possible. And I shall do that."

"I'll pay my debt, I'll pay," he told himself. And like a debtor who holds in his hands money enough to pay all his debts, so he now held his life in his hands, ready to pay. That gave him strength and allayed a little his humiliation.

"I'll pay, I'll pay," he almost shouted, as if he were defending himself against some one.

"But I must leave a few words for my father, something like: 'There's no need to grieve for me; this is the best way out.' " His father, too, seemed now unattainably above him: "After all he's pure according to his lights; he has his own code of morality. But what about me?"

Of a sudden he felt that he had no right even to think of such things. Every minute that he went on living and meditating was mere cowardly hesitation.

"No more reflection. Do it now! At once!" Once more his resolution hardened into validity, he felt that he had the money in his hand to pay, and for a moment his courage returned.

Should he write to Olga Michailovna? He dared not open the door to that thought: "Certainly not to her! She expects to find the news in the morning paper without any comment."

Now he felt he had come to the end of the short stretch left to him, that he had reached the gap. Now the moment had come to take the leap!

Very slowly, as if goaded, he rose from the sofa. How was he to do it? Until now he had never thought of that. A shot from a revolver would be the best way. But there was no revolver in the house.

"Does a suicide bother about how he's to do the deed? Are there so few ways of doing it? One simply flings oneself under the first convenient tram, or jumps into the river. Anyhow, I can always climb up on the window ledge and fling myself down into the street!

"No, not into the street, not into the street, not among the snow and filth! People would trample on me," he said to himself, as if asking some one to excuse him.

"Does a suicide think of what will become of his dead body? All this is mere cowardice."

He recalled having once read of a student who hanged himself with his braces on the chandelier.

He examined the chandelier: "Yes, that would be better, but it isn't the right way still. It would take too much effort and make too much noise. The maid might hear and interrupt me."

"After all, it's nobody's business how I do it, so long as I do it. And it will be done this very evening. I shall never leave this room again. The only thing left is to find a simple and quiet way, a noiseless, intimate way, as it were."

He remembered having read a novel where the hero took his life by cutting open his jugular vein, all the time keeping his eyes on his sweetheart's photograph. Yes, that kind of death was painless, even agreeable.

"Does a suicide think whether his death is going to be painless and agreeable?" he jeered. "These are the thoughts of a coward."

He decided for the opening of his jugular vein. "It is noiseless and intimate."

Slowly, as if driven by the lash of a whip, he began to take off his clothes. He took off one garment after another and did not forget to hang them up neatly, with the unspoken wish that the room should present an artistic appearance after his demise. . . .

When he caught sight of himself standing naked in the mirror of the wardrobe, all at once he became aware of the full significance of his act.

"My God, it's me, it's that body there that I'm going to kill! I've taken off my clothes and I'm standing naked, so as to make an end of myself!"

All his instincts rose in protest. Involuntarily he passed his hand over his body, over his breast, his shoulders, as if he wished to accompany himself with comforting caresses on his last journey.

"Must it be? Is there really no other way out?" Against his will the question rose in his mind.

"What a miserable coward I am!" he jeered at himself. "For my cowardice, if for nothing else, I deserve to die."

With hasty steps he went over to the toilet table and opened the blade of his razor. Then he regarded the veins standing out on his arm above the wrist: "That's where I must cut, cut deep and let the blood flow."

His head grew hot. The air in the room seemed to thicken and he suddenly heard his heart beating.

"No, there's no other way out. There's no way now! There's nothing left now!" he exclaimed to himself, almost in tears.

"I must do it! I must do it!"

On his way back to the sofa with his razor in his hand he paused before the mirror and contemplated his body. He told himself: "That body has been with me all my life, from the day of my birth. That body, that breast, that belly, those loins, all these are me, Zachary Gavrilovitch Mirkin." Now he was going to part from his body: "I, Mirkin, am one thing and my body, again, is another thing. I, Mirkin, am an idea that will perhaps go on existing when the body, that body there, is clay, corruption, dust."

The razor fell from his hand. He flung himself into a chair, pressed his hands to his temples and remained sunk in thought.

"How it is possible for me to go on existing after I have crumbled into dust?

"It seems impossible only because we are accustomed to look on death with the same eyes and in the same light as we look on life. But death is something different, something quite different. What is death?

It is the gate to that unknown eternal state of which we have no image and no knowledge. The road to it leads through annihilation. The speedier our annihilation, the nearer we are to that unknown infinite eternity which we do not know. So why am I hesitating? Why do I postpone the end? I should rather do my utmost to reach as quickly as possible the moment when this world will come to an end for me, to an end!

"I'll depart, then, to another country. Simply go away, because this place does not please me.

"Not for the sake of any idea, any human being! I simply *wish* it to be so. Of my own free will, I must be perfectly certain of that."

Strengthened by these thoughts, he picked up the razor from the floor and took a step across the room: "Where? Beside the desk? On the sofa? Yes, better on the sofa."

As he crossed from the desk to the sofa his glance fell on his mother's photograph, on which a warm melancholy glow was shed by the greenish light of the lamp. It was as if his mother with the white lace collar and cuffs on her black dress, with her young almost speaking face, was corporeally in the room.

Mirkin paused for a moment beside the photograph, astonished that his mother's face should be so alive. It seemed to quiver, as if her heart, nay, her whole body were concealed behind the frame; and from the empty oblong of cardboard his mother stared out at him with living eyes from a living face.

"It's a delusion. That's only a piece of cardboard after all. My will to live conjures up all these images to hold me back, to set obstacles in my path. There, I touch the photograph," he did so; "cold glass and behind that a piece of cardboard. There, now I touch myself," he put his hand on his chest; "warm and alive; my wits are not failing me yet.

"Yes, the body that I see there behind the glass, that face, those hands, are already moldered to dust. Where are they and what are they?" He tried to imagine his mother's body in the grave, but a tributary of his will to live kept on effacing the picture, so that it could not become distinct. "But in other people's thoughts she still lives. In whose? What does it matter? An idea can hover in the air even when the meaning it once had is long since non-existent. So mother has already gone the way of annihilation." And as his mother had already gone that way it seemed to him, in a sense, mapped out and known.

But then all at once—was it mere illusion? No, for it was quite clear and unmistakable—he saw his mother in her frame beckoning to him! Yes, she beckoned in a strange way, almost indecently, as if she were inviting him to something secret and obscene, inviting him to lay himself beside her in the grave to warm himself against her.

"My God, what thoughts to have! I'm having deathbed visions already," so a single little point of life within him told him, that had not yet been meshed in the net of death.

And so as to frighten away that last indecent blasphemous thought which had arisen in him in the last moment of his existence, so as to seek refuge in some other direction, he summoned up his memory of another body. While he thought of it he did not feel so depraved, as he had while thinking of his mother....

He had the vivid feeling that he was standing on an ice-block in the Neva. He had just leapt from one, which was threatening to sink, on to another; he had gained safety there and lingered a little to enjoy it. He saw himself again a child in the old house in Ekaterinburg. He longed for his mother, and as he was still a child everything was permitted him.

Naked, the razor in his hand, he fell on the sofa, buried his face in the cushions and, as if already everything were permitted him, dared once more to summon up in imagination the experience that he had enjoyed so recently, that very evening, the experience that his mother's dead face had again reawakened in him a moment before his death: "Yes, everything is permitted me now. What business is it of anybody's what a suicide thinks of to sweeten his pill?" he said, himself justifying his indecent thoughts and giving them free rein. In his imagination his experience now appeared deeper, stronger, more passionate, even though shadowy. The demarcation between idea and reality was blurred, the years changed place. He did not know any longer whether he was Mirkin, the young man, or the child Mirkin, little Zachary. And Maria Ivanovna was bending over his bed and clasping him protectively to her vigorous bosom. Yes, now he could feel it; some one was bending over him, was nestling his head, his face, in the marvelous warmth, the divine maternal glow that lies between the breasts of a woman. He could feel the blood flowing through the veins beneath that firm and powerful maternal breast. He could hear the blood beating. The breasts filled with milk, grew full and hard. And, lying between them, he had the feeling that all life had been conjured out of his corporeal frame and that between those breasts there rested now a naked soul. Every caress, every touch of that flesh, its coolness and its warmth, breathed maternal tenderness, mingled with unfettered feminine lust. Everything was allowed—to him, the child. And once more he repeated the words he had already said that evening:

"Mother, give me all, all!" And he felt that his mother gave him all.

His senses grew intoxicated with images, with scents; on his lips, on his eyelids he felt a hot breath, the touch of cool flesh. Involuntarily he stretched out his arms. Fiercely he clasped to his breast the form of a mighty mother, fashioned from all the women who had ever loved him, his mother, Olga Michailovna, Nina, Maria Ivanovna, and from many other women unknown to him, whom he had never seen. The whole being of woman was gathered up in the mother shape that he now clasped, in whose arms he now breathed out his life. . . .

He lay like this in a trance for several minutes, or it may have been for hours. He could not have told.

Until he awoke with the feeling: now I have achieved all. There is nothing more left; I have reached the gap.

"I must take the leap joyfully, courageously. With the taste of my mother's lips still on mine, and before the last hues of the vision fade away."

He got up, stretched out his left hand and clenched it; the veins at his wrist swelled and crept like blue worms from under the soft tissue of the skin. His wrist now looked like the plucked neck of a hen. To avoid seeing it he shut his eyes and with his right hand made a pass at the knot of veins.

He could not tell whether he was dead or still alive. He was merely surprised that he felt no pain. Then he slowly opened his eyes and saw that his right hand holding the razor had stopped motionlessly about two inches from his wrist, as if frozen there.

"God, I can't, I can't!" he cried in despair and began to rail at himself: "What a wretched coward I am! God, if the others knew how hard I find this, how they would despise me! Why can't I do it?"

And simply to punish himself for his wretched cowardice he made another attempt.

But the hand holding the razor refused even to move. It seemed to set itself against him, to rebel against his will.

"I can't! I simply can't!" In furious despair he flung the razor on the floor and screamed: "Oh, you miserable coward!" He walked up and down in desperation and sought some saving solution in his thoughts, some straw that he could clutch: "I can't either live or die. God, how terrible!"

His brain worked feverishly, his thoughts seemed to be trying to fashion a soft bed to catch his body when it fell.

"Since I can't die, it's clear that I'm not ripe for death yet. Nature won't let me die, my own fate won't let me die.

"But I'm a contemptible creature all the same; I can't, I daren't live. Everybody expects this of me, my own fate expects it of me. *She* expects too, to hear of it first thing tomorrow morning."

A devouring rage against himself flamed up in him. He seemed a pariah in his own eyes.

"And I'll fling my filthy carcass into the grave, come what may!"

He bent down to pick up the razor again.

Then the telephone on his desk rang loudly; with a strangely shrill and urgent note, it seemed to him.

"Oh, go to the devil! This is a fine time to ring!" he shouted, quivering with rage. Without paying any attention to the telephone, he tried yet once more to pick up the razor.

But the telephone bell rang as if mad and would not stop. . . . His knees seemed paralyzed, his hands trembled, he groped frantically for the receiver.

He heard Olga Michailovna's voice: "Zachary! Zachary! Thank God! Thank God! I don't know myself why—but I'm afraid! My heart is trembling with anxiety for you. For God's sake, don't do anything stupid! I implore you! Everything will come all right!"

In a voice quivering with anxiety and shame Olga Michailovna went on: "Why don't you speak? Promise me what I've asked, or else

I'll come to you straight away! I'm trembling from head to foot for you."

"I promise," stammered Zachary.

"Good night."

"Good night," he stammered.

CHAPTER XXXI

WHITE ROSES

IN THE last resort every man is fonder of his own hide than of anything else, and it is himself that he knows best. In every man the will to live is prepared at any moment to throw bridges across abysses, that the ground might not be cut from under his feet on his journey.

When, after a long and heavy sleep, Zachary got up next morning he had already found a justification for continuing to live, his thinking-apparatus having functioned in obedience to his will, which demanded that justification.

"Well, then, I'm a coward! What does that amount to?" he told himself. "What is cowardice after all? An instinct of self-preservation that nature has implanted in men. Just as it fills our limbs with the burning lust without which propagation would be impossible, so it has given us fear and cowardice that we mightn't throw our lives away. Just as egoism is the instinct that takes us to our goals, so cowardice is the preservative instinct that keeps us alive."

Deep in his heart he was aware of a fact which no explanation could dissemble: that he had made a virtue out of his wretched conduct of yesterday. Yet he had now a pretext for living through another day. To feel cowardice is the mark not of a sick but of a healthy nature; it evokes a strong current of life-energy which prevents us from putting our lives at hazard. It is men of feeble character, men weary of life who most often display heroism and readiness to sacrifice themselves; a healthy and strong nature guards his life like the apple of his eye.

"However that may be I've won a victory over death after all," he told himself not without pride. "But why have I won my victory over death, to what end? So as to live?"

Zachary sat down at his writing-table and supported his head on his hands. He had no desire to dress. Why should he? Why go down to the street and walk about among the people there? How could he look Nina in the face now? And, a thousand times worse, how could he now meet *her,* Olga Michailovna?

He was completely mastered by two contrary feelings, despairing resignation and unfulfillable longing. On his lips was the bitter savor of satiety, in his heart unsatisfied hunger. He felt like a man in whose body some poison was raging more and more powerfully; like a man infected by a contagious disease. Could he go about among people with that sickness, with that poison inside him? Touch Nina with his diseased body? His disease would infect both her and the children she bore him.

"Oh God, I know I can't die, but how am I to live? What will my life be like under the constant load of a heavy sin?"

As if he felt his limbs fettered he twisted and turned but could not free himself from the fear that pinioned him. "There will be no life for me, there will be no life for me," he kept on muttering these senseless words to himself, although he did not clearly know how or by what means he was to avoid life.

"It can't be, it mustn't be!" With these words he sought to fortify his decision. Yet even that did not help him to see his way clearly.

There was a knock, the door opened, and the maid brought in a small bouquet of roses wrapped in tissue paper.

"A messenger has just brought these roses. There was no card with them."

Zachary removed the wrapping and held in his hand three flawless white roses. Drops that looked like tears glittered on the white petals.

"Who sent them?"

"The messenger did not say."

"Where is the man?" Zachary rushed to the door.

"He's gone already."

Zachary held the roses in his hand as a grievous sinner might hold the Torah roll and feared to put them to his face: he knew from whom they came.

A desire awoke in him to touch the pure wet buds with his hands, as though that might purify him; but he did not dare to do so.

"Put the roses in water," he told the maid, but then thought better of it at once and added: "No, I'll do it myself. You can go."

Holding the roses in his hand he walked up and down the room and could not make up his mind what to do with the flowers. . . . He felt like a pariah upon whom the finger of some pure being had been laid. A trembling ran through his limbs; it purified and healed him.

The telephone rang.

Zachary was resolved not to answer it. He knew who was calling him. But the telephone rang imperiously and forced him to approach it; he went up to it with a deathly pale face, his knees failing him.

Her voice was no longer as resolute and energetic as the night before; it trembled. He felt in it the loud beating of her heart and saw her lashes shamefacedly veiling her eyes; quite distinctly, listening at the telephone, he could see the twin arcs of her black eye-brows.

"Is that you, Zachary Gavrilovitch? Thank God! Come and see me, I implore you, come just as usual, as if nothing had happened. No, come soon, at once; I must see you."

"How can I?"

"How can *I?* And I am only a woman. Why should I bear the whole burden alone?"

"Olga Michailovna, was it you that sent me the white roses?"

"Yes, I sent you white roses." Her voice had once more regained its firmness.

Zachary was silent.

"Zachary, come at once! I've been in anguish all night. . . . Come, be resolute, rise above all this. Come, you must come, or else—God knows what I am to do."

Zachary was silent.

"Why don't you speak? Why do you torture me like this? *I'm* to blame for everything, I, I!" she almost shrieked through the telephone. He knew that it was a cry from the very bottom of her heart.

"I'm coming, I'm coming, I'm coming at once!" he replied.

"Come straight to my room. I'll wait for you."

Zachary hastily dressed, gulped down a glass of spirits to give him strength, took a droshky and drove at a gallop to Olga Michailovna's.

She was waiting for him at the door of her room and stretched her hand out to him from the folds of her loose morning gown. She was, so it seemed to him, extraordinarily pale. He cast a glance at her face and scarcely recognized her. This was not the Olga Michailovna he had known; she had completely changed overnight. Her face was bloodless. White as it was it looked still more attractive than before. An unprecedented experience had set its stamp upon the woman; her face now was like that of a pale bride on the morning after her first marriage night. She looked at Zachary with such an unveiled glance that all at once he felt the full intimacy that enclosed them.

"I know everything, Zachary; I know what you have been thinking and feeling all this last night. I know everything. I've lived through the same torments and terrors. Look, my heart hasn't calmed down even yet," she put his hand against her silk dressing-gown. "It hammered like that the whole night, the whole night, until I had the relief of seeing you with my own eyes again. Thank God you're here!"

"What were you afraid of?" asked Zachary, avoiding her eyes.

"I don't know. My heart prophesied evil and I prayed to God for you. You're not to blame for this, you're not to blame. You're a child, a simple, innocent child. It's I who am to blame, I!" She struck her breast with her hand and reddened like a girl.

"Olga!" cried Zachary. "What are you doing? I'm a miserable creature, I shouldn't be alive! And I'm a coward as well who hasn't the courage to put an end to his wretched life."

"No, no!" she put her hand over his mouth. "You're pure and innocent, you're a child, a neglected child that I've taken to my heart. I'm to blame for everything. It's *I* that did it, I, so as to cure you, to heal you. And now you're whole and sound and cleansed; I'm not ashamed of having done it. No, I'm not ashamed. Any woman would have done it. I saw how tortured you were . . . and I had no choice." The last words were spoken in a shamed and almost inaudible voice.

Zachary bit his lips; he could not keep back the tears that rose to his eyes.

"But now everything must be forgotten, must sink in darkness, must be erased for ever, for ever, from your thoughts, from your memory, from all of you. Not a trace must be left of it, it must all be forgotten as completely as if it had happened with your own mother," she added in a low whisper.

Zachary was silent and a tearless sob twisted his lips.

"Do you promise me that?"

"Yes," he replied, nodding his head.

"For the happiness of our family?" she added.

"Yes."

She took his head between her hands and drew it to her breast, closed her eyes, and remained motionless for a while. Then she said, as if to herself: "Who will judge me for what I've done for my sick child?"

Maternally she kissed him on the brow and passed her embroidered handkerchief over her eyes. Zachary kept gazing at her like a dumb animal, incapable of speech.

"There! Now go to Nina! She's very dejected. Make your excuses for not coming to see her last night. Make any excuse you can, lie for the happiness of our family."

"Olga Michailovna, not yet, not yet!"

"You must. Everything must be wiped away at once, as if it had never been." Her bearing hardened, she straightened herself to her full height and said in a strong and assured voice, gazing firmly into his eyes, as if with that glance she wished to blot out everything: "Zachary Gavrilovitch, there has been nothing between us, you understand?"

"Nothing between us," Zachary repeated in a low voice.

She took him by the hand, led him to the door of her room and said with a firm and kindly maternal smile: "Zachary Gavrilovitch, Nina is expecting you," and she pointed to the door along the corridor. Zachary bowed deeply, left the room and stepped along the corridor to execute Olga Michailovna's commands.

When Zachary had gone Olga Michailovna remained standing inside the door with shut eyes and leant for a little while in thought against the door post.

Then she shook herself and with her old maternal assurance went about her daily tasks.

CHAPTER XXXII

AN EXCHANGE OF RÔLES

FORTIFIED by Olga Michailovna's words, Zachary knocked at his fiancée's door.

"Nina Solomonovna, may I come in?"

"It's you?" she asked in astonishment as he entered, and then fell silent.

Though it was late in the forenoon Nina was still in her morning costume, pyjamas and an embroidered Japanese dressing-gown; her hair wreathed her face in a thousand little curls. Zachary saw that her eyes were red with weeping. She did not even take the trouble to conceal it. Her face was not yet powdered and in spite of its unusual pallor showed the full freshness of her youthful complexion. She had crossed her feet in their embroidered slippers and was sitting like an oriental princess, her black curly head leaning against the delicate bright yellow pattern of the Bokhara rug, while she nervously smoked a cigarette fixed in a long holder, puffing deeply at it.

It was a quite new Nina that Zachary saw before him. Never before had he seen her so serious and thoughtful. His heart contracted when he noticed how pale she was.

"Nina Solomonovna, I've come to beg your pardon for having neglected you so shamefully yesterday. I was wandering about the streets and didn't know you were waiting for me," he began, and was surprised that the words came so easily to him.

"Oh, you needn't have bothered to come so early in the morning to tell me that! To be perfectly frank, I spent the time very enjoyably with your father."

The conversation flagged for a little while.

Suddenly Nina got up from the sofa, began nervously to walk up and down the room and seemed to be having an inward struggle with herself.

"I regret from the bottom of my heart that I let the opportunity lip," Zachary continued, without knowing what he was saying.

"And how did you spend the first day of spring?"

"I. . . . Oh, in lots of ways . . ." he sputtered.

Nina abruptly stopped in front of him and looked searchingly n his face.

"Admit it! Mamma sent you to me—you wouldn't have come of our own free will," and she added half to herself: "But things can't o on like this! An end must be put to it once and for all!"

"This time you're mistaken; this time I've come to you freely, ntirely of my own free will," replied Zachary, and his voice had a incere and convincing ring.

All at once Nina's bearing changed. The coldness and bitter aloof-ess in her face vanished; it became warm and alive. She drew in er cheeks as if she were going to whistle. She strove to conceal the ook of suffering on her soft lips and pointed chin, but she was unsuc-essful. Her face quivered, as if she had swallowed a tear. Her bright eautiful eyes were gleaming with unshed tears, and yet she miled.

Once more she paused in front of him and looked into his face, ot challengingly this time, however, but with a heartfelt, beseeching ook; in a broken voice she began: "Zachary Gavrilovitch, what have done to you? Why are you always hurting me?"

Zachary smiled awkwardly.

"I hurt you? What are you thinking of?"

"Yes, Zachary Gavrilovitch, yes, yes, you behave as if the Lord Iimself in person were your father and had sent you to earth to idge mankind. Why are you always judging me? Why are you lways hanging the scales of judgment over my head? I'm a sinful reature, certainly, I know it! But what can I do? Nobody could com-ete with you and Mamma! My nature is simply like that! And now llow me to be quite frank: If you think of me like that, if you do othing but criticize me and judge me, why don't you avoid me? It lmost looks as if it pleased you to think that I can never reach your evel. I don't know whether all pure people act like you, whether all ure people look upon others with the same eyes as you. But if they do, then I have no desire to be pure, then I'm quite content to remai as I am and go to hell in my own way as fast as possible."

She spoke hastily, excitedly and warmly, with a touch of bitter ness. Her curls shook; her dressing gown slipped, showing the roun curve of her bare brown shoulder.

Mirkin stood in the middle of the room and let her words ha down on him. When she had ended he began calmly and a littl phlegmatically, still smiling his embarrassed smile: "It's true, I hav judged you. I don't deny it. But you don't know this—that those wh have burdens to hear, who are laden with their own sins, are the firs to judge others."

She was astonished, more by the quiet and serious tone in whic he spoke than by the words themselves. She had once more taken u her position on the sofa and looked at him searchingly for a while all at once she broke into a fit of nervous, unreal laughter.

"You a sinner? You a lost soul? What nonsense are you talkin now, my little Zachary? Why, you're an innocent kitten, and all yo think of is to keep washing yourself clean with your tongue!"

Zachary retorted with a direct, smiling glance that was almos insolent: "How do you know what goes on inside me?"

She grew serious, but she still smiled: "Yes, who can tell There's a proverb that still waters run deep. But if what you say i true, I'm very glad."

"Yes," replied Zachary, "I've often thought of what you've sai about just people. Do you know, Nina Solomonovna, I've come to th conclusion that you're quite right: just people aren't always the pures in heart."

Nina grew rigid with surprise.

"What's wrong with you today? You in the rôle of a penitent You'd better give it up quickly, or else I'll be ready to believe you, she laughed. "You, Zachary, in such a rôle! Really, a quaint spectacle, she laughed loudly.

Zachary cheerfully joined in.

"But enough of this repentant groveling on the ground. I'r no father-confessor. If you've anything on your conscience, keep i to yourself—that's the best course. Now please come over here. Wh do you stand there in the middle of the room like a lost sinner? Come over here, seeing you've taken the trouble to look me up. And tell me what you did all day yesterday. We searched for you; but you couldn't be found anywhere. Such a pity! We made an excursion to Novaya Derevnya. Oh, how lovely everything was out there! Just think, the fields are growing green already! The snow is still lying on them and yet little green blades are peeping out everywhere. The young corn is springing up, and the ground is so lovely, so warm and fresh! How good it is to be out in the country in springtime! I never thought nature could be so refreshing. We two, Papa and myself, felt as if we were re-born. I never knew that Gabriel Haimovitch loved the fields and trees so much. He stopped whenever we came to a peasant and talked to him about the crops. And how the fields were stirring, how these people labored! The whole village was out in the fields, men, women and children. You know, Zachary, when one watches them all working like that—then one is ashamed of one's own idleness. For the first time I felt ashamed of my way of life. Really I'm just a parasite; we're all parasites! It does you good once in a while to feel the wind and smell the earth and see people working! You feel new born. Zachary, we must spend part of every year in the country. It's like worshiping, like going to church. One is cleansed of all one's sins in looking at a plowed field. Do you know why it is so lovely to do that? Because Nature is so sad. One has the impression that these naked fields feel a melancholy rapture when the snows of winter are cleared from them. You, Zachary, wouldn't understand that perhaps; you're always clean and brushed up at all seasons. But I and your father understood it. We people out of the smoky city, living all the year round in the reek of smoke and cabaret-scents—we need that purifying melancholy rapture of Nature."

With closed eyes Zachary listened to her gay childish voice. It sounded as if it had bathed the day before in the fresh fountains, been washed in the winds of which it told. It had a new ring. Zachary kept his eyes shut and gazed within himself; and—strange!—he was no longer gnawed by remorse. He felt cleansed by Nina's words.

"What are you thinking of, my little Zachary?" she asked, running her fingers through his hair.

"I was thinking of the melancholy rapture of Nature," he said, as if to himself.

"Yes, it is melancholy. I don't know why yesterday made such a deep impression on me. It's really absurd—but I feel as if I had been at confession! All night I lay awake thinking of my life. Now I understand you, Zachary; I see why you look upon me as you do, why you judge me. Yes, you're right; I was really a loathsome creature: how could you—with your beautiful nature—love me? Yes, now I can see myself completely—I'll reform, Zachary, I'll reform absolutely. Help me to do it." She hid her black curly head on his breast and stammered: "You're so pure; I'm not worthy of you."

Zachary was silent. A sentence, a dreadful sentence was on the tip of his tongue; but an inner instinct far stronger than himself watched over him as once before and sealed his lips. . . .

Suddenly Nina tore her head from his breast and wiped the tears from her eyes, which were still smiling.

"Forgive me, dearest Zachary; I'm a little fool! Do you know, Zachary, what I've decided? We mustn't live any longer in future like two quite separate people that daren't ask each other a question. Yesterday I saw everything quite differently: there must be no secrets between us. We'll live together in a quite different spirit from all the other people of our time. We'll be a real old-fashioned married couple, won't we, dear Zachary?"

Zachary smiled: "If you wish it . . ."

"Tell me, what did you do yesterday? I must know everything."

"Yesterday . . ." he reflected for a little, as if trying to remember. "Oh, nothing very particular. I strolled about the streets, watched the ice-blocks floating down the Neva, and then had a look at the Easter egg booths in the Nevsky Prospect. I spent the evening with Olga Michailovna."

Nina made to say something in reply, but was ashamed to utter it, and remained silent. Yet as she could not find any other words for those she had suppressed a short pause followed. The cessation of the conversation was painful to both of them; but neither was able to say anything to break it.

Nina fixed her great eyes on him and gazed at him for a long time. Zachary could not tell whether she was on the point of laughing or crying.

At last she said compassionately, running her fingers through his hair: And why are you so pale, Zachary?"

Zachary smiled: "Am I pale? I didn't know."

Nina broke out in a loud peal of laughter.

"Really, how sentimental I am today. It's yesterday that's to blame for it, that's all. It seems to me we've exchanged our rôles. The first spring day has had a sentimental effect on me, on you—a somewhat different one."

"In what way different?" asked Zachary curiously.

"I don't know. You seem so strange to me today, so different. I hardly recognize you. What happened to you yesterday?"

"In what way different?" Zachary repeated his question.

"That's hard to say," she gave him a somewhat nonplused look. "It's as if some one had . . . I really don't know, we must ask Mamma what happened to you yesterday." Thereupon she ran to the door and cried: "Mamma, Mamma, may we come to see you?"

"What are you doing?" cried Zachary in an unnatural voice.

Nina grew pale, gazed at him in astonishment, and said half to herself: "Forgive me, I didn't know it was so serious."

"What is serious? And why do you suddenly drag Mamma into it?"

Nina was ashamed, and remained silent.

"Forgive me. But you're so used to telling Mamma everything. You have more trust in her than in me."

Zachary did not answer a single word.

In the evening Gabriel Haimovitch called on Olga Michailovna. He had come to discuss family affairs. Without much preamble he began: "Do you know, Olga Michailovna, what I've told my son today? 'Young man,' I told him, 'you must get married now, and the sooner the better.' The behavior of the young people strengthens me, too, in the belief that we shouldn't delay much longer. Aren't you of that opinion too?"

"Yes, I think—that you are right," responded Olga Michailovna.

A faint blush like the last radiance of the setting sun flitted over her cheeks and quickly lost itself in the pure white of her complexion.

CHAPTER XXXIII

AT MADAME KVASNIECOVA'S AGAIN

Gabriel Haimovitch informed his son that he had heard from Count Akimov that the case of the Jewish soldier who had been sentenced to twenty years' penal servitude in Siberia for refusing to eat pork was to be laid before the Czar in a few days; Akimov himself was going to sponsor the matter at the audience already promised him; in some mysterious way information about the case had already penetrated to Court circles (Gabriel Haimovitch knew nothing about the "Pension Kvasniecova") and had roused a great deal of attention; there was every prospect of success.

"And now, my boy, you can tell your old woman from the Polish border—I can never remember her name—the joyful news. All she need do is to go on praying, and everything will come right!"

During the last few weeks Mirkin had been so occupied with himself that he had completely neglected his work and knew nothing about what was happening in the office. Since his first visit he had never gone near Madame Kvasniecova's house again. Now, at his father's encouragement, he set out to carry the news in person to the old Jewish woman for whom he had felt such a deep sympathy.

He found almost all the former inmates still at Madame Kvasniecova's. The legal actions and other affairs that had brought them to Petersburg proceeded but slowly and were relegated from one official department to the next—so the parties interested were often compelled to stay for months in Petersburg before obtaining a verdict or even a clear statement of their position.

Frau Hurvitz from Warsaw was also still at Madame Kvasniecova's. The translation of her son's notes must already have been sent in by the professor of ancient languages and was now in the hands of the police; but the case was far from reaching a settlement yet. It was not even known when the trial was to take place. Nobody was admitted to the accused, for the simple reason that nobody knew where he was. Since she had come to Petersburg, Frau Hurvitz had lost much weight and become a shadow of herself. Yet she showed not a trace of discouragement or despair; on the contrary, her optimistic bearing and her resolution gave courage to all the other lodgers. Her healthy good spirits infected her comrades in misfortune. Naturally energetic and industrious, she had set up a separate kitchen for the lodgers and with the help of another woman whose son was also a political prisoner she provided their meals every day. Frau Hurvitz seemed to take more interest in the unhappy fates of the others than in that of her own son. She knew the condition of every case and by her energy goaded her companions to take more vigorous steps. If any one folded his hands in despair she would try to encourage him:

"What a helpless creature you are! If everything doesn't go as you want it, is that a reason for folding your hands? That's just what they want—they want to torture us until we leave our children to their fate—they want to force us to give in! They'll find out their mistake! Don't give them any peace, make as much noise as you can! If they fling you out at one door go in again by another!"

And although she could not speak a word of Russian (the only language she knew was a country dialect of Polish, for she had grown up in a Polish village), she made her way through every door in the State bureaus and departments. She was simply everywhere. She visited the famous lawyer's office every day as a matter of course. But she also went to see the professor who was to translate her son's incomprehensible notes, and actually compelled him to produce a false translation. With all the means at her disposal she worked upon him, with her outraged maternal feelings and her feminine charm, with tears and with smiles. She actually managed to discover into whose hands her son's interrogation had been given, and had found admittance to the interrogator. Several times already she had been threatened with expulsion from Petersburg, but she was afraid of nobody and no official's uniform could daunt her.

The very tall Jew, the elder from the Jewish community of Tolestyn, Baruch Chomsky, was also still lodging at Kvasniecova's.

Chomsky had long wished to turn his back on the sinful city. He was tired of waiting in lawyers' ante-rooms, his quarters were an insult to his dignity (he, the father of grown-up daughters, had to live in such a house in his old age!) and the shameless insolence of the various officials, who tossed him like a ball from one ministry to another, completed his demoralization. He no longer believed that his efforts would meet with any success, and had he been there merely on his own business he would have submitted to his fate and left Petersburg long ago; but more and more urgent petitions kept arriving from his native town, asking him to move everything to preserve from destruction his community, which had existed for centuries. So, knowing his responsibility as the representative elder of his community, he did not wish to leave Petersburg without having tried every means he could.

He patiently bore his fate, ran from one patron, one advocate or State department to the next, endured all the rough jests and insults of officials as if he had to take them upon him for his sins, and remained steadfastly at his post, although he himself did not believe in his mission. Since Zachary had seen him last he seemed to have grown still taller and leaner; his huge beard was also longer.

This time the lodgers were not reciting their prayers when Mirkin arrived. They seemed to have grown apathetic and to have accustomed themselves to live in their strange quarters. It was evening when Mirkin appeared, and all the lodgers were sitting at the table under the chandelier, which, originally intended for gas, had now been furnished with electric bulbs; the milk-white bulbs cast a spectral light on the weary, troubled faces of the figures sitting round the table. They were all engaged in different occupations: two Jews with turned-up mustaches were playing at dominoes; the huge Chomsky, with his mighty beard, was sitting directly under the light writing a letter. In a corner a woman was sitting by herself eating out of a platter. Only Esther Hodel, the old woman from Poland, moved her lips perpetually, more out of habitude than piety. But it was Frau Hurvitz of Warsaw who ruled and managed the lodgers; her powerfully molded face, too, marked her out from all the others. At present she was standing in the improvised kitchen off the big room, and with her sleeves rolled up was ladling soup out of a great pot, shouting to each of the lodgers in turn to bring their plates.

"Reb Baruch, come here, please! Take your plate, or the soup will be quite cold," she shouted to the ruling elder of the Jewish community of Tolestyn.

"Well, Moskovitch, do you want your supper tonight or not? I'll come in a minute and sweep your dominoes on the floor. Do you think we're going to wash dishes all night for your sake?" she shouted at one of the players.

The lodgers were as afraid of her as of a stern parent, and each went over to the stove, received a plateful and bore it back to his place. Even the elder of the Jewish community of Tolestyn had to interrupt his letter and obey Frau Hurvitz's orders. While they spooned their soup they did not allow themselves to be disturbed in their occupations. The domino players emptied their plates without stopping their game, which they seasoned with observations delivered in a singsong, as if they were reading from the Talmud. The elder went on writing his letter while he supped, taking great care that no soup should spatter his beard or the paper on which he was writing.

The only one who refused to touch anything cooked in Madame Hurvitz's improvised common kitchen was Esther Hodel Kloppeisen from Dombrova in Poland. She put no reliance on Madame Hurvitz's ability to produce proper kosher food. Since with the inauguration of the kitchen she no longer received special favors from Madame Kvasniecova in the shape of food fetched for her from the kosher restaurant, she contented herself with dry bread. She was just devouring an old roll and an onion which she had drawn out of her bosom—other food than this she refused to touch in the iniquitous city of Petersburg. While she ate she muttered, more out of habitude than pity, her psalms, interrupting them now and then with sighing complaints, such as: "Joy to them that dwell in Thy house—eh, and woe is me!"

CHAPTER XXXIV

POLISH SOUP

WHEN THE lodgers became aware of the unexpected presence of Halperin's assistant they all jumped up inquisitively. They knew that something unusual must have happened, and each nursed the hope that the visit concerned him. They were bitterly disappointed when they learned on whose business Mirkin had come:

"Why should she have better luck than we? Was she born with a silver spoon in her mouth? Is her child the only one who has a mother, and did our children grow in the fields?"

The news that her case was to come before the Czar in person and that there was every prospect of a happy issue not only created a sensation among the lodgers, but jealousy and hostility as well. Of a sudden they all hated the pious old woman with her wig and hood. But she paid no attention to their envious glances. She piously rocked her body, her eyes glassy with joy, raised her hands and face towards the roof, and cried: "The rabbi has done this, long may he live! This is his work."

Madame Hurvitz issued from her improvised kitchen. In Warsaw she lived in a perpetual atmosphere of conflict with Jewish fanaticism—for she was a free-thinker—and now she could not refrain from putting in her oar; yet the words that came hissing through her clenched teeth were born of militant zeal, not of jealousy:

"Esther Hodel, would you like to know whose work it is? The work of those trollops over there!" She pointed with her finger in the direction of the "Pension Kvasniecova."

The others smiled significantly and exultantly. Esther Hodel did not understand Madame Hurvitz's words and went on piously: "With God's help you will get your wishes fulfilled, too. Every good mother who has pious children will get what she seeks, that's certain!"

"Yes, if we can find the right kind of influence," Madame Hurvitz added.

"The prayers of the holy rabbi."

"No, no, granny. People like us have to rely on the clients across the way!"

Thereupon she turned to the embarrassed Mirkin; her lively eyes danced and she almost shouted at him: "You can do nothing yourselves! It's only when somebody at Court helps you out that you can do anything: then you put on great airs!"

"She's quite right," added one of the domino players. "We've been sitting here in Petersburg for months, running ourselves off our feet and getting nothing. And then an old Polish woman comes with her case, a difficult case at that, she knows nobody in the town, finds favor in the eyes of a brothel-keeper and reaches the ear of the Czar himself! I wish to God I could get patronage like that!"

"Why, who are you, you fool? Have you got a pious son? All the pious lot stick together, even if they belong to different religions."

While the others were exchanging their views Madame Hurvitz stepped up to Mirkin, laid the bare arm with which she had just been ladling soup round his shoulder, and began, in a mixture of Polish and bad Russian:

"Young man, you're wasting your time sitting in that office of yours! Why do you let yourself be made a fool of? You should come to us in Warsaw and set about real work. Believe me, you'll do more good there than sitting in your office and fooling other people and yourself. Why, you know yourself that you'll never manage to do anything that way."

As she said this she looked at him earnestly with her strangely living eyes. Mirkin could see the movement of her powerful jaws with their flawless, strong teeth. The glance of her eyes warmed him, and her powerful arm held him as firmly and kindly as a mother holds her child.

His first impulse was to detach himself from the woman with an irritable shrug; for the rude tone in which she spoke to him annoyed him. But almost at once he saw that this was no case for annoyance: the words she spoke had a cordial and sincere ring, and a homely warmth radiated from her healthy body, her vigorous short neck and her clear, frank face, which was made expressive by the lively eyes and strong mouth. So Mirkin accepted her advice good-humoredly and asked with a smile: "Why, what could I do in Warsaw?"

"The same work that my husband is doing and that my son did. Why shouldn't a healthy young man like you, with most of his life still in front of him, help on the good work? What good are you doing here? You're only wasting your time rummaging among old papers; that does good to nobody, neither to yourself nor the others."

"What good could I do in Warsaw?" asked Mirkin curiously. As he did so he contemplated her animated face and asked himself in surprise why it should seem so familiar to him. He had the feeling that he had seen this woman somewhere before; more, that he must have been intimately connected with her. Her face was more than familiar to him.

"What good?" Madame Hurvitz repeated the question and winked slyly and coquettishly with a half-shut eye. "You know quite well what I mean! It's the kind of work that earns you night-visits from the police instead of sugar plums."

Zachary flushed under the coquettish play of her eyes as well as at her hint of the part he could play. He replied: "I don't know whether I'm suited for the work you mean."

"Then you could teach the young lads Russian at least, or prepare them for the secondary school. Whole droves of them come in daily from the country and one simply doesn't know how to deal with them: one would need four hands. Oh, there would be no lack of work; you've only got to be willing instead of sitting all your life with folded arms or pottering with trivialities! You don't get much satisfaction out of your job anyhow!"

"How do you know I'm not satisfied with my job?"

"Oh, one can see that straight away! Do you think we have no eyes? Your colleague, the other assistant, what's his name again—oh yes, Weinstein—Weinstein is very well pleased with his work, your famous lawyer as well. But you go wandering round like a shadow, as if you felt lost. One can easily see at a glance that your heart isn't in your work."

Mirkin flushed again; he stared at Madame Hurvitz in mingled astonishment and alarm: how did she know all this? For a moment the thought possessed him that he had already heard those words before, and from this same woman.

And as if Madame Hurvitz had divined his thoughts, she went on with genuine maternal sympathy: "I'm really sorry for you. You're such a nice fellow," and she smiled at him, her eyes glowing with cordial affection.

Again it seemed to Mirkin that he had heard such words somewhere, some time, uttered in the same tone, with the same deep concern for his fate. For a moment he felt he must be dreaming; but then he roused himself and asked with a smile: "How do you know I'm nice?"

"If you weren't you wouldn't come to see us, and you wouldn't have tried to help that old woman over there, either, and her son who's got into trouble with the army. Why doesn't your colleague or the famous lawyer himself ever visit us?"

"Do you really believe our office work is of no value? Why, we wage a continual battle against the bureaucracy; we stand up for law and justice!" Zachary tried to entrench himself behind these phrases.

"A fine battle, save the mark! Why, they simply laugh at you! And you only help them to keep up before the world the pretence that we can really get justice from them. No, young man, the fight must be waged in quite a different way—from below, against the foundations. The whole structure must be blown into the air, and with a bang that the whole world can hear!" Once more she glanced at him coquettishly, giving him a sidelong glance from her brown eyes; a soft smile flitted over her full lips; in the milky light of the lamp her face was half in shadow, and the keen profile stood out with strange force; this lent to her smiles and glances an ambiguous and yet pleasant and kindly expression.

Zachary could not hold out; her smiles were reflected on his eyes and lips and he replied smilingly: "I'll think it over. Who knows? It may be quite a good idea."

"Of course it is a good idea. You'll simply blossom out as soon as you stop playing the fool. Listen! If you come to Warsaw come straight to me. Don't hesitate, we're accustomed to stray visitors!

Every day young people like you come to us, young people who have fled from their homes, left their synagogue or their Talmud school, or their parents, or even their wives and sweethearts. Every day some of them knock at my door; they always tell me it's my soup they've come for." Once more she smiled her ambiguous smile. "Have you tasted my soup yet? Wait, you're still in time—wouldn't you like to taste it now?"

She took him by the arm and led him to the table. Mirkin made no resistance; he was already quite under her spell.

"Make room, gentlemen! Make room for the advocate to taste my soup!" She made him sit down and handed him a plate of soup.

Before he knew where he was, he was sitting, like an old acquaintance, among these strange people, and feeling quite at his ease, A warm comforting home-like feeling such as he had never known before enveloped him, making him forget all his worries, all his sorrows. He had the feeling that while he was in the care of Madame Hurvitz of Warsaw no harm could befall him.

"I've enjoyed your soup enormously. Thanks very much." He got up to leave.

"I hope you'll return soon to enjoy my soup again," retorted Madame Hurvitz; her warm, vigorous hand gave his a cordial squeeze.

"I hope so, too," he replied, and an inexplicable sense of happiness rose in him.

CHAPTER XXXV

PATERNAL WORDS

When Mirkin left Madame Kvasniecova's he was followed, as on his first visit, by Baruch Chomsky, the giant from Tolestyn with the long beard. He stopped Zachary on the stairs: "She's right, Madame Hurvitz—you can do nothing here. It's a waste of time to stay here."

"Oh, it's you, Herr Chomsky? Are you setting out for your evening prayers again?"

"It's better, at any rate, than running from office to office and being snubbed in them all. Perhaps my prayers will be answered some day yet. We'll go on praying until our prayers are heard. They must be heard and they will be heard." The Jew uttered the last words in an emphatic voice.

"How are you so sure of that? Our fathers prayed, too!"

"How am I sure of that, you ask? Do you imagine there's no justice in the world, simply because we see no sign of it? The Lord of the world lives for ever and can wait. He lets the vessel be filled first to overflowing. Because our eyes see only darkness, we think it is night. But behind us a light is shining, whether we see it or not. No, young man, God rules His world with justice, though we with our superficial vision may think it is not so. But finally and ultimately justice always conquers. Perhaps we won't see it with our own eyes—but, if not, then our children will. Man is like a jot or a tittle in the Holy Scripture, only visible for a space while we open the page where it is written; as soon as the page is turned it vanishes. But the Holy Scripture lives on, and man has his steadfast place on the page, in the chapter that he belongs to, and nobody can ever blot him out."

Mirkin did not quite grasp the old Jew's meaning, yet the words interested him and he felt he could learn something from them. For now he was interested in everything connected with Madame Kvasniecova's house. The mysterious Jew and his strange evening prayer had already made a deep impression upon him at their first encounter; now that he was hovering over an abyss, Zachary felt thankful for any straw to clutch at. He was searching for something, he himself did not know what. So he let himself be drawn into a philosophical discussion with the Jew:

"That may be so, my friend, but there is no guarantee that it really is so. We wander about and don't know in the least whether all this life of ours may not be a labyrinth, a maze without an end. We have no conclusive proof that the world is really ruled with justice, and that our affairs are really governed by logic. The examples that people cite can be interpreted in the one sense just as easily as in the other."

"You're talking stuff!" the Jew interrupted him. "I'm no great scholar and I don't know what the great scholars of the world say about it. Yet now in my old age I still take up a book now and then, just as I did as a young man. I know Hebrew, thank God—I was a well-known advocate of 'enlightenment' at one time—though today—well, who has time for such things?—But, after all, men aren't beasts; so at nights, when one can't sleep, one lies in bed and broods over the nature of the world. Sometimes, of course, one is assailed by doubt. And doubt has a far worse effect on an old man than on a young one. When you young people are assailed by doubt, which God forbid, you soon get over it. The strength of life in you draws you back from the abyss and bears you away on its current. But when an old man like me—God forbid!—falls into doubt, then it's as if he were knocking his head against a wall. You must see that—the grave is waiting and one must be prepared for the last journey, or else one is in a bad case. So some try to secure their place in the future world by prayers and intoning psalms—though that's no better than blind-man's buff! Others prepare themselves for the future world in other ways: by using their minds; they press on and on until they gain a certainty of some kind."

"And what certainty have you reached?" asked Mirkin.

"I've come to the certainty—with every faculty I possess—I've come to the certainty that there is finally a world order that binds everything together. I've come to that conclusion quite simply—one doesn't need to be a famous scholar to do that, one only needs to feel it, as I feel it. Often one says something without oneself being aware of the thought that lies at the bottom of it. A saying is like a fruit; one has first to eat it, so to speak, before one can know its taste. Take, for instance, the axiom set up by our logicians: 'From the particular can be deduced the general;' that means that we can draw conclusions concerning the community of mankind from the individual. Now, obviously logic governs the individual. If that weren't so, nothing, from the smallest to the greatest organisms, could exist; nothing either in the organic or the inorganic world would have continuance. Can you conceive that even the tiniest worm could live for a moment, the tiniest blade of grass become what it is, the smallest rock take shape, if there had not existed from eternity immutable laws and norms of life governing them? But if that is so, what reason have we to imagine that there is no logical meaning in the whole, in the world-order itself?

I've read very learned books on this subject, but I only saw their deeper meaning after I had myself come to this knowledge. Do you know what the world is? The world is a living entity just as much as the tiniest organism. Yes, the world lives, the great universe lives. We don't see it simply because we are a tiny strand in the great fabric, because we are so sunk in the emptiness, the petty nothings of our own individual existences, that we have no time to perceive the greater life. Like worms we have crept into the dark caverns, the narrow gloomy passages of our individual existences and have no time left to rise into the clear radiant world and to gaze at the mighty sun and the living light. Rise out of yourself, young man! Tear yourself free from the darkness of your own petty life; then you will see the great light, will feel the mighty pulse, the great heart-beat of the world!"

When the old man had finished Mirkin stopped and looked at him. For a moment he was in doubt: could the man have been speaking like that intentionally? Did he know of his, Mirkin's most secret experiences? Yes, he must know everything, and his words were directed intentionally at him! This feeling made the old man still more extraordinary in Zachary's eyes, as he stood now in the pearly radiance of the clear night.

The old Jew spoke Yiddish with a Russian accent, and employed many Hebrew phrases. Yet Mirkin understood him. It was as if words that had lived for a long time within him had all at once come to consciousness.

"I've never felt the pulse of the world," replied Mirkin in Russian, "never heard the heart-beat of the universe so clearly that I could say there was such a thing. I don't know whether it is absolutely certain that the whole must live because the individual lives. And it doesn't follow, because logic is present in the individual organism, that it must also be present in the total organism. And besides logic is not always in accordance with justice, for justice has no immutable shape. It is more a matter of feeling, and man does not judge by an abstract standard, but always with reference to his personal feelings and his comfort."

"Then how do you manage to live?" the old man almost shouted. "How can you exist, thinking such things? What on earth can they teach you in the schools, where you pass so many years of your life? All you learn is how to spend as comfortably and extravagantly as possible wealth that isn't your own, that has been earned for you by others. So you and your like grow into empty pots with many mouths to suck in wine that doesn't belong to you."

And after a short pause he added in a low, grave, almost beseeching voice: "Our wise men say that the thoughts of men bind the whole world together, bind every creature to mankind, even God Himself. We preserve the world by our thoughts. If one of us plays false to his thoughts, he plays false not only to his own life, but to the whole world, to God Himself. For our thoughts and our hearts—these are the foundation on which everything rests. How can any one renounce such a goal, and a young man in particular? How are you to live to the end the life that waits for you? On what will you support it?"

"The life that waits for me," Mirkin repeated the old man's words —"my life doesn't belong to me. I tried to cast it away and I could not. So I bear it like an alien burden," he confessed suddenly.

The old man stopped and gazed at Mirkin with such great, wide open eyes that Mirkin shrank at first. But then the Jew took him by the hand, held it firmly, and said:

"Young man, tear yourself free from the dark labyrinth of your own petty life where you have buried yourself! Where will it lead you? To suicide. It's dreadful! You are young, you're only at the beginning of your life. Why do you skulk in your own ego and gorge there like a worm in an apple? Get out of yourself! Then you'll feel the pulse of the world and unite your thoughts with the thoughts of the community! Then you'll feel a new man. Promise me that, young man! I'm sore at heart for you."

The old man held Zachary's hand and looked into his eyes for a long time.

"Who knows? Perhaps I shall try. Everything's indifferent to me, as it is," replied Mirkin.

"You'll never reach anything worth while on that horse. You mustn't try, but set out resolutely. And there's nothing that's 'indifferent'; there's only the way of those who help or fail the world by their thoughts. You must either unite your own life with all life or lose yourself in your own private little death. Do you understand me?"

"Yes."

"Do you give me your promise?"

"I give you my promise."

The old man let Mirkin's hand go.

"The different kinds of justice you spoke about—these are only the wretched human forms of justice. Eternal justice, no matter how different the forms it may take, rises from *one* source, the fountain of life, from the light that points to the great end of all."

"Blessed are they which believe."

"Without doubt there can be no belief, just as without darkness there could be no light. Don't be discouraged or deceived, if you doubt now and then. It will only strengthen your belief." The old man put his hand on Mirkin's shoulder before leaving him.

Mirkin looked after him for a long time. It seemed to him that the old man was wearing a white flowing robe. Robed all in white he strode through the streets of Petersburg. Mirkin was astonished that he aroused nobody's attention.

The last faint glimmer of day blanched the pallid sky: the white nights had begun.

CHAPTER XXXVI

A MOTHER'S HAND

A FEW DAYS later Mirkin was able to tell Esther Hodel Kloppeisen, the mother of the pious soldier, the glad news that the Czar had pardoned her son and not only commuted his sentence but completely absolved him from his term of military service.

Akimov told Zachary's father that the Czar had actually wept when he heard the story of the Jewish soldier. "He was so deeply moved," went on Akimov, "that he laid his hand on the badge of the Black Hundred (which he always wore) and cried: 'Jew or not, he is a pious man!' The Jewish soldier, Akimov continued, had found at Court a remarkable number of sponsors of every shade of opinion, among them very influential personages who had taken up his case and concerned themselves with his fate.

But, by a strange chance, on the same day that the son received his pardon, his mother, the pious Jewess, was arrested. It happened for the following reason. Esther Hodel had been given by her rabbi an infallible specific: during the time that her son's case was being decided upon she was to walk thrice round the place of judgment reciting passages from the Psalms. Madame Kvasniecova, who had been initiated by the old woman into this secret, conducted her piously to the Winter Palace, thinking that the affair would be decided there. She showed Esther Hodel the place and Esther Hodel began her march. But the secret agents who guarded the palace became suspicious of this figure dressed up in female attire. Taking her for a disguised revolutionist they arrested her.

The famous advocate had little difficulty in convincing the political police that Esther Hodel was neither a man in disguise nor a revolutionist. With Kvasniecova's aid he also succeeded in preventing the old woman from being sent back to her home.

On the evening of Esther Hodel's release a celebration in honor of her son's amnesty was held at Madame Kvasniecova's. Mirkin took part in it. By this time he was a frequent visitor at the house. Whenever he could he went there to pass his time in the company of old Chomsky and Madame Hurvitz, with whom he had become very friendly. In Madame Kvasniecova's he forgot the division in his soul and felt sound and whole again. It was a flight from himself—for in that familiar circle he felt quite different, quite well, as if in another world.

This evening he had a particular excuse for visiting the house: Madame Hurvitz was preparing to travel back to Poland with Esther Hodel. She had been able to discover nothing about the ultimate fate of her son, for the trial had been postponed till autumn. She did not even know whether he was incarcerated in Petersburg or in some other town. His case was still merely being inquired into and Madame Hurvitz was sick of "sitting idle" in Petersburg, while "her children" were needing her guidance at home.

When Zachary arrived he found Madame Hurvitz in a blue

flowered cotton dress such as she was accustomed to wear in her home. It was a warm spring evening. This time she was not standing in her improvised kitchen or supervising the supper; she sat in a corner, her clear-cut head resting sadly and forlornly on her hand. She was troubled by the uncertain lot of her son, whom she had now to leave to his fate, and also by the envy which she, like all the other lodgers, felt towards old Esther Hodel on account of her success. Her cheeks were flushed, her ears burned, in her eyes was a glassy, dangerous gleam: they reflected the savagery of every mother-creature robbed of her young. She paid no attention to Mirkin's entry. She did not even notice it, for she was oblivious of everything. Sunk within herself she sat in the corner, her teeth buried in her full underlip. Under the skin the movement of her strong jaws was distinctly visible; they seemed to be chewing something.

Mirkin gazed at her from the doorway and did not dare to approach her. He had become accustomed to her by now. He loved the sound of her firm energetic voice, and her assured movements. He liked it when she challenged him to have some of her soup. It seemed to him that nobody could resist her. Yet he had never before seen her as he saw her now. She, whose nature had always something cheerful and imperious in it, now betrayed her hidden helplessness and anxiety. Mirkin was filled with profound pity for her. Her maternal sorrow moved him. He gave no sign of his presence, so as not to disturb her. But after a while she became aware of him and through her tears sent him a cheerful smile.

Mirkin went nearer.

"Why are you sitting alone, Madame Hurvitz?"

"Why, should I be dancing?" she said bitterly, brushing her lips with her hand. "I must leave my son. And he's little more than a child still, he's only twenty-two. I was only a stick of a girl myself when I had him, hardly eighteen. Now I must leave him and without even knowing where I'm leaving him and what's happening to him, without knowing even where he is!"

"So you're really going home?"

"What's the use of my staying here? How can I stay here? At home I've got a whole houseful of children, one smaller than the other.

Who'll look after them? I'm here—but my mind is there. I have a daughter, it's true—but she must help her father in the school and distribute forbidden pamphlets as well. One day she'll be arrested, too, that's pretty certain!"

Her eyes gleamed with tears. Ashamed of them she hastily wiped her eyes with her handkerchief. As she stuck it back in her bosom again she said to Mirkin with a smile:

"I'm a silly creature; forgive me. Why should I cry, anyway? What good will crying do me?"

Mirkin was so moved that he grew pale. He took Madame Hurvitz's hand and said: "Madame Hurvitz, what can I do for you? Tell me! I'll do anything you ask."

"You ask, what can you do?" She smiled at him through her tears. "You can do nothing. You can't save my son; no one can. He must see what he can do for himself—wherever he may be. We're poor people, we have no influence and we want none!"

Suddenly she turned her eyes full on Mirkin and measured him—or so, at least, it seemed to him—with a contemptuous glance. There was no trace of tears in her eyes now; a savage fire burned in them. Her nostrils quivered and her mouth was twisted in a bitter and sarcastic smile: "My children aren't so delicate as you people here; they know what to do when anything happens to them. They're used to it; they know that they must be prepared to pay the price, once they've put their hands to anything. And I've no anxiety about them; no harm will come to them. And if anything does happen to them, then it can't be helped. We're used to such things. We know that if one wants to live one must be ready to die, must be prepared at every moment to pay with one's life. That's how it is with us—and I'm not afraid."

But her words belied her; once more her eyes filled with big tears which overflowed and rolled down her cheeks.

Mirkin could not bear to see a woman cry; it brought him almost to a state of desperation. Without thinking what he was doing he took her hand: "Madame Hurvitz, do stop crying, please! I thought you were strong!"

"Strong or weak—what can I do?"

She angrily brushed the tears from her cheeks with her bare arm and presently smiled at Mirkin again: "You see, that's what we women are like! We say one thing and do another."

Now she looked into his face maternally and smiled again.

What she had said about being ready to die rankled like a thorn in Mirkin's flesh: "So any one who can't die is incapable of living? I'm one of that kind."

Madame Hurvitz saw at once that Mirkin was in inward distress. She asked kindly: "Why are you so sad all at once? Was it what I said? That's just like us women, you see!"

Mirkin composed himself: "It wasn't that; I was just thinking over your words. You're right; you can only live if you are able to die; but if you can't die you—can neither live nor die."

Madame Hurvitz seemed to have guessed his meaning, perhaps from the tone of his voice: "To be able to die—yes, if it's for something, but not for nothing and less than nothing! Those that cast away their life for nothing, because something isn't to their liking—it isn't they who know how to die! To be ready to die means to be prepared to serve a great cause with all one's life and heart. That's what I call being ready to die."

"A great cause?"

"Oh, there are things in the world that are worth laying down one's life for."

"You believe that?"

"I not only believe it; I know it. Just come to us; then you'll find out for yourself."

Mirkin became thoughtful.

"But however that may be, it's a queer thing, at any rate, that a young man like you should take the time and pains to talk to an old woman in a great city like Petersburg," began Madame Hurvitz again. She threw him a grateful glance.

Mirkin reddened.

"It's because I like it; I love to listen to you, especially when you speak about your home," he said, adding with a smile; "And as for being an old woman—you're by no means as old as all that, Madame Hurvitz."

"You could be my son. Besides—do you know this?—you're a little like him. Only you wear a little black beard and he only a little black mustache."

"Well, then I'll shave off my beard; and then I'll look just like your son," Zachary smiled again.

"Do you lay such value on that?" asked Madame Hurvitz, flushing.

"Perhaps . . ." Mirkin broke off.

Madame Hurvitz also became silent.

"Madame Hurvitz," Mirkin began abruptly, "do you think work could be found for me with you in Warsaw? I've been thinking it over. I think I'll follow your advice."

"How? Are you serious? Stop talking such nonsense; you're only joking. You would actually leave Petersburg and your wealthy family?"

"Why not? I tell you I want to get out, and I mean it quite seriously. Do you think I could be of any use to you in Warsaw? Tell me frankly, Madame Hurvitz!"

His grave, almost imploring tone touched her: "You could certainly make yourself useful. You're an educated man, and we're always in need of educated people. But think what you're saying! You're a young man belonging to a wealthy family and accustomed to a life of comfort. What sort of life will you have with us? We're poor, and we never come in contact with people like you; our existence is a narrow one. How will you be able to put up with our way of living? You'll soon get tired of it! And then—what will you do then, do you think? Is that a possible life for you?"

"Yes, it's just what I want; I must have it! The other life disgusts me. I want to get out of my present life. I must, I must tear myself free from it! I've no other chance. It's the only salvation left for me, otherwise nothing remains but . . ."

Mirkin stopped in the middle of what he was saying. Madame Hurvitz gazed at him affectionately. He was deeply moved by her glance; with such a gaze she might look at her children! She laid her hand lightly on his shoulder; he felt a thrill of warmth running through his body.

"If you really want it—we'll welcome you with open arms. My husband will be delighted; you'll be able to help him a great deal with his Russian classes in our school, or with his night classes for the young lads from the country. You can help my daughter; you can practice your profession, too. Then we'll have a lawyer of our own, belonging to us."

"Do you really think that I can be useful, that I'll be of help to anybody?"

"No doubt of it! You're only beginning; you've still your whole life before you. Why you're only a child yet! A young man like you, healthy, educated—how can you fail to be of help? Come to us in Warsaw! My husband will soon find work for you, if you want it! And perhaps we'll find a wife for you too!"

Mirkin reddened.

"Why do you blush? You're old enough to get married. But wait; I've heard that you're engaged already, if I'm not mistaken, to the lawyer's daughter. What about that?"

Mirkin grew pale with astonishment.

"Oh, that, you mean?" he stammered. "Nothing has come of that, and nothing will come of it either." He was astounded that he could utter so lightly a thought which a moment before had seemed impossible to him. But now that it had crossed his lips he was absolutely certain that he would break off his engagement; the sooner the better.

Madame Hurvitz too felt embarrassed. To get over her embarrassment she asked: "And when do you think of coming to us?"

"Soon, very soon."

"Look us up when you come; you know our address: Hurvitz the teacher, Nowolipie, Warsaw—anybody will tell you at once where that is."

Mirkin got up: "When are you leaving? May I see you to the train?"

"That isn't necessary. We aren't used to such things. When one of us has to travel she has to find her way for herself."

Mirkin raised her hand to his lips.

"And you should be careful about things like that, too. Among people of our kind a hand isn't always in a state to be kissed; it has probably been helping in the kitchen," she laughed.

"It's a thousand times more worthy in my eyes just because of that." Mirkin once more seized her hand and pressed a kiss upon it.

"Do you know what else I must tell you?" began Madame Hurvitz, accompanying him to the door. "You're still a child, just a great child, in spite of your black beard! You need your mother still! I've never seen such a man before!" She passed her hand hardened with work lightly and tenderly over his beard.

When he stepped into the street he saw with surprise that all Petersburg lay in light.

CHAPTER XXXVII

BE COMFORTED

THE NIGHT seemed transformed into an overcast day; its pearly shimmer had faded to a sickly pallor. Everything seemed to exist behind a transparent veil. Everything was changed: houses, trees, human beings, animals. Ghosts walked the streets: ghostly horses, ghostly human beings, strange creations of an underworld, with faces such as those seen in dreams, with phantasmal bodies out of some feverish nightmare.

What could have happened? The ground under Zachary's feet seemed solid no longer, everything wavered, flowed, lengthened and shortened again, assumed fantastic shapes, floated, rose and sank. The houses grew tall and took on a Don Quixotish cadaverousness; pedestrians bore high pointed heads on their shoulders. Their shadows detached themselves, went their own ways and mingled with the corporeal crowd; actual body and shadow could no longer be distinguished from one another.

And as with actual things, so with one's thoughts and feelings. Desire became confused with fulfillment, dream with waking reality, and the one was indistinguishable from the other.

In a maze of shadows Zachary, himself a shadow, walked through the night. He no longer knew whether the events of the last few days were dream or actuality.

He talked to himself: "I've found my father and mother in the Kvasniecova's lodgings: isn't that strange?" For old Chomsky and Madame Hurvitz were as near to him now as if he had known them all his life. Yes, all his life they had been with him, though unknown to him, never seen by him; and yet they had been there, had shielded and preserved him till now.

Once more Zachary saw himself on a winter night in the house in snow-bound Ekaterinburg. The frost, breaking from the mysterious forests of Siberia, beleaguered the town and his paternal house. He was quite alone and forsaken, a small figure in his great nursery. He was lying in bed staring with wide open eyes into the cold night. Mamma was out there. A figure was sitting by his bed now, but it was only a governess or some one. . . . He could not see who it was. . . . But now he knew. Hidden by the darkness Madame Hurvitz had seated herself beside his bed, she was watching over him, shielding him with her mother's hands that were as strong to guard and keep as the paws of a menaced tigress—and she had tigerish, fire-darting eyes.

Such thoughts were fantastic, mere childish illusions. And yet, though childish illusions, they helped one. What business was it of anybody's what a grown man thought as he walked through the streets of Petersburg on a white night of summer?

What were one's actual parents? A physical cause. The little atom that they flung into existence was certainly the source of the whole that eventually developed, the original force that shaped it. But the tiny atom had long vanished, lost in the flood of experience that molded the organism. Every second in the life of an organism marked a growth into new and different worlds. Even though the organism might bear within it all the attributes of the original atom, yet minute by minute in its growth it created a thousand new attributes for itself.

"What connection, really, have I with my physical parents who brought me into the world? Mamma I never really knew; I myself created the image I cherished of her; it was an illusion woven by my own desire, a draught I brewed to still my own thirst. Perhaps in reality, in actual life, that woman was quite different, not Mamma at all? And my father? If I had had the choice I would certainly have sought out a father to my heart's desire, and would never have allowed myself to be bound to a strange man by family ties. Really father is quite strange to me, even repellent, and if he weren't my father would I ever have thought of becoming intimate with him?"

Every human being was born as lonely as a rock in the sea. There wasn't such a thing as family instinct. It was an imaginary conception created for purely materialistic reasons, so as to justify one's claim to accumulated wealth. Far more powerful in men were the purely collectivist instincts. Hardship had developed in mankind the need to live in herds, in communities. Their will to power and the egoistic desire to cling to hoarded wealth had produced the patriarchal form of society. The collective instinct roused them to heroic, idealistic deeds, gave them courage to sacrifice themselves for the whole. Family instinct, on the other hand, made them hard-hearted and strengthened their self-love. Consequently it must be fought and extirpated, just as one fought and eradicated other bad qualities in oneself.

Yet one's real parents existed in actuality. They lived somewhere, rooted in the soil of an unknown, secret life. Sometimes a human being encountered his parents, but that was a rare chance.

The old Jew who had held his hand so warmly and spoken the words he was in need of; Madame Hurvitz, who had recalled him to life again and given him a task to do—to Mirkin these two people seemed his real father and mother; chance had brought them to the Kvasniecova's house and a fortunate fate had led him to them.

"It sounds almost like a joke that I should have found my father and mother at the Kvasniecova's. But who are this new father and mother of mine? Who are all these lodgers at Kvasniecova's? They come from a remote, unknown world, from the darkness of Jewish settlements I have never seen, of which I know nothing. And yet, by a chance, one end of the thread that binds me to life is somewhere over there now.

"So it seems that I belong there; the path that I must tread is waiting there for me. The deeds I have to do are waiting there for me. There lies the meaning of my life. Through a pure chance, a senseless fortuitous error, I was born as the son of other parents and into another world. I must correct this error of nature as one corrects a fault, removes a deformity. Yes, that's it—I must correct nature. I've always belonged to that unknown life, and nothing was needed to tell me so but the clasp of an old man's hand, a woman's pointing finger: now I know what I must do."

All at once the streets of Petersburg became as bright as if it were day, brighter than day. A quite new radiance that came from some unknown source now touched the houses, the streets and the few solitary night wanderers who remained. The reddish-violet effluence of the northern lights was shed over the streets. It picked out everything, the houses and the passing pedestrians, with exquisite distinctness. Every natural perspective seemed to have fled, and things no longer cast a single shadow. All the shadows had vanished and everything emerged palpably in its natural dimensions. Contours rose sharply and angularly against the ethereal background, and just as everything was illuminated now from without, so Zachary's thoughts and feelings were irradiated from within. His thoughts, until now involved in phantasmal confusion, became clear, definite and firmly fixed.

Everything became clear to him: his previous life, his wrestlings with fate—all had arisen from an error in which he had been involved without his fault. But now he was free, with nothing in front of him or behind him to tie him; he was alone. Everything must have happened as it had done, and it was good that it had so happened. Now, still better than his actual deeds, he understood his cowardice.

His fight with death appeared to him now not as a wretched piece of cowardice, but as a mighty power making for its goal, a power that had conquered death. It had been a battle with dark shadows. He saw distinctly that he had conquered senseless, barren, unjust death for the sake of achieving a life clear of ghosts and shadows, a life that lay still uncreated away over there, far from the nothern lights.

In the white night he saw his way distinctly before him: at its beginning stood a woman. He saw her quite clearly. Her limbs were filled with strength and energy, with passion and love. Her generous body was confined within a black dress. He saw her ladling out soup for all her children in a great kitchen. At last, at last all the plates were filled; there was enough for all. All the rejected came to her. Her breast was full and strong, a mother's breast. Her face was boldly chiseled. He could see the line of her powerful cheek-bones. In her eyes gleamed tears of anger and of pity, glowed the compassion of the mother and the woman's heroic spirit. With the same tear-dimmed smile that she had given him when she spoke of her son's fate she now glanced at him again, and laying her hand on his hot wet brow said: "Be comforted."

The child felt safe and at rest on the breast of his mother. Nothing could ever harm him again.

That night Zachary slept for the first time for many weeks without being tortured by oppressive dreams. As he slept his pale face wore a smile as of purification and peace.

CHAPTER XXXVIII

A BOX AT THE THEATER

WITH THE spring the Moscow Arts Theater came to Petersburg for the usual season. Gabriel Haimovitch engaged a box for the night of Chekov's *The Cherry Orchard,* and invited the Halperins and the young couple.

The theater was packed. The galleries and half the stalls were filled with avidly expectant people. Students, men and women, were there, and the proletarian intelligentsia. It was by indescribable efforts that this class had succeeded in gaining admittance. Some of them had stood for twenty hours in a queue, others had paid fantastic prices for their tickets, prices which meant the foregoing of little daily luxuries and perhaps of urgent necessities for weeks or months. Even before the curtain had risen the tension of expectation so excited them that they could not sit peacefully in their places. This audience seemed to be awaiting, not a mere play, but an event of the first importance that personally concerned their own lives. The excitement, like an electric spark, communicated itself to the blasé theater-goers sitting comfortably in the boxes and the first rows of the stalls. So the whole audience were lifted into a sort of exaltation. Every pulse beat faster, and everybody was almost breathless with anticipation of something quite extraordinary to come.

In Gabriel Haimovitch's box the excitement was no less intense than in the rest of the theater. Besides, there was an additional and particular cause for agitation in the box: for it was only a few minutes before the rise of the curtain and young Mirkin had still not arrived. It was inexplicable to the whole party and they all felt on the verge of some crisis or other. During the last few days young Mirkin seemed to have completely vanished and he had not shown himself even at the Halperins'. Although all his friends were used to such behavior in him and put it down to his inert temperament, Olga Michailovna had been very disturbed by it during the past few days. His tactless lack of punctuality tonight (he had not even arrived to fetch Nina) announced to her the advent of a catastrophe. Yet outwardly she showed more composure than the others, far more than Nina in particular, who revealed her uneasiness by an exaggerated animation and an assumed interest in the play; more, too, than Gabriel Haimovitch, whose face was purple with fury; more even than her own husband, who was quite oblivious of everything and now and then asked quite naively: "Why hasn't Zachary shown up yet?" Smiling unaffectedly, and occasionally making some indifferent remark with a languid gesture, Olga Michailovna had a composing effect on the little party in the box. To her husband's question she replied with a shrug. "Zachary will arrive as usual after the play has begun, and he probably won't be admitted until the end of the first act, for that's a rule with the Moscow Arts players."

Although Olga Michailovna's calm bearing and animated conversation with Gabriel Haimovitch did much to decrease the tension, yet every one was relieved when the lights went off and the play began. The darkness absolved them from the necessity of looking each other in the face.

The occurrences on the stage held every one in their spell. Every single member of the audience seemed to have forgotten his own life and his own circumstances and to be drawn into the world of life presented on the stage. In Gabriel Haimovitch's box, too, the party

Why did I make myself worse than I am? I've driven him from me by my silly chatter and my sensation-hunting. I've only myself to blame."

Her eyes were gleaming with tears as she gazed into the dark auditorium.

"Yet it's his fault. What have I done that I should deserve to be perpetually reproved and judged? What gives him a right to be always suspicious of me? I've pretended, I've been a fool, just as childish as he is, but in a different way. Because of that do I deserve to be perpetually blamed by him and have such thoughts nursed against me?"

Of late Nina had again and again sought an opportunity for a talk with Zachary, so as to explain everything. She wanted to convince him that she was not what he took her for, that her relations with the Countess, the ballet critic and all their circle had become loathsome to her and that she intended to break them off, that she pictured their future life together in quite a different light from what he imagined, and that she wished to lead the same quietly modest life as he did, a life of simple domestic happiness.

But Zachary gave Nina no opportunity for this talk, since he persistently avoided her. His engagement to her he regarded, apparently, as a mere obligation which he had to fulfill. So whenever the pair met, Nina's wounded pride awoke anew, sealing her lips and locking her heart. And again, instead of uttering the sincere words that were required, she played the old comedy, an assumed comedy that was false and alien to her.

"This must end! He must be told! We must have an explanation—quickly, this very night! Things can't go on like this. Yet why doesn't he come, why does he torture me like this? What have I done to him? It must be done this very night, after the play! From tonight our relations must be put on quite a different footing—or else broken off. But why doesn't he come? Where can he be, in God's name? Perhaps Mamma is right: he's probably walking up and down in the foyer now, waiting for the fall of the curtain. How long this act is lasting; will it never come to an end?"

When the curtain fell the throng of late-comers poured through the doors into the theater and sought their seats. Nina's feminine pride forbade her to keep a look out for Zachary. The men impatiently scrutinized the new arrivals. But when they had all taken their seats and Zachary still did not appear the atmosphere in the box became actually oppressive.

Nobody even spoke except for Olga Michailovna, who had great difficulty in keeping up a semblance of conversation. Her remarks on the performance of the first act had a distracted sound. The others nodded agreement, hardly opening their lips.

Fortunately the interval did not last for long. The play presently began again and the four spectators in the box could once more conceal their thoughts in the darkness.

The scenery of the second act was so realistic that the audience felt themselves transported into the flowery meadows of midsummer amid which the action passed. The fragrance of freshly-cut hay seemed to float out from the stage, awakening, as in the hero, a longing to throw off one's clothes and take a cool swim. In some inexplicable way this scene evoked in Nina the conviction that she would never see the summer again, never feel again the scent of new-mown hay and the fragrance of meadow flowers. Her eyes filled with tears. Her efforts to keep back her sobs gave her a headache, and when the second act was over she had to leave. She drove home in company with her mother. The men remained behind, still waiting for Zachary.

CHAPTER XXXIX

MOTHER AND DAUGHTER

AT HOME Nina found a letter awaiting her. She grew pale as she picked it up. She had been expecting it and knew what it contained. She shut herself in her room, tore open the envelope with a trembling hand, and read:

"Something has happened that forces me to recognize that I have no right to approach such a pure being as you, whom in my wretched thoughts I have carped at again and again. So I beg you to blot me from your life. I implore you, forgive a weakling who could not find the strength to rid you in any other way of a connection that must be burdensome to you."

Nina's glance remained fixed on Mirkin's small, elegant handwriting. Her first feeling was: "It's lies! He's lying from start to finish! He's taking upon himself a fault that he certainly ascribes to me in his thoughts!" She was filled with rage and loathing at his touchiness and his disingenuousness.

"Why hadn't he the courage to say frankly what he thinks of me? Why does he take sins upon himself that are invented from beginning to end? It's a wretched Jewish trick!"

Trembling with loathing she flung the letter from her, as if it no longer mattered to her; she seemed to be inwardly relieved that the affair was ended once and for all and did not even feel any desire to seek out her mother for the moment, although she knew that her mother was apprehensively waiting to hear what had happened. That, too, was now a matter of indifference to Nina.

More out of curiosity than real interest she took up the letter again and read it a second time.

This time she was conscious of an indefinable feeling that made her cheeks grow pale.

"It isn't like Zachary to humble himself like that! Something must have happened to him!

"'I implore you, forgive a weakling who could not find the strength to rid you in any other way of a connection that must be burdensome to you.'—What does the phrase 'in any other way' signify? What does he mean by that?"

She tried to call up a picture of Zachary as he had been the last time she had seen him.

"What has happened to him? Why this change?"

And as if something had suddenly become clear to her she rushed to her mother's room crying, as she ran, in a voice that no longer had anything human in it: "Mamma, Mamma, Mamma!"

Olga Michailovna seemed to have been expecting this outburst; she advanced towards her daughter, this time it must be confessed not with her usual majestic composure, which nothing seemed capable of disturbing, but pale as death, with her knees trembling.

The daughter held the letter in front of her mother's terrified face and cried: "Tell me! What has happened to Zachary?"

More out of her habit of remaining calm in all circumstances than out of real inward assurance Olga Michailovna responded: "What are you screaming for? Have you lost your senses? How should I know what's happened to Zachary?"

Hastily she ran her eyes over the letter. Then with a furious and inexplicable rage, such as Nina had never seen in her before, she cried: "It can't be! No! No!"

"Why not? Why can't it be?" Nina seized her mother's hand, and as if she wished to extort something more from her she kept on crying: "Why not? Why can't it be? Tell me, you must tell me!"

Olga Michailovna's convulsive efforts to maintain her equanimity were successful; she gave Nina the required explanation in an outburst of ardent maternal indignation: "What can he mean by this? Now, just before the marriage, when all the preparations have been made, and the whole town knows about it, are we going to be made a laughing-stock and accept his pathological nonsense as the truth? You must see yourself: it's pathological!"

"No, it's the truth, the truth, the truth!" cried her daughter.

"What are you screaming for? The servants will be coming in a minute. What is the truth?"

"That something serious and fatal has happened to him." Suddenly Nina stepped up close to her mother and with her tear-filled eyes stared piercingly into Olga Michailovna's face, as if demanding something from her:

"What have they done to Zachary? You can see for yourself—he's quite dead! Some one has killed him! What has been done to him?"

Olga Michailovna grew pale and bit her lips. But her instinct of self-preservation came into action and censored her thoughts and reflections. She fought for her motherhood.

"I hadn't any idea that this tie meant so much to you. Calm yourself: I'm sure it's all a terrible mistake and will be cleared up."

Nina looked at her mother. The glittering greenish flame in her eyes had something of the beast of prey in it. The mother flinched.

"Nina, I don't know—what has gone wrong with you?" asked Olga Michailovna anxiously.

"You don't know? But I know, I know everything!"

Mother and daughter were panting. Both seemed to be shrinking from the same words. Nina seized her mother's hands and put them over Olga Michailovna's face, as if she could not bear to look at it. But the instinct of self-preservation was once more at work in Olga Michailovna. Like a marble statue she stood with high uplifted head before her daughter and looked her coolly and sternly in the eyes.

"Nina, you must be ill! I'm very sorry for you. Please, pull yourself together. Even the worst calamity couldn't excuse your behavior. I can understand your feelings, I'm sorry for you and I forgive you; but you don't yourself know what you're saying. Afterwards you'll feel ashamed of it. It's your despair that is speaking."

Nina was silent. Pale as death, her mother flung her a contemptuous glance. Then she began in a milder tone, at once sympathetic and offended: "I didn't know that this affair meant so much to you. Seeing that is so, it will be necessary to put it right again. Nothing really serious can have happened; the whole matter is probably pure childish fancy, caused by your distrust of each other. It can be cleared up, that's certain."

"No, no! Not that! Not that!" cried Nina, as though she were past her endurance.

Olga Michailovna grew pale again.

"It's impossible to speak to you in your present state. I'm afraid you may say things you'll be ashamed of later." With that Olga Michailovna turned away and slowly, with the firm step of grievously insulted pride, left the room.

When Solomon Ossipovitch, already in a very disturbed state, returned from the theater he rushed to his daughter without waiting to take off his overcoat.

"What has happened?"

Without replying Nina went up to her father and buried her face in his fur coat. There at last she burst into tears.

Deeply moved he took her head in his trembling hands and in the pathetic voice which came easiest to him, since he always used it in his speeches for the defense, he said: "My child, I shall demand a heavy reckoning for your honor, no matter from whom it may be!"

Nina left her father and went to her room to give free vent to her tears.

CHAPTER XL

THE ORDEAL

"How do you explain your conduct of last night? It's incomprehensible unless one is to assume that you've gone mad. Where are your good manners?"

With these words old Mirkin greeted his son in his office the morning after the theater party. He had summoned Zachary there by telephone.

Gabriel Haimovitch's face was still burning with shame and anger. One could see that he was boiling with rage, and that he was striving with all his might to repress it. He sat in his swivel chair and leaned so far back in it that it threatened to capsize; his fingers were convulsively clutching his great heavy paper knife; his watery blue eyes bulged and his ears burned.

In contrast to his father Zachary was completely calm. He sat opposite Gabriel Haimovitch in the spacious leather armchair that was reserved for wealthy clients. His face wore an almost indifferent expression, except for an almost imperceptible smile that flitted over his lips and was lost in his short black beard. It could equally have expressed inner peace and malicious triumph. He replied quite calmly to his father:

"That is not difficult to explain. I've decided to break off the engagement; besides, I'm convinced that that's what Nina Solomonovna wishes, too."

"To break off the engagement?" asked his father in amazement.

"Yes, my engagement to Nina Solomonovna; I've already taken the necessary steps."

"Taken the necessary steps . . ." the old man mechanically repeated Zachary's words. "What necessary steps?"

"I wrote to Nina Solomonovna last night telling her that I set her free from a burdensome tie. And I'm convinced—that the news was very welcome to her."

"What?" shouted his father in an unnatural voice, jumping up from his chair. "Have you gone mad?"

"I can't understand your agitation, father. This is my personal affair and I thought it right to handle it as I have done."

Gabriel Haimovitch went white in the face; he stepped up to his son and said—or so it seemed to Zachary at that moment—in an unusually calm voice: "You're a young cad and cads must be handled like this. . . ."

Thereupon a buffet resounded on Zachary's bearded cheek.

The father became far paler than the son; it was the extraordinary pallor of his face that made Zachary fully aware of what had happened. He remained motionless, sitting where he was, and gazed at his father in astonishment. His father looked at him with the same gaze. He noticed that Zachary was white. Only where the palm of his hand had struck Zachary's cheek was there a red mark like the brand of Cain; the impression of his fingers was lost in Zachary's thick black beard. And the fact that his fingers had touched Zachary's black beard dismayed the father most deeply of all.

"What have I done?" cried old Mirkin in horror; he put his hands to his eyes and stammered helplessly: "Forgive me! I've forgotten myself."

Zachary could really give no clear account of his sensations; instead of being indignant, he was seized with genuine pity for his father. In spite of the grievous insult, which he felt deeply, he simply could not feel any anger at his father; on the contrary, he was conscious of a great relief, as if the buffet had lifted a heavy and oppressive load from his soul. A strange content and peace began to invade him. Like a man who has found an intense inward happiness, he could not refrain from giving expression to his feelings: "I thank you for it, father."

Then Gabriel Haimovitch's anger burst out: "Why do you thank me, you fool, you irresponsible boy? If you were a man you would have hit back, instead of thanking me."

Zachary smiled surreptitiously and remained silent.

Gabriel Haimovitch once more seated himself in his chair, put his elbows on the writing-table, buried his head in his hands, and said to himself, as if there were nobody else in the room: "Here I've built up a whole life, and now comes a sprig of a boy and pulls it all down again! One had hoped to have a home to go to in one's old age, and now—into the streets again, live in a hotel! Then why all this labor? For whom?"

Zachary felt a profound pity for his father and longed to comfort him, but he could find nothing to say. It was a torment to him and he blamed himself inwardly, but he remained silent.

"Is it any wonder if one loses one's patience?" old Mirkin continued his monologue. "Yes, more than that—it's enough to drive one mad, enough to make one commit a crime, yes, an actual crime!" He screamed out the last words, staring at his son, but then he added softly, with an ashamed expression: "Forgive me, Zachary. I didn't mean it. How could I have forgotten myself so far?"

"You needn't worry any more about it. I've forgotten it already," said Zachary, half to himself.

"How can I help worrying about it? I've given my grown-up son a buffet in the face. You aren't a child any longer; you've a beard on your face!" cried the father.

Zachary was silent.

At last old Mirkin found speech again: "So you've really done this foolish thing? But why? For what reason? What has happened? All the preparations have been made. The house is ready for you. And now you go and bring shame upon a girl for nothing and less than nothing. Why, you've ruined her life!" The old man flared up again. "How could you do such a thing? How could you dare? Have you no heart in you? She's such a tender, sensitive thing! And what about Olga Michailovna? You've been taken into a family and you've brought unhappiness to it. How will I ever be able to look these people in the face? What really has come over you? The engagement is known to the whole town. What will people say to me?"

Zachary let his father's words fall upon him like blows from a cudgel; it was as if the buffet he had received had been only a first instalment; and the harder the blows were the better. Yet something cried in his heart: "No, no! I haven't brought shame upon her."

But he crushed down that cry and remained silent.

"And as for myself," the old man was muttering again to himself, "I was hoping to begin a new life. At last I saw the goal of all my labors. I understood at last why I had slaved all my life—to build your future, to build 'Mirkin House.' Then a puppy like you comes and turns everything topsy-turvy."

Zachary was still silent. But suddenly something rose up in his father, and, as if ashamed at his momentary weakness, he went on in a loud and calm voice, his eyes firmly fixed on his son: "But no misfortune, and you are one, can break me; I can try conclusions with greater people than you, and I shall do it with you too."

"Forgive me, father. I couldn't do anything else; I have acted according to my own lights," replied Zachary, getting up and leaving the room.

Old Mirkin gazed after him for a long time. The words rose to his lips and begged for utterance: "Are you really going to leave me? What will happen to me now?" But instead he shouted after Zachary: "You've acted according to your lights, and I shall act according to mine."

Without replying Zachary shut the door.

When Zachary reached his flat he felt inclined to take off his clothes and return them to his father as belonging to him. His heart swelled with inward satisfaction that now he no longer needed anything or wished for anything. It was as if with the buffet he had endured from his father he had paid all his debts.

He reflected how he should regulate his material affairs in future. He was firmly resolved to accept no further money from his father. A small sum lay in the bank in his own name; it was his mother's legacy to him, which his father had transferred to his name when he came of age. Zachary decided to make use of this capital; he would lift it from time to time in small instalments; it must last him out until he was able to earn his living. He would inform his father of this decision.

With the contentment of a climber who has just successfully scaled a perilous cliff Zachary proceeded to reduce his affairs to order. But soon remorse began to gnaw at his heart.

Suddenly he saw his father sitting forlorn and dejected at his supper table (the insult that the old man had inflicted upon him was already forgotten; it seemed to him that a stranger, and not his father, had paid him the wages he deserved). The sense of absolution which the blow had brought him helped to efface all the bitterness and anger he might have felt at it. Now he felt nothing but pity, perhaps actual love, for his father. Nina became in his imagination a pure angelic being against whom he had acted a wretched and dishonorable part. His feelings for Olga Michailovna were divided now, consisting on the one hand of vague and yet affectionate filial emotion, and on the other of a sinful and ashamed sense of satisfaction. Nevertheless she had remained pure and unsullied in his eyes, for ever bound to him by that ineffaceable deed. So his heart was sore for the three people with whom he had broken so suddenly and brutally; it was still bleeding from the wound, but these three people were not yet quite detached from him. It was a feeling similar to that after an amputation, when one can still feel for a time the nerves of the amputated limb. Zachary asked himself: "Have I a right to save myself? Isn't it already too late? What I'm doing is really cowardly and dishonorable—to run away like a thief? Here have I been taken into a family, have humiliated them through my evil instincts, and now I simply run away! That's not the way to set her free. I must pay with my life: there's no other choice! It's no use escaping from the hangman's rope—it will always pursue me."

His inward peace and contentment were gone. He seemed to himself now like a hunted dog: he ran and ran and ran again and again into the hangman's loop.

"How can I really run away?" he asked himself. "With what am I purchasing a continuation of life? What right have I to go on living?"

His head grew hot again, the room became as narrow and still as a tomb.

He remained standing helplessly in the middle of the room and once more could see no way out. He had a feeling as though he were stretched on a frame; the frame was life; beyond it was nothing but death and annihilation, and some one was perpetually driving him with a whip out of the frame; he desperately hung on, he did not want to go, but he must, he must. . . .

There was a knock at the door.

Without knowing what he was doing Zachary cried as usual: "Come in."

He turned rigid with astonishment. What he saw was so inevitable and yet so extraordinary, so understandable and yet a portent. Olga Michailovna stood in the doorway. It was really she! An uncanny, terrifying serenity lay in her pale face, from which she had pushed up her veil. She said nothing, but only looked at Mirkin. Overcome by weakness she leant against the doorpost and never took her eyes from Zachary. He seemed to become visibly smaller under her glance. He felt quite distinctly: that woman standing there has no connection with life; she has appeared to me as a spirit to give me some grave warning.

"Forgive me. I wanted to make an end of everything in a different way. I couldn't," said Mirkin, bowing deeply before her.

"Why an end?" she asked softly.

"I can't go on living like this," cried Mirkin in despair.

"Why can't you live with a broken heart, as we all—as I have to live?" she asked, and her eyes filled with tears. "Why are you so selfish?"

Zachary was more deeply moved by her tragic tones than by her words, which in his confusion he scarcely understood. The softness of her voice reawoke a feeling in him that he thought was dead. But it was not quite dead; her agitated voice evoked that sweet and sinful fragrance again. Zachary raised his eyes to look at Olga Michailovna. He saw the shadows cast on her eyes by the lifted veil, and he clenched his fingers.

Why not live with a broken heart, like Olga Michailovna? Am I of any more importance than the rest? With a broken heart—that's a possibility I had never thought of. And that it's selfish of me to wish to live differently from the rest—I had never thought of that either.

"Olga Michailovna, Olga Michailovna," he stammered the words inwardly without being able to utter them.

He felt all his resolutions tottering, collapsing, felt his heart changing under the influence of those downcast eyes. And he knew: I'll fall at her feet in a moment, kiss her skirts, breathe in her perfume and say the words that have been trembling on my lips: "Olga Michailovna, do with me what you will. . . ."

But a guardian was already standing behind him. He felt Madame Hurvitz's eyes fixed on him. She smiled at him through her tears; her strong right arm was stretched out towards him. He felt bound to her as if he were her child. Like a mother she had appeared to him, and he would do something pleasing to her, so as to win her praise and feel her hand caressing his cheek.

Now he could distinctly hear again the words she had said about her children: "My children are ready to die. Those who want to live must be prepared to die." He, too, would become worthy of being called a child of hers, would learn how to die. Yes, he felt the strength for it—he could die like Madame Hurvitz's children.

"Olga Michailovna, you can demand my life of me, but I cannot live with a broken heart."

For a long time Olga Michailovna gazed at Zachary without saying a word. Her look expressed astonishment and admiration; she did not seem to recognize Zachary in this man. She made to speak, but her trembling lips moved without uttering a sound. She turned round and hastily left the room.

CHAPTER XLI

THE OLD LION

When old Mirkin was left to himself boundless rage took possession of him. But at the same time new energy and self-confidence awoke in him. His anger reopened the founts of self-love which his paternal love had to all appearance buried under it.

"No use trying to alter the fact—for you there's nobody in the world but yourself; you have no family and no friends. And if you don't look out for yourself your own flesh and blood will give you your death blow."

He prowled up and down the room without a stop. While he was conducting his monologue his brain was occupied in disentangling the situation and deciding what was to be done.

"It's I who will be held responsible for everything: it is I who am chiefly concerned. Who is he after all? A silly youth."

He stopped in the middle of the room. A thought flashed before him that cast him into such agitation that he began to tremble from head to foot. Violently he put it from him, resolved not to let it a second time over the threshold of his consciousness.

"There's one thing I must certainly do—make over my property to Nina. She has more claim to it than he has, she's closer to me too—yes, closer, although he's my son."

Now he was astonished at himself: "Obviously fate decided from the first that I was to have no family. And I, old fool that I am, wanted to do by violence something that couldn't be done!"

In accordance with his custom of executing at once a resolve once made he went to his iron safe and took out a document. Briefly running over it, he seized his pen, drew two long strokes in red ink across the paper and wrote in the margin: "Invalid." Then he tore the sheet in two and put it in his pocket.

This somewhat appeased his rage. He sat down at his writing-table to recover. The destruction of the document (it was his will) had been a greater strain than his talk with his son. He had a feeling that along with the will he had torn in two for ever the bond that tied him to his son, and he now seemed in his own eyes a vagabond who had only one place of refuge, the hotel.

"Probably it's my fate," he told himself. For a moment he yielded to weakness, leant his head in his hands, sighed deeply and felt sorry for himself. His self seemed to have detached itself from him and to be sitting opposite him at the writing-table. Without his heart beating even a little faster he seized the telephone with his trembling hand and asked to be connected with Nina Solomonovna Halperin. He expressly added that he wished to speak to nobody but her. He had fixed upon his telephone call as a sort of omen: "If she replies, things will be all right; if she doesn't, then let things take what course they like!"

To his great surprise he succeeded in getting through to her far more easily and quickly than he had expected. Nina's ever-laughing voice came over the telephone: "Good day, Gabriel Haimovitch, here I am."

"Thank God!" exclaimed the old man, and he pulled out his handkerchief and wiped the sweat of anxiety from his forehead.

"Nina Solomonovna, I don't know what has happened between you,—but I must see you. I beg you, don't refuse an unhappy old man's request. I must see you, if it is only for this once."

Once more he was surprised, for she agreed more quickly than he had expected.

"Certainly, certainly: why not? When do you want to see me? And where do you want to see me, Gabriel Haimovitch? I'm ready to come."

"Where? In your house of course. I can be with you in a few moments if you wish."

"No, no, not in the house! My parents mustn't know I've seen you. And I don't want anybody to hear about it either. I'll see you alone, and only because I like you. I'm not concerned with anything else."

"Thanks! Thanks more than I can say! Of course, if you wish it . . . where would you like us to meet? What I've to say to you is very serious!"

"If it's agreeable to you we can drive out somewhere outside the town and have tea together. This is Sunday. I'll be at the corner of the Sadova at four o'clock; you can drive along there in your car and fetch me."

"Wherever you like and as you like! I shall be there. Many, many thanks!"

"I'll expect you at four sharp," said Nina, and to old Mirkin her voice seemed to have an inexplicable undertone.

He had pictured their meeting taking place in Olga Michailovna's boudoir, with all the trappings of gravity and solemnity. Accordingly he had intended to appear in black: "But she insists on giving a romantic turn to the business—there's nothing to be done but comply. The devil only knows what may come into the heads of these young people of today!"

He left the office and drove to his hotel. He had still two hours to himself. Stretching himself out on the sofa he ordered the samovar to be brought in. Hot tea had always been his specific for calming the nerves. Then he took a warm bath, had his whole body rubbed with eau de Cologne by his servant until it steamed, and thereafter rested for a little. He tried to get a few moments' sleep, but he could not. Then he changed his underclothing, put on his black morning coat together with a new tie, sprayed his side-whiskers with eau de Cologne and took his seat in his car, so as to be at the corner of the Sadova at the appointed time.

While he was still a good distance away he saw Nina walking along the Nevsky Prospect towards the Sadova. She was wearing a gray walking costume with a large bunch of violets at her breast. Under the broad brim of her black straw hat her face could scarcely be seen. It wore a sad and yet unnaturally animated look. From where she was Nina waved to him with one of her white gloves without troubling about the stares of the passers-by. The big car stopped. The heavy old man made an effort and assisted Nina to get in. But she had to help out his gallantry a little, and she did so with a smile from eyes which were glazed as after a debauch.

"To the 'Arcadia' again, as the last time," she said to the driver.

"Thanks, thanks, from my very heart for not leaving an old man alone in his despair," began old Mirkin gravely, and he kissed Nina's hand as the car started again.

"There's nothing to thank me for! It's only the son that I've fallen out with; I hope my relations with the father will remain the same as before," she replied with a spontaneous smile.

"I had to see you. I've something very serious to say to you," said the old man.

"Not now, not now! You can tell me everything when we're there. On the way I won't listen to a word," she answered, obviously with some annoyance.

During the drive nothing further was said.

When they arrived at the elegant restaurant, which was already veiled by the fresh green foliage of spring, old Mirkin asked: "Where would you like to sit—in the big tea-room?"

"No, we would be interrupted there. Ask tea to be served in a private room," she replied hastily.

Old Mirkin shrugged his shoulders; his ears became unnaturally red.

When they entered the airy and flower-decked room Nina fell into the nearest armchair, took off her fur boa and opened her coat. The fine lace border of her chemise could be seen under the open neck of her silk blouse. With her fingers she pushed back her short black curls, which had escaped from under her wide hat, and asked impatiently: "What have you to say to me, Gabriel Haimovitch?"

"Do you want to hear it now, before the tea comes in?"

"I've no wish to drink tea," she replied with mounting impatience. "I would like something cold. Ask the waiter to bring champagne."

"Champagne in the middle of the afternoon?" Old Mirkin was horrified, but he said obediently: "Waiter, a bottle of Monopol."

"And see that it's put in ice," Nina shouted after the vanishing waiter.

"Now, what is it, Gabriel Haimovitch?"

"Hm," the old man sought for the right words, "I don't know what has taken place between you, and I don't want to know either. Who can understand you young people of today? I thought everything was safely fixed up, and suddenly—but no more about that! I don't know what the next development will be between you. That is your own affair, yours and Zachary's affair. There's only one thing I want to say to you, and I beg you, Nina Solomonovna, not to misunderstand me! I am an old man, and all things considered I've had very little happiness in my life; I've only come to know what happiness is, I've only really understood what true happiness is since I've known you, since I've been able to tell myself that you belonged in a sense to us, belonged to Zachary. You were, after all, a member of my family, you were in a sense a child of mine, of my own blood, and I worked and labored for you. It was then that I first found a meaning for my life, my work, my struggles. And now suddenly—it's a calamity, a calamity! If I were twenty or thirty years younger—oh, I should know then what to do!" exclaimed the old man, tugging at his whiskers.

"What would you do then, Gabriel Haimovitch?" asked Nina, and from under her lowered lids she sent him a challenging glance.

"What would I do?" replied the old man half-jestingly and half-seriously. "If I thought I wasn't quite distasteful to you I would enter into rivalry with that young cub, my son, and beg you for the honor of your hand. Forgive an old man's silliness," he said, quickly gaining mastery over himself again; "it's my unwillingness to lose you as a member of my family that does it. You're not angry with me?" he asked in a tone of deep sadness, as he wiped something from his eyes.

Nina regarded him with a wry smile, but not without interest. She remained silent.

The waiter brought the champagne. Nina had the bottle opened at once and impatiently stretched out her hand for her glass. Thirstily she drank it down at one gulp. Old Mirkin merely touched his lips with his glass.

When the waiter had gone the old man began again: "Forgive my foolish words, Nina Solomonovna! I can't bear to lose you from my life. You yourself don't know how you've grown into my heart. Now I must lose you as my daughter-in-law—and I can't do anything about that, for it is not in my competence. But I don't want to lose you as my daughter—allow me to use that word, I've got so used to it by now; so don't take it ill of an old broken man. I would like you to continue to be one of us. That's the only thing that can give meaning to my work and my life. I know that my request is an unreasonable one, but I implore you not to reject it!"

"Gabriel Haimovitch, I still don't understand what you want of me. I would like to be your daughter, but others won't permit it. You know, surely, that it wasn't I who broke off the engagement. Tell me now what you want of me."

"What I want of you? This is what I want: I want to make you the heiress to my property, as if you were my own child. I have no child now, none! What I propose to do is not intended to make good an injustice committed by a silly youth—not at all! It is solely and entirely to give an unhappy old man the illusion that he hasn't lived in vain, struggled and labored in vain. I'll feel then that you're still in a sense a part of me. I beg you on my knees; don't refuse my request, Nina Solomonovna!"

Nina became very pale. Dark violet-shadowed rings appeared under her eyes. The rouge on her lips stood out with unnatural vividness. Shyly and haltingly she began, avoiding his eyes: "I, too, don't want to part from you, Gabriel Haimovitch. Couldn't it be arranged in some other way?"

"What way are you thinking of?" asked the old man in alarm.

"Why do you want me only as a daughter, a child?"

"Good God, Nina Solomonovna, what are you saying?" he cried, growing pale.

"I don't see why it couldn't be. You yourself said what you would do if you weren't distasteful to me. You aren't distasteful to me."

"But I'm an old man. I could easily be your father!"

"You're stronger, braver and better than all the young men put together and I like you better too—I've always liked you!"

Old Mirkin's brow grew damp.

"Nina Solomonovna, what are you doing? What can you do with an old man like me? How will it end? Why, you were my son's future wife. What will the world say? What will your mother think?"

The word "mother" released Nina's tongue again; she seemed resolved to be held back by nothing now: "I thought you were accustomed to do what seemed right to you without regarding what the world would say. And as for Mamma—my engagement to Zachary was Mamma's work and it has been broken off. My engagement to you will be my own work."

But Gabriel Haimovitch had collected himself again; he became cool and grave: "What you want to do, Nina Solomonovna, what you've just said to me—you must allow me to call it by its real name—is a mere counsel of despair: you're simply throwing yourself away! I would be forced to regard myself as a mean and wretched creature if I took advantage of such a moment of weakness—though for myself I look upon it, as you can understand yourself, as a precious gift from God."

"No, no! It isn't despair! I tell you quite seriously: Zachary has never meant anything to me, and I've always been fond of you." She took a step towards him and sank half-fainting into his arms.

Old Mirkin pressed a light paternal kiss on her brow.

"You can't mean this for good, seriously. You'll regret it later!"

"No, no, no!" Nina cried on his breast through her sobs.

When old Mirkin was driving back to the town with Nina, who was very pale and clung to his arm, the thought again flitted through his head: "Devil knows what one is to make of these young people of today! I can't understand them . . ."

And sunk in thought he wondered: "Can this be laid upon me in my old age?"

He answered himself:

"Obviously I broke too soon with Helena Stepanovna. It's easy for me to commit another folly even at my age!"

CHAPTER XLII

WORDS

About this time an event occurred in the Halperin family under whose influence the armor with which Olga Michailovna had seemed to bar any access to her inner nature suddenly melted like wax; for the first time she really felt she was a mother. It happened as follows:

As the Halperins were making arrangements to return the presents with which Nina had been overwhelmed by old Mirkin at the time of her engagement they suddenly discovered that a ring set with an unusually large bluish-white brilliant was missing: after the latest American fashion the clasp was of platinum. Nina had worn the ring only on rare occasions, because of its striking size; in her distracted state of mind she had not always locked it away carefully; as far as she could remember she had left it once either on her dressing table or in the bathroom. All search was in vain; the ring could not be found. Suspicion fell upon Anushka, the only maid who attended on Nina and had access to her things. Questioned by the advocate she grew more and more nervous and embarrassed, and Halperin's expert eye recognized at once that he was on the right track.

Nevertheless, nothing was to be extorted from Anushka but helpless tears. Yet as the ring, quite apart from its great value, had to be returned for reasons of honor, it was reluctantly decided, after an agitating scene with Anushka, to hand her over to the police, so as to force an admission from the unfortunate creature by more effective arguments than mere persuasion.

After three days the police brought the girl back to the Halperins'. Anushka bore on her body and her face palpable traces of the "arguments" of the police. Her eyes were sunk in their sockets so that they could scarcely be seen, and dark blue rings surrounded them. Her nose was unnaturally thick and swollen. When she opened her mouth gaps like broken window panes could be seen in her teeth. Anushka had admitted taking the ring, and had been conducted to the house by the police to point out where she had hidden it. But in the place indicated by her —her bed—nothing was to be found. Anushka caught at the excuse that the ring might have been stolen from there or got lost in the straw bedding. The lawyer and the police, who had experience of such things, did not believe this supposition, but suspected that Anushka had handed the stolen ring to some accomplice whom she would not give away at any price; a few more "arguments" would no doubt suffice to cure the girl of her romantic behavior and make her name her "hero."

Nina, when she saw the marks of the dreadful treatment the girl had been submitted to, burst into a passion of tears and implored the others to set Anushka free—she herself would go to Mirkin and explain everything to him. But it was of no avail; both the police and the Halperins (the lawyer on legal grounds, Olga Michailovna for the sake of her "honor" menaced by the missing ring) absolutely insisted that Anushka should be further interrogated, and, at no matter what cost, forced by every available means to name her "hero," whom she was so bravely shielding. As Anushka was being led out of the room to be conducted once more to prison she encountered Misha, the son of the house, who was breathless with running upstairs, his books under his arm, having obviously just returned from school. Although the meeting was entirely fortuitous and did not last longer than a moment, it roused the attention of one of the policemen, not so much because of the girl's bearing as the visible discomposure of the young man. On seeing Anushka, Misha grew pale and let his books fall. Anushka kept her head lowered; as Misha came upstairs she cast one glance at him from her deep, swollen eye-sockets. In that glance there was neither reproach nor repentance nor even regret, but affection and joy. Her swollen lips were twisted into a smile and her glance seemed to be seeking to reassure him.

The scene lasted only for a few seconds, for Anushka, who had obviously become aware that she was betraying something, sank her head again at once and defiantly drew her head-cloth further over her face. But Misha's nervous twitching, the circumstance that on seeing the girl he had become strangely embarrassed and dropped his books, and particularly his extraordinary pallor, awoke in one of the men who were escorting Anushka the vague suspicion that this youth must have had something to do with the theft.

The interrogation was next pursued in that direction. It was impossible to get anything out of Anushka; neither by blows nor other inquisitorial methods were they able to extort a word from her. Nor did the mention of Misha's name disturb her equanimity. She simply shrugged her thin shoulders and declared she knew nothing. So no adequate proof could be obtained to upset the celebrated advocate and involve his son in the painful affair, such proof as the Press, if it got hold of it, would work up into a great sensation. Nor did the police officially divulge this new turn taken by the affair, but contented themselves for the time being with shadowing the lawyer's son and making inquiries among the domestic staff concerning his relations with Anushka.

Soon they came upon a clew; it was discovered that Misha along with Markovitch had recently been visiting expensive and questionable night resorts in the company of persons of suspicious character. The Halperins' domestic staff on being interrogated made veiled insinuations regarding Anushka and Misha; they also revealed that Anushka had been borrowing money from everybody and was in debt to all the other servants.

The police, who now saw the possibility of dealing the progressive

Jewish advocate a shrewd blow, continued their inquiries in this new direction. Their investigations were carried on in strict secrecy, so that the lawyer might not discover them too soon. But Halperin's extraordinary keenness of scent in police matters and his watchful surveillance of the course of an inquiry in which his own prestige was concerned enabled him to guess in time the turn that the police wished to give to it.

And when one of the domestic staff confidentially informed him that inquiries regarding Misha were being made in the house, he knew with certainty that the police were set on engineering a slanderous campaign against his family. At once he summoned his son and shut himself up with him in his study. Misha was a far easier subject than Anushka to deal with; like an erring child, with tears in his beautiful eyes, he soon made a full confession. . . .

Olga Michailovna sat in the favorite corner of her boudoir; for the first time in her life she was not thinking of her appearance. For the first time the few gray hairs on her head, which were usually concealed beneath her heavy black strands, could be seen; tears flowed down her cheeks and cut furrows in the face powder without her paying any regard to their effect on her complexion. She actually held her hands clasped in the most unesthetic manner on her knees and sighed and murmured incomprehensible words to herself.

Solomon Ossipovitch, the celebrated advocate, nervously strode to and fro on the soft Persian carpet. His hair was still more disordered than usual, and suddenly it could be seen that he was an old man. He held up two fingers of his right hand—a sign that he was on the point of saying something very pathetic and impressive; for whenever a God-given inspiration came to him he always held up two fingers of his right hand, no matter whether he might happen to be addressing the high court or talking to company, no matter whether it was a public matter that he was discussing or his own private affairs.

"In my house," he began, and his voice swelled to its deepest register, "justice will always be upheld. Here has always been an asylum for the oppressed and persecuted, here protection from violence and injustice could always be found. And now the meanest, the most contemptible form of crime has crept into my own household. I shall root it out with my own hand and deliver it over to justice! Yes, even if the offender should be bound ever so closely to me—I shall tear him from my heart, though it cost me my life, and hand him over to his judge!"

Sunk in her own grief, Olga Michailovna did not seem even to have heard her husband's words. She kept groaning over and over again: "It's our fault, our fault!"

After a pause in which he had traversed the room several times, the lawyer continued his monologue:

"Only a few weeks ago I showed a man the door who was less to blame and had more right to protection and defense than my son. That man had harmed nobody, for he had not offended against any human being, but only against a dead principle. And I ruthlessly showed him the door. And am I to shield *him* and gloss over *his* offense because he's my own flesh and blood, and my own hide is in danger? No! Just because he's my own flesh and blood, just because I am responsible for him, I'm resolved to deliver him over to the law with my own hand. We must be an example to others. If we aren't, how can I find the moral strength to face the world and my opponents, and to fight for the things I stand for?"

"Words, words! Nothing but words!" The cry came from his wife. "I'm sick of all these words! We've built up our whole life on words, on beautiful, just, finely-turned words—empty phrases that have no effect, none! This that has happened is our fault, my fault and yours! All our life we have played a part, trifled with things. What have we done for our children? Nothing! I was occupied with myself, with my silly good looks; you were occupied with yourself, with your fine speeches, your liberal pretty-sounding phrases. We've both trifled with life. We've both been egoists, wretched egoists who never, never thought of our children, but always of ourselves, ourselves!"

Pale as death, Solomon Ossipovitch stopped in the middle of the room and gazed at his wife with wide, horrified eyes. He did not recognize this women; he had never seen her in such a mood before.

"What has gone wrong with you?" he asked in alarm.

"Nothing! A misfortune has happened. We have to save our child —and you—you make speeches! You know well enough that you won't do what you say!"

The lawyer remained standing where he was. His brow was deeply furrowed and his two fingers involuntarily sank again. For the first time in his life he was unable to find any answer to an accusation. Nor did he give one.

Touched by his helplessness, Olga Michailovna went up to him. She leant her face disfigured by weeping on his breast and sobbed like an ordinary woman of the people:

"Solomon, he isn't to blame; it's we! We're to blame for everything!"

VOLUME II

WARSAW

BOOK ONE

CHAPTER I

DAWN

THE AUTUMN nights in Poland are pitch-black. Sky and earth are wrapped in a close embrace within which broods the mystery of creation.

With the first glimmer of dawn the sky lifts from the earth and, receding upwards, leaves a fresh, untrodden layer of white frost on the fields and meadows. The trees drip. The earth lies silent. No animal is yet astir. Nobody as yet owns this earth, new-born under the ascending sky: like a foundling it lies outstretched with a bloom of dew upon it. . . .

From beyond the fields comes a metallic clinking like the trickle of single water-drops from some invisible gutter; out of the gray half-light, the first milk-wagons loom up and rattle over the stone bridge of Praga, an outer suburb of Warsaw. The clatter of the milk-cans resounds far and wide in the pure, clear emptiness and rouses the sleeping world.

When these have gone past, the gray half-light gives up other wagons; over the stone bridge appear high loads of cabbages and potatoes, carts packed with egg-boxes, with fowl-crates, with jars of plums, baskets of pears, casks of cranberries; all brought by Jews and peasants from the small towns and villages into the great city of Warsaw. The wet dew of the night-fields is still thick upon the wagons. From the lofty bales of hay, from hollows in the straw, there peer fresh, round-cheeked country girls, peasant women with weather-beaten red faces under bright head-shawls, shivering Jews muffled to the ears, dripping peasants in steaming sheepskins.

Weary, with hanging heads, drops of sweat frozen on their flanks, the horses set their hoofs on the hard stones of the bridge.

The long row of wagons winds through the streets of Praga towards the iron bridge that throws its mighty framework across the river Vistula.

Through the network of the iron bridge there gleams the shimmer of the hoar-frost that lies like a linen coverlet over the roofs and church spires on the other bank of the river.

That is Warsaw.

In the tenement where Hurvitz the teacher lived night still reigned unchecked. Garments hung spectrally over the chairs. A chorus of snores in all keys rose from the corners. The rooms were filled with the warm exhalations of sleeping bodies and bed-clothes. The housewife, her face still heavy with sleep, was the first to get up, stretching her foot cautiously from the bed. With inaudible, cat-like movements she groped in the dark for her clothes, anxiously trying not to waken any one. But the teacher was already awake. Silently he lit the candle on the bed-table.

"I can see well enough," objected his wife.

"Why so early?" grumbled the sleepy man.

"Winter's nearly on us, and it's hard to tell what to do first."

And all at once a stream of water began to splash from the tap in the kitchen. . . .

The marketing money—a few gulden—had been lying in readiness ever since the night before. It had taken a whole day to run round from one parent to another collecting the outstanding school fees. The housewife's daughter had contributed her own school earnings as well, money which should really have been laid by for the purchase of a new winter coat, but it could not be spared for that at the moment: there were too many hungry mouths to fill and a long, merciless winter was almost at the door; there had to be at least a few bags of potatoes stored in the house, some jars of pickled cabbage and a small cask of thick plum sauce.

While Frau Hurvitz hurriedly dressed herself, her eye ran appraisingly, like that of an experienced warrior, over the sleeping groups in the corners; she was rapidly reckoning up in her head how many people she had to feed. Involuntarily she frowned as she looked at the door of the "High School" (that was what she called the room where the young men slept who came wandering like pilgrims from the provinces to Hurvitz the teacher, and were boarded in the house for a mere pittance) : "How can they help it if they need to eat?"

But her feverish impatience left her no time for brooding: "In the market the women are at it already, grabbing the sacks out of the very carts, and the hawkers are buying up everything." Still nibbling at a stale roll of bread she threw her shawl over her head, hooked her arms into the handles of two huge baskets and scurried down the stairs.

Meanwhile the teacher settled himself in bed again, put out the candle and drew the warm blanket over his ears.

Hurvitz the teacher dearly liked a sleep. It was a bad lookout for any one who dared to rouse him when he was enjoying forty winks between two lessons. And last night he had been late in getting to sleep, for he had had a long argument with the Shachliner about the future of Poland. But Solomon Hurvitz simply had to come off victor and have the last word in any argument, more especially in an argument about Poland, or else the world would have come to an end. The Shachliner (the lodgers in the "High School" were all nicknamed after the towns from which they came) had made the teacher's blood boil by his ignorance of Poland's position, and, as usual, whenever ignorance and stupidity about Polish politics roused him to ire, Hurvitz had had to seek comfort in the prophetic words of Mickiewicz's "Funeral Dirge," a poem which he possessed in an edition smuggled across the border from Galicia (if it were discovered by an inspector he would run the danger of losing his teaching license). The argument and the reading of the "Dirge" had kept him up till two in the morning. And this would be a heavy day for him, without a free moment; lesson after lesson, down one stair and up another. But the sleep that he longed for would not come. Duty called him. . . .

The duty that called him was an examination on the four years' course of the Russian lower secondary schools, the passing of which would qualify him to hold a license for conducting an elementary school. A recent decree of the authorities had made the passing of this examination obligatory for all teachers. With laborious effort and much pulling of strings, Hurvitz had managed to have it conceded that his existing license should remain provisionally valid until he passed the examination. And so Solomon Hurvitz, who, when he was barely eighteen had been called to the vocation of Rabbi by the most distinguished Rabbis in the country, since even then he was famous throughout half Poland as an inspired expounder of the Jewish sacred texts, Solomon Hurvitz, who did not know one letter of the Polish alphabet when his first child was born and yet a little later had mastered three languages (which he did by way of learning whole dictionaries by rote), Solomon Hurvitz, who possessed a great store of philosophic knowledge, who kept in his head an enormous number of foreign words and all the more important dates in the history of the world—he, Solomon Hurvitz, had now to begin all over again and cram for an examination like a schoolboy.

But it was not the studying that he found difficult. He had learned by heart the whole of Ilovaysky's *Russian History*. Physics, Geography, Natural History, Mathematics—none of these subjects daunted him. It was a silly little Russian nursery rhyme that scared him. For he was very uncertain in distinguishing between the hard and the soft consonants in Russian. As a Polish patriot he naturally detested the Russian language. He could not relish even its literature, and for no price in the world could he or would he pronounce it correctly; his tongue simply refused to get properly round a Russian word, and the soft sounds slithered between his teeth and gave him nothing to bite on. But he knew that the school inspector would not ask him a single question in mathematics or in history; he would only be asked to recite the damned nursery rhyme that he now chanted morning after morning out of a tattered old anthology.

Yet Solomon Hurvitz was not a man to worry about things. All his worries had long been transferred to his wife's shoulders, indeed, ever since they were a newly married couple and were still being supported by her father. A Jewish wife of the old stamp, she had always assumed responsibility for the things of this world, leaving her husband to look after those of the next. That was how it was in their early days, when he used to sit in the synagogue making sure of his portion in the next world, and that was how it remained even after he became a renegade and began to study *trefe* profane books. And Frau Rachel-Leah still felt awed when from the tiny alcove that formed their joint bedroom she heard the voice of her husband intoning in the familiar Talmud sing-song some difficult chapter of "philosophy" (that word summarized for Frau Hurvitz the whole of her husband's new studies); she would go about on tip-toe and make urgent signs to the children to keep quiet... Solomon Hurvitz had only one preoccupation—study; once it had been the Talmud, now it was "philosophy." Everything else, now as ever, he left to his wife....

But on that morning, after Rachel-Leah's departure, he did not stay long in bed. His conscience pricked him. As once it had bidden him to rise early for his devotions in the synagogue, so now it bade him rise for an hour or two's devotion to learning. Hurvitz began to don his clothes. This he did with the same systematic orderliness that he displayed in all his actions. Properly folded, his garments lay one on top of the other in the order required for putting them on, and it was a bad lookout for any one who dared to disturb that order and to lay, for instance, the trousers a-top of the shirt. By this method the teacher could dress himself even in pitch darkness. Then he went quietly, walking on tip-toe so as not to awaken the children, into the kitchen to wash at the tap. As he passed his son, who was a pupil at the high school, he tugged at the boy's forelock which was sticking out above the bed-cover. In the kitchen he washed himself by rote and dried himself by rote, then he finished his toilet by rote, carefully polished his glasses and sat down to study.

The anthology with the children's poem lay open on the table and reminded him of his duty. But it irked him to think of wasting the fresh morning hours in twisting his tongue round Russian words. Pedantic as he was, he considered phonetically correct pronunciation very important, and yet it seemed to him an occupation too trivial for those good hours in the morning when the mind is fresh and receptive. He was burning to start on his pet subject, the collation of material for a scientific work he was compiling in secret; it was to be a thesis on the use of Polish names among the Jews during their settlement in Poland. He had brought some source-books home with him and wanted to copy out important extracts for his work.

And so the anthology, together with the impending examination, was relegated like everything else—like the rent, the provision of coal for the winter, the household catering—to his wife; Rachel-Leah would be able to devise something. . . .

From the dining-room, where the children slept, there came now a boy's voice reciting verses in a foreign tongue. The teacher's son, a pupil in the sixth form of the grammar-school, was rehearsing his Greek home-task; he was learning by heart the first hundred lines of the Odyssey. Hurvitz paused in his work and listened to the incomprehensible syllables. The boy was the apple of his father's eye. Ever since his eldest son, a philological student, had been put into prison for his secret political activities (disapproved of, moreover, by his father), the fifteen-year-old youngster had become the sole repository of his father's hopes. Solomon Hurvitz was a typical "enlightened" Jew, a Maskil, as the adherents of enlightenment were called among the eastern Jews; and he had brought with him from the synagogue an enormous thirst for knowledge. Exactly as his forefathers had passionately flung themselves into the profundities of the Talmud, he now dived into the river of learning. He willingly helped every one who wanted to acquire learning, but his passion for it was purely disinterested. In his younger son he saw the embodiment of his ideals; and with the same pride and joy with which his own father had listened to him as a boy learning the Talmud, Hurvitz the teacher now listened to the Greek declamation of his son. It must be admitted, however, that there was some envy mingled with his pride. He could not help envying the boy his chance of reading the Greek and Roman classics in the original; a piece of good fortune that lay as securely beyond Solomon Hurvitz's reach as wealth beyond that of a pauper. He envied the boy his youth, not for the sake of mere youth itself (Solomon Hurvitz had never been young), but because he had so much time ahead of him for study. Hurvitz, self-taught, had had to pay for every hour of study with a day of drudgery for other people, and from his earliest days had supported himself by selling to others the knowledge he acquired. As a boy he had had to teach other boys in the synagogue and in the Talmud-school, and he still remained a teacher later on when he pursued profaner studies. And although his natural bent for teaching and instruction disposed him to share with others the treasures he acquired and made teaching a genuine pleasure to him, he could not help regretting the countless days and long nights that he had had to waste. He kept on picturing to himself how much learning he could have absorbed had he been able to use for his own benefit the long summer days and the still longer winter nights. And as a pauper desires nothing but wealth, so Hurvitz the teacher longed for nothing but time, endless time, in which to study. That was perhaps why he had brought to a remarkable pitch of perfection the art of saving time. Nobody could dress so quickly as Solomon Hurvitz; nobody could keep pace with him in the streets when he was on his way to give a lesson; nobody could run up and down stairs so fast as he could, although he was well on in the forties. While he was in a tram he could concentrate completely on what he was reading and successfully take his ticket from the conductor between two sentences of Spinoza without expending a word or even a look—a shrug of the shoulders was all that was needed—and in the rush hours he could maintain his footing without so much as seeing his neighbors; his instinct told him when it was time to get out, and he could find the house he was making for without once lifting his eyes from his book. With the sureness of a somnambulist he could thread his way through the thickest crowd and he allowed nothing that happened in the street to detain him. This unceasing haste kept him as youthful and supple in his movements as he had been in the days when he first quitted the synagogue.

Now, as he listened to his son reciting the Greek lines, he was stirred by a paternal wish to go up to the boy and say a few kindly words. Yet he checked the impulse, for Solomon Hurvitz was not only a man of modern culture, but, like any pious Jew, he "kept the commandments" of culture; and, as a pious Jew avoids sin, so he anxiously avoided any infringement of accepted intellectual precepts. It was only for a moment that his paternal impulse struggled to get the better of pedagogic theory. "Sheer sentimentality towards an independent individual"—with that comment logic (a word to which he was much addicted) once more got the upper hand. Yet he had a great weakness for his son. Although proud of the talents that enabled the boy to attend the high school, he was still prouder of the diligence that urged him to learn today, for instance, a Homer task which had been set for tomorrow. He was sure that this son of his would never be seduced by political activities from the path which was the loftiest that a man could follow, the path of knowledge. And this feeling for his son was stronger than all his logic. Still, he could not sin against the laws of pedagogy, and so, instead of the kindly words that his heart prompted, he brought out a piece of criticism, shouting to the boy through the door: "David, David!"—all his children had Biblical names—"Why are you gobbling the words as if they were lumps of pudding? The Odyssey's not meant to be eaten, it's meant to be drunk slowly like good wine."

This remark satisfied both his fatherly love and his didactic disposition without transgressing a single educational precept.

The boy slackened speed and began to declaim the lines rhythmically, knowing what his father approved, but he said to himself: "It's all very well for him to say, don't gobble, but I have to learn a whole hundred lines if I'm to keep on the right side of that beast Vassily Andreyevitch, who's so keen on Homer."

For it was only by learning five times as many lines as had been set that young David Hurvitz could screw out of his form master a terminal report with "excellent" in every subject, and without such a report he need not come home, since that would mean the loss of the scholarship provided by a rich Warsaw philanthropist, which paid his school fees....

In a very short time voices came from all corners of the house, treble and bass, children's and adults' voices, breaking on the teacher's ear in a chaotic flood of syllables, some recognizable, some not, some making sense and others making nonsense: numerals, Russian grammar, laws of physics, geographical definitions; the names of African rivers and Pacific islands that would never be visited; astronomical calculations that would never be needed; formulas in physics that would never be applied; rules of grammar that would never be practiced; all invented merely to torment children and embitter their schooldays. In this manner the "High School" that lodged in Hurvitz's flat announced its presence.

When the day broadened and the gray morning light had superseded the gas-lamps, Rachel-Leah returned from the market. She was sweating, not so much from the burden of the two great baskets crammed with vegetables, cheese, and other eatables, as for fear that she would be late in getting breakfast for her husband and the children who had to go to school. Behind her an enormous rustic appeared, filling the doorway; he was carrying a sack of potatoes and a load of plums. Last of all came a nervous-looking young man, and this procession, headed by Rachel-Leah, advanced into the kitchen.

"Who's that?" demanded the teacher, rushing into the kitchen to heat water for the breakfast coffee. He pointed to the young man.

"No idea," returned Rachel-Leah. "I found him on the stairs, where he's been sleeping all night."

The young stranger, who was cowering in embarrassed silence behind Rachel-Leah, rose to his feet at the teacher's entry. His side curls trembled and his eyes goggled into a corner of the room as he asked: "Am I addressing Herr Hurvitz?"

"What do you want?" queried the teacher by way of admitting his identity.

"I want to study . . . I'm very anxious to study," stammered the stranger timidly.

"Quite so; very good! But what can I do about it?"

"They told me in Krasnyshin . . . I come from Krasnyshin . . . they told me . . . if anybody wants to study he should go to Herr Hurvitz the teacher in Warsaw, who helps people on . . . I'm very anxious to study . . . very anxious."

"I'm very anxious to study myself. To whom must *I* turn, do you think? Perhaps you can give me the address of somebody?"

The young man stood speechless; his side curls trembled more than ever; his whole body began to tremble and sway and he said as if to himself: "What am I to do?"

"How do I know? Why do you ask me? Am I the Minister of Education? Do I run an Academy of Sciences? If I were the Minister of Education or had an academy of my own I'd be very glad to help young students like you. But what can I do? Why come to me?"

"To whom can I go? To whom?" the young man said, again more to himself than to his questioner.

At this point Rachel-Leah, who had refrained from intervention out of respect for her husband, could no longer restrain herself; her warm sympathies were stirred. She reddened to the ears and cried:

"What are you jumping down his throat for? What else can he do, if he wants to study? He's not offering to steal from you or rob you. What are you scolding him for? You find yourself a chair, young man: I'm sure you're hungry. You might give him time to breathe, at least! He's been sitting on the stairs the whole night."

"Where are you going to find room for him? The house is full up already. Why do they all come to me?"

Meanwhile the presence of the stranger had roused the curiosity of the other inmates. A member of the "High School" appeared in the kitchen doorway to have a look at the newcomer.

"You're quite right, Pan Hurvitz. What has put it into your head to go in for studying, my lad? Work is much more important," remarked the man in the doorway, emphatically waving a withered arm.

"Aha, the renegade's on the stump next. As if anybody had asked you! He'll manage to go as far as you've gone, anyhow!" cried Rachel-Leah, and then with a friendly look she encouraged the alarmed young man: "Just you let them talk. Sit down and wait a minute; the coffee's nearly ready." With these words she took from the stranger the bundle wrapped in newspaper which he had been clutching all the time under his arm. She laid it on one side with a determined gesture that announced her resolution to keep the newcomer where he was. The teacher tried to say something but his wife cut him short: "What are you all doing in my kitchen? Clear out of it at once. I have to make the coffee!" —And with that Rachel-Leah ground at her coffee-mill so furiously that her husband and the Peeping Toms behind him took to instant flight.

CHAPTER II

RACHEL-LEAH'S DAY BEGINS

In the courtyard there echoed the characteristic cadence of the Warsaw street-hawkers: "Barrows! Barrows! Barrows!"

This cry told Rachel-Leah that the day had begun and she applied herself with redoubled energy to her coffee-grinding. Holding the coffee-mill between her knees, she tried to draw out the shy young Talmudist, who in spite of his desire to prove himself a man of the world was overwhelmed with embarrassment at finding himself alone in a room with a woman. But Rachel-Leah knew the whole of his history before he so much as opened his mouth. Early experience had made her thoroughly familiar with the kind of "past" that such young men were likely to have; the story hardly varied from one individual to another.

"Married, of course?" she shot at him in between turns at the coffee-mill.

"No, not yet," replied the young man, blushing.

"Thank goodness for that! But how does that come?" she asked in amazement. "Well, caught by your father reading *trefe* books, I suppose, thrashed and turned out of the house, eh?"

"He nearly half-killed me!"—again the young Talmudist reddened—"When he turned me out I went to stay with friends of mine... from one house to another... a different bed every night. What can you find to do in a small town? Nothing but stealing and getting into bad company.... Besides, if one door is shut to you, you have to open another for yourself.... One has to live!" cried the young man, his courage rising, although he still kept his eyes fixed on the corner of the room.

"And then they ask what makes young people flock into the city! Where else are they to go?" murmured Frau Hurvitz, and she turned again to her guest: "We'll see what can be managed."

She decided to call in at the leather-dresser's after breakfast; there might be some room in his store-cellar where a man could at least sleep on the hides. "If he has nothing then perhaps at the baker's; there might be room on the flour-sacks," she meditated while she shook the ground coffee into a pan of boiling water.

The whole house was waiting impatiently and in reproachful silence for its breakfast. The teacher was standing by the window, a book as usual in his hand, reading by the faint morning light; his son, swinging his schoolbooks in their leather strap, was prowling up and down the room.

"It's getting late," the warning rose from all sides. A minute later the table was covered, and Rachel-Leah was laying out fresh butter which she had brought from the market, and spreading enormous slices of bread with plum sauce for her son's school lunch. In the middle of these activities she pushed a jug of hot coffee towards the shy stranger with the friendly invitation: "Whatever happens, here's something warm first. Fancy spending the whole night on the staircase out there! . . . And we'll settle about the other things later on."

When the men were got out of the way, it was the turn of the two girls. They slept in the "dark room," a cubicle without a window that was cut off by a folding screen from the dining-room. The patter of bare feet in there was already audible, the singing cadence of girlish voices and the sound of squabbling; they were each laying claim to the morning paper with its new serial installment of a novel by Zeromski.

"Aha, they're up! Pan Shachliner!"—Frau Hurvitz never addressed her lodger as "renegade" when she wanted him to do her a favor, but gave him his full title, and so she now called to him through the thin partition-wall.—"Pan Shachliner, will you take the stranger in beside you for a moment? Helene's coming to wash." With that she urged the visitor towards the Shachliner, who appeared at her call, and then shut the door on both of them.

Sosha, her younger daughter, was already demanding from the dark room: "Is the coast clear, Mamma?"

Although barely sixteen the younger of the two girls was physically much more developed than her elder sister, and she lost no chance of advertising the fact. In the whole apartment there was only one place at which one could wash, the water-tap in the kitchen, but Sosha would run about half-clad all morning from one room to the other, scaring away the male occupants, whether members of the family or not, by her reiterated: "Is the coast clear? May I, Mamma?"

When the usual question was answered this time in the affirmative, two half-naked girls came rushing simultaneously into the kitchen. All the way to the water-tap they went on reading the serial story in the newspaper. The elder, Helene, was graceful and slender, a slim, virginal figure, a girl who loved to be prettily turned out. And the mother loved still more to see her elder girl well dressed; in Rachel-Leah's eyes silks and satins would not have been too good for her. But, alas! it was difficult to find even necessary clothing for the girl. Helene, with many tears, had had to leave the high school after her fifth year there in order to become her father's assistant, and in the afternoons she gave extra lessons so as to earn money for her clothes. This winter she should have had a new coat. Yet there was always some other pressing need to supply; the rent, or coal, or similar household wants had to be given the preference. But Rachel-Leah stinted herself wherever she could and devoted her scanty spare time to serving her elder daughter. This morning she fished out of an empty crock a corset that had kept her out of bed on the previous night: it had been hidden in the crock from the eyes of Helene's father, since there would have been trouble had he known that his daughter wore a corset and that Rachel-Leah herself had washed and darned it in the small hours. For the precepts of pedagogy strictly enjoined not only a cold sponging of the body every morning (a task which Helene was at that moment performing by the water-tap); they enjoined no less strictly and particularly the disuse of corsets. But Rachel-Leah, behind her husband's back, deviated occasionally from the straight and narrow path and sinned now and then against the laws of progress; she could not imagine a girl well dressed without a corset; and the teacher's lengthy explanations on winter evenings that the corset was a survival of barbarism, like the binding of Chinese women's feet, fell on deaf ears. Frau Hurvitz, remembering her own girlhood, now tenderly smoothed out the forbidden article and herself pulled the laces to rights.

Meanwhile Helene, having stripped, was proceeding with her morning wash. Her delicate skin, still brown with the sunshine that it had absorbed during the summer holidays in a country village, and strengthened by cool bathing in brooks and rivers, now reddened under the jet of icy-cold water. Wrapped in a towel, the younger girl waited her turn and in the meantime read aloud the last chapter of the serial. Her voice rose to a shrill scream, for the splashing of the water kept Helene from catching many of the words. It must have been an exciting story, for Helene kept on interrupting and insisting that the words she did not catch should be repeated; she stood listening with her eyes screwed up to keep the soap-bubbles out of them. Rachel-Leah, with the corset in her hand, kept urging her daughter to make haste; she was afraid that some one might come in and find her holding the illicit garment.

To her great relief the forbidden article soon vanished under her daughter's frock, and not long afterwards both girls were gone out of the house, Helene to her teaching and Sosha to her high school. Only then did Rachel-Leah find time to have her own breakfast. With a roll in her hand and the coffee-pot beside her she passed in review all her troubles. There was a sigh for her eldest son whom she had had to leave to his fate in a Petersburg prison; another sigh for David, her younger son, since her observations had led her to suspect that David was infected by the same disease as his brother. . . . On top of that came her household cares, for a hard winter was at the door. Another plague was the school inspector, who was continually grumbling because her husband had not yet passed the examination; Frau Hurvitz's blood ran cold whenever he appeared. And today, as an extra worry, the wealthy Frau Doctor Silberstein, one of the school patrons, had announced that she would pay a visit during class hours. Last of all there was this new burden, the task of securing a bed for the young man whom she had found at her door in the morning.

Whenever any such uncalled-for problem presented itself and she did not know what to do about it, Frau Hurvitz always consulted the Shachliner. He was the oldest occupant of the "High School" and Rachel-Leah's right-hand man; he knew more about her troubles than anybody else and helped her to solve the various difficulties that cropped up from day to day. Although she railed at him and called him a "renegade," the Shachliner was the one person in the house to whom she turned in extremity.

"Herr Weinberg, Herr Weinberg!" This time Frau Hurvitz gave her lodger his correct name; that happened very rarely and usually only when she needed his help. "Come here a minute, Herr Weinberg!" she called through the door.

Weinberg appeared in the door of the "High School"; his pointed little black beard stuck up almost vertically from his chin and his beady little black eyes were uneasy. He did not want to risk going into the kitchen, for her knew what was in the air and was unwilling to have a fresh burden thrust upon him. Like a dog he ran his little red tongue over his lips and asked: "What is it, Pani Hurvitz?"

"Oh, don't be frightened, I won't bite you! Come right in," cried Frau Hurvitz with a motherly gesture and a coquettish smile.

The Shachliner knew that this invitation would cost him dear, and he did not want to be entangled. But he could not withstand Frau Hurvitz's smile; he mumbled something incomprehensible and came in.

"Will you have a cup of coffee with me?" And she set a cup before him.

"No, thanks; I've had my breakfast"—he gently pushed the cup away—"I had some milk and a pound of bread left over from yesterday. What do you want me for?"

"I need your advice, Herr Weinberg. What can we do for this new young man?" asked Frau Hurvitz, laying her hand on his shoulder.

"Send him home again! There's no room for people like that here. If they really want to do something they'd much better stay away from the city. They can study in the provinces as well as here, and educated people are needed in the country towns far more than in Warsaw. That's where they should spread the light of knowledge and encourage the others to fight. What's to become of the fellow here? An external student? There's too many of them already. They should all stay in their provinces."

"And why didn't *you* stay in your own town, then, instead of landing here? It's easy enough for you to preach about other people!"

"I was a fool ever to leave it, you can take my word for it. I certainly could have done far more there than here. The trouble is that we all take the easiest way out, and that's the ruin of us. There's no sense in it. One should be able to turn oneself to account in the place where one lives."

"But you know well enough that his father thrashed him. How could he stay at home?"

"I was thrashed, too, yes, and crippled into the bargain. One should answer blows with blows. If one's resolved to fight, one can't expect an easy life."

"So you won't help me to find a bed for this young man?"

"I won't lift a finger. Why should I? What for? To add another piffling intellectual to the bunch? We have too many of them already. Fellows of that kidney live only for themselves and their own careers and never think of other people. As soon as they make good, they don't give a button for us and make common cause with the top dogs, with our enemies. When fellows of that kind get to the top, they just become new recruits to the class that supports them. They just play into each other's hands."

"But what's he to do, then?"

"Go home again! Go back to his kennel and live in it and fight fanaticism and reaction there! You needn't worry, he'll be well enough able to get books there if he wants to study. But the chief thing is to work, to earn his living by the work of his hands. That's the main thing; and if he has any time to spare after that, why, then, he can study, if not—then he can cut it out. This isn't the time to eat out of charitable people's pockets for the sake of becoming a pettifogging doctor or advocate; we have more than enough of these parasites. This is the time for work!— The day for 'enlightenment' is over."

Weinberg spoke with deep conviction. As always when he was wrought up his words came tumbling out pell-mell; his eyes were half shut, his goatee twitched up and down; his withered arm waved about queerly. Frau Hurvitz could think of no retort; she felt that Weinberg was in the right. But she was not to be seduced from that respect for learning which her husband had fostered in her, and, as usual when she was at a loss for an answer, she flew into a rage and took refuge in abuse: "You're very high and mighty now. But you sang a different song when other people helped you to live in the city. And now you're driving others away——"

"What kind of a life do I lead here? Am I running round to dances and studying at high schools? I'm working for my living, and it's only when I have a spare moment that I open a book. And if I have no time, I read nothing!"

Frau Hurvitz grew impatient: "So you won't help me to do anything for the young man?"

"I won't lift a finger. I won't do anything for parasites."

"You're a parasite yourself; you're just another of the pettifogging doctors and advocates. And if you aren't one yet you soon will be. You're making common cause yourself with the top dogs against the underdogs. You're a Lithuanian!" That was the worst of all insults in the Hurvitzes' house. "You're a heartless wretch, driving the young man away like that. You're crowing so loud that you seem to have forgotten you ever came out of an egg! I won't have anything to do with you; I'll manage by myself!"

With that Frau Hurvitz threw her shawl over her shoulders and turned to go.

But before she opened the hall door she called out to Weinberg.

"Shachliner! If you want any bread you'll find some on the table. And there's butter in the food-box."

Then she slammed the door.

CHAPTER III

NEIGHBORS

WITH HER shawl round her shoulders and a kerchief on her head Frau Hurvitz now set out on a round of her neighbors to seek some lodging for the young Talmudist whom she had found standing helplessly at her door.

The house in which the Hurvitzes lived was not in one of the shopping quarters of Warsaw, in Franciscan Street, for instance, or on the Nalevki Boulevard, but lay in the middle of the working class district in Bonipart Street. It was a typical tenement barracks with a labyrinth of courtyards where workshop leaned against workshop; there was no corner into which a small roof was not squeezed with four walls to prop it up. And the barracks surrounding the uncannily dark workshops were packed full of human bodies that worked at machines of some kind from morning lamp-light until evening lamp-light; weaving-machinists, knitting-machinists, bag-makers and strap-makers. From the open windows in summer issued the sad songs of apprentice work-girls who bartered their young eye-sight for halfpence during the long summer days and the longer winter evenings. For a few halfpence, makers of artificial flowers transferred the young red of their cheeks and the freshness of their lips to dead paper blossoms, while in other cages brush-makers breathed into their lungs the dust of the bristles and unskilful cigarette-makers absorbed the nicotine that brought them inevitably to the door of the sanatorium in the woods of Otvock. In almost every room there were also traditional seamstresses working their sewing-machines. The basement cellars were crammed with stores of leather, dyes, herrings, benzine and petrol, next door to bakeries and sausage-shops.

All day long the wide courtyards rang with the noise and movement of men, horses and enormous wagons unloading raw material for manufacture or carting away towering pyramids of cardboard boxes that contained the finished articles.

The "teacher's wife" was a familiar figure to her neighbors in the courtyards. If a woman lay in child-bed, or a child fell sick, or a bed had to be secured in the Jewish Hospital, it was always the teacher's wife who was called in.

Leather and hot sausage mingled their odors with the sweetish moldering smell of yeast and honey from the bakery. That was the prevailing smell of the courtyard which Frau Hurvitz was now traversing, qualified now and then by the pungency of decayed gherkins and herrings from the small provision shop; in winter at least, while all the tenement windows were shut, that was the prevailing smell, but in summer every other smell was overborne by the stuffy exhalations from the mattresses which were hung out to air at each window. Now, in the late autumn, there was an added rankness from the decaying vegetables in the provision shop. In front of the shop door sat old Pessie, herself like a gigantic gherkin, her apron plastered with glittering herring scales and crusted salt-brine. Her swollen fingers were thrust into an old much-worn fur muff; she had already assumed her winter toilet and wrapped a thick woolen shawl round her head, although the autumn sun was still warming the air with the last force of its bright rays.

When she saw the teacher's wife coming across the courtyard old Pessie assumed that Frau Hurvitz was collecting alms, as she often did, for some needy neighbor, and beckoned with her muff. Silently she drew out a torn and dirty four-mark note and offered it to Rachel-Leah.

"No, Pessie, it isn't money this time." Frau Hurvitz screamed into her ear through the shawl. "Do you happen to have room in your place for a poor young man that's come up from the country to study?"

"What? What is that?" demanded old Pessie, drawing the shawl aside and taking a huge plug of cotton-wool out of her ear.

"Room for a night's lodging!"

"Room? For the night? No, my dear." Old Pessie shrugged her shoulders as if it were useless to waste words on such a question, and to explain her shrug she waved her muff towards the surrounding herring-barrels and gherkin-casks.

Nor was there any room to spare at the leather-dresser's. In the first place the teacher's wife had begun to appear politically suspect to him, and in the second place his whole store-cellar was already occupied by the Talmud school from the second story; the scholars slept at night on his hides and so guarded them from thieves.

Benjamin the baker was a jolly fellow. He was always powdered white with flour and there was always a friendly smile on his lips. And he had long had a weakness for the teacher's wife. Benjamin the baker was a handsome fellow; but what good does that do one when one is always white from top to toe and one's black beard looks like a devil's brush in the midst of all that whiteness?

"O, Pani Hurvitz! You're a sight for sore eyes!" The baker made an elegant bow and scraped his foot. "Clear that dough away; let the lady have a seat!" he shouted to his apprentice as Rachel-Leah entered, and with his floury white overall he zealously dusted the chair on which the dough-tub had been standing.

"Benjamin, my friend, have you any place where a young man could sleep who has just come up from the country and has nowhere to go?" Frau Hurvitz asked with a smile that she knew would make the baker do whatever she wanted.

"There's nothing I wouldn't do for you, Pani Hurvitz!" replied Benjamin, putting his black beard to rights with a floury hand. "Would he care to sleep on the flour-sacks here? There are three people sleeping there already, my own two apprentices and another apprentice who can't be put up in his own place. But I don't mind if a fourth comes in, and I can let him have a dough-tub for a pillow." The gallant baker twirled his mustache and his black eyes shot amorous glances at Frau Hurvitz.

Rachel-Leah regarded the flour-sacks that were strewn with all manner of tattered and filthy bed-covers, shook her head and quitted the bakery without so much as a look at the handsome Benjamin. The apprentice burst out laughing behind her and delightedly scratched his curly red poll with his floury fingers.

Next door to the bakery was the establishment where Velvel the flesh-curer made his sausages. The whole courtyard trembled before him. His expression was always sinister: thick brows gloomed above his eyes, his bushy mustache, to which drops were always clinging, drooped morosely, and his eyes furtively avoided meeting anybody's look. Velvel always muttered to himself as if his conscience were secretly tormenting him. In his ragged blood-stained woolen waistcoat, with his chopping-knife in his hand, he looked like a bandit or some wild charcoal-burner just come from the forest. His children had early quitted their father's home: the sons had been thrown out, and the daughters, handsome wenches with thick black plaits of hair, full-bosomed and broad-hipped, had vanished of their own accord and were living, the devil knew why (so said Velvel), in the Argentine. For several years now gifts of money and cards wishing him luck had arrived from the Argentine every New Year's day. He laid the money and the cards (which he took to be another kind of money, since whatever came through the post was "money" to him) in his safe untouched, in their envelopes; for Velvel the sausage-maker had no need of money; he needed nothing in the world but his work. From six in the morning until late at night he chopped away at the enormous sides of meat that the butcher delivered to him properly sprinkled and stamped with the Kosher-mark of the Rabbinate. This Kosher-stamp had been already the cause of much scandal. The Rabbinate had several times pronounced his sausages to be *trefe,* for it had little confidence in his methods of preparation, and Velvel had rushed to the Community House and driven home with his rough fists the superiority of his "Kosher" wares. And now, whenever the butcher brought him a side of meat with the Kosher-stamp on it, he dragged it out into the courtyard and shouted at the top of his voice: "There's the Kosher-stamp for you, and devil take all of you!"

Velvel had no idea that breakfast or dinner could consist of anything but smoked meat; he fed entirely on the left-overs from his sausages. Thus he labored from one Sabbath to the next, and his only relaxation was a sleep on Sabbath afternoon. In summer he would put on his top boots, and together with his wife Neche, who was round and fat as a barrel and the only person he feared, since she did not scruple to box his ears for him, he would set out on foot for the citadel of Makatov near the Jewish Hospital, throw himself on the sun-bleached grass, lay his head on Neche's lap and sleep undisturbed by the yells of playing boys and squabbling girls right through the summer afternoon until the evening. Then he would waken, make a wry face and say: "Neche, let's go home, I have a bad taste in my mouth." In winter he took his nap beside his wife near the stove. Neche, who could read Yiddish, would open the Women's Bible and read her husband the chapter about Noah and the Ark. If Velvel interrupted her with an occasional belch, she would reprove him: "Velvel, you might at least show some respect for Noah."

"You're right, Neche," Velvel would sigh, oppressed by the thought that he was doomed to go to hell and had no chance of salvation. In utter dejection he would hide his hard head in Neche's full bosom and soon begin to snore; it never took long for Neche to follow his example. . . .

The only tenant in the building who was not afraid of the sausage-maker was Frau Hurvitz, and Velvel himself had a kind of respect for her. He knew that she was a woman who deserved to be respected, and whenever she made a collection for the consumptive cigarette-maker on the fourth story he would bring her of his own accord a juicy bit of meat, a piece from the breast such as he never allowed himself even on a Sabbath. When he saw her quitting the bakery in a hurry he came out to the threshold of his shop. The shop door was always open and emitted such a fog of steam that nothing could be seen of the interior, and in this cloud of steam the sausage-maker, in his ragged woolen waistcoat and blood-stained apron, with his shirt-sleeves rolled up and his chopping-knife in one hand, now waited for Frau Hurvitz. But when she hastened past without looking at him he called out sulkily: "What's this? Have the Jews disowned me? Is my house *trefe?* Why are you leaving me out if you're making a collection? Come in and I'll give you a bit of meat."

"No, Velvel," responded Frau Hurvitz, "I'm only looking for a lodging for a poor young man."

"For one that learns things?"

"Of course! Do you think I would be running round like this for the sake of an idler?"

Velvel scratched his head and shouted through the steam: "Neche, Neche, come here!"

The flabby mass that loomed up in the fog took shape as a woman when presently it emerged into the faint light of the doorway; a woman in a flowered dimity petticoat, with red stockings drawn over shapeless and swollen legs, and, instead of a head-shawl, a handkerchief tied round her enormous neck to supplement her chemise. One might have thought that she had just come from the wash-tub, but as a matter of fact she had been helping her husband to smoke the sausages that he sent out to cheap lodging-houses.

"What is it?" asked Neche, wiping the sweat from her massive face with her neckerchief.

"Do you want to do a good deed? Then take in a poor Talmud student as a lodger; the teacher's wife has one to give away," said Velvel, indicating Frau Hurvitz.

Neche's smoke-inflamed eyes regarded her husband with amazement.

"Eh, Velvel, have you begun to think of good deeds? When did this fit come over you?"

"Can't I do a good deed if I want to? Is the leather-dresser the only man that's allowed some credit? I want to earn myself a good place in the next world as well as everybody else," growled Velvel.

"It's hell-fire you deserve in the next world, for you eat without saying grace and without washing," retorted Neche; then she turned to Frau Hurvitz: "I'm afraid it can't be done. Where could he sleep? In the oven, beside the sausages? We have to sleep in the smoke ourselves."

"And I'll show you that I can do a good deed! Just a minute, Pani Hurvitz," shouted the sausage-maker, whose pride had been wounded by his wife's words. "Just you wait a minute! . . . There, that's a sausage made of the best meat off the breast; take it and give it to the sick woman on the fourth floor. Let her have something good for once! Her brats keep nosing round here all day like dogs trying to snatch a bone or a bit of sausage-skin."

"Velvel, have you gone crazy? A whole sausage! Some bones for soup would be enough."

"No, a whole sausage, and a piece of rib-beef as well! I want to be a decent Jew! I want to have some credit for good deeds!" screamed Velvel in a voice as pitiable as if he were being knifed. . . .

The whole tenement knew the consumptive cigarette-maker on the fourth floor. For every now and then the desperate shrieks of her children could be heard echoing through the house: "Mother's dying!" But that had been going on for several years and people had got used to it. On several occasions the house had subscribed money to send the sick woman to Otvock; but it's ill work filling a bottomless sack, and so she was still there, fading away, and every year, as she lay in bed spitting blood, she became a mother again and bore another child. Her husband was a ne'er-do-well who was supposed to be an excellent Talmud scholar; by profession he was a watchmaker but never got a job, and so he made cigarettes which the children sold on the quiet since they had no government stamp. Frau Hurvitz knew the family very well. Whenever the sick woman grew a little worse the children came rushing to the teacher's wife on the first floor: "Mother's dying." And then Frau Hurvitz would throw on her shawl and hurry up to the fourth floor.

Having received such an unexpected and lavish gift for the invalid—due entirely to the fact that Velvel had lost his head and remembered the next world—Frau Hurvitz ran upstairs to give her the sausage and the piece of beef. She found the sick woman in bed as usual; from the elevation, wearing her embroidered marriage-cap and with the characteristic red patches on her cheeks, she governed a troop of naked or half-naked children, one smaller than the other, who filled the tiny room, which was further cramped by a broad, heavy, carved cupboard, a remnant of the marriage outfit. The husband was not at home; he was out looking for odd jobs. But traces of his activity were visible, for on the table that stood in the middle of the room lay a large heap of tobacco. That did not hinder the children from eating at the table; they dabbled their crusts and spilt the coffee-dregs into the tobacco. The smaller children's toys were also bedded in the tobacco, filthy rag dolls that had been made by their mother.

The consumptive woman lay in bed and unceasingly chewed pieces of orange rind. When Frau Hurvitz entered the children grew quieter and the hubbub in the narrow room subsided a little. More and more little heads popped up from every corner; like hungry mice they were drawn out of their burrows by the smell of the sausage under Frau Hurvitz's arm.

"Here's something for you! Just fancy, Velvel the sausage-maker sent this up for you. Well, Gitel, how are things going?"

"Long may you live, Pani Hurvitz, for the goodness of your heart! What should I do without you?"

The invalid stretched out a pale skinny arm, eagerly grabbed the sausage and hid it under the blankets.

"But why put it away? Give the children a bit," said Frau Hurvitz, moved by the greedy look in the wide, wondering eyes of the children, who had gradually surrounded their mother's bed.

"In a minute, yes . . . but surely something should be saved for later . . ." stammered the invalid in embarrassment. "Go and play, children, go away, children," she concluded, in a weak voice.

But the children did not budge from the bed-side. If they weren't to have any sausage to eat they wanted at least to enjoy the satisfying odor of it.

"Give them all a bit now! You, my boy, bring me a knife," commanded Frau Hurvitz.

Then she divided the sausage among the children, much to the chagrin of the mother, who had to watch her booty vanishing piece by piece.

"They've just had something to eat. They should be thankful, and so should I, for they've just had something to eat. They're not hungry at all—isn't that so, children?" The mother stretched out her hand for the butt-end of the sausage. Her agitation brought on such a severe fit of coughing that she seemed to be on the point of dying.

This affliction of their mother's, an ordinary occurrence in their lives, did not interfere in the least with the children's enjoyment of the unusual tit-bit. Frau Hurvitz attended to the invalid. But the spasm of coughing grew so alarming that she was at her wit's end to know what to do. At that point Sheindel, the oldest girl, came to her assistance; still munching the delicious sausage she went coolly to the water-tap with a matter-of-fact air and brought a glass of water; she clutched the sausage in one hand and between bites held the glass of water with the other to the mouth of her mother, who was half-suffocated and weak with coughing.

Frau Hurvitz was alarmed and shocked. But the sick woman seemed to think nothing of the incident. When she felt a little better she merely turned in a matter-of-fact way to her visitor: "I'm glad you've come in, Frau Hurvitz; I was just going to send for you." Then she lowered her voice and whispered, with a shamed but pleased smile on her fever-flushed face: "Do you know, I think I'm near my time; it won't be more than a day or two now."

Frau Hurvitz stiffened: "What? And you in this state? How long is this kind of thing going to go on?"

"How can I help it? We're only sinful mortals after all." The sick woman smiled coquettishly. But the smile outlined with painful sharpness the bony skull beneath the drawn skin of her face.

CHAPTER IV

PAN KVIATKOVSKI

FRAU HURVITZ was not a woman to be deterred by obstacles. What she once undertook to do she carried out to the end. And so she was determined now that the young Talmudist who had fled from the provinces and knocked at her door should remain in Warsaw.

As she descended the stairs after visiting the consumptive woman she paused for a moment and reviewed in her mind all the neighbors, acquaintances, and friends whom she had previously persuaded to take in young country students. She soon gave up, however, for there was not a friend of hers on whom she had not already landed somebody.

On her way home she looked in on Henoch the joiner, not because she counted on his having room for a lodger, but because she needed his help. Henoch was a good friend of hers and she thought highly of him; he often helped her in very delicate negotiations of which mention will be made later. Besides, the joiner's workshop was in the part of the building where the invalid lived, and so within convenient reach.

The following was the domestic interior she beheld as she entered. Henoch the joiner was standing almost up to his neck in a turbulent sea of shavings and hammering away at a plank. But the hammering could scarcely be heard for the shrieking and yelling of a swarm of children of all ages who were playing about among the shavings. Near the open door stood a cradle over which Jochebed, the carpenter's wife, was bending with her naked breasts hanging down like udders, while from the cradle came a smacking, sucking sound. While she nursed her infant in this fashion Jochebed evidently found it quite easy to carry on at the same time a conversation with a loving couple sitting enlaced on a rumpled bed in the corner; the feminine partner in this alliance was her own sister, a source of shame to Henoch, who suspected her of following an ancient and none too honorable profession; and indeed the reek of cheap perfume and toilet-soap which emanated from her told its own story. Beside her sat a youth wearing the typical Warsaw cap with its patent leather peak. They were both eating pumpkin seeds out of a paper bag, and the floor around them was strewn with the husks. The conversation seemed to be about marriage; for as Frau Hurvitz came in Jochebed, stooping still lower over the cradle, was making a remark that obviously referred to some difference of opinion on the subject: "My sister's quite right in not wanting to get married. Why should she be such a fool? What advantage does one get, God help us, from being married? Nothing but *this* . . ."—and she indicated the cradle.

"And anyhow, do you think I don't know what he's after?" interrupted her sister. "He may talk about marriage but it's something else he means. I can't bear that kind of hypocrisy. If *that's* what you're after, you should say it right out and not try to bamboozle me with all this talk of marriage!"

Henoch the carpenter took no part in the discussion. He liked neither his wife's sister with her cheap perfumes nor the youth who was courting her; he regarded both of them with suspicion. So he withdrew into the middle of his shavings and worked with redoubled energy.

"Just look at him working himself to death!" cried out Jochebed, still bending over the cradle. "You would think to see him that I must be rolling in money and getting the best of everything. But with all his hammering and planing he doesn't bring in enough to give us a decent meal once a week on the Sabbath. . . ."

Henoch remained unruffled. He wiped his dirty, sweat-bedewed forehead and ran his plane furiously over the plank so that it screeched.

But Frau Hurvitz's arrival was now remarked and the discussion broke off. Jochebed rose from her stooping position and covered her bosom with her blouse. The couple shifted a little apart from each other. Henoch stopped working, left his work-bench, and came forward to the cradle beside the door where Frau Hurvitz was standing, the only part of the room that was well lighted.

"Oh, it's the teacher's wife!" cried Henoch with obvious pleasure, loosening shavings from his hair and beard.

"Yes, Henoch, I was just passing and looked in. Any news?"

"What news could there be? Everything's all right so long as there's some work to be had and a bit of something to eat. What else does one want?"

Frau Hurvitz liked Henoch; in all the neighborhood he was the only man who never complained and was always good-humored and cheerful.

"There's one man at least who's pleased with life! You never grumble, Henoch."

"Why should I? And if I did have cause to grumble—what would that matter? The world wouldn't come to an end: I should still go on living. So why grumble?"

"Dogs in the gutter go on living, too!" broke in his wife. "Of course he's quite content so long as he has his plane and a bit of bread and a book to read from his Union! And once he's buried in a book there's not a word to be got out of him—the devil knows what can be in these books! What does he care if his children have nothing to put in their bellies but potatoes, until they're all blown up? What does he care if winter's coming on and they haven't a rag to their backs?"

"Well, my dear, now you've brought out all your grievances; and to listen to you one would think the world was coming to an end. But meanwhile you have a roof over your head and a loaf of bread in the cupboard; there are plenty of people who haven't as much."

"What a comfort—to be told that there are people who haven't as much! Why don't you tell me about the people who live in fine houses and walk on Persian carpets and eat meat every day?"

Henoch calmly fished shavings out of his thick dark beard and replied with a smile: "Now, now, my dear, don't get excited. The palaces and the Persian carpets and the chicken broth will all come some fine day. Let Pani Hurvitz get a word in edgeways. She hasn't taken the trouble to come here for nothing . . ."

"Oh, it's nothing particular; I only looked in because I was passing. But tell me, Henoch, do you know by any chance where I could get a lodging for a poor young man who's come up from the country to study?"

"A lodging for a poor young man . . ." repeated Henoch. "If there's no room elsewhere, why not here? It could be managed. We could sweep the shavings away at night and put an extra bed behind the work-bench. A bed doesn't take up much room, does it, Jochebed?"

"And where are we to put Surele and Avreymel and Moyshle and the two littlest ones? Where do you think we could put a bed? On top of your head?"

"No, Henoch, you really haven't room for anybody. I wasn't thinking of you, but perhaps you might know of somebody willing to let out a bed?" asked Frau Hurvitz. "Of course it would have to be cheap, for the stranger's no Rothschild, but we could pay something amongst us."

"Half a minute, Pani Hurvitz, I have an idea; I'll run up and see Motche in the factory. If you need a bed you need a bed, and something must be done about it." And Henoch rushed away.

"Just look at him, how quick he can run! If he would only take half as much trouble for his own family as he does for strangers!" Jochebed shouted after him.

But neither Henoch nor Frau Hurvitz heard a word; they were already out through the door.

"Probably some *trefe* fellow," said the youth, cuddling in beside Jochebed's sister again. "And if he gets into trouble nothing will happen to *her,* you bet. Nothing ever happens to well-off people; but Henoch'll be put into jug. And I'd like to know who would lift a finger to help him?"

"Why did you let him do it?" demanded Jochebed's sister.

"How could I help it? That's just the sort of thing I've got to put up with. . . ."

The handbag factory was a story higher than the joiner's workshop. Motche, also called "the hunchback," was chief cutter-out there. He was a master of his craft and had, as the phrase ran in his profession, a "golden hand"; he knew how to cut out the leather so that not a square inch was wasted. For that reason he was cherished by his employer, all the more so as other factories were always trying to tempt him away. Motche was anything but handsome. Reared in the most bitter poverty, he had a deformed shoulder caused by a bad fall in childhood; hence his nickname. But Motche was obsessed by a devouring passion for handsome women with dark hair and large dark eyes—he called them "gypsies." And since in actual life he had little chance of meeting any, he had cut out of illustrated papers and advertisements all the pictures of such women that he could find, Amazons from the circus, dancers, lion-tamers, and these he had pinned to the wall above his cutting-bench; while he worked he would cast an admiring glance on them from time to time and heave a gentle sigh. His physical weakness made him want to pose as a strong character, and everything risky and dangerous attracted him. He belonged to a secret political organization and whenever he got the chance undertook dangerous commissions that might easily have cost him his life. Without employing the most elementary precautions, he would quite openly carry about or distribute revolutionary proclamations; in his lodgings he kept compromising documents and gave shelter to suspected members of his party. The more dangerous an enterprise, the more strongly he was tempted to test his strength on it. His recklessness had made him notorious in the party and among the working classes; everybody knew him, and anybody needing help turned at once to Motche: he did all that was required of him openly and under the very noses of the police. In this way he had endangered both his comrades and the party itself more than once.

Henoch briefly informed Motche that there was a job to be done. A simple member of the party rank and file, he was naive enough to believe that some important personage must be in question if the teacher's wife, who was so highly respected by the party, herself took the trouble of seeking a lodging for him. This conviction of Henoch's was at once apparent to the hunchback, who laid down his work and came downstairs to where Frau Hurvitz was waiting. He listened to her with close attention, but was extremely disappointed to learn that this time it was not a conspiratorial "job," and that the man for whom the teacher's wife wanted a lodging was not a political personage.

"I have lodgings, of course, but I need them for party purposes. I'm really sorry not to be able to help you this time. But in this case I can do nothing," he said, very gravely. "Tell me, was it the Shachliner who sent you?"

"No."

"Without instructions from the Shachliner I can do nothing."

Frau Hurvitz's hopes had sunk almost to zero; she feared that the Shachliner would yet be able to crow over her. But she was resolved not to surrender: "The young man must stay in Warsaw, even if the Shachliner has to stand on his head! But where am I to find a bed for him?" Once more she mentally reviewed the whole house from roof to cellar; she simply had to find a lodging for the stranger even if she had to keep him in the school for the night and so risk her husband's teaching license. . . . "And I won't stop till I've got lessons for him, too, and a new shirt into the bargain!"

But it was from an unexpected quarter that help finally came, from a direction Frau Hurvitz had never even thought of.

As she was going upstairs to her own flat, completely absorbed in the problem of the young man's lodging, she met Pan Kviatkovski coming down from the second story. Pan Kviatkovski was the sole Gentile tenant in the whole building. Why he had ever come here and what made him go on staying in a Jewish tenement scarcely remarkable for cleanliness were questions that no one could answer. His door was the only one in the building over which hung a holy picture and on which the three letters K. M. B., representing the names of the Three Holy Kings, were chalked every year. These letters filled the hearts of the Jewish tenants with a dull fear, as if they had been symbols of the Inquisition. Pan Kviatkovski was a "nature doctor" and cured people with herbs. Whole trains of countrywomen in their bright village costumes climbed daily up the stairs to the "doctor," carrying baskets filled with country products such as eggs, butter and fowls with which they paid the "Pan" for his medical advice and decoctions. The Jewish tenants were always eager to investigate these covered baskets and often asked: "Anything for sale?" But they were always met by a firm refusal which they accepted with a sigh, envying the doctor's good fortune. . . .

Naturally they all felt a great respect for their only Christian neighbor. Mothers made their daughters sweep the stairs, not so much for the sake of cleanliness as on Pan Kviatkovski's account: "Be quick now, the Goy will be downstairs in a minute," was the usual formula. . . . Pan Kviatkovski's own attitude to his Jewish neighbors was somewhat singular. He was often, indeed usually, very affable, courteously returned greetings and even stopped to gossip with a great display of Yiddish. When he was in a particularly good mood he peppered his Yiddish with Hebrew words that he had picked up somewhere or other and used with humorous exaggeration and without knowing what they meant. But now and then, without any reason, Pan Kviatkovski suddenly turned "cross" towards his neighbors, and then he would go downstairs scowling with his brows knit and his mustache bristling, ignoring every salutation and growling in his beard: "Lousy Jews!"

The Jews called this mood "the Pan's bad fit" and, whenever it came over him they avoided him, until suddenly without any reason his behavior would alter again, and just as abruptly as he had turned against the Jews he once more made friends with them. The Pan's bad fit always evoked the same remark from the Jews: "The worm's gnawing him."

Pan Kviatkovski showed more respect for the teacher's wife than for any of the other Jewish tenants. She was the only person with whom he talked Polish, a sign that he regarded her as an equal. And yet Frau Hurvitz was not certain when she met him now whether Pan Kviatkovski was in his "good" or his "cross" mood, and did not know whether to greet him or pretend she did not see him. But Pan Kviatkovski stopped of his own accord, swept his hat from his graying head and inquired with a smile: "Why so deep in thought, dear madam? Has anything happened?"

"Nothing has happened, but there's so much distress in the building, Pan Kviatkovski."

"Ah yes. Yes, there's a great deal of poverty among you as well as among us. Why don't you apply to me sometimes if help is needed? You only look to your own people to relieve distress, but am I not a neighbor, too? I like to be on good terms with all my neighbors whether they are Jews or Gentiles."

"On the contrary, your help is always most welcome, Pan Kviatkovski!—Can you by any chance take in a poor young man who has come up from the country to study and has nowhere to sleep?" asked Frau Hurvitz, more in jest than in earnest.

"Why not? I have plenty of room. Bring him to me; he can both lodge and board in my house. There's only the two of us, myself and my housekeeper, and the flat's large enough. Why not?"

Frau Hurvitz could not recover from her amazement: "Are you joking, or do you mean it, Pan Kviatkovski?"

"Joking?" cried Pan Kviatkovski, so deeply offended and so red with anger that Frau Hurvitz became alarmed. "Do you think I would permit myself to joke on such a subject? You are looking for a lodging for a poor fellow who wants to study, and you think I would joke about that? Do you fancy I'm incapable of understanding?—But that's just like you Jews; you think that nobody but yourselves has any fellow-feeling, and that you're the only people who help others—nobody else is allowed a look in! But we must all help each other, we must help everybody all round—not in the narrow way you set about it. You Jews turn only to your own people and never think of the others."

"Who says so? On the contrary, it was *I* who asked *you*, Pan

Kviatkovski. And if you are willing to do it, my very best thanks to you! The young man is very respectable; he has run away from fanatical parents and wants to be a student in Warsaw."

"Bring him upstairs at once, then. I'll go back now and have a bed set up for him. He can have his meals with me, too. Our country needs educated people; the more intelligence we have the stronger we'll become. And you Yiddishers have good heads on you," he added in Yiddish jargon. "I'll teach him Polish myself. Bring him right up, Frau Hurvitz. I'll go up and tell my housekeeper." And Pan Kviatkovski ran upstairs again to his flat.

Frau Hurvitz stood for a moment quite struck dumb. She could hardly believe what she had heard. Then full of joy and pride she entered her kitchen.

The Shachliner stuck his goatee round the door of the "High School" and his eyes danced mockingly: "Well, Frau Hurvitz—have you found a bed for your young man?"

"Just to spite you, you Lithuanian, I have—and not only a lodging, but board and lessons as well! You come with me, young man," commanded Frau Hurvitz. She took the Talmudist by the hand like a child and dragged him and his bundle wrapped in newspaper upstairs to Pan Kviatkovski.

CHAPTER V

FRAU HURVITZ COOKS PAMPHLETS

After Frau Hurvitz had thus absolved her public duties and established the young Talmudist in his quarters, she turned to the domestic tasks that awaited her. The chief meal of the day had now to be prepared, and Rachel-Leah betook herself to her cooking-pots. This she did with the energy and swiftness that characterized all her actions and were even more in evidence than usual on this day, after such a successful morning.

A couple of hours later the whole family was assembled round the table and Solomon Hurvitz made ready to instruct his children in the science of food values. He was always learning or teaching something;

but, since it was too dark in the room now to read a book either privately or aloud, he applied his time to telling his children how much iron there was in turnips and how much albumen in lentils. The teacher liked imparting information to other people and drew no distinction between his pupils, his children and perfect strangers whom he had never seen before.

The early dusk of the brief autumn day was already darkening the room. The weather had taken a turn for the worse, and the children, who had set out in brilliant sunshine that morning, had come back wet through and plastered with snow and mud. David and Sosha had to take off their damp shoes and sit at table in their stockings. The conversation inevitably turned to the urgent necessity for galoshes, and that depressed everybody, for it reminded them how near the winter was. The father behaved as if he had not heard a word, but the mother pursued in her thoughts plans of all kinds.

There was always some guest at Rachel-Leah's table and she had a unique skill in apportioning the food so that it always sufficed. She was sitting now as usual before the large dish, thinking out contrivances and at the same time ladling out portions; to one plate she added something, from another she removed something, according to the age and appetite of the recipient. Of course the newcomer had been invited to share the meal. He seemed to have been born under a lucky star, that young man, for he had won Frau Hurvitz's sympathy from the very first and the fact that she had found a lodging for him in such an unlikely quarter invested him with extra distinction not only in her eyes, but in the eyes of everybody else. It was almost as if they gave him credit for the fact that Pan Kviatkovski had suddenly gone mad and taken in a young Jew as a lodger. The guest, however, was a handsome youngster as well; unlike his predecessors, who had mostly been small and ill-formed, he was of a tall straight figure and had well-cut features of a provincial simplicity, beautiful large dark eyes and a soft down on his cheeks that looked like a continuation of his side curls and gave him a soft youthful charm. But what chiefly recommended him to Frau Hurvitz was the superior cleanliness of his garments, which in that respect were unlike those of all the young men who had previously turned up from the provinces. He wore the traditional caftan, but it was spotlessly clean. His shirt showing beneath his prominent Adam's apple was decently ironed. And the satin ribbon that he wore, in the Chassidic manner, instead of a tie, was smooth and neatly knotted round his neck. It could be seen that this young man came out of no poor family, and even in a house so democratic as the teacher's this fact did not fail to make an impression. The attention of everybody was centered on the stranger. And since Frau Hurvitz had managed to procure a lodging and all kinds of extra privileges for him in such an extraordinary manner, the teacher and even the Shachliner were reconciled to the idea of his staying in Warsaw, and all were curious to know more about him.

"Why do you want to study?" asked the teacher.

The visitor, who obviously found himself in such company for the first time in his life, and had to endure the additional ordeal of sitting at the same table with strange girls, blushed to the roots of his hair. The girls, observing his blush, nudged each other under the table and bent low over their plates to hide their smiles from their father. But the young man soon recovered his composure: staring at his plate like a schoolboy he answered with unexpected assurance: "I want to be an author."

This answer surprised and excited the company. The master of the house laid down his fork, took off his glasses, polished them thoroughly with his handkerchief so that he might examine the speaker better, and asked: "You want to be an author?"

"Yes, I want to write," replied the young man with conviction.

"What do you want to write?" the teacher went on with his cross-examination.

"I've written a drama already and I've brought it with me to read to literary men."

"A drama?"

"Yes, a drama in four acts."

"Have you studied the rules of dramatic construction?" inquired the astonished teacher.

"Rules? Are there rules? No, I haven't studied them."

"You haven't studied the rules and yet you have written a drama?"

"As you see," returned the young man, waving one hand as if he were displaying an ox standing before him in the market.

"Have you read the literature of classical drama?"—the teacher's voice became as severe as if he were examining a pupil.

"Classical drama? What's that?" asked the young man, growing red.

Everybody smiled. Sosha could no longer restrain herself and burst out laughing, until a glare from her father silenced her.

"I mean Shakespeare, for instance. Have you read Shakespeare?" the teacher continued.

"I've heard of him, but I've never read him."

"Do you know Molière? Have you read Molière?"

"Molière? Who's he? I don't understand—must I read all that before writing a drama? What has that got to do with it?" asked the candidate in surprise.

Once more Sosha lost control of herself. Her elder sister pinched her under the table to silence her. The teacher paused in his cross-examination, and his expression betrayed profound sorrow and misgiving. The young man divined that he had said the wrong thing; he blushed still more in his confusion; but his shy embarrassment won him the others' sympathy.

"Tell me, young man, have you ever been in a theater? Have you ever even seen a theater?" The teacher took up his catechism again.

"Yes, a Jewish theatrical company once came to our town and I looked in through a hole in the tent."

Sosha burst out laughing again. The guest sat as if on hot coals and did not know where to look. His guardian angel rescued him: "Look here, what do you mean by jumping on a stranger like that? Hasn't he come to study in Warsaw just because he doesn't know all these things? You should be trying to help him," cried Frau Hurvitz, and as a kind of compensation for all his humiliations she transferred a piece of meat from her own plate to his.

"Eat it up, young man. You'll have the laugh of them all one day."

The master of the house brought this painful scene to a close:

"There's nothing to laugh at. All our talented men have begun like that. We have no schools. The synagogue is all the university we have. I am very interested in your drama, young man, and I beg you to read it to me whenever you have time."

These words rehabilitated the guest before the whole company and Rachel-Leah cried triumphantly: "Aha, see that, now!"

But the meal could not be prolonged, for various members of the family had to go out again. The teacher had afternoon lessons to give in private houses. Helene, too, gave private lessons and so had no free time to herself, a fact that vexed her mother. But living was dear and the family was large. The school brought in very little, for it was mainly attended by poor children from the neighborhood whose parents could afford to pay only half-fees, and even to get these it cost much trouble and many fruitless journeys. True, a committee of rich Jewish ladies who moved in Polish circles privately supported the school, because it was the only place where poor Jewish children could learn the officially proscribed Polish language, which Herr Hurvitz taught them in secret; but the support of these ladies, like that given by most charitable committees, was moral rather than material. The committee was prodigal of good advice only. The chief patroness of the school, Frau Dr. Silberstein, appeared every Monday and Thursday to examine the children in Polish, and fate ordained that many a time while she was actually in the building the Russian inspector, who kept a sharp eye on the school because of its suspected Polish sympathies, made a flying raid on it and cross-examined the children to find out if they were learning Polish and had Polish text-books. But whenever an actual problem cropped up, such as how to pay the rent or get coal for the winter, the committee was never of any real use; Frau Hurvitz was kept trotting round from one lady to the next, and as usual it was on her shoulders that the whole burden fell.

Yet it would be a mistake to assume that all the worries, her own and other people's, with which Frau Hurvitz contended had furrowed her face or aged her prematurely. The contrary seemed to be the case; the more she had to do the higher rose her energy, strength and spirit. The inexhaustible reserve of nervous force that was stored in her—presumably an inheritance from generations of peasant ancestors—

made her young-looking, elastic in her movements and as fresh in her appearance as a country girl. When she went downstairs the whole house knew her step, for it was unmistakable; the stairs quivered under her tread and yet she always flew whether going up or down. Although she was over forty she looked like a woman of thirty. Sorrow and care had not bowed her proud figure. Full-bosomed and ripe she advanced like a soldier in an army of mothers, knowing her duty and her own value. She radiated courage, energy and self-confidence; it was as if destiny had challenged her to come out and do battle. The more difficult her circumstances the greater her strength and the more lightly she shouldered her burdens. It must be admitted that when her eldest son, the hope of the family, was imprisoned as a political criminal, Frau Hurvitz looked on the verge of breaking down, and for some time her health actually suffered. She, who had never been ill, began to complain of headaches and pains in her legs. But that lasted only while she was fighting for her son's release; as soon as she was convinced that nothing could be done she returned to her daily round, and was shortly in command of herself once more and as young and fresh as ever. To be quite honest, her clear-cut face showed a few furrows after her son's misfortune, and round the column of her neck three deep rings had appeared; but the furrows only gave a tender sorrowing look to her muscular features, while her gray eyes, which had previously gleamed like those of some wild animal ready to spring, now had a gentle, contemplative, mildly resigned expression that suggested a film of tears over the eyeballs. This mild look and the furrows of maternal sorrow scored round her neck formed a remarkable contrast to the proud straightness of her figure. It was as if her body lived a life of its own as far as the neck; it was controlled throughout by a unified force of will that brooked no obstacles.

Frau Hurvitz knew exactly what she had to do at every moment of her life. There was always new labor awaiting her. As soon as her husband and the children were out of the house she turned up her sleeves and set to washing dishes; she poured a pan of hot water into the large basin, threw in soap and soda, and began to scour her pots, her dishes, her knives and forks, with the same energy that flowed from her at all times like sap from a mighty tree.

But Rachel-Leah could not wash dishes mechanically; she dreamed to herself as she did so.

Her spirit was far away as she stood there with sleeves rolled up and hands plunged into the soapy lye. Her imagination drew glorious pictures. Where nobody else could see anything remarkable Rachel-Leah's eye perceived a light that irradiated all things with its golden beams; she saw everything through transforming spectacles. The simple, unsullied faith within her made her see things and happenings not as they actually were but in a kind of perspective, as if from the vantage ground of a higher reality. And in her fantasy the young Talmudist whom she had found at her door became a great and renowned man, and she was proud to have helped him. Just as she was firmly convinced that her husband was the greatest scholar in the world, that her children would be eminent, and that the Shachliner, whom she called a "renegade" and a "Lithuanian thief," would yet make his mark and become famous, so she now began to believe in the young stranger's future (her imagination made no distinction here between her own children and strangers). And while she was scouring her pots and plates sheer joy illumined her face, and an endless, incomprehensible happiness flowed through her because she had been able to help such a promising young man. She looked forward with great expectations to his future.

From her maternal forbears she had inherited the firm belief that men were born for the higher aims of life that lay beyond the trivial round of petty cares; the ordinary tasks of daily existence fell to women, but men lived to create spiritual worlds, spiritual values that guaranteed eternal life and the eternal meaning of the universe. For Rachel-Leah these spiritual values had once been embodied in the study of the Torah and a belief in heaven, but since she had followed her husband into apostasy she attached her faith to the new values of culture and progress, to a belief in a brighter future on earth that was bound to come as soon as humanity shed its stupidities and no longer submitted to slavery. She had heard much about this future from the Shachliner and the other young men who came in every Friday evening. And in her opinion women were intended to help men in the struggle towards that brighter future—just as her mother and her mother's mother had helped their men to secure immortality in the other world and a share in paradise.

It was already dark in the kitchen. A film of raindrops obscured the window that looked out on the courtyard. The large room adjoining the kitchen, by day dining-room, study and family sitting-room, by night the children's bedroom, was now half-lit by the milky glow of a lamp, within whose circle David was sitting doing his home tasks for school before going to his evening job. He, too, had to earn his own keep and school clothes; every evening from five to seven he read aloud to a blind man. It was now getting so dark in the kitchen that Rachel-Leah could not see the dishes, and she remembered the lamp in the big room (she was too thrifty to light a second lamp). So she called to her son:

"David, bring the lamp in here! You can work at the kitchen-table, I've wiped it clean."

David came in with the lamp and his lesson-book. When he saw that his mother was washing dishes he asked in amazement:

"Are you doing the washing up? Where's the concierge? Doesn't she come in to do that every day?"

"What an idea! The concierge indeed! As if I can't do it myself! We can easily use the extra shillings for something else. Don't say anything to your father, do you hear?"

"Well, why can't Sosha help you? Isn't she in?"

"I don't want her to ruin her hands doing housework, so I've sent her out to see a friend of hers."

"Let me help you then, mother; give me a shot at it."

"Go away; you have your lessons to do."

"I've only to learn a little bit of Cæsar, and I know it already."

"I'll do the washing, all the same, but you can dry. There's a dish-cloth."

In the middle of operations, however, Rachel-Leah made a discovery.

"For goodness' sake, just look at that hole in your trousers! And it's no time since I bought them for you." She indicated the seat of her son's trousers.

David was pulled up short in a dramatic sentence from the

"Bellum civile." Awkwardly he stuttered out something about an "accident" and then cried wrathfully:

"How can I help it if they get torn? Trousers are just like that; they always get torn. Cast-iron trousers haven't been invented yet."

"That's the kind you would need! Cloth trousers are evidently not much use to you. Come here, my learned scholar, and let me mend that hole."

She left her dishes, fished a work-basket out of the drawer of the kitchen-table and threaded a needle with the stoutest cotton she could find; then dropping on one knee she set to work on the trousers of her son, who did not allow this attack on his hind-quarters to interrupt him in the recitation of Cæsar's heroic deeds. Rachel-Leah's face was radiant with pride for a moment as she listened to the mysterious syllables rolled out by her son, but soon she was paying little heed to Cæsar for she was thinking: "All kinds of things are invented, but why has nobody ever invented untearable cloth for trousers?" And while she was meditating on this relevant question she noticed that the boy's pockets were crammed to bursting.

"What's all this?" she asked, feeling his coat-pockets.

"Nothing at all . . . something I mustn't tell you." David reddened with embarrassment.

But his mother's hand pounced like lightning and extracted a thick bundle of revolutionary pamphlets.

"This is the last straw!" cried Rachel-Leah. "You too? What do you think is to become of me?" she added despairingly.

"Mother, please don't tell father. I only brought them here for tonight; I have to pass them on to somebody tomorrow."

"Have I to keep my mouth shut as well? To have one son lying in prison is enough—and now *you*'re at it, too? Can't you wait at least until you've finished school?" Rachel-Leah was calming down a little.

"I only took them to oblige a comrade. I promise you, mother, I'll pass them all on tomorrow."

"You haven't the slightest idea how to manage things like this, you greenhorn. How are you going to carry them in your torn clothes? Look, just look here, they're sticking right out of your pockets; a blind man couldn't help seeing them. Hand them over! The next thing

I'll have to put up with is hearing you've been arrested in the street. There are police-spies at every corner!"

With that she emptied her son's pockets of the pamphlets, seized a newly-washed pot and crammed the papers into it, then laid a sheet of paper on top, shook over that a bowlful of peeled potatoes that were ready for next day's dinner and set the whole on the stove.

David laughed. "What are you after? Are you going to boil the pamphlets?"

"Boiling isn't enough for them, I'm going to roast them! I'm going to burn them to cinders! Don't let me catch you bringing things like that into the house again, you greenhorn. You can keep that kind of thing for later on, or else I'll tell your father. As sure as I'm a living woman, as sure as I stand here I'll tell your father!"

"Then I'll tell my father that you've been swearing again." (The teacher, who never stopped trying to educate his own wife, was at much pains to break Rachel-Leah of her habit of swearing.) "And I'll tell him, too, that you've been washing up the dishes yourself!"

"Will you hold your tongue, you greenhorn?"

"If you don't tell, neither will I. One good turn deserves another——" The boy ran off laughing, for it was time to go to his evening job.

"Stop!... Why are you flying off without your galoshes? Do you want to catch cold again? It's raining and your shoes are leaking."

"How can I put on galoshes? The ones I had are all torn."

"Come here a minute. There—I bought a pair second-hand at the market." With these words she threw a parcel at her son.

"Galoshes! Where did you get the cash for them?"

"Never you mind. Put them on and clear out at once."

CHAPTER VI

A SABBATH HOUR ON A WEEK-DAY

The evening hours between five and seven, since her husband and her children were then out of the house, belonged entirely to Frau

Hurvitz. The chief meal of the day was over, the dishes were washed up, and now the time for relaxation and dreaming came for the housewife, and she resented any interruption of it. It was reserved for one of two of her favorite occupations; scrubbing the floor or taking a bath. On this occasion she did both. Cleanliness was an obsession with her; as a girl in her country village she had been accustomed to see everything in the house shining, and to this custom she adhered all her life, honoring it even more now than she had done formerly. To scrub the floor was for her a kind of pleasant recreation, in a sense an escape from the troubles of the day, and whenever her burdens grew too heavy, whenever necessity pinched her too hard, Rachel-Leah betook herself to this favorite occupation.

She slipped off her shoes and stockings, dipped a cloth in a basin of soapy water, and on all fours crawled round the room, wringing out the cloth from time to time and scrubbing the floor thoroughly with a zeal that showed her pleasure in the job. The wet cloth traveled into every corner of the large dining-room, under the beds and the chests, and no crevice, however securely hidden, escaped its attentions. Rachel-Leah suffered no one to interrupt her; it was as if she were doing priestly service in a sanctuary; no one either could or dared enter the house; and if the Messiah Himself had knocked at the door, He would have had to wait until all the floors in the flat had been wiped with that wet cloth. Then every window was thrown open—summer and winter alike—to let the floors dry more quickly. After the scrubbing, yellow sand was strewn all over, and then no one dared to stir out of the kitchen, and it was in the kitchen that the teacher and the Shachliner had to fight out their battles over a glass of tea until the large room was dry and ready to receive its guests in a fitting manner.

When she had finished with the floors Rachel-Leah took herself in hand. She loved nothing so much as soap and water, and so not only her own body but everything that pertained to her had to make the acquaintance of soap and water pretty frequently. From time immemorial it had been an established law in the Hurvitzes' house that every member of the family had to face a tub of soapy water on Friday evening. The mistress of the house divided each victim into two halves; first the top half was dealt with, from the head to the middle, and then the lower half from the middle downwards. She made no distinction of age or of sex amongst her family: Friday's bath was obligatory. But in the middle of the week it might occur to Rachel-Leah to examine the ears of her children or the backs of their necks. And these attentions were not confined to her own family; she had even made it a law that every young man from the provinces who came to seek instruction from her husband should first of all face the tub of soapy water—to say nothing of her own lodgers, over whom she exercised a strict supervision. She would appear unexpectedly in the "High School" with a basin of hot water and a piece of yellow soap, and issue the command: "You must all take a wash, or else I'll have to come and wash you myself." It was the Shachliner who suffered most, for whenever Rachel-Leah was at odds with him or whenever he said anything of which she disapproved, she would call out, no matter who was present: "Herr Lithuanian, wouldn't you like to have a bath? As sure as I'm a living woman, there's a large kettle of boiling water ready."

But she loved most of all to apply soap and water to her own person. A bath was a kind of reward for the toils of the day and aroused in her new reserves of energy and courage. She locked and bolted the door, threw off her frock and underwear, and standing naked in the great tub poured water from a ladle over her supple athletic body. And just as thoroughly as she had previously scoured her pots, her dishes and floors, she now washed every portion of her own body with a hard loofah dipped in soap and soda. Her beautifully modeled back with all its hollows and dimples arched itself like a well-strung bow: her spine was as slim and delicate in its articulations as the backbone of a fish. Energetically and with great contentment she labored over the whole of her supple body from the breasts to the wide hips, nor did she forget to scour her strong and rounded knees. Every touch of the loofah left a red mark behind as if her blood had been awakened from sleep, as if it had been summoned from its farthest retreat and now was trying to burst through her transparent white skin.

But today was a special occasion, for Rachel-Leah washed not only her body but her hair as well. After such a day of trouble and running to-and-fro, it was a great comfort to her to wash her hair. Still naked, with her skin prickling into goose-flesh after her bath, she stood before a basin of warm rain-water and rinsed her long hair in it, squeezing out the soap; then she tossed her locks apart and poured the rain-water luxuriously over her head. A childlike innocence beamed from her face and her whole body at that moment, as if it were blessings that were being showered on her head. The dreams of her youth rose up again; green dells of her childhood, cool streams in which she had bathed as a girl, secret glades in fragrant spring woods; all lived again in her memory while she poured the lukewarm rain-water over her head. The sins of the intervening years were washed away, the sins of poverty and encroaching age; and Rachel-Leah quitted the wash-basin fresh and purified, as if new-born.

She sat drying her hair by the hot tiled stove in the sitting-room; she felt relaxed and drowsy in the green dressing-gown that had been made from her wedding frock. All the chairs and tables had lesson-books of some kind lying on them. But the floor was scrubbed white and strewn with yellow sand; so Rachel-Leah sat by the stove drinking tea in great content, new-born, purified, comforted; as happy as a child.

This was the sole hour of the day when Rachel-Leah heard her own heart, the sole point at which she became aware of her own life. It was the Sabbath hour of her day, the hour in which she dried her hair and drank tea by the milky light of the table lamp. As a shepherd passes in review his well-tended flocks, Rachel-Leah now reviewed her days and her dreams.... Long-forgotten and buried maiden dreams that had been shrouded in the darkness of the past rose and hovered as if in sunlight before her eyes; summer-green meadows, murmuring brooks, secret sensations, shadowy longings; almost bloodless and bodiless, they drifted before her, floated off and vanished. Following these came more sharply defined memories and actions more clearly retained in her mind....

Frau Hurvitz did not lament her destiny; on the contrary she was content. Could she have lived her life over again she would have taken the same path, the path she was now retracing in memory.... The first year after her marriage, when her husband had not been much in evidence. And then the children.... Her thoughts lingered with her eldest son, her child of sorrow, her darling. She remembered him as a nursling, when she was living in her father-in-law's house and was homesick because she did not care much for the new house into which she had been admitted; she liked neither her husband's parents nor their unfamiliar customs. She was regarded with suspicion because she could not adapt herself to their severe piety; locks of her hair would keep straggling out from beneath her marriage wig and hood, and she was always being caught in the breach of some observance or other. Her mother-in-law always had some fault to find with her and lectured her unceasingly. Her father-in-law grumbled at her beneath his breath. Even her husband had seemed a stranger. She had longed for escape, for her home, her village, the inn her parents kept, the country girls and country youths. Her only comfort was the infant she nursed at her bosom.... Then the whole course of her son's life unrolled itself; she saw him as a child playing, then as a school-boy in school uniform, with long trousers and a bulky satchel of text-books. What a trouble it had always been to find the money for his school-fees! What palpitations she had had over his examinations, wondering whether he would get "excellent" or not! She saw him shoot up: oh God! why did he grow so quickly? She did not want him to grow up; he should have remained a child, a little child, as when he lay at her breast....

Her eyes longed to sate themselves with the sight of her son. Where was he now? Alone, pacing up and down a gloomy cell. Or he might have been already sent to Siberia! Alone, and no one beside him. Was he yearning for her as she for him? If only the door would open, if only he would come in! Not tall and grown-up, alien and belonging to an alien world, as he had been in his last phase, but once more a child as in those days when he got his first pair of shoes.... Rachel-Leah remembered those shoes; it had pained her to throw them away when they became too small, for they still kept the shape of his little feet. She remembered how she used to hold him naked in her arms and bathe his small smooth body, how she used to hold him to her and give him the breast. The joy and sorrow of motherhood shook her; she had no wish but to hold him in her arms again and lay his little face, his open, warm little mouth, on her bosom. . . .

She did not know that tears were running down her cheeks. Her heart ached; her soul was empty. She yearned for something, she did not herself know what. It was not her husband she missed; she had a timid respect for him and looked up to him as beyond her reach; she took him for granted and never yearned for him, since he was always present, always above her head like a roof. It was something else she yearned for, something she had lost and no longer possessed, something that would never return again.

There came a knock at the door. "They're home already," murmured Rachel-Leah, still absorbed in her dreams. Involuntarily she asked herself which of them it could be; her husband? David? Perhaps Helene?

The knock was repeated.

"In a minute, in a minute," called Rachel-Leah imploringly, as if she were begging not to be recalled to the waking world. Then she rose slowly and opened the door. A man stood there who was a complete stranger and yet curiously familiar. He seemed to be known to her, an old friend, and yet she could not remember who he was.

"Don't you remember me, Madame Hurvitz? I'm Mirkin," said the stranger shyly, twisting his cap of Persian lambskin.

"Mirkin? Mirkin?" said she to herself in bewilderment.

"Yes. I hope I'm not disturbing you? I'm on my way through Warsaw and took the liberty of calling on you. You were once so good as to invite me," said Mirkin, somewhat disconcerted by her lack of recognition.

"Mirkin? Mirkin?" murmured Frau Hurvitz again, as if in a dream. She was not surprised to see him standing there so unexpectedly, for she had the feeling that she was dreaming.

"Come in, come in. . . . Please sit down . . . here, beside me. I'm all alone in the house; they're all out."

She led him into the room and set him beside her at the table without remembering that she had only her dressing-gown on and that her damp hair was hanging loose. Mirkin was at a loss. He felt he had arrived at the wrong moment. The woman was acting so queerly:

was she half-asleep? Her state struck him as uncanny: "Perhaps I'd better come at another time? I'm sure I'm disturbing you."

"No, no, not at all—I'm very glad you've come, very glad indeed. Will you have some tea with me?"

Still as if in a dream she went into the kitchen and poured tea for Mirkin into a coarse bowl such as she gave her children; then she brought the bowl into the sitting-room and set it on the table.

Mirkin did not know whether to accept it or not. "Now, tell me, how are you getting on? Where have you been all this while? It was high time you came . . ." she said, as if to herself, as if it were not a living man who sat there but a vision.

More and more disconcerted Mirkin said timidly: "I'm on my way to the frontier, and so I took the liberty of looking you up."

"You're on your way to the frontier? But why need you go farther? One of them has gone already, and now the other is going, too. . . . Why must you go? Stay here with us. Why must you wander about all alone? It's a shame, and you such a child!"

With these words she stretched out her hand and began to stroke Mirkin's hair maternally, as if she were hypnotized.

Mirkin sat motionless and white as death. He did not know whether this scene was real or a dream. He saw clearly enough that the woman beside him did not know what she was doing and was acting as if under some spell; once she woke up she would be ashamed of her conduct. He wanted to get up quietly and slip from the room, but her words, the smile that shone through her tears, the caressing movements of her hands, so affected him that he, too, sank under the spell; he felt that he was dreaming, and his head dropped lower and lower. . . .

How long this trance lasted who can tell? Frau Hurvitz suddenly started up as if out of a dream: "Who's this?" She lifted the head that was resting on her bosom and gazed with bewilderment into Mirkin's eyes: "Mirkin? Oh, it's you, is it? The assistant to the Petersburg advocate! I didn't know you were here! Where on earth have I been? My God, what have I been doing? I must have been dreaming!" She smiled in embarrassment. "It was you who came in, then? But look at the state I'm in! Excuse me, I must go and dress myself at once; my husband and children will be here in a moment!"

She forced the blenching Mirkin, who had jumped up in alarm, into his chair again and fled into the adjoining bedroom.

CHAPTER VII

MIRKIN RECEIVES INSTRUCTION

Not long afterwards the teacher returned from his lessons, and on his heels came the children. Hurvitz was introduced to Mirkin, of whom he had already heard from his wife, but he was interested in the visitor in any case simply because he came from Petersburg. The teacher had never seen Petersburg, but from all that he had read about it he imagined the Czar's capital as a kind of modern Babel in which a second Nebuchadnezzar sat enthroned. So he examined Mirkin with an expectant and judicious eye, as if the very cut of the stranger's clothes might provide some clew to the wickedness of Petersburg. The Shachliner, too, abandoning the mysterious business that occupied all his days, came into the sitting-room, introduced himself to the stranger, and at once engaged him in conversation.

After leaving Petersburg Mirkin had stayed for a few weeks in Vilna and there shared in the solemn Jewish festivities. Like every exiled Jew who has spent his whole life in a foreign environment and has neither seen nor known Jews, Zachary Gavrilovitch Mirkin was profoundly impressed by the Jewish tradition when he encountered it for the first time, and succumbed to this national Zionistic atmosphere which stilled the longings of his hungry soul. Like every one who first comes into contact with Jewish national feeling he, too, was wildly enthusiastic and even entertained vague projects of going to Palestine and doing pioneer work of some kind.

And he had a burning desire to discuss with somebody his new experiences in Vilna. Now that he met in the Hurvitzes' house people from the very heart of the Jewish masses, he poured out to them in fiery words all that he had experienced and all the new convictions he had acquired, believing in good faith that every person who belonged to the mass of Jews or had any connection with them must be filled with the same national sentiments that had fired him so instantaneously; he could not even imagine that any genuine Jew might have a different viewpoint.

So with the utmost enthusiasm he expatiated to the teacher and the Shachliner on the glories of Vilna and the festivals he had attended there. For the first time in his life he had seen Jews in their own surroundings praying to their God, and he could not find words to describe the lovely old synagogue in Vilna and its impressive services, especially those on New Year's Day and the Day of Atonement: "It's our religion alone that has preserved us Jews and will go on preserving us. Our religion is our sole heritage, our real fatherland. I simply can't understand Jews who don't appreciate that. As I stood in the Vilna synagogue on the Day of Atonement I was filled with a deep reverence for the piety and devotion of the worshipers. I felt as if I were witnessing a gigantic affirmation uniting mankind to a higher, invisible Being. I began to understand the meaning of Jewish history, and stood in awe before the generations that have transmitted the tradition, the spirit, the living word from the days of Abraham right up to our time. And when I heard the weekly portion read out from the Torah on the Day of Atonement, the mere sound of the Hebrew words stirred me, the sound of our forefathers' speech in the Holy Land, the language of the prophets. I discovered later what was the meaning of that chapter—a Jew found me a Russian translation in the synagogue—and as I read about Abraham's covenant with God and how he bound his only son to the altar, I realized that I was one of those for whom the patriarch made that covenant with Jehovah for all eternity. . . ."

Zachary was on fire with enthusiasm. At last he had found the longed-for opportunity to talk about his recent experiences and the change that had been wrought in him. Although he had never met these people before he felt as intimate with them, because of Frau Hurvitz who was sitting beside him, as if he had known them for years. For the first time he became fully aware how senseless and wrong his education had been; he had learned everything except how to know himself.

"I have made a beginning by starting to learn Hebrew. I know a little Yiddish already," he boasted. "But the mere sound of the Hebrew syllables affects me so much that I can't help trembling. I'm getting used to it now, but when I first began to learn the Hebrew words and pronounce them I was so struck by the thought that this or something like this was the language spoken by my own forefathers, that for sheer emotion I could hardly utter a word. Simply to look at the Hebrew letters fills me with awe. And now I'm thinking seriously of going to Palestine to start farming. I can't really understand why all the Jews in the world don't do that, and why the Palestine movement isn't supported by every single Jew. How is it possible to reject such an ideal? It's the only way out for us. Palestine is the solution for us as individuals and as a nation—to go back to Palestine would be to find oneself again. Since I've had that aim before me I've become a different person; for the first time I find that I can envisage and understand the life I have to live. . . ."

The teacher listened seriously and was silent for a long time. Every word of Mirkin's stabbed him to the heart. He thought to himself: "All those who come to us from outside, all those who have not shared in our sufferings, look on us as visions in a pleasant dream, figments of their imagination, and not real people actually existing with our good points and our bad points." A bitter smile played round his mouth. He felt impelled to refute Mirkin, but restrained himself because he was the host and because he was sorry for this young man who talked as if he came from the moon. The Shachliner, however, was less considerate; he had already felt like interrupting Mirkin once or twice but had refrained out of respect for the stranger. He waited impatiently until Mirkin had stopped speaking and then burst out: "The religion whose praises you're singing is no romantic tradition from the past; it's not a kind of benevolent grandmother sitting picturesquely reading the Women's Bible on a Sabbath afternoon. Nothing of the kind," he almost shouted, "it's an active and malicious stepmother that puts obstacles in our way to trip us up at every step. It's the Chinese shoe that cramps us like a vice and won't let us move. Do you see this useless arm of mine?" With his sound arm he lifted the withered one for inspection. "That's a gift to me from your religion, because I read a forbidden book. My father, a pious Jew, highly moral and cruel and intolerant like every wild fanatic, found me on the evening before the Day of Atonement reading a Hebrew critical work, and he thrashed me until he broke my arm. The ignorant masseur did the rest, and the result is that I'm a cripple for life. You people who have never lived in the 'mansions' that the Jewish religion has built for us, but in real mansions where you have enjoyed all the advantages you could desire, begin to have longings for 'indigenous values' when you're fed up with your luxuries or thrown out of your mansions; well, just you come and live the 'indigenous' life among us, and then you'll see where the shoe pinches! Come and take the ritual baths in a filthy bath-house, in the traditional 'Mikvah'; come and spend sixteen or eighteen hours a day in the synagogue studying such important problems as the egg that is laid on the Sabbath, or divorce and marriage—that's the order in which they come, you study divorce first and then marriage; just you come and plunge into the commentaries and super-commentaries, the glosses and explanations set down by every casuistical Jew who wanted to let future generations see how clever he could be; just you put the nice greasy velvet cap on your head, and then we'll see how you like it! How did *you* spend your childhood and your youth? Probably on the ice in winter and in summer roaming the fields and woods with your playmates. What did *you* learn at school when you were a boy? Probably all the countries and rivers of the globe, the great heroic deeds of history, the knowledge of the animals and plants in your neighborhood, the laws of nature. Through all these things your mind was enriched; every new lesson opened a new world before you, and you constantly traveled into new and unfamiliar lands, learning to know different peoples, customs, traditions. And apart from the usefulness of such knowledge, how much delight, how much sunshine it must have brought into your life! And you took it all for granted. Think of the works of the great poets that were put before you at school, the works of Poushkin, of Lermontoff and the countless others who sing of winter and summer and trees and flowers and people! O God, what a wealth of enjoyment you must have had in your youth! Every day must have been a feast-day!" cried the Shachliner, envy burning in his eyes. "But do you know how *we* spent our youth? Chained to those same letters that make you tremble with emotion, tied down to that alphabet that rouses you to such unnecessary enthusiasm! O, how I hate those letters! Yes, I hate them, for they have filched everything from me: my youth, my life, my enjoyment! Every morning at six—in the small hours while it was still pitch-dark—my father woke me; I had to hack away the ice in the water-barrel before I could dip in my fingers for the prescribed morning purification. And then I had to spend the whole morning reciting sentences that were of no earthly interest to me, and many of them were about things that one was ashamed even to mention; fortunately I didn't understand at the time what the words meant, but when I realized their meaning later they only inflamed my senses. And the only relief I got was to be switched over occasionally to the Haggadah, which at least illustrates the Jewish Law by parables and anecdotes in which a boy's imagination can expand a little and his mind find some rest. But that didn't count as learning. Learning meant to sharpen one's thinking powers, and to sharpen them on boring, irrelevant matter that wasn't of any use to any one, on problems that had no relation to contemporary life, none at all. And so it went on, summer and winter alike. How I used to long for a breath of fresh air on summer evenings! How I used to envy the boys at the high school when I saw them setting off in winter with their skates and toboggans. . . ! Year in, year out, until I was nineteen these Hebrew letters kept me prisoner; they robbed me of everything—my childhood, my time. I saw my youth slipping from me with nothing to show for it, cut off from all boyish pleasures—and now you come driveling about the holy Hebrew letters and the awe-inspiring sound of Hebrew words and the golden chain of religion! You only hearten and strengthen our enemies when you do that. This modern romanticism of yours only gives fresh license to the barbarous world in which all our young men, hundreds and thousands of our young men, are being tortured, and which they are all struggling to escape from. Don't smear your romanticism like a salve on our fetters to make them slip the more smoothly over our wrists! You're only giving our jailers an excuse for quoting you in their own justification: 'Look,' they'll say, 'even the graduates from the universities are coming back to our way of thinking.'—If you can't help us in our struggle, at least keep out of the way, as you've done until now!" shouted the Shachliner, trembling with excitement and frothing at the mouth.

Nobody spoke a word after this flaming outburst. The teacher only looked gloomier and more inscrutable than before. His own youth had been summoned up again before his eyes. That was two decades ago, and yet things were much the same still. In the towns and villages thousands and tens of thousands of young men were still being subjected to torments of the kind described by the Shachliner, and there was no prospect of help from any direction. And any one who came to them from outside, impelled by external circumstance or an inner need, came with shut eyes as if afraid to look the reality in the face. The teacher was sorry for this strange young man who came hungry from another world and found nothing to eat but his own words. And yet—the more quickly he came to know the truth the better it would be for him.

With a pale and quivering face and an embarrassed smile on his lips Mirkin sat at the table like a helpless child for all his downy black beard. His eyes that had been calm and serene now glanced uneasily round him. All at once the people sitting there had turned into strangers, and the thought flashed through his mind that things were not so simple as he had fancied. He felt afraid of the unknown world from which the Shachliner had lifted the veil. In despair he told himself: "I'll never understand it, I'm a stranger." The clew he seemed to have held had slipped from his grasp, and an inexpressible fear invaded him. At that moment Frau Hurvitz caught his eye, and her glance conveyed not only courage and hope but a peculiar intimacy, so that he felt once more admitted into the circle.

"After all I'm a stranger," he began, "and I don't know what Jewish life is like. But I've heard—and read—that even in the darkness of religious fanaticism, as Herr Weinberg calls it, there are gleams of light; the Jewish festivals, for instance. Every existence, however shut in, is bound to find pleasure in something. Did you have no pleasure at all in your childhood, Herr Weinberg?"

"I never knew what real pleasure was until I disowned my father's faith, and even then it wasn't merely because I had renounced my belief in God, but because I found in my books a belief in a better and juster world on earth. That's the religion I subscribe to like everybody else, and that's what I feel called upon to fight for along with the whole of mankind—the dawn of a better day. And the first blows I suffered for the sake of that faith gave me my first real pleasure. This arm that my father broke because of a book became my greatest happiness!"

"But did you have no happiness even when you were a child?"

But Weinberg's last remarks had restored the teacher's faculties, and he now broke in: "Weinberg's right; there can be no inherited faith. What we call faith must spring from our own experience. Every Talmud scholar among us who cuts himself off from his faith by his own act is being his own Moses—or better still, his own Abraham. Every one of us has found his own religion for himself and not merely taken it over from others. So the real believers among us are the renegades. 'Enlightenment' was the religion proclaimed once, and people became martyrs for it. And the gospel of enlightenment was abandoned much too soon, for we never needed it more than now. The great mass of Jews are still living in ignorance and fear and nobody does anything for them. Everybody's working now for political, not for cultural ends. Every political party wants to win over the masses so as to strengthen its own position, but nobody cares about the life these masses lead. Any amelioration of their lot is always postponed until later. All the reformers, from the Zionists down to this one here"—he indicated the Shachliner—"promise a future Paradise as soon as their political ideals are realized, but not one of them is concerned with the present. The only people who have done anything to uplift the masses are the 'Assimilators,' and they were shouted down and driven from the ghettos. But I say, and I keep on saying: let the 'Assimilators' be as bad as you like, they are none the less the sole heirs of the Enlightenment. They were the only people who brought a ray of light into the darkness, and they did it not in pursuit of egoistic party politics but from pure love of humanity."

Zachary had taken heart again, and ventured to say: "My standpoint is that Zionism, or rather the ideal of a country of our own subject to no alien domination, is a kind of common focus for all Jewish suffering, spiritual as well as material. How can one think of doing anything for the masses when one cannot take a step without running one's head against alien domination and alien interests? I have never been able to understand why Jews in the radical camp are so bitterly opposed to the Zionist ideal. Does it not mean the realization of all our aspirations to restore the Jews, body and spirit, to the status of simple humanity which other peoples have denied them? I am far more inclined to believe that all the Jewish suffering you mention will be quite naturally eliminated once we have a national life of our own." —Then, turning to the Shachliner, he went on: "I understand your personal sufferings and your regrets for the childhood you were cheated of, but how can you do anything for the unenlightened masses unless you have some means of influencing them? An administration set up by Jews in a free Jewish country is the only means of putting an end to the monstrous growths that have sprung up among us. I am convinced that all our ideals, even our religion, will return to health only when they have been filtered through an organized national life," he concluded, drawing a deep breath.

It was literally miraculous that the teacher suffered Mirkin to have his say out; for nothing upset Hurvitz more than this very idea that Zachary was championing. There are people who feel an actual physical repulsion from certain animals or human beings—such as those for instance who cannot endure the bodily exhalations of a negro—and in the same way there are people who feel an almost pathological repulsion from certain ideas. The teacher was one of these. He could not control himself if Zionism was so much as mentioned in his presence; it gave him almost physical discomfort and he could not help reacting at once. In vain Frau Hurvitz endeavored by nods and winks to dissuade Mirkin from enlarging on the theme; she even prepared to do something that her respect for her husband usually forbade, that is to take part in the discussion so as to divert it from the dangerous topic, but it was already too late; the teacher sprang up as if the floor were burning under his feet. Forgetting all canons of hospitality, forgetting his duty as a host, he advanced on Zachary, seized him by the arm and dragged his amazed guest to the window giving on the courtyard; then he flung the window open although it was a cold autumn evening, and pointing to the courtyard said with unusual emphasis:

"Look at this courtyard, look at all the small lights burning in these windows! In this courtyard there lives a hunted and tormented mass of people, in dirt, in ignorance, in contempt and disgrace, abandoned by everybody; ten, twelve, even fifteen of them crammed together in one room. And there are whole rows of buildings like this, whole streets, whole towns. Millions of Jews are living in misery like this. There is no Jewish nation but this one. This is our poverty and our wealth. Here is where one must begin; these are the people one must help, for these one must give up one's life. And what are you proposing to do? You want to begin with an ideal, with a theory. How long are we to remain in servitude to such false idols? They may satisfy a man here and there who wants to escape from suffering, from the actualities of life, from looking himself in the face; well and good! Let him trust to the paper bridge of theory and idealism! But as for you, young man, if you really want to do something, if you really want to be of use—here is the place for you. There's no Jewish nation but this one, and there's no asylum to which it can flee. Our forefathers had enough wandering through the world; we have to stay where we are and do battle for ourselves here!"

It is difficult to say where the discussion would have ended had not Frau Hurvitz, who had been waiting for a chance to break in and relieve the tension, interrupted merrily: "Now I think that's enough instruction for a poor stranger who has had the misfortune to land in your school. There'll be plenty of other chances of educating him, since Herr Mirkin isn't leaving just yet. Isn't it about time that we were thinking of supper? You'll stay to supper, won't you?" She turned hospitably to Mirkin.

Frau Hurvitz began moving busily to and fro between the kitchen and the dining-room. In honor of the visitor she spread a white cloth on the table and laid out all her dishes and cutlery. At the same time she warned Mirkin that he wasn't to pitch his expectations too high; there was nothing but plain bread and plum sauce. Yet as it was a special occasion she sent David, who had meanwhile returned, for a bundle of sprats (a great luxury in the Hurvitzes' house), a pound of sugar, and a half a pound of fresh butter. . . .

On the staircase merry laughter could be heard, and presently

Sosha burst into the room, threw her books on the table and at once began to talk eagerly to the stranger. A little later the elder sister came in almost inaudibly. All that Zachary could see was a black and white checked frock on a girl's slim back. The pattern seemed somehow familiar; he must have observed it somewhere already. But who else wore a black and white check like that? Mirkin could not decide whether it was in this life that he had seen it or in some other. Helene was holding a flowering plant in her arms, cradling it in her bosom like a child as if she was afraid to lay it down. Her mother grumbled: "How long are you going to carry around that flower-pot? The whole house is full of your flower-pots. Where are you going to find room for this one?"

The table was laid. Frau Hurvitz added bread, butter, sprats, plum sauce and steaming tea. Sosha helped to make everything ready and guessed her mother's wishes without a word spoken; she produced the starched table-napkins from the cupboard where they usually lay untouched from one Easter to the next, and to impress the guest still more set out the small silver sugar-bowl. This bowl, a wedding present from a rich uncle, was originally meant to hold a tomato at the Feast of Tabernacles, but now it served as a last resource in time of need. Whenever there was a shortage of funds in the Hurvitzes' house the pawning of the sugar-bowl was considered. Indeed, it often found its way to the pawn-shop, and only pure chance ordained that on this occasion it was actually in the house instead of in its usual quarters.

The teacher was ashamed of this display before his guest. Rachel-Leah knew it by his downcast eyes and burning ears; but she acted as if she had noticed nothing.

At table the teacher inquired what further plans Zachary had in mind.

"I'm not yet quite clear," replied Mirkin. "First I want to look round and find myself, so to speak. It's one's first duty to seek and find oneself in the infinite sea of existence. Otherwise we're bound to get lost in the flood of events that daily life washes over us."

"And in what way do you propose to find yourself?" asked the Shachliner.

"By being alone with myself."

"Where? In the forest? In the wilderness? Are you thinking of squatting in a tree like an Indian monk?" The Shachliner smiled sarcastically.

"Let us say in some remote and quiet place in Switzerland; I could put in a year or two there and find myself."

"Oh, of course—surrounded by books, and probably in the middle of a carefully selected and exclusive circle of acquaintances! People of that kind never know how much their ideas are conditioned by their interests. Without knowing or desiring it you and people like you base your philosophy, let it be ever so individualistic, even anarchic, on the assumptions that justify your own parasitic and idle existence. No, I don't believe that in the present capitalistic system it is possible for any one to live an innocent life without harming anybody. That might be possible in a backward and religious country like India, but in Europe people are bound to fall into one of two categories, whether they want to or not: those who work and those who live on the work of others; those who help the oppressed and those who help the oppressors. There's no third category, and you needn't persuade yourself that you stand outside. It's just the neutrals who think they stand outside that are the worst enemies of the oppressed classes. They help the exploiters, for their way of life can't be anything but a justification of the existing system, seeing there would be no room for them in any other."

Everybody smiled, for they all knew Weinberg's weakness. Just as Jewish traveling preachers invariably concluded their sermons by saying: "So may a Deliverer arise for Zion," Weinberg concluded every argument, whatever the theme, by a reference to Socialism. Frau Hurvitz called laughingly to Mirkin: "You'll hear a lot more about this if you come to see us again."

And everybody joined in the laughter.

When Zachary and the Shachliner left, Rachel-Leah's day was at an end. She pulled a bundle of underwear from a drawer and was soon busy patching and darning in her favorite seat beside the warm stove with the table pulled up beside her. The children sat at the table, too, over their school tasks, and the teacher as well, absorbed in a book. Their faces were illumined by the milk-white light of the large table-lamp. While Frau Hurvitz drew the end of a cotton thread through her strong white teeth she said to her husband: "Don't you think that the young man's to be pitied? What good will it do him to go wandering about the world? Perhaps he would be happy enough if he were to stay here?"

"I never advise anybody. Every man must do as he thinks best," answered the teacher, without raising his eyes from his book.

CHAPTER VIII

FEAR OF ONESELF

THE NIGHT after his visit to Frau Hurvitz, Zachary slept badly. He dreamed that he was standing before the entrance to an uncannily gloomy cellar inhabited by poor wretches, and these blended in his dream with the black, shadowy shapes of unknown demons lurking in himself. These creatures came running to the door and tried to push their way out, but Mirkin and some other people leaned their bodies against the door to keep them back. Suddenly Zachary's helpers vanished and he was left alone to stem the onrush; he braced himself with all his strength, all his will-power, against the door, but the pressure on the other side was too strong. The door was forced half-open so that he could see into the cellar. It was a deep and sinister vault, black-beamed and strewn—how extraordinary!—with yellow sand. The rigid figures in the corners began to come to life, and he could discern their idiotic, surly faces: they began to creep towards him, stretching out long hands with crooked fingers. "These are not poor beggars at all," the thought flashed through his mind, "these are the dark invisible shadows that haunt the depths of my soul and torment me so dreadfully; it is they who are stretching out bony hands to clutch me!" Nearer and nearer they came, creeping one by one out of the cellar towards him; he could see quite clearly their maniac faces, wild gestures and horribly distorted limbs. There were some still sitting motionless in the far corners, apparently waiting for a sign, and they glared at him threateningly. Mirkin hurled himself with all his weight against the door to shut them in, but inch by inch he was thrust back. And there was no one to help him; he had been deserted by everybody. "Help, help, help!" he screamed, struggling wildly to escape. He knew he was dreaming, but he could not waken himself; he tried to bite his fingers to rouse himself but his hands would not obey him. At long last a violent jerk of the head restored him to his senses and he awoke bathed in a cold sweat.

"Where am I?" Little by little he returned to consciousness and remembered that he was in a hotel in Warsaw and that he had been spending the evening with Frau Hurvitz.

He could not possibly go to sleep again. He lay awake with shut eyes and listened to the breathing of the world and its swift recession that every one can hear within himself in the silence of the night. He tried to recall the dream he had just had, but the details blurred and vanished like wraiths. Only the feeling of dread remained.

Mirkin put on the light and remained in bed with his eyes open. All that had happened in the Hurvitzes' house now emerged clearly in his mind, and he saw outlined with unusual sharpness everything he had felt and seen and heard during the evening. In the silence his vague impressions solidified into inescapable realities with a life of their own; nothing was spared him, nothing hidden; everything lay before him in complete and merciless revelation. . . . He understood with dreadful clarity why he had abandoned his original intention of avoiding Warsaw and traveling direct from Petersburg to the frontier.

"Oh God, what dark powers there are within me! Whither am I being driven? I am a sick man with sick visions; my body is saturated like a sponge with morbid fancies. A feeble, sick creature, the heir of unknown forebears who have bequeathed me a morbid tendency towards all that is unsound and horrible. . . . I escaped from *one* net by running away, only to entangle myself in another like a hunted dog. What need had I to come to Warsaw . . . ?"

But Mirkin remained in Warsaw. He did not visit the Hurvitzes again, for he did not dare. Several times he lingered near the house, usually in the dusk of evening, about the hour when he had found Frau Hurvitz alone. He had just sufficient strength to keep from knocking at the door, but not enough to leave Warsaw. His morbid obsession, as he called it to himself, for Frau Hurvitz could be kept under by force of will, but he knew quite well that he was deceiving himself and that it was only fear of his conscience that was holding him back: the slightest encouragement would be enough to make him burst all bonds. The only thing to do was to leave Warsaw. But he was incapable of that; a cold fear of a world in which he would be quite alone overwhelmed him. At the mere thought of leaving Warsaw his feeling of childish helplessness awoke again; the dreadful feeling that he was deserted and abandoned paralyzed him completely, and so he stayed on.

Meanwhile the days slipped past without purpose or meaning. Nobody knew him and he knew nobody except his father's agent, who gave him money whenever he needed it. By day he wandered in the streets of the Jewish quarter, observing the bustle of commerce, and now and then he stopped to look at a junk-shop or to enter a courtyard on the Nalevki Boulevard. Because of his astrakhan cap and collar the Jews took him for a Russian merchant, dragged him into stores and workshops and offered him wares of every kind to buy; one would try to get him away from another, and they would squabble over him and wave their hands. Once he was hauled into a house where stolen goods were laid out, and an unusually sly fellow even coaxed him into a brothel. . . . Mirkin understood very little of all that was preached at him; his Russian made it difficult for him to get into touch with the people. When he tried to stammer out some Yiddish he was met by astounded and frightened glances; these people seemed to be terrified when some one they did not take for a Jew spoke Yiddish.

Vilna with its crooked little streets, its poverty-stricken Jews and its fiery exaltation on the high feast-days, had made a profound impression on Mirkin. But he could not say the same of Warsaw. The Jews in their long caftans and small hats with narrow brims seemed to him like soldiers in uniform and for that very reason made an unpleasant impression on him. He knew that it was only a superficial impression, but seen from the outside these Jews, constantly hurrying and scurrying, always worried, always shouting and gesticulating, were unattractive enough. And whenever he tried to ask them a question he never got a direct answer. They seemed both close and inquisitive and replied to every question with a suspicious counter-question. Mirkin realized quite well that behind the exterior of these people there was another, more sympathetic, more attractive life, but he could not get into touch with it; for him they were as he saw them. "There is no Jewish nation but this one." The words of Hurvitz the teacher recurred to him. So these were men of his own flesh and blood, rich and poor, good and bad alike; this was the Jewish poverty he had heard of, and here was his salvation. . . !

Yet he felt completely alien to them. So far as he was concerned they were a book with seven seals. "I am a complete stranger," he said to himself, cursing his education, his past life, his isolation. It seemed as if he, Zachary Mirkin, were a nation in himself, unique and self-engendered; he had no kin. He had lost his own world, and the world into which he was now seeking to thrust himself would have none of him. For ever and a day he seemed condemned to stand alone, to be attached to nothing, to belong nowhere.

So his determined flight from home now seemed to him incomprehensible, its purpose and intent more and more obscure. He was bored with his present idleness and felt like a schoolboy who has run away from school in a fit of temper. How long can such an excursion last? A week or a fortnight at most. For the schoolboy must needs be drawn back again to the master's cane.

In Petersburg a whip had always cracked behind him; in Petersburg there were his father, Olga Michailovna and Nina, his fiancée. Whatever he did there had had a direction, whether he liked it or not; he had merely had to toe a line that was already chalked out for him. Even though the further horizons of his life had been obscured he had always seen the next step to be taken; day after day there had been something for him to do. But here? How long could he go on like this?

He discussed his troubles with nobody save himself, and even in his self-communings he had fallen into the habit of formulating nothing in words: he merely felt and brooded. During his sleepless nights he had the maddest and most morbid notions: for instance, he often had the strange feeling that he and his body were two separate entities. Then he would speak to his own body as if it were a stranger, caressing and comforting it until it dawned on him at length how childish he was becoming. . . .

During this period, too, the suicidal impulses returned which had apparently vanished after his attempt to do away with himself in Petersburg. Every night he brought himself to book for the preceding day, and propping his downcast head on his hand summoned himself to the bar of his own judgment: "Why do I cling so desperately to life? Why can't I let myself merge into the All, into the unending eternity which is what I conceive death to be? My entrance into life was determined by the will of another, but my entrance into death can be decided by my own! Why do I hang on to life like a withered leaf on a tree, waiting till death comes of its own accord to cast me to the ground? Why should I not be master of my own will, if not in life then at least in death? And if I have not the courage to be my own master and vanish at my own behest into endless night, what right did I have to flee from the sordid bed that life offered me to lie on? Why did I ever leave my father, my betrothed, Olga Michailovna—and leave them, too, with the proud boast that I could not live with a heart stabbed through and through? If my heart is riddled like a sieve it is with sinful and morbid desires and feelings! I ought to go back like a foolish prodigal and beg them to forgive me and take me in again; let them give me the humblest of corners in their lives so long as they only take me in!"

This verdict upon himself remained with him when he awoke in the mornings and he rose from bed without knowing why or wherefore; helplessly he drifted and tossed on the waves of his will like a plank on the open sea.

But in the morning hours, when the demons of the night quitted him, his thoughts became clearer. Then he would lay the blame for his unrest and childish helplessness on his upbringing, his motherless childhood and solitary adolescence devoid of all allegiance and kinship. That did not indeed give him any grounds for hope and yet it had a certain effect—like all weak people he felt heartened at shifting the responsibility on to other people's shoulders. But he still saw no way out except for him to return humbly to the place he had fled from, to submit without resistance to the net that destiny had so mercilessly made ready to cast over him.

"It amounts to the same thing, after all," he told himself. "A life that isn't shaped by one's own will but merely decided by chance and luck is much the same thing as death. Here there is nobody to shield me from myself, from those latent and alien instincts that dwell in me and lie in wait like bandits to carry me off to their den. Who is there that can help me to conquer them?"

He saw nobody; he stood alone on a wild and dangerous track, ambushed by sinister shadows that crouched in dark corners like the shadows in the cellar he had seen in his dream.

What was he to do?

Flee! There was no other way out. But whither could he flee? Perhaps the same fate awaited him everywhere. How could a man flee from himself, when the dark demons of night were in his own bosom? Or could he face the darkness with courage and bravely fight it? Could he remain in Warsaw and take up the fight against himself, this time with more strength than before?

Mirkin saw that he would never find in himself the strength to break from the net, to escape the claws of his evil spirits. He wanted to believe, he needed to believe in some higher strength that could rescue him from himself, and in the dark night around him he groped to find it. He recalled the old Jew who had once spoken to him on a dark night in Petersburg about the dependence of one's own ego on the thoughts of the world. And then he remembered the discussion in the Hurvitzes' house. It dawned on him that the teacher and the young man they had called the Shachliner had really been speaking of the same universal force as the old Jew in Petersburg. "Yes! it exists, that higher strength, in one form or another; and it lives in the poor dwellings of the righteous, it shines out and guides the heart of humanity!" Now he could see it all clearly: what Hurvitz called logic shed its rays throughout the world, uniting the heads and hearts of such men as Hurvitz himself, the Shachliner, the old Jew in Petersburg, and many, many others; that force was guiding them all in their own way towards some great end that was known only to the higher, directing will. . . .

"There is a higher will to which we must all give allegiance. Those who refuse to acknowledge its power lose themselves in the abyss of their own darkness, devoured by the shadows that lie in wait within themselves." If he were to be saved from himself he must become a minute cog in the universal machine, a tiny thread in the great web that was being spun. For only a world-wide thought could govern the individual.

"Only those who know their way and advance fearlessly along it whose hearts are bound to the World-Will, who are guided by its mighty force towards the common goal. Shall I try to fit myself into the scheme? Shall I stay in Warsaw and day after day look fearlessly in the face of danger? Shall I be capable of it? Can I withstand temptation?"

He flung his arms wide in the darkness and prayed to God: "Rescue me, rescue me from myself and shelter me in Thy Will as Thou hast done with others... !"

CHAPTER IX

MATERNAL COMPASSION

One evening when the sky and streets were drizzling wet Zachary stood once more before the house in which Frau Hurvitz lived; the pavement was filthy and crowded with hurrying people. He stood there because he did not know where else to go. In all the wide world this was the only house he was familiar with, and its occupants, whom he had seen but once in his life, were the only friends he possessed. Since he had come to terms with himself and decided to return to Petersburg his conscience no longer restrained him, and as a drunkard always finds justification for his weakness so Mirkin now found a plausible excuse for his visit: to say good-by. With beating heart he hurried up the badly lit staircase and rang the bell. It was some time before his ring was answered, but finally the door opened and in the dusk of the lobby a girl's shadow fell comfortingly upon him.

As he entered the familiar sitting-room he had an impression of warmth and festal splendor. The girl who had opened the door was Helene, the eldest daughter. He had obviously interrupted her, for she held a book in her hand with her forefinger between two pages, and she looked at him with surprise and bewilderment as if she had been roused from a dream. All at once she apparently remembered who he was and smiled: he could not see her eyes in the twilight, but the smile seemed to flit from her hair across her face. "Please do sit down. Mother will be here in a minute. Excuse me——" And with that she vanished, book and all, into the next room.

Zachary sat down at the well-remembered table. With some surprise he looked round the room. Nothing was changed, everything stood in the same place; the little book-case with the glass doors, the broad sofa of blue plush framed in red mahogany and battered by long service, chairs, cushioned and uncushioned, belonging to different suites of furniture and dating from different periods, some of them still looking trustworthy and others not at all, cheap reproductions in narrow frames hanging on the walls—everything was exactly as it had been on his first visit, and yet there was a novel air of warmth and festivity about the room which pleasantly surprised him. Was it an effect of the contrast between this comfortable home and the homelessness of his own soul? Mirkin could not account for the festal impression. Exactly as on his first visit the floor was scoured clean and strewn with yellow sand, but this time it all looked so much more stately, as if transformed by a new radiance, as if something had happened that made even the furniture feel solemn. But as he gazed round more intently Mirkin noticed that the table was covered with a white cloth on which stood two candles burning in polished brass candlesticks. Two cakes were on the table, covered with muslin, nor was the silver sugar-bowl lacking. He understood at last: it was the two candles that gave the festal radiance to the room. These were Sabbath candles and this was the Sabbath.

For although Frau Hurvitz regarded herself as a progressive woman, and although her husband was notorious in Warsaw as a "renegade" who seduced pious Jewish youths from the straight path, Rachel-Leah could not bring herself to deny her upbringing and to ignore the Jewish feast-days that involved her often enough in conflict with her "progressive" views, and yet—on Friday evening the Sabbath began for Rachel-Leah. To deny that would have meant for her renouncing something that betokened a higher life.

It was not long before she herself came in, and Zachary heard her firm step and her gay assured voice: "Where have you been hiding all this time? I began to think you must have gone off without bidding us good-by."

Like the room Frau Hurvitz, too, was transformed on this occasion. Her figure, clad in shining black satin, was more erect, more stately, more matronly than usual.

Once more Mirkin beheld the freshly-laundered lace collar that encircled her white neck, and a string of coral beads caught his eye. Her face looked fuller, gayer, clearer than before; her black eyes were larger and brighter; even her neatly parted hair seemed more firmly rooted to her head; her ripe bosom was rounder. Zachary eyed her with furtively desirous glances, and his mustached upper lip grew plaintive like that of a suffering child. . . . He made no reply to her query, but, avoiding her eyes, said with a double intention that his face betrayed: "You look very festive tonight."

"Why, don't you know that it's Friday evening? We're anything but pious and yet we always light candles on Friday evening. It's just a habit," she concluded shamefacedly, as if to excuse herself. "I'm glad you've come tonight. You'll have your share of the fish."

"Many thanks! I've never spent Friday evening in a Jewish house. In my childhood I can remember only the Christian festivals, and our maid decorated the house for them."

"But where have you been all this time? Why haven't you let us set eyes on you?"

"I haven't been feeling well."

"Then why didn't you let us know?"

Again Zachary was unable to reply. His eyes bored into her neck and the opening of her dress at the throat; his ears burned like his cheeks; his breath labored audibly. His furtive glances and his embarrassment infected Frau Hurvitz; she understood what they meant. Her cheeks began to burn, too, her bosom rose and fell quickly. With a laugh that could not conceal the trembling of her heart and her voice she said: "You're looking at me very queerly tonight!"

Zachary opened his lips with an effort and managed to say, smiling inanely: "You're looking so different tonight, Frau Hurvitz."

"Why, how do I look?" asked Frau Hurvitz anxiously, without quite understanding her own anxiety.

"I don't really know," replied Zachary, "so womanly, so motherly. . . ."

"Listen to me, Pan Mirkin, I must tell you something: for all your black beard you're just a child as far as I can see, a child that still needs the breast."

She was alarmed by her own words and blushed scarlet. Zachary sat as if turned to stone.

"Aren't you ashamed of yourself?" she went on. "I'm an old woman. A young man shouldn't look at old women; that's what young women are here for."

Zachary gnawed at his finger-nails in his extreme embarrassment.

"Forgive me, forgive me," he murmured in abasement. Everything reeled before his eyes and he did not know what to do with himself. They were both silent for several minutes.

Frau Hurvitz regarded him compassionately as if she knew all his sorrows, and began to speak in a warm and motherly voice: "If you would only begin to do something worth while you would soon forget all this nonsense. It's idleness breeds that kind of thing. In Petersburg you had evidently plenty of time to go in for nonsense like that."

"What am I to do?"

"Find some honest occupation, and do it this very night! You said once that that was why you wanted to come to Warsaw."

"I'm so unhappy."

"You're not unhappy; you only imagine you are; you're only spoiled. Your nurses must have spoiled you far too much. You'll have to be weaned from that like an infant. And if it can't be done in any other way you'll have to be smacked," she concluded, smiling.

"Don't drive me away," implored Zachary with yearning eyes that gazed out heart-breakingly from his pale face, those yearning eyes that could make such a deep impression on women.

"Why should I drive you away?" She was affected by his helpless look and her voice sounded tender and comforting. "You haven't done anything bad."

"I have nobody, nobody in the whole world," lamented Zachary, "and I'm so wretched."

"You're not the only one; there are plenty of motherless children! Have you any claim to more than the others, simply because you were brought up in a wealthy house where people gave in to all your moods?"

"You are right," whispered Zachary.

Then they both fell silent. When they found words again they spoke in low voices; their words sank almost to a whisper beneath the light of the Sabbath candles in the warm corner by the stove.

Zachary hardly knew what he was saying. He sat bent forward, feeling that blows were being rained upon him. But they were a comfort, for they came from a mother's hand. . . .

Suddenly Frau Hurvitz rose and as she turned to go she asked: "You're not angry with me, are you?"

"Not in the least, on the contrary—I'm thankful to you," he stammered, like a child who has just been chastised.

"Why should you be thankful? Because I've given you a good dressing down?" Frau Hurvitz smiled.

"I'm thankful for everything." He made a deep bow.

"There's something else I must tell you, Pan Mirkin," she said with a provocative smile. "You're a very dangerous young man, especially for elderly women. You must be more sparing of your boyish poses, for I'm only a weak woman after all"—and she ran her hand gently over his hair and went to the kitchen.

Mirkin started up with the idea of going away. He put on his coat and went into the kitchen to say good-by to her.

"But where are you going?" she asked in astonishment, busy with the fish.

"I think I should go now . . . Enough for tonight. . . ." he stammered, flushing with embarrassment.

"You're to stay here and have some fish! After that we'll have a talk with the Shachliner. Take off your coat and sit down!"

Zachary obeyed her like a boy who had been violently upbraided.

CHAPTER X

SABBATH MUSIC

IT HAS been remarked already that Hurvitz the teacher was a free-thinker and notorious in the small Jewish towns of Poland as a seducer of pious youth, but whenever Friday evening came he felt impelled to bathe and change his underwear as he had been accustomed to do from childhood. The blood of his forebears cried aloud in him, and, however sternly he called to mind the rationalistic explanations of how the Sabbath and other Jewish festivals had come into being, he could not help himself: whenever a holy day approached the ancient customs resumed their sway over his blood, and he was filled with the obscure mystical feeling that is evoked by the Sabbath.

As soon as he set foot in the big living-room after his last lesson on Friday evening he felt the Sabbath peace that his wife had spread over the house like a fair linen cloth. A feeling akin to exaltation awoke in him, and he was haunted by the desire to stand only once more in the silk caftan and fur-bordered Sabbath cap of the Chassids and welcome the angels that filled his dwelling and greet them with the old traditional salutation: "Sholem aleikem." He took off his spectacles, carefully wiping their misted glasses, and prowled up and down the room; gradually, against his own will, he sank more and more into a Sabbath mood. Solomon Hurvitz was fundamentally a religious man; he had changed one faith for another without losing a jot of the believer's purity and simplicity of soul. The complete faith with which as a young man he had held to the truth of the Jewish religion and the power of the Rabbi had later been transferred to the "Enlightenment" and the power of knowledge. He was firmly convinced that science and learning had laid the sure foundations of all truth and that it was impossible to doubt their doctrine or deviate from it; if anything was not yet clear it would be revealed in the further development of the more specialized sciences; the final balance could not be assessed until the human spirit stood on that supreme height which would be attained in some glorious future when all the fountains of knowledge were unsealed. Until then it was the duty of every man to help on the great work and to serve the cause of progress with all his might as once he had served God. A man could achieve nothing higher than knowledge; it would lead him upwards to his own purification. The partaker of knowledge not only drank from the source of all creation but shared in the work of creation itself, helping to unseal and develop the hidden forces of Nature. Therefore the intellect was the unique and sacred endowment of humanity—its promise of heaven. Through the intellect man was linked to the life of the universe, to the whole of Nature; it was therefore his first and supreme duty to enroll himself and his intellect in the service of knowledge and evolution.

Whenever Hurvitz rose to such lofty flights of thought he went over to his bookcase and fingered the pages of his books. During the week he had little time to dip into them, however he might yearn to do so. But on Friday evenings, before supper was ready, he loved to pick this book or that from the shelf and devote himself to it like a well-conducted Jew. His love for books was a passion which had already deprived his children of many a pair of shoes and cost the house more than one sack of coals. He believed in his books, and yet his daily toil left him no time to study them as he would have liked. So he let no spare moment go by without at least caressing them or browsing on a page or two; yet in general he could never enjoy this indulgence for long, since the hands of the clock were always warning him that it was time for his next lesson. On this occasion it was Rachel-Leah who cut him short.

She had been standing behind him for some time without venturing to remind him that the children were waiting for their supper and that "the crowd" would soon be coming in. Rachel-Leah's respect for her husband was most in evidence whenever he stood at his book-case; in her eyes he was then absorbed in a holy task which she dared not interrupt. Yet her Sabbath was dear to her heart, and not less important was the fact that the fish would be spoiled.

"Solomon, the fish is on the table. The children are waiting. I've filled a tub of warm water for you; go and have a wash," she said, in the gentlest voice of which she was capable.

When he had cleansed himself of the sweat and filth of the week, and put on the clean underwear that Rachel-Leah had spent half Thursday night in darning by the light of her lamp, the teacher felt more than ever in a Sabbath mood; indeed, he even felt moved to sing once more the traditional Sabbath psalms. On these evenings, therefore, he liked above all to read aloud to his family the poems of Mickiewicz or Slowacki, and in recent times he had included the works of Jewish writers like Bialik or Perez, which he either translated from the Hebrew or read in the original Yiddish. As might have been expected, he never omitted to add his own commentary on the poems that he declaimed.

When the master of the house entered the living-room the family was already gathered round the white-spread table. In honor of the Sabbath every member of it had made the acquaintance of Rachel-Leah's bath-tub, and the girls had also washed their hair according to program. On this occasion Mirkin was to share in the Sabbath fish. The Shachliner stayed away on principle; he disapproved of the Sabbath ceremonies, calling them reactionary and *bourgeois*. "It's only the fanaticism of other people that we cry out against, but we cling to our own," he reproached the teacher. He would not show face until after supper, when "the crowd" came in.

"The crowd" was a circle of young intellectuals who had gathered round the teacher. Most of them had run away from synagogues and Talmud schools, and a few had even left their wives behind them. To Hurvitz, and to Rachel-Leah even more, they were all indebted for having been able to settle in the city. Some of them had qualified as elementary teachers and gave private lessons or taught in the modernized Jewish Bible schools that were beginning to increase in strength; others with great toil and privation were preparing themselves for a high school course. But the majority, including the Shachliner, had not advanced very far in their studies, having been drawn into politics and into the life of the party, to which they devoted their lives and sacrificed their careers.

Hurvitz himself had never had much patience with political activity, and since his eldest son's arrest he had regarded it as the enemy of human culture. Despite the idealism and personal self-sacrifice for the common good which he could observe in the political struggle, he stuck to it that the liberation of humanity was not to be won by fighting but could be achieved solely through knowledge. "Once the human spirit is fully enlightened," he used to say, "evil will vanish; knowledge is the Messiah of humanity, and therefore we must all give it our allegiance. It's not the systems that are good or bad"—this was his favorite statement—"but only the people who use them; there's no such thing as an absolute 'good' or 'bad,' there is only knowledge and ignorance. A man who possesses knowledge is already ennobled; he may do evil once in a while but only by force of circumstance, never deliberately." Of course the teacher had no inkling of the secret ties that bound the members of his own family, with Rachel-Leah in the forefront, to the revolutionary movement.

On Friday evenings Solomon Hurvitz permitted no political discussion. These hours were sacred to the "Sabbath songs," as Rachel-Leah called the recital of poetic works which her husband liked to declaim before his friends and his children. Thus the Friday evenings had been turned into regular family evenings, and the homeless young men who came in could enjoy at least once a week the comforting atmosphere of a family and the homely warmth of domestic life. There were many differences among them, but all who came to the Hurvitzes' house on Friday evenings were united by the similarity of their fates into one family, and all were drawn to the house where they had been given the first spoonful of soup and heard the first kindly word on their first timid appearance in the great, strange city of Warsaw where their future was still obscure.

While supper was still proceeding the teacher felt impelled to read aloud—for at least the hundredth time—the great improvisation from Mickiewicz's "Lament for the Dead," which he always did whenever he felt more than usually exalted. In the days of Czardom this book was forbidden in Russian Poland, and Hurvitz kept it carefully hidden, together with other works bewailing the tragedy of Poland and summoning its people to action, works like "Konrad" by Mickiewicz, "November Night" by Wyspianski, and similar productions. No pious Jew ever treasured the Torah more reverently than Hurvitz treasured these books that had been printed on thin paper and smuggled into the country. They gave him courage, faith and enthusiasm in hours of depression; they were his subject-matter on Friday evenings when he was in an exalted mood. This time he was a little disturbed by the presence of Mirkin, whom he supposed to be ignorant of Polish. But his desire to read aloud became at length so overpowering that he brushed aside all considerations of hospitality and drew from his pocket the book which was waiting in readiness there. Besides, it was only at table that he had the chance of reading the "Lament," for "the crowd" which arrived after supper preferred other songs and other poems.

He began to read, his voice at first low, then increasing in resonance and trembling with sorrowful emotion:

"... O God, all Poland in the fresh bloom of its youth
Lies groaning under the heavy hand of Herod!
Yonder I see long white roads stretching away,
Crossing each other blindly in wastes of snow,
All tending northwards. In that alien North like confluent rivers
The many roads meet before one iron gate.
As rivers plunge headlong to an abyss
So do they vanish in a nameless sea.
And look! O'er all these roads there hasten on
An endless stream of wagons, endless,
Driven like cloud-rack, driven in the one direction.
O God—it is our children,
Driven north, driven out, O God!
What is to become of them? Wilt Thou suffer them
To be driven away, to be cast out, to be cast down,
To be cut off in their youth until all perish. . ?"

Hurvitz stopped. There was a lump in his throat, but he did not want to give himself away before a stranger. With a jesting air he turned to Mirkin: "All that's about the country you come from, Pan Mirkin—Siberia."

Mirkin flushed guiltily as if he were responsible for Russia's cruelty; he could hear a savage undertone in the teacher's words.

"But, Solomon, Herr Mirkin doesn't understand Polish." Rachel-Leah sought to smooth away her husband's discourtesy.

"Oh, but I do—not every word, of course."

"How's that?"

"As soon as I came to Poland I thought it my duty to learn Polish."

"Quite right—unfortunately there are others who don't do that and only strengthen our enemies," cried the teacher.

The fact that Mirkin was learning Polish raised him enormously in Hurvitz's estimation. He suddenly applied all his powers to explaining the situation to Mirkin, like a missionary anxious to make a proselyte. With a zeal that seemed to indicate sheer physical pleasure he poured out to Mirkin the whole tragedy of the Polish nation, the struggle for freedom in 1863, the fate of the rebels, their banishment to Siberia, and the meaning of Mickiewicz's poem. Having found a new listener in Mirkin he enjoyed this heaven-sent opportunity of giving voice once more to his concern for Poland's sufferings, fate, and hopes for the future.

The children had heard it all more than a dozen times already and knew it too well to listen with any interest. They had to make an effort to remain quiet, and contained themselves only out of respect and fear for their father. But just when the teacher was in the full flight of his eloquence, celebrating in flaming words the idealism of the rebels who had made the great sacrifice for their fatherland and "reddened the white snowfields with their blood," the schoolboy David whispered to his mother most disrespectfully: "What's all this rot about their idealism? The rebels turned into fat capitalists and grabbed all the wealth of the Siberian mines and exploited the Siberian proletariat for all they were worth."

"Hold your tongue!" his mother reprimanded him in a low voice. "Your father'll hear you."

Meanwhile the teacher's enthusiasm had reached its climax; he was aware of nobody but Zachary, whom he was trying to fill at one swoop with all his own devotion to the cause of Poland. He brought Zachary's chair nearer to himself and began to read another passage from the improvisation. His voice rose higher and higher and his eyes shone with enthusiasm, while he emphasized every single word of the poem.

". . . The Fatherland is my spirit's flesh and blood,
And should it die my body will die too.
I and the Fatherland are one.
In sorrow and in suffering I live
For millions of my people.
I look on my unhappy Fatherland
As a son looks on a captive father
Shamefully racked upon the wheel.
I feel the sorrow of my whole nation
As a mother feels in her own body
The suffering of her child.
So do I suffer and am racked with pain . . ."

He stopped, leaned his head on his hand and shut his eyes, as if withdrawn into another, spiritual Fatherland. . . .

But the schoolboy muttered: "I'd like to know if the Fatherland will buy me a pair of trousers when I need them."

"You need them now," retorted his sister in a whisper.

"The Fatherland only acknowledges those of its children whose bellies are full," went on David beneath his breath.

"Will you stop it?" His mother secretly gave him a slap. "Your father's only singing his Sabbath psalms!"

The bell rang. With a long-drawn "Good Sabbath!" the teacher's oldest friend, Solomon Königstein, came into the room.

Although Hurvitz was a violent opponent of Zionism and every mention of Palestine stirred him to fury, he could not live without his good old friend Königstein, who had been from the very beginning a faithful adherent of the Zionist movement and supported its modern developments with enthusiasm. Every encounter between the two friends ended in a catastrophe; they began with a debate in which all the old arguments were trotted out on either side, but the discussions soon branched into personal insults and were finally broken off in rage. Yet neither man could get along without the other. They might have been near to knifing each other, but the very next day would see them thick as thieves again, returning a borrowed book, or discussing the interpretation of some obscure piece of philosophy, or studying Jewish history, or even simply pouring out their sorrows to each other; from time to time they lent each other a little money when it was needed, or supplied mutual advice.

Their friendship had something touching in it. After their usual quarrel in which they heaped abuse on each other's sensitive heads, the door would not still have ceased vibrating from the slam given it by Königstein on his departure before Hurvitz would turn anxiously to his wife: "Rachel-Leah, I'm rather worried about Solomon today; did you notice how ill he's looking? What can be done about him?" This remark would be accompanied by a sorrowful head-shake. "Is it any wonder that he should look ill when you're always trying to claw each other to pieces?" was Frau Hurvitz's regular answer.

The two friends shared not only their halfpence but even their books, which were more precious to them than life. At festival times they presented little volumes to each other. When peace reigned between them, when what Rachel-Leah called "this Zionist nonsense" was not working them into a fever, they would sit side by side and talk of their families, their professions, their daily joys and sorrows, which, like everybody else, they felt the need of communicating to someone. And, if either of them was in trouble, the first person he turned to was his friend; indeed, they confided in each other things that they would not have told their own wives.

"Good Sabbath!" called out a friendly but hollow voice, a voice that came from diseased lungs. A tall man walked over to the table, a middle-aged man with a short, graying beard and shoulders that stooped a little, obviously from too much sitting. The rounded back, with nothing to hold it up, was bent like a reed. Two red patches burned on the man's cheeks, and his frail skin was stretched tight over his cheek-bones; his unkempt beard made a bridge between two deep hollows on either side of his prominent Adam's apple.

"What's the news, Solomon?" asked the teacher.

"I've something for you to see—something that will please you."

"First let me introduce you: this is Herr Solomon Königstein, and this is Herr Zachary Mirkin from Petersburg," interrupted Frau Hurvitz.

"Ah, the young man you were telling us about, Rachel-Leah! Very glad to meet you." And with these words he stretched out to the visitor an unnaturally long and dreadfully thin hand.

This formality over, the two friends were left together undisturbed. Solomon produced a cutting out of a Hebrew newspaper from Palestine and held it under the teacher's nose.

"There, look at that . . ." he cried with a gleam of triumph in his lively eyes.

Hurvitz put on his spectacles and read the excerpt first in Hebrew, then translated it aloud into Yiddish for the benefit of the others; his good-humored scorn made him look merry.

"Listen, listen to this earth-shaking news! In the village of Chedera two cows have calved; one calf has been named 'Hashchorah' (Black) and the other 'Hanaavah' (Comely). And the newspaper takes the trouble to print stuff like that!"

"It's not just the calves; it's the names," cried Solomon gleefully. "One is 'Hashchorah' and the other is 'Hanaavah,' don't you see? That's delightful!"

The teacher regarded his friend mockingly and shook his head thoughtfully.

"Solomon, Solomon, you're nothing but an old baby; if two cows have calved in Palestine must all the Jews in the world hear of it? How many cows have calves in Poland every day?"

"But 'Hashchorah' and 'Hanaavah'—don't you see? That's from the Song of Solomon, that's bringing back the times of the Bible and the Prophets!"

"What are you thinking of? If a cow calves in Palestine, has that to be reported at once in a newspaper? Truly an important event if a cow in Palestine manages to produce a calf," laughed the Shachliner, who had meanwhile emerged from the adjoining room.

"Aha! You're there, are you?" cried Königstein. "But I tell you that, if a single cow in Palestine has a calf, it's an important event for the whole Jewish nation. Every calf in Palestine is worth more for the preservation of the Jews than scores of Jews in the Dispersion."—The speaker's cheeks burned redder than ever as he shot out these words violently.

"So in your opinion one calf in Palestine is worth more than any

Jew in the Dispersion? Now we have it; that's the Zionist credo!" shouted the teacher.

"Have you started again? Can't this argument be a little more quietly conducted?" suggested Frau Hurvitz.

"Not any and every Jew," conceded Solomon, "but as far as Jews like that one are concerned"—he indicated the Shachliner—"a calf is certainly much more important."

"Here's a fellow-enthusiast of yours," said the teacher, pointing to Mirkin and speaking less aggressively seeing that Königstein had confined his animadversions to the Shachliner, who was a general scapegoat in the house. "He wants to go to Palestine too and break stones; for that's all one could do in a barren land like that."

"Don't you let him frighten you off it," said Königstein, laying his long hand on Zachary's shoulder to encourage him. "And I tell you, Solomon, you'll all end up in that stony country yet! It's the only country we possess on God's earth. We own nothing but these stones. And you'll come to them yet, as well as scoffers like him," and again he indicated the Shachliner.

"We'll let you keep the stones, Solomon; you can have our share of them, too, if you like," retorted the teacher.

"Hashchorah vehanaavah," murmured Solomon, shaping the words tenderly and paying no heed to his tormentors. "One needs to have a certain sensitiveness to understand the significance of these words"—he turned to the Shachliner—"they're a quotation from the Song of Solomon."

"Yes, I know: 'I am black but hideous,' " grinned the Shachliner, quoting an old schoolboy's parody.

Meanwhile "the crowd" was assembling. From the next room came a young man known in the house as "Itschele." He was out at work all the week and so was never visible, but he was the second lodger in the Hurvitzes' house, sharing the "High School" room with the Shachliner.

Itschele had seen a good bit of the world. His studies had taken him to Switzerland, Belgium and France, but he had grown convinced that study was a useless occupation and had become a bookbinder, having learned this trade on his travels. He was very proud of being a hand-worker and seemed to think that the whole Jewish nation should applaud him for it. He felt that it gave him at least the right to tell people what he thought of them at the first meeting, to recommend every one to enter a workshop, and to refer on every possible occasion to his trade. "I'm only an ordinary working man," was his refrain, and he announced the fact as if he should get at least a medal for it. Once upon a time Itschele had been ambitious, but he had been hindered from following up his plans by a too-early marriage; he never ceased to lament that he had been yoked to matrimony too soon. "If it weren't for my wife and children I'd have had my doctorate long ago," he was fond of remarking.

Itschele had brought with him a young Chassid in a ragged caftan, who could not be persuaded to take off his ceremonial hat. He was a pious working-man who drudged all week in a filthy stockinette manufactory in the courtyard of the Hurvitzes' tenement, and had recently been seeking admission to the teacher's circle, since his faith in the Rabbi was beginning to waver. Of course efforts had been made to "convert" him, that is to say, to detach him from his Rabbi and turn him into a free-thinker, but the Chassid had long withstood all temptation; it was only when he became a worker and saw and felt the injustice around him that the basis of his faith began to be undermined. The lives of his brothers, the Chassid workmen, as well as his own life stirred up in him the old question of good and evil, and he was now seeking an answer to it, seeking a new faith. Perhaps it might be discovered here, in this circle? Itschele had brought him several times already to the teacher's Friday evenings, and the young man always listened intently to the "doctrine" of his new Rabbi. He was desirous of coming to some understanding with the teacher, whom he took to be a Rabbi of a modern school, but could not summon up the courage to address him. So he lived in continual conflict with himself. While he listened to the discussions the thought kept on running through his mind: "There's something lacking here: this isn't like the Rabbi's teaching. There's no real joy; and that shows that they have no faith. . . ."

The recent newcomer for whom Frau Hurvitz had found a lodging —his name was Gedalje—had also quitted his comfortable quarters with Pan Kviatkovski to put in an appearance. He was almost unrecognizable. The beard and the side-curls had vanished; the caftan had given place to a Prince Albert frock coat. His long neck seemed still longer and displayed an Adam's apple of alarming size. The teacher had a high opinion of Gedalje, and since hearing him read his drama had taken great pains with him, devoting half an hour daily of his scanty spare time to studying the Polish classics with the new recruit. Hurvitz translated and expounded each word of the texts as if he were dealing with a commentary on the Bible or the Talmud. And Rachel-Leah was proud of her "foundling," who seemed to have been born under a very fortunate star. He had, indeed, as people said, the devil's own luck; not only did he have a room in Pan Kviatkovski's flat, but more food than he could eat as well, for Frau Antonia, the housekeeper, was literally cramming him with pork in the secret hope that he might turn into a Christian. Gedalje, however, whose stomach had not been trained to deal with such rich meat, had to retire after every meal to relieve its oppression; he would have given his life for a plate of *borscht,* the comforting beetroot-soup of his native town. But every now and then Frau Hurvitz regaled him with a plateful.

The Hurvitzes' living-room was soon humming like a Talmud school. Everybody was arguing at the same time with violent gesticulations. Two schools of opinion could be discerned, one of which was centered in the teacher and his friend Königstein, who, although they differed profoundly on the question of Zionism, were at one in their estimation of the value of enlightenment; they adhered firmly to the cause of "Civilization and Progress" and prized knowledge and culture beyond all happiness on earth or in heaven. The opposing group, which was of recent origin, comprised the Shachliner and Itschele the bookbinder, and preached hand-work as an ideal. Both camps fought obstinately for the new recruits from the provinces; the older contingent wanting to enlist them for culture, the younger for the workshop. One would be mistaken in supposing that the two factions showed very much tolerance for each other.

The young Chassid workman drifted from one group to the other and listened to the arguments. He wanted to ask a question of Hurvitz, whom he regarded with awe, but for a long time he could not screw himself up to it; finally he pulled himself together and with great deference advanced to the teacher and said timidly: "Excuse me, Pan Hurvitz, I'd like to ask you something. I have been listening to you. . . . It's all very reasonable of course, very fine . . . righteousness is an important matter . . . but all the same . . . I'd like to know . . . I'd like to put a question . . ."

Hurvitz, whose patience as a teacher was remarkable so long as Zionism did not come into question, encouraged the young man amiably: "Ask away, I shall be glad to answer you."

"I only want to ask one thing. . . . In your opinion, now, what do you think . . . is there any reward for us in a future world or not? Is there guilt and expiation in a future world or not? I've heard everything discussed in this circle except the main thing, the great fundamental question, what happens *after* our life; about that I've heard nothing at all."

The teacher sat petrified; this was a question for which he was not prepared. He drew the inquirer into a corner, made him sit down beside him, and summoned all his pedagogical patience. In stating his views he fell involuntarily into the Talmud sing-song which he had caught from the young Chassid. "All the knowledge we have," he began cautiously, "refers to this world. From the other world no one has ever returned to tell us whether it exists or not. But once humanity possesses enough knowledge and culture, once wisdom has spread like an ocean over the whole world, then, my dear friend, you can be assured that we won't need to look for Paradise in another world! Then all men will be brothers: national distinctions will vanish, frontiers will be swept away; every man will understand his neighbor. After our life Paradise will be in *this* world."

The young Chassid workman listened attentively, accompanying the teacher's words with an ecstatic rocking of his body. Then he grew melancholy and said with a compassionate sigh: "But if there's nothing to expect from a future world, what's the good of everything? Is *this* world"—there was mockery in his voice—"the kind of world in which it's worth a man's while to live?"

CHAPTER XI

KITCHEN SONGS

LITTLE by little the discussion died away, for "the crowd" began to drift into the kitchen, where there was food for the body as well as for the mind. Frau Hurvitz was now in her element and zealously dispensed tea and cakes she had specially baked that day for her guests. This collation had always its musical accompaniment; Itschele, a lover of singing, brought a new Yiddish song from the workshop regularly every Friday evening. The "boys" sat on the small kitchen chairs or on the floor if there was no room elsewhere, with Rachel-Leah, in her ample apron, gayly throned in the middle. Itschele sang the verses and the others joined in the refrain. The Shachliner, who could not sing a note, beat time like a conductor with his crippled arm. Besides him Pan Kviatkovski's new lodger and Mirkin and Frau Hurvitz's children, the two girls, and David the schoolboy had all settled down in the kitchen. The teacher himself remained in the other room; he objected strongly to the Yiddish that "the crowd" brought into the house, since it corrupted the correct Polish pronunciation of his children, but he could make no headway against it. Yet although he had given up the struggle, the times being too much for him, he held himself aloof.

Itschele led off one song after another, first the Yiddish folksongs that had a great vogue in Frau Hurvitz's kitchen, and then revolutionary songs, including the "Cradle song" that was very popular in those days and was sung in all the workshops:

"My child, my child,
Grow up and help your brothers
To fight for right and liberty.
My child, my child,
Grow up and help the others
To free our land from tyranny."

Itschele's new contribution this week was a weaving song from Lodz that had a strong appeal:

"Russia, we are weaving
A shroud, a shroud,
We twist around each silken thread
A threefold curse . . .

Weaving, weaving, weaving,
A shroud, a shroud for you."

The songs fired the singers to enthusiasm. Frau Hurvitz began to clap time with her hands, while the Shachliner took up the melody. He sang louder and louder, more and more out of tune, until he lost his place altogether and was several bars behind the others. Young David, who had but recently learned Yiddish, fought a hard battle with the unpronounceable words and finally contented himself with humming an accompaniment to the tune. The last item on the program was the great song of triumph:

"Then raise the scarlet standard high,
Within its shade we'll live and die!
Let cowards flinch, and traitors sneer,
We'll keep the Red Flag flying here."

While these forbidden songs were being chanted in the kitchen the two friends, Hurvitz and Königstein, sat in the living-room beside the little bookcase, lovingly fingering its contents and carrying on an earnest conversation.

"Do you know what I've been thinking?" began Königstein. "I've made up my mind to take a trip over there after Easter, God willing." (This extremely "unmodern" interjection was always cropping up in the conversation of the two "enlighteners.") "I'll go alone this time, for I only want to see how things are getting on; but perhaps I could find something to do."

The teacher looked astounded. This time, however, he made no attempt at a counter-thrust, for he could tell by the ring of Königstein's words that his friend was deeply in earnest, and so he merely inquired with an undertone of sympathy: "What could you do there? They don't need Hebrew teachers in Palestine."

"Teachers! I wasn't thinking of teaching, but of laboring in the fields with spade and plow."

Hurvitz stared at his friend and opened his mouth; but he saw the red flush on Königstein's cheeks, the fire of enthusiasm in his eyes, the profound solemnity of his expression, and so he uttered nothing but a deep sigh. This was the first concession he had ever made to the subject of Palestine, and he did it out of no regard for that country, but merely because he was concerned and sorrowful for his friend.

"What's your opinion, Solomon?" asked Königstein.

Hurvitz tried to find the right words and a tone that would hurt the other as little as possible.

"Well, how would that suit your lung? I mean, what would . . .?" He did not finish the sentence.

"My lung? It's not my lung that'll be the difficulty! Why, you idiot, Palestine will cure it—a man I know there wrote me that they had had consumptives whose lives weren't worth a snap of the fingers and the open-air labor cured them! You'll see, Solomon; you'll see me yet digging the fields of Judah; I'll cultivate the soil of Palestine with my own hands"—Königstein extended two meager arms whose emaciation was pitiful to behold—"you'll see, I'm healthy enough . . ." a severe and lengthy fit of coughing interrupted him.

The teacher sat silent, reflectively and ruefully he eyed his friend; he looked at the red patches on his cheeks, listened to the coughing, and said after a long pause: "Why shouldn't you be as fit for field work as anybody else? It's not farm-laborers that are needed for that now-a-days; there are technical inventions to do all the work, agricultural machines that need only common-sense and skill. That's how they farm in America."

"Solomon, listen to me," Königstein was so happy that he was near falling on his friend's neck—"if I can scrape up a hundred roubles, only a hundred roubles, I'll leave some of it behind for my wife and children and set off to Palestine to see what's happening. When I read about how they go out to work there singing in the mornings, I can't sit still in my chair! I want to see it with my own eyes before I die. Oh, God!" In his excitement he forgot his renegade principles and uttered the tabooed word with his hands before his eyes.

The teacher ignored this sin against "enlightenment" and encouraged him with heartening words: "And why shouldn't you realize your ideal? After all, Palestine isn't at the back of beyond in some mythical country. How far is it now-a-days from Odessa to Palestine? But tell me, are you really in earnest about it?"

"Solomon, I can't stand this place any longer. I simply can't. This life suffocates me."

"When do you think of starting?"

"Immediately after Easter—even if I have to walk all the way. I'll turn everything into money that I can do without."

"The journey isn't so very dear." The teacher, too, had now thrown his principles to the winds. "How much does it cost, taking everything into account? You should certainly go. Whether you stay there or not—at least you should have a look at what's being done! I couldn't think of it, for me it doesn't matter; but you ought to go."

"You would like to go, to! Believe me, you would go too if it were only half possible! You could have a look at it, too."

"Maybe I would"—the teacher was now agreeing with his friend in everything—"it wouldn't make me *trefe,* anyhow."

"Solomon, my dear friend!" Königstein fell on the teacher's neck. "Let us go together! Let us go together! Do you remember how we used to sit in Beth-Hamidrash and learn in the Talmud the laws for tithing the harvest? Solomon, the times of which the Talmud spoke have returned again! Jews are cultivating the soil of Palestine and tithing the harvests and observing the Sabbath year of rest. Two little calves are frisking in a byre, and one is called 'Hashchorah' and the other 'Hanaavah.' ... Let us go together, Solomon!"

The teacher decided that he had let his sympathy run away with him; he felt uneasily that he had gone too far, and quickly shook himself free.

"Listen to me, Solomon, leave me out of it where Palestine is concerned! You say you must go, and I agree. Since the madness is in you and can't be got rid of, go, and go in peace. As far as I can I'll help you. But leave me out of it! What has it to do with me?"

"I fear, Solomon, it has a lot to do with you!" returned Königstein, shaking his finger menacingly at his friend. . . .

When Hurvitz was left alone he arraigned himself; had he not sinned against Progress, and could he reconcile it with his conscience that he had been so weak, that he had not at once decisively opposed the "reactionary" step which his friend was contemplating? But, remembering the red patches on his friend's cheeks and the light in his eyes as he uttered the names of the two calves, the teacher made a resigned gesture with his hand. That was the first crime against Progress with which Hurvitz the teacher had ever burdened his conscience.

In the kitchen revolutionary songs were still being chanted with all the fervor of enthusiasm. When the teacher overheard the dreadful words "Russia" and "Red Flag" he rose quickly, went into the kitchen, and warned the choir: "Can't you sing a little less loudly? There are police spies everywhere!"

This chastened the vocalists, and gradually the singing ceased entirely. Frau Hurvitz now found an opportunity for a few words with her newest protégé, Pan Kviatkovski's lodger: "It's days since I saw you last. Evidently you like Frau Antonia's pork chops better than my soup. How are you getting on?"

The youngster blushed, but he had at least got so far as to look at a woman whenever he spoke to her. "Everything's well enough," he answered in a Talmud sing-song. "God be thanked, I have a roof over my head and plenty to eat. The *goys* are very kind to me. But are things to go on like this?" he asked wistfully, almost imploringly.

"Like what?"

"I mean—about my studies. At home we had at least the Talmud. Whether for good or for bad we believed that things had a purpose. Here there's leisure and no need to worry about food or sleep, but there's no aim in life. I'm often ashamed to face the *goys,* for I simply enjoy their charity and their house-room but have no occupation at all and go about idling."

"What do you want to do?"

"Have I come here just to see Warsaw? I want to study, to begin learning something! What's the good of just being comfortable? I'm not getting any further in the main thing. Herr Hurvitz gives me a lesson for half-an-hour a day; that's very good, but all the rest of the time I'm only an idler. Sometimes I think that I should never have come here. At home there was at least the Talmud, but here there's nothing. I've often wanted to ask you about it; you've always been so good to me."

Frau Hurvitz reflected for a little. Suddenly she had an inspiration and cried: "Wait a minute!"

Then she sought out Mirkin. As if nothing had happened between them she took him by the arm, led him up to the young provincial and said: "Here's something for you to do. Take on this young man and give him lessons."

"On one condition," replied Mirkin.

"What?"

"That he gives me lessons, too. I'll teach him *Goyish,* and he must teach me Yiddish." Mirkin managed to bring this out in Yiddish.

"Do you understand?" asked Frau Hurvitz of her protégé.

"If the gentleman is willing, I am certainly willing. When can we begin?"

"As far as I'm concerned, tomorrow. Agreed?"

"Agreed!"

"But that's not all," broke in Frau Hurvitz. "Shachliner, come here a moment!"

The Shachliner advanced cautiously.

"Here's a man with plenty of time and plenty of accomplishments, who's looking for a job. Give him work to do!" She indicated Mirkin.

"If he's only willing, he can have plenty to do."

"I'm ready for anything," said Mirkin earnestly.

"Good! Now I'll leave you alone to talk it all over." Frau Hurvitz left them together in a corner and turned to her other guests.

When Mirkin took his leave with the others he kissed Frau Hurvitz's hand. She made no objection and said in a low voice in his ear so that no one else could hear: "I hope you're not angry with me?"

"Why should I be?" asked Mirkin in amazement.

"Because I gave you such a dressing down."

Zachary flushed and replied quickly: "You did me good." Then he rushed away. Frau Hurvitz called after him through the lobby: "Don't make yourself so scarce again, or it's I who'll be angry!"

As Mirkin descended the staircase he saw Sabbath lights gleaming from every window in the large courtyard. The building in which Frau Hurvitz lived had always seemed to him unspeakably wretched and gloomy, but today there was a remarkable change; the Sabbath shone out of every Jewish dwelling. Zachary felt its radiance in himself as well.

CHAPTER XII

A THIRSTY SOUL AT THE SPRING

He who is hindered from living in the full current of reality takes refuge in fantasy—in worlds of his own creation.

Mirkin made the discovery that a man can do without other people, that all he needs is his own body. He was amazed that he had not made the discovery long before.

His nights were still sleepless, and he still felt in the darkness the crazy rotation of the world on its axis. It was as if he were falling through an endlessly long tunnel from one atmosphere to another, from one world to another. There was nothing, it seemed, to stop him, and he could go on falling indefinitely like a beam of light sent out by a planet. What was the purpose of this endless fall? None whatever; there was no why or wherefore. But he wanted to stop falling, to feel his own weight, his own mass. He was a center; the planets, the worlds, rotated around him and he wanted to discover himself.

Mirkin lit the lamp beside his bed. His surroundings took shape, formed relations in space and time; and he became master of all the worlds, for they had now projected themselves across the frontier of his intelligence. . . .

So he lay in the soft light of the night-lamp and contemplated his body exposed between the white linen sheets. White linen is the natural wear for the human body, being in a sense an extension of the skin. And he contemplated his body as if it were detached from him: he was merely an "idea," timeless, spaceless, and his body, lying there in bed, was the solid reality. He could possess it, control it, seize it, as if it were a separate "something." His hand caressed his body. The living pulse of the blood beneath his cool, smooth palm appeared to have an alien, a separate life. And he could control that alien life, he could compel it and soothe it with the touch of his hand.

Suddenly he felt that his hand and his body were two separate entities. His hand became an "ego," a personality in itself. His body, hips, breast, smooth skin, pulsing blood-cells, all belonged to some other creature with a will of its own, which the hand controlled by its hypnotic caressing.

The light intruded upon his secret, intimate experience. He put it out and sank into his self-created darkness as on the breast of a mighty, invisible mother. His body changed into a multiplicity of bodies; every limb had its separate, individual existence. His "ego"—it was his hand—caressed them all, and upon his eyes there fell as it were a dewy balm from cool mother-bodies. One after another he possessed them all. Whom did it concern if a man's fantasy created its own illusions to lull into insensibility his utter helplessness and loneliness . . . ?

But then shame awoke; he fell into an abyss of remorse, feeling himself inescapably caught in the trap of his curse; and to rescue himself he plunged into an alien world, the world Frau Hurvitz had found for him, so as to feel some connection at least with her. . . .

As if they were his sole chance of salvation Mirkin plunged into the new occupations prescribed for him by Frau Hurvitz. It was with a positive thirst for action that he began his coaching duties.

Frau Hurvitz first exerted herself to get him out of his lonely hotel. She engaged a room for him in the house of a doctor's widow, where he was much more comfortable. She arranged, too, that he should get his meals there and his other needs attended to, such as the washing of his linen and a regular provision for tea. Frau Hurvitz's kindness made a deep impression on Mirkin. His mood began to change, the visions and night terrors gradually ceased, and his life by day acquired significance. He now saw that his suicidal impulses came partly from the loneliness of the cold hotel rooms he had lived in since his departure from Petersburg, constantly changing one for another.

His interest in books also re-awakened, and the new life he was coming to know, aided by his new environment, strengthened his desire to study all the problems that concerned the people around him. Like a child he exulted over every step of his progress in learning the Yiddish tongue and the customs of the Jews, the modes of thinking and acting prevalent among the Jewish masses. He listened like an attentive pupil to the discussions on Jewish problems at the Hurvitzes' and elsewhere. With the young provincial Talmudist whom Frau Hurvitz had entrusted to him he spent a great deal of time over and above the allotted hours, asking exhaustive questions about Jewish life and observances. The knowledge of German which he still possessed from his school-days helped him considerably in acquiring Yiddish, which his pupil taught him by way of recompense; but he learned much more about Jewish ways of thought and customs from the Talmudist than about the language. His admiration for the old traditions made him appreciate doubly their beauty and dignity, as is often the case with those who return to the faith of their forefathers.

He soon became very friendly with Gedalje, the young Talmudist. His pupil amused and interested him, for he served as a window through which Mirkin got a view of the Jewish mind and its ways of reacting to impressions. The young man tried to apply to the new knowledge he was receiving the Talmud technique in which his mind had been trained at home; he posed all kinds of philosophical questions and entered into casuistical disquisitions. But he was greatly disappointed in the new science when he discovered from Mirkin how the solar system worked and that in relation to the cosmos our earth had no peculiar pre-eminence, that our sun was not even God's sole child and our heaven no heaven at all, since the universe contained endless solar systems with their satellites both large and small, some still incandescent, some already extinct, with or without a gaseous atmosphere, and that it was quite conceivable that on some other planet there might exist creatures more or less resembling ourselves, perhaps, indeed, given favorable atmospheric conditions, even more highly developed than ourselves. The young Talmudist was petrified with astonishment. He had believed that the new learning for which he had thirsted so much, for which he had abandoned his peaceful existence in the small provincial town, would provide him with a new faith that would explain in some natural way the mystery of creation; and now he was faced by the same "infinity" as in his old faith, except that behind the old "infinity" there had stood a mighty God in whose hand everything rested, while behind the new "infinity" there was merely a great and incomprehensible emptiness.

"What good is it to me to have the solar system explained if there is only the same 'infinity' behind it? The human eye has a limited range; it can see only this little earth and the few stars and suns that can be shown by a telescope, but beyond these, in the universe, as you call it, there are other suns with planets circling round them. An endless series. How can we live in an 'infinity' that has no God? That's simply dreadful!" cried Gedalje with a panic-stricken look.

The question behind this protest was one that Mirkin could not answer; all he could say was that science did not deny the existence of God: science was a kind of lamp illuminating the hidden mysteries of God's creation which were called "Nature"; but with our limited faculties we were not capable of explaining the concept "God," just as we were not capable of explaining or understanding the concept of infinity; our finest organs of perception, the brain and the nervous system, were only the products of certain chemical combinations which in their very nature were doomed to limitation, exactly like the earth on which we lived.

The young man's uneasiness, his unresisting search for a meaning in everything he learned, supplied Mirkin with an explanation of his own unrest and perpetual seeking. "That's a characteristic of our race," he said to himself, "we can't live from hand to mouth, we have to find out the why and the whither. . . ."

His interest in his pupil led him to an interest in Jewish philosophy and morals. Almost every evening he visited Hurvitz, the teacher, and discussed these subjects with him; Hurvitz also got for him various works by Jewish thinkers. The teacher, finding in Mirkin a favorable soil for the seed of instruction, gave him long lectures on Jewish history and the Jewish philosophy of the Middle Ages. He took delight in explaining the peculiarities of the Jewish religious philosophers of Spain and Germany, and Mirkin enjoyed listening. Hurvitz was thus able to bring into play all the knowledge he was always longing to impart; for he was never happier or more content than when he had a pair of attentive ears into which to pour his information. Mirkin, on the other hand, was an excellent listener and thirstily drank in all the copious commentaries supplied by the teacher. And whenever Rachel-Leah in her kitchen heard her husband and Mirkin studying the new "Torah" together, she felt a joy that was inexplicable to herself; a radiant happiness beamed from her face, as if it were her own son's lessons she was overhearing.

In addition to Gedalje, Mirkin instructed several outside students in the high school curriculum. Frau Hurvitz sent him every young provincial who turned up in her house. He gave all his lessons in his own room, taking his students singly or two at a time, so as not to arouse the suspicions of the police by too great numbers.

In the evenings the Shachliner would now and then escort him to various houses. Every time it was a different room in the poor quarter of the town, and there Mirkin taught the elements to groups of workmen or gave popular lectures on physics, botany, and other branches of science. The audience consisted mainly of working-class youths with a sprinkling of older people of both sexes; the lectures were usually given in workshops, so that, in case of a police raid, everybody could spring to the machines and work-tables and so allay suspicion.

In the dimly-lit room pairs of eager, shining eyes would gaze at Mirkin from beneath black Jewish hats; now and then he would catch questioning glances shot at him from under some girl's tangled locks; and these searching glances seemed to be looking for the clew to some mystery. The older workmen often fell asleep in their chairs and accompanied the lecture with loud snores. Many of the others simply stared childishly at the lecturer, more interested in him than in the subject of his discourse. Zachary himself had an almost devouring desire to become acquainted with his hearers, to speak to each one of them and find out what kind of people they were.

Yet he was never left alone with them. Nor did he ever know beforehand when and where his lectures were to be given. He was called for at his lodgings and guarded during the whole of his lecture; when it was finished he was taken home again. No attempt was made to conceal the suspicion with which he was regarded; it was impressed upon him that he was an alien from another world, that his help was acceptable only because he had nothing better to offer, and that he would be dispensed with as soon as his hearers could get on without him.

This suspicion was incomprehensible to Mirkin and wounded his feelings. He noticed, too, that he was kept in the dark as much as possible; he was admitted only to his own lectures. It was not difficult for him to gather that his motives were suspect; the very manner in which the others addressed him showed that they did not regard him as one of themselves, for nobody, from the Shachliner down to his hearers, omitted to prefix the word "Herr" to his name. Indeed, they all addressed him with a kind of shy deference. He very soon noticed, too, that in his new circle he was the only one who was well-fed. Almost all his students came hungry to the lectures. Mirkin was often ashamed not to be hungry, but he did not know what to do about it.

In the beginning he was too shy to offer any kind of help to his pupils, since he was naive enough to think that they might feel offended. But when he nerved himself to do it (encouraged by the fact that some members of his audience approached him of their own accord) he discovered that those he would have liked best to help and who most needed it evaded or refused his well-meant offers, and usually in a manner that made it clear that they were unwilling to accept help from him because he was not of their own class.

Ever since leaving Petersburg Mirkin had been under the watchful eye of his father. Wherever he was, on the first of every month he was informed by an agent of his father's that so and so much money stood to his credit. Mirkin had drawn only what he needed for his modest way of life, and by the Warsaw branch of the business he was now informed that it would be considered a favor if he were to exhaust his balance or even ask for an overdraft. Like every man who has never known cold and hunger Mirkin had no understanding of such things. The iron bridge that supported him and the walls that sheltered him were accepted by him as a matter of course, so completely, indeed, that he could see no reason why others should envy or mistrust him. His condition seemed as natural to him as the sky overhead or the air he breathed. He did indeed recognize that all the people in his new environment were from the gutter, men without a home, men who owned nothing but their sordid lives, their own bodies; yet he thought that he himself was in the same case, and had no idea that the mere food he ate, the nourishment he got without any bodily effort, could be of such great importance as to set him apart from the others.

Legends began to gather around him. He was said to be a millionaire's son who had left his father's house and come to Warsaw for the sake of living among the poor Jews. This tale was embellished with all the detail that human fantasy untiringly invents wherever it finds a favorable opportunity. And so it happened that the wildest stories about Mirkin went flying round, and wherever he was known conversation stopped as soon as he appeared and everybody became embarrassed. This hindered him from making new acquaintances, and he felt just as forlorn and deserted as before.

The only house he knew in Warsaw was that of the Hurvitzes. And yet even there he felt that it was only Frau Hurvitz who welcomed him with real kindness. All the other members of the family, the teacher, the daughters, and above all the youngest son David, displayed a marked coldness that betrayed the mistrust they felt for him. If Frau Hurvitz was not at home he never could stay for long; their looks seemed to be driving him out. At the very door he was generally met by the words: "Mother will be in soon," or "Mother isn't in," as if to let him understand that she was the only person in the house who was interested in him. This mistrust hurt him and increased his sense of forlornness.

CHAPTER XIII

THE FIRST DOUCHE OF COLD WATER

Mirkin was being escorted by the Shachliner to a lecture. He was supposed to give a popular address on social economics based on certain forbidden treatises to an audience of unemployed whose hunger was to be allayed by facts. The lecture took place in a room the purpose of which was far from clear to Mirkin, for it might have been either a workshop or a poor man's hostel. It was a cellar, apparently furnished as a joiner's shop and filled with long tables, tools and wood-shavings; countless glue-pots gave off an odor as of sour, stale food. But in the corners stood rows of iron bedsteads, some of which had been pulled out to serve as seats. On the wretched bedding and the dirty gray blankets sat figures whom Mirkin could not identify in the dim light, for the incandescent gas had been shaded with pink paper. As soon as he came in he was aware of hostility in the looks he met. By this time he spoke Yiddish with fair fluency, but still very incorrectly and with a strong admixture of Russian. He made careful preparation for all these lectures, and tried to deliver them in his very best Yiddish: the result, however, was really a hash of Russian and bad German, which he mistook for Yiddish. And since he took the lectures very seriously he always tried to enliven them with illustrations of his own invention. Yet this time he had hardly said two words in his bad Yiddish before listeners in the corners began to laugh, making it impossible for him to establish any contact with his audience. Taken aback, he apologized for his Yiddish with an embarrassed smile and promised to improve it in time. Then he attempted to go on with his lecture. But his audience would not listen to him. The rowdies in the corners mimicked his bad pronunciation and kept up a continuous disturbance. Mirkin, who believed in the importance of what he was doing and regarded his work as a kind of mission, tried to ignore their open contempt and work up his usual dramatic fervour. But the hungry men in the corners, who seemed to Mirkin like one monster with many heads, continued to make loud remarks. In a challenging voice someone called out: "Who's this clod-hopper?" The answer, provided in the same loud tones, was anything but flattering. Mirkin grew pale, went on smiling, and could not think how to extricate himself from his predicament. He continued speaking as if he had heard nothing. Suddenly a man in the back row—it was Motche, the humpback—rose to his feet and cried: "I don't understand this. . . . We thought we had come here to listen to a decent speech, and instead they've sent us a silly bourgeois who fancies himself as a philanthropist. He should trot off to the Community House; they might find some use for him there."

"Hush, he'll hear you!" Henoch the joiner, whose kind heart could not bear the thought of hurting Mirkin's feelings, pulled at the interrupter's sleeve.

"I don't care if he does hear me; I'm not afraid of anybody."

Mirkin stopped, stared round him in confusion with his mouth open, and plucked with trembling fingers at his mustache. He wanted to say something, but could think of no suitable retort.

However capable a mob may be of inspiration by ideals, it can become cruel to the point of brutality once it finds a victim. The fact that Mirkin's respectable clothes set him apart from his ragged associates may have added to the gathering hostility. At all events, the more he lost his composure, the paler and more embarrassed he became, the more the audience jeered.

"I'd just like to know what he had for dinner today!" shouted a pasty-faced boy, showing his toothless gums as he laughed. "Take my word for it, a chap like him gobbles up at a sitting as much as would keep one of us for three days," was the next contribution to the discussion.

"One of us?—a whole family," added a drowsy, unshaven, middle-aged workman with red-stained hands, speaking in a phlegmatic voice without even bothering to smile.

"Oh, do stop it; you should be feeling sorry for him! Look, he's as white as chalk," put in a tired girl.

"Why do they send us objects like that?"

Without having finished his lecture Mirkin walked home with the Shachliner through the snow-covered streets under the reddish light of the shop lamps. The Shachliner tried to excuse the attitude of the meeting:

"The people are desperate. For two months there hasn't been any work in the leather trade, or in the woven goods, or in the cardboard box-making. You shouldn't take it ill of them—they're simply desperate with hunger."

"How can I help it if they're hungry?" asked Mirkin sourly.

"Have you ever gone hungry, Herr Mirkin?" demanded the Shachliner, standing still.

Mirkin thought it over and answered hesitatingly after a moment or two: "No."

"Well, that's just it; these people can tell that you've never known what it means to go hungry."

"The fact that they're hungry is no excuse for their behavior to me. Would it make any difference to them if I were hungry too? After all, it was from the best of motives that I went to them and I didn't deserve to be met in that way."

"Herr Mirkin," returned the Shachliner, "between you and us there's an iron barrier. You'll never be able to understand us. How could you, since you've never been in the same case as any of us? Whatever motives brought you to us," went on the Shachliner, who loved rhetorical declamation and never lost an opportunity of indulging in it, "and I'm not questioning the sincerity of these motives, you'll never understand us, never realize our lot, never sympathize with us. And why? Precisely because you've never gone hungry, because you've never experienced in your own body what it means to stand alone and forlorn in the street, owning nothing but your bare life. Have you ever had to rack your brains one single time to think out where you were to rest your bones when night came? Have you ever known how it feels to go through the streets and see houses all round with lighted windows and realize that there isn't a door anywhere that you have the right to open? There has always been a warm bed waiting somewhere for you, and you have never been homeless for a single minute. Do you know what it means to be houseless and on the streets? You've never had to worry about your daily needs; it seems as natural to you as the sun and the sky that food should appear to nourish your body. But if you were to be locked in an airless box for a day, for an hour even, you would think of nothing but how to knock a hole in it and get a mouthful of fresh air. That's what it's like to be hungry; you can think of nothing but food and shelter. That's the wall between you and us."

"Well, since I've never suffered from these deprivations, isn't it possible that I've been moved to come to you by some higher ideal, some inner impulse that's stronger than mere necessity?" countered Mirkin.

"There's no stronger impulse than bare necessity. It's stronger than any ideal motive. It's the sole passport that admits a man among the proletariat, the only guarantee that his entry into their circle is sincere and irrevocable, that he has once for all cast in his lot with theirs. For what is there to prevent you from taking yourself off some fine day just as you came? You didn't come to us out of necessity, but out of caprice, let the caprice be as idealistic as you please: to-morrow another caprice may whisk you away again. There's always an open door for you somewhere and a warm home waiting."

"Is that why you distrust me? Only because I have the barest necessities of life? I can't believe that men should be judged by the fullness or emptiness of their stomachs. To be full or hungry is a superficial matter, and whether he's hungry or not a man can still be good or bad, just or unjust. Besides, if men are to be condemned simply because they try to provide for themselves, all God's creatures would have to be damned: there's not a living thing that doesn't stick to the bourgeois tradition; every bird, every mammal, every flower, every plant is concerned exclusively with the getting of nourishment and the propagation of its kind."

"But God's creatures don't lay up an inheritance, don't live on the accumulations of others, the hoards of their parents. They fight for their own food tooth and nail, and hunt for it separately or together by their own strength."

"That's our advantage over the beasts. Up till now we have had nothing but our hoarding and our inheritances to thank for the whole of our civilization."

"For what you call civilization!" threw in the Shachliner bitterly.

"Humanity hasn't yet discovered any other civilization, and so long as we have no other point of reference this one is all we have; without it we should become savages again."

"I'm not so well educated as you are," retorted the Shachliner, "but one thing I do know: it's just this accumulated wealth that is the barrier between you and us, and we can't get over it."

They took a cool leave of each other.

CHAPTER XIV

THE LAST BRANCH IS SAWED OFF

Not long after this an event occurred by means of which the branch on which Mirkin sat so securely was sawed off behind him; it happened much more quickly than he had expected, and he was cast on his own resources before he had time to prepare himself. As usual he had repaired at the turn of the month to the office of his father's agent in Warsaw so as to settle up his money affairs, and this time was handed a letter that had arrived by post.

"We've been trying to find you everywhere, but without success. The letter's been lying here for some time. You didn't give your new address to the last hotel you were in."

The sight of the letter agitated Mirkin, for he recognized his father's handwriting on the envelope. This was the first sign of life from his father since his departure from Petersburg, and it roused old memories. To escape from them Zachary thought for a moment of sending the letter back unopened; yet his curiosity overcame his fears and he tore open the envelope. There were only a few lines in his father's flowing handwriting:

> "I have felt it my duty to finish what you left undone. On the 30th of November Nina Solomonovna and I were married."

The blood rushed to Zachary's head. His hands shook and his teeth bit angrily into his lip. He asked for paper and pen and hastily dashed off this answer to his father:

> "You are a cad, and I don't want to have anything more to do with you."

He sealed the note and requested the agent to forward it.

"What's to happen to the money that's standing to your credit? The Petersburg office has instructed us to pay you a thousand roubles monthly. But since you haven't used up all the earlier remittances there's a considerable sum in your name."

"Do what you like with it. Send it back, for all I care. Yes, send it back along with the letter."

The agent, himself the director of a transport agency, regarded Zachary sharply through his glasses; the stiff collar above his carefully ironed shirt-front shone immaculately. After an attentive inspection he observed: "I'll keep the money here at your disposal, just in case. One never knows . . . you might find a use for it."

Mirkin, who had never known want, could not understand the meaning of this remark and replied: "I told you to do what you liked with it."

"You're not changing your address for the present?" asked the agent, obviously not merely at random.

"What do you need my address for?"

"Well, anything might turn up . . . a letter from Petersburg, perhaps."

"I shall be expecting no letter from Petersburg," said Mirkin, and with a bow he took himself off.

"In any case, we're always at your service. It will be a great pleasure to us," the director assured him, escorting him obsequiously to the door.

With the collar of his greatcoat turned up Mirkin strode on through the snow flurries; he felt relieved.

Towards evening he arrived once more at Frau Hurvitz's. It seemed as natural to him to go there as for a child to seek its home. She was in the kitchen raking the glowing coals in the stove with a hook as a preparation for cooking supper. The red gleam of the stove lit up her sharply-cut features. Zachary's arrival embarrassed her a little and she hurriedly wiped the beads of sweat from her brow with her apron.

"Madame Hurvitz, whether I want to or not I must earn my living now or else go hungry."

"I thought there was *one* man at least I should never have to provide for," said Frau Hurvitz with a smile. "What's happened?"

Mirkin did not answer. He searched through all his pockets, pulled out all the money he could find, coins and paper together, and flung it into the fire.

"Don't be a fool!" cried Rachel-Leah, quite forgetting herself, and she gave him a sharp slap on the hand. She was more upset by her action than Mirkin was, and stammered: "Oh, forgive me, I forgot myself. . . . I thought you were one of my children." This last word made her blush still more furiously.

Mirkin did not dare to look at her; he stared into the fire and said, half to himself: "Thank you."

That evening there was a great discussion in the teacher's house about the aims of learning and the meaning of life. As usual it was provoked by Gedalje, the young Talmudist, who was impatient to get to the bottom of everything in the universe although he had acquired scarcely the rudiments of worldly knowledge yet. In this new realm to which he had fled from the limitations of the Talmud he looked for the same purposiveness and certainty that the faith of his childhood had given him, and since he had not found them he felt a great emptiness. He poured out all his doubts before the teacher; his audience included the Shachliner too.

"In the ancient books at home," he began in his accustomed Talmud sing-song, "there would flash out now and then like a beam of light a divination of man's destiny and what he must do to fulfill his place in the universe. There was an assured place for him. But here, in this new faith, one is simply left hanging in the air. Let us suppose that I know all the islands in the Mediterranean, that I can recite all the rivers in Africa, that I know everything about the structure of plants or insects; all that is only a trifle in the huge totality; all that belongs to the Biblical six days of creation, and there are countless other particular details of the same kind; indeed, there are nothing but particular details. But in this new science where can we find a great scheme embracing the whole universe? What direction are we going in? I often feel quite panic-stricken, as if I were in the same predicament as the woman who said: 'I have thrown away the bedding and now I have to recover the feathers one by one.' We are left without anything to depend on but ourselves, and I feel as if I were being launched alone and entirely unsupported on an endless journey into infinity."

With his usual patience Hurvitz listened to the points raised by this new adept in the science he loved so much, slowly took off his glasses, polished them elaborately, and replied:

"All that you learned at home was a kind of Blind Man's Bluff, mere scriptural orthodoxy. The great aim of life, its real purpose, lies in these," he pointed to the rows of books. "Only through these books can a man learn his place in the universal scheme. Only by the power of the human intellect can the individual rise to a height where he can view the whole. By absorbing the learning of such great minds as Spencer, Darwin and their fellows we become a part of them; our own intellect leaves its narrow prison and soars in the mighty radiance of the World-Mind. Thus we bind ourselves to the sole, eternal Purpose, to understanding and knowledge; thus we become partakers in creation. We are not wretched blind slaves in the service of some prescribed ritual, trying to placate some imaginary power which every nation thinks is its own particular property. That's fetish-worship, not a living aim. The great purpose of our lives was formulated by Spinoza in these words: 'Thou must thyself partake in the six days of creation.' That purpose can only be fulfilled by contact with the Universal Mind as it is revealed in the greatest human intellects. What we call God or Nature is blind until the human intellect gives it eyes to see."

"But who created the human intellect?" persisted the young man, refusing to give in.

During this discussion Rachel-Leah sat at the table darning stockings by the light of the lamp. When the men's argument soared into the higher regions she paused in her work, propped her strong chin on her hand and listened with knitted brows. Although she did not understand what it was all about she felt her whole being uplifted. And she nodded grave assent to all her husband's conclusions.

As usual the Shachliner declared that these were bourgeois ideas.

"How can one rely on the intellect?" he inquired. "Where does it lead us? Only where the stomach wants to go. The intellect has no independent existence. It's only a part of the body, and it employs its cleverness and its acuteness to procure for the body what the body wants. Some people use their intellect to fill their stomachs or their pockets, others to satisfy some caprice or the evil impulses that exist in all men. The individual can free himself from that subservience only by shedding his individuality and recognizing himself as a part of the community. Then he knows that he is attached to a purposive force and not left to his own resources, not left alone with nothing but his own existence to fall back on."

Mirkin smiled at hearing the clear, dogmatic statements that the teacher and the Shachliner made so confidently in answer to the young man's questions about eternity. For them there was no such thing as doubt, no vague skepticism; they saw their paths clear before them and advanced firmly. Mirkin could not help thinking: "I would be happy if I could think as they do. That's the rub; I haven't got a nose-ring to lead me on. They all have a nose-ring, the teacher, the Shachliner, Königstein the Zionist; I'm the only one left to my own resources. And I'm tired of being alone. Perhaps that's the only thing to do, to let oneself be led by the nose! It doesn't matter what nose-ring we choose so long as we are led somewhere; nor does it matter what path we follow if only it is a straight one."

He did not, however, divulge this idea; he merely remarked with a smile: "You're all giving wonderfully clear answers to a question that's as old as the world and has never been answered yet. How can we give a clear answer when we still haven't sufficient knowledge to illuminate all the dark places? We can't even shine the light of reason into the obscurities that we come up against or feel instinctively to be there, not to speak of those that we know nothing about, the shadows that lurk beyond our own darkness. What is intellect, after all? And what is instinct itself, what is the most delicate instinct we possess, such as intuition, for instance? How far can it take us? Beyond our own world there are millions of other worlds, the endless infinity that our young friend here speaks about, and all of them are hidden from us in perpetual night. Besides, there's no need to look as far as that; for can we say that we know even ourselves? Do you know all the mysteries within yourselves? And can you give any explanation of those that you do know? Have you any certainty about what you will be doing in an hour's time? The Shachliner tries to get out of it comfortably"—Mirkin smiled—"by delegating responsibility, by preaching the suppression of one's own will and a blind adherence to the will of the community. That's very practical, and I'd like well enough to do it too. But what is this community? To begin with, there's more than one community on the earth, and secondly, how am I to know that the community is doing the right thing? The community is guided by human reason just like the individual. Many a time the community is more obviously wrong than the individual. And one can at least deal with an individual face to face, one can protest against him or lead a revolution against him; but what can one do against a community, however unjust its actions?"

Mirkin's words had the full effect of a bomb. The teacher denounced his ideas as dangerous and anarchistic, the Shachliner condemned them as typical of the smug, individualistic mysticism of the idle bourgeoisie. Both of them agreed that mankind ought not to concern itself with any world except the world in which it lived; and that this world could become a paradise if men only ceased to be egoists, concerned merely with the happiness of their own egos or of their families instead of considering the collective happiness of the community.

"The community has to bear everybody's burdens, the community suffers for all its members! Leave the other worlds to the astronomers!" shouted the Shachliner, in an ecstasy of passion. "Leave your inner life to the psychologists, and try to live decently in this world; take some trouble to become a help to your fellow-men as well as to yourself or your family! Then you'll enjoy the happiness of knowing that this world we are now living in can give far more to you than any other one."

A little later, when Mirkin found himself alone with the Shachliner in a corner, he said, still smiling: "Really, I envy you; believe me, I would be glad to take my place in the team beside you, for that's really the only way out for me. Won't you take me with you?"

"Take you with me? Where to?"

"Into the team."

"Do *you* want to do team work?" asked the Shachliner in amazement.

"I've thought of it often; for it's the only way of escaping from oneself."

"That won't take you far. Team work is only possible for those who must take it up, who are forced to do it by necessity."

"It's not a question of being forced, it's a question of being able," said Mirkin earnestly.

"If you can conquer yourself you'll be able enough. That's the first commandment."

"That's just what I'm trying to do," replied Mirkin, flushing. "Won't you help me to do it?"

"The doors are open for everybody who wants to enter."

They shook hands and resumed their former seats.

When Mirkin took his leave late in the evening Frau Hurvitz drew him aside: "Tell me, do you have any money for your tram? You threw all you had into the fire, you know."

Mirkin was astounded when this problem presented itself. It seemed very strange to him to be in such a position.

"This isn't much, but it's a few roubles anyhow."—Frau Hurvitz tried to push a few silver coins into his hand.

"But, Frau Hurvitz!" Mirkin blushed to the roofs of his hair.

"Well, if you're going to be so fussy you'll just have to go on foot."

Mirkin set off in great confusion.

"And don't forget to come here for dinner tomorrow! I'll have a talk with my husband—to see what can be done for you. I'm afraid you'll have to turn crammer like all the others," Frau Hurvitz shouted after him.

When the door was shut Rachel-Leah turned on the Shachliner; she suspected that he was to blame for Mirkin's extraordinary conduct, and that under his influence Mirkin had committed some folly or other, as a result of which he would now have to starve. In her irritation she shouted at the "Lithuanian": "A fine way you have of setting the world to rights! I suppose you couldn't bear to see another man having enough to eat? And when he's as hard-pressed as we are the millennium will dawn, what? It isn't as if he were used to it."

"Then he can just get used to it! Why should he be better off than us? Anybody who wants to join in with us can suffer as we have to suffer."

"But it's *his* money; he inherited it from his mother."

"Inherited? What right has he to inherit anything? What has he done to deserve it? And what do you mean by saying it's *his* money? It's stolen money! Money robbed and squeezed from the bloody sweat of his father's workmen! Bread that has been snatched from little children!"—the Shachliner boiled over again.—"His money? Do you know how fortunes are made? Just you read about them! By hours of forced drudgery wrung from hundreds of human beings, by their sleepless nights and joyless days. Hoarded human blood is what fortunes are, hoarded human sweat!"

"Now, now, this isn't a workers' meeting. I've known for a long time that you have a fine gift of the gab. But there's only one thing I want you to tell me: Would *you* renounce an inheritance?"

The Shachliner hastily betook himself to his room.

CHAPTER XV

A HUNGRY GUEST

"In the long run every man is fonder of his own hide than of anything else," Mirkin told himself, "and perhaps the Shachliner is right, perhaps brutal necessity is the only real factor in life."

Since he had cut the navel cord (that was the phrase he had found for his final break with his father) and was confronted with the question of how he was to make his living for the next few weeks, he had been able to take no thought except for the satisfaction of his daily needs. The problem of food and shelter and what he was to do next day drove out all other thoughts. They dulled even his rage against his father and made him forget everything else. For now all his thoughts were exclusively concerned with where he was to get the money for his next meal; everything else was pushed aside and had to wait for a more suitable time.

He had still a roof over his head, for his lodgings with the doctor's widow were paid for up to the end of the month. Yet he already felt homeless. A crushing sense of inferiority weighed on him; he had a curious sinking feeling, as though his being, his very existence had suddenly fallen in value so much that it could find no buyer. He felt all this although his situation was by no means as desperate as he tried to make it out. People who are unaccustomed to worry about their daily wants become as helpless and lost as children flung for the first time into the water when they are suddenly confronted with need. Formerly, when he had no necessity to worry about his daily bread, he had never been aware that a dinner might be a matter of crucial importance with which one must seriously occupy oneself. When he was invited to dinner at the Hurvitzes' he had accepted their hospitality as casually as he would have accepted a drink of water. But now it seemed to him that everybody must see from his face that he was hungry, and that as soon as he entered the teacher's house they would read from his brow the reason why he had come. Accordingly when he was asked to dinner by the Hurvitzes, he would go for a long walk that lasted until the dinner hour was well over, and only then make for their house. But as soon as he reached the door his nostrils would be assailed by the penetrating odor of turnip soup, which made his mouth water, and he would find the family still in the middle of their meal. Never did Madame Hurvitz's dining-room seem so warm and friendly to him as then. All the family sat round the covered table and the milky radiance of the lamp fell on faces and plates. Madame Hurvitz, her frank motherly face beaming, stood in front of a huge dish filled with potatoes and greens. She seemed to know at a glance that he had not eaten anything that day and was very hungry. Vigorously wielding fork and spoon she doled out the portions from her great dish. An odorous steam ascended from the plates, and filled the whole room. The smell of the turnip soup and the potatoes and onions fried in gravy penetrated Mirkin's whole being and released all his senses: all the pores of his skin drank in the odors, the fragrance of the food, and so he quenched his hunger in that way at least. Warm saliva gathered in his mouth; his nostrils quivered, and all his senses, all his thoughts were filled with an overpowering desire to plunge a fork into one of the plates and eat his fill. He felt ashamed of himself. Never had he guessed that food could be so important and set all one's nerves afire; that a roll strewn with caraway seeds, such as he saw before him on the table, could be a delectable morsel; and that salted beef and potatoes or the last drains of turnip soup in a tureen could make a human being forget everything else and even be prepared to commit a crime to gain possession of them.

"It's good that you've come; we kept dinner waiting for you; but you were too unpunctual even for us and we couldn't wait any longer. Sit down now at once," cried Madame Hurvitz, setting out a fresh plate for him.

A lust to eat awoke in Zachary; he felt like a starving dog who sees a bone before him. He swallowed down the saliva in his mouth and said: "I'm sorry—I didn't know you were waiting for me. I've just had dinner in my lodgings."

"What nonsense is this you're talking? You know you've given up having dinner in your lodgings! Sit down at the table!"

Mirkin flushed. He felt that he had given himself away. With a great effort he crushed down his craving for food and replied in a calm voice: "You may be sure I wouldn't think twice of eating with you if I were hungry!" and he tried to smile naturally.

Madame Hurvitz flung him a penetrating glance and asked laughingly: "And is that true?"

"Mamma!" The eldest daughter pulled her mother by the apron.

Mirkin had now conquered his longing for food and gravely contemplated the tips of his fingers.

"I'm quite sure that Herr Mirkin is old enough to know when he feels hungry," the teacher came to his assistance, "but that's what women are like; they've a habit of making us eat whether we want to or not."

To help Mirkin over an embarrassing situation and change the subject the teacher went on: "My wife has told me that you want to devote yourself to our profession."

"Yes, that's so, though I really don't know whether I'll be able for it. But I think I would like to try."

"That's a great deal in itself. You won't find it very difficult, seeing that you've a university education. Of course, you'll have to take an examination and get a certificate from the inspector of education; one isn't allowed to teach without that."

"But he'll have to have some more private pupils to begin with, that's the first thing to be thought of," Madame Hurvitz threw in.

"Oh well, I can afford to wait a little while longer!" Mirkin blushed as if doing penance for his lie.

"I'll make inquiries in the families I have connections with. It shouldn't be difficult to find people who want private lessons," said the teacher.

"It's very kind of you; but there's no hurry; things aren't so bad as all that with me yet."

Mirkin brought out the last words with such embarrassment that it gave away his whole position. There was a sudden silence.

In the midst of the silence, while everybody was desperately searching for some other subject, Helene said:

"Wouldn't it be possible for Herr Mirkin to teach Russian in our school? Our Russian teacher is only an ignorant army sergeant. The children learn nothing from him. If we asked Madame Silberstein to use her influence with the inspector we could easily get permission for Herr Mirkin."

"The inspector appointed the Russian teacher for the sake of the salary, not because he can teach. I can't believe that he would tolerate a second Russian teacher in our school."

"Then we can pay him the salary, and let Herr Mirkin do the teaching. All that the fool cares for is his salary," interrupted Sosha, who was inventive in such matters. "The children will at least get some good out of their Russian lessons then."

The teacher remained silent. His daughter had touched upon a painful and delicate subject. For the school was always in difficulties and perpetually short of money; a new burden would create heavy hardships.

Mirkin sat on needles while his future was being discussed. His face burned. Everybody could see his distress. To put an end to the painful situation the teacher began to talk of domestic affairs.

All the time that Mirkin was taking part in the talk round the table he had felt the warm glance of two eyes resting on his face. While they were regarding him he was suffering acutely and reproaching himself for his childish weakness and helplessness. He was on the verge of loathing himself: "Tens of thousands of people are in the same position as I am, and they don't complain!" He flushed still more deeply and searched for an excuse for leaving; he was resolved never to return again, thinking in that way to punish himself for encumbering strangers with his difficulties. "After all can I expect any one to share my worries? Why do I rush about and blurt them out before everybody?" he asked himself and felt that he had sunk to a still lower level than he had reached when he had arrived starving with hunger. His desire to get up and go grew stronger every minute.

Then he felt that strangely warm glance resting upon him. It almost burned his face with the profound warmth of its sympathy, its almost painful participation in his trouble.

"What does she mean by looking at me like that? What does the girl want?" he asked himself almost with exasperation.

He raised his eyes to encounter that regard and quell it once and for all by his own indignant pride. But he was strangely held by what he saw, for two clear frank blue eyes were gazing at him; they looked out from a pale girlish face. The glance she gave him was not one of mere pity, but one that sought, literally sought and sought, as if it were trying to discover something. And the girl's face was profoundly serious. The more Mirkin tried to stare her down, the more gravely and profoundly she gazed into his eyes, so openly and intimately that he was afraid the others might notice it. He hastily turned his eyes away, but they returned to her again and again. He regarded her slender neck and the scarcely perceptible curve of her girlish breasts and the black and white checked dress which had seemed so strangely familiar to him on his very first visit. Looking at the frail and delicate lines of that girlish figure, he felt a sudden pity for her as for a defenseless bird. Her form was thin and almost fragile; the faintly rounded breasts and the slender drooping arms awoke his compassion. He felt as though he held between his fingers the thin feathered throat of a dove, which the slightest pressure would hurt. He was afraid of looking at the girl, or even at her dress, lest he might wound her by his glance. So he set himself to think of something else and fixed his eyes on the remnants of the meal that were still standing on the table. But his hunger had vanished and his thoughts returned again to the girl's eyes: "How does this delicate girl come to have such a strong, profound look?" And to escape from those eyes he got up hastily as soon as the meal was over.

At the door Madame Hurvitz stopped him: "I must tell you frankly, Pan Mirkin—the way you're behaving may be all very well in the circles you've left, where people have nothing better to do than stand on ceremony! but it would be a fine thing if we had to feel embarrassed about such things! How could we go on if we did? How will we be able to turn to you when we're in need, seeing that you make such a fuss over a trifle like a meal? Rich people can afford to do such things, but people like us, no!"

"You're right," Zachary admitted.

"I had a few roubles a little while ago, and you wouldn't accept them. At present I've only a few copeks; here they are; go to a dairy and get something to eat." She took a few coins from her apron pocket and pressed them into his hand. "You're hungry, I know it."

Mirkin took the copper coins.

"Don't you need the money yourself? I'll borrow some cash somehow or other."

"Where will you borrow it? I know better than you how to make shift with things."

"Thank you."

"Keep your thanks to butter your bread! And let me tell you again—if you're hungry and you're invited to eat you've got to eat. If you don't you'll just have to go with an empty stomach."

Mirkin said nothing in reply and turned to go.

"Just a minute! Here's an apple to eat on the way!" She handed him an apple out of the kitchen cupboard.

Zachary smiled shyly and stuck the apple in the pocket of his overcoat.

CHAPTER XVI

CONQUERED PRIDE

MIRKIN's face was red with shame as he descended the stairs from the Hurvitzes' house. He still clutched the hard copper coins in his hand,

and he could feel the apple in his pocket. He felt like a beggar who goes from door to door. All his family pride rose up; he felt as if he had committed a shameful action that must outlaw him from his family circle for all time.

He angrily scolded himself: "A fine pampered little gentleman I am! What right have I to these aristocratic airs now? Why should I concern myself with what's past and gone?"

He felt a wish to do something that would cut once and for all the ties binding him to his past. It was like a need to punish himself, to stifle within himself his absurd and superfluous feelings of family and personal pride. "What is pride?" he asked himself. "A superfluous and useless piece of ballast, acquired by money. What is honor? An instinct of the privileged. The millions of people who have only the barest necessities of life can't afford the sentiment of pride or the luxury of honor. What need have I for such feelings? Can't I live without them if I have to?"

He sought for some way of humiliating himself, and hit upon the idea of stationing himself on the pavement with outstretched hand like a beggar. His reason also told him that that would be a quite natural action. Human beings lived communally; alone, as isolated beings, they could not exist at all; and that gave the individual a right to demand help of his fellows. Only the rich lived like lonely animals amid their piled up wealth; the poor, who were forced by necessity to work day by day, hour by hour for their livelihood depended after all on the collective help they gave each other in the form of money and provisions, hoping that when hard times came help would be given them in turn, as Madame Hurvitz had said; only the rich were ashamed to show their poverty to one another, because there was no group feeling, no sense of community among them; but the poor did not know that shame, for they shared a common social life, though they were not aware of it.

But Mirkin quickly rejected his first intention: "I shan't beg, for I have no need to; I still have these copper coins that Madame Hurvitz gave me for my supper. A poor man shouldn't worry as long as he sees his next meal before him. This money in my hand will be enough for a meal in the dairy."

So Mirkin turned his steps towards a dairy he knew. But he still felt a desire to do something to break his pride and, as he phrased it, conquer the fine gentleman in himself, as it were violate himself. He had it! He would go to a municipal kitchen!

His blood began to flow more quickly through his veins. He felt something within him rising against his will and knew that he would have a struggle.

On the way to the dairy he was making for, there was a municipal kitchen. Whenever he passed it and saw the tattered, ill-smelling crowds of men standing in queues before the entrance he always crossed to the other side of the street so as to avoid the nauseating sweaty stench that the place exuded. He could not even have pictured himself standing in the same row as these figures waiting for a cheap meal; he would have died rather than do such a thing. But now as he neared the place he defiantly resolved to cross over, take his place in the queue of beggars and swallow a three-copek meal. It was not hunger alone that drew him to the place; but hunger acted as the spur. The apple, which he had already eaten, had dulled his craving only for a little. Then it began to work in his empty stomach like an acid; he felt still more keenly his emptiness, and his stomach contracted with yearning. When the sourish sweaty smell of the kitchen struck his nostrils his mouth watered; and now it seemed to him that the stale stench was by no means so repellent and disgusting as he had thought before. It intensified his hunger still more and fortified him in his resolution.

All his instincts rose in horrified revolt as he turned his steps towards the place. He joined the row of waiting men. Every feeling within him now joined in one outcry, one protest. The stench filled his nostrils, and the heavy, oppressive atmosphere made him feel as though he were stifling; but he disregarded it; it was necessary to prove himself, to force himself to combat his inborn inclinations and his customary habits of comfort. They must be destroyed now, once and for all, forcibly humiliated; standing here in this row with beggars and homeless men, he would break finally with all his past. So he violently dragged himself with all his shrinking susceptibilities towards the municipal kitchen, despite their protest against the outrage on their long refinement that he was about to commit. He paid his three copeks, received a tin plate and a worn, suspiciously black spoon, used before him by God knew whom, and took his place in the queue. In front of him beggars were standing, through whose tattered clothes and ragged shirts he could see their dirty skins covered with hideous skin diseases. He looked into weird besotted faces whose eyes were glazed and whose noses were reddened and swollen with alcohol; their breaths bore a stench of sour drink and stale sausages. From the kitchen, where the cauldrons were bubbling, came a dense heavy smell, reminding one more of dirty washing and lye than of food being cooked. At a long table on which smoked a paraffin lamp there were sitting, in a cloud of steam, figures which looked like halves or three-quarters of human beings: the rest of their bodies was missing. . . . With almost pathological greed they hastily spooned the last scrap of food out of their plates and solicitously gathered up and swallowed every crumb that had fallen on their clothes.

When the waiting queue became aware of the well-dressed gentleman, all sorts of sarcastic comments flew round Mirkin's head. He pretended not to hear them and, with his plate in his hand, gradually advanced to the window where the food was being given out. But his neighbors maneuvered things so expertly that he had perpetually to fall out of line, and instead of advancing he found he was being pushed back. He bore this also with patience, and, squeezed between filthy bodies, forced his way forward until at last he reached the window.

The cook, a fat Pole whose mustache was half singed off with pipe smoking and whose cheeks had an unhealthy flush, blinked at Mirkin with the eyes of a habitual drinker, shook his head and opened his mouth, as if he wanted to say something; but without remark he doled out to his guest a bigger portion of soup than the usual one, and then picked out a juicy bone and a huge hunk of bread for him. Mirkin sat down at the long table along with the others and addressed himself to his soup and his bread though they filled him with disgust. He forced himself to eat and hunger came to his help; so he persuaded himself at last that he actually liked the food and told himself that it was not so bad as he had expected and was, indeed, quite appetizing.

When he had satisfied his hunger he was as happy as a boy who has just passed his school examination. He decided that hunger was by no means such a bad thing as it was called.

After finishing his meal he went outside again. The fresh cool wind made him feel better, and he inhaled it in deep draughts. Suddenly something rose up within him that was stronger than all his philosophical justifications, and more powerful than his will. Everything went round before his eyes, a warm stream of saliva gathered in his mouth and he felt sick; like a child he vomited in the middle of the street all that he had eaten in the kitchen. . . .

The passers-by avoided him and shook their heads. "Such a fine looking gentleman, and so well dressed; he should be ashamed to get drunk like that," said a Jewish woman as she passed.

Others made a wide detour round him and shrugged their shoulders in disgust.

Covered with shame Mirkin wiped his clothes hastily and hurried away like a thief.

"I'm an incorrigible mother's darling!" he raged at himself. "I can accept alms all right, I can take advantage of the town's benevolence, but even that I can't carry out to the finish."

He was once more overcome by a feeling of hopeless resignation.

"What good to us are all our principles and theories if we can no more escape from our way of life than a cow in a field? A small alteration in our lives, and we perish like flies. We are all tethered by a rope to some stake or other, and we go round our circle once, or perhaps twice, so long as our accustomed food is there. But we can't escape the tether that our social environment inflicts upon us."

Ashamed of his graceless behavior he at last told himself: "But all the same I'll conquer the fine gentleman in me, even if I've got to thrash him with a cudgel!"

CHAPTER XVII

THE CLUB AT THE DAIRY

IN THE DAIRY Mirkin met a few people he knew. The usual hour for dining, when the place was filled with customers, was over, for it was already late. Now there sat at the tables only a few intellectuals, politicians or semi-politicians, a sprinkling of teachers, day scholars and young people who had no home, no warm or lamp-lit table of their own where they could find refuge from the cold streets. They all exploited the hospitality of the dairy proprietor, who belonged to their own class, for he was himself an intellectual with literary aspirations. The room was half dark. As it would have meant a loss to waste light on customers who consumed so little, the main switch had been turned off and only one electric bulb burned over the table where Mirkin's acquaintances sat. The proprietor, a stately man with a broad gray beard, a finely cut scholar's face, a high gleaming brow and glasses, sat at the counter occupied with his great work, on which he had been engaged half his life. It was to be called "The Way to Everlasting Peace" and was to save mankind from the horrors of war. Now and then as he wrote he would glance up from beneath his jutting eyebrows, push his glasses up on to his forehead and contemplate the little cheeses, cream cakes, radishes, herrings and other eatables ranged before him on the counter, as if he were trying to extract from them some idea about everlasting peace for his book. In it everything was so arranged as to assure the world the blessings of peace: there were to be an international court of arbitration before which the disputes of states were to be brought and a voluntary army whose task it would be to compel states when necessary to recognize the verdicts of the international court. (Indeed he had already begun to enlist volunteers for that army, chiefly from among the intellectuals who frequented his dairy.) Only one trifling obstacle still remained to be overcome—to persuade the peoples and states to translate into reality the peace plan of this Warsaw Jew as he had outlined it in his book. This is what he was thinking of as he pushed his glasses up on his high gleaming forehead and contemplated long and piercingly the eatables in front of him. Then he noticed that Mirkin had entered, and smiled a welcome to him. Although Mirkin seldom came to the dairy he was known there and highly esteemed because of his rich connections, which were familiar to everybody; his mysterious appearance in Warsaw also contributed to his prestige.

At the intellectuals' table a violent debate was just starting, in which "The Philosopher" took the lion's share. He was a very queer character, and from the first had roused Mirkin's curiosity. It was to listen to "The Philosopher" that he made his occasional visits to the dairy. But "The Philosopher" was not always inclined to enter into conversation or take part in the debates that were conducted with great violence every evening. Mostly he sat by himself at a little table with a glass of warm milk and a biscuit in front of him, reading a book or staring, sunk in thought, at a spot on the table. His body, which was thin and boyish although he was middle-aged, was generally curled up as if he wanted to roll himself into a ball, and one leg was usually twined round the other with almost acrobatic skill. With his thin arms wound round his undeveloped, almost childish body, he would sit for hours on his chair staring like a Hindu priest at one point, his pallid face lit up by a smile of simple kindness which seemed to come from the world where his thoughts were lingering. . . . When he took part in the conversation it was always with a philosophic calm in complete contrast to the excited animation of the others, and his detachment had an almost exasperating effect upon them. Nobody knew on what means "The Philosopher" lived, where he stayed and from what class he came. He never borrowed money from any one, although the others knew that he was often in need of it. On the other hand if any one ever asked him for a small loan he never refused. Where he got the money for these loans nobody knew. It was generally believed that he had some friend who looked after him. His needs were certainly few, but the fact that he always had a few coins in his pocket when any one went to him for help proved that he had independent means. In that he was an exception in his circle —an exception, it must be added, that was not entirely approved of.

This happened to be one of his loquacious evenings. But for the small group of intellectuals there was scarcely anybody in the place. A waitress was sleeping in a corner with her head resting on a table. Another stood with her hands buried in the pockets of her white apron beside the table where the intellectuals were sitting, and listened along with the others to "The Philosopher."

When Mirkin entered he was just discoursing on the harmony between the body and the soul, and explaining at length that man was the mediator between his body and his soul and must make his soul live in harmony with his body instead of flying out at it, no matter in what circumstances he might find himself: "Generally it's the soul that gets stiff-necked and kicks. The body can endure far more than the soul both in good times and bad times. For myself I've established peace between them and attained calm and harmony."

"And what if one is hungry?" asked one of his listeners, who was irritated by "The Philosopher's" serenity.

"There isn't such a thing as being hungry," explained "The Philosopher" calmly, stroking his thin mustache with his frail hand. "Hunger is merely a state just like satiety, and there's no state to which a man cannot accustom his soul. It isn't the body that suffers, but the soul; but the soul can be diverted from a state in which it doesn't feel at ease and raised to a higher state. Let us keep to the example of hunger: do you know, gentlemen, that hunger has a music of its own? Every state has its own particular shadow, so to speak, which accompanies it as a man's shadow accompanies him. That's what I call the music of the particular state. And just as sages in the orient withdraw from the sun into the shadow, so as to get peace in which to commune with their souls, so one must withdraw from the state in which one finds oneself into its shadow. For a state is uneasy and produces a burning heat—in short, it's a torment to man. But its shadow is cool: there one can master and subdue the state itself. The wise man never finds himself in the state itself, but always just outside it, and in that way he is the master of every situation that may come his way."

The proprietor, standing behind the counter, once more pushed his glasses up on his forehead, a sign that he had ceased writing; he was about to address a question to "The Philosopher" from where he was standing, but one of his customers forestalled him.

"Will you allow me to ask you a question?" It was the Shachliner who spoke. "Have you ever been hungry, really hungry, not as a mere amateur so to speak, but simply because you had nothing to satisfy your hunger? Have you ever wandered the streets without enough money in your pockets to buy a roll?"

"I can't give you an answer to that question," replied "The Philosopher" in his calm voice. "I don't know what hunger means, any more than I know what satiety means. As I've explained already, I never find myself in the state itself, but always outside it."

"I've philosophized like that, too, when my stomach was full. But I know now that what you call the shadow of a state doesn't exist: there are only two real states, to be full or to be empty. And the world is divided into these two states."

Everybody looked up at the speaker. They could hardly believe their ears: it was Mirkin.

But Mirkin met their glances firmly and—wonder of wonders!—did not blush like a girl this time. A chance glance flung at him could no longer discompose him, for he had lost his timidity.

The others saw that something decisive must have happened in Mirkin's life. The conversation turned to other subjects.

A little later the Shachliner came up to Mirkin. With unusual warmth he asked: "What's been happening to you lately, Mirkin?"

Mirkin looked at him in surprise and replied with a smile: "Nothing, nothing in particular."

"Really nothing?" asked the Shachliner, and he added in a lower voice: "Look here, Mirkin, have you had anything to eat today?"

Mirkin's blood, not yet used to his new position, rose in revolt at this question and flew to his face. His family pride, not yet quite chastened, also rose in protest. But he soon appeased both as one soothes a recalcitrant child. He asked himself: "After all, what does it matter?" Then he replied defiantly, and yet calmly, resolved to adapt his feelings to his new station and to chasten himself: "Yes, I've dined in the municipal kitchen."

Something rose up in the Shachliner. Mirkin in the municipal kitchen, along with vagrants! He said nothing but simply looked at Mirkin in astonishment. Zachary understood his questioning glance and said: "Why are you so surprised? Aren't the people that eat there human beings?"

"No, no, I wasn't surprised," the Shachliner hastened to reply. "I only wanted to ask you, do you know the proprietor of this place, Herr Schneïrsohn, personally?"

"No," replied Mirkin.

"Then come along, I'll introduce you to him. He's one of us. That may be of use to you. If you're ever without money he'll give you credit. We all help one another in that way. Herr Schneïrsohn, here's another volunteer for your army of peace. You know him already by sight, of course. Our friend Mirkin, Zachary Mirkin."

"Of the rich Petersburg family?" asked the proprietor, combing his long beard with his fingers. Schneïrsohn knew the genealogy of all the Jewish millionaires in Russia.

"No," replied Zachary, shaking his head.

"What are you thinking of? What connection has he with such people?" the Shachliner exclaimed. "He's one of our circle."

"I just thought . . ." said Schneïrsohn.

"This is how matters stand, Herr Schneïrsohn. Herr Mirkin is looking for work, he wants to give private lessons to begin with. To-morrow or the day after he's bound to find some, but in the meantime—you understand—he needs a little credit."

"Well, what can I do for you?" With a deep sigh the proprietor lowered his glasses on to his nose again and turned once more to his work on everlasting peace.

"Comrade Manya, a portion of cream and cheese, the master knows about it," the Shachliner shouted to the waitress.

"No, a glass of tea would be better," Mirkin interposed diffidently. "I've a bitter taste in my mouth."

"That comes from fasting all day—that's the taste of hunger. I know it!" said the Shachliner with a laugh.

After that evening Zachary became a member of the little circle in the dairy. He was welcomed warmly, for he was no longer the elegant stranger. The others ceased to treat him as an object of curiosity and looked upon him as one of themselves.

CHAPTER XVIII

IN THE SCHOOL

MADAME HURVITZ's foster children were increased by a new addition, the young man from Petersburg, as she called Mirkin. She saw to all his needs. She succeeded in finding a room for him in the house of a better class master-tailor. Mirkin had nothing to pay, but in return for his lodgings he coached the tailor's son, who attended the high school, in Russian and mathematics. He generally had his chief meal at Madame Hurvitz's and for the time being she also gave him a little pocket money for his daily expenses, until he should receive the first fees for the private lessons that the teacher had got for him. In return Mirkin tried his hand at teaching in the school. There his abilities were welcome. The school was perpetually short of teachers and those allotted to it by the inspector of education were official spies more than teachers. As Mirkin possessed a doctor's degree from a Russian university the inspector had no hesitation in giving him permission to teach, with the proviso that the former Russian teacher should still receive his salary.

He taught all sorts of subjects: Russian, physics, mathematics and natural history. Hurvitz had prophesied at the very beginning that Mirkin would find it difficult to get on with the children; for he did not know how to maintain a due distance between himself and them, involving himself too often in general discussions. In this way he loosened the discipline that Hurvitz had managed to impose on his school. Sometimes, too, he lost his temper, for instance when little Moischele, nicknamed "The Spider" by his school-mates, an intelligent but turbulent boy notorious for his exploits in the whole school, put all sorts of saucy questions to the new teacher so as to make him look foolish. Hurvitz took Mirkin aside one evening and gave him a lecture on education: "There's a world of difference between talking on equal terms to grown-ups and teaching children." He concluded his long harangue on the fundamental principles of education: "The teacher must always and in every situation comport himself before the children as an authority, and must never show any sign of weakness. Children are little despots who watch for every opportunity to fall on the teacher and make him appear a fool. That being so, the teacher must always be vigilant and fully armored when the children are present, always ready to counter-attack, as it were."

Mirkin listened attentively and impressed Hurvitz's words on his mind with the intention of acting on them. But during the first lesson that he gave without supervision he recognized that he would never be able to keep strict order in his class; and this discouraged him so much that he became convinced that he would have to give up his new profession and seek another.

The children in the school belonged to the poorest Jewish class in the neighborhood. The majority of them were so poor that they could not pay their school fees. These were paid for them by a committee for the dissemination of education among the Jewish poor, who subsidized the school more or less regularly without the inspector of education's knowledge. These children were the most easy to deal with: their spirits crushed by poverty, always hungry and cold at home, they regarded the school as a paradise and the teacher Hurvitz was their idol. It was easy to keep them in order. But it was far more difficult to do so with the children of the better-off parents, the badly brought-up boys and girls of ignorant fish dealers, butchers, market women and small grocers. To get the school fees out of these parents was a hard business, and Madame Hurvitz had to put up with much annoyance before she could collect even a part of them in the form of meat, fish and vegetables. The people seemed to think that they did a great honor to Hurvitz by sending their children to his school, instead of the other way about; and in their opinion it was he who should have paid them. Infected by their parents' views, the children considered themselves better than their poorer comrades who paid no fees, and arrogated all sorts of liberties. Only the skill and infinite patience of Hurvitz were responsible for the moderate degree of discipline and order that prevailed in the school.

Mirkin's first lessons passed off in tolerable peace and good order. The children were still under the spell of the curiosity awakened in them by their new teacher. But a slight loosening of discipline very soon became perceptible, mainly caused by the tricks that the two ring-leaders, Moischele "The Spider" and Chaim "The Flea," played behind Mirkin's back. The inexperienced Mirkin noticed nothing and the children burst out laughing. He saw that their laughter was at his expense, but did not know quite how to deal with the situation.

He took his new calling very seriously. That was due chiefly to his enthusiastic temperament. While he taught the children the rudiments of physics and natural history he himself grew excited by his theme; he felt now more keenly than he had ever done in his school days the greatness and the wonder of nature, and he lived through his boyhood years a second time. When he spoke about the stars he grew so worked up that he forgot the children sitting in front of him, who were watching for any opportunity to make him look ridiculous and so shake themselves free from the fetters of discipline. They had nicknamed their new teacher "The Locust," because in his first natural history lesson he had in his enthusiasm for the subject given a long lecture on the structure of insect life, using the locust as an example. After that the children seized every possible opportunity of asking him questions about the locust. In the midst of a lesson on the law of gravity in which Mirkin was doing his best to explain Newton's experiment to the children, "The Spider" raised his hand as a sign that he wished to ask a question.

"What is it?"

"Please, sir, how many legs has a locust?"

Zachary turned white with rage. "The Spider" had asked the question in the most innocent voice possible and accompanied it with such a candidly inquiring look that Mirkin was powerless. But all his enthusiasm for the wonderful phenomenon of gravity, the mysteries of nature and her sublime laws which he was so eager to explain to the children, had vanished in a clap, and in its place had appeared—a locust.

"What has the locust to do with what I've been saying?" he asked in an exasperated voice.

"Chaim and I have been arguing about it ever since yesterday. I say that a locust has six legs and he says that it has eight legs—so I thought it would be best to ask you, sir."

Mirkin bit his lip and continued his lesson, but his enthusiasm and the attention of his scholars had vanished.

"Please, sir, has a woodpecker one head or two heads?"

This time it was Chaim who asked the question, it being his turn now to torment the teacher.

This was too much for Mirkin. Completely losing his temper he rushed up to the boy and gave him a buffet. Chaim jumped up indignantly; a moment later teacher and scholar were locked together and the whole class was in confusion.

In the next room Helene was giving the girls in her class a lesson in Polish. When she heard the din she realized at once that her father was out and that the new teacher must be in grave difficulties. After a brief struggle with herself she left her class in charge of one of her scholars and went next door to see what had happened.

Mirkin was anxious that Helene, above all, should not see him in his helpless plight. If a hole had opened in the floor he would certainly have vanished into it. It took him all his time to fight back the tears that started to his eyes. He stood there, blenching and helpless, far more embarrassed than his class.

"Forgive me . . ." he stammered, pale as death.

"Please, ma'am, please, ma'am, the new teacher has struck us, and Herr Hurvitz has forbidden it," cried a few of the boys, taking heart.

"Back to your places, back to your places at once!" Helene cried imperiously. And—wonder of wonders!—the boys obeyed her command like cowed young lions and sat down in their seats.

With a reassuring smile she turned to the pale and trembling Mirkin and whispered: "Things like this often happen."

"It's my fault," said Mirkin awkwardly.

She made him a sign to be silent. Then she turned to the boys and said in a severe commanding voice that astonished Mirkin by its power and authority: "The whole class must now apologize to the teacher! Stand up!" The words rang out like an order.

The boys obediently stood up.

"Ask the teacher's pardon!"

The boys bent their heads and recited in chorus:

"We beg Herr Mirkin's pardon."

"And as a punishment you will have no more lessons today. Pack up your books and go home!"

"Please, ma'am, it isn't our fault. It was 'The Spider' and 'The Flea' that did it," began some of the boys in a beseeching voice. "We want to stay. Herr Mirkin was just telling us a lovely story about the earth and the stars."

"Not a word more! You are to go home at once!" said Helene sternly.

With bowed heads the boys packed up their school-books and slunk out like thieves caught in the act.

Mirkin still stood in the middle of the floor, completely crushed, and did not know where to look. When the boys were gone Helene went over to him and looked gravely and seriously into his eyes, as she had done a few days before when they were sitting at dinner.

"This is my fault," he began. "I'm afraid I'm no use for the work. I'll have to tell your father so."

"Don't say anything to father."

"Why not?"

"It isn't necessary. I'll speak to him."

"I'm afraid I'll never be able to teach children."

"Of course you will!" With these words she took his hand and drew him towards the door.

"Come and see my class. You'll see how I do it."

She led him by the hand into the girls' class and introduced him to the children.

"Children, this is our new teacher, Herr Mirkin. Stand up."

The girls obediently stood up.

Helene told Mirkin to sit down and continued her interrupted lesson.

Mirkin was still unable to detach his mind from the incident that had just happened. "What a wretched failure I am," he told himself and he came to the conclusion that he was fit for no occupation. "It's labor lost. It seems that I've been trained once and for all to be a 'fine gentleman.' "

But there was another impression, too, still more recent, that he could not banish from his thoughts; he could still feel the cool smoothness of Helene's hand; he felt as if he had washed his hand in new fallen snow.

But all these thoughts soon faded, for a host of children's eyes were fixed on him. No other living creature has such a sad, hopeless, forlorn gaze as can sometimes be seen in the eyes of children. On these benches were sitting young girls from the poorest Jewish families in the neighborhood, girls of from eight to fourteen years. Yet no one could have determined their age. Lost eternities looked out of their sad eyes embedded in their sharp and bony sockets. Their gaze seemed to express the complete uselessness and hopelessness of their existence. For what had they been summoned out of the eternal silence of nonentity into an empty life? But no, their glances did not question, but were merely resigned and indifferent. The melancholy dejection in these children's eyes was not caused merely by the perpetual anxieties of their fathers and the unending worries of their mothers, by the cheerless hovels in which they lived, by hunger, by pain and illness, by poverty and loneliness: it was a deep eternal groundless sadness; on the lids of these eyes there still seemed to lie that terror of the eternal night which they had brought from the other world whence, only a few years before, they had come. . . .

Most of them were clad in clothes once worn by their parents and now made down for them; some had bandages over their ears, others had swollen hands; from the dowdy clothes made up of fantastic bits and shreds that hung clumsily round them emerged emaciated childish limbs, thin, puppet-like legs, helpless birdlike heads, pitiably delicate necks which seemed to be begging one not to wring them. But the faces blurred, these poor little bodies vanished in clothes far too wide for them, and now all that Mirkin could see was a host of eyes. . . .

And amid those eyes stood Helene, herself become one of her class. The black and white checked dress that covered her fragile body also looked as if it were made of old scraps and patches. And as on the children so on her, too, there lay, from her parted hair to her finely shaped feet, a fresh dewy bloom like the bloom on a peach, which a touch might destroy; and her head, just like the heads of the scholars, drooped helplessly to one side on the slender stalk of her neck.

She went from form to form, and addressed one girl after another by name. Mirkin listened to her familiar laughing voice, which seemed to come from some fresh and inviolate spring. He saw the sadness gradually fading from the children's eyes, saw them beginning to sparkle and laugh. Their little faces grew animated, took on a flush as of health, became bright and merry. Their bodies quickened and grew younger and more childlike, and even their shapeless clothes took on as by magic a sort of childish grace. Here and there a sound as of a little brook murmuring could be heard: it was childish laughter. Little arms rose and waved like blossoming sprays. Gradually the whole class awoke to merriment and careless play. . . .

"How does she do it?" Mirkin asked himself without noticing that he himself, carried away by the magic of the children's voices, was laughing with them and had become a child. All his troubles were wiped away; his adult life had vanished. He, too, was a child sitting on his form.

"How do you do it?" He did not even notice that he had seized her hand as she turned to him.

"Do what?"

"You laugh, you play, you dance, and the children laugh with you."

"They're my friends," said Helene seriously. "Gitel and Miriam" she indicated two of the children, "Eva Taubenschlag and Schönchen Pomeranz; we've known one another for a long time," she went on with a touch of pride, "from the first day that they came to school we've been great friends. We haven't any secrets from each other, have we, Eva?" And she nodded to one of the girls.

A girl's head in one of the forms nodded back.

"But how do you manage it?"

"It happens of itself. Children soon know when any one wants to be friends with them and respond at once. There's a little friend of mine over there, for instance; Mirele, she's only eight. When she came to school first she was afraid of everybody. She had been perpetually beaten at home; her father and mother, as well as her brothers and sisters, had beaten her for every little trifle, and when she came here she was always putting her arms over her head to shield herself from blows. She thought everybody who came near here was going to strike her. It took me a long time to convince her that I didn't want to hurt her and that she needn't put up her hands when I came near her. At first she didn't want to believe me, but one day I made her come to me, looked in her face and said: 'Mirele, I won't strike you, I'll never strike you, never.' She looked at me questioningly for a long time—and believed me. So I've weaned her from her fear of me. Shall I show you? Mirele! Mirele! Come here for a moment!" she shouted into the din made by the playing children.

A little girl detached herself from the others and tripped up to Helene. She wore thick heavy shoes on her painfully thin feet. In her dress, which was made out of an old skirt of her mother's, she looked as if she were masquerading as an ancient Jewish crone. She approached cheerfully; but when she noticed the stranger her steps lagged apprehensively and she fixed her great terrified eyes piercingly upon him as if she wanted to strike this new foe with a look.

"Have no fear, Mirele. Come nearer!"

In spite of her teacher's encouragement, Mirele looked suspiciously at Zachary, obviously prepared to defend herself with her arms. At the same time she directed her course in such a way as always to have Helene between herself and Mirkin.

Once she had reached Helene she stood in the natural position of a child at its teacher's knee, with her hands by her sides. But when Helene asked her to make her bow to Mirkin and gently pushed her towards him, she raised her arms at once and put them over her head. Her great black eyes darted apprehensively around her and they blinked rapidly as if in fear of a blow.

"Mirele, this is our new teacher; he is a kind gentleman, he won't strike you, Mirele, he'll never strike you. Now take your hands away from your face."

The child still looked suspiciously at Mirkin and could not summon the courage to approach him with her face unprotected.

"Mirele, if you like me take your hand away, else I'll be angry with you," said Helene.

It was clear that Mirele was able to obey her teacher's command only by a great effort of self-control; hesitatingly she lowered her arms, but still held them in readiness for any emergency.

Zachary lifted the child on his knee. She looked in his eyes, seeking to read his intentions there, and once more raised her hands to her face.

"Mirele, haven't I told you that this is a kind gentleman, and that he would never think of striking you? Don't you believe me?"

Sitting on Zachary's knee Mirele searched Helene's face. At last she believed her and let her arms fall.

"How do you do such things?" cried Mirkin, quite carried away.

"It isn't so very difficult; one must just love the children."

"I see. I'll never be able to do that."

"Oh yes, you'll do it all right. You can do it now. Why, don't you love children just as I do, just as we all do?" Once more she looked deep in his eyes.

"Certainly. What else have I left in life?"

Helene's steadfast, almost stubborn gaze remained fixed on Mirkin for a long time, as if she were challenging him to withstand it.

"Who are you really?" she asked all at once.

Mirkin was taken aback by the question.

"Why, can't you see for yourself? A human being, if one may be allowed the title," he replied with a smile.

"There's some secret in your life," replied the girl with conviction.

"What makes you think that?"

"There's a look in your eyes—as if you had nobody in the world but yourself."

These words filled Mirkin with astonishment. He felt inclined to rise up and leave the room, but then he saw that he had no cause to be offended. The words were uttered with such affectionate sympathy that he could not resist them; he felt as if an invisible bond held him fast to the girl.

"Why do you look at me like that?" he asked, for she was still gazing at him.

Helene did not seem to hear the question. She said: "Come for a walk with me in the park after the class is dismissed: it's on the way to the place where I give my private lessons, and I would like a stroll."

CHAPTER XIX

BOY AND GIRL LOVE

HITHERTO Mirkin had not paid any particular attention to the teacher's daughters. And whenever, in his shy, reserved way, he did so, it was the younger one that he singled out. Sosha was a few years younger than her sister, yet her firm, vigorous body already gave promise of womanhood. She had the special attraction, in Mirkin's eyes, of resembling her mother. Her neck, still that of a young girl shrouded in her girlish dreams, had yet that delicious cool whiteness that fills one with a longing to bury one's face in it. For her age Sosha was unusually mature in character as well as in physique. Her breasts were firm and powerful, and every movement of her arms was full of vigor and decision. When Mirkin occasionally saw her, bare-armed and bare-legged, scrubbing the floor, the exquisite whiteness of her limbs agitated him and sent a rush of blood to his face. . . .

It was not only physically that Sosha reminded one of her mother; she had also the same decisive voice, which compelled attention just like her mother's. She never begged, she commanded, and not only in speaking to girls of her own age but to her elders as well. Her mother was forced to remind her more than once that she, and not Sosha, was the mistress of the house. In return, however, Sosha wielded almost absolute power over her elder sister. She made Helene work for her and do her school exercises, and exploited her sister's kindness of heart in every way. She wore Helene's best dresses, hair-ribbons and shoes, to which the elder sister had the prior right.

As was natural in a man of weak character, Mirkin was attracted by Sosha's energy and abounding life. On the other hand he had hardly noticed the elder sister at first. Helene belonged to the class of human beings who go through life unnoticed. There are people who seem able to turn their existence, as it were, into thin air. They live with us—and yet they remain hidden from our eyes. They hide themselves, so to speak, in a shadow that always accompanies them, and pass by us unobserved. But if by chance we should discover such a being and know how to lure her out of her concealment, then we cannot understand how it was possible that we never noticed her before.

Helene knew how to conceal herself and become invisible although seen—how to be hidden, although present. Above all she knew how to be silent, so that one could feel quite alone in her presence. Everything within her seemed to be asleep. Sleep wove a shroud round her young, still unripened girlish body. Her thin birdlike head slept between her slightly rounded shoulders. And these shoulders themselves seemed to be quite sunk in slumber; sleep seemed to lie almost palpably on them. And it lay, too, on her hair, neatly parted in the middle. She held her arms pressed close to her body like a mother shielding the child she is carrying within her, and seemed to be afraid to stretch them out. Sleep lay on all of her, on her undeveloped, almost boyish breasts. Her walk was a sort of sleep-walking. . . .

There was nothing in the girl calculated to rouse Zachary's attention. Nevertheless it would be untrue to say that he had never noticed her. He saw her, but her appearance roused no desire, no happiness in him, but something perhaps more like fear. He was afraid of Helene. The reason was that in certain ways she reminded him of his mother. This was what his mother must have looked like as a girl, enveloped in just such a cloud of slumber. This fancy awoke in him for some inexplicable reason a disagreeable, almost apprehensive feeling. Everything that reminded him of his mother had become painful to him. Why this should have been so he could not explain—but the figure of his mother, which had ruled over him in his boyhood, now roused him to annoyance, almost to hostility. No matter how hard he tried to master this strange feeling, he had to admit that it overcame him again and again. It seemed to him that his mother was to blame for his fate; it was she, and she alone, whom he had to thank for his weakness of character and his unsureness about himself. And as he hated his own character, so he hated now his mother also and everything that reminded him of her.

Zachary did not look forward to escorting Helene through the park to her private lessons: indeed the prospect was in a sense painful to him. Nevertheless he went, driven by a compulsive force that he could not understand, as if fate were leading him. He had a vague premonition that if he should ever share his life with another human being, it would not be with a woman such as he himself longed for, in whose protective tutelage he would find complete fulfillment,—a woman, for instance, like Madame Hurvitz; he divined, on the contrary, that it would be with one of those beings who have within them the seeds of submissiveness and weakness, in other words a being like himself and like his mother. And he apprehensively sought to avoid such a fate.

Nevertheless he went with Helene, though without taking the matter very seriously. He did not expect anything very much from such an innocent walk; yet the way that Helene looked at him and the incident during his morning class roused within him a vague sense of fear. Like every man of weak character he mistook the shadow for the object and his imagination magnified the "danger."

And after all, what would have been easier than to have ignored the request of a timid young girl? And yet he obeyed it though inwardly protesting and fuming at himself.

So when in the afternoon Helene set out for her private lessons she found Mirkin waiting for her at a little distance from the house. She was wearing her one and only coat of a shabby indeterminate gray with the worn and patchy russet brown fox collar, and a broad-brimmed felt hat curved downwards at one side that she had fashioned out of a man's old hat. So Mirkin had seen her daily with her hair combed down over her ears, her animated finely drawn brows, her exquisitely proportioned nose and sharp cheekbones and her girlishly slight figure. Yet now it was as if he had caught sight of the rough gray frieze coat for the first time. The old coat seemed to live, seemed to follow all the movements of her girlish body, her whole girlish being. The refashioned hat he actually found original and—a thing he had never noticed before—even coquettish. The knitted woolen gloves on her hands, which were clasping a packet of books, even they had now a strange girlish charm. Zachary was about to speak, but with a blissfully happy glance Helene whispered to him: "Not now! Come into the park! I've half an hour!"

Winter had already begun. The dirty pools on the roadway and the pavement were frozen hard. Winter twilight. The electric lights from the shop windows transformed the snowy air into a yellow cloud in which everything sparkled.

When they reached the park a new world opened before them. Still unsullied, the snow lay in regular layers on the tree branches and flower beds. The measure and weight that God had given it was still untouched. In the glimmering dusk everything looked real and yet unreal. The electric lamps, casting their radiance on the white snow, gave the park a still more fantastic appearance. A cold wind passed over the top of the snow, sweeping before it a dust of fine snow crystals; and in the light of the lamps these were transformed into a cloud of flying jewels. The atmosphere was charged with electricity, in whose mighty current millions of sparks gleamed out and faded again, as though hordes of glow-worms were whirling in the air. Happy voices rang through the twilight. People walked faster than usual in the dim paths. But no human being and no shape could be distinctly seen; every palpable form was erased; there remained only dark silhouettes, voices, movement. The trees, the crowds, were shrouded in a pale wintry mist. . . .

Zachary could feel Helene's hand cool in his, and yet it warmed him. In silence she led him towards a short and unfrequented path. There they sat down on a bench.

From this point they had a splendid view of the brightly lit skating rink, from which floated up the sound of gay voices. A confusion of lights, mingled with echoing cries, came through the network of naked twigs. The radiance from the ice rink lit up the tree tops redly; in that clear brightness they looked like glittering and fantastic dream shapes. Zachary and Helene sat side by side; fanned by the same cool wind, the same cool air, they felt as if they were safely wrapped away. Zachary became a child again, and Helene too. Everything else forgotten, he longed only to know one thing, what it was she saw in his eyes, since she was always seeking them with hers. But simply because he was so eager to hear something about his own eyes she would say nothing about them, but began to talk about the trees.

"I love the trees in winter far more than in summer. In summer they disguise themselves and don't show their true faces. . . . But in winter they throw off their disguise and look like human beings that have been bound for ever to one place by a spell. They stretch imploring fingers towards the sky. Just look how many fingers they've got!" She pointed at the naked trees.

He could feel her nearness to him while his hand stroked her cold rough coat.

"Do you know what the trees do at night when nobody sees them?" she suddenly asked.

"No, I don't know," Zachary smiled.

"In the religious books, father says, it's written that the trees pray at night when nobody is there. But I think that they move about then and pay visits to one another." She laughed merrily. "They all visit their wives and talk about the life they used to lead. Don't you believe that, too?"

"I've never thought about it, and I'm quite indifferent to the trees just now. The only thing I want to know just now is why you look so deep into my eyes. What is it you want to find there?"

"I like looking in your eyes, for they're so childish."

Zachary did not understand. "Childish?" he repeated.

"I had always thought you were so sure of yourself and that nothing could touch you. But recently—it was that day you came to us while we were having dinner—I happened to catch sight of your eyes and there was such a bewildered look in them, as if you were a child still. Your lips trembled. Then you seemed like a child that had got lost."

He smiled to himself when she came to the word "child." What could it be in his expression that was so childish, seeing that every woman could detect it?

"And you're grown up yourself, I suppose?" he asked, seizing her hand again.

Helene looked at him in surprise.

"Do you think I'm a child? Why, I teach a class!"

"But why do you take *me* for a child? After all I'm older than you and have had more experience of life."

"I don't know why it is," she replied. "But when one looks at you one can see that you look like a child in spite of your beard, like one of my little girls when she comes to the school for the first day feeling quite lost."

"I must be a very stupid fellow, seeing that everybody looks upon me as a mere child."

"Children aren't stupid," she said gravely. "Children are the wisest creatures on earth. When children want anything they always make sure they get it. You're a child." She gently withdrew her hand and passed it caressingly over his face.

Zachary grew pale. He caught her hand and said in a low voice: "What are you doing?"

"I don't know what I'm doing."

They were silent for a while.

"Children are strong," she said half to herself.

"They certainly aren't that," replied Zachary.

"Oh yes, they are, I know. Aren't you strong?"

Zachary smiled: "I?"

"I know all about you. You've broken with everybody and made a new start, standing on your own feet, all by yourself."

It was like a discovery to Zachary: "Standing on my own feet? Was that what you said?"

"Certainly. You've put everything behind you and gone away to begin again all by yourself. Would many people have done that in your place?"

"I doubt whether that was what really happened. People don't act well or badly; they do what necessity, what the circumstances force them to do."

"Do you regret what you've done?" she asked.

"I don't regret it, but I see no necessity in it, no object either perhaps. . . ." He did not finish.

Helene seized his hand: "Why do you think that?"

"You say I'm starting anew, but it seems to me as if I were at an end. People who start anew know what they want and make straight for their goal; they have no doubts and see no shadows. Your father is a man of that type, so is his friend, the Zionist, and the Shachliner, and your mother certainly. They all see their road clear in front of them. With me it's different: hardly do I begin upon something when I see its dark side and begin to doubt. I'm always telling myself: 'Perhaps those who think otherwise are right too.' In your circle everybody is quite certain of what he says: I never am."

"What's bad in that? It's a good thing you should feel like that!"

"It may be good for people who stand aside, but not for those who want to take part in life and be of use to their fellows."

"And why can't you walk your road alone as you see it?"

"That's all right for the strong; but the weak need a bridle and a whip, otherwise the demon inside them will drive them God knows where."

Helene's heart was moved more by the sad voice in which he said this than by the words themselves. She felt the incomprehensible grief that seemed to cry out of him. Her hand seized his, she pressed her body close against him, gazed lovingly in his eyes and said with a beseeching glance: "What is it that you want? Why do you talk like that?"

"I don't want anything."

"You do want something. You're so sad, so tormented. Sometimes I can hear an infinitely sad music in your voice. What is it that's wrong? Tell me!"

"I suppose there must be an orchestra inside me that plays without my knowing it." Zachary laughed.

"Don't talk like that, please don't talk like that! You're suffering."

"It's very good of you, but I assure you that my sufferings aren't worth your pity."

"Why do you talk like that?"

Suddenly she bowed her cold face over his; Zachary felt the warmth of her breath on his mouth and eyes.

"What are you doing?" he asked in alarm.

"I don't know, I don't know," the girl whispered with shut eyes, nestling close to him and pressing her lips to his face.

"Don't do that! Don't do that!"

"I want to . . . I want to," she whispered and she kept her open lips thirstily pressed to his cheek.

Zachary felt a strand of her hair brushing his face; it had escaped from under her hat and fell over her eyes. He saw her slim throat beneath her bowed head; his arm stole round her thin shoulders.

Two wide open eyes, pure and fresh as if they had only now opened for the first time, gazed at him in painful rapture.

CHAPTER XX

HOURS OF TORMENT

In spite of all he could do Mirkin's desires were too strong for him, stronger even than his fear. He began to wander through the muddy streets by himself; Helene and he sat in the frost and cold in the city park and held hands like youngsters of fifteen. He had not only become young again, but like every lover, stupid as well. Whenever

Helene went to give her private lessons he accompanied her just for the pleasure of being with her. For hours he would stand in a doorway in the bleak street opposite the house into which she had disappeared, and wait until she came out again. He paid no attention to the weather or the risk of getting a chill; to be with her, to see her cheeks flushed with the cold—they were all that was visible to him between her fox collar and her soft felt hat—was an end so high and so well worth striving for that it made him neglect his work. The touch of her rough, weathered coat had for him the seductive charm of smooth naked flesh; and if he was allowed to gaze at her smoothly parted hair when she took off her hat the final pinnacle of happiness was reached. . . .

At dinner the glances they cast at each other were no longer open and frank, but stolen. They imagined that all the world knew of their love, took notice of everything and read their thoughts; so they only exchanged glances fearfully and at long intervals, and that itself awoke suspicion. The teacher himself became aware of this play of glances one Friday evening while he was reading out the customary lesson, and later questioned his daughter about it. But Rachel-Leah saved the situation by her presence of mind, exclaiming indignantly: "What are you going on at the girl for? She doesn't mean any harm. And Mirkin is a decent fellow and I'm sure his intentions are of the best. What do you expect? A young man and a girl have eyes in their heads after all, and they're bound to use them. You used your eyes too when you were younger." Thus she made fun of the matter and of her husband at the same time.

Zachary would assuredly have taken long before this the decisive step that his desires and his conscience dictated and asked Helene's parents for her hand, if his respectable upper class upbringing had not stood in the way; for it told him that he had no right to assume obligations which he could not carry out. And that upper class upbringing, which had accompanied him to the threshold of the Hurvitzes' house, which not even his meal in the municipal kitchen had been able to eradicate, persisted in posing the question: "What right have you to think of marriage when you can't provide your wife with everything she may need? What right have you to think of happiness when you have no real home to bring her to, no roof to shelter your happiness, and no money for a sack of coal to keep it warm?" His upbringing, in short, did not tell him that happiness very often has no roof and has to freeze, although he himself had actually discovered this by experience. . . .

Later his egoism suggested to him the idea of demanding back the share of his mother's legacy that he had renounced so light-heartedly. The idea was not yet ready to be translated into action, but yet far enough advanced to convince him that his decision to return to his father the money that really belonged to himself had been premature, rash and dictated merely by his first impulse. "Father's behavior doesn't deserve, at any rate, that I should throw my mother's money at his head," he told himself. "I should have reacted to it in quite a different way; that's certain."

But soon his pride flamed up again and he reproached himself for even thinking of demanding back the money. He was seized by disgust and loathing for everything that smacked of Petersburg, for the family of which he came, for his upbringing and his former life.

"Not that, not that at least!" He shivered with disgust, as though he had touched something unclean.

But one day something occurred that made him think differently of these matters.

Hitherto his meetings with Helene, meetings when they could hold hands familiarly and be happy, had always taken place in the street and in the park, in frost and wind. All that he had of her was her rough coat, which, though it bore for him in all its folds the fragrance of her body, had in it too the chill coldness of the streets. The worn shabby fox collar represented still more; its mangy fur held the warmth of Helene's girlish throat. But her felt hat was dearest of all to him; it possessed something of her eyes and also something of her hair. Yet all these things had also in them the coldness of the streets.

Mirkin had lately moved into his new lodgings, a little box of a room whose one window looked out on a courtyard that even by day was artificially lit. This room was his honorarium for the tutorial lessons that he gave to the son of a master-tailor, who was relatively well-off; it was small but clean, and resembled a student's room. Helene had never been in this room. Zachary's upbringing forbade him even to think of inviting her there. . . .

One evening while he was sitting at his table over a book, reading by the light of the table lamp, he heard a voice asking for him in the passage. Before he had time to get up Helene entered without knocking.

She was wearing as ever her rough coat with the fox fur collar and the felt hat. In one hand she carried her school-books and exercise books, in the other a little bunch of violets, in the middle of which was a little yellow spray of mimosa.

"I wanted to see how you actually live," she said in an apprehensive and guilty voice in response to his glance of delighted surprise.

He took her books from her. The violets she clutched convulsively in her hand and for a long time did not seem to know what to do with them. At last she plucked up courage and laid the little bouquet on the open book under the lamp.

There was only one chair in the room, the one from which Zachary had risen. Behind it stood the bed, on which was spread a heavy woolen checked rug that he had brought with him from Petersburg (it was a souvenir of his father's luxurious house).

He sat down on the bed and pushed the chair forward for Helene. "Won't you take off your coat for a little? You'll get cold when you leave if you don't."

It was very warm in the room, and the green shade of the lamp threw a homely gleam on the table.

"Could you bring a glass or a vase for the violets? They'll wither if they aren't put in water."

He went to the kitchen for a glass of water. When he returned he found her in her black and white checked dress, her head bare, and her hair coiled in plaits over her ears—but instead of the hard chair she was sitting on the bed, pressed against the very foot and holding on with both hands to the bed post.

Zachary pushed the chair close up to her.

Like boy and girl they gazed into each other's eyes.

Instead of her coat—her house dress; instead of her hat with its memories of the street—her bare head, and best of all her face, quite uncovered now, with its wide-open apprehensive eyes. Glittering blue fires swam in her pupils. Cool fresh girlish cheeks, finely cut lips trembling with longing. A delicate white throat rising unprotected from the neck of her dress and begging for him to put his arms round it.

Dumb childish play of hands and fingers. Dumb childish gaze of eyes into eyes.

Their mouths found each other and drank deeply.

As he flung his arms round her he became aware of the firm flexible body under her dress. He had never realized before that a girl's body could be at once so firm and so yielding, that a girl's delicate arms could clasp with such boyish strength. He could feel all the longing of her taut body through the checked dress....

The violence of his embrace pulled the neck of her dress somewhat to one side. A young round shoulder appeared, white, downy, chaste. He saw the embroidered edge of her chemise and a glimpse of a tender girlish bosom: it seemed to hold a thousand girlish secrets....

Zachary drank in the girl's body deeply with his lips and eyes.

For an endless moment their bodies touched.

Then they hastily tore themselves asunder and painfully drew apart. Mirkin looked down with tormented bloodshot eyes at the girl and said: "Come, Helene, let us go!"

Her eyes opened wide in her pale face. Her outstretched arms remaining hanging in the air.

"Why, Zachary?"

Nevertheless she obediently put on her rough coat, which Zachary held out to her.

CHAPTER XXI

A WARSAW MANUFACTURER

In the block where Madame Hurvitz lived there was a weaving factory such as was to be found in great numbers in all the back courts of Warsaw. It was a "Chassidic" factory; that was to say, all the workers employed in it were pious Jews. It belonged to a certain Berl Korngold, who was known in the court and the neighborhood as "Berl the Manufacturer." The story of this "manufacturer" is worth relating.

Berl belonged to a Chassidic family, and as a young man wore the closely fitting caftan fashionable in Warsaw and one of those characteristic little Warsaw hats with the tiny brims that were produced by a firm in the Nalevki for the dandies of the town. Berl had been brought up in the traditional Chassidic fashion and had some knowledge of the Talmud. But presently his father's business began to fail, and so the son was obliged to become a hand-worker. Yet the term "hand-worker" is not quite appropriate, perhaps, for it was machine knitting that he set himself to learn, a favorite resource at that time for youths of Chassidic families who did not want to sink to the wretched level of becoming ordinary tailors and shoemakers. Berl worked for a pious Jew who had two knitting machines. One of them was supervised by himself, the other by his daughter, a girl of marriageable age who had only one wish, to get a husband; and the father desired this just as ardently as she did. She earned her own dowry by making her father pay her a wage, out of which she purchased in instalments the machine at which she worked. So half of the "factory" became her property. With this pious Jew, then, who attended the same synagogue as his father, Berl learned the business and soon became the manager of the "factory." For he mastered not only his own job, but showed himself clever at devising color-schemes which appealed to women.

In consequence he very soon had the whole conduct of the factory in his hands. From the very start he had made a deep impression on the daughter of his employer. She was a sumptuous blonde with full round neck which seemed to echo the cry of her overdeveloped body for a husband, a desire which indeed was justified by her years. Her impatient tempestuous blood had sown her face with countless spots and pimples. Very soon the two young people betrayed their mutual inclinations by silent glances, and long before any marriage-broker had been seized by the idea of making a couple of them they were going for long walks on their Friday evenings. Out of respect for his long caftan Berl walked in front as long as they were still in the town, with the girl following behind; but, when they reached the meadows beside the Jewish cemetery and the fortress, they sought the bushes for preference and there did things which were not always connected with their factory work. . . .

When at last a marriage-broker was found (actually Berl and the girl prompted him) to arrange the marriage, Berl's parents insisted that the girl should bring both machines as her dowry, the one belonging to her father no less than the one she had paid for herself. (The two lovers also had agreed upon this during their secret walks together.) In vain the father-in-law tried to defend himself against this attack: "How am I to live? I must eat like everybody else!" Berl shrugged his shoulders, his fiancée was deaf to her father's protests. At last her pious parents, whose sole wish was to see their daughter married, had to give in willy-nilly, especially as she kept wearing them down by floods of tears. Berl received both machines as his wife's dowry, and his father-in-law, who had hitherto been the "manufacturer," worked for his son-in-law for a weekly wage after the marriage. . . .

When this stage was reached Berl proceeded to "exploit" his machines. He took on an apprentice—it was actually a grown Jew with a beard and a wife and children, who wanted to learn the trade. In addition Berl employed several boys, whom he kept busy winding wool on the spools till late at night. He was indefatigable and had inspirations which were actually brilliant. Nobody was his equal in making up new patterns, and he always knew which colors were going to be fashionable. So he produced beige and orange fabrics for the young and a sober gray shot with black for the more elderly. He also concocted seductive trimmings and edgings of divers colors for the necks and sleeves of women's dresses, and fringes and flowers that became a great rage. His products were actually fought for and he was overwhelmed with checks which he deposited at a high rate of interest in a little Chassidic bank.

At the beginning he himself worked with the others; his zeal and energy spurred on his father-in-law, who now stood at one of the machines, the pious Chassidic Jew, who was serving his apprenticeship, and the younger apprentices whose task it was to lift the webs, fix the threads and throw to the machine workers the spools of different hued wools which in the "warp" had to be combined in all manner of fancy patterns. Presently he set up a few more machines in the little house he had taken over from his father-in-law, and took several more Chassidic apprentices into his employment.

In his neighborhood Berl had a good reputation; his products were eagerly fought for by the agents who bought for the shops in the provinces; and both facts helped to procure him credit from the factory where the knitting machines were produced, the wool dealers and the little Chassidic bank, which was situated near the Iron Gate. From now on Berl no longer worked, but contented himself with supervising and spurring on his Jewish workmen and apprentices, and with giving out and determining the colors to be used. For the rest he occupied himself with the financial side of the undertaking, which, aping the phraseology of the great magnates, he termed henceforth "my department." Gradually his caftan grew shorter and shorter, and he began to wear stiff collars and trim his beard. Finally he boldly adopted modern attire and appeared in a peaked collar and a bowler hat. His beard dwindled to an imperial, his moustache curled up at the points. Soon after their marriage his wife had begun to spread. Her sumptuous form, which until then had still, as it were, kept within girlish bounds, seemed, when at last she had secured a husband, resolved to take unbridled advantage of its freedom and burst all the constricting boundaries of her nonage.... Her neck, shoulders and bosom in particular gave free vent to their potentialities. For the sake of decency she still wore a wig, but it grew smaller and smaller, blending gradually with her own hair, which she brushed over and round it with the most consummate skill. She wore knitted dresses in fancy hues made in the factory, and summer and winter—for the sake of keeping up the family's credit—a long Persian lambskin coat just as if she were the wife of a millionaire.

Ever since the time when his father-in-law had run it, Berl's "factory" had enjoyed the reputation in Chassidic circles of being a pious Jewish house. Women were not employed; all the work was done by men. The master allowed his employees to stop work for their evening prayers. So pious Jews who were driven by necessity to take up hard work willingly went to Berl to serve their apprenticeship. Chassidic Jews never visited any of the workers' clubs; Marxism was a conception unknown in Berl's factory, and the sole existing workmen's association in Warsaw at the time, the "Unity" association, whose members consisted of youthful free-thinkers, had no access to the pious concern. There were no set working hours; one worked as long as one liked. If a worker grew tired he slept for a while, leaning against his machine; when he awoke, with renewed vigor, the shuttles began to whir again.

By now Berl's concern was already a large factory. It was still housed in his father-in-law's premises for the sake of keeping the luck that had always attended it; for since business had been so good in these rooms Berl was afraid of changing now out of fear of "the evil eye." The kitchen, too, was turned into a work-room and the father-in-law banished upstairs to a small garret.

Twelve machines stood in the place so close to each other that it was scarcely possible for any one to move. At the foot of each machine was a revolving spool; beside the spools, almost hidden by the workers' caftans, sat the boy apprentices winding the wool in darkness; their eyes had to serve them not only for seeing but as lamps too. Twelve Jews in long caftans, their beards tangled with wool, sat chained to the knitting machines, their long lath-like bodies bent over the shuttles. Their faces were invisible; nothing could be seen but black shoulders and backs swaying like black shadows; at either side of them rose a long iron bar with hooks which seemed like a part of their bodies. Half man and half machine: these human and mechanical bodies seemed to be interlaced and knit together. From behind these human bodies the smooth, oily rhythm of the machines, the clattering rise and fall of the hooks could be heard. A thin flame of bright colored wool flitted across nimbly as a mouse, picking up the stitch. Man and machine were so confounded in the darkness of the room and of the caftans that the oily panting of the machine seemed like the sound of men breathing. In the gloom the machines completely disappeared behind the men's dark bowed backs, and one might have thought that these Jews were standing over Talmud machines as they perpetually swayed from side to side day and night. . . .

The workroom was also the storeroom and the shop. Beneath the ceiling, on the window ledges, in every nook and corner, in every available place, could be seen woolen fabrics wrapped in dusty paper parcels; on shelves, on boards, behind curtains. Woolen threads saturated with oil floated over the machines and spools, lighted on the men's faces, got caught in their beards, settled on woolen bales, covered the floor, the ceiling, the windows, the electric lights, every crack, every nook, every protuberance; they filled the whole room. The men breathed in wool along with the air, ate wool along with their food, exhaled wool when they spoke. . . . Here one literally lived in wool.

And amid this woolen snow Berl stood at his "office desk." His "office desk" was an ingenious contrivance adroitly fitted in a tiny space between an excised door panel and a machine. Whoever entered the factory knocked first of all against the "office desk." Behind the desk, that protruded a little beyond the door panel, stood Berl with his imperial, in the stiff collar to which his neck did not yet seem to have accustomed itself, and negotiated with his customers from the provinces. These had to stand outside the door in the passage. In consequence there was a standing feud between Berl and the landlord, the latter holding the view that Berl had no right to the use of the passage, while Berl argued that it could not matter to the landlord if his customers used the passage, for it did not cause the landlord any expense.

Business went splendidly. Berl was soon known to all Warsaw as one of the "great." He greeted men who were richer than himself, and let those who were not so rich greet him. He extended his business steadily and carried a pocket-book full of bills of exchange, which he called his "portfolio." So things went on prosperously, as if they had always done so and must always do so.

One day Berl complacently entered the Chassidic bank beside the Iron Gate in his fine fur coat, so as to hand over his "portfolio" of checks and bills and in return lift the money he needed to pay his workers. But Herr Grützhändler, a highly respectable figure with his elegantly fitting frock coat and his elegantly groomed black beard, pushed the "portfolio" back and said in an indifferent professional voice, without even taking his five copek cigar from between his teeth: "We cannot do anything for you, Herr Korngold."

"Why not?" asked Berl in mingled astonishment and offense. "I've a whole bunch of checks here, all good."

"Even if they were from Rothschild it wouldn't make any difference," retorted the banker, calmly wiping away some cigar ash that had fallen on his beard.

"What? Is it going to cost me another half per cent? Impossible, Herr Grützhändler, I simply can't do it!" cried Berl in his usual bargaining voice.

"Even if you paid two per cent more it wouldn't matter," replied the banker, once more flicking with his fingers the ash from his beard and the broad silk lapel of his dress coat.

Berl became uneasy.

"What has happened?"

"A crisis. There's a shortage of money."

"But, Herr Grützhändler, I must pay my workmen!"

"You can see for yourself that I've no time to speak to you, my dear sir!" replied Herr Grützhändler impatiently and he disappeared between the heavy double doors of his safe.

Berl rushed from one bank to another, offered one, two, five per cent interest per month, but everywhere he received the same response: "A crisis."

Berl wondered to himself: "What's that: a crisis? I've work enough in hand, thank God, my storeroom is full, the buyers for the shops in the provinces keep simply rushing in and pressing bills into my hand. I can't understand it—what has happened? Who has done this?"

At the "black exchange," where he offered ten per cent and a mortgage on his factory to get himself out of the noose he was caught in (he had one or two bills for raw material, too, that were almost due), he was given the explanation: "The situation is this. For economic reasons the great banks have stopped giving credit to the small ones. If the great ones refuse it, where are the small ones to find it?"

Berl could not still make out what the "economic reasons" could be that had forced the great banks to refuse credit.

"And because of these reasons I, Berl, am worth not a farthing? What about my bills? And isn't my shop a shop still, are my machines not machines still? What has happened in the devil's name?" He tugged at his imperial and simply could not understand in what these "economic reasons" could consist.

So this time Berl returned without any money from "the banks." (This was the standing formula for his absences from the factory; for his wife always said, when some one called and he was out: "My husband is at the banks," a sentence which in her opinion greatly enhanced the estimation of the concern.) When he returned he looked like a plucked fowl. The roses had faded from his cheeks, his mustache had lost its curl and drooped sadly, his little hat that usually sat so neatly on his skull (Berl was very particular about his clothes) was all to one side. His arrival was not announced as usual by the imperious tapping of his walking stick; he stole unobtrusively into his own factory and began to speak to his workers at first timidly and almost guiltily, then with more spirit: "What can I do if the banks won't give me any money? I can't pay you your wages this week!"

"But that won't do! How are we to get food to eat?" a dejected voice came from behind one of the machines.

"What can I do? There's a crisis!"

"How can *we* help that?"

"How can *I* help it? Here, take these bills! I get nothing but bills; I'll have to pay you in them too!" And he shook the bills out of his "portfolio."

"Are we to cook bills and eat them?" asked the Chassidic worker who had already spoken, getting more hardy, and in his indignation he made his machine spin violently.

Berl fought against his fate and struggled for a little while longer like a fish flung by a wave on dry land. His wife's Persian fur coat, his gold watch, a few silver candlesticks and a few bales of finished goods were disposed of to turn aside the approaching disaster, but soon Berl was "dead."

Now the machines in the two rooms stood silent and motionless;

they did not stir, and all life seemed to have faded from them. They became scrap iron. Wisps of wool fell on them like a snow shower, stopped up the eyes of the shuttles and spread like a spider's web on everything. Berl walked about in his factory, generally so full of life and movement, as in a mortuary.

He regarded his silent machines now as if they were corpses that should be carried away; the great bales of finished goods in which once he had seen his accumulated wealth seemed to him now like heaps of rags that nobody would touch; his "portfolio" crammed with bills that had been as good currency as gold contained scraps of paper; and he himself with all his skill in striking out new patterns, ribbons, collars and tassels that turned all the women's heads, seemed a wretched worm which was being trampled beneath the feet of the great and the small bankers.

Day after day, whenever she passed the court, Rachel-Leah could see Berl's workmen, pious Jews all of them, standing shivering and hungry in their black caftans before the factory. They came daily from old habit and sat down on the stairs leading to the workshop, stood about all day in the wind and cold and went home again at night. Whenever Berl issued from his factory he would fling them a dark glance and say: "Why are you standing there?"

"What else is there for us to do?" they would reply timidly.

The same fate as Berl's befell Schmul, the leather dresser, Chaim, the confectioner, and Jossel the cardboard-box maker.

None of them understood what had happened. Employer and worker went about helplessly, their eyes filled with dazed fear. Somewhere or other was lying a rotting corpse that spread pestilence over the whole city; it was "the crisis."

Then the frost set in and bound the city in its icy arms.

CHAPTER XXII

IN THE ARMS OF HUNGER AND COLD

Soon, like a true mother, hunger took the poor population of Warsaw to its arms. From the warrens of the Warsaw tenements, in which previously the ceaseless hum of machines and the clang of hammers were heard, rose now one single cry of lamentation. The whole Jewish factory and home industry which produced wares for the Russian and Asiatic markets was at a standstill. Not a single branch of that industry was organized. It depended entirely on the money markets. . . . Without any ostensible cause it would suddenly find itself busy and prosperous, not because there was a great run on its products, but simply because bank credits could be obtained at a cheap rate. But when there was the slightest sign of money shortage the whole industry would just as suddenly come to a stop.

The crisis in the clothing and leather goods industries soon involved also the smaller tradesmen who catered for the domestic population, the tailors, joiners, cobblers, saddlers and others. Presently the town was full of unemployed, hungry, shivering people, who with wide staring eyes and trembling limbs wandered about the streets as if driven on by some strange sickness. These aimlessly straying crowds stood with their noses pressed to the frost-rimed windows of the shops where food was to be had and regarded longingly and with watering mouths the sausages, herrings and other delicacies that were so dear to the people of Warsaw. While the cold was still endurable the unmarried workmen lounged about the Labor Exchanges, where agitators and political propagandists assailed their ears with the various fighting and strike policies that their parties advocated. But when the first severe frosts came everybody crept back into his hole and tried to warm it by burning the remainder of his furniture or wood stolen from some fence. The streets were quite dead. At a corner here and there a few policemen and street walkers could be seen warming themselves round an improvised fire. Now and then a shivering housewife would run across the street, driven out by the bitter cold, by the chill shroud that lay over the rooms. Women carrying half-frozen children wrapped in tattered rags hopped from one foot to the other, blew on their hands to warm them and slipped into a shop to breathe freely for a while and get a little warmth, but were soon driven out into the street again.

Rachel-Leah had long before said that she did not like the look of that winter. She had her particular reasons for thinking so.

When the first frosts came there had been loud complaints among the people who lived in the tenement.

Old Chaye, who lived with her grand-daughter in a garret, was the first to issue from her room and seat herself on a step before the front door beside the grocer's shop, where the people who went into it must pass her. She had wrapped herself in all the tatters she possessed, and stretching out her hand begged from the passers-by: "Good people, give me something to buy a blanket!"

Rachel-Leah, whose eyes nothing escaped, stopped beside the old woman. Old Chaye had never done anything like this before. She had always managed to keep going until now, along with her fifteen-year-old grand-daughter who helped her to sell the rolls, biscuits and other "tit-bits" that she hawked about in workshops and factories.

Rachel-Leah was particularly struck by the fact that the old woman did not beg for bread, as was usual, but for a blanket.

"Chaye, what are you doing?" she asked. "You'll get your death of cold here."

"Better freeze to death here than up in my garret; nobody will know about it if I die there."

"Where is your grand-daughter?"

"That's just the trouble. Up to now I've slept with her in the same bed and she kept me warm. Ever since she left me I've been cold. If I only had a blanket it wouldn't be so bad, for I could stay in bed; but it's so cold as it is that I can't stay there."

"Why has your grand-daughter left you?"

"Why shouldn't she leave me? God knows I've nothing to give her! At best she could only freeze along with me in my garret. After all she's grown-up now and can get on without my help. She'll look after herself all right!"

On the same floor as old Chaye lived Chaim, "The Horse." He was a porter; and he had got the nickname of "The Horse" because he did a horse's work. For he drew a cart. He had a partner, another "talking horse"; this was Moses, whose nickname was "The Cudgel"; he pulled the cart along with Chaim.

These two men were prodigiously strong. When they were harnessed with straps to their cart they could have pulled a house from its foundations. All week they were yoked to their cart transporting bales of cloth, crates of crockery, iron bars, in short all that was transportable, from one place to another. Amid the rattle of wheels on the bridges spanning the Vistula they dragged their cart, their backs pouring with sweat. Only one thing distinguished them from their four-legged brothers. When horses pulled a cart loaded with iron bars across the miry bridges they did so in silence; but when Chaim and Moses dragged their cart over the frozen mud they accompanied their work with curses by means of which they encouraged each other. So they were horses and drivers at the same time.

"Pull, you shirker! Have you gone to sleep? Do you think you're lying in bed with your wife?"

"Don't you worry about me. I'll pull all right when the right time comes."

"Just look how you're trying to get out of it! This is how to pull, you lousy beggar!"

Fired by these inspiriting words of his comrade, little Moses would stem his short powerful legs in the mire until his feet found firm ground, bow his short thick neck with all his might and drag the cart forward.

Now and then these two human horses would converse about their "fodder" as they walked side by side in harness.

"The potatoes have gone up again six copeks; and cabbage has gone up, too, a plague upon it! Soon a man will get nothing to eat for his money!"

"Don't I know that! I've eight mouths to feed!"

One day Rachel-Leah noticed that Chaim "The Horse" wasn't yoked to his cart as usual. He walked about the court idly, and behaved as if he had cast off his harness once and for all. Chaim "The Horse" was not exactly an Adonis: his right eye had watered ever since his childhood and had grown smaller and smaller ever since, and now there was a dried scar on the half shut lid behind which his pupil peeped out. From beneath the ragged leather peak of his cap a black shock of hair fell on his low forehead. Under the peak of this cap Chaim would look at you first with his half-shut eye and then with his open one, and so menacingly that he seemed to be waiting for a chance to get you in a dark corner, seize you by the throat and revenge himself on you for all the filth and misery of his childhood passed in dank cellars, which had left their traces in the great pock-marks that covered his face. He looked like an animal that has to fight its way through some thorny thicket and at the same time defend itself against the teeth and claws of its kind. No single part of him was complete and whole: his nose was broken, his ear was split, and down his neck ran the long scar of a knife-wound. With his tattered lambskin coat open, showing his gay knitted muffler and his shirt and vest, he walked about the courtyard swaying slightly as if he were drunk. But that was not the case; he was merely unaccustomed to walking without his "harness." His hob-nailed boots stamped angrily in the hard ice and he spat and cursed to himself.

At a safe distance, her arms raised defensively, her eyes filled with fear, his wife followed him. Beneath her tattered wrap it could be seen that she was pregnant, though a dirty infant's head peeped out from her shawl. Without heeding the other tenants she screamed: "Chaim, you blackguard, do you want me and the children to starve?"

Chaim gave no answer. His eyes glittered dangerously beneath the peak of his cap. He clutched his short bony nose in his fingers as if he wanted to tear it out by the roots, spat at the nearest heap of snow and gave a lump of ice that lay in his road such a mighty kick that it flew clattering against a door.

"We're freezing. The last chair has been broken up for firewood and the stove has been taken away. What am I to do now?" The woman turned to some people who were passing.

"You can go and hang yourself!" Chaim said between his teeth.

"And what about the children?"

"You can take the whole pack with you!"

Rachel-Leah, who was just crossing the court, was drawn in spite of herself into the domestic dispute, for Chaim's wife turned to her: "I ask you, Frau Hurvitz, isn't it disgraceful? He takes a holiday in the middle of the week! There isn't a lump of coal in the house, I and my little ones are freezing, and he's put off his harness and refuses to go to work!"

Rachel-Leah was looked up to by the whole house and so even Chaim "The Horse" thought it necessary to justify himself before her: "What good does it do if I drag the cart from the Nalevki to Tvarda Street and back again, half dead with hunger and cold, until my shoulders are all swollen? You slave yourself to death and you don't make enough even to buy coal! The last chair is burned—so everything can go hang for all I care."

Chaim looked like a stubborn horse. Even Rachel-Leah's kind glance by which she tried to appease him and coax him into harness again remained without effect.

"How can I do anything to help her? Yesterday I pulled the cart all day and brought nothing back but a rouble. And she spent it on coal. When I got up this morning she hadn't even a crust of bread for me! Just tell me yourself, Frau Hurvitz," he turned to Rachel-Leah, "how can I pull a cart on an empty stomach?"

"And what can I do? The children are freezing!" The wife now sought to justify herself before Rachel-Leah. "How could I help it? I *had* to buy a little coal. Was I to let the children die of cold?"

"She's right. The house must be kept warm first of all," said Rachel-Leah, taking the wife's side.

"But even a horse gets its fodder; it can't work without its oats," shouted Chaim. "That's right, isn't it?"

Rachel-Leah could say nothing in answer to this argument of the "talking horse." With a deep sigh she turned away; she had worries of her own to deal with at home.

But she felt sorriest of all for Henoch the joiner, her neighbor. He was waiting for her in her kitchen when she returned. He scratched his head dejectedly and said nothing.

"What is it, Henoch?" she asked in surprise when she saw him; for Henoch had never come to her for advice before.

"I'm afraid I'll have to do it. There's no other way," said Henoch half to himself, without raising his eyes.

"What has happened?"

"Nothing for it but the jemmy. I'll have to take a jemmy with me and do some night-work along with my brother-in-law."

"What are you thinking of, Henoch? What has happened?"

"Frau Hurvitz, there's no other choice left for me, I'll have to do it!" cried the joiner desperately.

Rachel-Leah went nearer and looked searchingly at him. She could hardly recognize him. This childish fellow who was always laughing and had borne his lot with careless gayety was completely changed; his face was white and gloomy. He gnawed at his mustache; his eyes, usually so frank, evaded her.

"What has happened?" Rachel-Leah asked once more in alarm.

"As long as the children were well I never complained and bore everything. But when they begin to die round me like flies I can't stand it any longer. I'll have to do it!"

"What will you have to do?"

"What my brother-in-law advised me to do: get hold of a jemmy and break into some house. It's the only thing left."

"What are you thinking of, Henoch? Aren't you ashamed of yourself?" Rachel-Leah stared at him in astonishment.

Henoch turned his face to the wall as if he wanted to hide it there, snatched the door-handle and rushed away without answering.

Rachel-Leah saw that she must act. She did not know what she should do, and being able to think of nothing sat worriedly seeking a solution in her kitchen chair. The Shachliner appeared. Recently he had always been on the go, remaining away sometimes for whole days and very seldom appearing in the house. When he did appear it was only for a short time; then he vanished again. He had changed greatly. This was no longer the Shachliner whom Frau Hurvitz had been so fond of, but a silent and morose man. When he entered the kitchen Frau Hurvitz was sitting in her corner gnawing her nails in impotent rage and muttering to herself: "A fine world! It should be exterminated!"

The Shachliner's coming was very timely, and she vented all her anger on him: "Oho, here comes my world redeemer! All you can do is spout! People are dying like flies, and a fool like you never thinks of lifting a finger."

"What can we do? There's nothing left for us but to lie in our holes and rot until the whole town is infected," growled the Shachliner, gesticulating violently with his paralyzed arm. "The position is getting worse and worse. These capitalists have vamped up this crisis, and in the middle of winter, too, so as to get the workers where they want to have them." He had soon found his usual scapegoat. "The workers are ready now to work for a crust of bread; they would beg for work to keep a little warmth in them. Up to now we've been able to keep them together at the Labor Exchange at least, but since this last spell of cold has set in we've lost sight of them altogether. We have no halls to meet in."

"And what are you doing?"

"What can we do? Perhaps you can tell us!"

"Break in a few of the shop windows. Send a bullet or two into the houses of people who have warm rooms and the fashionable hotels and the banks! Words won't do anything!"

Rachel-Leah wheeled round to see who had spoken; it was her son David who attended the high school. He held a school-book before his mouth to muffle his words, so that his father in the next room might not hear them.

It was not her son's words that made Rachel-Leah turn pale, but his dead white face and his trembling lips. The boy's rage and pain had brought a slight foam to them.

"What new catch-word is this that you've brought home with you?" asked Rachel-Leah in alarm.

"A good one! It calls for real action and not merely working with one's tongue as our Jewish parties do. I'm sick of all this talk! People are starving and freezing in the houses and the streets, and you rack your brains over how they're to get coal! Use the discontent of the workers to some purpose, get them out into the streets, and they'll help themselves with their own hands!" cried the boy furiously.

"Will you hold your tongue, you greenhorn? I refuse to listen to such anarchistic nonsense in my house! If you aren't silent I'll put you out of the house along with your catch-words!"

"What else can you suggest? You can only beg for crumbs and sponge on charity, all of you, as mother always does."

"Are you trying to teach me what I should do, a boy like you? Where will you get, do you think, with these ideas of yours? I'll tell you where you'll get. . . ." And his mother indicated her neck significantly.

"I don't care. You won't frighten me with that. This everlasting timidity, this endless talk; I can't bear it, I can't listen to it any longer. Words, words, nothing but words!"

"Have you ever heard the like?" said Rachel-Leah, turning to the Shachliner. "What does the boy want me to do? Haven't I enough trouble already?—And on the top of that I've got to listen to your rant! Will you be silent? If you don't, you'll feel the weight of my hand!" She lifted her hand.

"That's mother's notion of argument! When I'm right and she can't think of a reply she falls back on blows," said the boy undauntedly. "You would like well enough to follow my advice!"

"For God's sake will you hold your tongue! What am I to do with the boy?—His father will hear him!"

David began to read his book again, his lips moving, and Rachel-Leah sat down in her corner. She leaned her head on her hands, her face was twisted into a grimace of pain, her lips trembled, her nostrils twitched as though it were a labor to breathe. There was a moist glean in her eyes, kindled there, it seemed, by the sufferings of her fellow-creatures, which she was forced to see and could not help.

Suddenly she sprang up: "I know now what we must do! We must gather together a few dozen starving workmen with their wives and children, lead them to the Guardians' officers, and demand coal. If they don't give it to us we'll break their windows for them!"

"Ha, ha, ha!" laughed her son.

"What are you laughing at?"

"Charity! Here, Mr. Socialist," the boy turned to the Shachliner, "you go, lead the starving workers to the Jewish Community House! Fall on your knees and beg! That's about what you're fit for!"

The Shachliner turned pale, bit his lips, and replied:

"If I only knew that it would be of any help! For starving workmen I'm prepared even to go begging."

CHAPTER XXIII

THE ATTACK ON THE COMMUNITY HOUSE

It is impossible to say now who had spread in the chill tenements of the workers the rumor that people were marching to the Community House to demand coal. Probably the thought came to them all simultaneously, for the Jewish Community House was the only place in Warsaw to which the poor could turn in times of distress. When Rachel-Leah, escorted by her neighbor, reached the building in Grzybovska Street, she found there already whole crowds of unemployed workmen from all the quarters of the town. All Berl's workmen were there. Reinforcements had also arrived from the suburbs. The crowd surged round the door of the Community House. The two attendants and the single policeman, stationed there as if in mockery to protect the strong, securely barred main door, were powerless against the crowd, whose shivering bodies, pressed so closely together that they formed a wall, came on menacingly. At last with a gesture of resignation the doorkeepers opened, and the crowd streamed into the spacious entrance hall. It was deserted, and all the doors leading to the rooms of the higher authorities were firmly locked.

The crowd had imagined that all they needed to do to gain the assistance they demanded was to reach the entrance hall. Now that they were there they shook and tugged at the locked doors and stared blankly at the bare walls. There was great confusion and shouts and cries; weary mothers carrying their children in their arms sank on the long benches; others, half frozen with waiting in the cold street, flung themselves on the floor and breathed in greedily the warmth sent out by the stove, the warmth they had not known for such a long time. Everybody crowded to the warm stove as to a sun. But nobody knew what to do, where to turn, with whom to speak.

Rachel-Leah pushed her way through this confusion of closely packed bodies. A path was made for her. A part of the crowd knew her, the others regarded her with respect, for, compared with the other women, she was comparatively well dressed; she was wearing a short coat with a fur collar and on her head was a hat instead of the head-cloths worn by the other women. On all sides rose a cry: "Let her through! She'll do our business for us!" "Good luck to you, little lady, for taking our side!" "Bless you, lady; do something to help us poor people; we badly need it! Stand aside everybody. Rachel-Leah will help us."

Rachel-Leah was leading in either hand the two children of the consumptive woman who lived in the block. Several of her other neighbors who had come with her to back her up acted as her body-guard, chief among whom was Henoch the joiner. Chaim, "The Horse," had also lumbered along; when he heard that they were going to the Community House for coal he picked up a stout cudgel "in case there was a dust-up" and joined them. Motche, "The Humpback," was also there, for he loved rows. The Shachliner, however, was absent; at the last moment he had drawn back, evidently put off by the term "charity" which David had flung at him. But the flesh-curer Velvel, moved by pure sympathy for the tenement, had come instead. He himself needed no charity: on the contrary he had more than once slipped a sausage into Rachel-Leah's basket when she was particularly hard up. And now he wanted to help; for, in the first place, he had long nursed a grudge against the Jewish authorities, since they had several times declared his sausages to be *trefe,* and, in the second, he had come to a time of life when he wished to assure himself of his part in the next life by helping the poor. True, his wife Neche had warned him: "Velvel, don't push yourself forward; the affair is none of yours. Let them go that need to go!" But Velvel left her standing, drew on his short fur coat, put his cap on his head and armed himself with a stick loaded at the tip with lead, as if he were going to the wars. Rachel-Leah had also enlisted Selig the baker; she had done this by flinging him a friendly glance, clapping him on the shoulder, and saying: "Selig, come along. Perhaps we'll need you there." The chivalrous Selig could never resist a lady and Frau Hurvitz in particular, for whom he had nursed a tender weakness for a long time. So Rachel-Leah stood, surrounded by her body-guard, amidst the crowd of unemployed men and hangers-on. But there was no human being within sight to whom she could turn. All the doors were locked and barred; the place was deserted. Without waiting too long

Rachel-Leah began to beat with both hands on one of the doors: "Coal! Coal! We want coal!"

That signal was sufficient; the whole crowd broke out into one wailing cry: "Coal!" Hundreds of hands beat on the doors and walls. Feet stamped in time. "Give us coal! Coal! We're freezing! Coal!"

The shouts and the din grew louder and louder. A broad-shouldered Jew with a back as broad as a door pushed his way through the packed crowd roaring: "Just let me get at that door!" He strode up to the door where Rachel-Leah was standing and ran with the full weight of his body against it. Chaim, "The Horse," helped with a few mighty kicks, Velvel with his heavy cudgel—the door gave way.

Inside the misfortune seemed to have been foreseen. Everybody had vanished; the rooms were deserted. One sole official had the pluck to show himself in the splintered doorway; his expression seemed to say: "Here I am! You see, I'm not afraid of you." He was a dignified man in a well-fitting caftan, under which bulged a round little belly; on his head sat the peculiar little hat favored by the Warsaw Jews; his long, broad, reddish beard was also very impressive.

This well-nourished gentleman confronted the crowd without any sign of fear. The roses in his cheeks, which were fed on good roast goose, did not even blench. Calmly he stroked his beautifully groomed beard with his plump hands and asked coolly and quietly: "What do you want?"

The surging crowd who a moment before had stormed the door became as still as mice at the appearance of the worshipful official and retreated a step. Even the burly Jew who had torn the door from its hinges recoiled in alarm, Chaim, "The Horse," and Velvel following his example.

Rachel-Leah alone stood her ground; she gazed steadily at the official and asked in astonishment: "You don't know what we want? Why, don't you know what's happening in the town?"

"Who are you?" the official pointed at her with his finger. "You're a spokeswoman for these people, I take it; you aren't a poor woman, one can see that at a glance."

"And what if I am the spokeswoman—doesn't that suit you?" asked Rachel-Leah.

"Oh, no! On the contrary, it suits me splendidly. Just come into the council chamber; we can discuss the matter quietly there."

"Dear sir, take pity on us! We and our children are dying of cold!" cried a woman in the crowd, bursting into tears.

That was the signal for the others.

"Our very hearts are freezing within us!"

"We're dying of cold. We're freezing limb by limb!" lamented a pious Jew, in the cadence of the synagogue.

"It can't go on any longer like this! We're on our last legs!" shouted a dignified Chassid in a tattered caftan, waving his arms.

"What's the use of all this talk? Coal! We haven't anything to warm us! Coal!"

"You'll effect nothing by shouting and noise!" said the councillor composedly. "You have a spokeswoman of your own; let her take her seat with us at the council table; and then we'll see what can be done."

"Go, go, kind lady! Go!" the crowd shouted encouragingly to Rachel-Leah.

Motche, the hunchback, pushed his way to the front. Whenever a delegation was required he was sure to be there. He turned to Rachel-Leah: "Frau Hurvitz, come on! We aren't afraid to talk for our people."

When Rachel-Leah and Motche entered the council chamber they found it empty. Obviously all the other officials had cleared out, leaving their bold colleague with the red beard to hold the fort. The long green baize table was quite unoccupied.

"Where are the others?" asked Rachel-Leah.

"Why should you bother about the others? I can discuss the matter with you. Be seated." The official indicated two chairs standing at the table.

"They were afraid of the revolting workers!" cried the hunchback in a triumphant voice, throwing an exultant glance at Rachel-Leah.

"Why should they be afraid? Aren't you Jews just like ourselves? Are you thieves and robbers?" replied the crafty councillor in sugary tones. "Take your seat, young man!" he again waved to the hunchback to sit down. "The council has empowered me to treat with you."

"Aha!" cried the hunchback again, giving Rachel-Leah a significant glance; then, turning with a contemptuous gesture to the red-bearded official he added: "I can stand."

"Well, what message have you for me? What is it that you really want?" asked the official as if he had just dropped from the clouds.

At this prelude to the negotiations Rachel-Leah lost her patience entirely.

"You don't know what it is we want? Are you a stranger in this town? Don't you know what is happening in it? The people are freezing with cold!"

"Well, is that anything remarkable, that people are freezing with cold? Is that any reason for crying out at once and making such a noise, and setting the whole world in an uproar? In my house we feel the cold too. Who can help doing that in winter? Why, it's a universally accepted fact. After all, we're human beings and not wild beasts. What will the Goys think if we fall foul of each other, as if something unspeakable had happened?" the official said in a reproachful voice.

Rachel-Leah was no diplomatist, and she had not the patience requisite for such interviews. The man's full, well-fed cheeks, which seemed to gleam with the fat of winter geese, were themselves enough to make her lose all patience. Besides, she was exasperated by his cool, almost cheerful voice which told that he liked the sound of his own words, and the way that he kept on stroking his beard with his plump fingers. She felt a strong inclination to seize him by his read beard, shake him thoroughly and shout into his face: "Do you know what it is to freeze? Do you know that?"

She bit her lips, so as not to lose mastery over herself and said:

"You talk to him, Motche; I can't!"

"Very well then. Will you give us coal or won't you?" Motche burst out, growing pale at his own boldness.

"Where are we to get coal? Do you think we have coal mines of our own? Here you are! Here is the key to the safe if you like, undertake the distribution yourselves, take over our job; then we'll see whether you'll be any more generous hearted than we are! Do you think you've got the sole monopoly of pity? I feel pity too; I'm just as kind-hearted as you are. You seem to think you have a corner on all the kindness in the world."

"Do you know what it is to freeze? These people can't work, they're so cold. They've burned up the last scrap of furniture in their houses, can't find any warm place they can creep into—do you know that? Have you any notion even of that?" cried Rachel-Leah.

"Of course I know it. How shouldn't I know it? Well now, advise us what we should do."

"What, the council has no money?"

"I've told you already you can have the key; undertake the distribution yourselves, take over our job."

"Words are of no use with you, the only thing you understand is . . ." Rachel-Leah raised her fist and went.

"Oh, I didn't expect that of you! After all you belong to the better class," the official shouted after her.

While the crowd were impatiently awaiting the issue of the interview they indulged in all manner of dreams; the council would distribute not only coal, but potatoes and cabbages as well, perhaps even bread. They were convinced that inside there in the council room all these things would be got for them, conjured from the ground, as it were. And although their tongues contradicted this and one whispered to another: "Nothing will come of it," their thoughts were full of hope and their empty stomachs already yearned in longing for the anticipated food.

So it was natural that angry cries of disappointment should arise when Rachel-Leah shouted at them, as they stood with mouths and eyes wide open with expectation, the crushing words:

"There's nothing doing! The man has a heart of stone!"

For a moment the crowd stood in helpless silence; then a cry was heard. It came from Motche, who had entered behind Rachel-Leah: "There's only one help: violence!"

At the word "violence" a flame seemed to mount in the agitated crowd. A fire flared up in their eyes. Even the Chassid Jews, usually so quiet, rocked their bodies violently as if in prayer, savagely gnawed their beards and muttered in agitation: "It's unheard of!"

"Why, even a Tartar wouldn't have the heart to see people dying without helping them!" the women groaned.

Chaim, "The Horse," pushed his way to the front. With his hands shoved in his trouser pockets he lurched up to the door. His eyes gleamed menacingly, particularly the half-shut one with the dried scar. He walked up to Rachel-Leah and growled:

"What are we to do now, Frau? You tell us. . . ."

"Don't you know that yet?" shouted Velvel. "Wait till I get my hands on that official!"

The fury of the crowd went on mounting; at a word or a sign from Rachel-Leah they seemed prepared to tear the red-bearded official to pieces as soon as he showed himself.

And he showed himself. All at once he was standing in the doorway. With an unctuous face he gazed benevolently at the crowd, rubbed his hands and bowed courteously. Hundreds of eyes turned towards him; they had a phosphorescent glitter; they were like tinder that only needed spark to go up in flame. Yet the crowd remained silent; speechless with agitation and expectant curiosity, it waited to hear what the official had to say. Without paying any attention to the gloomy faces and the menacing glances fixed on him, he began with the innocent question, meanwhile rubbing his hands ingratiatingly:

"Is it coal you want, or what is it?"

"Coal! We said so!"

"Then all you need to do is apply for it! The council has already made all the necessary arrangements. Coal tickets are already being issued."

The crowd heaved an immense sigh of surprised relief.

"And what about potatoes, dear sir?" came a hopeful mother's voice.

"We shall distribute potatoes too," replied the official. "Give us time, and you'll have other food supplies as well. Did you fancy you'd get anything out of *them?*" Thereupon he pointed at the astounded Rachel-Leah and Motche. "Do you imagine *they* care whether you get coal or not? It's *something else* they're after." He emphasized the "something else" significantly, bringing it out in a sort of Talmud sing-song, meanwhile winking eloquently at the crowd and bursting into a thin laugh: "Hee, hee, hee!"

The crowd, which a moment before had been prepared to tear the councillor to pieces at a sign from Rachel-Leah, now left her in the lurch at the first hopeful words he had uttered and went completely over to him. To curry favor with him they hastened to take up his sarcastic "something else" and a few even joined in his laughter.

Rachel-Leah was struck rigid with astonishment. She did not understand what had happened, and felt as though a chill breath had touched her. Her faithful guard still stood by her, the hunchback, Henoch the joiner, even Velvel the flesh-curer. Chaim, "The Horse," alone had forsaken her and was already among the crowd of pious Jews, women and children surrounding the official. The women lifted up their babies to see him, and the movement displaced their tattered clothes, so that bare shoulders and breasts could be seen.

"May you live to be a hundred, kind sir!—When will the distribution begin?"

"At once, at once, of course. We won't keep you waiting! Do you think you'll ever get anything from *her?*" Once more he pointed, more boldly now, at Rachel-Leah, who had withdrawn into a corner. "Do you think she cares about your coal? It's something quite different she's after, hee, hee, hee!"

A hoarse tuberculous voice laughed hysterically along with him: "Hee, hee, hee, it's something quite different she's after!"

"Oh, kind sir, you're our only helper!" cried a woman, holding out her dirty child towards him.

"He's a father to our children, the kind gentleman!"

"May God bless you, may God bless you!" the women stretched out their hands towards the red-beard.

Rachel-Leah and her guard ignominiously withdrew.

When, sick and trembling with impotent rage, Frau Hurvitz reached her home, she sat down in her favorite corner in the kitchen, took her head in her hands, bit her lips and kept on muttering to herself.

David entered. When he saw the state his mother was in he guessed at once what had happened and began with a triumphant smile: "I told you not to have anything to do with charity. There's only one weapon. . . ."

Rachel-Leah, who was now of the same mind as her son, but did not dare to admit it, by good luck caught sight of a new tear in his trousers and flung herself upon it: "Be quiet! Look at these trousers of yours! They're in such a state that I really don't know where to begin on them. . . ."

CHAPTER XXIV

FRAU HURVITZ "PUTS SOMETHING IN THE SOUP"

RACHEL-LEAH was sitting with her head in her hands. She felt overwhelmed with grief and shame. Whenever she came in contact with misery she suffered intensely, although that happened to her almost daily. But the things that she had had to witness and hear during the past few days had been beyond anything in her previous experience. The worries that the misfortunes of her neighbors brought her were enough in themselves; but the scene in the Jewish Community House that afternoon, the helplessness and servility of the crowd, the way they had gone down on their knees to the official for the sake of a bag of coal, filled her with such bitterness that she began to lose her faith in mankind. Her strong will, which had always stood up to trouble and hardship, tottered. All her blood seemed to have withdrawn in shame to the inmost cells of her body, and refused to issue out again. Rachel-Leah saw no prospect for the future. Every hope was dead and she told herself: "It will always be like this, always, always, until we die, and after we are dead."

Her heart contracted so painfully that her face changed. Frank and cheerful usually, it became gloomy. Her large eyes grew small, were hidden behind countless puckers that suddenly appeared. Her lips, tightly clenched, became almost blue with rage. There was a dry whitish foam at the corners of her lips. Then they began to work and she muttered curses between her teeth, not caring who might be present, even if it was her husband: "This accursed world looks on calmly while people die of want. It should be wiped out, a dirty world like that!"

Suddenly a passion of tears burst from her eyes. She wiped them away with her handkerchief. The only hope that her primitive mind could see was some accident that would put her in power and give her the right and the chance to deal out blows right and left and force the whole world by violence to obey her orders: "Why haven't I the power? Why is it in the hands of wretches and fools who have no need of it and don't know what to do with it?"

There was no dinner cooked that day. When Hurvitz came home he was afraid to set foot in the kitchen. Rachel-Leah had her whims and moods. When she was in a good mood she would submit to anything; but one had to beware when she was in a temper, as she was now after her return from the Community House; then it was a wild beast that sat in the kitchen, and everybody without exception had to be prepared for rough treatment, her husband no less than the children.

On such days everybody avoided her. This particular day Helene improvised as best she could a meal out of hard-boiled eggs and other scraps and in that way appeased the family's hunger. A feeling of calamity filled the house.

"Why are you so upset, Mamma? It's nothing new, what's happened today," said Helene timidly, as she fried potatoes at the kitchen fire.

"Please leave me in peace!" cried her mother.

But David kept on whistling a tune to himself, kept on coming into the kitchen and whispering to her, so that his father in the next room might not hear: "I told you, Mamma, how it would end."

Rachel-Leah did not reply.

But it was the Shachliner that felt the keenest edge of her anger; she would not let him into the kitchen and shouted furiously:

"You're fine world reformers. You're great heroes in the kitchen, talking to Rachel-Leah!"

Mirkin was the last to arrive, and he found Frau Hurvitz in the worst of tempers.

He knew how things were. For the first time in his life he had come in contact with want and knew what it meant; lately he had gone about in silence, trembling with agitation, and often reflected how hasty his action had been.

Rachel-Leah's attention was so filled with all that happened in the street that she began almost to ignore Mirkin. But when she did take notice of him she would fling him such an unfriendly glance that it made him feel guilty in some way or other. He came to the conclusion that she had something against him; but what it was he could not think. As he entered now she looked at him morosely and muttered to herself: "That man might have done something, and then, of course, he had to send back the money his rich father gave him. No doubt he was afraid the old man mightn't have enough."

Mirkin grew pale. Frau Hurvitz regretted her words immediately. But to vent her wrath on somebody she fell upon the Shachliner: "You're to blame for everything! You put it into his head that he mustn't touch his father's money. But I say that one should accept money even from a rogue if one can help people with it! Since when have you grown so refined, so devoted to purity and decency? These people outside shivering in their hovels and hungering for a scrap of bread—they can't be so sensitive and delicate as you. They won't think twice of picking up whatever is thrown to them, even out of the gutter. You should have seen them licking that red-bearded official's boots, just because he promised them a bag of coal! And yet you have the cheek to be delicate and sensitive!"

"Are you in need of money, Frau Hurvitz?" asked Mirkin suddenly.

"That's really good! He seems to have just dropped from the moon! If we could only get a little money we could open a kitchen or a canteen where people could sit for a while and warm their insides at least. If we only had a little money for a start, we could begin with one or two kitchens and a few canteens: after that everything would go by itself."

Fired by her own words Frau Hurvitz felt her old energy returning again. She rose hastily and went on, addressing herself to her two "assistants," Mirkin and the Shachliner: "But what's the use of wasting my breath on you? Do you call yourselves men?"

With that she flung a wrap over her head and rushed into the court. Zachary followed her example, but took the opposite direction.

Frau Hurvitz went first of all to the baker's. Selig was standing in front of the oven; the furnace door was open, and the flames cast a red glare over him.

"Friend Selig, I need you! Leave your oven and come with me!"

"Just a minute until I take out the rolls first." With a long shovel he drew the batch out of the oven.

Rachel-Leah seated herself beside the oven without noticing that her one good dress, which she had worn that day at the Community House, was getting dirty. Laying her hand on Selig's flour-covered shoulder she said: "Selig, you're a nice fellow, you have a kind heart; I know you. Here are hundreds of people who are starving and can't work because they have nothing in their homes to warm them; they would give anything for a crust of bread."

"Do you think you need to tell me that, Frau Hurvitz?" asked Selig sadly, pushing his cap on the back of his head and supporting his arms on his long shovel. "I know that better than you do. The consumptive woman's children, the joiner's children, Chaim's children, gather here every day like half-frozen birds and beg me to let them warm themselves at the oven. How can I help things? I'm only a poor man myself! I throw them a roll and let them warm themselves; that's the most I can do for them."

"That's all right, but we must try to do more!"

"Certainly! Of course! But what are we to do?"

"Set up a free kitchen!"

"And where are we to get the money for it, Frau Hurvitz? The rich won't give anything and the poor have nothing to give."

"The rich can roast in hell! If the poor won't do anything, nothing will be done. My opinion is that we must make a start ourselves, beginning with our block. If we can only get the thing going, we'll be able to scratch the necessary money together somehow or other."

"That would be fine! Give me flour and wood and I'll bake bread all night through for these poor people. I'll put my oven at your disposal; all I need is flour and wood; as for the labor, I'll see to that. It makes one's heart sore to see all this misery, it's past endurance!" cried Selig.

"Friend Selig, come with me! I always knew you were a kind-hearted fellow." Rachel-Leah once more laid her hand on his shoulder.

"Just have patience for a minute more, Frau Hurvitz. I must shut the oven."

Selig shut the oven, clapped his trousers and his hairy breast to shake off the flour, flung on his short fur coat jauntily, fixed his cap more firmly on his shock of hair, and asked:

"Where are you going to take me?"

"Come with me to Velvel, the flesh-curer."

"But what are you thinking of? That man's a swine! He takes care to sleep on his money bags, and they're well lined too. You'll waste your words on him!"

"It isn't as bad as that. Velvel won't turn a deaf ear to us."

When they reached the sausage factory the heavy fumes from the ovens enveloped them at once, almost taking away their breath. The baker and Frau Hurvitz coughed as if they would never stop.

"Velvel, we've come to you on a begging mission," began Rachel-Leah. "Do you knew, Velvel, what's happening outside there?"

Velvel who, with his sleeves rolled up, was kneading a lump of mince-meat as if it were dough, raised his wiry thick eyebrows and glanced at the visitors with two little eyes: then he asked:

"Heh?"

"Velvel, do you know that people are starving out there in the streets?"

"Of course I know it: do you think I'm a brute beast? I've just made up a few sausages and a sack of left-overs for them. Take it with you, Frau Hurvitz!"

"Don't talk to us of your left-overs! There's something more than that needed here, my dear friend. Frau Hurvitz wants to set up a free kitchen. Now it's a case of producing your money bags and making the ducats fly," said Selig.

"My money bags? You fetch them; I've no objection!" retorted Velvel in a hoarse voice. "But Neche is sitting on them."

"No, no, Velvel, all we ask from you is meat and bones every day for the soup, once we've got the kitchen started."

"Meat? Meat? And where am I to get meat? I can give you as much bones as you like, though they cost me a mint of money."

"Don't talk to me of your bones. Eat them yourself!" began the baker severely. "He offers the starving people bones!"

"Well, then, I'll let you have some left-overs and fat every day." The second item in his offer Velvel pronounced in a lowered voice, so that his wife might not hear. Pointing to the door to the next room he added in a husky voice: "She'll make a fine scene, but as far as I'm concerned—am I a brute beast? Do you think I don't know myself what my duty is?"

A council of war was hastily summoned in Velvel's sausage factory. Rachel-Leah sent for Henoch the joiner. Chaim, "The Horse," appeared next, the women in the block gathered, and the discussion on the setting up of a free kitchen began. There was no lack of enthusiasm. Everybody wanted to help. The women were eager to cook, the baker was eager to bake, Velvel promised bones and left-overs and, behind his wife's back, fat as well. Chaim, "The Horse," took upon himself the delivery of fire-wood.

"You needn't worry about the fire-wood," he told the baker. "I'll bring you as many wooden fences as you like, and there's a good supply of barrels in the court," he jerked his thumb towards the herring barrels. "And if it's necessary to use violence I'm not afraid of that. The leather dealer has laid in a whole cellarful of coal and I'll see that you have some of it."

Rachel-Leah's proposal roused a mighty enthusiasm in the whole block. She was in her element. All the neighbors were eager to help. Both men and women came to her. Berl's whole "factory" appeared. Even Pan Kviatkovski descended from the second floor to attend the council. He soon learned that the Jews were engaged on some scheme and became inquisitive. Pan Kviatkovski was a queer card; as soon as the Jews in the house set about anything he wanted to be in it too. "When Jews start anything they know what they're up to," was the standing expression with him. As soon as he appeared he began to reproach them for not summoning him, too, and keeping the matter a secret among themselves.

"What does this mean? Am I not your neighbor?" he cried in a mixture of Polish and Yiddish. "Why wasn't I summoned? Jews always want to keep things among themselves, to 'keep their Sabbath' to themselves. That isn't nice! People must stick together! People must live in unison! This time our cause will prevail. I know all about your business! I know!" he said with a significant gesture, as if he were addressing a secret revolutionary association.

"What do you know, Pan Kviatkovski?" cried the Jews in alarm. "All we want is to set up a free kitchen for the poor people."

"A free kitchen? All right, let it be a free kitchen! But I insist on helping! I'm your neighbor after all!"

"Please, please! We'll be delighted to have you," cried the Jews in chorus.

"My housekeeper will help with the cooking and I'll pay my weekly subscription to the free kitchen like my other neighbors. That isn't right, you know, to keep your Sabbath to yourselves." Once more Pan Kviatkovski brought out triumphantly one of the few Jewish phrases that he knew and loved. "I insist on helping, too, I'm your neighbor."

"Do! We'll be glad of your help." The Jews invited him with courteous bows to collaborate with them.

So far everything had gone splendidly; but there was a shortage of money.

There were few tenants in the house who could give a weekly subscription. They consisted of the leather dresser, a couple of grocers and Pan Kviatkovski, who did not grow weary of declaring: "Whatever the Jews pay I'll pay too; I'm your neighbor."

The other neighbors, most of them "manufacturers" like Berl, were "dead," killed by the crisis, and so themselves needed help.

So the weekly subscriptions produced a sum that was quite insignificant. Money, however, was essential to buy a few sacks of flour to start with. (Selig the baker kept on saying: "Give me the materials, I'll work all right.") Over and above this, potatoes, groats, crockery, tables and benches had to be procured; but above all premises.

There was a vacant house in the block, consisting of two rooms and a kitchen; but the house agent, when approached, insisted that a quarter's rent must be paid down in advance, for he mistrusted the new scheme. Chaim, "The Horse," and a few others proposed breaking in the door and taking possession of the house by force, but the other tenants rejected this out of fear of the police. So there was a great deal of good-will available, but nothing, as Rachel-Leah expressed it, "to put in the soup."

"You see for yourself, you can't get money out of poor people.

If the rich people won't take the business up, it's certain that we won't manage to do anything." That was finally the unanimous opinion, and they all let their hands fall in despair. So the whole plan of the free kitchen threatened to come to nothing, for the tenants recognized that they could do nothing by their own efforts, and these were all that they could depend upon.

Rachel-Leah returned to her house in deep disappointment. But she had not yet given up all hope. Her instinct told her that she would find a way of getting together the money with which to start. How that was to be done she did not know; but she was of a sanguine nature, and when she put her hand to anything she did not look back. She exerted all her strength; her blood rushed from her heart to all her limbs, as though wanting to help her in executing her plan; she racked her brains to discover where she could find the first money, but she could think of nothing. There was nothing in the house that could be turned into money except her husband's books; but they were already reserved for another object. . . .

But as often happened in Rachel-Leah's life, this time, too, help came unexpectedly and in an unusual guise.

As she left the living-room, where for a short time she had stood gazing at the book-case, and with a troubled and disappointed heart entered the kitchen, Zachary Mirkin came hesitatingly forward to meet her in the early twilight and murmured in his beard: "You said you needed money. Please accept this thing here. . . ." With these words he slipped a superb ring into Rachel-Leah's hand.

"What's this?"

"I still have it from the old days," said Zachary, blushing, and he added shyly, as if apologizing for himself: "I had quite forgotten that I still had it in my possession."

"I can't take it. You'll probably need it for another purpose."

"I'll certainly never need it."

"One can never know!"

Rachel-Leah smiled at him archly.

"It's better that the ring should be used for *this,*" Zachary explained in embarrassment.

"We could find a good use for it," said Rachel-Leah, "and if it is intended for the one I'm thinking of, she'll be able quite well to dispense with it."

Deeply moved Zachary seized her hand. She merely patted him hastily on the hair, threw on her wrap and ran down the stairs to her friends. When she reached them she shouted in elation: "Children, we have something to put in the soup!"

When the ring disappeared in Rachel-Leah's hand Zachary felt a sense of great relief. The ring was the last tie that bound him to his mother.

BOOK TWO

CHAPTER XXV

EARLY SPRING

A CHANGE was taking place on the face of the earth. At first one could hardly tell what was happening. The pavements were still muddy, so that walking was a laborious business, the thoroughfares and bridges lay deep in dirty gray slush, into which horses' hoofs and wheels sank; and yet everybody felt liberated from a yoke and looked as happy as if they had unexpectedly come into money. One's winter clothing felt too heavy, one's winter underwear a burden. One wanted to have a good bath, put on fresh underwear and one's best clothes and go for a stroll about the streets. The sky, overcast one moment, was clear and blue the next. The sun smiled briefly and then was hidden again. Every now and then a hail-shower rattled down. One hour it was summer; the next it was winter again. One could feel the battle of the elements in the air. But it was waged not only in the sky, but also in the hearts and spirits of all living creatures; every living thing took part in the battle between summer and winter that was being waged all over the country.

In the Saxon Garden in Warsaw black patches suddenly appeared in the frozen blanket of snow; one could see again the familiar, fresh, damp earth. Cracks appeared in it, as if with a thousand mouths it were drinking in deep draughts the spring fragrance with which the air was filled. Yes, the black, glistening, familiar countenance of the earth could actually be seen again, which had seemed to be buried for ever beneath the white, barren, deathly monotony of snow; oh, the deep joy of seeing the black glistening earth again! The trees raised their blackened seamed trunks into the air and trembled in the fresh wind. Wet, bare and stripped, with not a single leaf to show, they stood there. But their branches, a system of limbs and muscles, were already filled with a current of life, and looked like the powerful contorted fingers of a gigantic hand. A light fume hung round their crests, as if they exhaled a reddish violet breath. And behold—through the network of their new twigs the true countenance of the world once more became visible: the deep, flawless blue of the sky, a sudden glimpse of the familiar red of the roofs. A white-washed wall, unnoticed until now, suddenly stood out as if newly risen, and windows glittered. The air seemed to have cast off a leaden net that had been spread over it all winter, and suddenly everything appeared in its true shape: human beings had faces once more, objects had colors, as though the veils had been torn that had covered the earth for so long.

Mirkin and Helene wandered tirelessly through the streets. They had been everywhere, had tramped through the mud of all the streets. For hours they sauntered through the walks of the Saxon Garden, gazed at the cold black water of the pond, now freed from its covering of ice, tramped regardlessly through the soft slush until they were splashed to their knees, and sat on the wet benches; strips of dirty green paint, peeled off by the thaw, stuck to their clothes. They held hands and gazed into each other's eyes without saying anything. Like a boy and girl they wandered on; their hearts were beating apprehensively; they knew that today something decisive would enter into their lives.

Mirkin had given up his teaching, as he saw he had no ability for it. He had found employment with a well-known Warsaw advocate whose subject was civil and commercial rather than criminal law. Zachary was at once given a department of his own to look after, and granted a comfortable salary. He had secured the post apparently by chance. An old Petersburg acquaintance had sought him out and taken him to a restaurant; there he was introduced to the advocate, who at once offered him a post in his office. Naturally Mirkin did not know that all this had been arranged from Petersburg, and that his father's eye still watched over him from afar. But even when the suspicion occasionally awoke in him, he refused to acknowledge it. He no longer felt any hatred towards his father, and he could forgive himself neither his hasty action nor his insulting letter: "What business is it of mine whom he marries?"

Also he had learned of late to think more independently and was no longer so easily moved by the whispered arguments of the Shachliner and his circle of friends, who considered the possession of property wicked.

"I can't alter the world by my unaided efforts and as long as the present system of society lasts I don't see why I shouldn't use the advantages that fate or chance has granted me."

He knew that this was a poor excuse and he was ashamed of it; but his egoism was more powerful than his scruples and his doubts as to whether he was taking the right course. In any case he had the justification he needed, particularly as at the moment he saw no other possibility before him.

His occupation allowed him a great deal of leisure. So he devoted more of it to Helene than he had a right to do, took her away from her classes in the middle of the day, and wandered about with her in the streets and parks. Helene had to pay heavily for these excursions in severe reproofs from her father. There were violent scenes. Her mother shielded Helene as much as she could, inventing ever new pretexts and excuses. Mirkin and Helene were frequently astonished by Madame Hurvitz's inventive faculties.

At the Hurvitzes' Mirkin was now looked at askance—particularly by the father and Helene's brother. They could not decide what his intentions really were. The teacher made scenes and perpetually accused his wife of being to blame for everything, seeing that she had introduced Mirkin into the house. Partly from shame, partly from apprehension, Zachary avoided the father; he waited for Helene at the door until her school hours were over and she set out for her private lessons. As the days were already lengthening she had more time to herself. Today he had actually called for her in the middle of her classes. The day was so bright and festive that it had simply driven him out into the streets. He longed to wander about like a boy playing truant. For the first time he drank in with joy the spring fragrance and felt freed from all his cares; for the first time the suicidal thoughts that every spring had brought him since his childhood stayed away. He no longer felt the apprehensive unrest, the gnawing longing and remorse that had descended upon him at such times as if he had done a murder; his Petersburg feelings had vanished and now the spring wind blowing in his face gave him a really childish delight. He regretted nothing; instead, like a child waiting for a party, he was ready to greet the spring with all his senses.

So today he wished to do nothing but walk about the streets, be all day in the open, look at the black patches of soil appearing through the snow and the bare trees raising their powerful trunks like arms to the sky. He must not be alone; he longed to walk in Helene's shadow, to touch her shoulder with his, to feel her breath, to drink in her perfume.

At the risk of encountering Hurvitz and being given a dressing down he went straight to the school. To be with Helene was well worth it! He called to her from the passage and proposed a walk in the park, or if possible in the country. Helene was in a curious mood that was new to Zachary; she avoided his eyes and seemed to be trying to hide something from him. He felt it at once; he took her hand and said: "What has happened?"

She refused to tell him, nor would she go with him: "Father goes on at me enough without that!"

Mirkin remained dejectedly silent. His happiness, his ardent longing were suddenly quenched and he felt helpless and downcast. Helene could not hold out. She saw his face all at once drawn with profound grief, his lips twisted, and she could not help smiling. She was filled with pity and could not say no; one could not say no to a child! Let happen what might, she would come.

She told him to wait in the street for her. He waited for a full hour. At last she came. She was still wearing her winter coat with the reddish-yellow fox collar, but the hat seemed new. Really it was her old hat trimmed up afresh and embellished with a new ribbon. And Helene herself had suddenly changed, too, completely changed! She apologized for having kept him waiting; but while doing so she avoided his eyes, a thing she had never done before: "I had to wait for the Russian teacher, who's taking my class."

As they walked on Zachary managed to find out what had happened: her father had struck her the previous day for gadding about with Mirkin and neglecting her work.

"Struck you?" asked Mirkin in astonishment.

"Yes; he got into a dreadful rage and soon forgot all his advanced principles."

Suddenly Mirkin burst out into hysterical laughter; Helene gazed at him uncomprehendingly; he seemed quite strange to her all at once.

"It's nothing!" he said presently. "It was only something I remembered," and he took her hand and pulled her along.

After a while he began as if to himself: "Do you know that I was once struck by my father, too?" He grew pale, as if horrified at what he had said, and fell into silence.

Helene looked at him in surprise. He persisted in his silence...

Still under the influence of Zachary's last words, they walked the whole way back without saying a word. They were turned in upon themselves, as though each were on the point of coming to a decision in a separate world. Without exchanging a single word they came to the same resolution: they must do something now that would unite them for ever; and it must be done soon, that very day, before they parted. A strange happiness that seemed to rise out of fear filled them. Their hearts beat loudly, as if they had just decided to commit a crime. They apprehensively avoided each other's eyes.

In this state they wandered through street after street and strode like outcasts through the young spring day.

They began to feel cold. Mirkin proposed going into a coffee house near at hand. Helene silently consented; she was prepared now to do all he asked her; her own will was in abeyance. It was the first time she had been with Mirkin in a strange café; and that gave her pleasure. She ate the buttered bread and eggs and drank the sour milk with a good appetite. The coffee with whipped cream that concluded the feast tasted better than any he had ever drunk before. When they had eaten and warmed themselves, they continued their walk. How long were they going to wander about like this? She must sit down and rest some time or other! When evening came they found themselves once more in the Saxon Garden. How was this going to end? Helene said not a word about going home, but walked on in silence beside Mirkin. Both were waiting for something. They were afraid, and they waited for something, they did not know what....

The sun sank. Its afterglow lay on the park, the trees, the twigs, the snow. The tree-tops were violet. Everything was enveloped in a reddish haze. Soft shadows lay on the ground, the shadows of the bare trees. Mirkin and Helene wandered among them.

Suddenly everything grew spectral. Darkness was falling; the shadows vanished. The tree-tops melted into the thickening gloom. The trees and the night grew into a single mass, forming two walls and a roof for the path where they were walking. It was as if they were in a room.

Helene was the first to say it: "Let's go to your rooms! I'm cold."

They made in the direction where Mirkin lived.

Then they softly stole through the street door, up the stairs and into Mirkin's room, as if they knew they were about to do something evil.

Their hearts beat loudly; neither of them spoke. They entered and closed the door after them. In the dark room they sat down silently, Helene on the bed, Mirkin on the chair beside his table.

So now two pairs of eyes gazed at each other and were mirrored in each other's glance. Joy and fear were mingled in that gaze. His eyes avoided hers; hers sought his. It was she who looked him frankly, almost challengingly, in the face. Her glance was strangely potent, as if she had thrown all her power into it. Zachary understood it. The mystery that had enclosed each of them in a separate world was suddenly made manifest without the speaking of a word.... Trembling convulsive hands sought each other. From whence did this girl's slim, gentle fingers get such strength? Heavy sighs died in a faint apprehensive cry.

But before their two tense bodies had quite touched, Mirkin, summoning all his will, tore himself away, brushed her moist brow with his hot lips, and murmured half to himself: "No, no, Helene, no...."

A cry drowned in tears was stifled in the bed-pillows.

CHAPTER XXVI

THE CAFÉ IN DZIKA STREET

MIRKIN did not join the Socialist Party. He quickly recognized the narrow sectarianism of its disciplined members and did not wish to be forced into a Procrustean bed; he already felt so sure of himself and of the future that he was resolved to go through life without unnecessary paraphernalia. He found the courage not only to hold his own opinions, but also to express them openly, to stick to them and defend them.

Naturally this soon brought him into conflict with his acquaintances. They treated him contemptuously, ostensibly because of his simplicity, which was shown in his taking things and phrases in deadly earnest. So they laughed at him behind his back, jeered at his naiveté, turned his frank straightforwardness to ridicule, and held him for a narrow-minded fool, whom it was useless to argue with. Finally some one found for him the biting nickname of "the *petit bourgeois.*"

"You see, Pan Mirkin," he was told by everybody, "you're a typical representative of the *petit bourgeoisie*. Your whole psychology and all your ways of thought are *petit bourgeois.*"

Zachary could not quite make out why this title should be so damning. "In what way is a small *bourgeois* worse than a big one? What sense is there in the word anyway?" he asked himself. Yet as all the others regarded it as very cutting he did so too.

But more profound conflicts of opinion arose between Mirkin and his friends over concrete questions, as, for example, his work for the Jewish masses.

The party had a definite program, which in general outline depended on the collaboration of the world proletariat. It sought to drape its grandiose principles on the frail bodies of the Jewish masses. But the suit, which was cut to fit a strong and powerful body, that of the world proletariat, was far too ample for the sick and emaciated body of the Jewish population: a different measurement was needed.

The better Mirkin came to know the terrible lot of the Jews, the more deeply he understood their needs, the more clearly his simple understanding told him that his friends were mistaken in their policy. Nobody saw or heard, nobody took thought for the real misery these people were suffering under.

On all sides Mirkin found himself surrounded by the suffering of the Jews; it cried from every door, from every window, from every face, from every body. He felt he was in a huge hospital among multitudes of the sick. The first thing surely must be to make these sick people well again; after that it would be time enough to talk about a final goal for them. But at present they were ill; every one of them was ill!

Although he was living in one of the great cities of Europe he felt as if he were in some remote, Godforsaken, savage village in Asia. Far away the world was making with giant's strides towards its future, its bright dawn, towards civilization and progress. But this multitude precariously housed in the huge city had been left behind in a sort of swamp. A whole people had been left behind in the swamp: there it grew and multiplied. Nobody thought of rescuing it and uniting it with the great body of humanity, which was advancing with immense bounds. Now and then, it was true, a few single individuals tore themselves free, fled and saved their lives; but the multitude, the overwhelming multitude, remained sticking in the swamp for good. In such circumstances how could people talk of organizing the Jewish masses for positive action? How could people lump them together with the rest of the working population of the world?

Yet this was the program that was always being talked about in Mirkin's circle. "Whom are you to organize?" he would object. "For these people to be smelted into a powerful collective unit they must first represent something in themselves: they must be able to come under the heading of factory workers, let us say, farm laborers, railway workers, and so on. But as it is, what is there in these people to organize? Sickness and destitution? Who would miss it, who would even notice it, if these crowds of half-famished creatures were to stop working? In what does their work consist? In hurrying to and fro desperately looking for an existence; in petty chaffering. Even those that are engaged, save the mark, in business in some small way, are a fluctuating crowd continually changing their class; they may be comfortable today, but tomorrow they are penniless; workers one day, street vendors the next...."

Mirkin could see only one possible task: to restore these people to health, first of all, so that they might take part in the working, productive world. Certainly the road was long and difficult and could be traveled only a step at a time; yet it was the only road. It was immaterial who undertook this task and where it was begun. In all lands, in all continents, by various methods, it might come about. Whether in Poland or America, in Russia or Palestine—everywhere that the task of restoring the Jewish population to health, of making Jewish life productive in itself and productive for others, of uniting the Jewish workers with the other workers of the world was possible—everywhere that Jewish effort existed it was one's duty to help, to bear a hand.

Zachary visualized the scattered Jewish people as a waste field never yet cultivated, overgrown with weeds and bogged with standing water. From separate sides plows guided by strong hands tore up the barren, crusted soil. At first it seemed that these plows, guided by different hands from different directions, were proceeding at cross purposes. But that was merely an optical illusion—they would all meet in the end. The work of all those who plowed that field, wherever they started from, however feeble the hands that held the stilts—that work and those hands were blessed.

Mirkin saw his way clear before him, knew where he stood; his place was wherever a plow was being driven over the Jewish field, no matter in what direction. He must shake himself free from the seduction of theories, programs and all other superstitions in their various forms; he must cut himself free from strange idols and have the courage to be himself.

In spite of all their differences with him the socialists did not go the length of breaking with Mirkin. True, the Shachliner and his comrades regarded him as a hopeless case, yet they went on arguing with him: "And how are you going to restore the Jewish population to health?"

"By putting them into the factories: they must become productive."

"Splendid! Perhaps you'll manage to persuade the Jewish capitalists first to take Jewish workers into their factories? In a way you belong to their class, don't you? Could you talk to them about it?"

"Why not? I'm prepared to act, instead of merely talking. I'll do anything I can, and gladly, to realize that ideal."

"We'll take you at your word," said the Shachliner.

"You can do more than that! I'm ready to do anything you ask of me to realize that aim."

A few days later the Shachliner called on Mirkin and with an air of great mystery told him that Comrade Anatol would like to meet him.

Mirkin had often heard the name before. Comrade Anatol was one of the secret leaders of the party. But Mirkin had not till now been considered worthy of the distinction of meeting the celebrated man, whose name had become a legend. So he was greatly excited at the prospect.

Next day the Shachliner called for him and conducted him to the café kept by Schloime "The Bachelor."

The café was in Dzika Street. It's owner, Schloime, "The Bachelor," was, despite his nickname, a married man and the father of several children. It was his wife who had miscalled him because, in spite of his condition, he always sought the company of young unmarried people belonging to the organization, of which he had been a member ever since his bachelor days. In Schloime's café forgathered the heads of the party, the members of the "Central Committee," who were known to very few of their humbler comrades. A little kitchen opened off the café; it had only one window looking out on the backyard. In this kitchen, amid steaming saucepans and kettles and coffee pots, the party conferences were held, strikes were declared, and important manifestoes sent out to the working classes. Extreme reactionaries were in power, and so papers that might prove compromising dared not be brought to the café in case the police should make a raid. Such raids occurred frequently, for the police kept a vigilant eye on the place. Sometimes the deliberators succeeded in escaping through the kitchen window, but occasionally they were nabbed. In either case, however, Schloime "The Bachelor" was invariably dragged to the police headquarters. But since the police were never able to fix anything on him, he always had to be released again after a few weeks' confinement. Every time he came out he had a few less teeth to show, or a black eye or a broken rib, for which he had to thank the police or the hardened criminals into whose cells he had been thrown. But Schloime made light of such things. His face was bandaged; beneath his upper lip, which was covered with a dark mustache, the blood-stained gaps in his teeth showed like a succession of broken window panes; yet he was always cheerful and undaunted and seemed not to have felt the blows he had been given, and would say to the comrades with a smile: "We'll teach them sometime yet!"

After the Jews had managed in Bialystok to make a breach in the wall of the labor market and to have some of their numbers taken into the textile factories, a similar attempt was next made in Lodz, the center of the textile industry. There the fight was much harder. The Jewish manufacturers to whom the factories belonged, most of which were driven by electricity, would not hear of taking in Jewish workers. Uniting with the reactionary Polish workers, they erected a regular barbed wire fence round their factories and, like angels with flaming swords, guarded the gates of these modern paradises against the flood of Jewish labor. They condemned the Jewish weavers to sit at medieval handlooms all their lives and to perish along with them.

But the leaders of the Jewish working classes did not give up the fight. When the Shachliner told them that Mirkin was prepared to help them they sent for him. They set illusory hopes upon him; his parentage and his father's legendary wealth fed their belief that he could achieve something for them, that he would be able at least to work upon the Jewish capitalists. It was this assumption that Mirkin had to thank for being admitted at last into the circle that frequented Schloime's café.

He had already heard a great deal about the café. It was evening when he entered it. The heat and fug that filled the little room dimmed the panes of the glass door, which was covered by a filthy curtain. Inside people were sitting about just as in other cafés at not too clean tables covered with newspapers, and trying to forget the chilliness of the inhospitable streets over a glass of coffee, a dry roll, or a fragment of herring. Behind the flyblown counter, on which were piled up cheese rings and other doubtful dainties, stood a huge fellow with his face bandaged as if he were suffering from toothache. Beneath his mustache a battered chin stuck out. From the kitchen, which was divided from the café by a thin moldering wall, sounded a shrill dictatorial feminine voice. At Mirkin's entrance the fellow behind the counter became uneasy and cast anxious glances at the intruder, but presently seemed reassured when he recognized the Shachliner.

Mirkin was disappointed. So this was the famous café! He had pictured it in far more romantic colors, as a cellar which one reached by descending a dark stair. The nearness of the street and the sober appearance of the room actually offended him.

The Shachliner led him to a table where some young men were sitting. Most of them were in workmen's clothes; but one attracted Mirkin's attention: he had the look of an honest clerk or a tutor in a liberal-minded family. His fair beard was well groomed. He was not wearing a black shirt like the others. He sported a comparatively clean double collar; nor was he without the invariable pair of glasses, that badge of the intellectual. Mirkin soon put two and two together: this young man who looked like a petty clerk must, of course, be the celebrated Anatol, the theorist and leader of the party, the much sought, tirelessly pursued revolutionary, who had escaped so many times from Siberia.

The conversation at the table naturally broke off when Mirkin entered. Without greeting the others he and the Shachliner sat down at the next table. Some one presently shouted across at him, asking whether he knew what the business before them was, and if he could help.

Mirkin replied that he did not know.

"You've declared your willingness to support us in our fight to win a place for the Jewish textile workers in modern industry, to help them to change over from their antiquated hand-looms. How can you help us?"

"I don't know; I was really waiting for you to tell me," replied Mirkin; he did not address his answer directly to the questioner, but to the Shachliner, to whom the question had also been put.

"You could help us a great deal," he was assured from the next table.

"I'm eager to know how. There will be no lack of enthusiasm on my part; I'm ready to do anything, anything at all that I'm asked. But I would like to say beforehand that my possibilities of action are very limited," Mirkin explained to the Shachliner, as if he were only talking to him.

"We'll see about that," responded the next table. "Your possibilities of action are not at all so limited. You could help us a great deal, really a great deal; it depends on you."

"Tell me how I am to do it."

"There's a comrade from Lodz at our table. He tells us that the position is critical, even very critical."

"I know that. But tell me what I'm to do."

From the next table came the decision: "It's a matter of influencing the Jewish manufacturers, of exerting pressure upon them to get them to cease their opposition to the Jewish workers. This pressure must come from a quite different direction than it has done till now; from Jewish capital itself. It must become a matter of course for Jewish factory owners to employ Jewish workers, or if you like a racial obligation. These gentlemen may use what reasons they like for doing it, even racial ones—that's a matter of indifference to us if we can only manage to make a breach in the wall. We'll soon overcome the objections of the Polish workers; it's a matter of education, of understanding. But we ourselves have no access to the Jewish manufacturers and so we must seek other channels. Now, there may be a possibility of getting all this done with your father's help or your father's friends' help. Every capitalist has a great respect for the words of another capitalist. But the pressure must come from above, from Petersburg itself. Would it be possible to get your father to employ a given sum of capital in setting up a textile factory in Lodz and working it with Jewish labor? That would set the others an example. Is it possible for you to do that yourself, perhaps? We don't ask any great favor either from your father or you; the one thing needed is for some one to make a start, to provide as it were some experimental proof that the exploitation of Jewish workers is just as possible as any other kind. That is the real question. How can you help us?"

Mirkin was astounded by this proposal, and also somewhat insulted; it proved that in spite of everything he was still regarded merely as a millionaire's son. And he had considered himself reborn and belonging completely to his new surroundings! What connection had he now with his father's riches? But he quickly recognized that he had no cause to feel insulted. That man Anatol sitting at the next table had made his proposal so sincerely and without afterthought that Mirkin could only feel astonished at the naive ideas that prevailed in his circle about Jewish millionaires. Flushing, he replied hesitatingly: "I've no communication with my father; I've broken off all connection with him."

"It's a question of tactics," replied Anatol with a mocking smile. "While it suited your purposes you had nothing to do with him; but if it is necessary you can resume your relations with him again."

Mirkin gazed at him with astonishment, more, with distrust. The cynical ring of the man's voice was actually painful to him. But Anatol's eyes were so frank and clear that all suspicion of cynicism had to be banished.

Anatol seemed to guess what the stranger was feeling, for he hastened to make himself more comprehensible: "Each one of us serves the cause to the extent of his abilities. It would be mad to leave unused the possibilities which the influence and the enormous wealth of your father throw open to us, because of a silly scruple. We have no time to waste on silly 'tiffs.' We employ all sorts of means for achieving our object; in this matter you, and you alone, can help us."

"And you ask me to resume relations again with my *bourgeois* father?" asked Mirkin in amazement.

"Why not? One's justified in doing that even with a robber, if it helps our cause," replied Comrade Anatol with a smile.

After a short pause for reflection Mirkin replied: "The purpose for which you need my help I approve of completely and entirely. But your suggestion that I should resume relations with my father I must consider more carefully. However, I should like very much to have a talk with you." The last words were uttered in an almost childishly imploring voice.

"With the greatest pleasure. I, too, would like to have a talk with you, and as soon as possible. He"—Comrade Anatol indicated the

Shachliner with a nod of his head—"knows where I can be found. We can arrange it through him."

Thereupon Comrade Anatol got up and prepared to go, for he had observed a pair of eyes watchfully regarding him from a corner of the room.

CHAPTER XXVII

COMRADE ANATOL

THOUGH he thought for himself, Mirkin belonged to the class of men who are always looking for a leader and guide, a human being to whom they can look up as higher than themselves, and whose nobility provides them with a justification for their existence, encouraging them and giving a direction to their thoughts and actions. Mirkin saw in Comrade Anatol such a man, a man to whom he could bring all his questions, before whom he could freely confess all his doubts; that was why he desired so keenly to know him better.

Comrade Anatol had no fixed residence. He led the life of a political suspect with the police always at his heels; he perpetually changed his quarters and never slept under the same roof twice. Mirkin had already tried several times to arrange a meeting with him, but it had invariably been postponed "for unforeseen reasons." One day the Shachliner at last called for Zachary and conducted him to the house of a young married couple. Anatol was awaiting him in a newly furnished room. The Shachliner left them to themselves.

Anatol greeted Mirkin as if he were an old acquaintance. The socialist leader's face consisted of two halves, each with a quite distinct expression: the one centered in the eyes, the other in the mouth. It was the mouth of a very old man; all the bitterness of a life filled with care and suffering weighed on that horribly twisted mouth with its perpetual cynical smile. Whether Anatol talked or was silent, the smile was always there. It was by no means a pleasant smile; there was something sarcastic in it. On his lips, on his neatly groomed blond mustache seemed to lie the moldering damp of the dark dungeons in which he had spent the best years of his life. Anatol's smile was a perpetual accusation of everybody who did not follow its owner's example. But the upper half of his face, his eyes in particular, had a childlike candor. His eyes never ventured to look at any one frankly and openly; they always seemed to be slyly hiding behind their half-shut, deeply arched lids; from there they glanced out with a child's sense of guilt, with an almost imploring plea for forgiveness. It was not affection that one caught in that glance, but a prayer for sympathy, for forgiveness of all the bitterness that fate had graved on the man's lips. Everybody who spoke to Anatol glanced quickly aside from the disagreeable smile on his lips and took refuge in the warm humanity of his gaze. Mirkin, too, did so now.

"Well, young man, have you decided yet to take the step we talked about the last time I saw you?"

Mirkin did not answer at once. Under Anatol's glance he could not overcome his shyness. He had not yet lost the naive curiosity about all Jews that he had acquired in his early life. Every Jewish beard he saw awoke confused feelings in him, for he assumed that the deepest mysteries of divine mysticism must reside behind them. Whenever he came in contact with Jewish idealism, whether in the lives of the older generation or the revolutionary fervor of the younger, he was overcome with agitation; he imagined he stood before an inexhaustible well, from which he could draw the answers to all his torturing questions.

So Mirkin felt before Comrade Anatol like a schoolboy before his master, and it was some time before he could find words: "I wasn't thinking of that at the moment, and it wasn't about that that I wanted to speak to you. That's really only a secondary matter. I want you to explain other things to me, to tell me about the whole business, the greater . . ." He broke off in the middle of his sentence.

Comrade Anatol looked at him in surprise and smiled.

"What do you want to talk to me about?" he asked, throwing Zachary a friendly and encouraging glance.

"About the whole problem . . ." stammered Mirkin.

"What is troubling you?" Anatol sat down at the table and rested his white, almost bloodless hands upon it; Mirkin, too, sat down. "You mustn't fancy that I myself am quite clear about everything. But we'll see if we can't understand each other."

The warm human glance of Anatol's eyes, which seemed suddenly to have grown brighter and larger, gave Mirkin confidence and he began: "It won't be an easy business. I don't know whether I'll be able to make everything clear to you, or if my heretical ideas mayn't annoy you. I am what people call contemptuously a *petit bourgeois* or a *bourgeois*. I've tried to root that cause of offense out of myself, but I can't. Nobody can escape from his own nature. I haven't come to you for any political reasons, but driven by an inner need like so many others of our generation, the need to find a new content for my life, or if you like to call it that, a faith. Life is a difficult business without a faith. For you 'class-conscious' people it's easier; for you the altering of conditions is an end in itself, satisfying your egoism and your desire for revenge. Many of you lose yourselves in the labyrinth of the means required for your goal, so that you see nothing else, and ask for nothing else. But we *petit bourgeois,* who come to you driven neither by thirst for revenge nor by self-interest, but for the sake of a fuller life—we can't live without having before us the great goal that we feel stands at the end of every road as the reward for all our striving. But what is that goal? What can replace for us the heaven of our fathers and grandfathers? Sometimes I can envisage it, but at other times I have the feeling that it isn't there at all, that there is nothing but a long dark corridor in which we stumble forward blindly, with nothing at the end of it—and we stray purposelessly and vainly from one 'means' to another. You may laugh at me as the others do—but I've come to you because I believe you know the goal and see it before you. Forgive me for my naiveté but please tell me what awaits us at the end, what it is that can give us the strength to travel the hard road. . . ."

Anatol patiently heard Zachary to the finish. While Zachary was speaking he could not detach his mind from the double and contrary effect his words produced on his companion's face. Anatol's eyes were profoundly serious and seemed to follow with genuine sympathy his passionate outpourings. But simultaneously the exasperatingly cynical smile on his lips seemed to express pitying contempt for those same outpourings.

"What are you really trying to say? Who asserts that one must have a 'goal' before one can go our road? The road to the social revolution isn't paved with marble slabs or set with trees in whose shade we can take a pleasant philosophical promenade. The road to the social revolution is a yawning tunnel into which we shall all be sucked whether we want to or not, driven by the rushing storm of time and circumstance. We do not go this way voluntarily. It is a decree determined by immutable laws. Some try to resist it. They are fools. We are just a little cleverer, seeing that we go voluntarily. We only help on the course of events a little, so that it may proceed more quickly. We do our duty by the coming generations, just as the previous ones did their duty by us. But as for the goal—who knows what it is, who can really speak of a goal? Who knows whether or not any goal even exists?"

Mirkin gazed at Anatol uncomprehendingly with wide-open eyes, like a disappointed child whose sweets have just been snatched from it by its mother without its knowing why.

"And that is all?" he exclaimed with a sigh.

"Yes, comrade," replied Anatol. "All these beautiful things such as idealism, goals, faith, have simply been invented by us intellectuals so as to smooth the road a little and make it easier. We, feeble and sickly as we are, need this balsam for our weak limbs. The masses, I mean the ordinary poor people, the oppressed people, who bear the burden of life—they have no need for idealism, they have no need for a faith; they are driven on by a far stronger and more effective motive power, namely the satisfaction of their own simplest needs, which every living thing demands. In real life there is no room for idealism. It is determined by pitiless laws, the same laws that govern the beasts in the jungle. Do you think that the masses are seeking to achieve power for any lofty purpose? That is only a comedy played by us intellectuals. The masses desire a revolution because they want to be masters over life, and wish, instead of being beasts of burden, to be drawn on the car of civilization to their own egoistic enjoyments. Yes, that is the situation, and the real and permanent factor to be counted upon; all the rest is talk concocted by idlers like us. The whole edifice of human idealism is mere dead lumber, a plaything for the intellectuals. The masses know nothing about it; they are as rude, primitive, and pitiless as the necessity that drives them."

Mirkin could sense in Anatol's last words a certain dissatisfaction and even pain. They made him feel that this man was trying to conceal his real thoughts behind the opinions of others.

"But you can't mean that seriously!" said Mirkin in disappointment. "Everything according to you proceeds of itself, without reason or goal, simply in obedience to necessity, simply through the primitive agency of the mass? And what is the mass really? What is this new idol you have fashioned for yourselves? Simply an anonymous Czar with a thousand heads. The mass is not an independent body, but merely a fortuitous conglomeration. At certain moments of exaltation it may, no doubt, have a psychology of its own. But you haven't yet found the furnace in which the masses can be smelted into an independent entity. They yield to the slightest temptation and crumble again into individuals who think of nothing but their own selfish ends. But I'm seeking the very opposite, and I've come to ask you about the loftiest goal of all, a goal that can transmute us all into one body as religion transmuted the first followers of Christ. From what source are we to draw the strength for our struggle?"

"There is necessity," replied Anatol quietly.

"If physical necessity is the sole motive power that determines our actions, and if no other moral power exists at all—what motive power for our actions will remain when physical necessity, as you assume it will be, is satisfied by the realization of the socialist state?"

"Then the world can look round it for some other factor! For our generation I fancy necessity will suffice." Thereupon Anatol withdrew again behind his wall of defense. But Mirkin did not give in; he was resolved to make this man come into the open.

"Then seeing that you reject all idealism, allow me to ask you a frank question, Comrade Anatol. I beg your pardon to begin with, for the question is a personal one. How do you justify your own way of life? How did you come to take up your life-work? I know about you; I've heard a great deal about your past life. It is a long chain of suffering. Yet all that wasn't called forth by necessity, but by something else that you don't dare to name. How do you explain that?"

"Oh, that's the kind of thing you mean?" Anatol smiled. "We do them really for nobody's sake but our own. Our motives may be various. Some of us are 'professionals.' There exists in humanity a desire, inherited from long dead generations, to display heroism. Those who have no opportunity to do that elsewhere come to us. It is the 'professional' revolutionary type that does that mostly, a type very common among us Jews. With us this desire is a desire for martyrdom inherited from our forefathers, a natural need, nurtured through generations, to sacrifice oneself for the faith; one might also put it down to romanticism. Those of us who have lost the old faith fashion a new god to whom we can sacrifice ourselves. But you can be certain of this —at the first temptation that assails such a group it will become as feeble as the intelligentsia after the abortive revolution in 1905. The masses have no time to feel disappointed. They don't join our movement because of inherited romanticism, for the masses have no inheritance; they join us so as to fight the bloody present. The ordinary people aren't 'professional' revolutionists; they are being driven by the force of circumstances towards revolution, and as long as these circumstances last . . ."

Mirkin impatiently interrupted:

"Allow me to doubt, Comrade Anatol, that your devotion to the movement rises from a longing for heroism or from inherited feelings. I fancy that far deeper and far more profound motives come into play there, motives that you probably can't yourself bear to explain."

Anatol remained silent for a little. The smile had suddenly vanished from his lips, and his face became profoundly serious. His eyes wandered as though trying to avoid Mirkin's gaze. After a pause he replied:

"It is our fate. It is faith that drives us into the movement. Perhaps you're right, perhaps all we do is only a means to an end—but I believe in spite of that there is a great and real goal at the end of all our striving: a life in common, a collective creative effort. We shall win eternal life when we die as individuals and are reborn into the community. The individual is transitory, the mass is eternal. It is the ground on which we, as individuals, grow. Year after year new grain sprouts—but the ground is eternal!"

Anatol's face was irradiated by the light that shone from his eyes. As he uttered the last words his whole body swayed like that of a pious Jew absorbed in burning prayer. In a grave, exalted tone he continued:

"Even the consciousness of being one among many brings happiness. One must know how to feel the truly human happiness that radiates from the community of all men. To feel it properly one would have," he smiled, "to belong to the Chassidim. They reached the highest plane where the individual becomes a part of the whole sacred mystery, feels within him the full power of all humanity, and becomes capable of great deeds. Yes, I believe this universal joy will fill all the world and make our life worth the living. I can't express it in mere words; one must feel it."

A thrill ran through Zachary. He thirstily drank in Anatol's words.

But presently Anatol seemed to become ashamed of his sentimentality and to regret his lapse into idealism; with a contemptuous smile he went on: "Nevertheless, young man, you must resign yourself to the fact that our rôle—I mean us intellectuals—the rôle of all those who join battle merely out of idealism, as you call it, is a wretched one. We are fated to destruction. When the great moment comes the revolution will crush us, for with our useless baggage, our idealism and romanticism, we should only be in the way. We must be prepared to play the rôle of negro slaves, whose labor is welcomed as long as it is of use, and cast off when it is not. Among us Jews there are saints, Zaddikim, who renounce all reward. That must be our rôle. We must give ourselves to the cause, whether we are paid for it or not. At the moment all that we can know is the 'process' and we must dedicate ourselves to it entirely and with all our faith. Whatever happens we shall have had our share in the common happiness."

After a short pause Mirkin said with a smile: "What do you wish? What am I to do?"

"Go to Lodz and find out what the situation is there. Then you will know yourself what you should do."

"Very good. I'll go. To whom must I address myself?"

"Our comrades will be expecting you."

CHAPTER XXVIII

LODZ

A COVERING of snow still lay on the fields; only here and there did the imprisoned earth peep through the rents of its white blanket. At several places it had already flung off its icy robe and stretched itself in freedom under the sun.

The woods were rejuvenated; the tree-trunks and branches quivered with new life. The thatched roofs of the little houses were wet with the winter snows which had blackened the walls and palings, and were hidden in a network of reddish new shoots. Peasants in huge boots tramped over the soft miry ground and looked on with approval while their barefooted wives bore heavy sacks home from the potato pits. Now and then a cart could be seen slowly lumbering over the roads; here and there a young colt pranced about in a field. At the stations Jews in long caftans whose tails were spattered with dry mud crowded eagerly into the carriages. Women flung packages to one another with much noise. Such were the pictures that Mirkin saw from his compartment on his way from Warsaw to Lodz.

The landscape was just as strange to him as its occupants; and yet it attracted him. There was no countryside that he could call his own, for he was a city-child. True, in far distant central Russia there had once been a street that he regarded as his own, the snow-covered road from his parents' house to the school; but a whole landscape extending to the horizon—that he had never had to himself. A country, a language, a people can seem strange to us, but a landscape never. Mirkin drank in the scenes he saw passing before his eyes down to the smallest detail. This landscape belonged to him, because he could understand it, because he had it in his blood; and he felt himself growing along with it.

It was Russian earth, a soil for potatoes, cabbages, turnips and man's daily bread. The homely appearance of everything, the thawing snow in the village streets, the low glistening thatched roofs, the walls blackened by the winter snows, the thin bare quivering trees, brought the people who lived in this landscape nearer to him, these strange peasants in their outlandish clothes, their queer four-cornered hats and the high boots which they wore in place of the usual sandals.

Looking at the countryside speeding past him Mirkin felt at home, as if he belonged to it. And his heart was filled with gratitude that he could love and feel at one with this landscape and these people: "I'll establish myself firmly here and refuse ever to be dragged away again."

The streets of Lodz, which Mirkin now saw for the first time, seemed to him still more strange, chaotic and marvelous; these were neurotic streets, neurotic shops, neurotic people! The lean painfully thin bodies of the men seemed actually in danger of falling out of their caftans which were far too long and wide for them. The caftans looked like tents, the bodies that were hidden in them like mere laths. From head to foot these people seemed to be cut out of one piece: they gesticulated with their hands, their beards wagged when they spoke, the atmosphere was filled with restless movement. A nervous fluttering; waving beards, anxious eyes flitting about, eyes that questioned, implored, sought, a sea of caps. . . . A forest of thin black Jews. Some passed hastily with rolls of cotton under their arms; others stood comfortably in groups before the shops and flourished their thin walking sticks. Amidst all this appeared now and then a patch of color from a peasant-woman's headcloth, the bright gleam of a peasant's coat; they relieved the colorless monotony of the black caftans and the dark buildings like a cluster of flowers in a sandy waste. . . .

On the bridges, which were still covered with dirty white snow, was a perpetual noisy traffic. There were piles of freshly made peasant clothes in wagons. Dragging the wagons were horses and human beings. There were pyramids of bright-hued undressed cotton and wool, pyramids of worsted yarn, pyramids of raw cotton; and among the wagons and barrows—hats, caps, bare-heads, beards, eyes and bundles of yarn, countless bundles of yarn. . . .

Charged with power like a great dynamo, overladen with human energy, covered with sweat, blackened with coal-smoke, the city quivered with perpetual movement, with constant haste. Driven by electric motors of lightning speed, the people seemed to race with the belts in one single revolution, one shriek, without surcease, without a moment's pause.

As evening fell in the dark and noisome Jewish alleys, far away, behind the Lodz plain, the sun was sinking, strange and unearthly. And the streets of the city were filled with the powerful, smoke-blacked figures of workmen. The tramways were packed with human bodies; the narrow pavements disappeared beneath the streams of home-returning workers. Their bodies exuded the specific smell of the Lodz factories which they had breathed in during the day. The whole city reeked of machine oil and worsted yarn. On one's lips, in one's eyes, one could feel the pungent stench that came from the bleaching-yards.

The shops were brightly lit. From back courts mothers of families with baskets and sad gray headcloths streamed towards them. At the street corners, pressed against the house walls, prostitutes in starched dresses and with freshly-washed hair kept their watch; their exposed necks gave out the penetrating smell of strong scent.

In the evening, after the factories were closed, a young man called on Mirkin at his hotel and introduced himself as Comrade Motel, and said he had been sent by Comrade Anatol.

Mirkin recognized him immediately; he was the same young man who had sat at Anatol's table in the café in Warsaw and had been pointed out to him as the delegate from Lodz. In Warsaw, Motel had worn the clothes of a better class workman with a soft hat or a cap, had, in any case been distinguished in no way from the other comrades. But now a young man in Chassid costume stood before Mirkin, a young man who could easily have been taken for a diligent Talmudist, because of his long caftan and his queer shaped hat, although he had tucked his ritual curls away behind his ears.

"Don't you know me? I'm Comrade Motel. I remember you quite well from our meeting in Warsaw. I wear Jewish clothes here for reasons of expedience; circumstances force me to do it," said the dark young man with the youthful beard in the dry and matter-of-fact tone of a soldier making a report. "My parents are fanatically religious and it's necessary for me to keep in with them."

"That's all the same to me. What difference can the clothes one wears make?"

"Oh, it makes a difference! Seeing the others are so fanatical, we, too, must show that we can stick to our principles. But it won't last much longer now: my circumstances will change presently."

After a pause Comrade Motel went on: "I've received instructions to tell you about the situation here."

"I'm very grateful to you."

"Shall we take the tram, comrade?" asked Motel.

"I would rather go on foot; one sees more then."

"It's a pretty long way and the executive committee is waiting for us," said Comrade Motel in an official tone.

When Mirkin heard the words "executive committee" he immediately agreed to take the tram.

Comrade Motel conducted him to a little one-storied house in the outlying Balet suburb; a feeble light issued from its shuttered windows. Through a dark entry and an uneven, pitted courtyard Mirkin reached a low-ceilinged room, whose roof with its three massive rafters seemed almost to touch his head.

Before he had time to take in more of the dark and shadowy room his eye was caught by a tall clumsy shape standing in a corner; and though he could not distinguish any human face he was greeted by a voice coming from somewhere: "Aha, another young calf for the shambles! When are they going to drag you to the slaughterhouse?"

"Don't answer him, comrade! He isn't in his right mind. He talks to everybody like that. We hold our meetings here because of the police."

Comrade Motel led Mirkin to a table where a workman was sitting in his shirt and trousers, having obviously just risen from his handloom, along with a younger man with a strikingly intelligent face. This was the executive committee.

"And these people think they can get something done. They'll get nothing done. A set of cattle, that's what you are, oxen, cows, calves—you'll all be dragged to the slaughterhouse, some of you sooner, some later."

"He's out of his mind; don't mind him, comrade!" They turned once more reassuringly to Mirkin. A member of the executive committee got up and went over to the corner to pacify the madman.

Mirkin was so astonished that he could not say a word. He looked more attentively towards the corner from which the words had come and saw, sitting on a chair beside the hand-loom, which took up almost the whole breadth of the room, a spectral figure, all skin and bone, from whose twisted mouth saliva was dribbling; a pair of unnaturally bright eyes were measuring him with the piercing glance of an insane person.

"What would you like to be told about first, comrade? About the general state of the textile workers, or the special question that you're interested in, the problem of transferring the Jewish textile workers from hand work to factory work?" the younger man asked Mirkin in a businesslike voice.

"Comrades, I'm a stranger to these things. This is the first time in my life I've come in contact with Jewish workers, known what Jewish destitution is. I implore you; don't address me in that official tone! I want to be told everything, to know everything," replied Mirkin beseechingly.

"What do you want to know, comrade?" the intelligent young man asked again.

"What kind of house is this?" asked Mirkin.

"The house you're in now, comrade, is the house of a Jewish weaver. Two families live in it, and three fathers of families work at the looms that are housed in it; a father, his married son and his son-in-law. That's the father sitting over there; he's having a doze at his open loom before he begins his night work." The young man pointed towards a face with a gray beard that now became visible in the dim light of a lamp hanging on a cord above the loom. Then the speaker went on: "There's only room for two looms in the house, but there are three families to be fed; so the father takes the night shift after the son is finished for the day. The son is the comrade sitting here at the table beside us. The son-in-law has gone to get raw cotton. The other members of the household have been sent to neighbors until our conference is over. What more do you want to know, comrade?" asked the young man in an energetic voice.

"Do you mean to say that two families live here in this small room?" asked Mirkin in utter astonishment. "Where do they all sleep?"

"On the looms, under the looms, wherever they can. Do you see those boards there beside the hearth? A whole family lives there, a man, wife and two children. The table we're sitting at is pushed out into the passage and a bed is set up in the free space; the second family sleeps in that. Seeing that the father has no place to sleep in at night he sleeps during the day. But that gives him the chance of earning a few roubles at night, seeing that the looms are unoccupied. What more do you want to know, comrade?" asked the young man once more in an energetic, almost rough voice.

"The madman—who is he?"

"He isn't mad, he's only deformed. He's been lame since childhood through the doctor's carelessness when he was born; that man over there is his father, too. Opposite this house there's a cattle market. As there's no place for the cripple to sit here during the day they lead him outside; there he watches all day oxen and sheep being driven to the slaughterhouse, and he's taken it into his head that human beings are nothing but oxen and sheep. When he sees a funeral procession he says: 'Aha! There's an ox being carried from the slaughterhouse!'—What more do you want to know, Comrade Mirkin?"

Mirkin was silent.

"Well, do you know all you want to know now?"

"Yes, now I know all I want to know," replied Mirkin. "And he's right . . ." he added after a pause.

"Who?" asked the young man.

"Him there." Mirkin pointed towards the cripple, who was staring at the table with an idiotic gaze from his corner.

"No; for a man has a far harder time of it than an ox. An ox is provided with fodder, at least, while it lives; for otherwise it would be of no use as food. But graveworms can't feed up the bodies they live on to make them nice and fat. The worms are like us, you see: the rich get all the fat and the poor content themselves with skin and bone." The young man laughed bitterly.

When they were out in the yard again Mirkin suddenly stopped. Through the closed shutters of a room near by came the sound of a Chassid melody with its peculiar mixture of joy and melancholy, accompanied by hand-clapping and the shuffling of feet dancing in time to the rhythm.

"What place is that?" asked Mirkin in surprise.

"A Chassid prayer-house. They're enjoying themselves in there. There's nothing much to see. A set of wild fanatical Dervishes, a running sore on the body of Jewry," replied Mirkin's escort.

"I would like to have a look all the same; do let me have a look."

They opened the door. A dense heavy gust of warm air met them in the face. A ring of Jews in black caftans, holding one another by the shoulders, were going through a dance. In the light of the burning candles pale faces could be seen bowed over Talmud folios. Some were absorbed in study, others were asleep. A man with thin bony hands walked about wakening the sleepers and offering them spirits and pastry.

At the far end of the room, enveloped in thick obscurity, flickered a single tiny light. It looked like a candle at the head of some enormous corpse lying in impenetrable darkness.

"Why all the gayety, Baruch?" Mirkin's companion asked the man who was dispensing the spirits and pastries and whom he seemed to know intimately. "What occasion is it?"

"Why, you ignoramus, don't you know that? This is the anniversary of the great Rabbi's death. Besides, must one have some occasion before one can be merry?"

"We're just happy, just happy—occasion or no occasion," agreed another man, who had put on his cap backside foremost, waving his glass in the air.

"There's something I want you to do for me," said Mirkin in an imploring tone, suddenly turning to his companion.

"What is it?"

"I would like to live in this house. Try to get lodgings for me here!"

"Here, in this wretched slum?"

"Yes, here, in this slum, among these people. I want to know them, I want to know them!" said Mirkin almost in a shout, seizing the young man's hand and gazing at him with beseeching eyes.

"Good. We'll see what can be done."

CHAPTER XXIX

BACK COURTS

A FEW DAYS later Mirkin was installed in Weaver's Court in the suburb of Balet. Comrade Motel had got him lodgings in a flat on the first floor, facing the courtyard. It was the cleanest and roomiest house in the whole building. Mirkin quickly struck up an acquaintance with his neighbors and was soon on friendly terms with them.

The two-story wooden building lay opposite the great cattle-market to which from all Poland came the meat needed by the working classes of Lodz. All day the rooms resounded with the squealing of pigs, the lowing of oxen and the bleating of sheep being driven past. In the filthy city court these sounds seemed extraordinarily strange; the piteous voices of the animals brought memories of green meadows, lush grass and autumn mists into the forlorn place. The house was not a big one; in style it resembled a thousand others to be found in Poland. The courtyard was rambling and full of nooks and corners. Everywhere round it extra rooms and sheds had been set up. They crowded against and on top of each other, making one feel that they had been knocked up only for a few days. The owner of the building had not had enough money to finish it, and so he had been forced to complete the ground floor in great haste and rent it out before he was able to roof in the upper story; the bad material of which the house was built was crumbling, the walls had rents, the roofs leaked. . . .

In all these half-finished, badly-roofed flats stood great, clumsy wooden hand-looms; they almost filled the rooms and reached to the ceilings.

As if in a medieval prison the weavers sat fettered day and night to their looms. The looms were like gigantic spiders; at them, like flies caught in a web, half-naked men, their hairy chests bared, moved the treadles all day with their naked feet, making the shuttle continuously fly through the warp. Beside the looms sat youthful assistants, almost all of them children under fourteen, winding the thread on reels. The wives and older daughters spun the colored worsteds for the "fancy" webs. All day human beasts of burden brought in on hand-barrows piles of raw material, various hued wools, yarn and cotton. On the same little barrows the finished rough webs were carted away to the pressing factories or the warehouses, thence to be dispatched to the great distant markets of the Russian empire.

On the yellow faces of all the hand-weavers there was a constant look of anxiety, as if they felt condemned to death. More and more chimney stacks were rising in the new suburb which in the last few years had spread over the wide Lodz plain. Parts for new mechanically-driven looms kept rolling in on the trains to the railway station of Lodz. But not for these men were the mighty chimney stacks being erected, not for them were the new spinning-machines being introduced; they were forever condemned to sit at wooden hand-looms and to go down to destruction with them. The old men told themselves: "It will serve our turn; after all we'll soon be in our graves." The young men just starting life thought of nothing but emigration; they saved up penny by penny, painfully stinting themselves, for their ship fares, and dreamed of cotton mills in distant lands. . . .

The dull wooden thud of the hand-looms, reminding one of the sound of planks knocking together, was not to be heard in all the rooms. From many windows came the hasty importunate rattle of sewing machines. Out of bad shoddy material, out of factory left-overs, winter coats, suits, and peasants' trousers were put together for sale at the weekly market. All day the sewing machines flew as if hurrying towards a point that they would never reach. . . . In other rooms sat shoe-makers, hat-makers, furriers. In almost every family the daughter had a knitting machine. Every mother wound yarn; every son was a weaver or a tailor.

So there was perpetual activity in the court. From every window came a rhythmical clatter, now rising, now falling. Sewing machines whirred furiously, as if trying to overtake one another. All the windows gave out a choking smell of raw webs, raw wool, worsted yarn.

The court seemed to exude oil and sweat, and the sour stench of sweating bodies, stale food, moldy mattresses. Yet all these smells were drowned and lost in the specific smell of Lodz itself—the effluvium of insanitary courtyards. . . .

Mirkin's landlord was called Moses Pokrzyva; his surname in Polish meant "the stinging nettle," and nobody seemed to know clearly whether it was his official designation or whether he had been given it as a nickname. In any case it suited the man, for Moses Pokrzyva knew of no better occupation for his days than to make stinging remarks to people. At home his wife and daughters were victims of his sarcasm; none of them could ever please him. When he appeared in the court itself he let fly at all and sundry. If he saw a boy playing there he would at once take him to task: "Why aren't you at school?"

In the middle of the day he would rush into the synagogue to see that the young lads studying their Talmud were earning their free meal. He would start quarreling even with Christians; if a peasant's cart stopped before the door he would play the policeman: "Don't you know that you aren't allowed to stop here?"

It was Moses Pokrzyva's daughters who were responsible for his bitterness. He had four of them, all of marriageable age. Although he lived on his daughters (he never lifted a finger, but existed on what they could earn with their sewing machines), the fact that they could not find husbands and were growing into old maids caused him deep suffering. He knew, of course, that if they married nothing would be left for him but to go and beg; yet he would have put up even with that, if he could only have got them married off. But the young men nowadays married only girls who had dowries; and so Moses Pokrzyva's daughters were left sitting, worked hard to keep themselves alive, and sweetened their bitter existence by reading romances.

The oldest was an angel of goodness; Gitele, a dried-up emaciated creature, had a face that consisted mostly of two great eyes. Her head rose from a thin, bird-like neck. She was a passionate novel reader. Her whole life was involved with the destinies of people she read about. She stayed awake half the night over books that she borrowed from the lending library for three copeks a week. She got through a different book every day. She read while she was eating, while she walked about, while she stood, even when she was sewing. With his perpetual scolding her father had quite broken her, sucked all her strength; for Gitele was the only one in the house who showed respect towards her father and did not answer him back when he spoke. So she alone was made to feel the full wrath that he nursed against her sisters and had all day to hear that she would come to a bad end and that he begged to remind her that the Jews did not approve of nuns. . . .

Gitele kept silence; her father's words no longer evoked even tears from her. Her sick mother, whom in spite of his nettlelike disposition Moses nursed as tenderly as a child, was continuously confined to her bed. Moses gave her her food, even put on her spectacles for her, and stuck the prayer-book in her hand when she wanted to pray. Whenever she heard him at his scolding she would sigh from her bed: "Why do you torment the child? Why do you go on at her? Is it her fault?"

But the father was convinced that Gitele was to blame for everything, not only for her own lot, but her sisters' as well; for while the oldest daughter was unmarried the younger ones could not marry even if they were ostensibly in a position to do so. The three other daughters, however, were not deceived in the least by this argument. The second oldest one, the stocky Sarah, went her own way; for she had—at least so she said—"prospects." She was engaged to a Jewish soldier and was waiting until his term of military service should be over. She disappeared with him every Sabbath. He came to the house and ate there as well, but of marriage he never mentioned a syllable. The youngest two daughters acted like their sister, but without having "prospects." On Sabbaths and holidays they went walking in the Helenover Park with weaver and tailor lads and stayed out for half the night. When their father made a scene and told them they were "going too far," they would reply tersely and conclusively: "Can you tell us what else we can do? Get us husbands, and we'll be only too glad to marry!"

Moses Pokrzyva was a pious Chassid Jew and came of an extremely respectable family; he was distantly related to a rabbi. That itself was sufficient ground for him to be outraged by his daughters' way of life, and so he tried to subdue them first by scoldings and reproaches. But his daughters shouted him down. Then at last one day he snatched up a flat-iron, whereupon his daughters left the house and remained away for quite a long time. Moses' poor sick wife wept bitterly in her bed: "Who will look after us?"

The words frightened Moses; things might be even worse after all! And he set out to search for his daughters. One of them remained unaccounted for and did not come back again; she had left, so he was told, for Buenos Aires or somewhere to live among the "Blacks." The others returned to their home. . . . Since that time their father had swallowed down his anger and said nothing. When evening came there was a great dressing up, a rouging and powdering, and then his daughters set out on their usual walk with their young men, who were already waiting outside for them. Sarah walked out with her soldier, the second sister had no constant escort—one night it would be this youth, the next it would be another. The father stood in front of his door and regarded everything in silence; his face was thinner, his nose as sharp as if it had been ground on a grindstone; his beard had grown ragged and the sharp angles of his bones showed beneath his tattered caftan. The old man dumbly gnawed without ceasing at the end of his beard. At last he turned back into the house and all the rage gathered within him was poured out on the head of his eldest daughter, the meek dove who never answered back; on her he laid all the blame. Gitele merely turned her emaciated face towards him and looked at him with her great eyes. That glance was heart-breaking. And the mother groaned on her sick bed: "Moses, Moses, come here!"

The man went nearer: "What is it, Beile?"

The sick woman bent forward painfully and whispered: "Moses, what are you doing? Why do you torment her so ceaselessly? Just because she's so soft and defenseless?"

Moses saw that his wife had spoken the truth, and his heart was touched by his daughter's fate. He tried to say a kind word to her, but he could not; it went against his grain. So he rushed to the little synagogue, took up the first book he could find, and as he read began to sway his body so violently and make such a disturbance that he confused all the others. . . .

But when Sabbath Eve came Gitele, too, found a recompense for all her sufferings and humiliations. Her father slept over his Bible, her spectacled mother nodded over her prayer-book, her sisters, having washed themselves down to the hips with perfumed soap, were out walking with their young men. In the whole house reigned a paradisal stillness. Then Gitele would put on her wrap and sit on the narrow wooden balcony that looked out on the court. That was her ivory tower; she herself became the noble Rebecca waiting with beating heart for her true knight Rudolf who might return any moment from the chase, a bouquet of flowers for her in his hand. She then lived in another world.

From the weaver's shed opposite the old father led his cripple son and lowered him on the doorstep. The cripple had a sharp tongue and there was a saying about him in the court: "If a cat could think and the cripple could walk the world wouldn't have much chance of lasting."

Although he looked so stupid and forlorn as he sat there, the cripple knew everything that happened in the court and where the shoe pinched everybody. He tried to fix slanders on every one, and did not spare anybody who came within the range of his voice. But of Gitele he made an exception; she was the only one in the court towards whom he had a soft side. When he saw her smoothly parted hair and the great inquiring eyes in her thin pale face warmth streamed into his heart and his lips grew moist. He longed to say a kind word to her and so give utterance to the emotion that filled his heart. But his tongue always betrayed him; instead of a kind word he said something spiteful; it was as if some one took the kind words out of his mouth and substituted others for them. This happened in spite of himself and he could no more help it than the moisture on his lips, the sight of which filled Gitele with disgust. Yet she felt the warm glance that gleamed in the boy's idiot eyes and basked in it. Everything would have been well if the cripple could only have kept silent. But he could not curb his tongue; for a long time he thought over what he should say to her; at last he found it. "Good Schabbes, Gitele."

Without glancing up from her book Gitele replied: "Good Schabbes, Samuel."

The cripple was boundlessly delighted at having succeeded in saying something kind. "I did that splendidly," he told himself and made another effort, like a child who is learning to walk for the first time and totters on slowly, step by step.

"Is that a nice book that you're reading?" he shouted from his doorstep across to the little wooden balcony.

"Yes, Samuel, it's a lovely romance; it's about a Count and a Countess."

Once more the boy was delighted that things were going so well; full of joy he exclaimed: "Your sisters live romances and you read romances!" And an idiotic laugh like the cry of an animal escaped from his mouth and seamed his face in a thousand wrinkles.

Without speaking a word Gitele got up and went in. The cripple followed her persistently with his glance, as though he wanted to keep her from going. But he was as unsuccessful in that as he had been in keeping back the spiteful words that had involuntarily escaped his lips.

Dumbly the cripple fixed his eyes on the bare wall opposite and tried to get up. Again he wore the helpless expression of a child learning to walk, and he impotently fell forward from the step where he was sitting.

CHAPTER XXX

"THE POOR MAN'S GOD"

IN THE court stood a little edifice made of new planks with a shingled roof. There lived the poor occupants' "God." His dwelling was just as wretched as theirs; nor was it any more distinguished by cleanliness. The shelf where the Torah was kept was curtained off with a strip of cheap cloth. On the wretched Almemor burned a candle in a broken candle-stick. Copies of the Talmud lay about on tables, and just as the other houses were filled with the clanking of hand-looms and the whirring of sewing-machines, so here could be heard all day the gray monotonous sing-song of poor Bible scholars, impecunious free-meal Talmudists and lugubrious Jews, that spoke of hopelessness.

If Mirkin happened to be in the court contemplating the poverty that surrounded him he often went into the little prayer-house of "the poor man's God" to get a nearer glimpse of those Jews and listen to their prayers and their readings from the Talmud. The poor man's God exerted an inexplicable attraction on Mirkin: he doubted whether he was acting rightly in troubling himself about the prayer-house and its God, but he went on doing so; he, a radical, a believer in progress, a bit of a socialist although he belonged to no party—he had to admit to himself that these things interested him, that something attracted him to the poor temple. Curiosity drove him to inquire what happened there, who the young people were who studied there with such wild zeal. Often he would visit it in the evening, sit down in a corner and listen; he watched the poor Jews arriving for the evening service; they appeared in their ordinary clothes, came straight from their work, from haggling, quarreling, cursing. The hands of the fish vendors were still covered with the scales of the fish they had been selling in the market. The fleshers from the neighboring cattle-market had still round their wrists the ropes with which they led their beasts. The tanners and cobblers were black with their work. The bakers' clothes and hats were covered with flour dust. Ends of thread hung from the beards of the tailors. They had all come from their work without making any preparation, without any show of reverence, as if their God were one of themselves. With Him there was no need for ceremony; He knew at once what one wanted of Him, and one very quickly settled one's business with Him too: a worshiper would wrap himself in a filthy prayer-mantle and in a hoarse perfunctory voice hastily reel off the prescribed prayer; the others repeated it after him, scarcely able to keep up with him.

So they said their prayers, rendered to God what was due to God, spat, and—were gone again. Nobody remained but a few idlers, one or two old people who had nothing better to occupy themselves with, or people passing through the town; they pattered over a few chapters of the psalms by the feeble light on the reading desk. Here and there a sleeping Jew could be seen with his beard spread over an open Bible. A shivering, famished-looking youth with a bloodless face swayed his body as he read the Talmud. And many long ritual curls swung to and fro, some with burning ardor, others with weary boredom.

In a corner a white-bearded Jew sat in front of a candle. Under his hat gleamed a lofty forehead; he piously swayed as he read his book. Sometimes in a dark corner Moses Pokrzyva or Chaim Klopot was to be seen; they leaned their faces against the cold wall of the prayer-house and murmured: "Father in Heaven, help me!" Beside the book-case near the door sat a little manikin whose effeminate appearance was still further emphasized by a headcloth. From out of it peeped two infantile blue eyes and a little snow-white beard. The old man looked like a child who had been forsaken by his mother. In one hand he held a little candle and cast its light on the book of psalms that he was reading; he was capable of nothing now but reading psalms, he was aged and longed for death and, with "the dry bread of heavenly comfort," strove to earn for himself his part in the next world, that he might not arrive there with empty hands. . . . The world held nothing to detain him longer.

Mirkin was overcome with a strange feeling when he beheld such scenes. Unutterable pity seized him not only for the human beings but also for the God that lived here. This Jewish God seemed just like the men who came here, a poor Jew just like them. He had left His glory behind Him in Heaven, and had come down among these people to dwell with them in their stinking court. Here, among weavers, cobblers, tailors, fleshers and fish-dealers, He had set up His house. They had hung before the shrine in which His Torah was kept a wretched filthy strip of cloth, a garment such as they wore themselves. They lit for Him a poor candle such as lighted their own rooms. They shared with Him the scanty bread that they themselves ate. When they had time they came hastily running to Him in their working clothes, hurriedly recited a psalm in His praise and rushed away again. He understood them. They had no time for Him, for they had a hard job earning bread for their wives and children. This God knew how painfully the Jew scratched together his subsistence, and He, the Jewish God, accompanied His Jews when they went to the market, stood humbly with each of them before the doors of the wealthy, helped them to rent a field, or bargain for a fish-pond or a cow; the rich man might tweak the Jew's beard with impunity, and in doing so he tweaked the beard of the Jewish God as well, and He let it happen, for He was humble and subservient like the Jews. And when things were desperate, when a Jew returned from some village with his sack empty, because the peasant refused to sell him a calf, then he asked his God, who walked by his side: "Well, what are we to do now?"

And the Jewish God answered him: "Do not trouble, my dear brother, things will presently get better!"

From his earliest childhood Mirkin had had a disgust for filth; it caused him actual physical nausea. When he saw evidences of uncleanliness he shrank. Hard as he had tried, especially of late, to overcome the "fine gentleman" in himself and conquer his repugnance, he was unsuccessful. He had grown accustomed to certain things, but he had to have cleanliness about him, no matter how poor his surroundings might be. He often thought to himself that personal uncleanliness was the only thing that could drive him to suicide.

The room he lived in now was comparatively clean. The reason for that was probably because there were daughters to attend to the house. A further reason was that the eldest had fallen in love with Mirkin at first sight. (She was overcome by this weakness, it must be admitted, whenever she happened to come in contact with any young man; the countless romances that she read so inflamed her imagination that she saw in every man a disguised prince.) However that may be, the eldest daughter kept Mirkin's room in order and saw that it was clean, and every time he returned to it he was surprised by some attention or other: a gay ribbon bound in a coquettish bow round the handle of the lamp, or a paper flower left on the cushion of the little sofa.

But outside his room everything was in terrible filth. And it was worst of all in the prayer-house that stood in the court. Just as in their own houses so in the house of their God, the occupants of the court paid no great attention to cleanliness. At the very entrance, at the place where the worshipers washed their hands, lay a heap of dirt that was never cleared away. The walls, the tables, the books were thick with dirt.

While in Warsaw Mirkin had often talked to his friends about the universally bruited filthiness of Jews' houses and expressed his surprise that nothing was done about it; but his words had always been greeted with incomprehensible head-shakings and his "ideas" laughed at.

The only one who had shown any understanding for his notions was Madame Hurvitz, but even she had been somewhat at a loss. The Shachliner had comforted him by pointing to the day when the social revolution would triumph and everybody would live under conditions in which they would naturally consider such things as cleanliness. When Mirkin brought up the matter again in Lodz his new neighbors looked at him in amazement, as if he had gone mad. "We only wish we had your worries! Give us some servants, then we'll be clean enough," they answered.

Things became unendurable to Mirkin. It seemed to him that the whole Jewish people were stifling in a gigantic lake of filth, and he could actually see the universal filth rising round him like a deluge and choking him.

One day he had an inspiration. An almost mad thought shot through his brain: "Everything depends finally on cleanliness. First of all things must be cleaned up. That is the first task, and I, I must take it upon myself!"

When this thought became too much for him Mirkin rushed to the market and bought a broom. Thereupon he went into the prayer-house and began to sweep the floor. The whole population of the court gathered in front of the prayer-house and gazed in astonishment at the mad "Russian," who, after living there for such a short time, was sweeping out the place.

Laughter and jeers rose from every side. With obstinate defiance Mirkin stood in the middle of the dust cloud raised by his broom, and swept from the walls and out of the corners this dirt and filth in which, it seemed to him, he was in danger of smothering. Suddenly some one took the broom out of his hands with a timid smile.

"Do go away: this is no work for you."

It was Gitele, Moses Pokrzyva's eldest daughter. She snatched the broom from Mirkin and set herself to continue cleaning the filthy prayer-house.

"He's quite right, too!" sighed an old woman who was standing among the lookers on.

But in spite of these approving words Mirkin was known thenceforth in the whole court as "the mad Russian."

But once every week Mirkin saw the wretched little synagogue in its glory. That was on Friday evening. Then all activity ceased in the court. The looms fell silent and the hasty monotonous whirr of the sewing-machines ceased. The court was swept and the dust-bins whitened. Suddenly children streamed into the court, little girls with heads newly washed and gay ribbons pranking in their carefully combed hair, and boys with clean faces showing under caps which, for a wonder, were not tattered. This unusual apparition gave the court a quite different look. From the houses came, instead of the usual stench of machine oil, the appetizing smell of fish being cooked. The sharp biting odor of cut onions brought tears to one's eyes. As soon as the stars appeared in the darkening sky the windows were lit by the flame of candles burning in shining brass candlesticks upon the festively decked tables. In the glimmering dusk the walls of the houses seemed all at once to be changed; they suddenly looked quite strange and unreal, like illustrations out of a picture book. The Sabbath preparations transformed the scene completely.

The presence of the Sabbath could also be felt on the little wooden balcony. The light from the window fell upon it and showed there Gitele's pale face. Her hair, like that of the little girls, was carefully brushed, and fell down in two plaits. She held a book in her hand. And in the house with the little balcony, through whose window with its cut paper curtains the light of the candles came, one would not have thought now that there lived a Jew called Moses Pokrzyva, who was worried over his daughters; no, on the balcony sat a pale princess looking out from the tower of her castle, a daughter of King Solomon to whom an eagle was bringing food at her father's command; and on his wings he would also bear the king's son who was destined for her. Gitele's eyes, gazing out of her pale face into the darkness, seemed to be awaiting him. . . .

Gradually the little prayer-house was thronged with bearded Jews. They exuded the fresh scent of soap and lye. Hair, beard and ritual curls were still damp with their ablutions. From the breasts of their caftans gleamed clean newly washed shirts surmounted by high collars. All the hanging lamps in the prayer-house were burning. The newly scrubbed floor was still wet. In front of the Torah shrine hung a new velvet curtain. In a clear voice a man sang the hymn welcoming the Princess Sabbath.

Mirkin stood in a corner. Amazed, almost terrified, he contemplated this transformation. A mysterious splendor irradiated everything, lifted it from its poverty into another, fantastic world. Everything was real, and yet unreal, the broad-shouldered Jews in their new caftans with their rough red faces no less than the shrine up there lit by its new candle and veiled by a curtain of red velvet. Mirkin had a feeling that God had thrown back one fold of His wretched raiment, and through the opening gleamed the royal garb which He wore beneath His beggar rags.

CHAPTER XXXI

A JEWISH MAGNATE

Mirkin was sitting opposite the well-known Jewish textile manufacturer Henryk Flachs in the latter's cold inhospitable office in the huge manufacturing town of Zavieruchov. Out of respect for old Mirkin's name, which opened all doors, Flachs had consented to receive him. Zachary had imagined he would see a strong stern man; the man who had built up, by his own efforts, this enterprise which gave work to a whole town must certainly possess an inflexible character that must show on his very features.

But before Mirkin sat a Chassid Jew; he might even have been a rabbi who was obliged by the legal regulations to wear "German" clothes. His finely cut face showed both intellect and that apprehensiveness which is peculiarly Jewish. His exquisitely groomed black beard threaded with gray made his scholarly face with the lofty rabbinical brow seem still gentler. But out of his lively black eyes, whose animation the half-lowered lids tried to conceal, glinted a restless dark fire that betrayed hidden energy. His "German" clothes, his stiff collar and elegantly cut West European suit did not sit comfortably on Flachs; he looked as if he were not yet at home in them. His slender hands were in ceaseless motion, he cracked his long fingers and kept Mirkin from getting an opening.

Mirkin had addressed himself to Flachs as the greatest Jewish manufacturer in Lodz, a man who had built up one of the largest textile businesses in the country and employed thousands of workmen, in the hope of discovering why he employed no Jewish workmen in his factory. Mirkin wished to discuss with him what could be done about that most vital of all questions for the Jews, and how the idea of a power-driven factory of their own could be realized, and so make possible the transition from hand to machine labor. His efforts to lead him to commit himself on this point had so far failed.

Flachs evaded the question and kept on talking round it without allowing Mirkin to get in a word. In vivid detail he described the enormous labors he had achieved and related the whole story of his factory, the catastrophes he had survived, the dangers he had overcome, how often he had been on the edge of ruin and how he had always saved the situation in the teeth of everything. The credit for his rise, however, he ascribed neither to luck nor to his own abilities, but to a higher, almost divinely mystical power that had made everything succeed and had watched, so to speak, over him, Flachs, in particular. From the story one might have thought that King David had risen again and was telling of his battles with the Philistines. He wove into his tale quotations from the psalms and applied them to his own battles and victories. While doing this he piously rolled his eyes and passed his hand over his beard with the typical rabbinical gesture. The psalm quotations he interpreted in his own fashion and so aptly that one might have thought the author had written them specially for him or even at his express instructions. The story of the founding of his factory he told in a grave exalted style, as if he were not talking of a private enterprise, but rather of a matter of significance for world history, upon which, at the very least, the peace of the world depended: in short, he spoke in the tone of a Field Marshal describing one of his most decisive victories.

"What am I, after all, God help me? Nothing but a feeble creature —and I started as a young man from a Chassid household. It's all the work of God."

After Flachs had described his success in great detail, Mirkin thought at last the moment had come for him to corner his opponent and force an answer from him on the question of employing Jewish labor.

Mirkin spoke with all the ardor and indignation that his late experiences in Lodz and his life with the poor Jewish weavers had awakened in him. He spoke of the death sentence that threatened the Jewish masses, cast out as they were from the community of the workers and fettered to antiquated hand-looms with which they would have to perish; of the malice of other people and the indifference of people of their own blood, of the wrong that was being committed against the Jewish population simply because they belonged to the same race as Flachs himself. He spoke also of the necessity for the Jewish masses to become participants in the progress of the whole world, the necessity to raise them from their medieval existence and find them a place in the modern world: they must become a constituent part of the creative force of the world and must not remain in the filthy kennels where the world had confined them until they perished and had to be swept away along with the rest of the filth in which they lived.

It could not have been said with certainty whether the great manufacturer was listening to Mirkin's words or not. That he was listening could be guessed from signs of strong inner agitation on his face; yet he behaved as if he were not listening, for he was afraid of admitting that the matter interested him lest he might be forced to give a concrete answer, show his cards and involve himself in some way, a thing which as an experienced negotiator he did not wish to do. So he put Mirkin off with evasive words.

"Oh, come now," he said affably, bending forward. "Is working in factories really an occupation for Jews? Every Jew likes to be his own master, likes to work in his own house, where nobody can order him about. We are king's sons," he added with a smile, "we are incapable of being slaves. And how are we to compromise with the Sabbath? We manufacturers are in the minority and we're forced to ignore the Sabbath; we manage as we can and employ Gentiles who don't keep it. I may as well say, however, that I wouldn't set my foot in the factory on the Sabbath, no, not for a million! I've never yet opened a letter or a telegram on the Sabbath, not even if a fortune was involved. And yet I know very well that my position isn't quite what it should be, for my 'beasts of burden' work on the Sabbath. Otherwise we couldn't exist; after all we're a world-wide business! It's a matter involving the world market. But take a purely Jewish factory—who will accept the responsibility of forcing the workers to give up their Sabbath? No, it isn't so simple as you think. We Jews are a chosen people; we were created for something better than that. We're king's sons, you know that as well as I do—and we must pay for it."

Mirkin's patience gave way, and he resolved to try what a personal attack would do: "Who benefits by your energy except yourself? A people takes years and centuries to produce a vital creative force such as you. When a man like you appears among other races he changes the life of half his nation, gives work to thousands. But what benefit have *we* from your strength? Who gets anything from it?"

Mirkin's question produced an almost overwhelming effect. In a voice from which one could divine a whole tragedy of isolation and loneliness the manufacturer replied: "Do you imagine this factory really belongs to me, and that I can do what I like with it? No, no, I'm not master in this place, but only director. I'm a slave who does his work—and must keep silence."

"That's only because you're alone. The Jewish masses are pariahs left behind by the rest of the world, but the Jewish manufacturer is in a still worse position. Let me tell you something. Without the Jewish working-classes the Jewish manufacturer is like a withered shoot that has been stuck into the ground. Your position is a miserable one; and even if your energy were a thousand times more productive it would be slandered as parasitism and exploitation. It's because you stand alone that you have no power."

These words were like needles jabbed into an open wound. Flachs' delicate face suddenly grew white, his long beautifully groomed beard seemed to tremble and the nostrils of his long thin nose quivered; his upper lip twitched and his slender fingers drummed nervously on the table. Suddenly from his eyes shot such an intense fire that it seemed to Mirkin as if all the power hidden in the man's feeble, bowed body as behind a veil were concentrated on it.

For a long time Flachs regarded Mirkin with a piercing glance. Then his thin lips twisted in a lugubrious grimace and he replied: "Perhaps you're right. I'm even certain that you're right. There's no point in concealing the fact from you. My position, the position of a Jewish manufacturer, is a thousand times worse than that of the wretched people. For they are many, and we are alone. Have you noticed that the back of my office chair is pushed close to the wall and that my office windows are hermetically closed? The reason why I burn electric light all day isn't because I can't stand sunlight, but because I'm afraid that some day I may get a bullet in my back from outside there. Yes, I sit here with my back guarded against the dangers of my factory, of all this town I have summoned to life; for I'm afraid of a shot in the back. I was a poor Talmud scholar once. My father was a clerk in the little factory that used to be here. By my own efforts I've turned it into one of the greatest textile factories in the country, yes, in the whole world; I've done that with nothing to aid me but my own hands. On the credit of my bare word England sends me machinery, America and Egypt send me flax. This city of labor grows every year. Thousands of wretched, landless, starving peasants from the villages come to me and I give them work. My travelers journey all over the world, even to the most remote and forsaken places. I've put our linen on the markets of Siberia, Turkestan and Bokhara. I bring together England's machinery, America's flax, and Poland's labor power. I clothe millions of people. I have done all that simply by my own energy. And yet I sit here like a criminal and am afraid to venture into my own factory that I built myself. And if I should venture out for once in a way, with an escort of course, I'm greeted with black looks as if I were a thief and robber. What am I really? A prisoner in my own factory, a prisoner of those for whom I sow and reap. Tell me yourself if there is any help for me!"

"Yes!" cried Mirkin. "Take Jewish workers into your factory! Come out of your isolation; don't stand aside any longer! Fight side by side with the Jewish people to win for us a place in the progress of the world! With your energy, with your influence, you could bring thousands of Jewish families into the life of this country and in that way into the life of the whole world. But what do you do instead? You skulk in your tent. Fear is always the reward of the coward—forgive me for being so frank. A man of courage will live or die with his people. You had enough daring to climb the ladder alone. You've fought your way through your enemies by your own strength. Why haven't you the courage to stretch out your hand to your brothers and draw them, too, into the path of world progress, the path that you are walking upon now?"

"Jewish workers?" The magnate smiled. "Jewish workers?" His smile became ironical. "Would I be any more sure of my life among them? I fancy that if I had Jewish workers in my factory—the first stab in my back would come from the dagger of a Jew."

"But the stab wouldn't be that of a Jew but of a class. The whole world is in conflict. But the bullets from outside that you're afraid of now; they're not intended merely for the manufacturer but for the Jew as well."

"My dear young friend, what difference does it make whose hand fires the bullet, or for what reason it is fired?"

"Oh, it makes a great deal of difference, and you yourself know very well what that difference is. The dagger blow of the Jewish worker would be meant for the manufacturer; but a bullet from outside there would be aimed at the heart of the whole Jewish people."

"You may be right," Flachs admitted despondently. "But however that may be, I am powerless, I can do nothing," he concluded in a hopeless voice.

"Whether you help us or not," cried Mirkin, "we shan't let ourselves be imprisoned in a new ghetto! The Jewish masses will fight for their freedom! We'll fight with tooth and nail for an existence and our share in the progress of the world. We shan't let ourselves be driven back again into our filthy courts to rot there! Whether you help us or not we *will* live in spite of all our enemies outside and inside the gates! We'll board the car of progress and drive it wherever it may take us: into the factories and into the fields, both in this country and elsewhere! We shan't give in without a hard fight. The Jewish masses have wakened to life and they shall live in spite of the whole lot of you!" cried Mirkin, on fire with passion.

The youthful ardor of his visitor both interested and amused the magnate. The faith that spoke out of the young man warmed his heart and evoked simultaneously the painful knowledge that he himself no longer possessed belief in the power of any idea. This vexed him, for he had persuaded himself that with his success he had achieved all the noblest human virtues. But much as vanity obscured his eyes, he now recognized nevertheless the emptiness within him, and suddenly he was overcome by unavailing regret and a longing for a faith such as this young man possessed.

"And what will you do if the great world refuses you admittance?" he asked with a faint ironical smile.

"If we have to perish—we'll drag down the world with us!"

"How will you do that?"

"It's quite simple. Every power seeks an outlet for itself; if it is not employed creatively, then it is transformed into a savage need for destruction," replied Mirkin, also with a smile.

But the magnate would not hear of this; such assertions made him nervous. Nor did he like Mirkin's smile; it was the same smile that he could feel behind his back through the shuttered windows of his room, yes, even through the walls; it pursued him perpetually; gave him no peace.

"Very well, we'll leave it at that for the time being; we'll find time later to continue our argument. Would you like to see Zavieruchov? You won't regret it. Afterwards we'll finish our talk. Perhaps something might be done after all." Thereupon he pressed a button.

A tall Polish count with a thin face and a monocle entered. Flachs employed him exclusively for dealing with the outside world.

"Allow me to introduce Count Zarycki, our intendant," said the manufacturer in an indifferent tone, taking up a letter in which he became immediately absorbed.

"Count, you will be so good as to show Pan Mirkin round. Of course he won't have time to see everything," said Flachs, raising his eyes from the letter and giving his count a complacently condescending smile, "but I should like you to show Pan Mirkin the two most important branches; the cotton mills and the machine foundry. Please report to me afterwards. . . . Right?" he added with a faint smile that was quickly lost in his graying beard; then he became once more absorbed in the letter, which he held before his eyes in his soft, white, slightly trembling hand.

CHAPTER XXXII

THE CITY OF STEEL

On the wide flat plain there stretched a city. Its central point was the huge square from which rose the gigantic chimney stacks of the power houses. Uncannily long streets radiated from it. Not a blade of grass, not a woman's shadow to be seen, not a child's voice to be heard—unsmilingly the houses stood side by side, all of the same color, all wearing the same uniform rusty red hue. No sound of human life came from them; through their doors and windows no sign of household activity was to be seen. The whole city was covered with a layer of chalk dust like frozen snow. The air was penetrated with the sourish smell of carbolic from the surrounding bleaching-yards.

No human voice was to be heard in the great forlorn city; but instead rose without ceasing the uncanny voices of invisible animals confined to their cages. Ceaselessly came the regular, gasping sound of distant dynamos, ceaselessly fluids bubbled in cisterns somewhere or other and steam whistled through pipes. Tanks spluttered over, little wagons shrieked on rails, chains rattled, cranes groaningly lifted up bales of flax as if they were toys and deposited them in their destined places, in the huge boiler houses could be heard the ear-splitting whistle of escaping steam. The whole city seemed to be inhabited by bizarre creatures made of steel and iron, who breathed through belts and chains instead of lungs and moved on steel limbs. . . .

Mirkin was first shown the dynamo houses from which electric power was distributed to the looms. Like steel dogs on leather traces the dynamos crouched in their recesses; at the command of a human being dressed in leather and covered with oil they made their leather belts spin without cessation like blind Samson turning the millstone. The rows of docile steel dogs ran away endlessly; always on the stretch, they accomplished their tasks zealously and swiftly, without stopping, without ever taking a breath. Round these curse-laden slave dogs men in leather overalls, men like cattle drivers or prison warders, were always busied; they held huge oil cans in their hands and now and then comforted a thirsty animal with a drop of life-balm.

From the dynamo houses ran, immediately under the roof, the leather belts that kept the looms going. Like beasts with their fells flayed off these looms of steel stood side by side in the machine room; their intestines were visible, and the structure of their sensitive mechanism could be clearly distinguished; their wheels, all their complex "nervous system" lay exposed; stringy tendons of steel rope ran from their invisible hearts, regulating the motions of their limbs, which were almost human in appearance and action but many, many times more efficient.

From time to time one of these skinless mechanical animals would slowly stretch out, as at a word of command, several steel arms furnished each with a dozen fingers. From every finger tip hung a tiny hook, so small that it could scarcely be seen; these hooks caught up the stream of threads that poured ceaselessly from the intestines of the machine. The arm made an almost human motion, the fingers crooked, the hooks caught the threads and connected them with the mesh of the linen weft that the flayed steel creature span out of itself like a gigantic spider. The human being who stood beside this mechanical beast was nothing more than a slave and had to serve it like an idol. White-faced girls ceaselessly bore, like priestesses, spools of woolen thread to the machine to feed it; now and then they tied a thread that had accidentally snapped during the complicated evolutions of the mechanism. The high priest of these mechanical gods, the foreman, kept vigilant watch, now and then with ceremonious dignity put the warp to rights, saw to a screw that was not tight enough, wiped away like a solicitous mother the oily sweat that the machine exuded, and occasionally flung a severe glance at the priestess allotted to him, his assistant, to see that she was fulfilling her duties blamelessly. . . .

Room after room was filled with these uncanny creatures which consisted solely of steel intestines. They filled story after story, building after building, ranged in rows and platoons like soldiers on parade. When Mirkin saw these creatures stretching out their thin steel arms simultaneously, as at the word of command, a shudder ran through him; here man was only an inanimate machine and the machine had taken his place!

In department after department he saw steel fingers carrying out the finest, most complicated human tasks; the men stood beside the machines simply to serve them.

In the spinning department he saw hundreds of iron fingers burying themselves in bales of wool and picking out threads which, entirely of itself, without any outside help, the machine drew into its bowels, where they grew thinner and thinner, until at last the machine produced its most brilliant conjuring trick—it drew all the threads through a little flame, where wooly tufts so tiny that they could not be distinguished by the naked eye were all burned away; but the threads went unscathed through the flame.

In huge furnaces infernal fires blazed, casting a glowing red light on human faces and naked bodies glistening with sweat. The men did not dare to approach those smoldering hells; with a clatter of chains steel cranes sank their iron arms into the white heat, seized with hooked hands an incandescent bar that scattered blazing sparks round it, and laid it on a steel bench, round which human bodies gleaming with oil swarmed like vermin.

Into the bleaching houses streams of linen flowed from the weaving rooms and fell in abrupt cataracts into the huge lime and starch baths; of their own volition they emerged again and flowed on into the drying rooms and slipped into the ironing machines. This stream of linen went on perpetually, as if it were resolved to drown the whole world in a sea of linen.

The machines looked like mighty giants; the men who moved about them like sweating insects were small and puny. In the bleaching rooms Mirkin saw human bodies eaten by chemicals until they had an unnatural blue appearance, as though they were made of the same material as the linen. The bodies of the forge men were covered with steel filings as with a shroud, and their sweat had a metallic look; as they moved round the flaming furnaces and bubbling pans they looked like glow-worms. And how impotent did the women workers appear compared with the incessantly busy bobbins and the arms of the looms.

Mirkin felt as if he were in a fantastic magical city in which perilous creatures lived. By some magical spell thousands of human bodies had been robbed of life and energy, feeling and understanding, that these might be incarnated in inanimate steel. These steel creatures possessed arms, fingers, eyes and brains, and they performed human labor. Men who were turned to stone served them. The magician who had achieved all this was a little Chassid Jew who sat with his back to the wall of his office behind securely barred and shuttered windows, working by electric light and in perpetual fear of being shot in the back. He never dared to venture into the light of day out of terror of the Golem he had himself created.

And to that magician Mirkin had just come to plead for his brother Jews: "Here are human bodies, human hearts; take them, take their lives and breathe them into these new machines!"

When he stood beside these machines man looked small, impotent, lonely and forsaken. But presently Mirkin was to see him in his full strength, his true shape.

Hooters shrieked from the chimney stacks. From every door and gate poured streams of men and women, filling the streets of the work-city as if it were market day. Through the huge iron gates of the factory, which night and day were guarded by watchmen, streamed a new river of human beings hurrying to their labors. Two opposite energies met and evaded the encounter; the one pressed in, the other out.

These were no longer the sickly, acid-eaten, blue-dyed bodies he had seen in the bleaching rooms, the insect-like forms he had seen in the foundry; no, here was a stream of human strength and human will! It was the power. For it all this had been fashioned; it ruled over all this. By its volition the dynamos ran, the belts flew, the dead automatons stretched out their steel arms, the cranes with their hooked hands lifted the incandescent steel out of the fiery furnace. And, if that mighty stream willed it, all this city would become a cemetery, the machines would be dead automatons, and all the devices that the magician had thought out would collapse like a child's house of bricks. For that stream was the only real, living, moving and thinking agency to whom a will and a soul had been granted.

Involuntarily Mirkin thought of the bent bodies of the Jewish hand-weavers. He saw them like prisoners fettered to their looms, like flies perishing in the spider's web, and set against them the power that now streamed through the work city under his eyes. His heart was wrung with pity. They had been forgotten by everybody, these weavers at their hand-looms! And it seemed to him that it was not only the Jewish weavers of Lodz who sat there, condemned to death, but that along with them the whole Jewish race was fettered to these looms. The whole Jewish race was chained there, sat before these looms, forgotten by everybody, doomed to destruction....

With envious glances he contemplated the two opposite powers that streamed from and towards the factory. In vain he sought a face among these faces that might belong to his fellows.

He felt no ill-will against these men; no, he accompanied them with his heartiest blessings, for justice and power were on their side. Yet he could not fight down the hostile feelings that rose within him; for they had everything by presumptive right: the fields outside there in winter and summer, the cattle in the meadows, the trees in the forests, the cheerful brook and—these great dumb machines as well. They and they alone ruled over the dynamos, the gigantic energy of the forges, the fine mechanism of the looms and spinning machines. Everything belonged to them! To the Jews they had left nothing but the forlorn streets lying beyond these mighty gates!

Mirkin was consumed with envy, and stronger than ever grew his resolve to strive with all his might for the inclusion of his brothers in this great world.

When he once more entered the magnate's office to say good-by he found Flachs sitting as before at his desk. Now Mirkin was really struck by the fact that the room was lit by electric light in the middle of the day, a fact that had made little impression upon him the first time. The window shutters were closed and secured with iron bars. In the glow of the green-shaded electric light Flachs's face had a parchment-like appearance. His eyes seemed to be still more deeply sunk in their sockets and had an inward look. He greeted Mirkin with a faint smile which gave his sensitive lips a wry expression, and passed his fine thin hand over his beard. Mirkin felt that it was not a man who was sitting there, but a mystagogue, a magician, who had set a Golem in motion and was afraid now lest his creature might turn against him. ... In spite of his immense power the man awakened pity; it was as if he were suffering grievously from a secret sorrow.

After Flachs had asked Mirkin what his impressions were, he began:

"While you have been looking over my factory I have been thinking over your words. I've always held that Jews are born for a higher fate than to look after machines, for in my opinion every Jew is himself a complicated machine.—You agree with me there, don't you? But your words have made an impression on me. In our factory, as we have established it, your ideas can't possibly be realized. We aren't free, for we're really nothing more than servants of the machine. But, to cut matters short—I'm prepared to help in founding a factory for Jewish workers exclusively that will close on the Sabbath instead of Sunday; I'm prepared to do that, providing that you or your father will find the necessary capital. I can't say at present just how such a factory could be established, nor am I in a position, of course, to say anything about the organization and carrying out of the whole idea. But if your father shows sufficient interest in the project, I'm quite willing to put my experience and my energy at his disposal, and I hope..."

In the excess of his joy Mirkin broke in before the manufacturer could finish. He seized Flachs's hand and cried, his eyes shining like those of a ship-wrecked sailor who has just caught sight of land: "Father will certainly be interested—I know him— And you'll take charge of the organization!— Do you know what that means? Do you know? We'll become a part of the great creative force of the world at last...."

CHAPTER XXXIII

SON TO FATHER

THAT SAME evening Mirkin wrote to his father:

FATHER,—In a moment of frenzy I insulted you; in a fit of madness which your behavior roused in me. But what does a momentary outburst matter compared with the unquenchable feelings rooted in my heart that I have inherited from countless generations, the feelings in my very blood?

Father, forget if you can! But if you can't, then I implore you, don't think of these things now, and now, when everything that happened in Petersburg seems so far away to me, is so remote to me, that it seems no longer to have any connection with me or my life. The narrow little circle of my own ego in which I lived made me blind to everything outside it and magnified infinitely my own insignificant existence, making it seem a thousand times more serious and important than it was. Every little obstacle became a mountain in my eyes, blocking my way, and I magnified every danger beyond recognition. How small and petty now everything seems to me that I took once for walls confining the course of my life!

Yes, father; I can talk of all that now without blushing or turning pale, without agitation. I feel neither angry nor pleased with you because of the step you have taken. Probably it had to be. It is a matter that concerns you alone. Believe me, I can send you now my sincerest congratulations without a trace of rancor, purely animated by my natural desire to see you happy. The same applies to your wife. I assure you that my feelings for you have always been the purest and best of which I am capable. And they are so still. I can understand that it would be very painful for her to meet me in person, otherwise I would come to Petersburg at once and show her the respect and consideration which is her due as the wife of my father.

Now that I understand myself rightly at last I can say that my feelings for her were never of a kind that need give rise to jealousy. I felt nothing for her but friendship and the profoundest respect. She felt this intuitively at once and so the thing happened that was bound to happen—fortunately for us all. I can speak quite frankly of that now, and I assure you that in doing so my heart doesn't beat more quickly, nor my hand tremble. I can say this now, for fate has chosen for me, too, and chosen that I should live among a class of people whom I never knew before and of whose very existence I was unaware.

You can congratulate me, father. I have found something I had never hoped for even in my dreams, a thing that I fancied would always remain locked away from me: joy in being alive. I am filled with energy and desire for life. I feel as if I were newly awakened to life out of the dark night that since my childhood has wrapped me in its arms. Now I see how childish and weak I have been. But don't forget, father, that my upbringing and my constant longing for my mother were bound to bring such results. All your exhortations, telling me it was time for me to be a man, were useless. I was afraid myself to say this frankly; for I was ill. But I confess it to you now: I thought that the ordinary feelings, the simple natural desire for the opposite sex with which nature has endowed all living creatures was denied for ever to me because of my motherless childhood or for some other reason; and that, because of a sin that had never been expiated, a curse lay upon me, binding my hands and feet, casing my heart in iron so that the beams of human happiness could never penetrate into it. Often I have been on the point of seeking death. Often I have wandered on the very frontier between life and death. If I never took the final step, it was not because any hope drew me back to life again, but simply because of my cowardice, my childish weakness and helplessness. But now I am sound and whole, and I can declare it openly, can cry it to the whole world: I am sound and whole, I feel it. I am full of life, I feel all the gradations of rising happiness; my heart, my nerves, my feelings vibrate at every contact with human life. I am filled with energy and creative desire; and I feel that I could lift the world from its hinges. Yes, now I can see it: I was sick and now I am sound. And I tell you quite frankly, father, that I have regained my health and found the meaning of my life, the idea of my existence, the subject matter for my creative force, among the most wretched of the wretched, the most forsaken of the forsaken: the Jewish masses.

You must not think, father, that my happiness exists merely as an idea; oh no, it exists very actually in a slender girlish body dressed in a little black and white checked dress; it exists in two great blue eyes, hair parted in the middle and gathered above the ears, round girlish shoulders and all the rest that goes with these—forgive me, father, for that touch of cynicism! You cannot conceive how much joy can radiate from such a little, gentle, modest creature! Where does she find it? Often it seems to me that happiness itself dwells within her; and as she passes she gives some of it to everybody.

The house she belongs to is poor but kindly, father. It is an honest and virtuous house. You don't know what happiness is if you don't know that house, and the people who visit it are happy too. The life they lead lifts them above the stinking, disease-ridden stews in which they sit, and spurs them to creative deeds. Their life is not the brief and fleeting life of their own insignificant egos, but the eternally creative, eternally inflowing life of the community. Though it is a long chain of suffering, it will be raised above all sorrow yet by the joyful events that are preparing in it.

Along with my happiness I have found my life ideal, or perhaps my ideal has brought me my happiness. I have found it in the Jewish masses. Father, I am living in the midst of deepest poverty, among outcast Jews, but I have found happiness there. From my room I look round and see the inexpiable wrong that the world has committed against us, and still more clearly the wrong that we ourselves are committing, we, who surely should and must understand where we are at fault. That sin is like a noose round our necks, whose end is in the hands of all these oppressed and insulted people; and one day they will draw the noose tight. . . . You must not be alarmed at my words; they are only a natural result of the feelings that must rise in any one who sees poverty and suffering before his eyes and observes the almost criminal indifference of those who could and are in honor bound to remedy that poverty. Father! Day after day the Jewish masses are being burned in a slow fire. Their life is a long chain of torture and misery. You must not think that I am in favor of violent measures. I haven't come to that stage yet; but I confess that now, living in the midst of poverty and seeing its daily wretchedness with my own eyes, I understand the wild popular outbursts of savagery during times of revolution. They are not a mere discharge of the dark senseless powers that always slumber in the depths of humanity; they are only a puny retaliation for the long and unnecessary anguish which the rich inflict on the poor day after day, and have inflicted for generations and centuries.

But it is not fear of their coming vengeance that has drawn me to them, but love and the need to do something, to find something in this existence to which I can hold. And now I am bound to them, by gratitude if nothing else—yes, by gratitude; for they have delivered me from my wretched, wearisome existence; they have healed me, just as my love has healed my sickness. I feel my life filled more and more with courage and power to act and do, because it belongs to them. I want to do all I can and may for their good. Not only for their sake, but for the sake of my own happiness. For through them I shall find salvation.

After a long and thorough study of the situation I have come to the firm conviction that the heaviest misfortune that rests on our poor people consists in this: that they are shut out from productive life. They are forgotten, left to their own fate. The energy, ability and extraordinary perseverance in following out a single line to its goal which certain isolated figures among us show so uncontestably, alleviates in no way the state of the Jewish masses. With every other people the creative powers given to the individual fertilize all that surrounds him as well; with us talent sheds its benefit on other peoples, leaving our own people to molder in oblivion. I am convinced that one of the chief tasks waiting for us is to restore the Jewish masses to health, to bring them as quickly as possible into the general progressive course of the world, to develop their powers creatively, and as quickly as possible, and wherever they may happen to live; as it were to harness them to the car of the world, so that bit by bit they may be able to pull it into their own fields like the other peoples. I want to devote myself to this task with all my energy. I haven't the ability to do great things, and am not so presumptuous as to regard myself as a leader; but I have come to the conclusion that every one of us, no matter how small his capacities, can be of use to the great cause. Whether great or small—I am resolved to do this task in which I find both my meaning and my happiness. At any rate I think I would be capable of running a factory.

To come to concrete proposals, this is the idea I should like to carry out. I want to open a textile factory in Lodz, a model factory that might be a forerunner of others and would help to transfer the Jewish worker from hand-loom work to machine production. In Lodz there are tens of thousands of Jewish handworkers who are condemned to perish along with their hand-looms, at which they still labor as in the middle ages. This melancholy state of things is caused chiefly by the fact that this class of workers are refused access to the factories because of the ill-will of others and the indifference of people of their own race; they are refused this although more than a half of the power-driven factories belong to Jews. These men all look on calmly while the great mass of the Jewish people perish in filth and misery, while more and more of them are thrown on the streets every day; and those who could help do nothing. The few, on the other hand, who really concern themselves for the lot of these people only see the dead principle and forget the living human being. To break through this wall of indifference a power-driven factory employing Jewish workers must be found. The plan is not at all so fantastic as you might have expected of me. To realize it I have approached the greatest textile firm in the country, whose owner himself originally came from these forsaken people. So the matter is in good hands, the hands of a man with much experience and great success hitherto. According to what you have often told me there must still be a considerable sum of money in my name: my mother's legacy. Until now I have had no occasion to use that money. But now I am convinced that that capital—I don't know how much it amounts to—and perhaps your help as well (if I may venture to hope for it) would give me the opportunity of setting up a business that would bring much good to others but still more good to myself.

CHAPTER XXXIV

A MEETING

Shortly before leaving Lodz Mirkin paid a last visit to the little prayer-house in the court where he lived. He did not suffer from the Jewish religion as Shachliner and others of his circle did, that is by violently hating it; on the contrary, like everybody else who has "found his way back," he could not but feel a certain piety towards the ancient institution for which the Jewish people had made such sacrifices for so many generations. In the forms and customs of the Jewish religion he saw the Jewish nature itself, whose peculiar character exerted a deep attraction on him.

In Warsaw he had had no occasion to visit Jewish prayer-houses and schools, so that he was resolved to make use of his opportunity in Lodz where the Chassid prayer-house was at his door. There was the added advantage that here he had no mentors anxious about his "soul's good." So in the evening he would unobtrusively enter the little prayer-house, sit down in a dark corner and with his eyes and ears open take note of everything that happened, as though he were resolved to drink in all the mysteries of the Jewish soul to which his upbringing had given him no key, and come to learn by immediate contact all that was incomprehensible in the Jewish mind.

This particular evening Mirkin sat unobserved in his dark corner and watched the old and young people swaying ecstatically over the Talmud or standing about in groups and talking. But his attention was still more powerfully attracted by the other half of the prayer-house, which lay in complete darkness. In that impenetrable gloom the separate flames in the everlasting lamp before the Torah shrine flickered like the lights of a ship on the sea; a few tapers were also burning. They seemed to make the part of the room where they were still darker, as though they radiated obscurity instead of light. Like every other stranger Mirkin felt an incomprehensible terror before that mysterious darkness, and to him the whole mystery of the Jewish religion seemed to be hidden behind that veil of night, the great mystery of the Jewish soul to be slumbering there; that challenge to the world which had lasted from the beginning of all time until now.

Feelings and thoughts that had lain dormant in the obscurest cells of his blood reawoke again without his knowledge; feelings and thoughts which he had never known. All at once he felt bound up with powers rooted in remote worlds, in the beginning of things; powers that came to him from ancient and unknown books; powers of whose nature he knew nothing. And he, Mirkin, was a drop in an infinite ocean stretching away to that starting point where was the fountain of all life. All at once he felt as close to the Jewish patriarchs, to Abraham, Jacob, Moses and the others, as if he had lived in their day and generation and had actually known them. Generation after generation buried in time arose before his eyes and moved beside him. But not only did the past become alive; the generations of the future to the end of time rose before him. They all lived at that moment, the moment of his own life. It was as though in an endless chain all that had existed before his time was unrolling within his mind. Abraham walked in his field with God, the cloud covering him; Jacob wrestled with the angel in the ghostly evening light; in remote distance Moses stood on the Mount, the Torah in his arms. Wherever he looked he saw the spirits of the old and the new; the spirits of all the generations—those that he knew, those that he did not know were there, united in a life that was not of this world, nor of any other, like the light, which is not of this world nor of any other, but a reflection of eternal being....

Mirkin was terrified by his own thoughts and shrank from carrying them to their conclusion. He turned his eyes away from the mysterious corner where the Torah shrine stood and contemplated once more the living sitting on their benches at the table lit by the hanging lamp and piously swaying over their books. Over there—who could that be?

His eyes were attracted by a man whom he seemed to know. Yes, he knew him quite well, had seen him somewhere before either in actuality or in a dream. He knew that long unnaturally huge face with the high forehead and the thick eyebrows overhanging the deep-set eyes; he knew those eyes which seemed an epitome of all the Jewish eyes in the world, those eyes full of infinite apprehension and unshakable faith. Where could he have seen that brow and that mighty beard? Was he dreaming? No, this was real; he, Mirkin, was sitting there alone on a bench in a prayer-house, and over at the table, less than ten paces away from him, was sitting a man whom he knew, whom he had met somewhere!

For a moment it seemed to him as if the ten paces to the table where the man was sitting were a journey of many years, the span of a whole life time. He, Mirkin, a man of the present, was sitting in his corner, and over there sat a ghost.

No, it was no ghost, but a living man! Mirkin jumped up and rushed hastily over to the man at the table, as though he wanted to catch him before he melted into thin air.

"I'm sure I know you, Pan . . ." Mirkin began, overcome by a feeling of mingled fear and happiness.

Two heavy eyelids were slowly lifted towards him beneath their heavy brows; two grave eyes regarded him at first without recognition, then with delighted surprise: "I know you too; we met in Petersburg."

"Oh, now I remember! You are—wait a moment, just a moment!" Mirkin tried to remember the name.

"Chomsky, an elder of the Jewish Community of Tolestyn," the stranger prompted him.

"Of course, Pan Baruch Chomsky."

"And you're Pan Mirkin, the lawyer's assistant."

"What are you doing here?" asked Mirkin in surprise.

"There's nothing unusual in my being here. I'm a merchant and I'm in Lodz to make some purchases. There's nothing for me to do in the evening, so I came here to the synagogue to read a few pages of the Talmud. But what are you doing here? How do you come to be here, in a synagogue?" Chomsky's question also expressed surprise.

"I'm here on a matter concerning the Jews," Mirkin smiled.

An inquisitive circle had gathered round the two speakers. Even the Talmud students left their handkerchiefs lying on their open books and came nearer.

"Would you like to go for a walk? We could talk then without being disturbed," the old Jew said to Mirkin, who was still dumb with astonishment, so as to escape the curiosity of the others.

"Yes, let's go. I should like to have a talk with you too."

Only when they were outside did the impression made on them by their extraordinary encounter begin to fade. Chomsky was less astonished than Mirkin and behaved as if he had just met the young man in a Petersburg street instead of in a Chassid prayer-house in Lodz. Mirkin expressed his surprise at this: "Aren't you surprised, Pan Chomsky, to meet me in a prayer-house?"

"Of course I am," replied Chomsky. "People like us find distraction in a prayer-house, but surely not a young man like you! On the other hand, who can tell what may be happening in a Jew's heart?" The Jew smiled.

"I want very much to ask you a few questions," began Mirkin

abruptly. "Up to now I've had no chance to talk to any one about them, for I don't know these Jews here. Tell me, Pan Chomsky, what satisfaction do you find in your reading of the Talmud, over and above the fact that you hope to be rewarded for it in the next world? One can see that you do get a great deal of satisfaction from it, a pleasure of this world; you study the Talmud with as much ardor as if the act gave you physical satisfaction. I've never been able to understand that! What do you really get out of it? In the last resort it's nothing but arid casuistry, a barren dialectical exercise of the mind. What pleasure do you really find in it over and above, of course, the prospect of being rewarded in the next world?"

"You're very much mistaken, young man," said the old Jew gravely. "I don't know how others feel—but to me the reading of a page of the Talmud gives just as much pleasure as you get, say from an evening at the theater, perhaps even more. Whenever I'm free of an evening I go to the prayer-house, and not merely so as to gain my reward in the next world—though of course that comes into it too—but far more that I may forget myself, that I may enjoy myself. We Jews have no country now, and so I study the laws and customs that we once had when we possessed a country. We Jews have no fields and gardens of our own; so I study our way of life when we did have our own fields. You can believe me, while I read the laws about tithes, rights of possession and the like I feel myself transported, at least for an hour or two, to our ancient Palestine; I can almost taste the fruit and vegetables that grow in my fields; I reckon the tithes, I pay my due portion of income to the poor. It isn't empty words, what I'm saying—while I sit over the book I actually believe I am transported to the times when we lived in our own country. What do I care then for all the enmity and hate that we are bogged in up to the very neck? The world and all its malice no longer exists for me, for I am living in a different world. You may believe me—that pleasure is so great that I can't describe it to you in words. One must be a Jew, and suffer like a Jew, to be able to feel it. That in itself is abundant reward for such studies, and I ask no other. . . . So much for my concerns. But how do you come to be in Lodz? And what are you doing in a synagogue?"

Mirkin briefly explained the object of his stay in Lodz and told the old man of the plans he hoped to realize; also that he had first visited the synagogue by accident and afterwards returned, drawn by pure curiosity. (His other feelings during those visits he did not divulge, out of a sense of shame.)

Chomsky listened with sympathetic interest, stroking his long beard, and murmured in a pleased voice: "Very good! Splendid!" When Mirkin had finished he turned to him and said approvingly: "That isn't my road, it isn't the road of us who belong to the older generation, but it is a road. I can understand it. My children too are taking it. That has often caused me a good deal of sorrow, but it's caused me joy too. The only important thing is to do something. What does it matter how one serves God? But one mustn't be for oneself, like a robber in the woods."

"What do you mean by that?" asked Mirkin, somewhat disappointed. "Do you think my work won't succeed?"

"I was thinking of the plan you've told me about. You're preparing to undertake a great task; you want to carry through a change that will affect the whole world. May God aid you to carry it out! Of course, it may turn out—which God forbid—that you won't be able to achieve your end—that doesn't depend on you alone. If that should happen don't lose courage: that's all I wanted to say. Then you must try to serve the community in some other way. Believe me, there are countless little things one can do that are just as important as great and glorious deeds. After all, what does our whole life consist of? Of our daily actions. The actions of every single human being are woven into the total life of the world. Our sages say: "In every drop of the ocean all the attributes of the whole ocean are contained, for the ocean consists of drops." It's the same with our actions. In every task, even the pettiest, that a man carries out, all the attributes of the greatest and most heroic deeds are contained, though it may appear of no consequence at a superficial glance."

Mirkin was silent. He could not quite make up his mind whether the words he heard had been really uttered or were an hallucination. He was still sitting in his corner in the little prayer-house gazing at the shadowy Torah shrine; and it was there that the ghost of old Chomsky had risen and lifted its voice. And as though afraid of shattering the dream Mirkin said nothing and let the old man finish what he was saying.

"The main thing," Chomsky continued, "is to believe in everything one does. God does not care in what fashion you believe in Him, so long as you believe there is a power for good directing the world, and resign yourself to it so as to serve its purpose, and do what you can to increase it. In doing that you become a part of the pure creative force and touch eternity, passing beyond death to the morning after death; you become a part of Nature. For what is Nature? The learned say that God stands completely outside all natural being. Outside being and the course of Nature: that is a delusion. God and Nature are one, and Nature and faith are one—so *our* sages hold. Just as every day brings forth the bread that you need to nourish you, so God has given spiritual food for you. Your future tasks are ripening for you in invisible fields that God has sowed for you, and God has chosen you as His servant that you may carry out your tasks, which are His also. That is why it does not matter whether the things you have to do are small or great; they all come from *one* source, they all have *one* purpose: to accomplish God's work on earth. That is our life, the life of God in God, the eternal and only life, the life of all the worlds from eternity to eternity. Except for that life there is nothing, there is only death and nonentity. . . . Do you hear, young man?"

Mirkin seemed both to hear and not to hear. He was still rapt in his vision, and it seemed to him that he was under the spell of some incredible and unnatural being. Suddenly he caught the old man by the arm and cried in terror: "Who are you? Tell me at once, why are you here? What is all this? Where am I?"

"What is wrong with you?" asked the old man in surprise. "This isn't the first time you've seen me! And as for who I am—what does that matter to you? You know me as I am. But don't let us talk about me! I'm an old Jew—what does it matter who I am? Soon I shall be nothing! But who you are matters a great deal; for you're only beginning your life. And so I'm glad, I'm very, very glad that you've torn yourself away from your old life. Thank God for that!"

"You helped me to do it," said Mirkin.

"Not I, but One up there." The old man pointed to the starry sky. "Walk the road, young man, that God has forced you to take. There's one other thing I should like to say to you. If you shouldn't have the strength—which God forbid—to carry your task to the end, don't despair. Our sages say: 'Accomplishment is not given to you.' All that we can do is to help the cart forward. In the brief time that is allotted to us each of us must work with a will. But we are not destined to accomplish what we set out to do. . . . And perhaps there is no final end, as certain of the learned men hold."

Only after the old man had disappeared did Mirkin waken out of his trance. He was struck by the strong resemblance between the old man's ideas and those of Comrade Anatol: it was only the words that were different. Probably it was Chomsky's remark that his children were going the new road that now inspired in Mirkin the groundless notion that the mysterious Anatol was the old man's son. But he quickly rejected this absurd idea with a smile at his foolishness.

CHAPTER XXXV

FATHER TO SON

MIRKIN had not to wait long for his father's reply. A few days after his return from Lodz he received it, as usual through the Warsaw agency of his father's firm. The style was flawlessly matter-of-fact, without rhetorical flourishes or superfluous sentimentality; it was in his father's usual style. Nevertheless Mirkin was cast into astonishment by the calm tone of the letter and the assurance that spoke out of it. The tone itself more than the actual letter showed the great change that had taken place in his father's life.

The contents of the letter may be summarized as follows:

His father was very pleased (Mirkin was struck by the fact that he employed the expression "pleased," and not a stronger one) to hear that his son's health had improved and that Zachary now himself recognized that he had been really and gravely ill. All the incomprehensible things that he had done in recent years had been simply an outcome of his unfortunate and strange illness of mind. His father had known of his state for a long time, but had remained silent so as to spare his feelings. Consequently the dreadful words that Zachary had flung in his face not so long ago had neither wounded nor offended him, for like everything else they had simply been caused by Zachary's state. That Zachary himself now admitted that was the best proof possible of his recovery. As a father he, Gabriel Haimovitch, felt boundless gratitude towards the lady, mentioned by Zachary, who had worked this miracle. She and only she had been able by her good influence to restore Zachary's health. It did not matter to him what class she belonged to, whether she was rich or poor; the fact that she had been able to work such a miracle was the best proof that she was the destined wife for Zachary. He was very pleased (once more the cold word annoyed Zachary) that it should be so, and was prepared to recognize her as his daughter and accept her as a member of the family.

Since Zachary, as his letter proved, was now cured, the writer might be permitted to write to him frankly, as man to man, without any of the sentimental frills in which he had been accustomed to wrap his communications hitherto. He, Gabriel Haimovitch, desired to declare quite frankly that his life with Zachary's mother had never been a happy one and that it was an unfortunate fate that had united him to her, peace be with her. There was no point in trying to hide this from Zachary. He himself desired to push the blame upon no one, and took it all upon himself; but the fact remained that, for the greater part of the time they might have been leading a genuine life in common, he and his wife had been parted; she had lived abroad, he himself in hotels in various big cities. So he had never really enjoyed the simple joys of family life, to which every hard-working man had a right. He had always longed for that simple happiness. The hopes he had set on Zachary had not been realized. He had no wish to refer to the question of who was responsible for that, for Zachary himself recognized that clearly now. Yet what had happened had happened, it was certain, not without the will of higher powers and must inevitably have turned out as it had done; in no other way could he explain the course of events. At the age he had reached he had had no thought of beginning family life anew, but had imagined that he would never taste such joys again. So, homeless himself, he had desired to realize the happiness that only a family can give, that happiness he had never experienced, in his son's life, despairing of it in his own. His son had said no, had shattered an old man's hopes for his last days, and brutally driven him from the door of his new home. Only after that had a voice spoken within the father's heart: "Start over again yourself!" Yet even then he had fought against the alluring temptation, had tried to ward off the happiness that knocked so belatedly at his door. Not that he was lacking in strength and self-confidence; on the contrary, after his son had forsaken him God had filled his heart with fresh youth, new sources of energy had opened within him, as if God had wished to comfort him by remaining with him in his old age. Nevertheless he had fought against his own happiness for his son's sake and in deference to the world, which might interpret his motives wrongly. But his fight against his happiness had been in vain, for every path had led him back to it. And after profound consideration, after a thorough search of heart and conscience "I came to the conclusion that I had no right to reject the helpful hand that God stretched out to me, and that I should and must drag myself out of my loneliness. So I thankfully accepted the grace reserved for my old age by divine Providence. God Himself gave his consent to our union that I should be preserved from breathing my last hours in the arms of some paid stranger. Divine providence has been gracious to us and blessed our union with a hope which my wife and I look forward to with deep gratitude; we praise God for the unmerited grace that He has shown us . . ."

At this point Zachary stopped reading. He wanted to laugh, and was filled both with shame and annoyance at himself. He began to read again.

"I do not know," the letter went on, "whether you and your present friends, who certainly have great influence with you, will understand me when I say that in my opinion it is not only you nihilists (forgive me for the term, but I take it from your letter that you belong to them) who have ideals that uplift you above the petty trivialities of life—an expression of your own in your letter, which gave me, I assure you, great joy. We bourgeois and capitalists have also our ideals, to which we dedicate our powers, yes, if you will, our lives. They make us forget all the follies and the pettinesses, uplift us and give us a boundless will to be up and doing. Your grandfather and I devoted all our capacity and energy to the firm not merely for the sake of the money that it brings in. Great as the seduction of money and the power it gives may be, it would not have sufficed to fill our lives had not our labors been irradiated by an ideal. The ideal of every firm is, if I may so express myself, to found a ruling dynasty. Yes, I have always dreamed of creating a 'Mirkin dynasty' similar to the dynasties of Morosov, Ginsburg and other firms. That was also the wish of your grandfather, which I took over, brought nearer to realization and did all I could to carry out. I thought I would be able to leave to my son a firmly established business which would support our dynasty for generations. You would have nothing of that and chose a different path. Your father's best wishes follow you upon it. But God has blessed my old age with a new hope, and to that hope I intend to devote the rest of my life. I shall give the child I hope for the upbringing that I was unable to give you; I shall awaken in him the powers and capabilities necessary for carrying your grandfather's work and my own to fruition, and so secure the Mirkin dynasty."

Only at the end of the letter did his father refer to the matter that interested Zachary most and had spurred him to write—the textile factory for Jewish workers.

Old Mirkin advised his son against it. It was not the money (which would pretty certainly be lost) that he was thinking of. That, it was true, must also be taken into account, for money was precious and important not only because of the value it presented, but also as it were in itself, as money. Money to the merchant was as precious as a violin to a violinist; business was to him what art was to the artist. "No artist," old Mirkin declared, "can risk a public failure, or dare do so. The plan of a factory for Jewish workers sounds very philanthropic, perhaps, but it sounds by no means businesslike."

Old Mirkin went on to say that it had always been a principle of his to keep business and philanthropy separated from each other by an iron wall. "Business is a value in itself, is itself an ideal," he informed his son, "and I do not think that your abilities lie in that direction.

You have never shown any inclination for business; and that your friends will be of much use in it I cannot believe."

In the following paragraph his father expressed the opinion that Zachary should turn to some other vocation, science, for example, and advised him to get married as soon as possible and settle abroad, if possible at some university town in Germany or Switzerland; there he could devote himself to scientific study in whatever line he chose; it would be more in accordance with his whole disposition.

"As for the considerable sum," old Mirkin concluded, "that you look forward to as your mother's legacy, I must tell you that it never existed. I have informed you once or twice already that your mother received no dowry of any consequence from her parents over and above the small sum that I later put in her name, and her jewels, the most valuable of which, the pearls, I shall send to you, reserving the others as a present to your fiancée. I am sending you also the small capital of a few thousand roubles which your mother herself looked after until her death."

Old Mirkin added that of course he would be prepared to secure his son a life-long income from the firm, which would make it possible for him and his wife and children ("if you have any" the old man did not forget to add, and Zachary saw in these words something approaching raillery) to live a comfortable if not luxurious life. He, Gabriel Haimovitch, felt in duty bound to do this. He also begged his son to buy out of the sum he was sending separately through the firm a present in his and his wife's name for Zachary's fiancée, to pass on to her their warmest greetings, and to thank her in both their names for making their son happy.

After the signature came a postscript in which Gabriel Haimovitch regretted that he had to say all this by letter. It would have been far better if they could have met and talked. But his wife's condition made it inadvisable for Zachary to come to Petersburg at present. He himself could not receive Zachary anywhere except in his house and so he had been compelled to write all that he would have liked to say.

Mirkin's first response to his father's letter was a burst of helpless laughter which he could not account for to himself; it came over him like a hysterical fit: "What good terms he stands on with God, just like a patriarch! My father in the rôle of Abraham! Marvelous!"

As always when he came in contact with his father he felt as if he were back in his childhood; he seemed like a child trying to grasp a ball too big for its tiny hands. The inexplicable and incomprehensible riddle of his father's character once more disturbed him: "Who is he? Actually I know nothing about him! Nothing whatever!" And like every weak nature confronted by a strong one he was seized with impotent rage against his father; he shouted: "You're a devil of a fellow, aren't you?"

For an almost ridiculous feeling had now taken hold of him, and yet he could not throw it off: jealousy of his father.

He was jealous of his father's strength of will and confidence in himself: "And when he can't take the responsibility for something himself he summons the Lord God Himself from heaven, orders Him to lay aside all the tasks that He has to attend to in all His countless worlds, so as to settle the personal difficulties of Master Gabriel Haimovitch Mirkin! He's coöpted God Himself as his partner! A patriarch!" Zachary laughed hysterically. "My father in the rôle of a patriarch! God Himself sees to it that he is provided with an heir in his old age!"

Zachary knew that his laughter was hateful, called forth simply by jealousy of his father's ability to execute with an iron hand whatever he considered necessary, without regard for anybody, content that the future should justify what he thought right to do in the present. Zachary measured himself against that picture, contemplated his own impotence, his dreams, his doubts, his relation to Helene: "Why haven't I the strength to do what my father has done? What prevents me? I have far more right to do it!"

Like every only child he was jealous of the new intruder whom his father, according to his letter, was expecting. He felt that this would detach him far more fatally from the bond to which he clung than all that had happened already. He could not resist the mean feeling that he had been freed from all responsibility by the news of this "rival" to whom his father was resolved to transfer all his love. And then he suddenly saw that he was still bound to his former world like a child by a navel string, although he had thought himself free. The very violence of this feeling, however, was sufficient to show him, as by a knock on the head, the absurd position he had got himself into: "Have I fought with myself all these years only to find at last that I am still the weak, incapable, only child that I have tried to conquer?" The powers that he had wakened to life and nursed within himself at last came to his help and gave him the energy to shake off all those thoughts once and for all and send them packing, as we shake off the evil spirits that come to us in our dreams.

"What does all this matter to me? Is it any business of mine?" He burst out laughing at his own foolishness.

"No! I shan't let myself be carried away by hysterical sentiment as I used to be! If you aren't sentimental, I'm not either. I'll fight with your weapons," he said aloud, as if he were addressing somebody, "and I have a better right to them than you, for I don't employ them for the vulgar egoistic end of founding dynasties, but for a higher end, to help mankind. If you're sly, I'll be sly too! Your money, father, will come in very useful. If it doesn't give me the help that I expected of your generosity of heart, it will help in other ways. Madame Hurvitz will find a use for it all right, not to speak of Anatol and the Shachliner. And it will be of use here! Yes, father," he cried with a laugh, "I'll let you see how well I am! I'm no longer sentimental, I won't throw your money back in your face with a silly grand gesture, as you no doubt expected! I accept it with thanks and will employ it as well as I know how to. And I no longer envy you, father, for your resolution and firmness, I no longer regret I am not like you, that I don't ruthlessly make straight for my goal like you. I have other methods: I want to be weak, for in that I will find my life's happiness."

"Good-by, father!" The cry burst from him, and he himself was terrified by it; for it sounded like the last farewell with which one might greet the dead.

Zachary sat down at his table and wrote a correct, matter-of-fact letter to his father. He accepted with many thanks all his father's suggestions, except for the journey abroad, which under various plausible pretexts he postponed until a later date. He thanked his father more particularly for his interest in his health and the kind things he had said about his fiancée. He gave his father the assurance that he would buy a worthy present out of the money sent him and give it to his fiancée in his father's name.

A few days later Mirkin managed to have a talk with Anatol, who was waiting to hear the result of the correspondence between father and son about the factory for Jewish workers in Lodz. Mirkin began with a shy apologetic smile: "I haven't enough money for construction. He refused that. But I think I'll have enough for destruction. Here's something to begin with." And he handed Anatol the sum that his father had sent him for Helene's bridal present.

Comrade Anatol smiled good-humoredly: "Destruction is a part of our program too. Those that are incapable of constructing we use for destroying. As things stand, we'll include your father in the latter part of our program."

"Between us and him there's an iron wall. I was stupid enough to imagine I could burst through it; but I see now that the attempt can only result in breaking one's head," replied Mirkin gravely.

"I'm very glad you've come to that conclusion at last. This is your graduation fee. At any rate you may be certain that we'll employ your father's hard-earned cash faithfully and honestly; you can tell him that too!"

CHAPTER XXXVI

UNDER THE TREE

In the courtyard of the block where Hurvitz the teacher lived stood an old chestnut-tree, a survival from earlier days. How it could have gone on flourishing in the court and reach an old age is a riddle. It was like a faithful old dog, who, kicked out into the street, has to starve and yet keeps on doing his duty, guarding the house and barking watchfully whenever a stranger appears. All the year the tree stood in a rubbish hole which was quite frozen over in winter and in summer was choked up with stones, bricks and refuse; and yet it lived and flourished. It was, so to speak, the scapegoat of the whole building. "Cudgel" Moses tied his cart to it when he returned home; Selig the baker beat his flour sacks on it all the year round, and Note the leggings-maker hung his wares beneath it. As a consequence the few chestnuts that hung from the tree in late summer had the same leathery smell as the leggings. But the tree also served for all sorts of other purposes; boys made upon it their first attempts at carving; all the children in the block found it necessary to leave their names upon its bark for future generations; in autumn the women hung out their winter clothes upon it to air; every week mattresses were flung on its branches and beaten; and if wood was scarce in winter the householder visited the tree for faggots.

Nevertheless every spring the chestnut-tree did its duty and attired itself in thick green foliage. When the tenants saw that new shoots were again bursting from its bark scored by ropes and the sides of carts, they all assembled to behold the miracle. It was an uplifting sight to see that the tree bowed with age and labor unfolding a green umbrella of foliage and showing at the very top, which was scarcely visible, half a dozen candles like a memory of the tree's vanished prime raising themselves aloft. When the tree was in blossom it was treated as tenderly by everybody in the building as a pregnant animal. "Cudgel" Moses leant the shafts of his cart cautiously against it, and the baker beat his flour sacks as gently as he could. And if any one treated the tree unceremoniously there was a shout from every window: "Leave the tree in peace!" In spring, then, it served the purpose for which it was created, and became the garden, the park, the wood of the building. The children who lived in the top flat led down their consumptive mother to the court, spread out a couch of cushions for her beneath the tree, lowered her, panting for breath, down upon it and left her there to enjoy the "fresh air"; in the evenings the work-weary women in the building fled from their hot rooms to the tree and used it as a "summer resort"; the children tore off the leaves and played with them: in short, for the dwellers in the tenement the tree was the sole substitute for Nature.

When spring came Helene was accustomed to teach her children their lessons in the open air. They were too poorly clad to be allowed admission to any of the Warsaw public parks, into which at that time only persons who wore "respectable" and "European" clothes were allowed to enter. So Helene conducted her children to the chestnut-tree in the court.

One day as Mirkin was entering the wide front door, intending to visit the Hurvitzes and take Helene for a walk in the Saxon Garden, he heard a merry din of children's voices rising in the distance like the gurgling of a fresh brook. . . . When he reached the court he saw that the familiar monotonous gray that he had been accustomed to see there had suddenly vanished. The court had put on festal robes. Children were dancing in a ring round the tree. Their happy shouts actually drowned the screams of the housewives and the clatter of the carts. The children's arms were in even more violent motion than their feet; one might have thought they were swimming. Mirkin caught the white gleam of a dress that seemed known to him. A familiar black head bobbed up among the children's heads and then suddenly disappeared again. The white dress gleamed out and then vanished among a crowd of children's dresses.

Mirkin remained standing in a corner and regarded the scene. Helene was racing about in a throng of children. They were the girls in her class, her little friends whose faces he knew so well; but the children of the block had joined them: the consumptive woman's children, "Cudgel" Moses' children, all the other neighbors' children. That had always been the way in the building: whenever a mother did not know what to do with her children she sent them to the "young schoolmistress," as if Helene were a public benevolent society to which they all belonged. Some of the children were still wearing their thick winter clothes with clumsy down-at-heel boots; others, however, were wiser: they had flung off their heavy clothes and shoes and hopped about in bare feet which were not all of them very clean. But who notices a thing like that in children? Children are always clean and keep their fragrance even when they are covered with mud. Many of their faces were not washed too thoroughly, but what did that matter? For they were spring blossoms, happy and full of life, their little bare arms in perpetual movement; and their laughing voices rang like a silvery brook.

Children can transform a muddy trickle into a clear rill, a rubbish heap into a garden. They changed the gray dirty court now, where chests and crates, carts and hand-barrows stood about, into a fragrant shadowy wood, a scented meadow. They were little nymphs, pixies and fays. But Helene was the goddess. She marshaled the children into a ring and sent them circling round the tree, herself taking part in the dance and singing a nursery song in which the clear happy voices of the others joined. Spring had blown away all their winter rheums and catarrhs, and their voices were as clear as a bell. The old chestnut-tree with its leafy branches almost touching the ground let them do with it what they pleased. They climbed up on it, tugged at its branches, tore off its leaves so as to make garlands for their heads. Like a faithful old dog the tree obeyed them as far as its strength would permit it to.

Mirkin looked on entranced from his corner. Helene had not noticed him. She was so absorbed in playing with the children that she had become one of them; she had, as it were, cast off her own life and stepped into theirs. Mirkin gazed at her in astonishment as if she were an apparition from some other world, and it was as though some one had spoken to him. The words of old Chomsky now returned to him clearly and he recognized that human tasks were quite easy and simple; they lay, as it were, at one's feet, and all that one needed to do was to lift them up. . . .

"Who can say that there are greater life-tasks and smaller ones? In what we do nothing can be called great or small; there are only tasks to do and a will to do them. Every man has his own niche and does what is destined for him to do. The results of all human labor are united in a total which is our process of growth, our ascent step by step to the heights. Our growth is not hastened by attempting more than our strength is equal for, by trying to appear more than we are. That's only but outward ostentation, borrowed plumes, false trimmings. Just as base metal can be made to glitter like gold, so it is with our ideals. I'm no hero," Mirkin told himself, "nor do I want to be one. All I want is to be a humble servant of the cause, one of those who carry bricks, drag loads and wind threads. The main thing is to sit diligently at one's loom and weave, for finally we all weave the same garment. . . ."

He did not want to disturb Helene, so he stole softly from the court without her having seen him. For a long time he wandered, feeling rich and happy as though he had discovered a great treasure, through the sunny streets.

Later he returned and found Helene by herself in the school, and pressed something into her hand. She examined it: it was a proclamation summoning the Jewish workers to go with all the other workers to the demonstration on the first of May.

"What is this?" asked Helene.

"The bridal present that my father has sent you."

"What?" cried Helene, not having understood his words.

"This proclamation has been printed with the money that my father sent me with his instructions to buy a bridal present for you. You haven't anything against the present, have you?"

"Certainly not," replied Helene. "But why did he send me a bridal present?"

"Oh, of course, you don't know! I wrote to him saying that we are engaged and intend to get married soon."

"What?" Helene did not yet understand; a burning flush dyed her face.

"Yes, I mean it! I intend to ask your father this very day."

Helene gazed at him for a long time; two great tears stood in her eyes: "You've written to your father about it; you intend to talk to my father; it's only to me that you've said not one word!"

Mirkin was taken aback. He smiled awkwardly, and, as he could think of no reply, repeated mechanically: "No, I haven't said one word to you."

Only then did Helene seem to grasp the situation. There was an imploring look in her eyes as she asked: "Why have you never said anything to me?"

"I don't know," replied Mirkin, smiling, and after a while he added: "Because I didn't think I needed to say anything to you: for you know all about it."

Helene remained standing where she was as if turned to stone. Her face grew quite white. Defiantly she looked him straight in the eyes: "And why do you try to avoid me?"

Mirkin shrank as if he had received an electric shock. His fingers clenched. He, too, grew pale and looked Helene in the eyes: "Because I was afraid of you."

"Of me?"

"Yes, you're so like my mother, and so I tried to run away from you."

"But why?" asked Helene, and her expression changed from defiance to anguish.

"I don't know. I can't explain it."

"And yet you want to marry me?"

"Yes."

"Why?"

"Because it's my fate," replied Mirkin hastily, lowering his eyes.

"I thought I was your happiness! And I don't see why I should bind my life to a fate that isn't mine." With these words Helene made to leave the room.

"Don't you see that without you I shall be lost?" said Mirkin half to himself. He did not move and made no attempt to hold her back.

It was not so much Zachary's words that made Helene stop as his forlorn helplessness as he stood there before her. She walked quite close up to him, looked deep in his eyes and said slowly: "If you don't love me—why do you ask this sacrifice of me?"

Mirkin bowed his head and answered: "You're used to it; it's your fate."

Tears burst from Helene's eyes and choked her as she murmured: "And yet you run from me!"

He buried his face in her cool neck and whispered: "It's because I love you, Helene!..."

CHAPTER XXXVII

THE FATHERLAND

Hurvitz's friend, the Hebrew teacher Königstein, thought seriously of going to Palestine. But neither he nor anybody else saw clearly how this plan was to be carried out. He had no money for the journey; nor did he know what was to become of the wife and children he would leave behind him. Nevertheless his whole mind was absorbed by the idea; he neglected his classes, did nothing all day, and was hardly to be recognized as the same man. In the evening he sat with his head in his hands and by the dim light of the lamp studied all sorts of Hebrew books and calendars in which the holy places of Palestine were described; he learned by heart the number of inhabitants and cattle in the few Jewish colonies, and sighed with yearning as he did so. Deep shadows lay under his eyes, which had a veiled look. His pallid face was irradiated with bliss; red spots burned on his cheeks. In the dark little house there lived, besides himself and his wife, their numerous family, among them a grown-up daughter already of marriageable age. She was a milliner, but had been out of work for two months, and could not leave the house, in any case, as she had no winter coat. Königstein's wife must have been beautiful once; from her prematurely aged face there still smiled, even now, the charming girlish dimples and beauty spots that had once ensnared Königstein's heart. But on that face with its traces of former beauty were also inscribed the six-and-twenty laborious years of her married life. Every winter, every rent day that had to be met, every illness among her children had engraved a furrow there; but the deepest of them all, those round the mouth and eyes, had been caused by her fears for her twenty-five-year-old daughter; the gray strands that ran through her thick dark hair were also due to those same fears.

Frau Chane Königstein sat at the table opposite her husband and helped her younger daughter to make up a wig composed of hair taken from the close-shaven heads of Jewish brides, which was used frequently for that purpose. Now and then she cast a glance at her unfortunate husband, who was still absorbed in his books about Palestine, his head resting on his hands. She felt that he was sick with longing for the Holy Land, and saw that the red points on his consumptive cheeks were burning like hectic roses. She shook her head over her own misfortunes and said in a complaining voice, sighing deeply as if she were standing beside her mother's grave in the cemetery of her native town Lenczyca:

"But you must have gone clean off your head, man! This new calamity, this Palestine idea of yours, is past endurance! I never heard such nonsense!"

"What harm has Palestine done you?" asked Königstein in an

indifferent Talmud drone, without deigning even to glance at his wife.

"What harm has Palestine done me? You sit there lost in a dream! Is it any wonder that you're losing your classes? Your thoughts are never with them; all day you've got nothing but Palestine in your head, you're as good as buried in Palestine!"

"Do you think it would be a bad thing to be buried in Palestine? Many a pious Jew would be glad of it," retorted Königstein jestingly.

"That may be all right after one is dead. But what if one isn't considered worthy of that favor and has to drag on one's sinful existence for a long time still? You haven't brought a penny into the house for several weeks. If this child didn't earn a little money making wigs we should have died of starvation long ago. We're bleeding her white as it is. Have you no heart? Have you no regard for anything?"

"People aren't buried in Palestine today; they live and work there! They're building up new things in Palestine!" Königstein got to his feet, and it seemed to his wife as if he had grown taller. The sickly roses in his cheeks burned still deeper, and there was such a fire in his black eyes that his wife, as always when he was "seized" by this mood, was terrified lest he might have a stroke. She regretted having started upon him with her reproaches and tried to repair the damage. This she did by shrugging her shoulders resignedly, but it had no affect: Königstein stood there like a knight resolved to vindicate at the spear's point the insulted honor of his country:

"And I tell you, my dear woman, that we lie buried nine fathoms deep in the earth *here!* I am in exile here among these ignorant people into whose greedy, stupid children I must hammer a little Hebrew, among these dirty wigs that you sit all the night over, among these hats and all this wretchedness generally. What is a life like ours worth, in God's name? It's a joyless, hateful, miserable exile! And to what end, for whose sake? What do you hope for? What do you expect to happen? What will you get by remaining here?"

His wife and children bowed their heads as under cudgel blows at these words. He had revealed to their eyes the eternal night of darkness stretching before them.

"You're certainly right there, man. But what way out have you found? Perhaps you can tell me that?"

"We must emigrate to Palestine, mark off a farm and till the soil! We must work under the free sky, live on God's good earth as our fathers did. Then we'll breathe freely, then we'll revive, I, you and the children: then we'll be new beings! We'll drink the milk of our own cows, we'll return home from our fields in the evening singing, tired with our day's work, sit in our own garden, eat the fruit of our own trees!"

"But in heaven's name where are you to get the money for the journey? Do think of the money for the journey!" The woman could no longer restrain herself and screamed at her husband. "How is one to make the man see it? I say nothing about what it would cost us to buy our own trees and cows, but what about the money for the fare, the money for the mere fare?"

"The fare money? The fare money?" Königstein stood as if struck by lightning when he heard his wife's words. Driven out of his paradise, he kept on stammeringly repeating like a child the question to which he could find no answer.

"The fare money, you say?" All at once he rose to his full height. "If you'll only make up your mind firmly to go we'll soon find the money!"

His wife was about to retort; but her glance fell on the red spots on her husband's projecting cheek-bones and she was filled with terror. Königstein's whole face was aflame. She was seized with pity and bowed her head over the heap of curly hair-strands before her, which would in time become wigs for young Jewish matrons. She was silent. Soon Königstein was wandering once more through the holy places which his books opened out to him. So it went on evening after evening . . .

One day Königstein went to see his friend Hurvitz and began:

"I'm stifling in this place! I can't stand it any longer! Solomon, what am I to do? This life here has become disgusting and loathsome to me, it's an unendurable burden and I really don't know why I go on bearing it. My only hope is Palestine. I know that I would be able to achieve something there. And even if I failed, I would rather wander hungry through the streets if I could only be there and breathe a different air! There I would know at least what I was living for, why I suffer, why I bear this yoke! Here I'll go to pieces; I feel it! There's nothing for me here but suicide!"

Hurvitz listened to his friend without jeering as usual at his "dreamland" or making a single sarcastic remark. He saw that Königstein was suffering, and suffering for an ideal. Besides, in the last weeks Hurvitz had resigned himself to many things that he would not have tolerated in his younger days. His own life and that of his dependents had brought him to that point.

"You're well off; you have an ideal at least, something to strive for. But what about those that don't even have that?" the teacher said with a sigh.

"What use is all my striving if I haven't the means to make it succeed? I see my goal before me, it's always there before my eyes: but how am I to reach it? If I only had enough money for the fare, at least!"

The teacher remained sunk for a while in silent reflection; then he asked: "Assuming you had the money for the fare—what would you do about your family? Whom could you leave them with?"

"What good am I to them, while I am here? I earn nothing in any case. They live as they can on wig-making, millinery and other jobs. If I were to go it would actually be easier for them; and who knows, perhaps after a time I might be able to send for them."

Hurvitz made no reply and silently shook his friend by the hand.

That evening—the children had finished their school exercises and Rachel-Leah as usual was concluding her day's work by darning stockings beside the stove—Hurvitz began rummaging in his book-case. There was nothing extraordinary in that, for it was a common occurrence for him, after his long day's work, to occupy himself with his books, and often he would not be torn away from them. But then Rachel-Leah suddenly noticed that he was pulling out one book after another and lovingly fingering and regarding them as though in deep thought; after that he put them all together and tied them in a package. This conduct of her husband's alarmed her: "Why is he bundling up these books? What does he intend to do with them?" Hitherto no emergency, frequent as these were in the house, had ever driven the teacher to touch the books he kept in his book-case. One's last suit of clothes might vanish into the pawn-shop, but the books had always been immune. It had never even entered Rachel-Leah's head to pawn the books, no matter how bad things were in the house; even when she had to scrape up money to go to Petersburg after the arrest of her eldest son she had left the books untouched. They were inviolable. What on earth could have happened to make Solomon Hurvitz lay his hands upon them now? Rachel-Leah was filled with alarm, but she did not dare to question her husband. She felt how painful such a step must be to him. Silently she laid down the stocking she was darning and gazed at him in wordless surprise.

Hurvitz felt her eyes upon him. He ceased fondly contemplating his books and jauntily tied up the package as if it did not contain his precious books but worthless scrap-paper; then he said: "Things are very bad with Solomon; he was telling me about his troubles today. I'm afraid of his doing something to himself."

"Who can help it if he has convinced himself that he absolutely must go to Palestine—as if the world will come to an end if he doesn't?"

"It isn't my ideal, but it's an ideal, after all," replied the teacher.

Rachel-Leah would have liked to retort, but old habit prevailed, and she merely bit her underlip and resumed her darning so energetically that she pricked her finger with the darning needle.

Hurvitz spent a sleepless night. He did his best to lie quietly so as not to disturb Rachel-Leah or betray his feelings to her. But she could not sleep either; she heard every sigh and every uneasy movement of her husband. It was not the books that robbed Hurvitz of his sleep. Naturally he was sorry for their loss, for every single one of them had been procured at the cost of painful renunciations; Rachel-Leah had had to go without new shoes and Hurvitz himself without warm winter underclothing. Every book represented a great sacrifice, a victory over poverty, a battle with and triumph over care. And every book contained also a holy message, an article of the religion of progress; each one held for him a dream and a reality: Taine and Spencer, Rousseau and Darwin, Mill and Kropotkin—they were to Hurvitz shining angels opening to him the paradise of Nature. But his pain at losing his books he had quickly overcome. In future he would content himself with borrowing a book now and then. It was something else that robbed him of his sleep: it was the disturbing, torturing doubt whether he, a man who believed in progress, in the triumph of civilization, in the brotherhood of all men, whether Christian, Jew, or heathen, should lend his assistance to such a "reactionary" step as this that was driving his friend to Palestine, a step that in his opinion would tend to stiffen the conservative and separatist tendencies in the world. But finally his mind was comforted by dwelling in the idea of "the fatherland" that was bound up with his friend's ideal. The idea of "the fatherland" justified everything. Hurvitz thought of the new generation, of his own children; they no longer possessed any ideal of a fatherland. He sighed deeply: in his lack of a fatherland ideal he saw another proof of the materialism in which the younger generation was immersed so profoundly and said to himself: "Palestine or any other country—the fatherland ideal is still there. The young people no longer possess it. We of the old generation are the only warriors it has left and we must stand by each other, whether the particular country should be our ideal or not."

Next morning he carried his bundle of books to the "modern" bookshop run by Israel Aronsohn in Tvarda Street, where the supporters of the Jewish "enlightenment" met every Friday evening to smoke cigarettes and argue over the new Hebrew literature.

After much haggling he got enough money for his books out of the surly and greedy book-seller to pay for a third class ticket to Odessa and a third class boat ticket from there to Jaffa. Full of elation he went with the money to his friend Königstein, handed him the bank-notes with shining eyes, and said: "It's all nonsense, I know—but it's an ideal after all!—a pleasant journey!"

CHAPTER XXXVIII

THE FIRST OF MAY

THE SPRING was celebrating its advent. And as in every other year began, along with the coming of the new leaves and tender blossoms on the trees and the warm moist spring wind the season for police interrogations, police raids and arrests . . .

Warsaw was menaced with military law. Nobody knew whether he might not be in prison next day; the whole population lived in fear of dreadful things to come. Patrols marched through the streets, stopping pedestrians and examining their papers. There were police raids in the open street in which all passers-by were arrested, and in the coffee houses, where all the customers were marched to the Town Hall. It presently became a familiar spectacle to see whole crowds of civilians being escorted through the streets by armed patrols; and no distinction was made between man and woman, Christian and Jew. Nobody dared to go out at night; at every corner stood police inspectors in civilian clothes; spies and gendarmes stopped everybody and led them away. But it was just as dangerous to sleep in one's house; every family which was suspect was wakened by a loud peal of the doorbell, accompanied by the familiar shout: "A telegram!" Everybody knew what that meant. In the silent streets could be heard every now and then the rattle of droshky wheels on the cobbles; it told of citizens dragged out of their beds and conducted between fixed bayonets to prison.

At the Hurvitzes' as in all other "suspect" houses a visit of the police was expected every night. Rachel-Leah, who had experience of such matters, made a "general clean up" every evening before going to bed, and saw to it that nothing suspicious was left in her son's pockets. Night after night she awaited the unasked-for visit; but it seemed as though they had forgotten her. All her acquaintances had already received these night visits; Rachel-Leah alone was spared; it was as though they wished to inflict on her the disgrace of going scot free. . . .

"They seem to have forgotten us this time," said Hurvitz at supper one evening. "They've been at all our friends already."

"I don't like this peace," replied Madame Hurvitz reflectively.

Meanwhile the first of May was approaching and the whole police force of Warsaw was being mobilized. Troops were concentrated in the surrounding villages, and presently the rumor spread that the bloodthirsty Volhynian regiment, notorious for its ruthlessness towards the civil population, had recently been given a double supply of ammunition with the order to fire on the crowd at the least sign of resistance. But that did not cow the demonstrators. Silently the opponents marshaled their forces and armed for the conflict that seemed bound to come.

On the first of May all Warsaw was out in the streets early. Both forces had completed their preparations. The broad streets were filled with military patrols, police officials and gendarmes. Cossack cavalry troops, with their rifles ready and swords at their belts, from which hung the red holsters containing their revolvers, barred the ends of the streets. The pavements were thronged with a gay crowd in their holiday clothes, a crowd drawn from all classes and conditions of the population. Amid groups of workers in their dark clothes could be seen pale intellectuals, well-dressed gentlemen and elegant ladies in full fig. Little red ribbons flaunted in many of the men's buttonholes. The more stylishly dressed intellectuals with their eye-glasses and soft hats wore blood-red carnations. Here and there could be seen a smart young lady displaying coquettishly a bunch of red poppies that gleamed provocatively amid the gray, dense, slowly moving throng of working men.

At first the battle was waged in silence, without incident or a word spoken. The police stood at their posts, the crowd at theirs, and neither took any notice of the other. The streets had a holiday appearance; no droshky or tram was to be seen; it was as though they had withdrawn so as to give room for the conflict that must soon burst into flame. The shops in the main streets were shut. Here and there a gendarme would beat against a shop door with his scabbard as a sign that it must be opened. The side streets leading towards the Marszalkovska—the street traditionally reserved for May Day demonstrations—were guarded by police and military patrols, as well as the Saxon Garden: by this means they hoped to prevent workers from the outer suburbs of the town from reaching the place of demonstration.

But like a mighty stream that leaves its bed the crowd broke a free course for itself to the Marszalkovska; through courts, backyards and alleys that the police had forgotten to guard they swept to their goal. So quite early in the morning the pavements of the Marszalkovska were crammed with gray-clad, serious-looking workmen, among whom could be seen here and there the animated figures of stewards and other officials. The drabness of the picture was relieved by crowds of pale working girls in white dresses trimmed with red ribbons and small groups of fashionably dressed ladies.

The Marszalkovska was guarded on every side. At the end where it ran into Krolevska Street beside the Saxon Garden stood a heavily armed military patrol supported by Cossack cavalry. At the other end of the street, before the Vienna Railway Station, stood a similar guard. All the side alleys and courts had also been suddenly barred. The householders had the strictest orders to keep all doors or other ways of escape shut. Groups of Cossacks were concealed in many of the back courts; every rider held a knout or a revolver in his hand.

The shops were shut. The shuttered shop windows and the barred doors gave the spacious street the appearance of a long prison-courtyard from which there was no escape. The festively clad crowd were there as in a trap. On the men's faces lay uneasiness and apprehension, but also the fierce resolution that filled them.

It need hardly be said that Rachel-Leah and her children had been in the Marszalkovska since the early morning. The first of May was a traditional day of rejoicing in her house. Her husband, naturally, never joined in the rejoicings, and this time, too, as in former years, he had brought up all manner of objections and tried to keep his family from taking part in the demonstration. But on every first of May he was powerless; he let his wife do what she pleased, for he knew that all opposition would be vain.

The evening before Rachel-Leah had had a great washing up, using much soap and soda, and as was usual on the eve of a holiday or feast day, she and her daughters had finished by washing their hair. Now red ribbons gleamed in Helene's and Sosha's plaits. Rachel-Leah considered that she herself was too old for such adornments, but she had put on her best dress, the dark one, and wore her hat with the feather, which Helene, who was very skilful in such things, renovated every first of May, and had trimmed now with a new black ribbon. On her bosom she wore, like a knight errant his colors, the red carnation that Mirkin had given her in honor of the day. She had sat up late the night before darning her young son David's trousers and oiling his shoes so as to hide the cracks in the leather; instead of his school cap, which would have given him away, he was allowed to wear a soft hat for the occasion. The Shachliner, Itschele and the other inmates of the "High School" had also of course to be there; they vanished to find their own groups of friends, and David soon followed them; he had come with his mother but very quickly disappeared. So Rachel-Leah walked along beside her two daughters; Mirkin followed close on their heels, filled with curiosity to see what would happen. . . .

For a while a deadly calm reigned in the Marszalkovska. The crowds walked backwards and forwards on the pavement as though they were taking their Sunday promenade, without daring to set foot in the roadway, where the gendarmes and military patrols were stationed. Nor did the latter either stir from their allotted posts. Sparsely distributed over the uncannily silent street with its holiday crowds, these men seemed to be paralyzed by the emptiness around which they stood; fear looked out of their eyes and faces. Police inspectors with red fleshy necks stood nervously, with flushed faces, at their stations; stout and unwieldy in their tight uniforms, they looked every moment as if they were about to have an apoplectic seizure under the strain. The gendarmes were apprehensive and worried; their faces had the helpless and stubborn look of cattle being driven to the slaughter. They seemed to be longing for the day to end as soon as possible. The military patrols paced boredly to and fro with stiff wooden strides, contemplated with the indifference of soldiers the moving crowds, and now and then showed their white teeth in an awkward smile. So neither party dared to attack the other or to attempt to set foot in the enemy's territory.

But presently a dense knot formed at one point of the pavement. It grew dark and purposeful. In the confusion of thronged bodies and heads some one raised a red banner which he had drawn from beneath his jacket, and to the grave strains of a song that sounded almost like a dirge, mingled with a shout sent up from agitated and apprehensive throats, the dense knot pressed on to the roadway. Their arms linked together, their bodies pressing against one another as though seeking mutual protection, they timidly raised their voices: "The people's flag is deepest red."

Now from the pavements the whole crowd streamed to join the

little singing group and formed up into line behind it. A second man unfurled a red flag as he ran. Singing—but the words could hardly be made out and the song was more like a cry—they all rushed towards the demonstrators, trying to outrun the police and the patrols. But the others were quicker. From a back court galloped a group of Cossacks and flung themselves against the crowd. The more timid jumped back to the pavement again. The dense procession that had already formed fell into confusion and crumbled away at the edges. More and more of the demonstrators fled from the roadway back to the pavement. Only a small remnant of the procession was left; they crowded together helplessly, and the nearer the Cossacks came, leaning over the necks of their foaming horses and swinging their knouts, the more shrilly and heart-breakingly rose the song of the crowds: "The people's flag is deepest red...."

Already the knouts were whistling like a rain of fire about their heads. The frightened horses plunged madly, like an unleashed torrent, into the crowd. Here and there a hand appeared above the heads of the throng and tried to hold back the maddened horses. The knouts fell. A woman's hat flew to the ground, a cap rolled over the cobbles and was carried away by the wind. The red flags vanished in a mass of human bodies and the crowd scattered like dust, forced its way back to the pavement again and mingled with the others.

But soon the same stratagem was repeated on the other side of the street. Rows of men formed up at a point which was for the moment free of police and soldiers. Once more a red flag fluttered in the sun and a crowd gathered round it. Those who were on the pavement hastened to it and joined the procession, which grew broader. The densely packed mass took up a greater and greater part of the roadway every minute. It grew like a stream pouring from an open sluice. Everybody rushed to the place where the new procession had formed. They were like drops of water swelling the dark stream to mightier strength. Already red banners with all sorts of inscriptions were fluttering in the wind. Songs rose in different languages and grew to a great cry that seemed to come from *one* throat, from *one* heart:

"The people's flag is deepest red...."

The words rose in a solemn mighty chorus. But not far off came waveringly, timidly and hesitatingly, the strains of the Jewish hymn of the workers:

> *"We swear, we swear,*
> *Our vow of blood and tears . . ."*

A little while passed before the police grasped the situation. They ran towards the procession. Meanwhile it grew broader and longer, hands and arms were linked, shoulder pressed against shoulder; an impenetrable wall was formed, over which fluttered the bright red banners. Inspired by the hoarse singing, the crowd's mood rose higher and higher. When at length the panting police inspectors, swinging their naked swords and followed by their armed men, reached the procession, they found themselves confronted by a dense impregnable wall of bodies and heads, which moved onward with unshakable tread.

For a moment the police officers and their men were overcome by panic fear; helplessly they glanced back at the Cossacks, who were occupied in dispersing the crowd at the other side of the street. They apprehensively retreated a few steps. That gave the procession courage. It marched on. The singing grew louder, clearer. It lost its undertone of despairing fear and became a shout of victory.

Here and there a hand would shoot out and pull a police officer or man into the procession, where he disappeared as quickly as a pebble in a torrent. The other policemen started back hastily and in frightened voices shouted for help to the Cossacks. But the Cossacks never stirred, although they could see clearly what was happening. They stood at their posts beside their horses as if rooted there. They paid no attention. Voices shouted: "The Cossacks have mutinied; they refuse to shoot on the crowd!"

A great wave of enthusiasm flowed over the demonstrators. Their voices rose in a pæan of triumph. A forest of red flags shot up over their heads, almost hiding them. Seized by panic, the police fled like rats into the side alleys. The whole breadth of the Marszalkovska was left free to the triumphant crowd, now drunk with victory. Every face shone with rapture. Eyes sparkled, hands waved, the crowd marched on. It burst through barriers that were invisible and yet real; it passed through firmly-barred portals into worlds that were invisible and yet real, set foot on new worlds. It bore onward with its deliverance not only from the Czar and his satraps watching it, but from the inward bonds that enslaved it as well; it was a river that had burst its cover of ice and now poured from its long confined bed great waves over the fields and meadows of spring.

CHAPTER XXXIX

IN THE RAT TRAP

SUDDENLY an impregnable wall towered in front of the unleashed flood. Nobody could tell how it had arisen. Conjured up as if by magic, an impenetrable line of soldiers, shoulder to shoulder, had sprung from the ground and now blocked the way of the onward moving crowd. In open formation the soldiers advanced and without haste occupied one point of the street after another. Their rifles were no longer shouldered but held ready in their hands, the bayonets pointed at the crowd. Without hurry, quite leisurely, they advanced point by point. As if they were quite certain of their victims, the ranks of death approached with a cool leisureliness that was almost uncanny. Absolute silence and deadly seriousness rested upon the murderers as well as on their victims. In the front rows of the procession the songs and shouts of victory fell silent; farther behind the singing still went on but soon the terror struck there too; it was as if everybody in the crowd had seen a ghost. Every heart stopped, every face grew pale; feet refused their office and eyes looked into eyes for help. The terrible words "The Volhynians!" flew from mouth to mouth.

Suddenly the procession seemed to bunch up. Those on its fringes pressed inwards and tried to hold it back. Every one tried to lose himself in the throng, to find cover behind the others' bodies. The crowd condensed into one rigid mass. Body was crushed against body, but the procession did not stop. Magnetically attracted by the angel of death towering before it, it went on. The knees of many were tottering, and the procession moved forward spasmodically, reeling as if drunk. As a serpent holds its victim with its motionless stare, so the soldiers seemed to draw the crowd towards them. It marched straight towards the rifles and sang in a trembling voice that betrayed its terror:

"The people's flag is deepest red . . ."

In front a silent command was given; an officer waved his sword. The rifles, which had been idly hanging at the soldiers' sides, were suddenly jerked upwards, and the mouths pointed straight at the wall of human bodies in front of them. The soldiers grew pale: it was a proof of the deadly seriousness of the moment. But—wonder of wonders!—the crowd showed no sign of panic. There was merely a dead silence. The singing ceased, the procession halted. These thousands of bodies seemed to have become one body, these thousands of lives one life. Pressed together for protection so closely that each could feel his neighbor's heart beating, all these thousands seemed to melt into one like the flames of a conflagration. Instinctively they took one another by the hand, as if each wished by doing so to instill his own life into his neighbor.

Suddenly something unexpected happened. A boy's face appeared above the men's heads. Only the deathly pale face with the wide quivering nostrils could be seen. The boy seemed to be supported on some one's hands or shoulders in the front row, and was on a level with the wall of soldiers. He stretched out two white hands towards the line of rifles and began to speak in Russian in a voice almost inarticulate with agitation:

"Brothers from Volhynia! . . ."

But before he could finish his sentence there was a dull report. It was so feeble, so almost soundless and smokeless, that the demonstrators did not know at first that anything had happened. A perceptible interval elapsed before they became aware they were being fired on. They stood motionless where they were; they simply wondered why people here and there were crumpling up, falling to the ground, or sinking against some one's shoulder.

After the first volley the soldiers, too, remained motionless, as if in doubt whether or not they had received a command to fire again. At all events they did not fire, but gaped stupidly at the crowd, which never stirred, which neither advanced nor retreated. In this way a minute or so passed. It seemed an eternity. During that dead pause the boy, who was still sitting where he had been, breathing heavily through his quivering nostrils, suddenly fixed his eyes on the fair, beautifully trimmed mustache of the young officer who had given the signal to fire with his sword. The boy's glance fell on the golden-fair lashes shadowing the young officer's beautiful blue eyes. For a moment their glances met. The boy took a good look at the officer, as if he wanted to remember him for ever; then with lightning speed he drew a revolver from his pocket and a well-aimed shot blotted out the handsome young officer's golden lashes.

The boy's act was like a signal. It awakened both the staring crowd and the motionless soldiers. Like maddened demons the soldiers flung themselves upon the procession and fired right and left. In their hysterical terror they attacked whoever happened to be near. The crowd, which a moment before had been a single body, wavered to every side like a flame driven by the wind.

They climbed over each other, trampled over fallen bodies, fought their way out with tooth and nail. Dreadful shrieks and wails filled the street. Into this chaos white-faced soldiers kept on firing ceaselessly and madly, their eyes and tongues protruding with terror. In a moment the roadway of the Marszalkovska was empty. A deathly silence lay on the spacious cobbled street. Here and there bodies lay about as if forgotten; they looked as though they had lain down of their own accord like children playing at being dead.

The panic-stricken demonstrators tried to escape the wild rifle fire. The pavements on both sides of the street were instantaneously crammed to bursting. Everybody crowded round the house doors and tried to force their way in, but in vain; all the house doors were locked and barred from inside. Men shook and pulled at the door handles, screaming and sobbing, and kicked the doors with their feet; but everything remained silent, impassive, unresponsive. Some ventured to make a run for it, so as to try their luck at the next door; but the rain of bullets falling in the street soon drove them back.

The Marszalkovska from end to end had become a death-trap, the crowd helplessly rushing hither and thither—the prey of the hunter. There was no escape. The house doors remained shut; the side streets were barred by mounted Cossacks supported by armed police, who with knouts, revolvers and drawn swords drove the surging crowd back again into the deadly trap.

Among the fugitives were Rachel-Leah and her daughters. When the catastrophe happened she kept her head; she gave each of her daughters a hand, told Mirkin to follow her closely, and took refuge in the deep embrasure of a door, hoping she would manage to get into the courtyard. But the door was firmly shut like all the others. In vain eight hands whose veins stood out with the exertion shook at the door handle; the door, secured by iron bars, held fast. Inside no sound was to be heard; the whole house seemed dead. More and more people thronged from the perilous pavement to the only door whose deep embrasure furnished some protection, and in a few minutes the place was crowded. Hundreds of bodies flung themselves with all their strength against the unresponsive door; but it was stronger than they. Out in the street the bullets sang past; they flew past the doorway like a hurricane. Any moment the maddened soldiers might appear and shoot down everybody who had sought refuge there. Rachel-Leah glanced round her and saw nothing but frightened, panic-stricken faces. She must get away from here, but to venture out in the street meant almost certain death. One thing was clear to her: if one was to escape one must break through the cordon of Cossacks in some side street. To do it single handed was impossible. Rachel-Leah looked round for someone who would dare to risk it along with her. She looked and looked. But she could see nothing but a helpless, despairing, panic-stricken crowd. A new stream of fugitives was pouring towards the entry; and in front ran a pale youth without a hat, a revolver in his hand.

"God in heaven!" cried Rachel-Leah. She elbowed her way forward, shoving aside every one who stood in her way, and made a narrow path for herself. Dragging her daughters after her she ran up to the new group. Seizing the youth she gave him a buffet in the face and then a blow on the hand, so that his revolver fell to the ground.

Then she tore her shawl from her shoulders, threw it over the boy's head and in a ringing voice cried to the terrified crowd: "What sense is there in staying here? They'll shoot holes in us! Follow me! We must break into Zlota Street through the Cossack cordon at the next corner."

Thereupon she gave a push to the youth with the shawl round his head and took her daughters by the hand. As if hypnotized the crowd followed. Rachel-Leah prepared to cross the street, first giving her daughters' heads a shove to show that they must keep them lowered. A few steps at a mad run—the end of Zlota Street was reached.

"Where are you going? Where are you going? . . . Back! Back there!" panted a police officer, running towards her with a revolver in his hand.

"Come on! Shoot me, stab me, murder me, you murderers!" Rachel-Leah flung like an enraged lioness at the police, who recoiled rigid with dismay. "You've murdered one already"—she pointed at the youth wrapped in the shawl—"Come, kill me too, you murderers! Your time too will come some time!" And she shook her clenched fist in the officer's face.

The inspector's congested face grew pale with apprehension, and he instinctively shrank before her uplifted fist. Thinking that the muffled youth was wounded, and alarmed by the woman's savage outburst, he retreated a step. Instantaneously the crowd that had followed Rachel-Leah swept past him, and the mouth of Zlota Street was filled with hysterically shrieking women and men prepared to risk anything.

The crowds, still hearing the ceaseless firing behind them, seemed instinctively to have guessed at the path of escape that Rachel-Leah had blazed for them and with the irresistible violence of human beings fighting for their lives flung themselves upon it, trampled down the police, refused to be stopped by the knouts of the Cossacks hastening to intercept them, and—burst through. . . .

When Rachel-Leah arrived home with her children she hastily seized her son's blouse and trousers, tore them into a thousand shreds, and flung the bits into a pailful of water; then she wrung them out vigorously and began to scrub the floor with them.

"What's Mamma doing? Why, that's my new trousers that she bought for me only the other day!"

"Don't you worry! They'll recognize you even in your patched ones," retorted Rachel-Leah. And with a heavy sigh she added in a low voice: "In God's name, where am I to get the money for a new pair?"

CHAPTER XL

A MOTHER'S CRY

IMMEDIATELY after the May Day events the Shachliner left Madame Hurvitz's "High School." He had not returned in the evening; next day he sent a boy for his belongings, and since then he seemed to have completely vanished. From this Rachel-Leah concluded that she might expect trouble and should send David away. Yet she could not send him away, for his absence from school would rouse suspicion. Besides, his father must not guess anything. So, making some pretext or other, she sent the boy for the night to Mirkin's flat. Whatever happened they would not find him at home if they came for him. After the first few nights had passed quietly without anything happening, David went home again, for his father's attention had already been roused by the fact that he was not sleeping in the house. Only after his return did Rachel-Leah receive the long expected and unwelcome night visit. The house was searched from top to bottom; even the girls were dragged from their bed on flimsy pretexts, the cupboards and chests were searched, the floors torn up, the pots, pans and plates in the kitchen thoroughly examined. At last they found among the books in David's school-bag a bundle of revolutionary leaflets. He admitted at once that they belonged to him. Thereupon he and his father were led away.

When the police ordered the boy to put on his clothes and accompany them, the grim Rachel-Leah observed that his trousers were in an impossible state and she snatched up needle and thread to mend them hastily. But suddenly she let her hands fall. Deep hopelessness overcame her and to darn her boy's trousers seemed no longer worth the trouble. For the first time in her life Rachel-Leah completely lost heart.

But then she was seized with sudden, blind fury: she itched to give her David a thorough thrashing before he went. The last words she flung at him were ones of angry exasperation: "You simpleton! You might at least have given the things to me to keep for you! Sticking things like that in his school-bag!"

At that moment she was quite indifferent to the fact that the police could hear her.

"Sticking such things in his school-bag!" she shouted after her son again on the stairs.

Next morning Helene hurried to Mirkin to find out if anything had happened to him. Obviously he was not suspected, for he had not been visited.

When he went along to the teacher's house he found Madame Hurvitz for the first time in a dispirited and despairing state. A wet cloth bound round her head, she sat impassively on the chair beside the stove, stared dully before her and kept on muttering:

"Now the second of them is in for it."

Later she said in a low reproachful voice: "Why did I let fly at him just when he was leaving?"

Then with bitter defiance she justified herself: "Isn't it enough to drive you mad? Sticking things like that in his school-bag! If he had only given them to me to keep for him at least! The little simpleton!"

A few days later appeared a group of officials from the school authority who sent the children home and sealed the doors of the school.

The house of Hurvitz saw downfall awaiting it.

Then Mirkin awakened to unaccustomed energy. It was clear to him that the first and most important task was to save the school. The work at which Hurvitz had labored for so many years must not fall to ruin. To Mirkin this task seemed so important that he would have been ready to give his life for it; it was as though on the fate of that one school depended that of the whole world.

So he forced his way into every office of the education authorities of Warsaw, and employed without scruple every means that seemed suitable in his eyes. Where bribery was necessary he bribed; where influence was needed he obtained it. As he possessed a university education and was an advocate he succeeded in a very short time in securing a school license in his own name.

With this license he continued to carry on Hurvitz's school, adding to it and conducting it in a more modern and hygienic fashion. He engaged new teachers and himself took over the management. Under the spur of necessity he soon found the right attitude to adopt to the teachers and children. His voice acquired an authoritative ring, his gestures a decisiveness that impressed not only the teachers and children, but Helene and her mother as well. In a little while he had completely assumed Hurvitz's rôle, whose substitute he was for the time being.

He undertook also the organization of David's defense. Nobody knew what the boy was charged with, or whether the part he had played in the May Day scenes was known. Nobody was allowed to see the two prisoners. Mirkin told Madame Hurvitz to be of courage and tried to reassure her: the fact that David and his father had been put in the "Paviak," the prison for slighter offenses, was itself sufficient to show that the inquiry was still in its early stages and that the authorities certainly knew nothing about the May Day incident. As the prisoners were allowed to have food brought in to them, and father and son were both in the same cell, Mirkin's theory seemed to be plausible enough.

Presently, however, Mirkin learned that David's case was to be tried not in the civil court, but by court martial. The man who would have to decide the boy's fate was Skalon, the Governor General of Warsaw, a man notorious for his cruelty who, by virtue of the powers granted him by the Czar and the exceptional state of things in Poland, could if he wished sentence David to death even without giving him a trial.

From this Mirkin concluded that the authorities had come to know of David's part in the May Day Demonstration. He saw what that would mean, but concealed it from the family as best he could, pretending that David's case was still in a preliminary stage and that nothing had yet been proved against him. Every day Mirkin opened his paper with a beating heart and searched the shorter notices to see if he could find David's name among them. He had given Helene instructions to hide the newspapers from her mother, so as to forestall any sudden shock.

Every day Rachel-Leah prepared food for her husband and son and carried it to the prison, which was not very far away. There, together with other mothers and wives of political and other prisoners, she waited until her turn came to hand her bowls and plates through the little grill in the iron door.

Every time she approached the prison it seemed to her that she could see a hand waving to her through the bars of a window just under the roof. She did not know whether the hand belonged to her son or husband, or to one of the other prisoners, or even to one of the detested warders. But gradually the hand became a symbol to her. She began to look for it; and when she saw the fingers (it was impossible to get one's whole hand through the bars) her heart grew lighter; it was a sign that everything was still well.

One day when she arrived at the prison she found a great crowd standing in front of it and stretching into the neighboring streets. Curious faces looked out of the house-windows. Rachel-Leah's heart began to beat loudly, and sweat broke out on her brow, over which her thick hair had by now turned grey. As she came nearer she suddenly heard, behind the walls of the prison, cries so horrible that they seemed scarcely human, cries like the death shrieks of hens being strangled. The old fathers and mothers, the sisters and sweethearts of the captives stood outside the prison door and gazed at one another helplessly. Here and there an old woman could be seen furtively wiping the tears from her eyes with the end of her headcloth, her face red with impotent fury. Secret curses were muttered behind upraised hands and presently a loud angry murmur ran through the crowd:

"They're flogging some one in there!"

Rachel-Leah gazed round her in puzzled surprise. At first she could not make out what was afoot and kept on asking: "What has happened?" Nobody gave her an answer; but the white faces of the crowd, twisted with pain and compassion, the groaning sighs of the women, the hopeless head-shakings told her all. Yet she had not yet realized what was actually taking place; she simply felt that every one behind the prison walls, including her son and husband, had become one body, and that it was being tortured.

Rachel-Leah dropped the food she was carrying wrapped up in a napkin, pushed her way through the crowd and flung herself with all her might against the iron door, beat upon it with her fists, and screamed in a hoarse hollow voice that no longer sounded human:

"Murderers! Dogs! You're torturing our children! Robbers! Dogs! Murderers!"

Her cries awakened a many-voiced echo, and soon the muffled sounds of sobbing in the crowd were changed to a loud cry of lamentation. An inhuman yell arose, and it was taken up by every one, both friends of the prisoners and strangers:

"Dogs! Murderers! Dogs!"

Crowds rushed in from the side streets as at a shout of "Fire." Soon the square was dark with drab figures. Incessantly the mob hurled itself against the iron door and the prison walls, shouting:

"Open! Open! Open!"

Above the crowd rose the head of a woman. Her thick black hair streaked with gray had escaped from her headcloth and fluttered wildly in the air. Her great eyes burned in her dark face. Her arms, which seemed to have grown longer, were uplifted above the people's heads; rising angularly from her black sleeves they waved like dark flames, like fluttering banners above the sea of heads and roused it to fury. Presently other arms were lifted. A forest of hands beat against the cold iron door, fingers convulsively clutched at it, nails scratched at the pitiless steel. But still more violently than their hands and nails their wild cries beat against the prison:

"Dogs, open the door! Open! They're killing our children!"

The cry seemed to have been heard within the walls. Presently there rose like a muffled echo the dreadful sound of voices that seemed to issue from endless cold damp corridors and to be crying for release from the hangman's rope and the bestial hands of the torturer. The sound was subdued, stifled, sometimes scarcely audible, but that only incited the crowd to still greater rage. That distant echo whipped their pity to madness, their grief and indignation to fury:

"Dogs! Hangmen! They're murdering our children!"

The shouts became so wild that the prison authorities could not ignore them. The little iron portal in the huge impassive door, which until now had stared out at the raging crowd like a motionless sentry, suddenly opened. A little prison official appeared, escorted by armed warders. Before he had time to open his mouth Rachel-Leah flew at him savagely, shouting: "You dog!"

A blow with the stock of a rifle drove her back. She tottered: she swayed backwards and forwards and almost fell. But, then, summoning all her strength, she straightened herself and rising to her full height confronted the little prison official. A thin stream of blood trickled from beneath her hair, and with eyes blazing with anger, she stared at the man. Her glance was so frightening and uncanny that the official and his escort, who had appeared with the intention of pacifying the crowd, started back. Apprehensively they retreated before Rachel-Leah as before an apparition and quickly vanished again through the iron door.

When Rachel-Leah was brought home her children were terrified by her appearance. They took off her clothes and put her to bed. Mirkin ran for a doctor. On examination the wound proved to be deep, but not dangerous. The doctor washed off the blood, cleaned the wound and bound it up.

Her children resolved that she should not in future carry the food to the prison. Nor was it necessary, for the very next day father and son were transferred to the notorious Tenth Pavilion of the Warsaw Citadel. There it was forbidden to visit the prisoners or bring them food. They were dead to the world of the living.

CHAPTER XLI

IN THE CAGE

Father and son had been put in the same cell in the "Paviak." But they were led away separately for examination. The authorities did not bother much about the father; after a few brief questions they left him in peace. But the son was dragged from one examining judge to another, conducted back to his cell and then suddenly sent for again. Sometimes they dragged him away in the middle of the night, rousing him out of his sleep. Every time David returned from these interrogations he was exhausted and tense; his face was ashen pale, his mouth convulsively working, his eyes unnaturally brilliant and blood-shot, the lids red and swollen. After every examination the boy flung himself on his pallet and was asleep before he had closed his eyes; he breathed so heavily that his nostrils quivered. He said nothing about the accusations that were brought against him, nor did his father ask. Hurvitz was not one of those people who are unable to repress their curiosity; so now, too, he waited patiently until his son should speak.

In the cell the teacher had divided up his time in such a way that his son and he had something to occupy them all day. Hours were reserved for various subjects of study. In the forenoon the father took David's Latin and Greek lessons along with him; he was resolved to learn these languages during his confinement. In the afternoon he recited passages from Mickiewicz's *Pan Tadeusz* and other Polish classics which he knew by heart, or lectured his son on the Jewish philosophies of the middle ages. Every now and then an eye would appear at the observation hole in the cell door and take a look at them. Very soon they had grown so accustomed to this recurrent eye that it no longer disturbed them in the least. For them the man outside to whom the eye belonged was no longer a human being like themselves, but a domestic animal before whom one is unashamed whatever one may be doing...

But the program of the day could not be strictly kept. David was taken away for examination more and more frequently; sometimes he had to spend the whole day with his interrogators; and he was often fetched during the night as well. When he returned he was quite exhausted, had black rings round his eyes, and breathed heavily through his wide nostrils; and his forced smiles and challenge to his father to continue their lessons could not conceal his condition.

"I'll recite the first hundred lines of *The Odyssey,* father, and then you repeat them in Polish."

"You're tired. Lie down and take a sleep."

And indeed David soon threw himself on his pallet and was asleep at once.

The father wandered restlessly up and down the cell and muttered:

"What do they do to him there? What are they doing to him?"

Then he hummed to himself songs he had known when he was a Talmud student. They were so filled with melancholy sadness that they transported him into another world and comforted him and made him forget his sufferings. . . .

Once, as he was prowling about the cell like a sick wolf while his son was sleeping off the effects of another examination, he stopped, for David had said something in a loud voice. The boy was cursing in the filthiest language. Most of his curses were directed against the little prison doctor. Some of the words he used horrified his father and made him wonder where the boy could have heard them. He went up to the bed to waken David. The light in the cell was dim. The tiny window high up under the green, projecting ridge of the roof gave no admittance to the sun. Hurvitz was short-sighted, so he went quite close up to his son's bed and bent over him. Quite by chance he noticed through the rents in David's tattered trousers angry red stripes running like bands of fire over his naked skin. It was incomprehensible to Hurvitz how such unnaturally red swollen stripes could have come there on the flesh of a living human being. He felt that his boy's body must be in a still more pitiful state than his trousers.

He put his hands before his eyes and did not waken his son. Reeling to the window, he climbed on a chair and leaned his head in despair against the window ledge. He stood there quite motionless for a long time . . .

When David woke—the prisoners were just being brought their food—he looked fresher, was in the best of spirits, and even joked with his father (during their imprisonment they had become very intimate and a sort of camaraderie had arisen between them, so that David occasionally ventured to chaff his father, a thing he had never dared to do formerly). Hurvitz went up to his son, who was still lying on the pallet. Now he realized, too, why David hardly ever sat. He laid his hand on the boy's forehead, which was damp with sleep and terror, and kept it there for a long time without saying anything.

David blushed a deep red; it was as if he were inwardly on fire. Gently pushing away his father's hand, he asked in surprise:

"What's gone wrong with you, father?"

"Why haven't you told me what they do to you?" Hurvitz covered his eyes with his hands.

The boy became pale as death. The dark rings beneath his eyes seemed to have swallowed up the fiery flush that a moment before had flamed up in his cheeks. He breathed painfully through his quivering nostrils.

But that lasted only for a moment. A forced smile appeared on his lips and lighted his sunken eyes. He answered carelessly:

"That's what you're bothering about? I told them what I thought of them, and in return they walloped me a bit."

"Why did you do that?" asked Hurvitz, taking his son's hand.

"It's this way, father. The little prison doctor has such a disgusting highbrow air that I want to spit in his face every time I see him. And he wears pince-nez too!"

The father was silent.

On David's last night with his father he already knew his fate. That day, after the interrogation, his sentence had been announced to him; by virtue of the special powers granted to the Governor General of Warsaw by the Czar it would be carried out without his having to stand his trial.

After the announcement of his sentence David was conducted back to his father, so that—as they put it—he should say good-by to him.

That day the boy had not been tortured, and so he was not so tired as usual when he returned.

Indeed he was unusually animated. He did not fling himself on his pallet as usual, but began to pace quickly up and down like a young caged lion. His father guessed that something extraordinary must have happened, and waited for David to tell him. But David said nothing.

He had still four hours with his father. During them he recited a hundred lines of *The Odyssey* in Greek, and with such fire and animation that his father was amazed.

Hurvitz was still waiting for what his son had to tell him. David said nothing. But he broke short his recitation to change his shirt. He chose the darkest corner of the cell for this purpose and carefully kept in the shadow so that his father might not see his naked body. Hurvitz asked in surprise: "Why are you putting on a new shirt in the middle of the week?"

"They may separate us today. They said something like that at the examination. They're going to send me to the Tenth Pavilion."

The father padded up and down the cell with hasty steps. His voice, as he muttered to himself, grew more and more hopeless.

"It's a good sign, anyway, being sent to the Tenth Pavilion. It means that the examination is over. After that we'll know at least what the charge is," David began again.

"Yes, you may be right."

Then they were both silent. But they could not endure the silence for long.

"I would like you to tell me something more about the mediæval Jewish philosophers, father, that you were talking about yesterday."

"About Solomon ibn Gabirol and his conception of the Godhead, you mean?"

"Yes. Yes."

Hurvitz gave David a long and exact educational lecture on the philosophical system of Solomon ibn Gabirol and his conception of the idea of God.

"And do you believe, father, in a life after death?"

Hurvitz grew pale.

"Why do you want to know that?"

The boy, too, grew pale.

"I just wanted to know what the Jewish religion thought about it. Is there another world? As far as I know there's no mention in the Old Testament, in the Bible, of another world. Is that so, father?"

Hurvitz explained to David the Jewish conception of immortality, and told him that the belief in another world had not developed until later, under Roman influence, during the time of the second Temple; and he spun the theme out as long as he could. But he had a feeling that his son was not listening.

"What are you thinking about, David?" he asked.

"I'm certain," began David suddenly with burning conviction, "that it's only people who have nothing better to do, the rich and the mighty, that concern themselves about death or a life after death. After all it's simply a luxury to brood over death and the soul, and the only thing it's good for is to kill time. A poor man can't afford it; he accepts death when it comes for what it is, as a necessity just like life itself. After all what can death mean to those who know that they share the life of thousands and millions of people all making for the same goal? Those who believe in that try to wreck the moldy old world of the past, so as to create a new and more beautiful one for all men. If I disappear, if I am destroyed, I shall still live on a thousand times in the thousands of millions of human beings who will carry on my aspirations, my strivings, my fight, and continue it until they reach the goal. The only ones who are afraid of death are the powerful who stand alone, and the idle egoists who have nobody to live for but themselves. Any one who is caught up by an ideal, any one who serves something higher than his mere ego doesn't fear death, for he lives on far more strongly and powerfully in his ideal and grows along with it."

The father was more deeply moved by the rapture in David's shining eyes than by his words. The boy seemed to be fighting against something that he feared and trying by his words to give himself courage and strength.

Hurvitz bowed his head and replied not a word.

When they came for him, David drew from beneath his pillow a clean handkerchief that his mother had sent him, and pushed it under the blouse of his school uniform.

"Why are you taking nothing but a handkerchief with you?" asked his father.

"You can send my other things after me."

David shook hands with his father.

"When shall I see you again?" Hurvitz could no longer maintain his composure.

"Do you think they can separate us for very long, father? They haven't enough cells for that!"

Hurvitz did not understand:

"What do you mean by that, David?"

"There are millions outside there who will take our place when we are gone," said David hastily, following the soldiers who had been sent for him.

After the boy was gone Hurvitz kept padding up and down the cell without stopping. In an exalted voice he sang the sorrowful melodies he had known as a Talmud student. Such despairing grief cried in his voice that the warder had to shout at him through the grille to be silent.

CHAPTER XLII

AT DAWN

The sky was unusually bright when David was led out of his silent condemned cell into the courtyard of the Tenth Pavilion. Nothing can kill youth, not even death itself. The fantastic light of the spring morning, which the boy had not seen for weeks now, intoxicated him and made him forget his situation. It was impossible for him to conceive that he was to die on such a spring morning; he could not believe that the soldiers were leading him to execution. The last trace of this feeling vanished as the escort issued with him from the courtyard. The short distance to the execution ground was changed for David into a life time. In a moment he lived through a thousand experiences. At every step he saw something that enchanted his awakened and hungry senses: the smell of the trees which he now felt for the first time this spring, the thick dew that his feet scattered on his way to death, the marvelous blue light in which the world was bathed. All his being was refreshed. With delight he gave himself up to the pure bright morning and felt re-born. As soon as he felt the first touch of the spring wind on his face he forgot everything; the world, the trees, the houses, all dreaming still, sunk in their night sleep, seemed to him so new, so unfamiliar, that they drove everything else out of his mind.

So he walked the short stretch from the prison to the place of execution as in a dream, as though the spring morning had lulled him to sleep. He knew that he should be thinking of something else; for soon something would happen that would put an end to all this, and something quite, quite different would begin. But that other thing of which he should be thinking, for which he should be preparing, was now only an unpleasant duty of which he did not wish to be reminded. That "duty" was like a knife in his living flesh; and yet he endured the knife in his flesh, and in the few minutes left to him drank in the marvelous world and the fresh, dewy spring morning.

But then it all abruptly broke off, like a violin melody when the strings snap. He knew: that gate was the end, the utmost bourne: he would enter but never return again. All at once he felt the stabbing pain of the cold knife in his flesh.

When the gate opened to admit him he stopped on the threshold and involuntarily leant for support on one of the soldier's shoulders to keep from falling. All his senses greedily seized on the extraordinary picture presented to his eyes. His feet refused to obey him. The soldiers who were guarding him humored him as if he were a sick child. Involuntarily they too stopped on the threshold, thinking that David was overcome by fear of death. That pause lasted only for a moment, but it seemed an eternity.

A marvelous panorama stretched before David's eyes. The whole world lay before him. He had never known that the world was so great and wide. For miles the green fields stretched away in front of him, bushes and trees rose amidst them to the very horizon. The shining ribbon of the river glittered between the bright and dark green of its banks like the back of a fabulous fish and its scales gleamed with a pearly shimmer. That long fish-back shone like a metallic mirror. And beyond it stretched fields and meadows, an endless level plain that was lost in the dim distance. On the dewy fields there was life everywhere: houses rose from them, trees, farmsteads, countless villages, a whole world.

And above that world arched another, heavenly world, a floating sea with thousands of cloud islands whose edges were tinged red by the unrisen sun.

David could not tear himself away from the spectacle. "Why have I never seen all this before?" he wondered. But before he could answer the question a soldier seized him by the arm: "Come, my lad, you should have been afraid before this: it's too late now!"

David walked on; his feet now were stiff and wooden.

The large "escort" allotted to him, the officers and soldiers who were waiting for him at the place of execution, he scarcely noticed. He was still sunk in contemplation of the world that had been revealed to him. Suddenly he felt a glance upon him that was like a pang, like a needle thrust under his finger nails. He raised his eyes and noticed, standing among the officers, the little prison doctor; he seemed to be afraid of the light of day and was hiding behind one of the officers' backs. Immediately David forgot everything else: in a clap the situation became quite clear to him. The whole bitterness of the moment rose into his throat and stifled him. The little man in the doctor's uniform seemed to be smacking his lips in complacent expectation. David summoned all his strength and tried not to look at him, but in vain. The mannikin had a short wrinkled face like a deformed ape. On his thin, razor-like little nose sat precariously a pair of glasses that threatened every moment to fall to the ground. He put up his hand to them every few minutes to keep them on.

David was filled with a feeling of crushing sadness. But he did not want to be sad now and exerted himself to master his dejection.

Hastily he turned his eyes away from the little man and gazed again at the endless world that spread away beneath him from the tree where he was standing. He thought: "If I could I would wander over all these fields and meadows now to the very Vistula. Why have I never done it?" He longed to bathe in the Vistula once more before his death; it would comfort him. He saw himself bathing in the Vistula, splashing the water over his naked body. Yes, he would die holding to that thought! But once more the little prison doctor spoiled his pleasure. The little man suddenly turned into a goblin and leapt into the water. David was disgusted with bathing and hastily made for the bank again. . . .

Meanwhile he could hear words being spoken. Something was being read out. That brought the boy's fear of death back again. The longing to bathe in the Vistula was still in his heart, but he knew already that he would never realize it. It was the same feeling that he had had as a child, when he asked his mother for another pear and knew that she would not give him one.

Suddenly his position became quite clear to him. He recognized that he must die, and it seemed to him that the whole world, the fields, the Vistula, would die with him. He felt more sorry for the world than for himself.

The soldiers led him to a slight prominence on which a tree stood. Now he could still better see the world stretching beyond the walls of the prison. Really it was very pleasant to stand there; it was a lovely spot and one could see the whole length of the Vistula!

But then some one stepped up to David and robbed his eyes of the sight of the world. He could no longer see the fields, the houses, the Vistula—he could see nothing. Night was round him. David ground his teeth, shouted something, and tried to put out his hand. Then he realized that his arms were bound to the tree. He shouted as loud as he could:

"Take that rag from my eyes! Take it away!"

A muttering of voices arose. The bandage was taken from his eyes and he saw the world again.

Then David wakened from his dream. He knew quite clearly where he was and what awaited him. But the world that he was looking at: they could never crush that. Neither the fields, nor the trees, nor the Vistula—never! "Everything will live on, will be there even when I am dead!" That knowledge comforted him.

In the world lay now all his hope: it would live in happiness and all that was upon it, the broad fields, the people in their dwellings, the boats on the Vistula, the children bathing in the river, who would perhaps bathe there that very day. A great love for mankind and for all the world awoke in him and now he saw quite clearly for what he was dying.

For that was his longing, that the aim of all his striving—that the world should live happily after him. That was the reason why he had shot one of their tyrants, and that the reason why he himself would be shot now.

David opened his eyes wide and gazed at his executioners. With the angry, challenging glance of a defiant boy he looked round him. A saucy smile twisted his full lips. His nostrils quivered as he painfully drew in his breath. With a white face he laughed. It was a gay guttersnipe laugh. Then, in the same unnaturally thickened voice with which he had addressed the soldiers on May Day, he shouted:

"You'll crush me, but you'll never crush the country, you'll never crush the world!"

He did not get any farther. A dull report. A surprised look came into his eyes, the look of a dumb animal. He kept his mouth open, as if a bone had stuck in his throat. Then he rose on his tip-toes as if to see better. But immediately his head fell on his shoulder and his eyes turned upwards. Slowly his whole body sank forward; but it did not reach the ground, for his thin arms were tied to the tree.

The broad surface of the Vistula gleamed brightly in the rays of the sun, which began to mount the heavens in splendor.

That night Rachel-Leah had a dream that alarmed her so much that she told nobody about it. She dreamed that she had sat down to mend David's trousers; but do what she would she could not find any black thread and again and again found herself holding a white thread in her hand.

"But we Jews only use white thread for a shroud!" she muttered in astonishment in her sleep.

CHAPTER XLIII

NEW PATHS

Hurvitz did not remain for long in the Tenth Pavilion after his son's death. No charge was brought against him, for he had been arrested simply because, in the opinion of the authorities, he, as the father, must bear the responsibility for the offenses of his young son.

As Hurvitz had held no communication with his family in the last few weeks of his imprisonment, he only learned of David's death after his release. He also felt certain that his school must have gone to ruin, and in prison his thoughts had been perpetually occupied with what he was to do next. To his great surprise he found the school in full activity when he returned, and enlarged and modernized, too, the class-rooms newly painted and furnished with new benches, and above all a good staff. He was deeply moved, and his opinion of "the Russian young man" (as he was accustomed to call Mirkin) radically changed. But as he could never bring himself to the point of praising his own children, he could not do so in Mirkin's case either, whom he already regarded as his son.

After the first labor of reorganization Mirkin had handed over the conduct of the school to Helene, and merely lent his name to it. In spite of his success he laid claim to no ability as a pedagogue and accordingly returned to his former vocation. He worked now in the office of a well-known free-thinking advocate who dealt almost exclusively with political cases. Zachary had by this time quite a different conception of the rôle of a defending counsel in the Czar's courts from that he had used to have in Petersburg; for he had come to the conclusion that the Czarist régime must be fought by every weapon that could be found. He threw all his enthusiasm into the case of the Hurvitzes' oldest son. He learned that the young scholar had been sent by the administration to Siberia and was now on his way there. That was the reason why no news came from him. Mirkin got in touch with the leaders of the Polish Socialist Party, to which young Hurvitz had belonged, hoping that with their help and the help of friends whom he had known in his school days in Siberia he might be able to arrange an escape for the exile when once he had reached his destination.

The "High School" in Rachel-Leah's house stood empty. The Shachliner, who had vanished for a long time after that eventful May Day, appeared in Warsaw again, but Rachel-Leah did not take him in as a lodger. She had other uses for the room, she said. Itschele, the workman with the high-school education, had emigrated to America, having changed his views, and being resolved to continue his studies. He imagined he could do that most easily in America, where the workers had an opportunity to attend scientific lectures in the evenings. Mirkin now occupied the "High School." Hurvitz no longer had any objection to this, for he already looked on Mirkin as his son-in-law. So

Mirkin and Helene now did not need to carry their love out into the streets and the city parks. Their love too found a home.

As already related, Hurvitz had not yet heard of his son's death when he was released. So his first words to his wife when he got home was a grumble about the boy's trousers:

"Rachel-Leah, you must really send a pair of trousers to David in prison! He can't possibly appear before the judge in the clothes he's going about in!"

Rachel-Leah replied with a sigh:

"They'll just have to take him in the suit he's wearing."

When Hurvitz learned the truth he was, though not entirely unprepared, so broken up for the first few days, that it seemed as if he would never recover from the blow or be capable of work again. But after some time he regained his balance. In that short period, however, he had aged greatly and his beard had suddenly turned gray. Yet his energy, which he seemed to have completely lost, soon returned and also his enthusiasm for education. With redoubled zeal he flung himself into his school work and his own further education. The unimpaired youthful energy that had remained with him ever since he had studied the Talmud in the Chassid Synagogue helped him over his great sorrow.

But the blow had had a quite different effect on Rachel-Leah. She had not wept a single tear when she heard the dreadful news, nor had her face shown any signs of weeping since. But a hard and bitter look had come on her mouth, and her lips had assumed a strange twist from which one could not tell whether she was smiling or crying. There was a blueness about her lips too, which did not augur well. Her eyes had sunk and the dark rings beneath them had grown. Although no tear could be seen in those great black eyes a perpetual moist glaze always covered them. Her low brow seemed to have shrunk still more and to have still more furrows. Her hair was thick and black as before, but almost in the exact middle of her crown there was a gray strand.

A great change had taken place too in Rachel-Leah's disposition. A calm had come to her such as she had never shown before. Often in the middle of her work, when she was cooking or washing, she would let everything slip and sit in her chair with folded arms, her eyes gazing into the distance and looking at things that nobody else could see. So she would sit sunk in profound thought for half an hour or an hour at a time, until her husband or one of her children roused her by saying: "Rachel-Leah, why are you sitting like that?"

"What?" She would start up, as if dragged out of some other world. She became indifferent to the things she had once taken up with fiery zeal. Among these was the revolutionary movement. She seemed, indeed, almost completely to have lost interest in the outer world. The Friday evening gatherings had ceased, although the Shachliner and a few other friends still sometimes called, though far less frequently than formerly. When they did come they talked far more to Hurvitz and Mirkin than to Rachel-Leah. From old habit she still sat in her chair beside the stove and listened to what was being said. But at the same time she gave the impression of thinking of something else.

She had not lost her interest in her neighbors, however. On the contrary she was more occupied with them than ever. Her chief concern was for the consumptive woman and her children. Often Rachel-Leah stayed away for the whole day. Her family knew where she could be found: she would be standing before the fire cooking supper for the sick woman's children, a supper she had managed to extract from the grocer or the flesh curer out of their left-overs. Sometimes too she would wash and mend the children's clothes. Recently she had been engaged in making a collection among her neighbors, so that the sick woman might be able to go to the sanatorium in Otvock for the summer.

She no longer showed her old fondness for Mirkin. For reasons difficult to explain her affection for him had grown cold. She regarded him as her daughter's fiancé, who would presently become her son-in-law or perhaps was already that. With that his connection with her was finished, so far as she was concerned. She felt that Mirkin no longer needed her, now that he had someone else. It was not exactly jealousy that made her affection for him cool. That of course might not have been out of the question—for who can fathom the depths of a woman's heart? But it was probably something more like envy that chiefly moved her; for she saw Mirkin assuming in the house and in the hearts of her children the place of the son she had lost.

On the other hand Rachel-Leah now showed a particularly warm interest in the Talmud student who one day had appeared on her doorstep. Since then he had become a writer. Although the "High School" was dissolved, the young writer no less than the Shachliner still remained faithful to their teacher and they were the most frequent evening visitors to the house. But Rachel-Leah no longer devoted her chief interest to the Shachliner, but to the young man from the provinces.

She tended the wants of the young writer, as she had once tended Mirkin's, devoted whole evenings to mending his shirts and darning his socks, and did everything for him that he needed. So the young man was now looked upon as one of the family. Some of the Yiddish periodicals that appeared frequently in Warsaw had published his first literary attempts and these had roused wide attention. A famous Yiddish writer living then in Warsaw and regarded by the younger generation almost as their mentor, considered that the young man had a brilliant future before him. So the former Talmudist from the provinces saw a great many literary people and soon had won a name as a short-story writer of whom much might be hoped.

When the young writer came to visit Hurvitz in the evenings he would often read out his latest story. Hurvitz thought very highly of him and devoted himself with enthusiasm to the general education of the young man, lent him books and frequently instructed him methodically of an evening in various subjects. Under the influence of the visitor the whole attitude to the Yiddish language both of the father and the daughter completely changed.

True, of recent years the "jargon" had already penetrated into the house, greatly to Hurvitz's annoyance, along with the talk about the "revolution." It had been confined, however, to Rachel-Leah and the kitchen, where revolutionary songs had been sung on the Friday evenings. But while Hurvitz was in prison the "jargon" had spread to the other rooms as well and soon had almost completely captured both house and school. The daughters, who formerly had held that literary expression was possible only in Polish (Hurvitz himself countenanced the "jargon" as a means for spreading enlightenment among the masses), were gradually won for the Yiddish language by the works of their mother's protégé. During Hurvitz's absence, while Mirkin was reorganizing the school, one or two reforms were initiated with the assistance of the young writer: the upper classes were given courses in Yiddish, while the lower classes were taught entirely in their mother tongue. On account of these reforms everybody looked forward to Hurvitz's return with a certain foreboding. But to the general astonishment the teacher not only accepted the changes that had taken place in his lifework during his absence, but actually declared they were important and necessary, and proceeded to develop them. Clearly a change had taken place in Hurvitz himself.

A few days after Hurvitz's release the papers reported that an Austrian Archduke had been assassinated. In the Jewish quarter of Warsaw nobody attached any great significance to the news; indeed, people were not sure whether the assassination had occurred in a Serbian or a Bulgarian town. Nor did the occurrence waken any echo elsewhere in Warsaw. There were people here and there who had nothing better to do than read newspapers, and they either expressed their compassion for the murdered man or said:

"It serves him right! What right had he to go pushing in where he wasn't wanted?"

There were also a few timid people who were afraid that the affair might have evil results, but by the generality the incident was soon forgotten. Everybody had his own daily cares and so left the incident to the newspapers and the idle, who had nothing better to do with their time than to waste it on politics.

In the Hurvitzes' house nobody had the slightest interest in politics at that particular time, and so nobody there paid any attention to the report.

CHAPTER XLIV

A RAY OF LIGHT IN THE DARK WOOD

At the time when he was still a Talmud student Hurvitz had had the habit of bathing in the river in summer; he had kept it up ever since, and neither his imprisonment nor the death of his son could lessen his pleasure in it, just as it could not crush his youthful energy. Like a pious Jew who will never miss his prayers, so Hurvitz never let a summer evening pass without having his bath in the Vistula. Formerly he had taken his son with him; now Mirkin accompanied him every evening to the banks of the river.

One beautiful summer evening as they were returning home, cool and refreshed, from their swim, they found the town unusually animated. The streets were black with people; groups stood everywhere debating with special editions of the newspapers in their hands and fear in their eyes.

The incident that had been reported ten days before and that nobody had paid any attention to was likely, it seemed, to produce unforeseen results. Austria had sent an ultimatum to Serbia, and the papers expressed the apprehension that a world-wide conflict might be expected. . . .

When Mirkin and Hurvitz got home Rachel-Leah was just finishing her preparations for the Sabbath. The floor was scrubbed and sprinkled with sand; the windows were wide open. Her sleeves rolled up, her arms and feet bare, Helene was helping her mother. At first the women were against letting the men into the house until the floor was dry. But when Rachel-Leah heard the news she gave in and let the men enter with the remark:

"It's all the same to me what happens now."

It was not clear whether she was referring to the threatened world war or the freshly scrubbed floor, or to both.

In a little while the Shachliner rushed breathlessly into the room with a special edition in his hand. He was in unusually high spirits, indeed almost elated. A new and incomprehensible glow shone from his restless black eyes. He did not seem to be able to sit still. Holding the paper in his sound hand he gesticulated triumphantly with his crippled arm: "Have you read it?"

Hurvitz and Mirkin had been seriously troubled by the news they had heard on their way home, and the women too had been seized by fear of the unknown menace. They were all worried and dejected; so they were all the more surprised at the Shachliner's good spirits, and they gazed at him in astonishment.

"It's possible that Austrian troops are crossing the Serbian frontier already to the sound of guns while we're sitting here. And there will soon be things happening here too!" With these words he turned to the two silent men.

"Why are you so glad?" asked Hurvitz in surprise.

"Why am I glad? The day of judgment is come!" cried the Shachliner. An incomprehensible triumph shone in his eyes, as if he were the originator of all that was now threatening the world.

"The day of judgment!" he cried again. "Vengeance for every sin, for every devilish crime! A flood, a flood will engulf the world and sweep everything away with it! Everything! And they have brought the flood upon their heads by their criminal deeds!"

"I can't understand yet why you're so glad about it," Hurvitz said in a voice of still greater surprise.

"Why I'm glad! Don't you understand? The whole business will cave in; the whole false, sinful world, false from its very foundations, will collapse like a house of cards! And I hope it will collapse, this hateful, blasphemous world; may it be buried beneath its own iniquities when the flood comes that it has brought upon itself! But then, when it lies in ruins, when it is crushed to powder, we, *we* shall creep out of its ruins and *we* shall build it up anew on new principles, principles of justice and humanity! Then there will be no oppressed and no oppressors. All of us, all of us will . . ."

Hurvitz did not let the Shachliner finish. Pale with agitation he jumped up, rushed to the Shachliner, seized him by the shoulders, and shook him. He looked as though he were about to strangle him. He was on the point of shouting at the Shachliner: "Out of my house!"

But instead he began to speak, pale, his whole body trembling, every word coming hoarsely through his clenched teeth:

"You would build your world anew on bloodshed? No, no, the blood that is shed will sweep *you* away and you will be buried beneath the ruins of the falling world. Out of evil no good can come!" Calmed now that he had got rid of his first wave of anger, he let the Shachliner go. He was ashamed of his outburst, mastered his emotion, and proceeded in his ordinary voice:

"Do you understand what you've just said? Human lives are at stake. Tens of thousands of innocent young men will be killed. Human beings will turn into beasts again: they will devour one another—and you think you can build a new world on that? No! No! I tell you what the end will be," he had quite regained his composure and sat down in his chair again. "The blood bath will cast us back into the middle ages; every memory of civilization and progress will disappear; we'll experience a terrible set-back. The world will be full of the poison of hate, it will become a primitive jungle again in which men hunt one another. I don't want even to think what the end will be!"

Hurvitz covered his eyes with his hand and went on in a voice filled with pain, as though he were speaking to himself:

"And one had thought that humanity had advanced God knows how far, believed that civilization had grown so strong that mankind would never employ such barbarous weapons again! It's enough to make one despair! It looks as if our generation had gone out of its mind! There's no logic in our development, no progress in our history. We move in a meaningless zigzag. What can we lay hold on? Where can we find a proof that we really are moving forward, when a man like him there"—he pointed at the astonished Shachliner—"a socialist, more, an idealist, a fighter for justice, a hater of oppression, can look forward to rebuilding his world on blood and corpses? What will any world look like that is built on such a foundation? It won't be a world, it will be a hell, do you hear me?" he suddenly shouted. "A hell, where wild beasts live! And it was the beast that spoke out of him just now, too, not the man, not the socialist! And if he speaks like that, what will the rest say? Oh, there's a wild beast hidden in all of us, and we're going back into the dark murderous jungle without seeing any other way and without hope!"

Deep silence followed Hurvitz's words. The Shachliner did not venture to open his mouth. It was not that he was at a loss for arguments for the other side; but Hurvitz's agitation alarmed him.

But Rachel-Leah who, with her cup of tea in her hand, was sitting in her favorite chair by the stove (a habit that she remained faithful to even in summer), pushed back the strand of gray hair that hung over her brow and said softly and calmly:

"You can do what you like to me, but I tell you that the Shachliner is right! Better a dark jungle than such a world as this!"

Her words gave the Shachliner back his courage and he began with a supercilious smile:

"Do you think the war has only begun now? It's been going on for a long time, let me tell you. What form it takes on is a matter of indifference. The main thing is to know what side you are on!"

"He's quite right!" cried Rachel-Leah from her corner. "Blood flows whether there's war or peace. It has flowed up to now in secrecy, without any one noticing; now everybody will see it!"

Hurvitz looked round helplessly, as if seeking for help. He was desperate. With a hopeless gesture he let his hands fall; on his clenched lips was a look of profound despondency.

But quite unexpectedly Mirkin came to his aid.

Sitting beside Helene in a corner he had listened attentively to the excited discussion, but had obstinately remained silent until now. He looked as though he had come to no clear conclusion and so contented himself with the rôle of the silent listener. But now he unexpectedly took the lead. He spoke in a subdued and quite calm voice that contrasted strikingly with the loud and excited tones in which the discussion had been carried on. This had the immediate effect of making the others listen.

"It seems to me that you're both mistaken, both Comrade Shachliner and Pan Hurvitz" (whenever he addressed the teacher he felt awkward, for he could not make up his mind whether to address him as "father-in-law" or "father"; so he always gave him his name, pronouncing it hastily and in a low voice). "You have both overlooked the most important factor in this sad business. Who will wage this war? Men. And I believe in man. Man can never rid himself of his humanity. By the mad whipping up of passion it can be suppressed or reduced to silence for days, for a year, perhaps even for several years; but it will awaken again, transcend all passion and redeem every sin. I don't know how long humanity will stay in the dark wood it is entering now." Mirkin's voice trembled. "I don't know either what awaits it at the other side of that wood, or whether it will really find there the new world of which Comrade Shachliner spoke. I believe no more than Pan Hurvitz that one can build on bloodshed; but I don't believe either that man will wander about forever in the dark wood. And do you know why? Because man takes his human instincts with him even into the dark wood. And these instincts will save him now just as they have preserved him hitherto and brought him to the stage that humanity has reached today. Man's humanity will soon refuse to tolerate the dark wood. Man will leave the wood with hands smeared in the blood of his brothers, with the hands of a murderer, but shame will burn on his brow and repentance in his heart. He will be like a child who has fallen in the mire and runs to his mother to be cleansed and comforted. A dark night is falling upon us, but I have no fear, because I trust humanity. It will emerge again from the dark night, the dark wood, and find its own path. No matter how crooked the course of humanity may be, it follows the laws of logic and is making towards a goal. . . ."

There was complete silence in the room while Mirkin spoke. Hurvitz's head was bowed in his hands. The Shachliner sat motionlessly in the same posture. All desire to utter the retort that he had prepared left him. The teacher too said nothing. Both felt that Mirkin had uttered more than mere empty words: the sacred faith of a human soul had been laid bare to them.

VOLUME III

MOSCOW

BOOK ONE

CHAPTER I

WHO ARE THESE BOLSHEVIKS?

No STALK of grass is motherless, and every blade is caressed by the soft arms of the wind. But no grass in the whole world is nursed for so long against the warm maternal breast of the snow as the rich, shadow-flecked grass in the birch woods round about Moscow. After the protective snow of the long winter has melted, and the sun first shines upon the young stalks, they are as fresh as carefully-tended nurslings. Each stem laves itself in the dewdrops that mother night sheds before she has to abandon them for the whole day. And when the wind blows over those lawns, the green surface is shaken in soft trembling waves like a lake....

The rich green beneath the young silver birches in the woods round Moscow keeps fresh the whole summer long until the first frosts come and the icy winds begin to blow again. The tender blades shiver in the cold mornings, but under their chill coating of frost their innocent green still looks out; they look like forsaken children left outside to shiver in the cold. . . . But then at last, the good white snow carefully covers them up, and beneath its kind maternal blanket they sleep the whole winter through.

Although it was late October, no snow yet lay on the soft green summer-like carpet of grass—as it generally did in other years. Vassily Andreyevitch, owner of Sapianka, an estate adjoining the Nijni-Novgorod railway line, breathed in with gusto the keen tang of frost as he looked out of the window of his compartment at the hills still dim in the dawn-light.

The black Moscow fur coat that enveloped his robust form was thrown wide open, and he stood pressing his red face with the fleshy nose close to the damp window pane and contemplated the landscape flying past him. The cool and yet warming sun that was rising above the horizon licked the dew from the field and tree like a mother cow licking her new-born calf smooth and clean.

And the awakening world really made one think of a new-born calf standing somewhat shakily on its spindle legs.

It seemed to be rubbing the sleep from its eyes, reluctant to leave the soft arms of the night, from which the reddening morning sky tore it with impatient summons. . . .

Vassily Andreyevitch remained happily absorbed in the golden stubble fields, the green lawns between the woods, the little brooks and pools, in which, though it was late autumn, ducks and geese were cheerfully splashing. Blue and green painted window shutters, curiously carved cornices and roofs of peaceful homes, peasant men and women at their morning's work, red spotted cows grazing in the fields, horses and foals tethered by the leg, who leaped aside awkwardly and tried to flee from the panting locomotive; these filled in and completed the landscape that rushed past the train.

Vassily Andreyevitch was a peaceable man, and he loved Nature. But good food he loved even better. After a sledge drive through frost and snow he always had to have a few good glasses of schnapps, accompanying them with half a calf's head in vinegar, a swine's ear with horse radish, or a pair of salted pig's-trotters.

And in summer, after he had taken his usual bathe in the river on some sweltering afternoon and was sitting on the veranda of his fine house, there always had to be a steaming samovar on the table beside him, a plate of raspberries and cream, or else a "chlodnik" as it was called, a green salad with gherkins and sour cream in it.

Next to good food, however, what the owner of Sapianka liked best was Nature. His greatest passion was to tramp through some forest swamp, in long boots reaching above his knees, on some autumn morning when the mists were still lying on the fields, and shoot wild duck; the happiest moment he knew was when his white spaniel retrieved some wild duck he had shot, and ran up to him wagging his tail with the bloodstained bird in his mouth.

Vassily Andreyevitch worshiped his dogs and horses; he would rather have let a pregnant peasant woman drag his loads of wood home for him than employ one of his horses for such a purpose. His cows were far cleaner than his peasants; their stalls were far more frequently swept, washed and scoured than the houses of his servants. When the sheep, after the reaping, were grazing in the stubble fields, he loved to sink his hands in their soft oily wool and feel their fat shoulders. It gave him genuine pleasure to have his hands, his chin, his mouth, his whole face licked by the tongues of his dogs, his cows and sheep, and he would often kiss with joy the moist nose of one of his favorite horses. . . .

The fields and woods were his kingdom. Part of his property he had inherited from his parents; the greater part, however, he had acquired by marriage. He loved best to walk over it in the gray dewy dawn, his short fur coat flung over his shoulders, and followed by his dogs (he had not the heart to use one of his horses). In great draughts he breathed in the fresh morning air. He would stand for a while in the woods listening almost voluptuously to the soft lullaby that the wind was humming in the branches of the trees. He loved particularly to stride in early spring over the newly plowed fields, now and then thrusting his hands into the soft black soil or breaking off a clump so that he might feel the softness of the mold between his fingers. He could never pass a corn or barley field without plucking a few ears and putting them in his mouth. Whenever a bird flew past him during those morning strolls, he felt sorry that he had not his gun. He knew the track of every wild creature on his property, though they were always changing, and with his gun and his dogs he pursued them to the end, so as to add to his trophies. The fields and the woods were dearer to him than a loved woman, dearer even than his mother had ever been.

And now as he stood at the carriage window and regarded the golden stubble fields, the green strips among the woods, the gayly carved wooden houses, the little lakes, he could not keep still. He wanted to touch everything that was flying past his eyes, to grasp it in his hands, to possess it. The mere sight of the landscape drew an appreciative sigh from his breast, followed by a melancholy exclamation:

"Oh, little mother, there's no land like you! We have a fine land, a great land—all that we lack is law and order!"

He thought of the evil time which he was passing through—for there was actually war and revolution in the country! The Czar was cast from his throne, the Governor of Moscow driven from his palace, and the peasants spoke insolently to their masters. The woods that had been such a cause of litigation between him and his peasants for so many years had simply been requisitioned, and the fellows were cutting the trees down right and left! They actually had the impudence to drive their cattle on to his pastures, and the bailiff was afraid to punish them for it. Even the women were rebelling; the servant maids would not do what they were told. Only yesterday his wife Maria Arkadievna had burst out crying because of one of those creatures. Once he would have had a recalcitrant trollop like that dragged to the cow stall, commanded two peasants to pull up her petticoats, and given her a good dose of the knout with his own hands; then she would have been ready enough to fall at her gracious master's feet and thank him! She would never have dared to complain about him, that was certain; and if she did, he had only to send the village magistrate a brace of ducks or a few bags of potatoes, and the girl would promptly be sent home to beg her master's pardon. But now one could do nothing but hold one's tongue—and God knew how much further things would go yet. The peasants were saying that the land was to be taken from the masters and divided up. No, no, the people in Petersburg would never allow that! They could never get along without the land-owners! Who would keep the peasants up to scratch and see that they worked the fields? There wouldn't be much farming done without the land-owners!

"If only this cursed war was finished! What need had we to go to war with the Germans? They've always been our best friends. It's these sly English that began the whole business! If only the war was over the soldiers would come back, and once they were packed off to their villages—everything would soon be in order again."

Vassily Andreyevitch tried to banish his uneasiness:

"It will come right somehow; they'll soon come to their senses yet in Petersburg. If only the generals were back again with their mounted Cossacks they would soon rid the towns of the most disturbing elements, and particularly of these Bolsheviks! These Bolsheviks are to blame for everything—all the papers say so. The others are reasonable, one can deal with them: the Bolsheviks are the only obstacle. German spies, that's all they are, brought here with German money in German railway carriages—all the papers say so.

"Yes, and who are these Bolsheviks?" Vassily Andreyevitch scratched his head in perplexity.

To this question he could find no answer, and as the name "Bolsheviks" awoke gloomy thoughts in him he discarded it in exasperation: "To the devil with the Bolsheviks!"

With that he turned his mind again to his own affairs. He thought of the reason for his journey to Moscow—of Natasha. Of course he always addressed her by her full name, Natalia Stepanovna, as is due to a lady. He could see again the strong white back, the sumptuous round breasts, the soft throat of his mistress Natalia Stepanovna, who lived in Moscow: he saw, too, Anushka and Simoshka, the two children that Natasha had borne him.

A broad satisfied smile widened his thick lips and vanished in his great mustache. Yes, it was as if his mighty belly were chuckling too with anticipatory pleasure and voluptuously quivering beneath his clothes.

The mere thought of Natasha and the children made Vassily Andreyevitch happy and drove away all his troubled imaginations and forebodings. Now all he saw was the comfortable little flat in the Petersburg Chaussee, quite far out, almost beside the race course, in the newly built suburb of Moscow where he had furnished a house for Natasha. . . .

Vassily Andreyevitch had a modern wife. Maria Arkadievna had read all manner of queer books and did not wish to have any children. "Woman is not a domestic animal," she said, "and does not exist merely to suckle and look after children." She actually had her bed removed from their common bedroom and set up a boudoir of her own. "A woman must live her own life," she declared. "A double bedroom robs a woman of her individuality." Every evening before going to sleep she came to Vassily Andreyevitch in her dressing-gown, pressed a kiss on his brow and said "Good night." And Maria Arkadievna's night attire was extremely seductive. Above all the trousers of her piquant pajamas. Her dressing-gown, too, was particularly interesting, as it had loose wide sleeves and was cut very low at the neck; it was always flying wide open, showing the pajama trousers, which were fastened with a coquettish red girdle. But if Vassily Andreyevitch took his wife's hand and did not show any disposition to let it go again she always said: "A woman isn't a chattel. For *that* one must be in the right mood and have the right atmosphere." And since the right mood and the right atmosphere could not be produced artificially, he had to content himself with a kiss on the brow. Thereupon she would release herself and go, giving Vassily Andreyevitch another glimpse of the pajama trousers. A pleasant perfume lingered in the room: Maria Arkadievna used particularly seductive perfumes.

Vassily Andreyevitch was a man with healthy desires; he longed for a sound strong woman who did not need the right mood and the right atmosphere, and he wanted to be a father, to have children, to send his children to the school, to examine them in their lessons, and now and then lay one of them across his knee and like a proper father give it a good drubbing. But the tale was always: "A woman isn't a domestic animal and wasn't created to bring children into the world."

Should he get a divorce? That would be a pity. Her dowry—the village and the forest that he looked after—brought in a good income. He could not live on what he got from his own property, and Maria Arkadievna wore interesting negligees. . . .

Maria Arkadievna had had a housekeeper Natasha, a healthy, well-developed woman. Her sumptuous bosom seemed in danger of bursting through her black working garb. And when Vassily Andreyevitch's eyes rested on her firm, superbly curved hips the thought rushed into his mind: loins such as these could bear healthy children.

At bottom Maria Arkadievna had no objection whatever to her husband's carrying on with her housekeeper. A healthy man must satisfy his natural impulses—and after all servant-maids existed to fill the rôle of domestic animals, so to speak. All that mattered was that Maria Arkadievna's "individuality" should not be threatened, that she should be allowed to keep what company she chose, that no objection should be made when any of her women friends spent the night with her—that her husband should not disturb her, but content himself with a kiss on the brow, a glimpse of her pyjamas and a whiff of her perfume. . . .

At last the housekeeper's condition could no longer be concealed. That was a nuisance, because of the domestic staff. So Vassily Andreyevitch—with his wife's full knowledge—rented a flat for Natasha in the city.

So his mistress became for him his real wife.

Natalia Stepanovna was a simple pious woman, loved as much as Vassily Andreyevitch himself a quiet domestic existence, and was devoted to her man and her children. So the pair led a peaceful God-fearing life together. Every two or three months Vassily Andreyevitch left the village and went for a visit to Natasha. From the station he drove direct to the Hôtel Métropole, where he also took a room in his own name—in case people might gossip. But he lived with Natasha and comported himself like an honest and respectable husband. In the neighborhood indeed, he was regarded as such, for he gave out that he was a bailiff from the country, who had sent his family to the town for the sake of the children's education. Every Saturday evening and Sunday he went with Natasha to the nearest church, and both of them bought consecrated candles and lit them in front of the sacred ikons. While Vassily Andreyevitch stayed with Natasha he interested himself in the housekeeping, went over her household books, inquired into everything that had happened during his absence, settled all the accounts, went himself to the butcher to get a good shoulder of beef for the dinner, and showed great zeal in chopping fire-wood.

They had already two children, the elder of whom was five. If she did anything particularly naughty, Vassily Andreyevitch would gravely and soberly lay her across his knee and show her what it meant to have a father. Before other people he and Natasha always called themselves man and wife. And when he was with her he actually felt like a real husband and father, and that filled him with joy. There was only one shadow on his and Natasha's happiness—that their life together was not blessed by the church. Often they considered what stratagem they could employ to obtain the priest's blessing . . .

As the train rushed on towards Moscow, Vassily Andreyevitch

had the feeling that he was nearing his home; a genuine feeling of domestic happiness and peace filled him. His illegitimate wife would wash him clean of the sinful life that he led with his legitimate one. All that life sank behind him now and he thought only of his happiness, of Natasha's clean dwelling, of her rosy sumptuous body, of the healthy, round-cheeked children that she had borne him....

It was more than three months since he had last seen her and the children, for that summer there had been many things to do before the harvest was at last safely under cover; he had also to put up with a great deal from the peasants, who refused to work as they had done formerly. Swearing at them had been of no use, and the village magistrate, too, had been less amenable than usual; the only recourse was to adopt different methods, to be sly and politic—and Vassily Andreyevitch was not cut out for that.

Hitherto he had had only one means of bringing his peasants to book: he would draw up his eyebrows and twirl up his huge mustache. That had almost always sufficed to bring them to heel. But the times were bad, and during this harvest the peasants had made his life a burden to him. Now, however, all the disagreeable things he had had to endure would have a rich reward; for soon, soon he would see Natasha again. He was filled with actual hunger for her: "And she, poor thing, must be longing to see me, too. I'm dying to see whether her summer holiday has done her good. She's certain to have got stouter—and I hope she has! It suits Natasha to be a bit plump!"

This idea gave Vassily Andreyevitch such pleasure that he smacked his lips.

"And, please God, the children will be flourishing, too. They're certain to have grown out of their clothes! The boy will be going to school now. And Natasha is sure to have everything in apple-pie order for my arrival, the house will be swept and scrubbed." He could see the night-cap that Natasha had embroidered for him hanging on one of the bed-posts; his slippers would be standing as usual in front of the commode. "Oh, Natasha is a good housewife! Everything must be in its place in her house. When I am not there everything is kept in readiness for me."

Every time he came she had prepared a surprise for him; once she had embroidered his name on a pillow "Vassily Andreyevitch," and the last time she had made him a warm dressing-gown. "What can she have in store for me this time? A sly wench, Natasha, she knows how to steal into my heart! Just do it, Natasha, I've nothing against that! And if only the dear Lord would grant us the priest's blessing, so that we may live together without sin. . . ."

He thought of the pickled pig that he had brought with him from the village, sewn in a sack: "That'll please her! It will taste lovely flavored with herbs!" And while his thoughts were still lingering on the pickled pig the train stopped in Moscow station.

Vassily Andreyevitch shouted for a porter, but in vain—there was no porter to be seen! He leaned out through the window and looked round him in annoyance: then he suddenly noticed all the people on the platform making pell-mell for the exit.

He called to those who were hurrying past him: "What has happened, friends? What has happened?"

No answer. Everybody was rushing for the exit, carrying luggage.

"But tell me what has happened, friends?" Vassily kept shouting in an almost imploring voice.

"The Bolsheviks . . ." some one shouted back and hurried on again.

Vassily Andreyevitch seized his luggage, ran after the other passengers, infected by the general panic, and pushed his way towards the exit. When he emerged on the square before the station he managed to secure the last droshky, over which several other passengers were already quarreling. He hastily flung his luggage into it, got in himself and shouted to the driver:

"Petersburg Chaussee!"

"I can't drive you there, it's impossible!"

"What has happened?"

"Why, have you been living in the moon, sir? The Bolsheviks have seized Petersburg, and they'll be in Moscow any day now."

"Then drive straight to the Hotel Metropole."

"That will cost you a twenty note today."

"Drive on."

As he was rolling through the panic-stricken almost empty streets,

Vassily Andreyevitch turned to the driver: "Tell me, who are these Bolsheviks?"

"Oh, well—I really don't know myself, sir."

CHAPTER II

THE HOTEL METROPOLE

AFTER the events of July, 1917, when the "German agents" (as the Bolshevist revolutionists who had come over the frontier in sealed German trains were popularly called) had made a sudden bid for power and General Kornilov's sally on Petersburg had failed, the more solid and wealthy classes had gradually left the capital and settled in Moscow.

Petersburg was at that time regarded as a sick town which had been seized by a dangerous malady, and whose ultimate fate was uncertain; and all those who could not keep up with the seven-league strides of the revolution and were ignorant where that furious advance into a dark future would end, fled from the dangerously infected town to the heart of Mother Russia. The very sound of the name "Moscow" awoke trust and a sense of security. So the inaugural meeting of the syndicate which called itself "New Russia" was arranged to take place at the end of October in the great marble hall of the Hotel Metropole in Moscow.

The syndicate was planned as the nucleus of a great industrial concern. Since the beginning of the revolution financial circles had become aware of a gradual withdrawal of foreign capital from Russian enterprises. It was known that the house of Rothschild had dropped its shares in Russian petrol and induced a number of associated Russian capitalists to do the same. Soon after that it became known that several Russian financiers had transferred their capital to foreign banks and industrial concerns. A financial scare followed, which was camouflaged for the time being, however, by the excellent business opportunities that the war had brought with it, and the sympathy that the revolution seemed to have awakened in America, which at that time was just making up its mind definitely to join the Allies (that sympathy in turn opened up immense opportunities for loans on a large scale). At this point the firm of Mirkin in Petersburg, the influential timber and banking concern, which had always been predominantly Russian, had a daring and happy inspiration. Old Gabriel Haimovitch Mirkin summoned a small gathering composed of his intimate friends and fellow directors, among whom was naturally included the celebrated advocate Solomon Halperin, who had once been on the point of becoming Mirkin junior's father-in-law, but was now Mirkin senior's. Gabriel Mirkin with his usual keen practical judgment made it convincingly clear to the gathering that now, when foreign capital was showing a tendency to withdraw from Russia, was the very moment to get the great Russian industrial concerns, which had for so long been exploited by foreigners, into Russian hands.

Mirkin's wisdom and experience and Halperin's patriotic rhetoric carried away the great magnates who were present, among whom, in accordance with the liberal temper of the time, Jews and Christians were to be found together. A syndicate was formed, which in all secrecy sent an emissary to London, and there secured the great iron mines of Michailovka, which had been exploited by an English Company ever since the time of Nicholas I. Made nervous by the "anarchistic tendencies" produced in the Russian people by the revolution, the English company let the new syndicate have the iron mines at a comparatively low price. The next step was to give the Russian masses an opportunity to participate, in accordance with the spirit of the new era, in the concern. For this purpose the "New Russia" syndicate resolved to issue shares at a low price to the extent of several hundred million roubles, so that in the words of that famous liberal, Solomon Halperin, "the great mass of the Russian people might be given an opportunity to enjoy the fruits of revolution."

The first general meeting of the "New Russia" Syndicate was to be held at twelve o'clock noon on the twenty-fifth of October, 1917, in the marble hall of the Hotel Metropole.

The chief promoters of the company already had been in Moscow for several days, for it had to be settled who was to have the predominant influence. "Who is to hold the shares and to what extent?" that was the crucial question. And for almost a week there had been active bargaining and haggling in the various rooms of the Metropole. Naturally all those interested in the new company were staying in the hotel itself, and could quickly get in touch with one another whenever it was necessary.

Accordingly the advocate Halperin and old Mirkin, his son-in-law, had also been in the Hotel Metropole for some time. Both had been somewhat affected by the war years and the recent upheavals; their hair had grown visibly grayer; yet they were well-nourished (for Nina looked after them splendidly), filled with confidence in the happy age that was beginning for Russia in general and themselves in particular (in spite of the obstacles and difficulties which the extreme left wing might possibly cause the new Russia), and tanned with the sun after their long summer stay in a comfortable health resort in the Caucasus, from which they had only recently returned. So they were in the best spirits and on the best terms with each other.

The celebrated advocate's interest in the new concern was a purely patriotic one. He insisted on emphasizing this fact at every opportunity, so as to leave no doubt that his sole object was to banish from the country all the foreign capital with which it had been flooded under the old régime. He left his son-in-law to settle with the other main shareholders the extent of his own share in the company, as well as his salary as a director on the board of management. He was like one of those rabbis who concern themselves only with their clients' petitions, but leave the reception of the ensuing rewards to their secretaries . . .

On the day that the solemn inauguration of the company was to take place (the advocate had undertaken to introduce it with a speech stressing the significance of the step), the Moscow morning papers came out with the disturbing news that the "German emissaries" had, during the night of October 24th and 25th, attempted a new stroke in the capital similar to the one that had been unsuccessful in July, and had occupied the railways and bridges. "The Provisional Government, however, is master of the situation," the papers confidently asserted.

Only the scrappiest reports had arrived from the capital of what had actually happened. The papers, therefore, could devote the greater amount of space to violent denunciations of the ringleaders in Petersburg, and they demanded the setting up of a "Committee against the general danger" which would deal sharply with any attempt that the Bolsheviks might make to seize the reins in Moscow.

Solomon Ossipovitch Halperin's morning paper was brought to his room in the hotel as usual with his samovar. As he read the reports, he grew so agitated that his glasses slipped from his sharp nose. Rage seethed within him. He could scarcely give himself time to throw on his clothes. With his hair in wild confusion he hurried to his son-in-law's room, but Gabriel Mirkin was no longer there. His newspaper in one hand, his glasses in the other, the advocate rushed with youthful haste down the stairs and into the hall of the hotel, and pushed his way through the excited crowd into the restaurant. There he found his son-in-law at last. Mirkin was sitting at his breakfast; the well-known magnate Koropotkin was with him.

"Have you read this, gentlemen? What have you to say to this? It's about the last straw, on top of our defeat on the Galician front! How can we face our allies after this for very shame? What will the world say? These people are a shame and a disgrace to revolutionary Russia!" cried the lawyer giving free vent to his indignation. There were red spots on his sharp cheek-bones, and his hair, rising wildly from his head, was like a barbed wire entanglement.

"Now, no excitement, Solomon Ossipovitch! It's bad for your liver—the doctor has impressed that upon you particularly. Your cure in Kislovodsk will go for nothing if you don't take care," Gabriel Mirkin calmly warned him.

Astonished at such coolness, the advocate stared long at him, but then burst out again:

"How can you take it so calmly? These people smuggle themselves into Russia with Germany's help and destroy everything we have achieved! It's German money that calls the tune, believe me! And these people call themselves revolutionists! How can you look on calmly? I am surprised at your indifference, Gabriel Haimovitch."

"And what good will you do by getting excited? You'll only damage your liver and undermine your health," retorted Gabriel Mirkin with unshaken composure. "Thank God we've left our wives and children in the Caucasus!"

"My liver, my health! It's Russia that is at stake! Gabriel Haimovitch, I can't stay here a moment longer: I must return to Petersburg at once! I'm very sorry I won't be able to be present at the meeting today—but Russia and the revolution are in danger! The Government needs me at this dark hour." Thereupon the lawyer took a few steps towards the door, but stopped when Gabriel Mirkin called after him:

"Where are you off to, Solomon Ossipovitch? Petersburg has been seized by the Reds."

"What? Petersburg seized by the Reds? And you say that quite calmly! No, I can't stay here another moment! The only thing left now is to get a rifle! Yes, get a rifle, and save the revolution!"

"There will be enough saviors of the revolution without you! And as for carrying a rifle, you're too old. Calm yourself, Solomon Ossipovitch!—Sit down with us.—Have you had your coffee yet?—Oh, of course—I've quite forgotten to introduce you gentlemen.—You've heard of my friend Koropotkin, of course, Michail Nikolayevitch Koropotkin of the Industrial Bank, one of the chief shareholders in 'New Russia.' Do sit down, Solomon Ossipovitch—they'll manage all right in Petersburg without us! We're needed for something else." Old Mirkin took his agitated father-in-law politely but firmly by the arm and made him sit down at the table where breakfast was set out.

"I'm surprised at your calmness, Gabriel Haimovitch!" The lawyer had not yet regained his composure, although, in obedience to Mirkin's gentle insistence, he remained seated. "Who can talk of business affairs now? Who can think of breakfast now?" and he pushed away contemptuously the coffee cup that Mirkin had set in front of him. "Civil war is starting: the Government is in danger! Russia, the revolution, are at stake! No, I can't go on quietly sitting here. I feel that they need me. I must go out into the street at least!" He tried to get up.

But Mirkin took him firmly by the arm and pushed him back into his chair.

"Solomon Ossipovitch, don't be childish!" Mirkin now assumed a severe tone. "Your behavior will only create a panic among the other people here. We can do nothing. Russia is off the rails, it's like a roundabout that's got beyond control, and we must prepare to live as we can while it's spinning round. Either the government will manage to deal with this business without us, or it won't manage to deal with it at all—

and in that case everything will go to the devil! Meanwhile we have *our* affairs to see to! Even while a ship is sinking people have to attend to their business."

The advocate was more daunted by the grave decisive tone in which Mirkin spoke than by his words, and he allowed himself to be persuaded like a child. He pettishly pulled the coffee cup towards him that he had pushed away before, hastily poured coffee into it and murmured with a hopeless gesture:

"Poor Russia! What will you have to put up with next! But we'll endure it, we'll endure everything that may come!" And he put the cup to his lips at last.

At that moment he heard a voice which seemed to come, not from his companions, but from behind his chair: "You'll admit now, Solómon Ossipovitch, that they would have known how to settle these people much more quickly under the old régime."

The lawyer pushed away his cup again in indignant agitation, while he regarded the man who dared to utter these horrifying words. It was Koropotkin.

It was not a human shape that Halperin saw, but a formless mass. A black, motionless, shapeless something showed above the table, and seemed to spread out on all sides. The first thing one could recognize in that mass was an enormous belly, that quivered and swung from side to side in front of the rest—but, what was worse, all the expression seemed to have vanished from the creature's face and settled into his prodigious globular belly. His eyes were not in his face, but in his belly. It may sound like an exaggeration—but that belly could laugh, actually laugh. The man's face was as impassive as a death mask, a brownish lump of flesh with no very definite features. But in compensation for that, his belly was lively and expressive; it quivered like a huge fish, expanded and contracted again, trembled, twitched, laughed, cut a wry grimace, in obedience to the momentary situation or the man's passing mood. The phrase "the old régime," pronounced by Koropotkin's lips, his belly accompanied with an expressive quiver and a significant smile. The lawyer guessed far more clearly from that belly smile than from the words themselves the contempt that this man felt for the new régime.

Halperin could not tolerate that. He felt partly responsible for the new régime. He took at its face value the famous motto: L'Étât, c'est moi." So he drew himself up, lifted his right hand impressively, not forgetting to raise two fingers as he always did when he came to some effective passage in his speeches before the courts, and retorted in a theatrical tone:

"Nobody, whether he belongs to the right wing or the left, will ever induce us to return to the methods of the old régime! The old régime is dead! And the revolution will never besmirch its glorious name with such methods! *We* shall see to that!"

Meanwhile the business of the hotel went on as usual; indeed the place was busier than was usual at that time of the day. For the morning of October 25th had brought a great rush of new guests to the hotel. The regular train service was still running, and in the great busy square in front of the hotel a succession of droshkies drawn by powerful gleaming black horses, stopped, one after another, bringing guests and trunks from the stations. The disquieting newspaper reports and the nervous atmosphere they produced had alarmed and terrified many a peaceable Moscow bourgeois; and a number of them who lived near the working-class quarter decided to move for a few days, until peace was restored again, to the Hotel Metropole, so as to be nearer the center of the town.

The manager and his staff naturally had their hands full making their excuses to the throngs of new guests who streamed to the already overcrowded hotel and reserving a little accommodation for important arrivals and old customers who could hardly be refused. Everybody was on edge and talked louder and more excitedly than usual. An elegantly-clad gentleman of a very energetic disposition had rushed in early in the morning, armed with a huge bouquet, and inquiring for a lady. He was by no means satisfied with the cautiously-worded information he received that the lady was not in the hotel. His bouquet in one hand, a telegram in the other, he demanded in a loud voice that the lady should be produced, and behaved as though he suspected the hotel management of having devoured her. With sweat running down their faces the hotel clerks went through the whole register of visitors; the attendants ran up and down the carpeted stairs looking for the lady or someone with a similar name. Soon the powerful voice of the temperamental gentleman attracted the attention of the other guests: for he insisted with extraordinary obstinacy on seeing his lady, not merely in words and by pointing to the telegram that he held in his hand, but also by gesticulating with his bouquet, so that the flowers peeped out of their paper wrapping like frightened birds terrified for their lives . . . and, indeed, the poor things finally came to a sad end.

In a little while Vassily Andreyevitch, whom we have already met on his journey to Moscow, also drove up; trembling with apprehension and lack of sleep, he arrived accompanied by his pig in a poke. There was no room ready for him. Thereupon he sat down in the hotel office on his pickled pig and declared that he would not stir from the spot until a bed was found for him in a bathroom, or, if that could not be managed, in one of the passages, he didn't care what happened. At last a corner was found for him where he and his pickled pig were accommodated. They were both in need of it.

The entrance hall of the hotel was very busy. Moscow merchants with brightly polished top-boots, wearing Prince Albert coats from which emerged high-necked Russian shirts, stamped heavily to and fro. Ladies of suspicious character, exuding penetrating scents, made their way through the tables in the dining-room and the breakfast-room, which were almost exclusively occupied by men; thick clouds of cigar and cigarette smoke filled these rooms and here and there a hoarse throat already, at that early hour, exhaled the reek of vodka. Waiters in white jackets and aprons hurried with full plates from the kitchen to the dining-room and back again: in a word, the morning was like any other morning, except that it was busier than was usual at that time of the day. It was almost unthinkable that any physical power existed capable of putting a stop, on that fresh and beautiful autumn day, to the customary rhythm of all that busy life with its almost automatic progression.

The reports in the newspapers about the events in the capital, the rumors about the Moscow Revolutionary Committee that were going from mouth to mouth, seemed to concern some foreign city and to have no connection with the life inside the hotel. . . .

"If the Provisional Government asks me, they should hand over the power to these people! Then we would see what these Bolshevist gentlemen are capable of. They wouldn't last out twenty-four hours. . . ." With these words the tea magnate Rosamin, who had also been invited to the inaugural meeting, approached Gabriel Mirkin's table. He looked as though he had slept well, and was immaculately dressed and groomed. He made a custom of letting nothing excite him too much and pedantically observed his doctor's orders: "Take nothing too much to heart." Even the words with which he greeted the gentlemen sitting at the table he uttered, true to his guiding rule, in a voice quite devoid of any trace of agitation, the voice of a detached spectator, as though the whole business did not concern him in the least; and he emphasized this fact by complacently stroking his thin silky beard with his fingers.

"It's easy for him to talk. He's transferred his head office to London, his money is already safely lodged in American banks, and his tea grows in China. But everything that we possess is here!" cried the advocate, who had found again his old energy. "Twenty-four hours, you say? In that twenty-four hours these people will bring Russia to ruin!"

"It hasn't come to that yet, and there's no good in getting excited!" Gabriel Mirkin said soothingly to his father-in-law. "The Russian army is still on the front, and the inland garrisons are strong enough. And you're only spoiling your liver, Solomon Ossipovitch. . . ."

"The burgomaster has telegraphed to all the towns in the province of Moscow to come to the defense of the city. Kerensky is with General Krassnov. Cossack transports have been summoned from the front. The whole business will soon be settled. . . ."

"Young man, where did you get this news from?" The lawyer seized the speaker by the arm; he was an elegantly dressed young gentleman, scented like a woman.

"That is my secret—most esteemed Solomon Ossipovitch," replied the young man, regarding his manicured finger nails with an air of mystery.

But before Halperin could find time to reward the strange gentleman with a few kind words for the pleasure the news had given him, he felt Mirkin's strong hand tugging vigorously at his sleeve:

"Don't have anything to do with him!"

Halperin gazed in astonishment at his son-in-law.

"My news will be very useful to you yet, take my word for that, Gabriel Haimovitch," the young man flung at the table and hastily disappeared.

"That's the sharper Misha 'Molodyetz.' He's ferreted out information about our meeting and followed us. But it won't do him any good," Mirkin explained to the lawyer. "Well, it's getting near time for us to be stirring. It isn't long to twelve."

"Do you really still think of holding the meeting, now, at a time like this?" asked the lawyer in amazement. "God knows my heart won't be in it!"

"Yes, now, especially now! And we expect you, you, Solomon Ossipovitch, to say some inspiring words to us to fortify our hearts in this critical hour."

"Perhaps you're right. Now, especially now!" Halperin repeated. Thereupon he rose and went to his room to prepare himself for his solemn appearance before the important inaugural gathering.

CHAPTER III

NOAH'S ARK

EVERYBODY was agreed that in his opening speech at the solemn inauguration of the "New Russia" Syndicate in the Hotel Metropole the celebrated advocate would surpass himself.

At the stroke of twelve the shareholders were present in full force, in spite of the disturbed times and the dark news from the capital. It was a brilliant gathering where met the best-known and most reliable names, the most highly esteemed leaders of Russian finance and industry.

Apart from the figures we already know there were present Goldstein, the great petrol magnate, Koropotkin, president of the Industrial Bank, and Arkasov and Meyersohn of the Eastern Bank, personages of sufficient weight to find a hearing. The advocate's address was of a semi-official character. He claimed to speak in the name of "influential personages," and expressly emphasized the fact that, while he had no direct instructions, yet he could, if necessary, back up his statements by the utterances of these influential personages, which he had at first hand.

His speech convinced the magnates gathered together that they were predestined to fulfill a patriotic duty of the first importance, namely to deliver Russian industry out of the clutches of foreign capital, into which it had been betrayed recklessly under the Czarist régime; it was "a duty of the revolution" to enlist the great Russian masses in the industrial regeneration of the country:

"Let us bring the treasures of the Russian soil, with which God and Nature have so richly endowed us," he exclaimed melodramatically, "into the poorest Russian houses! Let us bring our people oil from the Caucasian oil fields, iron from the Krivoyrog iron mines, silver from Baikal! In fraternally sharing your profits with the masses, you will put an end to this fratricidal butchery in the streets. That is the only way in which the age-long conflict between capital and labor can be reconciled; that is our socialism! And Russia must set the example, Russia must be the forerunner of the whole world in this respect. Just as we have abolished despotism in the State, so we must abolish it in industry!"

With that impressive peroration Halperin concluded his speech.

The enthusiastic applause that followed his brilliant speech had not yet died away, and the gathering was still cautiously reflecting how his words could be translated into action—when outside in the square scattered shots rang out. The first bullets hit the plump bottoms of the charming Cupids that decorated the beautiful rococo fountain in the square.

They were the first shots fired by the Red Guards of the Moscow Revolutionary Committee as they emerged from the Governor's Palace to seize the most important strategic points in the city. They were scattering fanwise in the center of the town, to wreck the offices of the bourgeois newspapers.

An organized committee of defense did not yet exist in Moscow. Consequently the burgomaster called out the city militia, supported by the cadets from the military college, to drive back the Red troops. The first clash came in the Theater Square outside the hotel, which both parties wished to occupy. An irregular firing broke out.

These first shots came as a thunder-clap to the people gathered in the marble hall. Mirkin, who was in the chair, nervously rang the bell in front of him, but in vain. The majority of the meeting, the famous advocate at their head, hastened to the great windows and, hidden behind the heavy curtains, peered down into the square. There was not much to be seen there. The square, usually so busy, was suddenly as deserted as in the early morning or on a great holiday: far and wide not a droshky, not a horse, not a human being was to be seen. In solitary state the plump bronze Cupids sat perched on the edge of the fountain. Opposite, at the other end of the great square, the bronze horses stood motionlessly on the roof of the brick-red Great Theater.

Only behind the pillars in front of the theater could any movement be seen: small groups of men were crouching against the walls there, trying to find cover. The separate groups could be clearly distinguished, for in addition to the dark gray of workmen's clothes, one could make out soldiers in field gray and blue sailors' uniforms. And the fact that civilians and soldiers were fighting side by side simultaneously awoke in the watchers delight and terror. To see soldiers and civilians on the same side was a sight so strange, so unprecedented, that with a clap it brought home to the watchers at the windows the gravity of the moment and the uncertainty of the future.

"Where's my overcoat? Where's my hat? My overcoat! My hat!" the celebrated advocate suddenly shouted to no one in particular; obviously he had quite forgotten where he was. "I must go out there, they need me!" he almost screamed.

"Solomon Ossipovitch, where are you going? You'll get killed if you go out there!" Someone nervously seized him by the arm.

The chairman energetically rang his bell again, but in vain. The meeting was nervous. The more cool-headed, such as Goldstein, the petrol king, and the bankers Koropotkin and Meyersohn, as well as some of the Christian shareholders, had remained calmly sitting in their chairs. But the tea magnate Rosamin jumped up. His plump, well-nourished face suddenly looked green and fallen in, and great dark brown rings had appeared under his eyes. He cried in amazement:

"The position is really serious!"

"Gentlemen, I implore you to keep your seats! The meeting is not yet adjourned! The meeting is not yet adjourned!" The chairman obstinately went on repeating the familiar phrase and seemed incapable of getting away from it.

But the first one to lose his head and raise a general panic by his behavior was the celebrated advocate himself. He could not restrain his agitation and kept on shouting:

"My overcoat! My hat! Gentlemen, let us arm ourselves and sally out!"

Suddenly there was a loud dull crash, somewhat like a short peal of thunder. Simultaneously there came the sound of splintering glass. A number of window panes had fallen from their frames.

"Get away from the window!" A confusion of frightened voices arose. And more than one reverend gray head in the company vanished hastily behind chairs and tables, where they sought cover.

The advocate with a grand gesture rose to his full height. He looked taller than usual and resembled a startled wild beast emerging from a thicket. His disordered hair stood up defiantly, his eyes glittered; stretching out his thin arms he shouted hysterically: "I can't stay here any longer!" With that he made hastily for the door.

But someone abruptly stopped him; it was Gabriel Mirkin, who was also alarmed, but, as in every emergency, had kept his composure:

"Where are you going? Where are you going?" He roughly took Halperin by the shoulders and forced him into a chair.

The door opened. The elegant hotel manager entered, clad as usual in his faultless tail coat, and bowed to the pale and frightened company:

"Gentlemen," he began in a calm voice, "fighting has broken out in the streets. The Bolshevists are trying to seize the square outside. Meanwhile our gallant militia and our brave young cadets are defending it. The commander of our gallant defenders has given me express orders to clear my guests out of their rooms during the action and accommodate them in the basement—otherwise he cannot vouch for their lives. I beg you, therefore, gentlemen, to proceed to the billiard-room. We have cleared it and arranged it as well as we can under the circumstances for our guests' reception. You will not have to stay there very long—just until our gallant defenders have rid the square of the rioters. I beg you to follow me, gentlemen. This room must be vacated and locked."

"Jamais!" Halperin's dauntless voice could be heard. "Hide from these people! Only over my dead body. . . ."

But two strong hands seized the advocate and forced him to follow the manager.

The elegant and spacious billiard-room in the basement occupied, along with the side rooms appertaining to it, the whole length and breadth of the great hotel.

As the shareholders of the New Russia Syndicate descended the stairs, they encountered other hotel guests hurrying from the various floors bearing with them their most immediately valuable belongings.

Some were carrying hand bags, jewel cases, toilet requisites, night attire; others—the majority of them women—were carrying pet dogs, mainly Pekinese; several elderly women had plump cats in their arms, a few were actually equipped with cages containing parrots and canaries; some laughed shrilly, others were crying; among the crowd of dejected faces were sprinkled a few looking strangely elated. All the guests had been swept out of their normal course of life and infected by the general hysterical panic.

As the shareholders accompanied by the advocate—who was still struggling, though with considerably decreased energy, to escape from the firm clutch of his escort—reached the billiard-room, the hotel staff were hastily removing the huge billiard-tables and bringing in armchairs and sofas for the reception of the ladies and basket-chairs and small tables for the gentlemen. In such situations the same qualities are evinced by people of the highest and most elegant breeding as by the poorest and most wretched; everybody, the ladies in particular, thought of nothing but how to occupy as much space as possible and monopolize the most comfortable of the seats. At first good manners prevailed, but the need of the moment soon made everybody forget the maxims of their upbringing and minor battles for the remaining places presently took place. . . .

One never has an adequate conception of the number of human beings and objects that a huge hotel houses in its countless rooms, each unknown to the others. In normal circumstances it resembles, regarded from outside, a single banknote or, say, a check for a big sum, which one knows to represent so and so many thousand roubles, although it is very simple and convenient to handle and dispose of. The hotel now, however, looked as if that check had been fully cashed in nothing but copper or nickel coins, which were so countless that they rolled away on all sides and could not be kept in hand. A whole town streamed into the billiard-room. New arrivals appeared every moment and those who had already taken possession of places regarded with fear and alarm this immigration of fresh tribes: "When *will* this procession ever stop?" And among the arrivals were the strangest specimens of humanity, the most queer types! All Russia seemed to have settled in the billiard-room. There appeared not merely young and old, men and women, but other creatures as well, creatures belonging to some third species, for whom there is no name, although they exist.

A gentleman and a lady entered arm in arm, accompanied by a serving man carrying a traveling case in one hand and a cage with a parrot in the other. The couple advanced in a solemn measured tread, as if they were going to some imposing church service. The gentleman, who was very tall, looked as though he had swallowed a ram-rod. Not for a moment did he lose his stiff bearing and he neither hastened nor lengthened his step. In the chaos that reigned the appearance of this figure had an extraordinarily reassuring effect, and his measured ceremonious bearing calmed down the more excited. For even in these abnormal conditions he retained a consciousness of his dignity as a human being, begged with exquisite politeness that a place might be made for his wife on a sofa, and when she was seated stationed himself behind her as if he were attending a fashionable reception. The serving man, for his part, posted himself behind his master with calm and respectful bearing.

A regular boarder at the hotel, who had occupied the same room for many years, was now led in by her maid. She looked like the wife of a general, or the widow of a rich land-proprietor. Her face twitched hysterically and she groaned aloud. A countless collection of large and small cushions was borne behind her; when she had found a place, the maid ceremoniously deposited the cushions in turn on the seat, and behind her back and head, until, enthroned high above all the others, the old lady seemed almost to be floating in the air.

A charming young lady enveloped in a cloud of perfume, obviously a cabaret singer or a cocotte, arrived in semi-deshabille, escorted by a whole regiment of elegant young men of the dandy type, who carried her bags and pet dogs; she tripped gayly into the room, as though she were going to a picnic, and her clear laughter—greatly to the indignation of the more respectable ladies—trilled continuously through the room.

An hysterical, moody young wife, with a headache and a wet bandage round her head, was led in by her exhausted husband. His very appearance proclaimed how heavily the yoke of matrimony weighed upon him. His pale, worn face almost implored pity and help. Without ceasing he tried to comfort his wife, holding smelling salts to her nose and laying wet handkerchiefs on her brow. With piteous glances he besought someone to give his wife a seat, and got one, also, since everybody felt sorry for him.

A handsome young man in top-boots, a dress coat, and a dark-colored, high-necked Russian shirt appeared, followed by a whole harem. He had the look of a provincial white slaver, and the way, too, in which he treated his companions pointed to that profession. With his fists he conquered a whole sofa for his harem and when he encountered resistance pushed up his sleeves and assumed a pugilistic attitude.

There arrived superannuated generals in faded uniforms with frayed epaulettes, their breasts covered with orders; they could not refrain from giving loud expression to their contempt for the new régime. One could see high State officials with aristocratic airs; and the high stiff collars of diplomatists; they took no pains to conceal their malicious, cattish delight at the discomfiture of the Provisional Government.

A plump, comfortable, red-cheeked old gentleman set himself zealously to cheer the ladies by facetious remarks and to raise their dejected spirits by ambiguous stories; and the ladies showed their appreciation by loud bursts of laughter. An extraordinarily polite and amiable young man, fair-haired, with an elegantly curling mustache and dazzling white shirt cuffs, evidently regarded it as his special duty to make himself useful to the ladies and see to their comfort. He begged the gentlemen to give up the upholstered chairs to the ladies, brought footstools for the older ladies, and kept on asking the younger ones if there was anything they required, though, in the chaos that reigned at the beginning it would have been difficult, indeed impossible, to fulfill their manifold requests and needs. But the young man was in perpetual motion, nevertheless, kept running excitedly to and fro, and so had a constant occupation.

The orderlies of the old generals fought with the civilians' servants for comfortable seats for their masters. Vendors from the provinces sat in dark corners and with apprehensive faces verified that their money and papers were still safe in their breast pockets. The room was like a veritable Babel. . . .

Meanwhile it had become clear that it was urgently necessary to establish a little order, and above all to end the war that had broken out among the domestic animals. For the dogs were chasing the cats, and both were attacking the canaries and parrots which belonged to the various ladies. Soon the room was filled with the furious barking of dogs, the shrill, ear-piercing mewing of cats, the angry screaming of parrots, and the wretched twittering and wing-beating of the canaries in their cages.

The ladies pressed their darlings protectingly to their bosoms and loudly reproached the men for not taking the part of their poor helpless pets as men should. But, whenever a man intervened on the side of one dog, the cavalier of the lady who owned the opposing dog entered the fray in his turn. Those who had no dogs raised a protest against the barking and the din. So the quarrel spread and spread and finally developed into a universal war of all against all. An end could be put to this confusion only by reducing the animals to order.

An elderly gentleman—by his looks a Jew, who obviously had no particular understanding or love for animals—made the proposal that the quadrupeds should be removed, since they only caused confusion and aroused contention among the "Citizens of this tiny Republic" (such was his expression). In accordance with the spirit of the time this proposal was put to the vote and passed by a majority.

Now followed touching and heart-breaking farewell scenes, accompanied by passionate caresses and tender endearments, bringing tears to the eyes of many a spectator. At last peace was established in the billiard-room.

As often happens in such cases, the hotel guests now felt that they were extraordinarily hungry. It was as if their stomachs had instinctively guessed the approaching danger far sooner than they did themselves, and were resolved to lay in food for the bad times that were coming. And now the guests were insatiable; the whole staff of waiters and assistant waiters in the huge hotel were kept constantly employed in carrying plates of sandwiches, cold roast beef, salads of all kinds, gherkins, pickled mushrooms, caviar, smoked fish, into the billiard-room.

The more they ate, the stronger grew their appetites. Gentlemen of the most polite manners actually fought for the dishes and victoriously bore their trophies to their famishing wives. Only when they were assured that the hotel had abundant provisions, sufficient, indeed, to hold out during a siege of several days, only when the waiters presented them with the bills for what they had consumed, the price for which the manager, taking the extraordinary state of things into consideration, had multiplied several times over, did their hunger relax somewhat. They resolved to nurse their appetites until dinner time.

But at least eating together had somewhat allayed their agitation, and nerves that had been set on edge by the unpleasant episode of the dogs began to calm down again. People started to make each other's acquaintance, and presently the common situation in which they all found themselves created among them almost a family feeling.

CHAPTER IV

THE BOLSHEVIKS ARE SUMMONED FOR TRIAL

A LITTLE later such a cheerful and animated atmosphere prevailed in the billiard-room that a chance observer might have thought that the people assembled there had not been thrown together fortuitously, by the pressure of events, but were voluntarily attending a social reception, a rout, let us say. All that was lacking was evening dress.

The national Russian warmth of feeling, but still more perhaps a few glasses of vodka, soon established such warm relations between the guests that they all felt like old acquaintances. Not only women, men, also, were perpetually embracing and kissing each other every few minutes, swearing eternal friendships and clapping one another familiarly on the back.

Naturally enough the profound gravity of the moment, their patriotic emotions, their mutual love for Russia and hatred of the common foe who was trying with German gold to strangle the revolution and all it had achieved, bound them together still more firmly.

Soon an animated, almost violent debate on the aims of the Bolsheviks was in progress.

No one, of course, took seriously their attempt to seize power, and everybody was convinced that the "Reds" would never be able to hold out. Some regarded the whole business as an electoral dodge of the Bolsheviks, an attempt to gain as many seats as possible in the republican constituent assembly, which was shortly to hold its first session.

A young man in a student's cap (he kept it on ostentatiously, though all the other men were bareheaded, but his clothes and appearance were more like those of a successful profiteer than of a poor student) kept on repeating, so loudly that everybody could hear him, that he had just returned from Siberia, liberated by the revolution, and was afraid of being sent back there again, all through the Bolsheviks' fault. "I've had enough of Siberia!" he cried. "I won't go back there again!"

The high spirits that infected everybody had also had a good effect on the famous advocate. His first attack of painful agitation soon passed; more, the gay and animated scene in the billiard-room poured oil on his fiery temperament, which quickly flamed up again.

His energy awoke anew and his social instinct imperiously sought for an outlet in action. He felt completely in his element—like a fish in water—and zealously set about organizing, in the spirit of the times, "the besieged garrison" (as he called the collection of people driven by necessity to take refuge in the billiard-room) and to transform that fortuitous gathering, as he put it, "into a social organism complete with all the functions essential to it."

With the help of a collaborator he formed a "Defense Committee." What the function of this committee was to be was not quite clear, it must be confessed, for nobody had any wish to intervene in the shooting-match between the Bolsheviks and the city militia that was now in full swing outside; besides, the officer defending the square would not have allowed any one to leave the hotel. But the committee was duly constituted, enrolled volunteers in the billiard-room and even called an ambulance corps into existence. And soon many of the ladies —particularly the younger and prettier ones—were wearing nurses' caps which they had improvised with their skilful hands out of wraps and shawls. It need hardly be mentioned that there was a Red Cross division as well, which all the older gentlemen felt in duty bound to join. And so most of the gentlemen wore arm bands or badges showing the division to which they belonged, while the women went about in nurses' caps, which made the young and pretty younger and prettier —and the old, still older and uglier.

But soon the committee found itself without an occupation. Yet Solomon Ossipovitch could not remain idle, and so he struck the brilliant idea of organizing a "People's Tribunal" to try the Bolsheviks, expose publicly their wretched crimes, and brand their names for all time in Russian history. But no one would act as counsel for the defense, for it was obviously difficult in such a gathering to find anybody who would stand up for the Bolsheviks.

Soon, however, this diversion proved quite unnecessary, for Comrade Galenko, after entering by force the offices of the bourgeois newspapers and smashing the setting machines, was routed by the city militia and the cadets from the Theater Square and driven back on the Governor's palace, which the Bolsheviks had made their headquarters. Street fighting was still going on sporadically, but in the square before the Hotel Metropole there reigned absolute peace.

And so the hotel manager permitted his guests to return to their rooms, although the city militia refused to allow them to leave the hotel, since there was still occasional firing in the streets. A number of the guests—the older and more timid—received the reassuring news with joy and took prompt advantage of it. The more belligerent—mainly young—had no great desire to return to their rooms, and secretly, indeed, were a little annoyed that this pleasantly exciting episode had passed so tamely and come to an end so soon.

They were keyed up to new emotions and excitements; besides, they had enjoyed the social life that had begun to unfold so interestingly in the billiard-room, and they were not willing to give it up again so quickly. Consequently the greater number of the guests remained in the billiard-room and the buffet; after all there was no other way in which one could pass the time, for one was forbidden to go out.

But soon the fraternal spirit produced by enforced proximity and the common peril vanished. The guests once more withdrew within their personal dignity.

The more exclusive among them, the rich land-proprietors, the one-time high State officials, the men about town, the beautiful young ladies with their hosts of admirers, who had lost their composure on the first threat of danger, regained their calm superiority when things became quiet, and kept their distance from all the more "suspicious" elements in the room.

As there was nothing, however, that they could do—they could not go out and they had no desire to seek their rooms—the guests adjourned to the little chambers off the billiard-room to sweeten the "siege" with champagne or cognac. Soon from all these rooms issued sounds of subdued laughter, women's merry shrieks, men's drunken voices. Never before had the waiters received such ample tips, never before had the hotel done so well as on that day—and never had the manager been so pleased by the good spirits of his guests as on that very noteworthy Moscow Wednesday, the twenty-fifth of October, counting by the old style.

A figure who contributed not a little to the general amity and merriment was the man who went under the name of Misha "Molodyetz" or "the financial genius," the pale young man dressed with exaggerated elegance whom we have already met.

The hotel was cut off from the outer world; and the Theater Square had meantime been occupied by the officers of the Moscow

Garrison, who had been posted there to prevent any attack on the Municipal Duma. To leave or to enter the hotel was alike impossible. But Misha was fully informed on everything that happened in the city and could tell in detail which strategic points the Bolsheviks had been able to hold and which they had been dislodged from; which important buildings and points were in the hands of the Duma and which had been conquered by the Reds.

He retailed information on the progress of the struggle from hour to hour. But he was not only exactly acquainted with all that was happening in Moscow: he seemed to have a private wireless connection with the whole world, or to receive his news by some other mysterious channel, perhaps it was the wind that brought it; for he knew all that was occurring in the capital and the provinces, how the soldiers at the front regarded the recent events, how the railways were functioning, which classes among the population and which socialist groups had declared for the Bolsheviks or repudiated them.

Everybody asked himself in astonishment where Misha could get his information, and all doubted its truth. Nevertheless they listened attentively to the bulletins which he issued, as it were, on the heels of the events, as for example:

"The Provisional Government is now besieged in the Winter Palace. . . . A Cossack Division is deploying from the front in the direction of Orska. . . ."

The usual comment was: "Oho, Misha is drawing the long bow again!" And yet they all longed for more, so as to satisfy their thirst for sensational news. When there is no clear water to be had, one has to put up with muddy—and so Misha's reports went from mouth to mouth. Soon every one turned to him when they wanted information on the state of affairs.

During the rest of the day and all evening Misha's "wireless station" kept on sending out reassuring and glad tidings: "The burgomaster has called a special meeting of all loyal elements in Moscow for tomorrow. . . . The burgomaster has appealed to all the town councils in the neighboring towns to mobilize their available resources for the defense of 'Little Mother Russia'; countless train-loads of volunteers are already on the way to Moscow. . . . The morale of the province is excellent. . . . The complete breakdown of the Bolshevik adventure is expected this very night. . . ."

As all the news given out by Misha was reassuring and in accordance with the desires and hopes of the hotel guests, he soon became a general favorite; the ladies in particular declared that he was a darling, and this made him a dangerous rival in the eyes of the younger gentlemen. "That nice Misha"—so he had been baptized—was in short worshiped by the fair sex, envied by the men, and soon became the cynosure of the company gathered in the billiard-room. People sought his acquaintance and even elderly and dignified gentlemen pressed his hand warmly and said affably: "It gives me great pleasure to make your acquaintance."

At every table he was invited to drink with the company: to his credit, however, it must be said that he refused all these invitations very politely but firmly. This heightened his personal prestige among the guests still more.

In the general good spirits that prevailed in the hotel only one group struck an inharmonious note by their obvious dejection. They held themselves completely apart from the others, sat by themselves and talked in subdued voices. The whole gravity of the situation was to be seen in their despondent faces.

This was the group of Jewish capitalists who had come to the Hotel Metropole to attend the first general meeting of the "New Russia" Syndicate: old Mirkin, Rosamin the tea magnate, and Goldstein the petroleum king from Baku. But while the latter two evinced a certain outward assurance at least, as if to imply that these recent happenings did not concern them, old Mirkin seemed to be quite broken. The whole weight of the heavy cloud that was gathering over Russia seemed to press on his shoulders. His face had suddenly turned a sickly yellow, his eyes had sunk behind their slack, dark-rimmed lids. Flaccid creases of skin hung from his cheeks and his neck, as if they had been suddenly deflated, and his impressive two-pointed beard, whose reddish fairness had until now fought triumphantly against old age, had turned gray. The great Gabriel Mirkin who had held himself so proudly was now bent and small, almost shrunken.

In vain the other two magnates argued with him in lowered

voices, telling him that it was not yet too late and that everything would "come right." He did not listen, but muttered to himself despondently, as if they were not there: "It isn't that; it isn't a question of property—no, it's a question of Russia, of my existence. All my life I have been building, and I thought I was building on firm ground. No storm, no upheaval could daunt me, for I trusted the foundations—do you understand?—the foundations. I firmly believed that beneath the surface rubbish there was rock that could withstand anything. But in reality there's nothing but rubbish, and everything will sink and vanish in it. . . ."

Rosamin, whose mind was occupied with the problem of how he would be able to continue his tea transport, which stretched from the remotest borders of China to his central depot, replied loudly, in a sort of chant, thinking all the time of his own interests: "We're surely bound to find some way of keeping in touch with foreign countries!"

"For what purpose?" asked Gabriel Mirkin.

"To put our capital in safety."

"That would be treason," retorted old Mirkin, grinding his teeth, which were still sound.

"But, but—treason to what?" cried the petroleum king.

"To Russia."

"To which Russia? If there will be a Russia at all, that's to say! I've always warned you, Gabriel Haimovitch, against staking everything on one card!"

"It's all the same to me which Russia it is," replied old Mirkin. "This is the only home I have, and I'm too old now to take my staff and wander elsewhere. And I don't regret it either that I've staked everything on one card—I believe in Russia."

"Oh, you Jews!" the cheerful voice of the lawyer suddenly broke in on their discussion; he bore down on their table arm in arm with a member of the new army of defense. "I'm ashamed of you. You're sitting here like hens waiting to have their necks wrung! The struggle hasn't properly begun yet, and you've lost heart already! It's the opposite with me: the battle gives me fresh powers. 'The storm is my steed, I ride it elate,'" he quoted from a Russian classic. "Don't set the others a bad example by being so downcast! Courage! Courage!" The famous lawyer was now bursting with energy and enthusiasm in sharp contrast to his earlier mood.

"If courage were the only thing needed to drive the Bolsheviks from the square, you wouldn't find us wanting!" interrupted the petroleum king.

"But we'll drive them out all right," Halperin went on. "Yes, we'll see who is the stronger! They're going to be had up for trial, yes, this very night!

"We've actually got a counsel for the defense," he went on, enraptured with his latest idea, and pointing to his colleague. "Here he stands! Fedor Arkadievitch Smirnov has taken on the ungrateful task, and is sacrificing himself for the general good. We shall brand them tonight for all time and relegate them to their fitting place in the history of Russia."

"Good! A regular casting out of devils that will be," observed the petroleum magnate with an ironical smile.

But Halperin did not hear this jeering remark. Arm in arm with his Christian colleague—obviously as a symbolic gesture demonstrating that in times of peril all must stand together—he went from table to table inviting the guests to attend the "Trial," where the fitting verdict on the rôle of the Bolsheviks in Russian history was to be pronounced once and for all.

Many tables responded to the invitation. People engaged good seats for themselves and thronged to the corner of the room where the hotel staff were improvising a tribune for the "judges" and the "jury." Suddenly the electric lights went out and everything was plunged in Egyptian darkness.

Immediately a panic broke out. The room was filled with the hysterical shrieks of women. Then electric pocket-torches flashed out here and there and voices from various points in the room strove to recall the guests to reason:

"Quiet there! Silence! The lights will soon come on again."

"What is it? What does it mean?"

And all eyes were turned on the sole person who could provide an explanation: on Misha.

"It means that the Bolsheviks have seized the electricity works," declared Misha.

Scarcely had he finished speaking before the lights went on again.

"Ah!" All eyes stared coldly and suspiciously on Misha.

"And that means that the Bolsheviks have been driven out of the electric works," he stuttered lamely.

"As quick as that?" asked an elderly gentleman in amazement. "Your reports don't seem to be very reliable, my dear sir!"

It could not be gainsaid that Misha's authority was somewhat shaken by this little incident.

"Gentlemen, the trial of the Bolsheviks is just going to begin; a counsel for the defense has been found!" shouted the lawyer, now filled like the others with the feeling of heightened confidence which the restoration of the electric supply had produced.

We must here make the confession that only a small proportion of the guests, and these almost exclusively of the younger generation, who were "infected" so to speak by modern thought, responded to the summons and showed a fitting interest in the important "People's Tribunal" which the advocate had set up to judge the Bolsheviks. The others—and they were the overwhelming majority—did not attach the importance they should have to a verdict that was bound to be so important for the future history of Russia. They refused to interrupt the card parties and carousing that they had begun; more, the great relief they had felt when the lights went on again had now for the first time put them in the most excellent spirits. So they left the complicated problem of Bolshevism, which had so suddenly been presented to a great empire, to "Jewish brains," and the Jews could tear each other's hair out over it if they liked! It was a hard business to know what one was to think about all these theories.

The servants brought in a long table, covered it, in accordance with the spirit of the times, with a red cloth instead of the usual green, and then set two gigantic candelabra on it, and lit the candles. And it must be confessed that when the celebrated advocate took his seat in the high-backed gilded chair between the two fellow-judges he had hunted up, his head with its thick gray mane gleaming in the shine of the candles commanded respect and esteem.

The red cloth and the massive candelabra added dignity and decorum to the spectacle, and one might actually have imagined that it was an important trial. To complete the impression all that was wanting was a colossal portrait of some crown prince on the wall behind the table; but the advocate's head with its gray mane was an effective substitute. And his voice trembled in full response to the importance and solemnity of the moment when he presently began:

"Gentlemen! The Bolsheviks shall now be summoned for trial!"

CHAPTER V

IN THE GOVERNOR'S PALACE

THE PALACE of the Governor General was in Skobelev Square. It occupied nearly the whole middle frontage of the great square on which stands the monument to Skobelev, and it extended as far as Tverskaya Street.

The red stone that is characteristic of Alexander I architecture, and of which almost all Russian governmental edifices are built, has always had an intimidating effect on the population of the great empire. But the red of the Governor's palace in Moscow was like freshly shed blood. The uncanny effect of this hue of murder was heightened still more by the fixed bayonets gleaming above the thick sheepskin coats of the innumerable Cossack and police sentries that constantly patrolled in front of the building; and in addition to these, suspicious-looking men in civilian clothes were always to be seen prowling round the walls.

Whenever the inhabitants of Moscow had to cross Skobelev Square they did so on the side opposite the palace, so as to give rise to no suspicion that they were prying into the huge courtyard which stretched away behind the wide-open, heavily barred gate of the Governor's palace.

Since time immemorial this palace had been occupied only by men of the blood of the Romanovs or relatives of the Imperial house. But when, after the February revolution, scattered and sporadic troops of deserters from the front lines penetrated into the hinterland, and marauding bands from all parts of the country streamed into Moscow to make their "center" there, they took up their quarters—as if in ironical comment on the age—in this awe-inspiring palace, which had stood empty ever since the Governor's flight. All its wings and floors, all the rooms, public and private, were packed with soldiers of all sorts and conditions. It was a Babylonian confusion of all the peoples and races that inhabited Russia: fair, laughing Great Russians, dark-haired Little Russians with soft cow-like eyes and dull faces, gloomy melancholic slit-eyed Asiatics with Mongolian faces, black-eyed Poles with potato faces, small, animated Jews. But most numerous of all were the Letts and Lithuanians, heavy-blooded and lowering, and clothed in a miscellaneous assortment of military garments, fur caps, top-boots, blouses of various kinds and shapes, whatever they had happened to lay their hands on.

Along with the soldiers a considerable collection of other people had found lodgings in the palace, people who had no immediate connection with the army, the majority of them agitators and active members of the various socialist and revolutionary parties. They wore civilian clothes, it was true, but with a military cut: short fur or leather coats, top-boots and fur caps that resembled the ones the soldiers wore. All without exception had a filthy stubble on cheek and chin, an eight to fourteen days' growth.

The Governor's palace was the headquarters of the revolutionary war committee, and this committee was trying to win over all the revolutionary parties to its side. So for many months the soldiers in the palace had been plagued to death with meetings and discussions, speeches and proclamations emanating from all the parties. The Residence had been transformed into a sort of Talmud school, and the soldiers into Talmud students, into whom every party drilled their particular theories and preached their particular programs without intermission. Naturally enough the soldiers very soon could no longer make head or tail of anything.

After each of these debates a corresponding resolution was of course passed and the constitution of the revolutionary war committee changed, so that finally the soldiers could no longer recognize their leaders by sight, and every man resolved to be led by nobody but himself. . . .

And now, on the evening of October 25th, there was to be held in the huge reception hall of the Residence, where once the grand balls of the Russian aristocracy had taken place, a great meeting which all the socialist parties represented in the revolutionary war committee were to speak.

The gigantic hall with its marble pillars and walls hung with red damask, its ceiling where goddesses and muses sported against a sky-blue background, was crammed to bursting with soldiers and workmen. The marble balcony where once military bands had played music was now packed with shock-haired soldiers' heads.

Here and there a strip of silken tapestry was missing from the walls. Some bayonet had been busily occupied with it, but had been stopped in time by the "house commission"; so the silken strips remained hanging where they were and one of them now draped loosely a great lamp fixed to the wall.

The bronze-gilt nymphs and amoretti who sported on the chandeliers still served their turn. Just as once they had illumined the naked shoulders and backs of beautiful Moscow ladies at the Governor's ball, so they illumined now—a little dimly, it was true, because of the dust and dirt that encrusted them—the faces of the soldiers.

The marble pillars were misted with dense exhalations from the throng of hot, closely packed bodies.

In the embrasure where the platform stood, behind which had once shone the dull brown or parchment white of some portrait of the Imperial family, red flags with various inscriptions now hung, framing the enormous tangled beard and the mighty gleaming brow of Karl Marx. The leaders sat at a long table covered with a red cloth, and the speakers stood a little to the side.

Weary, apathetic and bored, many of the soldiers sat half asleep with their heads on the shoulders of their neighbors. For weeks, for months, these debates had been going on, and nobody actually knew what they were really about. A promise had been made that the soldiers from the front would be sent home after the deposition of the Czar, and that the land would be divided among the peasants. The

Czar was already deposed—but men were still being driven to the front, and of the land's being divided there was not a whisper. These men were already heartily sick of drifting like vagabonds from town to town. They had had enough of whoring and boozing. . . . They longed for their homes, for their villages, their wives, their own people, their own cattle and pigs. And here! Nothing but talk, talk without end, quarrels and division, and no hope of coming to an agreement. The devil take the lot of them! . . .

The men's faces were hot and angry. Sweat ran from their thick, matted hair down over their foreheads. Their nostrils quivered as they breathed. A man opened his mouth wide, so that his teeth and tongue showed, and shouted without knowing what he shouted. Some drank in the speeches silently as a sponge absorbs water, listened in an almost religious ecstasy, and nodded their heads approvingly after every word. One or two seemed actually dazed by the hail of words that fell about their heads from the tribune; every word found its mark like a well-aimed bullet; and every speaker hit the mark as well as his predecessor, the one was right and the other was right: the last speaker was always right. The closely packed men sent out such a heat that their shirts stuck to their backs. Their throats were dry, their gums sticky with the badly baked bread and the heavy fatty groats they had eaten—and there wasn't enough tea to go around. If one could only get a drink of water, at least, to wash away the taste of rancid dough! And this awful stench on the top if it! And the heat met one in the face as if one were in a Turkish bath!

Above, on the tribune, at the table with the red cloth, *they* sat, familiar and unfamiliar figures, soldiers and civilians: a soldier from the 56th Regiment which was posted in the Kremlin, and two sailors. Daring dogs, these sailors, who had boldly started it all—but clever devils! They understood the business and knew what was what. Side by side with them were civilians in workmen's blouses and unshaven faces, but the devil only knew what was up with these civilians! When they spoke you couldn't understand a word, and they were always hoarse, too, devil take them!

There he was on his feet again, the civilian with the flat chest and narrow shoulders. One couldn't hear a word he was saying. That voice of his—hollow as an empty cask, and the man was as hoarse as a tom-cat wailing on the tiles! And if you did catch a word by chance, he got beyond your depth next minute. There he was again, spouting "the revolution is in danger" and "we must defend it with our breasts!" Whose breasts was he talking about? If it was a woman there would be some sense in talking about breasts.

They all wanted you to lay down your life. First they called on you to defend the Czar, then the fatherland, and now the revolution. But what will you get out of it yourself if you give your life? The revolution won't bring you to life a second time!

"Silence, you son of a bitch! Don't you hear what the man's telling you? The Whites want to send you to the front and these folks here won't give in to it; they say: 'Don't go, it isn't necessary. Down with the war!' "

"But what do I get out of it if these people here order me to go out in the street and face the Whites' bullets? It's all the same to me whether I'm shot here or out there."

"And if you don't go out in the street, you fool, the Whites will take you by the pants and send you to the front again. Don't you see that? But these chaps on the platform won't have it. They're on our side! . . . It's a Bolshevik that's speaking now. Don't you know that?"

"The devil take all of them! They should all be strung up together on the same tree, Kerensky, Lenin and the other Jews. We must get hold of some trains and go back to our villages. The land was to be divided up—and they spout all the time about the revolution! God, but I'm sick of it! The devil take them all!"

"Make him shut his bloody mouth! He must be drunk."

Tangled beards, dejected faces. Eyes with gray rings round them gazed dreamily and yet despairingly out of round sockets. From many a soldier's breast a deep groan was wrung as he listened to the hoarse, discordant voice of the speaker.

"Hi, comrade! Tell us, won't you, what Bolsheviks really are?" From a corner came a deep ringing voice, whose possessor kept on munching a slice of black bread even while he was making his interjection.

At first this question was greeted with surprise and hostility. The speaker lost the thread of his argument; on the tribune and among a part of the audience there was visible uneasiness and astonishment, which made it quite impossible for the speech to go on.

"Why, you fathead, these men are Bolsheviks! This is a Bolshevik meeting," some one retorted to the questioner.

"I know that—I'm a Bolshevik myself. But nobody has told us yet what the Bolsheviks are. What do we want and what do they want?"

This question broke the spell. All at once the audience became aware that questions were allowed, and voices were raised on every side.

"Hear, hear! Perhaps the comrade will explain that to us once and for all!" another man cried; he was very short, so that his head could scarcely be seen above his comrades' shoulders. "What *is* a Bolshevik?"

The speaker—he was a typical intellectual just returned from abroad, dressed in foreign-looking clothes and wearing a very filthy collar and shirt—grew pale; the question took him completely aback. He tried to continue his speech, addressing himself more to his comrades on the tribune than to the audience. Then the soldiers began to shout him down and he had to leave the platform.

The revolutionary war committee still consisted, at the time when the Bolshevik revolution was beginning, of supporters of various revolutionary parties; both social revolutionaries and Mensheviks belonged to it, though most of them had been driven out. And although street fights had already taken place between various socialist groups, the moderate parties were still attempting to achieve a unified program by means of discussion. Their supporters now took advantage of the tumult in the hall to enlist the soldiers' sympathies for the moderates, whom the Bolsheviks wished to exclude from the revolutionary war committee; and this only added to the confusion.

Comrade Ryshkov was sitting at the table on the tribune; his prodigious clean-shaven skull gleamed under the electric light as if it had been polished.

The whole meeting knew Comrade Ryshkov. He kept gnawing the nails of his blunt fingers and said not a word. He was no speaker; he was a listener. An inveterate listener. Not a muscle of his face stirred; it was as though the whole meeting had nothing to do with him. From time to time he merely scribbled a few words on a piece of paper and pushed it across with an indifferent air to Comrade Karpilov who was sitting at the other end of the table.

But if Comrade Ryshkov was quite calm, gazing out indifferently with his cold composed eyes on the audience, Comrade Karpilov was correspondingly nervous. His body was like a dried-up bundle of nerves stuck into a black frock-coat of foreign cut that was far too wide and long for it. From his dirty stiff double-collar rose a long stiff neck, which had a wiry look. Comrade Karpilov took endless notes in a little book, pressing his pencil vigorously on the paper. While doing so he knitted his dried-up face until it looked like a compressed sponge, and repeatedly adjusted the glasses that balanced precariously on his thin bony nose.

While the audience went on shouting, a brief cool glance of understanding passed between Comrade Ryshkov and the chairman. The chairman was a Lettish soldier with a lowering expression and dead eyes. From the bluish tinge of his cheeks and the dark holes in which his slate-gray eyes were hidden, the gloomy discontent of the whole man could be read. Although the hall was stiflingly hot, he wore a new and heavy military greatcoat which had not been made to his measure and trailed round his feet with every step he took.

The chairman understood the glance that Comrade Ryshkov flung him; he rose to his feet and introduced to the audience Comrade Karpilov, the theorist of the party, who would explain to them the ideas of Lenin.

A burst of applause, hand-clapping and shouts of "Bravo!" greeted the deserving theorist of the party. In the general enthusiasm the protests of the opposite party were drowned. A voice began to sing the Internationale, and the whole audience joined in.

At last silence was restored. Subdued coughs could be heard. The audience prepared to listen and to understand. The soldiers stretched their naive heads as docilely as lambs, animated with the sincere desire to receive the Bolshevist teaching at last from the lips of the theorist, and so to know once and for all why they should take arms and go out and fight and stake their lives.

The little bent man on the platform spent a considerable time in cracking the joints of his fingers, clearing his throat, and trying to dispel the dryness in his mouth. Then he pulled out his notebook, cast a glance at it and began to speak.

His voice was just as hoarse as those of the other speakers, and nervous as well, so that it often broke. Then it gave out a sort of whistling sound like that produced by the violent escape of steam.

He began with the history of Russian socialism, went extensively into the split that took place at the London Conference and proved conclusively that the theories of Martov, the leader of the Mensheviks, deviated from orthodox Marxianism, and could not stand "a criticism from the point of view of historical materialism." The only valid conception of Marxism was that of Lenin.

But for the audience, whose sole wish was to learn why they were ordered to fight, why they were asked to arm themselves and go out in the street and fire on people and into houses, Bolshevism did not mean theories and arguments about theories. For every soldier in the hall the question was one of life or death. Why were they to risk death by the bullet of an *enemy* who was also their *fellow countryman,* here, in the middle of their own country? But the things the speaker was saying seemed to these simple men empty talk concocted by idlers to cause dissension; and for the sake of these empty words they were asked to stake their young lives, with which they had just escaped from the muddy trenches!

The infinite patience of the soldiers that had enabled them to bear their lot in obedient silence gave way and they revolted:

"To the devil with Lenin! To the devil with Martov! To the devil with your theories! Tell us why you ask us to fire on other men!"

This outburst became contagious; it touched the soldiers' hearts on the most sensitive spot, and immediately there were shouts from all sides: "Why won't you let us be? Why do you order us to shoot? That's what we want to know! Who must we fight for? What must we fight for?"

A menacing murmur rose and there was a rush for the platform.

Uncomprehending and helpless, Comrade Karpilov stood on the platform, looked about him with terrified astonished eyes and pale quivering lips and could not make out what was happening and why the audience were so excited.

In vain the chairman tried to restore order, promising that the speaker would try to speak more loudly and clearly; the soldiers were no longer to be controlled, they refused to listen to anything more. The chairman glanced coldly across at Comrade Ryshkov, but he was calmly regarding his short bitten fingers as if nothing had happened. The chairman understood. That meant: Wait! Let them have their fling!

Comrade Karpilov left his post, still blinking his eyes nervously, and sat down at the table with a shrug of his shoulders. And suddenly another figure stood on the spot that he had left.

A murmur ran through the audience and rose until it was like the roar of waters.

"Just look who's up there now!"

To their astonishment they saw that it was Comrade Anatol.

The chairman cast another glance at Ryshkov; but he was still contemplating his finger nails. Then the chairman stepped up to Comrade Anatol and said in a heavy voice: "Comrade, it isn't your turn to speak."

"Let him speak! Let him speak!" shouted a few voices.

"Traitor! Judas!" The answer rang through the hall.

The man against whom all the audience was shouting now stood as if rooted to his place and let the angry cries pass over his head. Calmly he contemplated the furious crowd, who flung savage curses at him, and the contemptuous smile on his twisted lips did not fade for a moment although his face remained grave as ever.

"Be silent, you fool! Don't you see who's standing up there? That's Comrade Anatol!"

"Who's Comrade Anatol, anyway, that his feelings should be considered?"

"Where have you lived? He's been in Siberia, he's printed proclamations defending you, and he had to do it in secret too! Don't you know who Comrade Anatol is?"

"And now he's gone over to the other side!"

"He tries to justify his treachery by pointing to what he's done in the past. He strengthens our enemies by his fine-sounding lies! Down with him! Down with him!"

Once more a tumult broke out among the audience and they made a rush for the platform. The opponents of the Bolsheviks still seemed to have a numerous following among the soldiers, for a thick wall of soldiers and civilians soon formed round Comrade Anatol, prepared to defend him from attack.

The chairman threw yet another glance at Comrade Ryshkov. The man with the gleaming skull made a sign in return; his face was clouded.

"The representative of the Mensheviks has the floor. I call on Comrade Anatol," cried the chairman.

The speaker exerted himself to speak loudly and clearly, though his voice, like those of the others, was already hoarse. The seriousness that could be seen in his face and heard in his voice soon secured him general attention:

"If you pour water into your own cannons, that won't bring you peace by a long way. For peace two parties are necessary. If our soldiers forsake the front and by doing so throw open the gateway of the country, it isn't peace that will enter by that gate, but the iron fist of German militarism, and instead of the Russian knout we'll have—the German sword. No, you yourselves don't want a peace of that kind. And you know very well that it is not in your power to bring a real peace. You only talk of peace, and in the meantime you are doing something that will bring about the bloodiest fratricidal war. . . ."

"Traitor!"

"Let him speak!"

"You aren't out for peace, you're out for the social revolution—you want to smuggle revolution in under a false pretense of peace. . . ."

"War-monger! Reactionary!"

"Nothing is easier than to be a revolutionist in times of revolution. Nothing is easier than following your wishes. But I'm no toady," he shouted, "and you need expect no pleasant lies from me! I've a tough skin and I'm not afraid. . . ."

The audience calmed down.

"For us the revolution isn't an adventure or a stroke that may come off and may not. A revolution isn't a lottery or a game of chance. A revolution breaks out because it must break out! And if it does break out it must be controlled by a strong hand and not handed over to any charlatan at a street corner," his voice thundered now. "What you are setting your hands to is a mere adventure! You know it just as well as we do," at this point he turned to the men sitting at the table. "The whole of socialist literature is concerned with the question of how the transition from a capitalist to a socialist society can be accomplished, what roads to take, what stages must be gone through—and you propose to effect all that with a leap in the dark! That means simply running your heads against a stone wall. You're exploiting the ignorance of the masses!"

These words made an impression and won sympathy for the speaker, as could be immediately seen by the attitude of the audience. The chairman glanced across at Comrade Ryshkov again. Ryshkov passed a note to the man sitting beside him, and one of the sailors sitting at the table rose and interrupted the speaker by asking: "Then how would you behave in the present state of things, comrade? Would you take arms against the proletariat?"

"That would depend on the decision of my party." Thus Anatol smilingly avoided the unpleasant dilemma into which the sailor wanted to drive him.

"There you see for yourselves, comrades, what this martyr of the revolution is like! And if your party," the sailor once more turned towards Anatol, "should decide to go in with the nobility—you're something of a democrat, aren't you?" he added contemptuously, again trying to corner him.

"Yes, I'm a democrat," replied Anatol, laughing. "I admit that I believe in the principle of majority rule. But I'm neither a pacifist at all costs, nor a democrat at all costs."

The adroitness with which Anatol avoided the snare set for him once more left the leaders on the platform at a loss. They all turned helplessly to the man with the gleaming skull.

Comrade Ryshkov calmly wrote something upon a piece of paper; but as he handed it over he could not repress an energetic gesture of the hand.

Then suddenly something quite unexpected happened. A woman appeared on the platform and before any one had realized her intention was standing on the speaker's dais.

Agitation on the platform. Someone pushed Anatol aside. Where he stood the woman was standing now.

"Comrade Sofia! Comrade Sofia!" came shouts from the audience.

The soldiers gazed greedily at the platform and in their curiosity forgot to shout and protest; indeed they did not even remark that Anatol had disappeared. All their attention was absorbed by the feminine figure on the tribune, by her powerful girlish bosom, whose form showed beneath her leather jacket, by the neck and shoulders displayed by her low-cut blouse, by the thick strands of hair falling over her brow.

Comrade Sofia's face was extraordinarily pale. Her nostrils quivered with excitement; the veins showing on her strong neck stood out distinctly. She tried to overcome the trembling of her knees by walking to and fro on the platform. One could see her breast agitatedly rising and falling beneath her blouse. In a girlishly high voice quivering with excitement, a voice at first so powerless that one could only guess at it by the movements of her hands, she began in somewhat foreign-sounding but good high-school Russian:

"Comrade soldiers! You want to know what Bolsheviks are! Bolsheviks—you are Bolsheviks, you, the down-trodden and suffering Russian masses, who since time immemorial have been enslaved and scourged. Formerly by Czars, by tyrants and officials; now by patriots and war heroes. First you were ordered to sacrifice your lives for the Czars, now you are ordered to do it for the fatherland. *You* are Bolsheviks, you, the poor, the suffering, the enslaved! You, whom they have torn from your homes, your mothers, your wives, your children, stuck into uniforms, doomed for years to barracks and muddy trenches, and exposed to the bullets of your enemies, without food and without clothing! They have promised you land—and they have not given you it. They have promised you freedom—and they drive you back to the front with bayonets, force you at the point of the revolver to attack the German proletariat, who are peasants and workers just like yourselves. And nobody benefits by it but a few empty-headed climbers, who want to gain the reputation of heroes at the expense of your blood. You have nothing to gain by the war! Whoever wins the war—you can only lose it; in any case you'll have to bear the burden, whatever happens, whether it is the yoke of a Czar or a general or a patriot. Down with the war! Down with the patriots!"

The slight pause that Comrade Sofia had to make after almost every sentence to wipe her mouth, the pounding of her heart, the hasty fluttering rise and fall of her breast, clearly visible through the thin fold of her blouse—all this fettered the listening soldiers as with a charm; with open mouths they stood and gazed at the girl.

She had to make a longer pause so as to take breath. This pause worked like dynamite on the excited crowd. The feminine softness of the girl's figure touched them and carried them away. Their faces grew pale with excitement, their eyes glittering; with quivering nostrils and lips they breathed in deeply the hot and stifling air. The strands of hair falling over the girl's brow and ears, her defenseless throat and delicate white hands, completely won the hearts of the soldiers and made them forget their doubts and their despair.

But the words she spoke also did that: for the soldiers could read their own lot in her words, and that made them surrender unconditionally to her.

"Go on, comrade! Go on! Speak!" a soldier shouted.

"What are you bawling for? Can't you see? Give her a breather!"

"Hi! Give her a drink of water! What are you sitting there for like dummies? Give her a drink!"

"You couldn't understand when the men were talking—but you understand a petticoat all right!"

"Don't you sneer at a petticoat. A wench like that one is worth more than a whole brigade."

"Hold your jaw there! I can't hear a word!"

"Go on, comrade!"

Comrade Sofia took a deep breath and continued her speech, with less sign of agitation now, but just as emphatically:

"And suppose you win the war—what will you have won? What will come after that? The revolution? No! The generals will come, Kornilov, Russky, or whatever they call themselves. They'll set the Czar on the throne again. You know yourselves how carefully they guard him, how tenderly they treat him. . . ."

"We'll see they don't manage that!" cried a soldier heatedly.

"A few minutes ago a Menshevik stood here and told you—what did he tell you? Go back to the front and defend the gate of Russia with your bodies! Why doesn't he go himself? Why does he send you? Oh no! *They* sit in their warm rooms and they send *you* to your death. They want to destroy your young lives, for that will rid them of you. For them the war is a melting-pot into which they pour the forces of revolution so as to burn them to ashes. That's why they all want war: the officers, the social revolutionaries, the Mensheviks. They want it, for they hope to stifle the revolution by means of it!"

"Down with the traitors! Put them against the wall!" the soldiers shouted furiously.

"Comrades!" The girl's voice rose above the din. "In Petersburg our friends have risen, and they are winning. The people have joined them and driven out the 'provisional traitors.' Now they're fighting these other traitors, the generals. We must do the same thing here in Moscow: we must arm ourselves and drive out the enemies of the people, all of them, no matter what they may call themselves, and get the supreme power into the hands of our councils."

"That's the stuff! All power to the councils! Hurrah!" the soldiers shouted rapturously.

Meanwhile at the table the leaders were occupied in drawing up a resolution in accordance with the feeling of the meeting and making out a new list of members for the revolutionary war committee, from which naturally the "traitors" were excluded.

The resolution which, as usual, had been drawn up by the man with the wrinkled face, and the names of the new members, who were now exclusively Bolsheviks, were read out as a matter of form to the seething audience. They were greeted, without being clearly heard, with loud imprecations against the "traitors." The crowd in the hall were now quite indifferent to what it was all about: they thirsted for action.

The soldiers surrounded Comrade Sofia, and she had a struggle to escape from them. When at last she could breathe freely, a man who had made his way unobserved through the soldiers went up to her. It was Zachary Mirkin. A few gray hairs showed now in his short black beard. His face was pale and thin but extraordinarily alive. His eyes radiated energy, as they had seldom done formerly.

"Did you hear me?"

"Yes."

"Why don't you say something?"

"I liked your speech, because it stirred the crowd to action. But surely it isn't necessary to tell lies?"

"Lies?"

"Well, you weren't too scrupulous in your treatment of the truth," he smiled.

"You'll never win them with other arguments. One must talk to them in a speech they understand. You can't carry on a revolution with kid gloves."

"But you can't do it with tub-thumping either."

"Oh, you bourgeois! You've come with us to the very gate of the Governor's palace—but you've kept your sentimentality."

"My conviction is that the Bolsheviks are so just in their demands that it's quite unnecessary to use questionable methods. It's sufficient to tell the people the truth: that the other parties want to continue the war and to postpone the harvest of the revolution until victory has been gained. But we hold that every extra day that the exhausted soldiers are kept at the front is a crime. And the war is not only a crime against humanity, but also the death sentence of the revolution."

"Do you fancy that it's intellectuals you have to deal with?"

During this argument Comrade Anatol had stepped up to them. Still smiling his twisted sardonic smile he turned to Comrade Sofia: "I heartily congratulate you, comrade. Your arguments were incontrovertible."

Comrade Sofia reddened.

"What do you mean by that, comrade?"

"It was your temperament I was thinking of, of course. Who could stand up against you?"

"What are you thinking of doing, Comrade Anatol?" asked Mirkin.

"I'm going—and you?"

"I shall stay," replied Mirkin calmly.

"You, too, Mirkin?" asked Comrade Anatol in a jesting voice.

"Yes, I, too," Mirkin said firmly.

The smile on Anatol's lips grew still more bitter. Almost inaudibly he said: "I expected this."

Mirkin and Comrade Sofia watched an old, bent man walk to the door with his head between his shoulders: on his shoulders seemed to weigh the whole heavy burden of the approaching and still unknown time.

CHAPTER VI

NIGHT SHADOWS

IMMEDIATELY after the enthusiastic passing of the resolution in which the assembled soldiers affirmed their solidarity with the Petersburg proletariat, they proceeded to organize rebellion in Moscow.

Those who disagreed with the resolution left the palace; only a few wavering Mensheviks resolved to wait until next day. But the great majority of the soldiers put themselves at the disposal of the new revolutionary war committee. They remained in the Residence. Among them was Zachary Mirkin, and naturally Comrade Sofia. (She was no other than Sosha, the younger daughter of the teacher Hurvitz.) That night no one thought of going home.

The huge governmental building was transformed into a living organism. Its head, its brain, functioned in the top story, where the rooms of the various committees were. Comrade Ryshkov and the Executive Committee occupied the former study of the Governor. In the great rooms in the lower stories were accommodated the members, the arms and legs, of this living body. One comrade after another appeared with a written sheet of paper, picked out a few soldiers or Red Guards from the crowd of armed workmen, and vanished mysteriously with them.

Comrade Burshanov, the Lettish soldier with the gloomy expressionless face and the long army coat who had taken the chair at the meeting, walked about among the soldiers. Pale, almost dumb, making his orders known by silent glances, he posted sentries at doors where meetings were being held, as well as at all the outside doors of the building.

After that he dealt with the huge crowd that still remained, asking each man whether he wished to stay, and sending away those who had no business there.

Comrade Ismailova, a woman of the intellectual type with a solicitous nun's face, went about in a respectable black dress that reached to her very chin; even her fringed white silk shawl was decently closed with a safety pin. With the cool unobtrusive efficiency of a good housewife she took over the running of the house, supported by a regiment of women, some of them intellectuals, some of them simple peasant girls, and among them Comrade Sofia; she examined the store-rooms and took a note of the available supplies of flour, bread, groats and other means of life.

In this journey of investigation linen sheets were discovered. Under Comrade Ismailova's supervision these were cut into strips and rolled up to serve as bandages. She examined also the medicine chest, posted sentries everywhere with loaded rifles, gave the educated and the peasant women instructions what tasks they were to undertake, and set them all to work. A soldier who could draw, now unreproved tore great pieces of taspestry from the walls and with a brush, hastily improvised out of hair taken from a broom, wrote on the red silk in Indian ink all sorts of inspiriting proverbs, appeals, hopes and wishes, as well as the names of the various committees. He embellished every inscription with a picture drawn out of his own fancy.

But on the top floor, in the Governor's workroom, sat Comrade Ryshkov, the brain of the movement; he spoke into the telephone, replied to questions, and gave out commands and passwords.

He ordered the 193rd Infantry Regiment to join the 56th Regiment, which was stationed in the Kremlin, and to take possession of the arsenal: "The commandant of the Kremlin arsenal is a party comrade. He will distribute rifles to the proletariat."

And Ryshkov summoned workmen from the suburbs, and sent comrades out to the barracks of the Moscow garrison to persuade soldiers who were sympathetic to join him. The gunners were completely under Bolshevist influence, and now the problem was to waken them in the middle of the night and smuggle them along with their artillery into the headquarters of the revolutionary war committee.

But the most important thing was to get at the arms in the Kremlin arsenal; the more rifles, machine guns, ammunition that could be had the better:

"Bring it all as quickly as possible to the palace!"

And soon shadows were creeping through the darkness, keeping close to the walls; they bore rifles and ammunition from the Kremlin arsenal to the Governor's palace.

There was a rattling of arms as bundles of rifles were stored away in cellars by the light of pocket lamps. Sentries armed to the teeth stood guard over them.

Comrade Sofia worked tirelessly. Her face was flushed. She had thrown off her leather jacket. Over her full, heaving breast ran diagonally the red leather strap that held her revolver holster. She ran indefatigably from room to room, rushed up and down stairs, hurried to the room where the Executive Committee were sitting, returned immediately with a piece of paper in her hand, took a comrade aside and whispered something to him. Immediately afterwards she was standing in the midst of a group of soldiers who looked at her with tense excited faces, she addressed them with fiery gestures, and her girlish form with its continuous animation swayed her listeners like a field of corn in the wind, and made them do her will. Oh, Comrade Sofia (as she was called here) was in her element! Not for nothing was she the daughter of her mother! For years she had waited for this hour, for this night. And now all within her was in a wild turmoil; everybody was infected by her fiery energy—Rachel-Leah's energy. She was everywhere—in the cellars, in the kitchen, in the soldiers' canteen; she collected the bread that the soldiers brought her, that it might be distributed equally on real communistic lines. One never knew; they might have to stay here for a long time, they might have to stand a siege.

In this building filled with unfettered energy Comrade Mirkin walked about with hesitating steps like a sleep-walker, as if he were in a dream. Everything seemed to him real and unreal at the same time, clear and yet indistinct; he knew what was happening round him, and again did not seem to know. A thought leaped up in his mind: "This is the last battle and these are the last men that are waging it."

That very night the workmen began to assemble in the palace; they came from cellars and hovels, they came from outlying suburbs, their hands black with smoke and soot, their bodies scarred with drops of molten metal from the foundries. The firemen came straight from their furnaces, only waiting to fling their workmen's blouses over their naked gleaming shoulders. Their shaggy locks fell jauntily from beneath the peaks of their ragged caps, and their strong arms swelled with contained lust for battle. Every face shone with solemn joy. Only the men's eyes glittered vengefully, and that glitter was like an electric spark that spread like wildfire. The whole room was as if charged with electricity.

Mirkin saw the huge palace turning into a human power station, saw the frozen, distorted, death-like faces of these men coming to life again and filling with new energy the room with the great gallery; he saw the pain and rage of generations that had hitherto found no vent but impotent muffled curses suddenly unfettered in that huge space; he saw death-dealing eyes and powerful arms that snatched weapons of death. These were not human beings any longer: the ghosts of many generations who had perished in misery crept, demanding salvation, out of their hidden graves and grew to flesh and blood in the bodies of these powerful, steely-muscled workmen, gazed vengefully out of workmen's eyes, filled the swollen veins of workmen's strong right arms, charged these workmen's rifles. The seed of vengeance shot up, grew and grew, and ripened towards the great Judgment Day that was at hand.

Mirkin was seized with terror before these armed shadows who, with their rifles between their knees, sat in pitch-dark corners. Certain of their victims, they waited patiently for the hour of vengeance. And side by side with these shadows there crouched, waiting in readiness, the penalty. The penalty for the sin whose name was Russia.

At that moment Mirkin became aware where he stood.

In the gray of dawn the armed shadows slept, drugged by the hot and stifling atmosphere of the previous night. Weary of waiting for something to do they sank down one after another, each where he happened to be. Soldiers in uniform lay outstretched on the floor, in the dust and filth, with pyramids of rifles stacked beside them. With their heads resting on the breasts, knees, backs or arms of their neighbors, they drank blissfully of sleep, breathing deeply and heavily the while. Intellectuals slept sitting at their tables, their heads lying on their arms. Here and there among the men's bodies a woman's could be seen. The workmen dozed in the corners, their rifles between their knees.

At last Ryshkov, their leader, came down from his room. He walked slowly up and down among the sleeping shadows. His weary tired face twisted in a painful grimace, which gave it a still more gloomy expression. He muttered thoughtfully: "And still they haven't come! Nothing but a lot of young lads! No sign of the older workmen. And not many soldiers either. And not a single big gun! And I thought the town would rise in one night!"

He cast a glance at the great windows and added sadly:

"And it's morning already. . . ."

But the opposite party had not been idle either.

The Burgomaster had summoned an emergency meeting of citizens for the early morning in the Town Hall for the purpose of forming a "committee of defense against the common danger," whose task would be to defend Mother Russia from the "forces of evil."

And Russia responded. The old double eagle of the Czars tried once more—and for the last time—to spread its wings.

Everybody came. Men of the right wing and of the left joined hands: old Czarist officers whose tongues had not yet forgotten the Czarist anthem rubbed shoulders with revolutionary terrorists whose bombs had sprinkled the pavements of Moscow with the brains of Grand-Dukes and Governors: all prepared to fight for Russia, which now, in accordance with the times, was subsumed under the term "the Revolution."

All the officers from the Moscow garrison zealously put themselves at the disposal of the Burgomaster. Even the soldiers, who were under the thumbs of the Social Revolutionaries, sent delegates. The cadets from the Moscow Military School appeared in force; members of the Democratic Party fraternized with Menshevik socialists just returned from Siberia. The students and intellectuals were particularly strongly represented. And the province of Moscow, to which the Burgomaster had appealed the day before for assistance, had sent representatives.

But the party who set the tone of the meeting and carried most weight were the Social Revolutionaries. No single party in revolutionary Russia had attracted such a large body of adherents from the most diverse classes after the February revolution as this heroic organization. For this its romantic past was certainly partly responsible, but what counted still more was its patriotic attitude to the war, which was gratifyingly popular.

At the time of their revolutionary activities under the Czar, while their members were still carrying out the most daring attempts on the lives of the Czar's satraps, the fighting organization of the Social Revolutionaries as well as the party itself had regarded themselves as a national and secret military association, whose task was to combat the absolute rule of the Czar, but not the Russian bourgeoisie. They had been more concerned with organizing political associations, manufacturing bombs, procuring dynamite, spying on ministers and governors, than with socialistic problems. They left this to a few "do-nothings," the party theorists; these could occupy themselves if they liked in wrangling with the theorists of the other parties. Their solution, "The land for the peasants, the factories for the workmen"—a legacy that the party had taken over, with much other traditional ballast, from the "Narodovolsen," one of the first secret revolutionary organizations formed in Russia—was at that time no more than a pious wish whose realization was postponed to a golden age, till the time when the Messiah, that is the social revolution, should come. When after the revolution of 1905 the Czarist régime showed a very slight trace of clemency, the party leaders of the Social Revolutionaries abandoned at once—much to the annoyance of the terrorists—all terrorist methods. At the outbreak of the War in 1914, and indeed up to the last days of the Czarist régime, the party was animated with a strong patriotic sentiment. But when the revolution triumphed and the leaders of the Social Revolutionaries became the predominant members of the Provisional Government, the party became a patriotic party pure and simple. The pious wishes embodied in their solution of the economic problem were postponed until the time when a "final victory" should be achieved; the leaders of the party visited the front and harangued the soldiers with eloquent socialist patriotic speeches, in which they exhorted them in the name of the revolution to go on fighting their brothers.

Their romantic revolutionary past and their present patriotism, which their power and influence enhanced still more, rendered the Social Revolutionaries and their party an excellent field for concealing and nurturing people of the most diverse types.

Every Russian, no matter how reactionary the class he belonged to, nursed at the bottom of his heart a certain respect mixed with envy for liberalism and for the life of a revolutionary, consecrated as it was to a holy cause. This feeling no doubt arose from the dualism which is so characteristic of the Russian, and from a deeply hidden desire that the revolution might triumph.

So that when the February revolution broke out even those who until then had been completely on the side of the ruling régime passed over to the victors. That was not a difficult matter for them, for a Russian had only to consult his soul to discover that he had always in fact been an enemy of despotism, always had sympathized with the revolution, and had stood aside from it hitherto only for this reason or that.

After the February revolution the whole of Russia suddenly became socialist and revolutionary. Steady and respectable citizens marched through the streets of Petersburg with radiant faces and red ribbons round their arms or on their breasts, uttered broad sentiments about socialism and accepted the solution, "The land for the peasants, the factories for the workmen," without troubling to consider whether it could be reconciled with their interests or not.

The patriotic sentiment that prevailed in this bourgeois socialist class had been evoked on the one hand by the triumph of the revolution, but on the other by an extraordinarily exaggerated ambition to demonstrate to the world that the revolutionary régime was better than Czarism, which had suffered nothing but defeats in the war, while the new government would achieve victory. And so this particular class in revolutionary Russia began to strike up a friendship with army men, even to court them. Everybody's ambition was to become an officer. But the middle-class Jews, for whom in the Czar's time an officer's life had been a shut and barred Paradise, sought most keenly of all to satisfy their longing desire for glittering epaulettes.

The officers' colleges were almost swamped with youths from middle-class Jewish families. Any one who wore an officer's uniform found all the doors of the better middle-class houses thrown open to him. But since, at the same time, one was anxious to commit no offense against the revolution, to which one was indebted for all the liberties one enjoyed and which was the sole guarantee of safety and security, all the dogmas and postulates of freedom were generously acknowledged. In this way there arose a strange type of revolutionary, partly militaristic and patriotic, partly socialistic. On the one hand, people proclaimed that the war must go on "to the last man" and wanted to lead the soldiers to an attack "for the glory of the revolution," whether it was expedient or not; while on the other, they destroyed the whole military organization by practicing the freedom which was the fruit of the revolution, undermined the discipline of the troops, and thought that they could keep the soldiers in the muddy trenches with patriotic speeches.

The majority of the military participators in the meeting, which the Burgomaster had summoned in the Town Hall to form a "committee of defense against the common danger" and to protect Moscow from the Bolshevik menace, were just such men as these.

Things did not go at all smoothly. First of all there was a violent difference of opinion about the composition of the committee, whether, that is to say, it should be composed of representatives of political bodies or of military institutions.

After their bad experiences with General Kornilov, the majority were chary of giving too much power into the hands of the officers and the nobility. They were resolved to defend themselves against the "Reds," but at the same time to preserve the fundamental principles of the revolution, and not deliver themselves into the hands of men who after victory might try to seize power for themselves. This reciprocal mistrust led to endless arguments, and the meeting quarreled and wrangled hour after hour; at last the command of the whole defense forces was confided to the social revolutionary Colonel Karamzov.

The new commander immediately took the necessary measures to organize the town against attack by the Bolsheviks. He occupied whole sections of the town, surrounded the Kremlin, where the troops lay that favored the Bolsheviks, began to cut off the governor's palace, and drove back from the suburbs the Bolshevik workmen who were seeking to reach the center of the town by side streets.

Wherever the opposing troops encountered each other there were isolated conflicts during which both parties fired on each other—not officially, but, so to speak, on their own responsibility.

Civil war had not yet begun; for the Whites were still unresolved, and the Reds not yet armed for it.

Before the Governor's work-room stood armed sentries and would not allow anybody to enter, for an important conference of the Executive Committee was taking place. The commander of the Whites had sent an ultimatum demanding that the regiments who favored the Bolsheviks should be evacuated from the Kremlin. This ultimatum was now being discussed.

The former work-room of the Governor was a spacious high room with four windows looking out on a garden and a view of the monument to General Skobelev, that heroic fighter for the Russia of the Czars.

It was as if the builders of the palace had known who would one day occupy this room and what purpose it would serve; for they had seen to it that the great walls were completely covered with blood-red damask, of which, however, large strips were wanting now, having been cut out for more practical uses. Huge vacant golden frames hung on the walls; the portraits had been torn out, but golden crowns still embellished the tops of the frames. And as if in derision a photograph that had not been touched stood, framed, in one of the corners; it was a photograph of one of the former occupants of this room, Grand Duke Sergius surrounded by his family. The faces, no doubt from shame at the desecration of the room, were quite faded; this, probably, was the reason why the photograph had escaped attention. . . .

The floor of the great room was literally covered with cigarette butts, mainly the fag ends of hand-made cigarettes. Long since the supply of tobacco and cigarette paper had given out. So the members of the committee tore pages out of books and documents and in these or in some other scrap of paper rolled cigarettes made of the mixture that was popularly known as "machorka roll." This consisted of dry tobacco leaves and all sorts of other plants grown by Russian peasants. As even the most hardened smoker could not for long endure his "machorka roll" and its wrapping, he soon flung it away, and the smoldering butts lay about everywhere on the tables and window ledges; but most of them served to decorate the marble frame of the great mirror and the moldings of the marble fireplace.

In the room silk-covered sofas and countless iron army beds stood side by side. Everywhere sat serious anxious-faced men, soldiers and workmen: occasionally one saw a woman's profile. Some gloomily rested their heads on their hands, which were holding the barrels of their rifles. Naturally enough the intellectuals had been the first to lose their nerve. The shortsighted man with the wrinkled face and the thick glasses lay groaning on one of the many sofas; he had been attacked suddenly with severe pains in his limbs and a tearing colic dug deep furrows in his waxen yellow face. Beside him, on the edge of the sofa, sat a little old man with a grandfatherly look, who kept on stolidly munching black bread which he broke off in tiny morsels from the loaf lying on his knees.

At the Governor's gigantic bronze-inlaid desk sat the man with the gleaming clean-shaven skull, Comrade Ryshkov. Before him lay a map of Moscow; upon it stood a whole battery of tea glasses filled to the brim with cigarette butts, ashes, spent matches, bits of paper and other refuse, although—unnoticed by any one—there were many huge metal ash-trays in the room. Ryshkov's hard well-cut chin with the deep cleft in the middle moved vigorously while he said briefly and sharply: "One thing is certain. Our position isn't rosy."

The gloomy Lettish soldier silently nodded his head in agreement. Even now, during the conference, he was still wearing his long army coat which reached to his toes and seemed to be a sort of second skin. He was not sitting like the others, but stood beside the writing-table and with gloomy, downcast eyes contemplated his toes.

"I wish the comrades to understand the situation clearly before we take the vote," the man with the close-shaven skull began slowly in a metallic voice, as if he were weighing every word. "We have no ammunition. The comrades we sent to the barracks to fetch artillery have not returned. Also, it's very uncertain whether it will be possible for them now to break through the White lines. We have a few rifles and machine guns, but we haven't a single big gun. The White Defense Committee, on the other hand, have the help of all the officers in the garrison, the cadets in the infantry school, the students, the intelligentsia and—most important of all—the Social Revolutionaries, and probably of the soldiers that follow them as well. Their artillery can reach us. What do you think, comrades?"

For about a minute there was a dead silence in the room. In the light of the hanging lamps the men's faces, rigid with anxious thought, were like parchment masks. Some bit their lips; the faces of others were twisted in a grimace of impotent despair. The eyes of others seemed to withdraw deeper into their sockets and from there shoot out angry fires. Their nostrils rose and sank as they heavily drew the air into their lungs.

This silence seemed an eternity, though it lasted hardly a minute. At last Comrade Ryshkov broke the frozen silence and struck the table once with his hand, which was like a hammer:

"Comrades, we do not know how many are prepared to support us. We have not reckoned our forces. But we believe that countless generations of slavery and oppression have made the masses ripe for our cause and theirs. We have the working class behind us. We shall take the vote now, comrades. Those who wish to yield to the ultimatum of the bourgeoisie to the proletariat raise their hands."

An anxious silence followed this command. Not a single hand was raised.

"Those who think that we should reject that shameful ultimatum with indignation signify their agreement by knocking on the floor with their rifle stocks."

There was a thump of a rifle stock on the floor. Slowly one dull thud followed on another, sending an echo to the farthest corner of the great room. At every thump the crystal on the bronze chandelier rang faintly. The chairman of the Executive Committee counted the blows.

"The decision has been taken," he announced.

There was the sound of a woman's loud sobbing. It was followed by that of a kiss.

"This isn't a meeting of romantic terrorists, but a revolutionary war committee," said the chairman reprovingly in his hollow, guttural voice. "And now—to work! Call in our comrades!"

But it was not necessary to summon the others. The door was flung open and a dense crowd of soldiers and workmen in civilian clothes burst into the room, all with rifles in their hands. They roughly and unceremoniously pushed the armed sentries aside and impetuously poured in.

The news that the Executive Committee had decided to reject the Whites' ultimatum and proceed to action had spread like wildfire through the building.

"The most important and urgent task," began Ryshkov, "is to get hold of points we can hold. We must smuggle ourselves into the Whites' territory and get machine guns posted on some roof. For that we need an intelligent leader, a man of self-control who can keep his men from firing too soon. The greatest caution is required. The point we want to seize is a very dangerous one."

Among the little group that stepped forward from the gray mass of human bodies was Mirkin; blushing, he hesitatingly made his way forward to the writing-table where Ryshkov was sitting and said: "I fancy I..."

The chairman contemplated him sharply: "Who are you? Whom do you know here, comrade?"

"Comrade Mirkin worked with us in Warsaw," shouted Comrade Sofia.

The Chairman shut one eye and gazed inquiringly at Mirkin: "Mirkin—Mirkin—I've heard the name somewhere.... Didn't you help Comrade Anatol in his work once?... How do you come to be with us?" he added in surprise.

"Since Kerensky's disastrous offensive on the Galician front...."

"Are you a member of our party?"

"No, but I sympathize with it. For I believe that you are the only people who can bring peace to our miserable country."

"It's all one—you're with us now: that's your best legitimation! Will you undertake the task of getting these soldier comrades on to the roof of the theater?"

"To tell the truth, I've never conducted military operations in my life, but I think I could carry that out."

"Don't worry! The revolution will educate you! And you're intelligent enough to understand what is required to be done."

"Yes, I think I understand."

"This is your job. You must steal through the White patrols till you reach the theater, when you must give the password to the door attendants in the building, who are on our side. They'll open the door without making a noise. You must lock up the other attendants. The machine guns must be set up in such a way that they can't be seen by the officers who are posted on the roof of the Hotel Metropole. It's important that strict discipline should be enforced on the soldier comrades; they mustn't show themselves on the roof or start operations prematurely. We'll send you word when to start firing. The object is to get the Theater Square into our hands, drive the Whites out of the Hotel Metropole, and occupy the hotel itself. It's occupied at present by rich people: they must be driven out. Unnecessary bloodshed and acts of revenge by the soldiers must be avoided at all costs. It is essential for us to gain the sympathies of prospective colleagues. Comrade Burshanov will put a machine gun section at your disposal. The comrades must put on civilian clothes so as to escape attention. You don't need written instructions; if you should be caught, you needn't admit who you are. I repeat again—this is a difficult job; you're going into the very stronghold of the Whites!"

"That's what I'm here for," replied Mirkin.

"Very well. Comrade Burshanov will give you your further instructions. Comrade Burshanov, take this comrade along and allot him a machine gun section. Good luck, comrade!" Thereupon Ryshkov bowed his head once more over the map of Moscow.

As Mirkin turned away from the table along with the Lettish soldier Sosha hurried up to him; she was far paler than he.

"Zachary!" she cried, seizing his hand.

"What is it?" said Mirkin, looking up.

"Nothing!" But then she seemed to remember something, for she pulled off her short leather jacket and threw it over his shoulders. "It won't be too warm up on the roof."

"Comrade Burshanov, see that the men have enough bread," Ryshkov suddenly shouted after the two men without raising his eyes from the map. "The pretty Moscow ladies won't send up sandwiches on pulleys to the roof of the theater, as they do to the White officers."

The soldiers laughed at this remark of their chairman.

When the comrades had left the Governor's work-room to take leave of the departing patrols whose return was uncertain, there entered the old serving man Vassily, who in his long life had had the privilege of serving countless Moscow governors. Like genuine Russians the comrades had not driven out the servant staff when they occupied the palace. They regarded these men as members of the proletariat, treated them kindly, and shared their food with them.

Old Vassily still wore, as in the good old days of the governors, his scrupulously groomed two pointed beard, but no longer his red official livery; this the comrades had peremptorily refused to allow him, as in their opinion it was an offense against human dignity. But Vassily's true servant nature made it impossible for him quite to give up the traditional usages to which his former masters had accustomed him; consequently he had hit upon a compromise and now wore an ancient frock-coat with gold buttons.

In these last days old Vassily's back had grown a little bowed. But when he reached the door of the Governor's room he straightened himself as of old and passed his fingers through the points of his gray beard as he had always done whenever he entered the room, no matter whether the Governor was there or not. Vassily carried a brush and a duster in his hand. He entered and coughed loudly. Then he began to pick scraps of paper and cigarette ends from the floor and the marble mantelpiece. But there were too many of them, and soon he gave up his task with a sigh.

Then, faithful to old habit, he went over to dust the Czar's portrait with his duster. For this purpose he mounted a little ladder that stood ready in a corner. But as the portrait was no longer there he contented himself with wiping the dust from the frame.

Old Vassily returned to this task again and again, whenever the comrades gave him a chance by leaving the room. But his pleasure in this accustomed work never lasted for very long, for one comrade or another was always sure to come in, give him a severe lecture on his sycophancy to the Czar, and send him out of the room.

This time a longer spell of pleasure was granted him, and he had time to go over the frames more thoroughly. While doing so he discovered the faded photograph of the Grand Duke which had been unnoticed by the comrades. For a long time he remained standing in front of it, straining his old eyes to make out what it represented. At last he recognized his old master, His Imperial Highness Grand Duke Sergius. Full of joy he contemplated the faded lineaments and murmured with his toothless mouth: "Ah, little father, little father! First they shed your blood, and now they're doing the same with Mother Russia!"

CHAPTER VII

ON THE ROOF OF THE THEATER

SHADOWS crept through the streets of Moscow in the darkness. They crouched against walls, hid behind buttresses, sent keen glances into the darkness, listened for footsteps and voices, crept like animals on all fours. Noiselessly shadow after shadow crept on, with ammunition belts wrapped round their bodies and hidden beneath their overcoats; after them came shadows with machine-gun parts, shadows with hand grenades, shadows with revolvers, ready for any emergency. The way was not far. A square, a narrow street—and the theater would be reached. But the short way held a thousand hidden dangers. The streets were wide and strongly guarded by enemies, for this was the frontier between the Whites and the Reds. But the churches were friendly helpers; they had buttresses and hidden niches which provided a constant refuge for beggars and homeless people. When danger threatened one could plunge into them and be swallowed up in darkness. There were strict orders to avoid any noise or do anything to rouse attention; so when one came to a street crossing one ran quickly across with one's sack of bread on one's shoulder. So these shadows flitted from house to house, from niche to niche, and filled the empty night with their anonymous presence.

There was the theater. A side door, hidden by huge pillars, was open. A young theater attendant had seen to this, so that the Bolsheviks might seize the theater noiselessly and without a stroke. The other attendants were locked into a distant room. Posts were set up. Helpful attendants showed the way to the roof and the rooms immediately beneath it. Over terraces, up ladders, on shoulders, the machine-gun parts were heaved up, and before the morning dawned in the streets of Moscow the machine-guns were posted on the roof, in niches and garrets, under cover of the bronze horses, their muzzles trained on the Theater Square.

As soon as dawn came a thick mist rose, enveloping all Moscow. The Red Square, the Kremlin, the thousand churches with their crosses seemed to have been swallowed up. The mist lay low; but above it the air was clear, and out of the smoke-gray wreaths rose a pair of golden eagles, resting on golden pillars, showing where the Kremlin was.

Wrapped in Sosha's leather coat, Mirkin lay beside one of the machine guns; with his head concealed like his comrades' behind one of the bronze horses, he contemplated the golden eagle of the Czar hovering in the air and felt that it was flying from the Kremlin towards him. . . .

It all seemed to him like a dream: that he should be there in a garret window beside a machine gun whose muzzle was pointing at the Theater Square. . . .

How did he come to be there? What had he to do with machine guns? He had always striven to avoid force, always fought against the use of force—impotently enough on the physical plane, but how powerfully, how ardently in all his inward being! His deep and bitter anger at the violation of innocent men led like a flock of sheep to the slaughter had brought him in spite of himself to the gate of the Governor's palace in Moscow! The violation of the human will had brought him to this step—because they were all without exception arrogating to themselves the divine right to dispose of the lives of their fellows, whether in the name of the Czar or in that of a wretched obscure lawyer who had climbed to power on the shoulders of the suffering people only the day before, or in the name of some other idol.

And now he himself was lying beside a machine gun! A vicious circle from which there was no escape! He had escaped one abyss and now found himself on the edge of another. And no escape! He had avoided all violence—and suddenly he was taking part in a war and busying himself with guns whose muzzles were pointed at enemies, at human beings!

He wanted to be quite clear in his mind about the step he had taken, to justify himself, and he set himself to recall again to his memory the long and bloody path that he had trodden since the beginning of the War.... That might account for the fact that he was here on the roof of a theater in Moscow, with a machine-gun by his side.

The War had not drawn him into its clutches. As an only son he was absolved from military service. But he very soon volunteered of his own will for "the Jewish front."

For in the War there was, in addition to the others, a "Jewish front" as well. It was a front where there was no hope of victory, a front which was perpetually chosen as the point of attack both by enemy and friend—indeed, by friend more than enemy.

Before Mirkin had time to look round him and orient himself to the universal conflagration that had burst out everywhere so suddenly, "the Jewish front" had already engulfed him and he gradually found where he belonged.

One day a procession of peasant carts rolled through the streets of Warsaw loaded with children and Torah scrolls. There walked behind it a long train of Jews with bundles on their backs and lamenting mothers leading children by the hand or bearing them in their arms. The confused lamentations of women who had lost their children in their wild flight over the countryside still rang in Mirkin's ears; on his eye-balls was still imprinted in letters of fire the spectacle of their wide-open mouths and distorted faces; he could not forget the cries of despair that filled the court of the Community House. There groaned and sobbed whole families of Jews who had been driven by the Russian authorities from their houses, their streets, their towns, their shops and synagogues like cattle from their stalls, and hounded naked and destitute along the whole front.

They would be turned out suddenly in the middle of the night, given a few hours and sometimes only a few minutes to pack their belongings, get the sick out of their beds, and the children out of their cradles. There were no wagons to transport the sick; the few that the peasants still had in their possession were worth their weight in gold. So every Jewish commune hired one or two wagons to carry their Torah rolls and women who were with child, and all the others followed on foot. As there was firing on the main roads they would have to pass, they made their way through impassable forests and across rocky fields, exposed to the hail of shots that whistled through the air. In their terror they took to their heels and in the panic and confusion that ensued many of them lost their children.

Mirkin could still see the faces of these bereaved women and the madness in their eyes; they were engraved for ever on his memory. He saw them now, their tangled hair escaping from beneath their wigs, their dumb, wild, half-mad gaze; and as he looked at the eagle of the Czars rising above the mist that lay over Moscow, a curse escaped his lips that were blue with the cold; he clenched his fist and muttered, trembling with rage: "Nikolay Nikolayevitch, the muzzles of our guns are trained on that eagle of yours! Now begins the hunt of the hunter!"

In these days at the beginning of the War blood flowed in rivers in the streets of Warsaw. And Mirkin had rushed about literally trying to dam it with his own hands. Once more he saw the famous Jewish poet standing with his gray shock of hair in the courtyard of the Community House among a crowd of lamenting mothers, helpless in the presence of such grief and misfortune; he had but just dealt with one group, and allotted them quarters secured by hastily requisitioning a few empty houses, much against their owners' will—when another group was waiting. Was the whole Jewish population of Poland streaming to this one place, to the courtyard of the Community House in Warsaw?

Frau Hurvitz was kept very busy during those days. She was

never at home except at night, and not always then. For Rachel-Leah was helping to find lodgings for women fugitives; she gathered together a band of young lads and at their head broke forcibly into empty houses, made war on house agents and their satellites, and threatened owners with her fist. Now she had to see about getting straw for her refugees to sleep on, now potatoes for their kitchen. Who had time to think of one's home and one's own personal affairs? Not to speak of love and marriage!

Mirkin could hardly get even a glimpse of Helene at that time, although they were engaged. She was kept completely occupied with her work in the school. "Whatever may come, the school must be kept going," was her father's watchword; in such a time it was more necessary than ever. As for Mirkin, he threw himself with all his heart into the relief work. From the very first day he devoted himself to it. He did what he could to help the poet in the Community House. He got together a committee; hunted up subscriptions; organized the younger people; started classes in the children's homes; obtained work for the men fugitives; and zealously collected linen and leather to make into shirts and boots.

The local subscriptions in money and kind were insufficient to deal with the problem. The stream of fugitives never stopped, and the danger became acute and spread like fire. Support would have to be obtained from the capital. Mirkin traveled to Petersburg, interviewed old acquaintances, and appealed to the conscience of politicians and other public men. He actually came in contact with his father, not directly, but through a committee that had been formed. But personal things left him completely indifferent at that time; all private matters and all feeling for them were drowned for him in the general misery. The events in Warsaw had so tempered his heart that it no longer responded to past things.

In Petersburg a great Relief Committee was formed. The danger was daily growing vaster; Nikolay Nikolayevitch's red beacons could be seen flaming up in Jewish settlements along the whole front. The farther the Russian army retreated, the more Jewish towns and communes were destroyed and laid waste. Shelter had to be found for the fugitives. So Mirkin was perpetually on the road from town to town, penetrating more and more deeply into the country, founding local committees for the housing of the fugitives.

Events came rushing on each other's heels, hurtling with the speed of a bullet into unknown space; and humanity was swept along with them, and human feelings and thoughts, human faith. One no longer proceeded from one stage to the next, but was driven helplessly on, urged by driving, impotent rage, as if by a whip. So people broke all their bridges behind them, threw away all scruples and doubts, and surrendered themselves to be driven by despair instead of by calm reason.

Private causes—apart from despair—had also helped to drive Mirkin along the road that had ended on the roof of the theater.

To Helene he felt united by indissoluble bonds of intimacy which he rarely troubled to think about, since he took them for granted as a part of himself. Sosha, on the other hand, the younger sister, had begun to exercise on him a strong attraction which he himself could neither understand nor explain. Physically Sosha had the same potent charm as her mother, the same energetic maternal ways, and a throat of gleaming whiteness rising out of her low-necked blouse. In whatever company she found herself she took the lead. Her imperiousness had long since subjugated her more quiet, somewhat dreamy elder sister to her will, and gradually she began to acquire an influence over Mirkin too. She regarded him as her tool, imposed her views upon him, as she did on everybody else she knew, and bit by bit involved him in her revolutionary activities.

Long before the War Sosha had already belonged to the party, but after the death of her brother David she had flung herself body and soul into revolutionary work. She hardly ever slept at home, was often not seen there for days or weeks, and during those absences occupied herself in carrying forbidden propaganda from town to town. One week she would be conducting an agitation among the factory workers in Lodz; the next she would be in Bialystok or somewhere else. She actually was daring enough to convey forbidden pamphlets, wrapped next her skin, to the soldiers at the front. Gradually she drew Mirkin, too, into this work, employing him to establish new connections, convey instructions, and sometimes even smuggle packets of literature that smacked of high treason, during his perpetual excursions to the front and to Petersburg. . . .

Sosha and Mirkin were brought closer together by their work and the common danger they incurred. When they met they had always secret matters to talk about. Helene saw this but made no sign. She knew the real state of things. And although at the bottom of her heart she felt something akin to jealousy stirring, she showed no trace of it; more, she did all she could to make it easier for Mirkin and her sister to be together. Whenever during the mid-day interval they sat in the school-room talking in lowered voices, Helene would stand on guard so that they might not be surprised by the unexpected appearance of her father.

In the letters that Mirkin sent to his fiancée he never failed to ask her at the end to give Sosha the date of his return to Warsaw. And Helene scrupulously saw to it that her sister returned home from Lodz or any other town in which she was "working" by the date given by Mirkin. Nor did Sosha ever fail to do so. During these stays in Warsaw Mirkin spent more of his free time with Sosha than with Helene. That, too, Helene accepted as if it were quite natural, and much as she suffered she never allowed any reproach to escape her lips. "They've serious and important things to discuss." This thought always comforted her.

When on occasion a faint doubt rose in her mind she was ashamed of her pettiness.

But sometimes she yielded to weakness and would say, half-jokingly, half-seriously: "You've so much to say to each other that I'm almost beginning to feel jealous!"

But Sosha would gaze at her sister in astonishment and reply, with a pitying shake of the head: "In these times there are more pressing things to do than staging sentimental love scenes!"

Then Helene felt deeply ashamed and unworthy.

Through Sosha, Mirkin came into contact with Comrade Marek.

Comrade Marek belonged to the Polish county nobility, but did not in the least share the sentimental longing for an independent Poland that on the outbreak of the War became the watchword and the animating force of the Polish Socialist Party and permeated all its activities. He had nothing but contempt for the socialists who were taking part in the formation of the Pilsudski Legions, and regarded all effort devoted to the liberation of the Polish fatherland as reactionary. Consequently he was in a state of constant warfare with the patriotic socialist parties. His fatherland was the world revolution, his millennium the world order *after* the social revolution. How his own fatherland would come out then was a matter of complete indifference to him, so long as the dictatorship of the working class was secured. Any fatherland without the dictatorship of the proletariat was for him a bourgeois state of exploiters, which it was one's duty to fight from the start. At the outbreak of the War he immediately got in touch with the central branch of the party in Petersburg, took his instructions from it, and began a double campaign of propaganda, in the factories and at the front.

For this man there was only one parallel: a high priest of some idol in ancient Babylon.

In our age it not seldom happens that figures out of long vanished epochs arise again and take part in the life of the present. Even Marek's outward appearance awoke this impression: he had a pale ascetic face, and only the reddish-yellow copper miter was lacking from his unnaturally narrow, cylindrical skull. From his face it was hard to tell what age he was. He might be in his forties; he might also be much younger or older. Through the waxen-yellow skin stretched over his cheek-bones the bones of his skull were clearly visible, and they seemed to be on the point of cutting through their parchment-like covering. Attached to this skull thinly covered with skin was a short, reddish-hair, and as it were dead beard. When Marek spoke the many branching blue veins in his high forehead started out, and one had actually the feeling that one could see his brain working.

His eyes alone gave life to his yellow frozen features. But their effect was due to their striking resemblance to the eyes of a corpse. The pupils, which were deeply sunken in the great eye-sockets, emitted the icy, metallic-greenish glitter that can be seen in the eyes of drowned men. The sharply jutting ridges above them, leaving them in deep shadow, seemed to emphasize still more that strange gleam. When Marek looked at any one, his eyes seemed to retreat still farther into their sockets and peer out suspiciously as from an ambush. They seemed to retreat like a man preparing for a spring, to leap immediately afterwards with a malicious, green, catlike glance on their object and seize it by the throat. . . .

He never spoke in a natural tone; either he screamed discordantly (generally at conferences and popular demonstrations) and raged so wildly that one was afraid the veins in his forehead must burst, or he spoke almost in a whisper, seriously and urgently; this was when he was addressing a single listener. While doing this he held his interlocutor tightly by the lapel of the coat, or if it were a woman, by the blouse, talking in a deep, hollow, solemn voice, pausing ever and again as if he were counting his words and each was a burning spear that he wished to thrust into the heart of his listener.

Women were drawn towards this man like moths towards a flame. The young and beautiful no less than the old and ugly surrendered to his charm; among them, girls of good family, factory girls, and domestic servants; but, most numerous of all, women wearing a heavy crown of black hair and with emphatically Semitic faces. Some magical power innate in him seemed to give him an irresistible power over women.

When he talked to women in his soft, grave, almost pious voice, his bony face quite close to their cheeks, his dead eyes fixed on them, they experienced a sort of religious ecstasy and felt they were being admitted to some secret and divine mystery. They were ready to walk through fire for him: more, they begged him for the privilege. And he fulfilled their wish. Without turning an eyelash, without saying a single superfluous word, without even thanking them with a smile, he sent them—to their death. He spared nobody, not even his own wife, whom he sent when she was far advanced in pregnancy to agitate among the miners in the coal mining district; she never returned again. This fact was universally known; but that did not frighten or deter other women and young girls; on the contrary, it attracted them all the more to him. Like a high priest of Moloch he offered up the women and girls who crowded to him. He would send one with forbidden propaganda to the front, which meant almost certain death, others again with guns to some manufacturing town. If by good luck a girl should return more than once with her life from those perilous expeditions, Comrade Marek at once became suspicious and submitted her to a strict and almost inquisitorial examination. The result of these interrogations was always the same: Comrade Marek either left the girl behind in a locked hotel bedroom with a revolver and orders that, to resolve all doubts, she should take her own life, or he sent her off on a new journey from which he was certain she would never return. . . .

Sosha had succumbed to this man like all the other women. In spite of her managing and imperious nature she obeyed Comrade Marek with doglike devotion and trembled at his very shadow. To Mirkin, Marek's influence over her was inexplicable; and it may be added that he had come actually to hate Comrade Marek because of this power.

Perhaps an auxiliary cause of that hatred was the sense of weakness that Zachary felt when confronted with Marek. "What is this power of his?" he kept on asking himself. He tried to crush down this feeling, of which he was ashamed, and tried to justify Marek. "It's the revolutionary will that radiates so strongly from Marek. That's what enables him to rule everybody, even Sosha."

And through Sosha, Mirkin, too, like all the others, came under the spell of Comrade Marek. Although he could never overcome his antipathy for Marek and also a certain secret suspicion of him, he carried out all his orders, in doing which he frequently risked not only his life but the existence of his own work, the relief committees. He knew that he was committing a crime against the suffering refugees, knew that he had no right to do what he was doing—but he did it nevertheless. Gradually Mirkin became, so to speak, the liaison officer between Marek and his comrades at the front, which he frequently visited in the course of his relief work.

Partly for personal reasons, and partly because their work demanded secrecy, Mirkin and Comrade Marek never communicated directly; Mirkin received his instructions through Sosha, with whom his relations bit by bit became more intimate. . . .

During one of his journeys the Germans broke through the Russian line at Gorlice. The Russian front was pushed far back and

Warsaw was occupied by the enemy. Mirkin was cut off from his fiancée and her family.

CHAPTER VIII

APOCALYPTIC DAYS

AND THEN the war revealed all its brutality. Nikolay Nikolayevitch took revenge on the Germans by glutting his impotent fury on the Jewish population, who were helplessly delivered into his power. After the break-through at Gorlice, the right wing of the Russian army at Kovno had to withdraw also. During the retreat Nikolay Nikolayevitch evacuated the Jews from the Lithuanian towns with fire and sword.

The things that had already happened in the Jewish settlements of Sochatschew, Skierniewice and Grodzisk in Poland were child's play compared to the inhuman cruelties committed on the defenseless Jewish population of Lithuania by the imperial butcher. Large towns such as Kovno had to be evacuated within a few hours at the command of the General Staff. Some thirty thousand Jews along with their wives and families were driven with bayonets and rifle butts out of their dwellings and crowded in wagons like cattle. Sick people and women far gone in pregnancy who could not leave their beds were summarily shot by officers where they lay, in order to "facilitate the escape" of their families, as the brutal jest of these butchers ran. These wretched people were packed indiscriminately like herrings into the railway wagons: grown-ups and children, sick and sound, without air to breathe, without food or drink, pressed limb to limb, a dense confusion of human members and variegated scraps of clothing. Coupled to hastily-stoked locomotives, these wagons raced with their wretched cargo through fields and woods towards a destination which nobody knew. It was not man that seemed mad, but the world itself; the blooming fields, the budding woods revolved in a mad circle round the heavily laden trains.

The Central Relief Committee did all in its feeble powers to alleviate the suffering. Mirkin was journeying perpetually from town to town to organize local relief committees.

The poor Jewish inhabitants of the little towns through which these packed trains passed bore their last scraps of food, apronfuls of bread, cans of boiled water, jugs of milk, to the railway stations and reached them up to the confused remnants of humanity in the wagons, which, strangely enough, though packed together like inanimate freight required food. . . .

The shrieks and screams that came through the locked doors of the wagons along the whole line awoke a panic terror in the Jewish population of some of the villages; for it sounded as if these human beings were being crushed like grapes in a wine-press by the weight of their own bodies. And from the doors and cracks of the onward rushing wagons blood dripped and human entrails were scattered on the gray fields of Lithuania.

Mirkin never forgot the faces of half-insane mothers who, through the iron bars of the small windows or the inadequate openings of doors, handed their gasping and dying children to the Jews on the platforms.

Soon the trains spewed out at every station the corpse of some one who had been stifled or had died of some illness without any one being able to help. Mothers and relatives trustfully confided their children and their dead to strangers in unknown Jewish villages, whenever the police—against the strictest orders—were humane enough to allow it. The most forsaken among the forsaken, they had at least the comfort of having entrusted them to the hands of their own people. The sense of community inoculated into the blood of the Jews by centuries of suffering borne in common awoke to life again. That blood became the blood of *one* mother and beat in the same pulse through all their bodies. A common furnace smelted all Jewish life into one.

Although Mirkin was rushing from town to town in the region of the front, he had never once come in direct contact with death. Countless times he was stopped by the military police, for his activities drew upon him the suspicion of being engaged in espionage or revolutionary propaganda; but his coolness and his indifference to death always saved him, giving him the assurance that is required in such emergencies. He showed the same indifference to infection by typhus as he did to violent death. The transport trains crowded with Jews often stopped for whole days at the stations of small villages. The dreadful over-crowding and the filth that had accumulated in the wagons during a journey that had lasted for several weeks caused contagious diseases of all kinds to break out among the passengers. Whenever food was handed into the wagons at these stops, half-decayed corpses had to be removed at the same time. This was usually achieved only by giving heavy bribes to the railway officials and the local police.

Mirkin entered the wagons polluted by typhus and did what he could for the sufferers. He was in constant expectation of catching the disease, but death did not seem to want him. He was prepared to die at any moment; for of what consequence was his own insignificant life in a world given over to destruction? But simply because he dared to court death he was spared.

When he saw the essential communism of the life of the Jewish masses, which the hour of need had revealed so clearly, he often asked himself the old question: Why was it that the idea of a communal life did not seize all humanity? For the blood of the whole human race had the same chemical constituents. Probably the impulse to live in common was once an elemental force in human character, but step by step man had deviated from it and left it behind. This deviation had no doubt already begun in primitive times through the rise of the family system and the clan. But it was the raging fires of religion and of patriotism that had finally killed the communal impulse. If a great Messiah should ever appear, his first task must be to awaken from its long sleep that feeling of universal kinship through the mother-blood of humanity. Only then would the real redemption of the world come, the redemption from one's individual prison and the rediscovery of the communal whole. Only then would the empire of evil cease and the kingdom of good begin. And that was what one had to work for even now, had to seek even now, in the midst of this holocaust of fratricidal murder, in the midst of a world war. . . .

One day Mirkin found himself at a little railway station and suddenly noticed an eddy of excitement on the platform. He went nearer to see what was happening: a train-load of Austrian prisoners, who were being sent into the interior from the front, had stopped at the station. The local population, peasants and Jews, were thronging round the carriages, gazing at the frightened enemy soldiers in their strange tattered uniforms, and seeking to recognize in them the bestial animals, so frequently described in the papers, whose cruelty was supposed to be an ample justification for all the hatred that the war had roused. But the curious villagers were quite unable to see anything extraordinary in their enemies. They were just human beings like themselves: sad, dejected men, who looked as if they were relieved to be taken captive and at the same time apprehensive of the unknown fate that awaited them in a strange land.

"They're just like us—no difference at all," said someone in the crowd.

A peasant woman was carrying on her arm a basket filled with eggs and butter, which she had brought to the village to sell. She pushed her way forward to a carriage and handed her basket to the astonished and frightened prisoners.

"Don't you know they're enemies?" cried a timidly reproachful voice.

"We must give them something to eat. And then their mothers will give our sons something to eat if they're taken prisoners," replied the peasant woman in her simplicity.

The others saw the point and nodded approvingly.

This simple scene made a deep impression on Mirkin. His heart was always touched by any human action which shone like a beam of light athwart the red and lowering day of fratricidal murder. Every act of humanity that occurred between enemy soldiers at the front awakened in him new hope and faith whenever he heard of it; was for him a sign that humanity still lived, still breathed under the mountain of corpses that was piled upon it.

Mirkin longed to go up then and there to the peasant woman and thank her with a reverential bow for the happiness that she had kindled in the hearts of men during such dark times. But he refrained, for he wished to avoid notice. He waited for her, however, outside the station, and when she appeared again, walking serenely, he hurried over to her, stopped her, seized her heavy roughened hand, pressed a kiss upon it and turned away without saying a word.

The peasant woman gazed after the stranger in alarm, then she spat and crossed herself.

And then came the "days of the Apocalypse." The impossible happened: a power that had seemed so divinely ordained, so god-like, that to struggle against it was like trying to take the heavens by storm, now lay trampled in the mud, spurned beneath the feet of the people, trembling for its life like the meanest of creatures. A god fell from his heaven, the Czar was hurled from his throne; the millennium was dawning, the miraculous coming of the Messiah was nigh. And then there followed these February days in Petersburg! In clear sunshine—for in truth the sun shone every day in Petersburg during that February; let snow smother the world elsewhere, let storms darken the sky, in Petersburg the sun was shining—crowds of joyful and liberated human beings thronged the streets everywhere; red on the white snow, red fluttering above the dark heads of the crowd, red banners over snow-covered processions, red in buttonholes, red armlets, red shawls sparkling with snow crystals. And the white earth black with human beings.

Whither led the way? What did that matter? Whatever the proclamations, men's blood glowed anew as they listened side by side. Man—the Father; the soldier—the Son; and over both of them hovered the Holy Ghost in flaming red.

The same feeling everywhere. From the Duma to the Taurian Palace, to the soldiers' meeting in the Catherine Hall, to the people's palace and the former villa of the Czar's mistress Kreshinska. What did it matter whither the processions were heading? The wills of all had been fused into one; irresistible forces had been released, the forces of a millennial age, prepared to carry out the will of each, the will of all.

Mirkin was once within a hair's breadth of being torn to pieces by the crowd.

A mob had gathered threateningly round a fur-capped man with a clipped black beard. Some of them claimed to have recognized him as the detested governor of the Petersburg Prison, Platonov.

His protruding eyes staring with childlike terror, the man lay on the ground surrounded by the maddened crowd, holding out his arms appealingly and stammering helpless phrases. The stiff black hairs of his beard trembled as he spoke and seemed to be begging for mercy.

In the Messianic hour of redemption the heart is rich in mercy and forgiveness.

And Mirkin added his prayers to those of the man lying in the snow, helpless as a child for all his strength: "Let him be, comrades! He can't do any harm now even if he wanted to."

The crowd retorted: "That is Platonov! The swine! The torturer!"

Once more Mirkin appealed for the man: "Let him be! You mustn't hurt him."

A sailor pushed his way through the dense crowd till he reached the man lying in the snow; still keeping his cigarette in the corner of his mouth, calmly, without any sign of hatred or anger, he drew a revolver from his pocket and put it to the man's temple; and before the man had time to shout "Don't!" his head fell on the snow, his glazed eyes staring in dumb amazement at the crowd, now transfixed with terror.

"And what about this fellow?" Several hands pointed at Mirkin. Revolver in hand, the sailor walked up to Mirkin and contemplated him indifferently, still puffing at his cigarette.

Mirkin laughed in his face: "Shoot me if you like!—It's all one to me—the revolution is here!"

The sailor pushed the revolver into his leather holster and made his way out of the crowd. That saved Mirkin's life; the others let him go unmolested. On his lips he could feel the bitter savor of death, as if he had eaten poison; but the sun shone and the snow was falling on red banners and streamers.

Processions of demonstrators, choirs singing through the streets —he lost himself in the crowd, grew drunk with the white snow, the red banners, as with strong wine; but the bitter taste of poison on his lips would not go away.

Since his childhood Mirkin had sensed the sadness hidden in all joy, the everyday anxieties lurking in all feast days. So now in the songs of the marching crowds he felt a hidden sadness—and an emptiness. He could not explain the reason for this to himself. It was as if a worm were gnawing at his heart.

When the honeymoon of the revolution was over this feeling of emptiness became more insistent, gnawing more deeply into him. The rejoicings were over—and it was as if everything remained the same as before. Sledges drove through the streets of Petersburg with a gay ringing of bells, the great restaurants were brilliantly illuminated, the cinemas were open as usual; and through dark side streets homeless, ragged soldiers crept towards the magnificent, brightly lit Catherine Hall, which the revolution had confiscated, to attend meetings of officers and men, meetings summoned by the politicians.

The new gods sat in the high places, on the tribunal. An aged leader of Russian liberalism preached in unctuous tones: "And now, my dear children, my gallant soldiers—we must organize our victory. The first task of the revolution is to insure that iron discipline is maintained within the ranks. The German challenge will not shake our unity! We cannot and dare not enjoy the fruits of revolution until a decisive victory is won over our enemies."

A democratic politician, smirking complacently, seconded him:

"The goal is not yet achieved. The revolution is only the first step; the final one is—Constantinople! The revolution must realize at last the aspiration of centuries!"

The high priest in person next got to his feet. He was a little man and his stiff, bristly hair was cut too short—a Czarish cut. Rising on his toes so as to look bigger he shouted in a voice grown hoarse with public speaking:

"For the greater glory of the revolution we must convince our allies that while the outworn and moldering fabric of Czarism could achieve nothing but defeat we, the heirs of the revolution, shall bring victory!"

And the red banners waved in the brightly illuminated marble hall. Rounds of applause rang through the room and broke on the white ceiling. The high priest of the revolution was seized by a group of officers and hoisted on their shoulders. Postcards with his portrait were handed to him, and with the air of a prima donna he autographed them and handed them back to the flushed and rapturous young ladies who surrounded him. But the red banners waved as before, the red banners with their noble inscriptions did not burst into flames, were not consumed with shame.

Mirkin wandered alone, a prey to his dejection, through the streets, which still glittered in their festal attire of red banners and white snow, and murmured as if in prayer: "Messianic days—and no Messiah! Messianic days—and nobody has a thought of delivering the world from the curse of war, which like a rapacious wolf has sunk its teeth into their throats, and clings to them with its fangs and claws so as to tear them to pieces! Nobody has any thought of stopping this bestial slaughter. The high priests of the revolution are doing their utmost to sharpen the claws of the ravening beast."

But sometimes it seemed to him that the revolution itself was that bloodstained monster. Moloch had put on a disguise, had planted a red revolutionary wig on his head, so as to hypnotize his victims. The old methods of luring human bodies into his insatiable maw were no longer effective: "Czar" and "fatherland" were already stale catchwords. So Moloch had discovered a new one, "revolution." And as for these men in their high places—they had embellished the maw of Moloch with flaming red banners, and stood beside him and lured men into his dreadful jaws—in the name of the revolution. . . .

In these days of inward despair Mirkin chanced to meet the advocate Halperin. The lawyer, who had risen high and was in close contact with the new government, went about making patriotic speeches at soldiers' and officers' meetings, ending with a final exhortation to "hold out until final victory is achieved." Most of all he appealed to the young Jews to show their patriotism in gratitude to the revolution for according them their new freedom. It was at one of these meetings that he encountered Zachary Mirkin.

Zachary tried to avoid him, for while in Petersburg he solicitously avoided all contact with his father's circle. But Halperin had recognized him, though not at once, for in the three years that the War had already lasted Mirkin had changed greatly and aged considerably. The advocate hesitated at first to renew his acquaintance with Zachary; but finally he walked up to him, put his hand on his shoulder and said in a reproving voice, as if he were quite used to meeting Zachary:

"Young man, you should be at the front! We must set the others an example by our readiness to serve the fatherland."

Mirkin stared at him in helpless astonishment, so he went on: "My son is at the flying school; Nina Solomonovna and her mother are busy all day making bandages. We Jews must give the others a lead!"

Mirkin left him standing. With head erect the advocate passed on. The phrase "making bandages" stunned Mirkin like a blow on the head. He saw little Nina, now his stepmother, and the quietly elegant Olga Michailovna sitting in their boudoir rolling up bandages. Probably "The Englishman" helped them, letting his smooth glance glide now and then over Olga Michailovna's half-exposed bosom.

When Zachary left the meeting he caught sight of the people for whom the elegant ladies were making bandages. Long files of soldiers in full kit were marching across the Neva Bridge towards the railway station.

They marched now-a-days without singing. Silent and serious they trudged on; the hoofs of the officers' horses rang dully on the snow-covered bridge.

Urged on by the ambassadors of the allies and the army commanders, Kerensky was making ready for the senseless offensive in Galicia, "for the glory of the revolution."

"The time for beautiful phrases is past; it's the turn of the bayonets now," thought Mirkin suddenly. And he added aloud to himself: "Messianic days—and no Messiah!"

CHAPTER IX

BEFORE THE FINAL VICTORY

THE SNOW vanished, all the earth was green, and with the soft airs came new courage and new hope—but the red remained, nay, it increased. There were endless street processions: soldiers with rifles and red arm-bands, soldiers with red flags. Who would have expected to live to see such things? It seemed like a dream or a Siberian snow mirage, and yet it was real: soldiers with rifles and red flags! And they did not appear for a day or two and vanish: they went on for weeks and months! Every day the bread ration dwindled and the bread grew worse. Sugar and salt were no longer to be had in the ordinary shops. But who paid attention to such trifles when soldiers with red bands on their sleeves and red flags tied to their rifles marched through the streets?

Mirkin rented a small room in a cheap hotel in the suburbs of Petersburg. During the war he had got used to wearing his underclothes until they dropped to pieces, his suits and shoes until they were in tatters; nor did he bother much about taking baths.

One day, while he was in this down-at-heel state, he met his father. He was not in the least put out. Old Mirkin made as if to walk up to him. But he saw by his son's bearing that he was not going to stop, and before Zachary had time to put on speed his father had passed him without a look.

Zachary's own needs were few; he ate in the communal kitchen, sometimes too at the soldiers' canteens in the barracks when anything was to be had there; and he had always his bread ration to fall back upon. And what more could one ask for when processions of soldiers with red arm-bands and red flags were marching through the streets?

Every day was a red letter day; almost every hour the trains brought famous men to the capital. With every train they arrived from all directions of the compass: from exile in Siberia, from foreign countries by way of Finland, yes, even by way of Warsaw in sealed German carriages. Every day demonstrators marched to the stations, and soldiers hoisted the heroes of the revolution on their shoulders. Banners fluttered in the wind; fiery speeches resounded in every language. Sight-seeing processions trailed through the city. The visitors were shown the Winter Palace and the throne of the Czars, visited the Duma and Taurian Palace, where the soldiers' and workers' committee held their meetings. But with every day the situation became more complicated and serious, the bread ration smaller, clothes dearer and more difficult to get.

The people longed for peace and the fruits of the revolution: but nobody was capable of giving them peace. Like a sweet cake before a hungry child the fruits of the revolution lay before them: the land, the factories, freedom and all the other benefits that had been cried up so often at public meetings; they stretched out their hands—and yet could not reach what looked as if it were under their very eyes. . . .

During the first few weeks, the honeymoon of the revolution, when the impossible had become possible, everybody had expected and hoped that the miracle would happen elsewhere as well, that the enemy countries would follow Russia's example, and the peoples would stretch out their hands to each other over the heads of their rulers. The miracle did not happen. The hands that were outstretched to each other across the trenches and barbed wire entanglements were sundered with fire and sword. Every attempt at fraternization, every sign of friendship was cut short by the Germans with powder and lead. Kerensky's senseless offensive on the Galician front uprooted completely the fraternal feelings that the first weeks of the revolution had planted in the hearts of men on both sides. Kerensky's offensive gave the German militarists a welcome opportunity of fanning into flame the fire of patriotism and rousing in German men a murderous hatred against their Russian brothers.

What could one do? How could peace be won? Lay down one's arms and leave the trenches? That would mean leaving the revolution at the mercy of the enemy. So Mirkin like everybody else attended all the meetings in the great halls and assembly places in Petersburg, waiting for a message of hope from some of the speakers. All of them spoke in the name of the revolution; all were already hoarse with speaking; all wanted the same thing: peace. But none of them knew how it could be brought about.

One day, in the courtyard of the Taurian Palace, the headquarters of the Soviets, Zachary encountered the man with the high bald brow and the Kalmuck eyes whose name was at that time on everybody's lips.

He was at once the most hated and the most respected man in the whole empire. One section of the people regarded him as a traitor who had entered the country with enemy help in order to destroy the liberty that the revolution had painfully won and to clear a road for the spiked German helmets. Others again saw in him the Messiah who alone could bring salvation, a new Moses who had miraculously appeared to lead a helpless people out of the abyss into which their countless enemies had pushed them; for these he was a saviour, the only man capable of throttling the serpent of war which was strangling everything in its coils.

This man stood in the courtyard of the Soviet palace amid a little group of men in uniform and civilian clothes and one or two women; he seemed to be arguing violently, carried away by what he was saying. Mirkin went up to the group and took a look at the speaker. He was wearing a storm cape of foreign cut which had certainly not been made to measure, and crushing his hat in one hand sawed his arm jerkily with short, violent movements as if he were striking someone to the ground. His stocky body rocked in time to these blows delivered in the air: in proportion to his breadth of shoulder and his huge head it looked actually small. As he argued for his point of view, his wide nostrils grew tense, his lips twitched convulsively and seemed to gnaw at his thick mustache. His small Mongolian eyes were half shut, as if dazzled by a too strong light.

The extraordinarily powerful head of the man awoke genuine respect in Mirkin. The bald roof of the skull seemed to be a continuance of the forehead. Clouds were sweeping across that gleaming forehead with its network of bluish veins; one had the feeling that in the great vaulted head the huge mechanism of the world was revolving and that its workings could be read on that lofty brow.

Like the others Mirkin listened attentively and respectfully to the man's words. He was just talking about the war.

"One of two things must happen," he said. "Either the war will strangle the revolution, or, if that is not to happen, the revolution must put an end to the war—and at once, without shilly-shallying. But only one power can do that: the proletariat. The power must be taken completely into the hands of the Soviets. The Soviets alone can work the miracle and bring peace."

At that moment several well-known members of the Military Council emerged from the Soviet buildings: their high rank could be recognized by the number of officers who surrounded them. The most important figure seemed to be a little gentleman with very lively movements and gestures who was wearing top-boots and a sports coat of a strongly military cut.

When this group saw the man with the Mongolian eyes talking to an audience of soldiers they gave him the cold shoulder, shot angry glances at those who were listening to him and began to whisper among themselves. The circle of men round the man with the gleaming brow grew thinner and thinner. Those of his listeners who were wearing a uniform tried to dissociate themselves from him and inconspicuously went over to the other group.

The man's nostrils grew tenser and his lower lip twitched into a cold, disagreeable smile.

Mirkin seized this opportunity of stepping up to him. In a modest, almost shy voice he began: "Will you allow me to ask a question, comrade? How do you think all this can be done? How can the Soviets bring peace? The enemy. . . ."

Mirkin could not finish the sentence, for the suspicious glance of the other stopped him midway. The man screwed up one eye and his nostrils sharpened to a tense line. He mustered Mirkin suspiciously and penetratingly, not with his open eye, however, but with the other. Apparently there was something in Zachary's expression or voice that won his trust, for a cold smile widened his mouth, making his strong cheek-bones stand out prominently beneath his dusky yellow skin; then he replied, not directly, but with another question: "In whom, do you think, are our comrades, the German proletariat, likely to put confidence? In people who are beginning a new offensive against the German army? Only if the Soviets were to assume full power could the German proletariat have any guarantee that Russia desires a real peace without annexations and without empty patriotic phrases—and then the German proletariat will force their generals to make a just and lasting peace."

"Certainly. . . . But, comrade, we've all been waiting for the miracle to happen on the other side of the front. Unfortunately it hasn't. . . ."

Once more the man would not let Mirkin end his sentence: "Comrade, the war will do its work on the other side, just as it has done it here. The foundations of the bourgeois world are rotten through and through, and ripe for collapse. It only continues to maintain itself at all by means of bayonets and cannons. I have faith in the German proletariat, just as I have had faith in the Russian proletariat, and I have faith in the world proletariat."

"Faith?" asked Mirkin in surprise.

"Yes, faith. I have faith, and I shall work and do all that can be done to realize that faith. Things will turn out with them just as they've turned out with us."

"But, comrade, how can one work among the Germans while they are shooting down every one who goes over to their lines?"

"They've issued the command to take no prisoners," added a soldier, who had been listening.

The man with the polished skull was prevented by his friends from continuing the conversation. The angry lowering glances of the other group, who had remained where they were, boded no good to him. The little bunch of men and women who stood beside him whispered something in his ear, took him by the arm and led him away. He had just time to turn towards the soldier who had spoken, and again answered one question with another: "You're willing to risk your life to kill German workmen, to fire on your brothers; but to enlighten your fellow-men and give them your hand—aren't you willing to risk anything for that? Sacrifice yourselves for peace instead of for war as these people over there bid you do."

His companions dragged him away by force.

In the other group, which meantime had increased, indignant mutterings could be heard. An officer's voice now ventured to say quite loudly: "Is it a matter for surprise that our military operations miscarry when German spies are allowed to seduce our soldiers in the very capital?"

And another was still more explicit: "I wish to God the Provisional Government would only deal more vigorously with these traitors."

After that Mirkin became a regular visitor at the villa of the dancer Kreshinska, where the Bolsheviks had their headquarters. The word "faith," that the man with the Kalmuck eyes had used, took possession of Zachary completely: "Yes, that's it—faith in the conscience of the proletariat, which will awaken all over the world as our consciences have awakened! We must build on that; there's no other force to build on."

Mirkin found in the word "faith" the true meaning of humanity, the true human value, the one creative, ethical force. This the old Jew from Tolestyn had once taught him, this Comrade Anatol had also affirmed: that the most important factor in the shaping of human destiny was a faith in the innate moral force in man. It existed, it was there, even when it gave no hint of its existence. When the time was ripe that force would bestir itself. . . .

At the villa, which the last Czar had built with extravagant magnificence for his mistress, a Polish dancer, Mirkin found men of quite a different type. And here, too, as well as outside, it seemed to him that people were living in an unreal dream. From countless prisons, from countless places of exile an endless stream of men and women arrived: known faces and unknown faces which seemed familiar without one's being able to remember where one had seen them. And sitting on a sofa covered with rose-colored silk—Sosha! Sosha—she was called Comrade Sofia here—the sister of his fiancée, the girl with the milk-white skin of her mother, and the low-necked blouse which displayed it! Her black leather jacket was flung over her shoulders; over her full bosom ran a red leather belt from which hung a revolver. Her soft silky brown hair, now cut short, fell in thick curls beneath her mannish hat over her rosy little ears and on her gleaming neck, whose powerful lines reminded one so vividly of Rachel-Leah's. A revolver by her side in its bulky leather holster and her hands hidden as ever in long brown leather gloves, there sat Sosha on the silk-covered sofa, with her legs, encased in top-boots that came up to her knees, carelessly crossed, smoking "machorka," which she had rolled in a scrap of paper. A group of laughing soldiers stood round her. And as ever she was enthusiastically preaching her gospel to them.

"Sosha!"

It turned out that Rachel-Leah's household was well represented in Kreshinska's villa. Not only was Sosha there, but her older brother Jash was expected every day from Siberia.

Sosha herself had arrived by way of the neutral foreign countries. After the Russian upheaval the German authorities in Poland had given many of the revolutionaries permission to betake themselves to the neutral countries. They had actually liberated Comrade Marek from the prison in which he had been interned after the occupation of Poland, and provided him with a passport. In Stockholm he and Sosha had waited for official permission to enter Russia, and had promptly received it from the Soldiers' and Workmen's Committee. Now all these Polish refugees found themselves in Kreshinska's villa, and formed a separate Polish section of the Party under the leadership of Comrade Marek.

Mirkin felt again the atmosphere of Rachel-Leah's house. And Helene's picture rose before him.

"What is Helene doing?"

"Oh, Helene. . . . The school has grown, and the classes are taught now exclusively in Yiddish. It's packed with refugees . . . a slice of bread is worth its weight in gold in Warsaw. The people are starving, for the Germans are sending everything out of the country. The people are suffering frightfully. With us at home things aren't so bad, for the school has its own kitchen, provided by the relief committee. Mother is kept busy day and night hunting up provisions for it. She has to scour the whole town for them. All Helene's time is taken up by her school work. She has had to organize double classes, and she has so much to do that she has no time left to think of herself. Father shares the school work with her. Mother is on her legs all day, running from one committee to another to get provisions as well for the kitchens that have been set up for the poor people. She's almost breaking down under the strain. Lately she's been complaining of pains in her joints, a thing that never happened before with her. Some nights she gets no sleep at all. And yet she's up again and at work before sunrise. But who has time now to think of herself?"

"Helene, yes, Helene. . . ." Mirkin had of course often racked his brains to find some way of communicating with her through the neutral countries. He had also written two or three letters to her, but had received no reply. After that he had given it up. Who had time for personal matters? . . .

"Quite so—who has time for a personal life?" he assented loudly.

They linked hands and danced through the streets of Petersburg.

The sun shone. A marvelous spring, a marvelous summer. Everything was in full blossom. A white and red snow fell from the chestnut trees. The whole city was crammed with revolutionary soldiers and red banners. Demonstrators everywhere. Rapturous revolutionary speeches. At a soldiers' meeting here and there Sosha would jump on to the platform, and her brown curls, her hastily rising and falling breast, her milkwhite throat rising above her leather jacket, carried away her listeners; the soldiers applauded loudly and lifted her on their shoulders. . . .

Summer and revolution. The most impossible things became possible, all barriers were broken. On the mighty pinions of the new age, the new creation, one flew over mountain peaks, took every obstacle, cut through barbed wire entanglements, ruthlessly stormed over trenches. . . .

Once Mirkin kissed Sosha on her strong white neck. He could no longer restrain himself. It was after a meeting in which Sosha had addressed the soldiers. She had been borne on their shoulders in triumph, rising like a fluttering banner over their heads. Uplifted by her own words, upborne in men's arms, she at last found herself out in the street.

It was one of the white nights. A milky starlight lay over the world. Zachary and she walked on as in a dream. Sosha's breast rose and fell agitatedly beneath her leather jacket. Like a bride of the wind she flew with Mirkin through the streets of Petersburg in the white night. And in the middle of the street he flung himself as if intoxicated on her throat and buried his face like a forsaken child in the maternal warmth that streamed from it.

With her strong arms she clasped him firmly to her full breast, but then vigorously pushed him away again. "Helene!" she panted, while a sigh of ecstasy escaped her.

"Yes, Helene," he murmured obediently.

They went on in silence. After a while she pushed her cool hand into his and whispered: "Let's go up to your room."

There they sat together all night. Zachary made tea on a spirit stove; there was black bread too. Sosha drew a few lumps of sugar out of the pocket of her leather jacket.

"Where did you get that?"

"The soldiers gave it to me."

Then they both lay down on the bed in their clothes, held each other by the hand, and talked of the revolution.

Helene's name was actually mentioned.

Mirkin leant his head against Sosha's breast. She clasped him firmly to her like a forsaken child and went on talking about Helene, praising her beauty, her goodness and her enthusiasm for her work. As she spoke she pressed Mirkin's head closer and closer to her breast. They lay like this, clothed, until morning came. . . .

Then Sosha's brother Jash—so his sister called him—returned from Siberia. He was a dreamy, phlegmatic man with eye-glasses, a typical scholar. During his exile he had written a book on the Siberian tribes and their languages. He walked with his shoulders much bent and spoke in a very low voice. But a violent fire burned beneath this quiet and gentle exterior. He took part in all the phases of the revolutionary activities in Petersburg, but declared nevertheless that in actual reality they were indifferent to him, for he was a Pole, and not a Russian. He behaved as if he were a foreigner interested in the events in Russia only in so far as they touched his own country. He still belonged to that generation of Polish socialists for whom socialism was indissolubly bound up with the idea of the restoration of an independent Poland. And the revolution had interest for him only in that connection. He threw himself into the work of re-forming the Polish legions, was convinced that Pilsudski, who was interned at the time, would return again to power, and agitated for the mobilization and drilling of the Polish prisoners of war, that they might be prepared for the moment when the German army would collapse. He was at constant feud with his sister and treated her as if she belonged to the enemy camp. After a while he ceased coming at all, having discovered a circle of Poles who shared his ideas. "Really," declared Comrade Marek, "they should all be arrested out of hand, and Sosha's brother first of all, for he's conspiring with the Polish soldiers." Later Jash completely vanished from Petersburg, betook himself to the front, carried on propaganda there among the Polish soldiers in the Russian army, and spent long periods on mysterious missions in the prisoners of war internment camps. Then he suddenly appeared in Petersburg again, to vanish again as suddenly, this time for good. . . .

Events followed one another as swiftly as if they were whirled on a windmill.

After the abortive July *coup* the Bolsheviks were attacked in the streets of Petersburg. Kreshinska's villa became unsafe. Finally a systematic search for them was begun. The Bolshevist leaders who were not successful in getting away were arrested. Agitators dared not show their faces at any of the meetings. All who were connected with Bolshevism had to scatter to the four winds, seek refuge in cellars and garrets, and carry on their propaganda by subterranean ways in the working-class quarters. Comrade Marek hid in a remote workman's house on one of the islands and from there gave out his instructions to the Polish group of Bolsheviks.

But the universal longing for peace visibly thinned the ranks of the warlike Social Revolutionaries. Every day more soldiers and workmen went over to the Bolsheviks. The people became more and more convinced that only the Bolsheviks were able to exterminate the serpent of war that was threatening to strangle Russia, and thereby put an end for good to the acitivities of the belligerent patriots and the power of the generals who wished to impose the fetters of Czarism once more on the people. The abortive offensive on the Galician front was the beginning, the absortive advance of General Kornilov on Petersburg the end of the process of development that made the capital ripe for the Bolshevist revolution.

When things had reached this stage the Bolshevist leaders left their places of concealment and had very little more to do than let the ripe fruit from the tree of revolution fall into their mouths.

Petersburg capitulated when a cruiser arrived from Kronstadt and trained the muzzles of its guns on the Winter Palace.

But Moscow was doubtful.

Consequently hosts of agitators were sent there.

Comrade Sosha, who was called "Sofia" here, for nobody could pronounce her real name, was a popular speaker at soldiers' meetings, and always carried her audience with her. Consequently she was ordered to Moscow by Comrade Marek. Mirkin went with her.

And in Moscow he had stayed in the Governor's palace for a time, until at last he found himself here on the roof of the theater. . . .

And now he lay, wrapped in Sosha's leather jacket, in the gray morning, looking out through a window under the roof with a machine gun beside him, hidden behind the gigantic horses.

While he gazed musingly through a little opening at the double-headed eagle of the Czars which seemed to be taking off from the Kremlin, he felt as if he were hunting a quarry. The machine guns were trained on that eagle. Now he could see his way clearly.

He, who all through the war had striven against the horrors and bloodshed of armed warfare, was lying now beside a machine gun; he, who all his life had turned away in loathing from every weapon of destruction, now clasped one to his breast. It seemed to him that he had been caught in a vicious circle which he had been perpetually trying to avoid; he tried to find an explanation for his course, for what he was doing now; he sought to understand why he was lying there on a theater roof in the city of the Czars.

And he replied to his doubts with an answer that was at the same time a justification:

"It is the *last* battle before the *last* victory. And we Jews can only be redeemed by the last victory. For we are the last of all."

CHAPTER X

THE NEW DISCIPLINE

THE GIGANTIC bronze statue of Skobelev, the hero of the Russo-Turkish war, was swallowed up in the dense, drizzling mist that obscured the high windows of the former Governor's work-room in the Residence of Moscow. Yet one could divine the proximity of the monument, for every now and then it was lit up by the reddish glare that accompanied the firing of White troops not far from Skobelev Square.

Again and again the scimitar in the general's hand blazed out, throwing its uncanny reflection on the windows. The rattling salvoes re-echoed from the walls. Telephone in hand, Comrade Ryshkov sat impatiently at his writing table and desperately tried to get a connection with Petersburg. But it was of no use: the telephone was a mere dead instrument. Nor were the savage curses that Ryshkov kept muttering to himself of any avail—the telephone was deaf and dumb.

"The Whites must have driven our men out and seized the central telephone station," said the man with the wrinkled face, who, quite untroubled by the grave situation, was writing an abstruse article for the party journal.

"But I gave them the strictest orders to hold the central station, no matter what it cost, at least for the time being! We simply must know how things stand!" cried Comrade Ryshkov with unusual violence.

"Can our comrades in Petersburg have been captured by the Whites after all, do you think?" asked another anxiously.

"The fight must have been won, one way or the other, by now," said Comrade Ryshkov more to himself than the others. "The last news we had from Petersburg was that Kerensky had set out from Gatchina along with General Krassnov's Cossacks. They must have come up against our Red Guards by now. We must find out whether there was a fight or whether they managed to win Krassnov's Cossacks over to our side."

"How will the state of things in Petersburg help you? We must challenge a decision *here!*" said the man with the wrinkled face, still writing his article, and without raising his eyes from his knees, which he was using as a desk. "It seems to me that the Whites are seriously thinking of rushing this house. Just listen—the firing is growing louder."

True enough, a bright glare pierced the dense fog, lighting up now not only the sword, but also the huge brazen horse on which the general sat.

"They seem to be coming nearer," said someone in an apprehensive voice.

"And must we sit here with our hands folded?" cried a young soldier. "We must show them that we can defend ourselves!"

"With what, I should like to know? With our bare fists?" demanded Ryshkov. "We haven't a single big gun. Comrade Smirnov, who was sent to get artillery for us, hasn't come back. We haven't even enough rifles for all the soldiers, and we're cut off from our other bases in the town by the Whites. What do you think you're going to fight with? Do you think they'll be scared at the mere sight of you?"

"Well, what are we to do? Are we to give up the palace without a struggle and meekly let ourselves be butchered by the Whites?" shouted an indignant voice from a dark corner. "Let's take our rifles and fight our way through to our other bases. Once we're there we can try conclusions with the Whites."

"How are you to get through? We're surrounded on every side by White patrols!" cried a soldier.

"Time is what we need. And we can gain time, for they won't dare to begin civil war openly." Ryshkov cut short the other members of the Executive Committee. "We mustn't allow ourselves to be rushed into thoughtless action."

Suddenly there was a blinding flame followed by a loud humming sound, as if a gigantic top were spinning with incredible speed in the air. A rattle of broken window panes came from the top floor.

"There you see whether they dare to start civil war!" cried someone with a laugh.

"I repeat nevertheless—they'll never dare it. They'll fire and fire again, but they won't try to storm the palace," Comrade Ryshkov stuck obstinately to his opinion. "They've seized the greater part of the town, they've forced their way into the Kremlin, they're firing on the workmen who are trying to slip through to us here—but they won't touch the palace itself.

"For that would be too much of a crime against the revolution to take on their consciences. . . ."

"Comrades, this room is getting unsafe. Let's go down to the ground floor," said someone.

When Ryshkov and the other members of the Executive Committee entered the great ball-room, they found it almost empty. As if nothing were happening outside a few soldiers were sitting calmly round a kettle which they had fetched from the kitchen, drinking boiled water in default of tea. A few workmen of the Red Guard were walking up and down with their rifles in their hands; they turned expectantly to their newly-arrived leaders. Other figures rose hastily from the corners where they had stretched themselves, exhausted after their sleepless nights, and crowded round Ryshkov and his companions.

Presently soldiers appeared from the courtyard and the various other rooms and streamed into the ball-room, thinking that the alarm had sounded. All eyes turned to Ryshkov, literally imploring him to give an order.

Ryshkov gazed at the shadows moving about him and asked hoarsely: "What is it?"

"We can't go on like this any longer, comrade. We must do something!"

"For the moment there's nothing to do," replied Ryshkov shortly.

"And if they come?"

"They won't come," replied Ryshkov in a confident voice.

At a table a group of women was sitting, among them Comrade Ismailova with her clever aristocratic face, which neither her stormy revolutionary past nor three sleepless nights had been able to rob of its housewifely calm. Beside her sat Comrade Sofia and a village girl wearing a red peasant head-cloth, a constant inmate of the palace, where she made herself useful in the kitchen. The women were working busily by the light of a wall lamp.

"Comrade Ryshkov stepped nearer and saw that soldiers were tearing strips of silken tapestry from the walls, while Comrade Ismailova and Sofia were writing words on the strips with India ink.

"What is this?" asked Ryshkov in surprise.

"This is to make sure that the Whites won't miss you when they come," replied Ismailova; and she took up a band inscribed with the words "Revolutionary War Committee" and bound it round Ryshkov's sleeve.

"They'll recognize you *now* at least," she added with a hint of malice in her voice.

"Good," Ryshkov smiled.

At the end of the table he caught sight of a young soldier, who, because of his skill in drawing, had been appointed to design the posters for the palace; he sat a little distance away from the women and was busily occupied in painting in beautiful flowing script an inscription on a large piece of red silk.

"What slogan is that you're writing out, Comrade Ivanov?" Ryshkov asked the young soldier.

"Read it, comrade," the soldier pointed at the inscription which he had just finished.

"Peace in the cottages, war on the palaces," Ryshkov read. The inscription was surrounded with little vignettes drawn from the artist's fancy; on the left was a peasant's cottage with a peasant sitting peacefully in the doorway, on the right a country manor in flames.

"Where did you get the phrase?"

"I heard it at a meeting. Is it a poor one?"

"No, no, not at all; it's very good! Have it put up somewhere, comrade. You're doing the only kind of work that's of use at present," said Ryshkov approvingly.

Meanwhile the first victims of the civil war had fallen in the Red Square.

Some three hundred Bolshevik soldiers, who called themselves Dünaburgers after the town to which their regiment belonged had attempted an armed rush from their barracks, hoping to fight their way through to the Residence. In the Red Square they were surrounded by a troop of cadets who had lain concealed in the ten towers of the Kremlin walls, and shot down from every side. The Dünaburgers could find no cover from the White bullets and several dozens of them fell beside the walls of the Kremlin. The remainder lifted the wounded on their backs, and bearing in their midst their commander Sopranov, who was literally riddled by sword-thrusts, cut a bloody path for themselves through the White chain of patrols till they reached the Skobelev Square and the Governor's palace.

Desperately they hammered with the stocks of their rifles on the gate. The soldiers inside thought it was the Cossacks or the White Guards and did not want to open.

When they reported to Comrade Ryshkov that White Cossacks were hammering at the gate and trying to rush the building he laughed heartily: "Cossacks? Maybe even the police! They would never dare!

No, it's comrades. Hurrah! They've come to help us!" he shouted in elation and went himself to open the gate.

The Dünaburgers bore their wounded comrades, of whom many had died on the way, into the great ball-room and laid them down on the tables.

A great storm of indignation and despairing rage burst out among the men in the palace at the sight of these first bloodstained victims of their enemies. Comrade Ismailova, Sosha and the other women immediately set about the work of nursing. Bandages were fetched, and warm water from the kitchen. Among the men was an army surgeon; he bound up the soldiers' wounds. Then they were hastily carried into the next room, which had been hurriedly transformed into a hospital ward. Only the dead were now left lying on the tables in the ball-room and the mutilated commander, whose body was like a stuffed sack slashed with holes; his blood-stained top-boots stuck out uncannily over the end of the table.

From all the rooms in the huge building every one streamed into the ball-room—soldiers, workmen, Red Guards, intellectuals, as well as comrades belonging to the various committees that were in session on the upper floors. On all their faces could be seen the dumb fury that was boiling within them. The spectacle of the blood that had been shed called for instant vengeance, and they felt that they wanted to hurl themselves on their enemies, even if it was with their bare fists.

Soldiers gathered in the corners, their rifles in their hands. Their faces were dark, their lips twisted with rage. They all stood silent, gazing expectantly at their leader.

Ryshkov stood, pale as death, under a wall lamp, bit the nails of his blunt fingers—and said not a word.

Her eyes fixed on the floor, Comrade Ismailova walked about the hall as if she were searching for something. As if by chance she walked close past Ryshkov and flung him a furious glance from beneath her lowered eye-lids. "Well, what have you to say now, comrade?" Her glance spoke more eloquently than her subdued words.

"What do you expect me to say?" replied Ryshkov loudly, so that everybody in the huge room could hear him. "You want to cause trouble and divide the members of the Revolutionary War Committee against one another. But we shan't allow ourselves to be divided. We'll take up the challenge when it suits *us,* not when it suits our enemies."

Angry, uncomprehending looks came darting at Ryshkov from the corners where the soldiers were standing. He felt them, and was aware too of the menacing fires kindling in the eye-sockets of the gloomy and silent soldiers.

"Comrades, we must keep our heads!" shouted Ryshkov. "We aren't in a position to take up the challenge; we haven't a single piece of artillery."

But how could they keep calm when dead, murdered soldiers were lying in the room beside them with helpless hanging unshaven jaws and wide-open lips behind which their teeth gleamed piteously? Here and there one could see hairy breasts, still young and powerful, beneath their open shirts; white skin, that still seemed full of life, clotted with blood; gay shirts stained with dark and dreadful spots. How could they remain calm when they saw these bodies lying motionlessly and crying in letters of blood for vengeance?

"Take them away! Take them away!" Ryshkov said between his clenched teeth.

Soldiers and civilians, men and women, drew together in one group. Ryshkov saw that Comrade Sofia was climbing up on a chair to make a speech. He rushed up to the group and shouted sharply: "No speeches! Comrades, bear the victims of the revolution down into the cellar, and cover them reverently. The revolution will presently find the right way of avenging them!"

Dead silence reigned in the agitated throng; it was as if they had all lost the power of speech. No one stirred a finger to obey their leader's command.

Suddenly, from the marble gallery where in the times of the Governor gay dance-music had been played, there came horrible shrieks and cries of grief: a whole regiment of screaming women seemed to have gathered there to raise their lamenting voices to heaven: "They have shed the blood of our soldiers! They have murdered our children!"

All eyes were raised towards the gallery.

"Who is that screaming there?"

It was Comrade Maslova. She had managed—God knows how—

to get into the gallery and was beating her peasant skull against its marble panels, her hair straggling from under her red head cloth, while she screamed, in a strangled voice like nothing human: "They have shed the blood of our soldiers! They have murdered our children!"

Comrade Maslova was an ordinary peasant girl. But she had obviously lived for a long time among soldiers, for the only thing that suggested her peasant origin was the red cloth which she now tore from her head. The rest of her attire was military: she wore a long army coat, top-boots and a revolver swung on a strap round her shoulder.

Nobody knew where Comrade Maslova came from. She had been in the palace ever since the Revolutionary War Committee had been established; very probably she had come along with some band of marauding soldiers and after that had stayed on. Like all the others she was given her "payok," her daily bread ration, and a rifle; the soldiers taught her how to handle her weapon and looked upon her as one of themselves. Naturally Comrade Maslova was a Bolshevik from the very first day.

Her laments infected the other women and made the soldiers nervous: they shouted up to her from all sides: "That's enough! That's enough, Comrade Maslova!"

But Comrade Maslova's sobs rose until they seemed the grief-stricken wails of a defenseless tortured animal. And her dreadful keening, and the way in which she kept beating her head against the wall, penetrated like a fiery ether into the blood of the lookers-on in the ball-room and awakened their primitive instincts. Their thirst for revenge awakened, drawn from the profound depths of their natures by Comrade Maslova's shrieks.

Her cries suddenly changed to a dull, hoarse moaning as of a great tree being sawed in two. And monotonously, like the howling of an animal, came the words: "They have shed the blood of our soldiers! They have murdered our children!"

Comrade Ryshkov stood, deadly pale and helpless, down in the ball-room. The atmosphere was stifling, as if the air had been pumped out of the great room, and it was filled with burning ether.

"Silence! Enough now! Take her away!" shouted Ryshkov.

Nobody stirred. The men gloomed menacingly in the half darkness.

"Take her away, or else I'll shoot her down!" Ryshkov drew his revolver. "This is a revolution, not a hysterical melodrama. Comrade Burshanov, arrest Comrade Maslova!" And he took aim with his revolver.

The Lettish soldier made a dumb sign. The leader's order was obeyed. The new discipline had begun.

"The Executive Committee will meet at once," said Comrade Ryshkov.

The Executive Committee betook themselves at once to a distant room.

CHAPTER XI

COMRADE RYSHKOV AND COMRADE ISMAILOVA

COMRADE RYSHKOV was the child of poor parents. His mother died while he was still a small boy. As his father, who was a droshky driver in Moscow, could find nobody to look after him, he kept him with him in his droshky all day. At night he made a bed for the child beside him in the straw of the stable. Through all the course of his stormy life Ryshkov never forgot the tender warmth with which his father had surrounded him in his boyhood. As he grew older he had to fight tooth and nail like a young animal with the other children of the street to keep himself alive, and he grew up like a savage animal, waging war on the great.

But through all the years of want and struggle his father's face went with him.

Whenever he shut his eyes he could see before him the simple peasant face with the kind eyes, which were embedded in a leathery skin furrowed with a thousand wrinkles. Moscow snows and frosts had chiseled these furrows as in stone. Ryshkov could see, too, the little goat's beard on his father's chin, which moved up and down like his flat, hard breast when he spoke, could see his blue-veined neck rising out of the collar of a peasant shirt; he could feel his father's blue, thick-veined hands that had wrapped him in the torn carriage rug as he sat on the driver's seat, could feel his father's hard, hairy breast to which he had been clasped night after night lying on the straw in the stable. A pleasant warmth still ran through Ryshkov's powerful limbs when he shut his eyes. . . .

The street was his home; his father's face all that he knew of a mother's love.

And that face drew him on, raised him out of the street, which otherwise would certainly have been his fate for ever; it filled him with the desire to strive for something better.

His ambition drove him into an iron foundry. There many blows and little food taught him to have no fear of fire. He learned to seize glowing iron with his hands and to endure the drops of molten steel that sputtered in his face. His father's memory next led him into the revolutionary camp. He zealously learned to read and write. His innate intelligence, his ambition, his unbending will, his hand tested in the fire, his boundless love for the class out of which his father and he had come, made him one of the leading spirits of the party and had brought him to the position where he now stood, a leader among his fellow-men.

He drew his power from two sources: the street, and his father's face.

From the street he had taken his almost animal need to rely upon himself, and his instinctive independence in matters both of thought and action. His pitilessly hard childhood had taught him to meet everything with absolute fatalism and to be grateful to nobody and for nothing. But his father's face and memory, which still lived on profoundly in the grown man and bound him to that sole human being with something of the feeling of a child for its mother, gave direction to his strivings, subordinated all his powers and gifts to one end—the good of his father's class.

From the street he had taken, too, his hatred of everybody whose childhood had been brightened by a warm home. He hated the intellectuals, but still more those who had helped in the revolution not from necessity but merely out of philanthropy. Whenever during his party activities he encountered intellectuals who, so to speak, had marched to revolution with warm, fur-lined gloves, he was seized with overpowering rage. If he had had his will he would have twisted these people's necks and flung their bodies to be devoured by dogs. . . .

Comrade Ismailova was the direct opposite.

She had joined the forces of the revolution not because she was driven by necessity but out of pure idealism and romanticism. She came of the high aristocracy, but had nevertheless taken up the cause while she was still a schoolgirl. She dedicated her life to it like a nun to religion; and she had, indeed, the look of a revolutionary Sister. At first she worked with the romantic Social Revolutionaries and was an active member of their terrorist organization, supervising the transport of explosives and undertaking the most perilous tasks.

For her the revolution was a sort of divinity, and her own work in it the service of God. In her eyes revolution had its own ethic, an unbroken romantic line; it was the ideal of future generations, the final goal.

Her terrorist comrades reverenced her like a saint, came to her to confess their sins and draw new courage and ardor. When, after the granting of the constitution of 1905, the Social Revolutionaries discontinued their policy of terrorism Ismailova cried like a child: "Why have they killed the soul of the revolution?" As she always longed to be at the point where the danger was greatest, she left the Social Revolutionaries, who were now too moderate for her, and joined the extreme left wing of Russian socialism, the Bolsheviks.

For a long time a tension had existed between Ryshkov and Comrade Ismailova; but the glory of the great hour obscured the division and both parties did their best to suppress their hostility.

Yet whenever they met, it was as if two opposing streams of energy clashed together. They strove to avoid any explosions, but in the Revolutionary War Committee the latent tension was discharged in open conflicts.

Comrade Ismailova despised Ryshkov's measures, his diplomatic policy, his negotiations with the opposite party to gain time. Like everybody who came under the influence of Ryshkov's strong personality, she could not but trust him, yet was convinced nevertheless that this time he was not equal to the occasion.

The tension broke out openly during the meeting of the Executive Committee that Ryshkov had called after the incidents following the arrival of the Dünaburgers.

The committee met in full force. Comrade Ryshkov listened in silence to the separate speeches bearing on the situation, but his thoughts were occupied with quite different matters. His strong, firm hand was outstretched before him and he gazed at his blunt fingers. For a long time his glance rested on the nails, bitten down to the quick. One could see how feverishly his brain was working inside his powerful, copper-brown skull, how violently his blood was pulsing in the blue veins standing out on his broad, sharp-angled forehead.

Whenever Ryshkov found himself in danger he contemplated his fingers. They reminded him how he had acted at other times in a dangerous hour and counseled him what he should do now.

This time they brought to his memory a day when—it was before the war, in the time of the Czar—he was held up at the frontier with a passport made out in a false name. The gendarme officer gave him into the custody of two of his men, with instructions to guard him until word came from Petersburg that the pass in the name of Antonov, which he had shown, was genuine. Ryshkov knew that the reply which might be expected would mean death for him, or a life sentence in Siberia. While he sat in the guardroom with the two gendarmes he had an inspiration, lured one of them aside, and persuaded him to visit a brothel in his company. There he rid himself of the man by violent means and escaped.

Since then he had acquired the habit of biting his nails when he was in a dangerous fix.

Now his nails suggested a similar way out to him: "I must act just as I did then. All the same, I'm sorry for the soldiers," he added in thought, "but there's nothing else for it."

"We'll have to lure the Mensheviks into a corner and dangle peace in front of them," he began suddenly, turning towards his colleagues.

As they did not understand, but stared at him with astonished and disapproving eyes, he went on to explain: "We aren't strong enough to take up the challenge. The Whites could take the palace at any moment. The only reason why they don't do that is because their left wing, above all the Mensheviks, won't agree to it, out of fear of the responsibility that they would have to shoulder in the name of the revolution. We must exploit that. We must do everything we can to deprive the other side of the initiative, paralyze their energy, and create a division in their camp. To secure that we must telephone the Mensheviks and dangle our lure before them. We'll ask them to work for peace and begin negotiations for the setting-up of a combined executive committee for the whole of Moscow. Of course, we'll use all the means we can to linger out these negotiations, until the situation in Petersburg is clear. And in the meantime we mustn't interrupt our own work; on the contrary, we must stick at nothing to mobilize the forces of the Moscow proletariat."

These words brought Comrade Ismailova's indignation, which had been simmering ever since the ball-room scene, to boiling-point. She could no longer restrain herself and cried in a voice trembling with rage: "That kind of trickery is unworthy of the revolution! The revolution has its own morality! More than any other party we are in duty bound to keep our flag unsullied! We cannot and dare not stoop to trickery, it would be unworthy of our sacred cause and the martyrs who have died for it! If we cannot live as revolutionists, then we must die as revolutionists, revolver in hand!" Pale and trembling in every limb she panted out these words.

By now Ryshkov's self-control was also at an end. He bit his nails till they bled, spat, and shouted: "What do I care for morality? To the devil with your morality! Are we in a girls' school? Only the bourgeoisie can afford the luxury of having a morality. Is the revolution an idol? My God, I want no revolution that is a mere fetish. I want the dictatorship of the proletariat—the power in our hands. And it's quite indifferent to me how we get it. If we must use diplomacy, then we shall use diplomacy. What's the meaning of all this stuff? Are we a set of romantic intellectuals, who do acts of terrorism to prove that they have courage? We aren't romantic; we're the despised and enslaved proletariat!"

Comrade Ryshkov spat again and sat down. The others were pale and silent. The intellectuals kept their heads bent; Comrade Ismailova, too. Their black shocks of hair trembled like the combs of angry cocks. Their eye-glasses slid from their noses. Malicious satisfaction sparkled in the eyes of the soldiers and workmen. . . .

The chairman nodded silently.

"I move that we take the vote, comrades," cried Ryshkov, when he had regained his composure.

The workmen and soldiers belonging to the Executive Committee voted unanimously for Comrade Ryshkov's proposal that negotiations should be started with the Moscow Duma through the Mensheviks. Several of the intellectuals also voted for it, but the majority abstained. Comrade Ismailova was the only one to vote against the proposal.

Ryshkov rang up the Town Hall and asked for Comrade Anatol: "Comrade Anatol, your present friends have shed workmen's blood, soldiers' blood, on the Red Square."

The other voice seemed to be objecting to this statement, for Ryshkov went on more loudly and emphatically: "Yes, your friends! You went in with them and you must be held responsible for them! In the name of the revolution I implore you to do all in your power to save the revolution in this critical hour. The White officers are singing the Czar's anthem in the streets already. Think well of what you're doing—before it is too late! For the sake of our common cause we suggest that military operations should be discontinued on both sides, and also that authorized delegates should meet to try to set up a coalition committee for all Moscow."

The answer was obviously displeasing to Ryshkov, for he knitted his high gleaming forehead and exclaimed: "No, no—that would never do! You mustn't resign from your 'Committee of Defense against the common danger.' The revolution must be represented as strongly as possible on it so as to keep an eye on the Whites at such a crucial moment and see that they don't get out of hand."

Once more there was an objection from the other end, and Ryshkov went on in a calmer voice: "Not at all, comrade! I have no wish to dictate to you, I merely took the liberty of pointing out to you that what you proposed wasn't advisable for the good of the revolution. That was all. Do what you think best!" And thereupon he put back the receiver and turned to his companions: "Well, we've driven a wedge into the enemy's ranks! The Mensheviks are going to send their allies an ultimatum, demanding the immediate cessation of hostilities and the setting up of a non-party committee. If their demands are refused they will leave the Duma. That's all we need at the moment. . . ."

At that moment loud hurrahs and shouts of rejoicing could be heard coming from the ball-room. Ryshkov and the others jumped to their feet in astonishment and hurried down.

In the ball-room their eyes encountered the following spectacle:

On the shoulders of the rapturously cheering soldiers and workers a pale, exhausted figure was sitting; it was Comrade Smirnov, who had been sent out on the twenty-fifth of October to bring in artillery, and since then had not been heard of, so that everybody was convinced he had been captured by the Whites. He could hardly hold himself erect; he tried to speak, but could not bring out a word, and waved his hand towards the courtyard.

There stood three batteries and in front of them a majestic armored car. How Smirnov had succeeded in getting with them through the White lines remained a riddle.

At the sight of the guns an indescribable passion of enthusiasm seized the soldiers, hitherto sunk in impotent fury. The fire that had been almost quenched in them by enforced inactivity now flamed up with redoubled force.

The Dünaburgers who had had no opportunity of revenging themselves for the death of their comrades, the young workmen who had arrived at the palace so eager for battle and had been condemned to sit idle, yes, even the women threw themselves with shouts of joy on the guns. The soldiers kissed the steel barrels and stroked the gun-carriages. The women pressed to their breasts the cold muzzles that would soon spew fire and destruction. Comrade Maslova broke out in hysterical shrieks of joy. "Children, children, *they'll* revenge us for the blood that has been spilt!" she cried. She was no longer under guard and could express her elation without hindrance.

"Oh, they'll revenge us all right! Their mouths will let the world know what the Whites did to us!" shouted a jubilant Dünaburger.

"Help is pouring in! We're growing in strength!" So they infused new courage into each other.

Comrade Ismailova, her head high, walked over to Ryshkov and flung him a challenging glance. Comrade Sofia was the first to climb on to the armored car, revolver in hand.

But Ryshkov took the situation firmly in hand. "Where is Comrade Ivanov and his new banner?" he cried.

"Comrade Ivanov! Comrade Ivanov!" was shouted on every side.

Comrade Ivanov ran up, in his hand the red banner with the inscription.

Ryshkov unfurled it and by the light of hastily lit pine torches read aloud:

"Peace in the cottages, war on the palaces! "

Then he fixed the banner to one of the guns and gave the command: "to work, children! Get the guns in position in the square and set to! Meanwhile I'll look after the peace negotiations!"

The streets and roofs of Moscow began to spew fire. From Skobelev Square came deafening roars, accompanied by flames. A shell struck a chemist's shop, exploding the benzine and alcohol stored there, and a pillar of fire rose over the houses.

The armored car, manned by Red Guards, among them Comrade Sofia and Comrade Maslova, rolled proudly through the White lines into the working-class quarters, bringing reinforcements to the already threatened supports. The young revolutionists, who had waited so long and so patiently, could now give full vent to their repressed lust for battle. A newspaper stall was overthrown in Sucharevskaia Square, a few empty barrels piled up, house-doors torn from their hinges, all sorts of articles of furniture flung out through the windows—and Comrade Sofia found the dream of her childhood fulfilled: a loaded revolver in her hand, she stood, with heaving breast and flying hair, at the head of the Red Guards on a barricade in the city of Czars.

From roofs, out of basements, poured a hail of fire. All night the golden cupolas of the Moscow churches glittered in it like gigantic stars. Here and there bells could be heard ringing from the towers calling despairingly to God to save Mother Russia. The metallic tongues of the bells mingled with the sound of the firing. . . .

In the Governor's palace Comrade Ryshkov sat calmly at his writing-table and negotiated with the Committee of Defense against the Common Danger over the terms of peace, to the musical accompaniment of the brazen tongues of the guns standing before his window.

Comrade Ismailova stood in one of the great windows of the Residence; she saw fiery sparks rising from the house roofs and became fearful for her beloved Moscow. The patriotic feelings of her ancestors awoke. Pale with terror she rushed into the room where the Executive Committee were sitting, and cried: "What are you doing? You'll destroy all Moscow! Tell the gunners to stop!"

"Calm yourself, comrade; they won't destroy Moscow!" Ryshkov comforted her. Then he calmly put the receiver to his ear and called up Comrade Anatol, who was still in the Town Hall: "Comrade Anatol, this is our answer to the bloodshed in the Red Square. But we are still prepared as before to treat with you for the setting up of a coalition committee and the immediate cessation of hostilities. . . ."

The people who suffered most during the fighting were the populace of Moscow. They were terrified of going into the streets, in case a chance bullet might hit them; but they were terrified still more of falling into the hands of the opposing parties. . . .

Both the Red workmen and soldiers and the White aristocrats wreaked their martial fury on the civil population. . . . Both sides demanded papers and documents, both carried out house-to-house searches and pocketed gold watches and the new roubles coined by Kerensky whenever they found them; and by both sides one might expect to be ordered to lay down one's life on the altar of the revolution, so as to be commemorated by the victorious party as a hero in the annals of history.

So the wretched and tortured people shut themselves in their houses, and could not make out whether they were on the side of the Reds or the Whites. They eagerly awaited help from the front, for an obstinate rumor went about that trainloads of Cossacks had left from there and would be let through by the railway workers to save the holy city of Russia.

For a long time already there had been a food-shortage: the rich lived on the ample stores they had laid in during better days, while the poor hungered as usual or crept by back ways at the risk of their lives to some shop where food was sold and begged for a few grains of meal to keep them from starving. So the poor did not care which side won, and left the hostile parties to fight it out between them.

The people were so exhausted by the events that had trod on each other's heels since the February Revolution, and so weary of the quarrels and open feuds of the various parties, that they were already indifferent to the outcome of the struggle and merely wished to see the end of it and the establishment of some authority in the country, under whose protection a return to normal conditions would be possible. The rich, on the other hand, did their best to make as agreeable as possible their enforced confinement to their houses, which resembled a regular siege; for the rich can extract pleasure from any situation in which they find themselves.

For them the siege became a sort of game, a kind of amusement. Their houses were warm inside, the weather was fine, the electric light functioned. And the telephone—the telephone remained, so to speak, neutral during the civil war that raged in Moscow: it served the Whites no less than the Reds and actually found time as well to transmit the conversations of elegant ladies who inquired into the state of each other's health and retailed piquant gossip concerning the handsome White officers quartered in their houses. The telephone—since there was nothing better to do—became a pleasant recreation, and to its credit it must be said that during those dark days it functioned far more punctually and well than it had ever done in the good, normal times.

People also passed whole nights at the card-table, playing preference or poker; in short, they did everything they could to pass the time amusingly. And the pretty young ladies and girls of Moscow—this must be said in their praise—contributed as best they could to maintain the general gayety by allowing the gentlemen to pay court to them, as it were "pro bono publico," so that these gentlemen might await with composure the moment when Kerensky and General Krassnov would be able to send troops from the front to Moscow's assistance. The handsome young cadets, the suckling lieutenants and students, Moscow's gallant defenders, who were welcomed everywhere and received with grateful warmth after their self-sacrificing labors in the cold streets—these handsome youngsters provided the ladies with ample opportunities for fulfilling their "patriotic duty." Many ladies actually risked their lives in fulfilling it; wrapping a few sandwiches in paper they ventured bravely out into the streets so as to transmit these love gifts on cords let down from the roof by their heroes.

As may be seen, Moscow did not take the Bolshevik rebellion very seriously. Everybody thought that it was a transient episode, a sort of bad joke. The great soul of Russia, which existed in the revolutionaries just as it did in the moderates, must be allowed to give vent for a little to its exuberant powers; yet very soon it would return to the normal again. . . .

But then people became weary of the game, for it had lasted too long.

Gradually Moscow became ripe for the Bolsheviks: the long siege, the six-day-long enforced confinement at home, the uncertainty of the situation and the deadly fear that towered over the heads of all soon effected this. In vain people waited for the decisive stroke which, they were assured every day, might happen at any moment and clear up the situation at once. In vain came one announcement after another that the city was in the firm possession of the Whites and that they could now deal with the Bolsheviks at pleasure. In vain did reports follow one another that the Cossacks, led by a famous Hetman, were on their way to Moscow, that Kerensky himself, after having already reconquered Petersburg, was marching on Moscow at the head of an army to deliver the Mother of Russia.

But no help came, the situation was not cleared up, and on the sixth day after the Bolshevist rising the people of Moscow were still confined to their houses with no prospect of relief. Their food stores were exhausted and their hopes were unfulfilled. So, when they saw that the battle was tending to the advantage of the Bolsheviks, a sudden slide towards the left resulted among the people.

The first to rebel were the people in the working-class quarters on the outskirts; they drove out the officers and cadets and took the part of the Bolsheviks. But in the central districts, too, where the rich lived, the saviors of yesterday were now greeted with oblique, contemptuous, even menacing looks. The word "White" that had the day before been a term of praise and admiration now changed into one of contempt.

The Moscow young ladies, who had made a cult of worshiping the handsome young officers, now scoffed at them. They began all at once to recognize the ancestry of many of these heroes and jeered at them as "Jewish trash." And at last Moscow awaited the Bolsheviks with actual impatience.

CHAPTER XII

CAVIAR AND CHAMPAGNE

In the Hotel Metropole the panic caused by the disturbances of the first day was followed by an equally complete reaction. After the storm of the twenty-fifth of October had passed, the life in the hotel might have been described as almost normal.

It was not, of course, quite normal, for the guests' freedom of movement was confined to the hotel rooms. The great building was cut off from the outer world and the inmates were thrown back completely on their own society. And as their life together in the hotel was an enforced one they soon grew weary of it. Every face they saw round them quickly became as familiar as a worn coin. They had the feeling of being herded together in a small ship for a boring voyage. Every one of them would gladly have given a fortune to see a new face, if it had been possible to discover one.

But here a qualification must be made; for not all the inmates of the hotel were so completely bored as this. Certain ladies fulfilled their duty of maintaining the good spirits of the party so conscientiously that violent scenes took place between their husbands and some of the other gentlemen. The one who provided most subject for gossip was the piquant young lady who on the first day of the "siege" had made her laughing entry into the billiard-room under the escort of a troop of admirers and thus excited the voluble disapproval of the older women. "They say actual orgies go on in her apartment at night," people whispered. All sorts of other scandalous tales went round, too, of a scene where two gentlemen had come to blows, indeed there was actually some talk of a duel between two gentlemen of high position, each of whom considered that the other had insulted his wife; the execution of this affair of honor had, however, to be postponed to a more suitable time.

But these great and petty scandals, no less than the piquant and thrilling affairs of honor, had also their good side: they relieved a little the monotony of life.

Yet there were other difficulties, for instance in providing for the needs of the guests. Already on the second day of the siege it became clear that while the hotel was very well provided with all sorts of delicacies and rare wines the supply of necessary everyday food essential for nourishment, such as bread and potatoes, was getting very short. Now, as everybody knows, bread is the favorite food of the Russian, whether he be rich or poor. And when it threatened to give out altogether it became a precious delicacy which nobody could do without, and all the arts and wiles that are usually expended only in great transactions were now devoted by the guests to persuade the hotel staff to part with their meager bread-rations.

In compensation, however, there was a superfluity of the finest delicacies of every kind, smoked salmon of all varieties, Astrachan sturgeon, enormous herring from the Baltic and the Crimea, but above all—caviar. Huge jars of caviar of the most diverse hues, shading from deep black, through gray, to rose and pearly white, fresh caviar and pressed, were brought to light. One might have thought that the hotel had an inexhaustible reservoir of caviar at its disposal, or possessed secret fountains of caviar. In spite of the uncertain situation one could have as much caviar as one wanted, providing, of course, that one paid proportionately high for it. But as money had almost lost all its value at the time, and the class to which the guests in the hotel belonged were accustomed to spend it freely, the question of the price did not enter into their calculations. They lived in accordance with the prophetic motto: "Let us eat and drink today, for tomorrow we die," and caroused and gorged with desperate indifference.

At the beginning they were given a piece of biscuit, and in exceptional cases, as a mark of quite unusual favor, a thin slice of black bread with their portion of caviar, as well as a little chopped onion if they cared for it, and of course a little carafe of vodka. But presently the supply of biscuits gave out too. Only an odd fragment of sweet biscuit now appeared here and there at table. But then the worst thing that could happen did happen: the vodka, a necessity in Russia, was at an end; and there was nothing left to drink with the caviar but—champagne.

Caviar is an excellent means for shapening the appetite; but taken as the main course, in large portions, without bread and without a glass of brandy, it left a lustful taste in the mouth and roused the glands to heightened activity; at the same time it immoderately stimulated all one's energies and desires. As the only thing that was left to wash it down with was champagne, that diabolical drink naturally helped to increase the passions awakened by the caviar, until they became quite unbridled.

Inevitably the outburst of youthful high spirits that followed among even the most sedate inmates of the besieged hotel, where no one could avoid another, led to all manner of painful scenes and disagreeable quarrels, which only the generally unpleasant state of things deprived of their sting. . . .

On the other hand the prospects that the painful situation in Moscow would soon be cleared up were almost brilliant. Every day there were new assurances that the patriotic defenders of the city were in full control of the situation, that the loyal troops occupied the whole town and at any moment would finally annihilate the Bolsheviks in the Governor's palace. On the other hand nobody could quite understand why this had not yet been done, and the "adventure" finished off once and for all.

The telephone functioned promptly and obediently, far better than in normal times. So most of the guests helped to pass their time by chatting to their acquaintances in the town. The electric light was in perfect order, and that made it possible to sit all night through at cards.

Misha "Molodyetz," who was still the best source of information in the beleaguered hotel, kept on sending out reassuring reports quite in the style of the official telegraphic agencies during the War: "The Bolsheviks have surrendered unconditionally. A general committee has just met to determine the terms of the capitulation. . . ."

At last someone had discovered where Misha got his information. But this discovery, instead of lowering his reputation in the eyes of the hotel guests, only served to raise it considerably.

Among the hotel guests was a lady with whom Misha was very intimate. In time the news trickled through that this lady was the legitimate or illegitimate wife (this point could not be resolved) of a prominent member of the Defense Committee, who was the commander of a neighboring district. This fact also procured her certain extraordinary privileges; for instance she was the only lady who had been allowed—much to the annoyance of the other women, who bitterly complained of such favoritism—to retain her pet dog at the time when every one had been forced to seek refuge in the billiard-room.

With the "commanderess"—as she was universally called—Misha stood on terms of the closest intimacy. She was a voluptuous brunette with a faint down on her upper lip and the most charming moles on her cheeks. Her figure, it was true, inclined somewhat to fulness, and her hips were unmistakably broad, but the piquant dark down on her upper lip turned the scale in her favor so that the general verdict was that she was "beautiful."

Naturally the "commanderess" enjoyed the public esteem of the whole hotel, and, with her, Misha, who never stirred from her side. Whenever she appeared in the common-rooms he was always to be seen following her. He had always a smile or a compliment ready for her, or, when she herself was not particularly receptive, for her pet dog with the little wet muzzle, which always peeped out beneath the curve of her warm bosom. The effect of Misha's attentions was the same in both cases, for the little dog was a part of its mistress.

Now since the commander very frequently visited his lady in her room, she naturally possessed first-hand information. And Misha's reports emanated from her.

"For God's sake, Misha, find out how things really stand!" Misha was importuned imploringly after every visit of the commander. And at once he would take his post, smiling his thin, obsequious smile, behind the "commanderess," and inquire after the health and digestion of the lady and her dog.

"Well, Misha—what have you found out?"

"Everything going splendidly, couldn't be better! The committee are just considering the formalities for the surrender of the Bolsheviks."

"And when will it all be over?"

"Just have a little patience, a little patience, ladies and gentlemen!" replied Misha severely in an almost official tone. . . .

As the situation seemed promising, the interrupted meeting to inaugurate the "New Russia" Syndicate was now resumed, in spite of the siege.

When the first panic had passed and the square in front of the hotel once more became quiet the founders of the syndicate assembled again in the marble hall and after two days of perpetual haggling over shares and profits the constitution of the company was worked out with the help of a notary who happened to be in the hotel; in addition, the shareholders pledged themselves by separate contracts to fulfill their responsibilities to the undertaking. And thanks to Misha's optimistic reports the shares began to rise there and then in the Hotel Metropole. They rose in the closed ring of the shareholders concurrently with all other stocks and shares, which were being watched and bought and sold even here not only by stockbrokers but by everybody who took an interest of any kind in the stock-exchange; there was an astonishing number of such people among the ladies and the state officials who lodged in the hotel. The traffic in stocks, the rise and fall of the "New Russia" and other shares in response to the reports given out by Misha, was both thrilling and profitable, and helped every one to forget the momentary unpleasantness of the situation. . . .

Soon it became clear that Misha had set up his information bureau simply and exclusively to serve his own interests as regarded the stock market in general and the "New Russia" company in particular.

For Misha had a burning ambition to belong to the newly founded company. But like a watchful house-dog old Mirkin kept him out. So to reach his goal Misha set up his information bureau, or more exactly two bureaus: the one was for the general public and gave mere reports without going into details or explaining the situation clearly or entering into future possibilities, while the others were confidential, and were passed from mouth to mouth only by the chosen few; they were expressly intended for the members of the "New Russia" syndicate.

"Gabriel Haimovitch, I'm in a position to be of use to you, and I'm eager to be so," Misha said, turning with respectful politeness to old Mirkin, the chairman of the new company.

Old Mirkin smiled wisely and ironically; thoughtfully he passed his hand over his long two-pointed beard, which was growing gray, but still retained its reddish fairness. He asked indifferently: "How can you be of use to me?"

"I've just received important information," Misha began in a grave voice.

"Information?" old Mirkin interrupted him. "That doesn't interest me. I have time enough to wait for whatever is coming, and have no need to rush out and meet it," he added with a smile.

"But, Gabriel Haimovitch, I want to help you."

"I don't need your help," retorted old Mirkin sharply; his smile vanished and his long beard took on an aspect of icy dignity.

"Not even now?" asked Misha with peculiar emphasis, looking old Mirkin in the eyes.

"Neither now nor at any time," replied the old man, leaving Misha standing.

"Well, we'll see about that yet!" Misha shouted after him.

But old Mirkin had already walked off and disappeared.

The guests in the Hotel Metropole were in the best of spirits. They flirted, did business, sought every amusing means they could find of passing the time, and waited in a mood of cheerful hope for the end.

Everybody was full of confidence except for one single man—and the very one from whom, by virtue of his nature and his position, one might most naturally have expected confidence—the celebrated advocate Solomon Ossipovitch Halperin.

It was not the general situation but an unpleasant personal experience that had caused his spirits to droop in such a pitiable fashion. For the famous lawyer had been the victim of a painful incident.

He had at last come to the unshakable resolution that he must act and by his courage give an example to the others. He saw that it was not in accordance with his dignity to sit like an old woman in a beleaguered hotel: he must exert his personal influence on events at such a grave hour, he must be at the post where he was needed!

Without divulging his intentions to any one he left the hotel one day when the streets seemed to be fairly quiet. He succeeded in passing the officer patrols that guarded the hotel. Whether they had recognized him or not (Halperin of course assumed that they had), in any case they let him pass. With erect head, firm tread and expanded breast the famous advocate crossed the dead and empty Theater Square and turned in the direction of the Alexander Military School, where the headquarters of the Whites were; there he hoped to find a crowd of friends and acquaintances.

But at the corner where Georgevska Street crosses Tverskaia Street he was stopped by a group of cadets. This point was highly dangerous; it was quite close to the Governor's palace, and the whole quarter was occupied by Bolsheviks. The Whites had fenced off the entrance to the Bolshevik zone with barbed wire. Their patrols were made up of young cadets and high-school boys whose downy cheeks had not yet been touched with a razor, but who stood at their posts with grave, self-conscious faces. They were armed to the teeth with rifles, swords and revolvers; a pile of hand grenades lay on the ground before them and each held one in his hand as well.

"Halt! Where are you going?" A young officer stepped up to Halperin.

"To the Alexander Military School to defend the fatherland," cried the advocate in a voice expressing all his consciousness of his own dignity and of the historic moment, and he made to go on without regarding the young lad.

"Show your papers!"

"I don't need any papers. I am . . ."

"The password!" the officer interrupted him quite rudely.

"I, I . . . *that* is my password," and he pointed to his buttonhole, where he was wearing his badge as a public functionary of the government.

The badge made but little impression on the young officers, for they did not know the badges given out by the new government. Besides almost everybody wore a ribbon or a badge in their buttonholes during those days, and so nobody could any longer tell what the various rosettes and emblems meant and to what party they belonged.

"It's a bad look-out for the present system of education if the young aren't taught to recognize their leaders. That should be one of the duties of a school!" muttered the advocate in an offended tone.

"A Bolshevik, I suppose?" one cadet asked another, without paying any attention to Halperin's remarks.

"Quite possible. Trying to slip through to the Governor's palace, probably."

"He looks like one anyway—a real Jewish mug."

"We'll show him some fun!" The youngsters nodded laughingly at one another.

"Listen, uncle," began one of them, blowing the smoke from his cigarette brazenly into Halperin's face, "you'll just go back the way you came, and look slippy too: we'll count up to four and then we'll fire. Now, get going!"

They spun the famous advocate round and pointed their revolvers at him: "One . . . two . . ."

Naturally Halperin started to run for all he was worth. In this race for life he quite lost his dignified bearing, and at seeing that ludicrous figure fleeing from them with wild leaps the young lads burst into roars of laughter. When they had counted four they fired in the air. At the report of the revolvers a convulsive trembling seized all the lawyer's limbs. The cadets laughed until they were aching.

Bathed in a cold sweat, the advocate reeled across the Theater Square with trembling knees and a wildly beating heart and at last, more dead than alive, reached the hotel. On the doorstep he fell down in a faint.

It was a long time before he came to himself again; he was carried to his room and put to bed. As life began to stir in him again he kept on stammering incomprehensible words to the people standing round him: "They've gone mad. . . . All Russia has gone mad. . . ."

Since that day his spirit had been broken. He never left his room, never showed his face in the billiard-room, and took no part in the business life of the hotel. His son-in-law Gabriel Mirkin tried to rally him: "How could you think of leaving the hotel at such a time!"

And the tea magnate, who during the siege had lost the roses in his cheeks and acquired great brown rings round his eyes, said in a reassuring voice, repeating his customary comfort: "It will all soon be over. It's said that they're already setting up a general committee in the Town Hall. . . ."

This was the universal formula of encouragement in the Hotel Metropole—until the night of October 31.

CHAPTER XIII

THE SERVANTS

Of a sudden the situation completely changed.

The street fighting that had started on the outskirts came nearer and nearer to the center of the city. The Moscow Bolsheviks had already received reinforcements from Petersburg, and these were now advancing from the suburbs along with their Moscow comrades against the Whites.

The officers and cadets secured all the routes to the Town Hall and the Kremlin, among them the Theater Square, with barbed wire and a thick chain of patrols. But already Mirkin's machine guns were looking down, unabashed and without concealment, from the roof of the theater, their muzzles trained on the Hotel Metropole.

On the evening of October 31, Mirkin's squad received the signal to open fire. From the roof of the great theater poured a hail of shot that swept the whole square. The inmates of the Hotel Metropole were alarmed by the rattle of the machine guns and the explosions of the hand grenades. Once more the manager and his staff ran from room to room and dragged the guests—some from their beds, some from the card table, some from still more pleasurable recreations—to the already familiar billiard-room, where chairs, arm-chairs, sofas and couches were ready to receive the alarmed and frightened crowd. But this time they were not allowed to go into the great entrance hall or the buffet; the rooms and alcoves off the billiard-room were also out of bounds, for they looked out on the courtyard. All the business offices were deserted, the buffet remained locked. The billiard-room alone remained available for the assembled guests, the assembled staff and the manager's lieutenants.

In their six days of enforced proximity even the politest among the guests had lost their good manners. They were all already so sick of each other and so worked up that they were ready to fly at each other's throats at the smallest provocation. The manager and the guests who still had their nerves under some control had a hard task calming down the others until finally there was comparative order in the room.

Scarcely had Misha entered the room when he was surrounded. Like people dying of thirst they longed for some word of comfort in their wretchedness, some ray of light in the darkness of their fears. All day Misha had indefatigably disseminated the cheerful news that at any moment the Governor's palace would be captured and the city delivered from the Bolsheviks—and now came this sudden turn-about!

"For God's sake, Misha, find out what can have happened!"

"Misha, go to your lady and ask her what the position is!" Thus Misha was assailed by imploring voices on all sides.

And even now he obstinately kept on asserting that this last turn meant nothing, for he had just received "a little report," quite confidential, according to which this attack was, indeed, a stroke of the Bolsheviks similar to that of the twenty-eighth, but this time it had been precipitated by the White officers, who were resolved to put an end to the whole business once and for all over the heads of the city Duma, infected through and through as it was by the "social revolutionaries."

Yet suddenly Misha's reports found no credence from anybody. All at once the guests felt what fools they had made of themselves in believing such a glib and untrustworthy phrase-monger. Everything he had said had given the impression that he was in close touch with responsible and authoritative circles; and now that his authoritative tone was exposed as pure pretense, those who had set their hopes on the old order lost all their faith in that too.

Misha's reports were now greeted with ironical headshakes.

"These are the people who are supposed to be protecting us!" they sneered. "*These* are the rulers of Russia!" And they pointed with open contempt at Misha.

He now resembled a worthless bill of exchange, a coin that had been withdrawn from circulation, and they all asked one another in astonishment how they could ever even have listened to the man.

Misha soon began to feel the insulting contempt of the whole room and shouted angrily: "This is really too much! You all fly out at me as if I were the government!"

So "that nice Misha" quickly became the scapegoat for all the sins of the former régime, of the tottering old world. . . .

But suddenly something happened that made them all turn to Misha once more. The electric light went out and in a clap the whole room lay in pitch darkness. And this time, against everybody's expectations, the light did not come on again in a few minutes, as it had done on the first day of the siege: the darkness continued.

"Lights! Lights! Lights!" the shout came from every side.

"Silence! This is a regular inferno!" someone cried in exasperation.

"Silence! Silence!" everybody began to shout.

The gentlemen lit matches. Several pocket torches, too, flashed out; for it was a fashion at the time for men to carry these. The manager shouted something into the din. In a few minutes a candle flame rose up. It was followed by a second, a third. Waiters bore in candlesticks with candles burning in them, also paraffin lamps held in reserve in case of a failure of the electric light.

"This is something we can't help, but we'll do all we can." With these words the manager, himself nervous by now, replied to the countless shouts for light.

"And I advise you to be sparing with the candles, too!" shouted a voice from the corner of the room.

"Quite right! Nobody knows how long this may last," the manager said approvingly.

"Well, Misha—what has happened now?" asked someone jeeringly.

"Don't ask me. I know nothing!" retorted Misha in an offended voice.

"I'll tell you what has happened!" cried another voice. "The Bolsheviks have seized the whole town. And they'll soon be here, too!"

"All the better! I hope they'll come soon and put an end to all this nonsense!"

The others remained silent. Everybody had the same wish....

Nobody knew what the new state of things would be like. But something of its grimness could already be read in the faces of the hotel staff.

During the whole siege the staff had been the barometer registering the various changes in the situation. At the beginning, when it seemed probable that the Bolsheviks would be driven out, the servants had been almost slavishly obedient, carrying out with that submissiveness so characteristic of the Russian the most arbitrary orders of the guests. In the last few days they had already grown more discourteous, but after the evening when the electric lights went out they became the masters. From beneath the masks of their flunkeydom all the horror that was approaching began to peer out, and on their faces could be read the sentence they had pronounced on their masters, their vengeance for their wretched lives passed in service, for all the insults and humiliations of many years of slavery.

The guests now handled the staff as gently and solicitously as they might have handled a cracked vase, and were careful not to wound them by a single word or even a sigh. And as once the servants had smiled cringingly and obsequiously to the masters, so the masters now smiled to them. It was a forced smile, an attempt to melt the icy armor, to drive away the dark clouds that brooded ever more darkly on the faces of these men, once so submissive....

But this new attitude was perceptible only in the hotel staff. The private and personal servants of the guests were altogether different. For many of the inmates had brought their private lackeys with them, servants who had been bred like domestic animals to obey a master and serve his various needs. These were already so depersonalized in their subjection that they took more to heart the inconveniences caused by the enforced confinement of their masters than did their masters themselves. On these private lackeys one could rely. Not the slightest alteration was visible in their attitude, except, indeed, that they exerted themselves to be still more devoted than before, as if they were trying by their personal submissiveness to recompense their masters for all the unpleasantness they had to endure. And indeed the masters found a certain relief in the fact that in their servants they had a safety-valve for the impotent fury that had gathered in them. It was the ladies of rank who made most use of this opportunity.

In the hotel there was a princess, to whom a poor baroness distantly related to her acted as "companion." The princess tormented this poor creature pitilessly. She showered the worst abuse on her, but never forgot, all the same, to give her her title of baroness.

"Baroness, you're no better than a yokel! A kitchen maid has a lighter hand and a gentler touch than you, Baroness!" she would scream at her companion before everybody.

To the annoyance of the whole room the baroness swallowed all these insults submissively, without stirring an eyelash, quietly went on with her menial work and even excused her mistress to those who witnessed such scenes, saying: "Poor thing, she used to go for a ride every morning to drive away her headache. She can't do that now, so she's always very upset in the morning."

The private servants did all they could to make the siege pleasant for their masters. They fought each other for the best places, quarreled over foot-stools, waged war in the kitchen with the cooks and waiters for an extra portion, a glass of tea or a hot water bottle for their patrons. If they were unsuccessful in their efforts they took the blame on themselves. It was as if they felt responsible for the critical situation and the evil times. They comforted their masters and mistresses like mothers comforting children, laid cold compresses on their brows, held smelling salts under their noses, or offered their shoulders as support to some tired head. With their backs, their chests, they tried to avert all harm from their masters: in short they spent themselves in trying to compensate by their physical assiduity, at least, for the unhappiness their masters suffered from the revolution and these accursed Bolsheviks.

With the hotel servants who came in direct contact with the guests —the waiters, house maids and attendants—one could also get on well enough, if not so well as with one's private servants. They carried out —from sheer habit—the orders they were given, and above all—one knew their faces. In the course of the siege, however, the sharp line of demarcation dividing guest and servant had been slightly effaced. In these days the hotel staff took liberties with the guests which otherwise would have been unthinkable; they ignored wishes, pretended not to hear orders and frequently answered back in a way that made the guests see red.

Yet, as we have said, it was possible to get on with this part of the staff, for it was always possible to bribe them. The staff exploited this opportunity without shame and made the guests pay through the nose for every amiable smile, every act of assistance, every order that they executed. And since—in accordance with the spirit of the time—everybody was eager to show that his heart was with the people, the guests were quite willing to make good by the size of their tips the sins that they had hitherto committed against the lower orders. So there began a sort of competition in displaying one's sympathy for the people: each man tried to outbid his neighbor by giving larger and larger tips. Some went even farther; they were not content to buy the people with money, but wished to draw them, so to speak, into intimate relations. The advances once made by the servants were now made by the masters; they inquired into the health of the staff, and took an interest in their personal circumstances and family affairs: "Are you married? . . . Children, of course! . . . And your weekly wage? Why, it isn't enough to last one from Monday to Thursday! . . . You should be more ambitious, my dear fellow! You must think of your wife and children. Come to my office when things have quieted down—we'll see what we can do for you. . . ."

But the more friendly, cordial and familiar the masters showed themselves, the more reserved, stiff and silent became the staff. . . .

All at once quite new figures made their appearance in the billiard-room, figures one had never seen or noticed before. They emerged from the hidden corners, from the cellars and garrets of the hotel, as the situation became more menacing. The cooks, the bottle-washers, the charwomen, the stokers, the lavatory attendants, the scavengers, in short, the "hotel rats," who dwelt unseen in the remote basements, cellars and garrets of the great hotel, now came to the light. The very appearance of these figures evoked an icy shudder and chilled the blood in one's veins. Faces white with flour and black with soot, half-naked bodies glistening with sweat, whose bareness was covered inadequately with rags or tattered sacks; and all exuding a sourish stench mingled with the smell of stale food which they brought with them from their hidden holes and corners.

In the dim light of the candles and paraffin lamps the appearance of these strange figures awoke in the weary and apprehensive guests a feeling that they were seeing devils or evil spirits as though in a nightmare.

And indeed any one might have had that impression, looking at the ragged and tattered intruders with their clumsy movements, their rough faces covered with dirt, and the idiotic grins on their mouths opened wide in dazed astonishment. One blear-eyed hag kept on gaping at the ladies, showing all her rotten teeth. With an insolent and yet vacant grin she contemplated them as they sat about half-awake, and even went so far as to shuffle close up to a young lady and feel her dress. "Silk," she said with a laugh.

The lady started back violently and fell into hysterics.

A shapeless colossus with legs like pillars, evidently a coal-heaver, for his naked trunk was wrapped in a blackened sack, stood motionlessly in the middle of the room; his face was covered with deep, badly-seamed scars, and his glittering eyes, in which there was a cold, menacing smile, kept straying challengingly from one guest to another; it was the glance of one surveying his victims. . . .

The newcomers went still further: they jeered at the hotel servants who still behaved with decorum, aped sarcastically the obsequious bearing of the private lackeys, and shouted insulting and gross remarks at them: "Tame poodles! Look how they creep on all fours at the noble arses of their masters!"

The appearance and bearing of these extraordinary figures created, excusably enough, a panic among the terrified guests, whose nerves were already in a bad state. They glanced apprehensively at each other and whispered: "What are these people? What can it mean?"

The coming horror could be read from the countenances of these threatening figures. It was as if the black abyss of the days to come opened before the hotel guests.

"Send these people away! Why have they been brought here?" shouted someone angrily.

The others hastily implored him: "Hush! For God's sake be quiet! Don't you realize the times we live in?"

Quite unconcerned, the newcomers mingled with the guests and presently tried to find places for themselves on the comfortable armchairs and cushioned sofas which were exclusively reserved for their masters; indeed some of them went so far as to rub shoulders with the ladies and gentlemen. The washerwomen carried their insolence to the length of squeezing themselves in between ladies sitting on the couches. And the unendurable smell of sweat and dirty linen that they exuded made many a terrified lady jump up hastily and rush away.

"What are they doing here? Why have they put them in here? Ivan! Ivan!" a chorus of voices shouted for the head porter.

"Here! Shift up and make room, gentlemen! You've sat on comfortable chairs long enough; now it's the turn of other people." The man who spoke these words sent out an unbearable stench that reminded one of dead rats and made one want to cough.

Fortunately Ivan now appeared; he marched up quickly to the man, his elegant, shining boots twinkling.

"What do you want? Don't you know that only the hotel guests are allowed to sit here? Come on, get out of that, go back to your own people!" the head porter began in as friendly a tone as he could summon up, though one could see what self-control it cost him to speak to such a fellow in a friendly tone. At the same time he seized the man by the arm and tried to pull him away: "You come with me. I can show you a much more comfortable place. You can see for yourself that there's no room here."

"Lickspittle! Just wait till our lot come—they'll soon show you!"

"Be quiet! Don't shout!" and Ivan dragged the man away.

In these evil days Ivan was the guests' sole comfort.

He was the head porter of the hotel, and he stood in an elegant posture in his gold-braided uniform, his silver-mounted staff in his hand, before the entrance of the Hotel Metropole and smiled amiably and invitingly, like the master of ceremonies at a wedding, on every one who entered.

He was a well made, strikingly fair-skinned man in his thirties. Beneath his gold-braided coat he always wore a snow-white embroidered Russian shirt which, in spite of its loose cut, outlined his unusually large breasts. His delicate fair complexion gave him the look of a strong, well-grown woman rather than of a man. His small, beautifully-shaped feet encased in boots that were polished until they shone, advanced with a light, almost inviting step that seemed to indicate a readiness for any service. The soft glance of his blue eyes attracted the men as well as the women. . . .

In spite of the heavy work he had to do carrying luggage, his hands were always groomed, the nails of his straight, slender and yet powerful fingers invariably clean and neatly manicured; he liked to make play with them, holding them in such a way that they were bound to be remarked. . . .

Only in a Russian bred through generations for slavish service could such an infallible feeling for the needs and wishes of his masters have developed as it had in Ivan. Like a trained dog he guessed with all his senses the most secret desires of his masters before they were clearly aware of these desires themselves. His light feet in their polished shoes were ready to walk through fire at a sign from his masters. In talking to them he avoided looking them straight in the face, as if he were concealing something, and instead glanced at them sidelong with an almost appealing gentle submissiveness. From this position his eyes glided caressingly over his interlocutor, whether male or female. . . .

Only Russian serfdom could have developed in human beings, side by side with an absolute renunciation of their own personality, that cunning which was so often to be found among the oppressed masses in Russia. Ivan never lost sight of his own advantage, not for a moment. For his advancement he employed the means that nature had given him: he used his feminine charm to extract tips from the men for the things he did for them; he turned on his masculine charm for the women. His every action was coldly calculated. Although in accordance with his obsequious nature he obeyed every demand made on him, he was no spendthrift with his touching glances, and saved them up for guests from whom he could expect a rich reward....

Submissive to the powerful, Ivan was just as tyrannous to all who were under his authority. He made his subordinates pay for all that he had to suffer from those over him. He tormented them with the morbid cruelty that is peculiar to his type, perpetually supervised them and pitilessly kept them at work. But his face, twisted in fury one instant, could transform itself at the sight of an approaching guest to a submissively smiling mask inviting to secret sin.

Naturally Ivan believed as little as his masters that the Bolsheviks could win. He was convinced that the present unrest would pass over presently, and that it had been caused by that accursed war (even Ivan and his like were enemies of the war). The world would survive it all right. Bad times came occasionally—and Russia was having them now. But things would quiet down again, the Czar, the Little Father, would return, and with him the old officials and the beautiful old roubles. (Ivan did not put much trust in the Kerensky roubles and always exchanged them for the old roubles, of which he had already a whole bolsterful.)

As Ivan knew that a gentleman never forgets a service done to him in misfortune, and as he saw that the hotel gentlemen were at present in misfortune, he set himself to serve them still more devotedly and humbly than before, so that when better times came they might remember him. And the guests felt instinctively that he was their friend. They consulted with him over what they should do and how they should comport themselves if the Bolsheviks came. Some went further, and actually arranged to pass their jewels and valuables to Ivan as soon as the Bolsheviks entered the hotel; a few, indeed, did that on the spot, and Ivan carried about in the tops of his patent-leather boots, in his bosom and in still more secret places more than one fortune....

Now that the flood of misfortune was already almost engulfing the guests, and danger in the shape of the new and strange inmates of the billiard-room threatened them ever more urgently, regular conferences were held with Ivan over what was to be done. He now assumed the position that had formerly been held by Misha. All the guests fought over him, and he was dragged from one sofa to another: "Ivan, a moment.... Ivan, won't you come over to us for a little while?..."

And with light foot Ivan hastened from one group to the next and cried in his soft clear voice: "I'll come presently, gracious sir.... I'll be at your service at once!"

His zeal for serving his masters gave Ivan a happy idea; under the seal of strict secrecy he entrusted it to a chosen few from whom he could expect with certainty a good reward. Later, it was true, people declared that it was Misha who had given Ivan the idea, for Ivan would never have hit on such an inspiration, which was worthy of Misha at his best. And indeed Misha, too, was an earnest advocate of the new idea; while the "New Russia" group were sitting together sunk in anxious and gloomy contemplation of the future, he suddenly addressed himself to them.

Misha was not one of those people who take insults too much to heart. He turned to old Mirkin: "Gabriel Haimovitch, the present moment is too grave for me to bear a grudge. Though you've turned me away twice already I want to show you that I'm ready to serve you at a pinch."

"I've already told you once that I don't desire your services—I dislike them."

"But, Gabriel Haimovitch, it's a matter involving your own life," replied Misha impressively.

"I wouldn't accept your services even if my own life were involved. Besides, where does my life come in?" asked old Mirkin in astonishment.

"Do you know what the Bolsheviks may be capable of when they find you here, and with a well-filled pocket book, too? In Petersburg there were cases of that kind...."

"I've told you already that I don't want your kind services."

"We might as well listen to what he has to say, at least," the others intervened. "Go on, Misha—what's going to happen?"

"It's already a *fait accompli*.... I can tell you in the strictest confidence," Misha lowered his voice to a whisper, "the Whites are going to evacuate the Theater Square at daybreak. The 'commanderess' has just told me.... There's no hope now...."

"We know that already," the financiers interrupted him.

"When the Red Guards and the drunken workmen break into the hotel we must be prepared for the worst. In their rage at having to take so long to reduce the hotel they'll be ready for murder. Don't forget that the wine cellar is still full. The manager refuses to pour out the wine. The only resource that is left is to keep out of their way so as not to rouse them to fury. Then, when they have quieted down again, something might be done...."

"Very good. But how are you to keep out of their way?"

"That's just our plan. I've discussed it with Ivan," Misha lowered his voice still more and almost breathed the following words: "He'll take a few of us into his room and dress us as servants. We'll each get a blouse, or an apron, or a waiter's coat, and we'll be washing dishes, or sweeping the passage or doing something like that to deceive the Bolsheviks. They'll believe that we're members of the hotel staff. And that will be a way of sticking to our little hoard of money, too. All that matters is getting over the first moment safely, shielding ourselves from their first fury—you understand?"

"Misha, you scoundrel!" shouted old Mirkin, and his huge face, which had grown quite pale in the past days, grew blood red now. "Get out, or else..."

The others were silent.

Misha quickly put himself out of old Mirkin's reach.

But not everybody was so sensitive as old Mirkin. From the "New Russia" group as well as from others a great number of gentlemen began to steal away, draw Ivan and Misha aside, whisper with them, and disappear into the hotel.

Yet as Ivan's supply of overalls, blouses and waiters' coats was not sufficient for the great demand, and he could not take the risk of dressing up too many people as servants, so that the hotel staff might not arouse suspicion by its numbers, the prices offered by the hotel guests for working clothes on that dreadful night, the last of October, rose to fantastic heights. A string of pearls was given for a workman's blouse, a whole fortune for a set of overalls.

When morning dawned the rifle fire in the Theater Square became louder. But in the hotel it was already known that the Whites were fighting a rear-guard action and that they were about to withdraw.

Old Mirkin sitting sadly in his chair suddenly noticed that the tea magnate Rosamin was wandering about the room in a comic disguise; he was wearing a Russian shirt and a green apron was tied round his fat belly; his ashen pale face was smeared with soot.

Old Mirkin turned away in disgust at this spectacle and burst into loud hysterical laughter.

Ashamed of himself the tea magnate tore the apron from his fat belly and awkwardly tried to justify himself: "What follies one commits in times like these!"

CHAPTER XIV

THE KREMLIN CALLING

EVERY man possesses a secret reservoir of powers and qualities of which he is not aware until the hour of need. One of those qualities is the sense of responsibility. It comes into action in every man as it were automatically when he finds himself unexpectedly in an important position. So it was with Zachary Mirkin.

He had always had strong sense of responsibility. That quality had grown within him into a sacred obligation during the time when he had helped the typhus-infected refugees. But now the task confided to him by the Revolutionary War Committee literally remolded his character. Now his sense of responsibility seemed to have mobilized in its service all the other traits that lay concealed in his nature.

From the moment when he took over the command of the machine-gun section with orders to clear the Theater Square and seize the Hôtel Métropole all his doubts and hesitations vanished. He saw only *one* goal: to carry out his task in exact accordance with his instructions, regardless of all obstacles and dangers. These dangers, even the possibility of death itself, were now nothing more than a part of his task.

As if all his life he had been exclusively occupied in handling soldiers, Mirkin, his revolver in his hand, gave the necessary orders to his men in a firm voice. He himself stood by the posts on the roof where the machine-guns were stationed and saw that his men, excited and eager for revenge as they were, made no attempt to open fire prematurely. He posted sentries and sent messengers through the White lines to the Governor's palace to report, receive instructions, and smuggle food and ammunition back to the theater.

His decisive, well-considered words, his firm voice, and the seriousness with which he bore his responsibility soon secured him power and authority over his men.

But the long inactive waiting became a torment to his men, and their impatience gnawed at them like a physical pain. Day and night Mirkin had to be tirelessly on his guard to prevent an explosion. For the squad on the roof must expect to be discovered at any moment by the White officers who occupied the square in force, and if the fight were to break out too soon there was the danger that they would lose their lives, for they would in all probability be shot down by the Whites; and at best they could not prevent the roof being rushed and the machine-guns lost even if they themselves managed to save their skins.

"They won't get us as easy as all that"—every man in the squad was resolved on this, and Mirkin knew that this time it was a case of fighting to the death. "But," he thought, "it isn't our lives that are at stake, but the triumph of the revolution, the end of war and the new day that will dawn on the morn of victory. And that is a thousand times more important and necessary than one's life; it is a holy thing and for its sake I must stick to my post come what will." This thought gave Mirkin the strength to command, to employ force and, if necessary, to set the muzzle of his revolver on a fellow-man's breast. And this strict sense of responsibility he transmitted to all his squad.

Once during one of his rounds he passed a group of soldiers who were resting from their duties on comfortable cushioned chairs that had been brought up from the theater boxes, and caught them talking of the unlimited wealth owned by the rich bourgeois in the Hôtel Métropole. The Czar's crown jewels were even mentioned; these, it seemed, had been given for the time being into the hands of the bourgeois in the hotel by the Provisional Government, so that they might be conveyed out of the country.

Mirkin divined at once that the impatient soldiers were comforting themselves for their torturing inactivity with dreams of the fantastic riches they would be able to seize in the Hôtel Métropole. He knew that legendary accounts of these riches had been going about among the soldiers, and that they rubbed their hands with joy when they thought of the opportunities that awaited them. And now he saw clearly that he would find it a far more difficult and perilous task to maintain discipline among his men during the occupation of the hotel and keep the name of the revolution from being stained by innocent blood and his sacred crusade from turning into an affair of private loot than to face the decisive fight that was inevitable with the Whites themselves.

Consequently he weighed all sorts of expedients for avoiding the danger. He had frequently explained the ideal aims of the revolution to his men; he was now all the more indignant at the cynical and open way in which they talked of robbery and murder. He came to a stop beside them and said: "Aren't you ashamed, comrades, to be talking of such things? What do you think we are? Red Guards, carrying out a revolution and conscious of our responsibility, or a band of robbers? I wish to tell you this, comrades: any attempts to compromise our sacred cause will be regarded as a counter-revolutionary act! And you yourselves know the penalty for that!"

The soldiers were ashamed and remained silent.

Knowing how difficult his task would be, Mirkin searched his mind, while he sat on the roof of the theater, for ways of preventing any breach of discipline. There was only one way, he decided: to educate the men and find among them some who really understood what the aims of the revolution were, who would support him.

Among his men was one who was called by everybody "Red Sumashko." He thoroughly deserved his nickname, for he had bright red hair that always looked as if it were newly washed; it fell in thick strands over his white freckled brow, and on the back of his neck, which was equally white. Bright red eyebrows made a thatch over his great blue childlike eyes. A soft golden-reddish down sprouted like young grass after rain on his healthy red cheeks and his chin. Sumashko's dazzling fair complexion seemed incapable of absorbing dust or dirt; in spite of the fact that he had slept for a week on a heap of tattered and dusty costumes once used in a performance of *King Lear* in the theater, Sumashko exuded a dewy fragrance reminding one of flowery meadows. He always looked as if he had just bathed in morning dew. His sound body called up in one's mind the countryside from which he came. He resembled some young white birch in a plantation in the fertile soil of his Volhynian home, its green gracefully-drooping branches wet with morning dew.

Sumashko was always laughing, always in good spirits. Even when he was engaged in his bloody profession he laughed. And in truth he had already terrible deeds to his credit. It was these that had made his comrades, who had originally called him "White Sumashko," christen him anew as "Red Sumashko."

In the three years that he had spent in the trenches he had got used to walking on corpses when he had to spring from one trench to another; this had taught him to set as trifling a value on human life as, let us say, a handful of the pumpkin seeds of which his pockets were always full. Sumashko would fell a man, set a revolver at his breast, or at a pinch strangle him with his own hands, as nonchalantly as he cracked one of his pumpkin seeds. He did all this without anger or malice, without his eyes losing their childlike glance or his red lips their friendly smile.

Mirkin chose Sumashko as his confederate. He divined that behind this foolhardy lad's frivolous nature there was concealed an instinctive, highly developed sense of responsibility which came into evidence whenever he was given a serious task, either as a sentry or a propagandist.

Originally, Sumashko had joined the Bolsheviks out of pure bravado. Why not? The Bolsheviks believed in disobeying their superiors, agitated in favor of leaving the front, and above all wanted to take the wealth of the rich people and share it among the poor! Sumashko had seen a great deal of poverty in his life; in his own home and among his relatives. Consequently he considered it entirely just to take their rich property from the landowners and give it to the poor peasants. But when later he heard the proclamations that were read out to him (to his great grief he could not himself read), and the speeches and debates of the various parties in the Governor's palace, he recognized that the cause of the Bolsheviks was a far more serious and important affair than he had thought. He did not completely understand it, certainly, but he trusted the people sitting up there on the platform; they knew what was what! And just as credulously and reverently as he had once gazed up at the black statue of Saint Michael, he gazed up now at these men with their unshaven faces and unkempt hair: "They know all about it. It's a great and important cause. You haven't quite understood it yet, Sumashko, but that doesn't matter."

"Comrade Sumashko," said Mirkin, "do you really know what we're doing?"

"Of course I know. We're making a revolution, a Bolshevist revolution."

"And what is a Bolshevist revolution?"

"I don't know that yet, you know I don't. But it's a serious and important thing," added Sumashko reverently.

"Comrade Sumashko, do you know that we're making the Bolshevist revolution for everybody, for all Russia—more, for the whole world? We're doing this for all the poor and oppressed, for all who have been hounded and tormented until now, to deliver them from the yoke of their masters. . . ."

"Oh yes, I know that," Sumashko assured him.

"The revolution is not merely for you and me, so that we may fill our pockets, but for everybody. Isn't that so?"

"Of course, that's quite clear," replied Sumashko with the profoundest seriousness.

"Yet today I've heard soldiers, our soldiers and Red Guards at that, talking of murdering the bourgeois in the Hôtel Métropole when we seize it, and pocketing their money and their valuables. . . ."

"That isn't right! That mustn't be allowed!" Sumashko agreed and a cold smile appeared on his lips.

"Nobody must touch anything belonging to these bourgeois unless expressly commanded to do it. We must simply send them away; that's all. The revolution must not be disgraced. Do you understand, Comrade

Sumashko? We must prove that we aren't brigands out for loot, but revolutionary Red Guards. We serve a holy cause, not our own interests. If necessary we'll make the bourgeois give up their property by lawful means. But there must be law and order—isn't that so, Sumashko?"

"Why, that's quite clear; that's what you're a commissar for! You command and we must obey you; that's what we've been told. We must act only on your orders. Discipline is discipline!"

"And will you help me to get that done?"

"Of course! You only need to command us. We're in duty bound to obey."

"Comrade Sumashko, you're a good soldier of the revolution. Very few understand what we're out for as well as you do. So we'll have to speak to the comrades and explain to them that they must do nothing to bring shame on the revolution. Do you understand?"

"It shall be done." Sumashko saluted and hurried away to execute the order. . . .

He translated Mirkin's words to the comrades in his own language, commenting upon them after his own taste, all the time smiling the cold smile whose meaning the others knew very well from experience. . . .

The machine guns stood ready in position on the roof of the theater. Day after day Mirkin waited in vain for the command to begin operations. No command came.

At the beginning he was able to remain in touch with the palace, for it was still possible for his men to slip through the White lines with messages. But since October 28, he had been completely cut off. The couriers he sent out never returned. The telephone, through which he was to receive the agreed signal, remained stubbornly silent. He himself did not wish to call up the palace for fear the Whites might intercept the message and discover his hiding place.

From his point of observation he saw the reflected glare of the palace bombardment. He knew that the situation was critical and that the Revolutionary War Committee were fighting for their very lives, but he had not yet received instructions to intervene. The coolness he imposed upon himself alone kept him from opening fire at once, and he decided to remain watchfully at his post whatever happened.

His days were spent in waiting, the nights in listening. His nerves were stretched to breaking point and threatened to fail him. His men were so demoralized by impatience and inactive waiting that only Comrade Sumashko's cold, menacing smile and cocked revolver could keep them in control.

And then came the night of the twenty-eighth, when the first cannon shots roared in Skobelev Square. They recognized that this was their own artillery. From where they were crouching they could see the shells bursting against the houses. Yes, that was the answer of the palace to the salvos of the Whites!

A shout of joy and relief burst from the soldiers' throats. They flung themselves on the machine-guns. Mirkin and Sumashko had to drive them back at the point of the revolver, for no order had yet come, and to begin firing without orders meant discovery by the enemy and death or imprisonment by their own fault.

But the torturing waiting paralyzed all their physical powers, killed their ardor, effaced every trace of their revolutionary nerve, and involved them in doubts and fears, so that they forgot their aims, could no longer understand their former enthusiasm, and saw their existence and their work as incomprehensible and superfluous.

Then—suddenly the agreed signal from the Governor's palace!

"Make ready, lads! They haven't forgotten us."

At last a sign of life!

The telephone rang.

"Certainly—everything ready."

"On with it, lads!"

Then one should have seen the rush on the hungry machine guns! It was as if every man were trying to fire his own life through the steel tubes.

From all corners of the great roof began a rattling accompanied by showers of fire. And the same Mirkin who had seen the horrors of war with his own eyes, who had denounced a thousand times the use of destructive weapons as the worst crime against humanity, who had regarded war as the breaking out of the beast in man, now felt the rattling of the machine guns as a joyful deliverance from his impotent gnawing rage. To his ears the hasty pattering noise sounded like music, like a triumphal march. His inspiriting shouts mingled with the yells of the soldiers, his atavistic longing for vengeance rose and satiated itself, and as a gambler is drawn irresistibly to the card table, so he was drawn in now by the bloody game of war. He felt delivered from all bonds, and became a spark in the rain of fire that swept down on the White patrols from the roof of the theater.

The fight for the Theater Square lasted through the whole night, all the next day and all the next night. At last the Whites were driven out with the help of the reinforcements which had arrived from Petersburg. They withdrew to the Town Hall and the Kremlin and the Reds advanced upon the Hotel Metropole.

The Hotel Metropole now remained without protection. Mirkin stationed a strong guard at the entrance, and standing there with drawn revolver shouted threateningly at the hungry and excited soldiers and Red Guards, who were savage with the long wait and the long fight, and were making to rush the place:

"Comrades, any one who dares to cross the doorstep of the hotel without orders will be shot down on the spot by the guard as a counter-revolutionary!"

As his words did not have the desired effect upon some of the more unruly of the men, he shouted:

"Comrade Sumashko, command the guard to fix bayonets."

"Fix bayonets!"

A jagged line of bayonets confronted the soldiers.

"Five paces back!" Mirkin commanded. "Comrade Sumashko, take three men and enter the hotel. Tell the manager to conduct you to the wine cellar. Break all the bottles, and turn on the taps of all the barrels. See to it that not a drop of alcohol is left in the place."

"Very good."

Sumashko picked out three men. They hammered with their rifle stocks on the door and presently disappeared into the hotel.

The guard stood motionlessly in the entrance with their bayonets pointed at the soldiers, Mirkin beside them with his revolver drawn. A little while, and along the gutters, ground high, of the little cellar windows, there was running a dark red brook flecked with white foam, which left reddish splashes on the asphalt.

A few soldiers ran across holding out their caps. Mirkin cried:

"It's a shame for Red Guards to drink out of a gutter!"

Two comrades posted themselves voluntarily before the cellar windows with their rifles ready. A few women and old boozers flung themselves down on the wine-flooded pavement and tried to lap up the stream with their mouths. Nobody paid any attention to them.

"Finished!" Sumashko appeared, his hands stained red; whether the hue that stained them was wine or something else could not be discerned.

"Comrade Sumashko, you shall take command here. You shall answer to me that nobody crosses the doorstep of the hotel without orders."

"Good." Sumashko posted himself where Mirkin had stood.

Mirkin chose a dozen armed Red Guards and entered the hotel. The manager ran up to him at once with an obsequious smile.

"Are you the manager?" asked Mirkin.

"Certainly, comrade."

"It will be as well for the guests to leave the hotel by a back door. Is there one?"

"Certainly, comrade!"

"Then go and open it. Where are the guests?"

"In the billiard-room, comrade."

"You will let them out one by one—do you understand?" Thereupon Mirkin descended the stair leading to the billiard-room along with his men. . . .

When he opened the door all he could see was a darkly moving mass, cowering against the walls.

"Citizens, you are free to go! To prevent any collision the manager will let you out one by one by the back door."

At these words the rigid mass scattered like peas emptied out of a sack. They all rushed towards the corners of the room; there they all picked up something and hastily made for the door. Mirkin's soldiers had to restore order with their rifle stocks.

Suddenly Mirkin caught sight of a familiar face. A pair of half-dead and horror-filled eyes were fixed upon him. Zachary's eyes did not waver before the other pair. Yet this deadlock lasted only for a moment or two. Then old Mirkin turned his head away with a vigorous jerk and hastily followed the others to the door.

"The old man has aged," Mirkin told himself.

"Arrest me! I am a sworn enemy of yours!" A head covered with thick, tangled gray hair appeared before Zachary.

"What do you mean?" asked Mirkin in perplexity. "Who are you?"

"I—I——"

But Mirkin suddenly recognized the celebrated advocate. He replied smilingly: "Why should I arrest you? You aren't dangerous."

Only now did Halperin see to whom he was speaking. Open-mouthed and incredulous he remained where he was standing and could not bring out a single word. A soldier roughly pushed him towards the door.

"Comrade, I've made up my mind—I'll stick by Natasha! Please keep that in mind!" A massive, square built man bowed to Mirkin.

"Have all the people here gone off their heads? Hurry up, comrades!" cried Zachary.

The soldiers drove out Vassily Andreyevitch and the other guests with the butts of their rifles.

Only when the last of the guests had passed through the back door, to scatter in all directions, did Mirkin give the command: "Now let the comrades in. They can search the hotel and see what they can find."

Like a herd of enraged elephants the soldiers and workers, grown savage with impatience and exasperation, flung themselves on what was left in the buffet and in the rooms.

A few days later the Red troops stormed the last bulwark of the Whites—the Kremlin. Among the attackers were comrades Sofia and Maslova.

In the Kremlin a very questionable wireless station was discovered, which the Provisional Government had begun to set up. Naturally the Reds immediately took possession of it. Comrade Sofia announced to the proletariat of the whole world that the red flag was flying on the Kremlin, and exhorted them with burning eloquence to follow that example in all lands.

After the other revolutionists had spoken in all languages to the proletariat of the world, Comrade Maslova, the peasant girl, also insisted on speaking to them. But when she stepped before the microphone—"the whole world" had been first informed that a Russian village girl was now about to speak—she did not know what to say, and in her agitation could not bring out a word. At last she screamed in a shrill, scolding woman's voice into the microphone: "World! World! The devil take you, world!"

The transmission did not function, and unluckily Maslova's memorable words did not penetrate farther than the Kremlin.

BOOK TWO

CHAPTER XV

THE COMMISSAR IS HERE!

IN PETERSBURG the damp mists had already begun which every year, rising from the canals, ushered in the first snows and like a sponge sucked up the whole city into them. The houses were but sparingly heated, for everybody had already exhausted the piles of fuel heaped up in the back courts. So the penetrating damp crept through the thick walls and the windows, and people lived in a mist.

Little had altered yet in the capital. The shops were still open, and any one with enough money could get abundance of food—at exorbitant prices, it was true. Even caviar and excellent fish was to be had in plenty as in the good old times; on the other hand there was a shortage of flour and potatoes. Many commodities could still be picked up in the street markets, though only on the sly, for the illegal vendors were always being hunted by the militia. Food was to be had, too, in the grocers' shops if one entered by the back door and brought enough money with one. It was almost the same as it had been before October 25; any one who had money could eat, any one who had none could starve.

All sorts of suspicious figures poured into the town. They came from the front and from the surrounding villages, charged with evil energy, prepared for anything, given new heart by the changed conditions. Everything was still in a state of flux; the old order was dead, but the new had not yet seized hold. Two opposing forces lay heavily on Petersburg, wrapped in mist: one had died there, the other was coming to birth there. Meanwhile, the capital and the empire remained without guidance.

A boycott began against the new régime. Everybody from the Mensheviks to the extreme conservatives joined forces to fight the insolent usurpers. The officials who still remained from the time of the

Czars tried to sabotage the new regulations; they forsook their desks, and the government offices, the courts of justice, even the prisons were left without supervision. The officials who actually stuck to their posts did so simply to undermine the Bolsheviks' influence. The socialist parties who in Kerensky's time had filled the government offices with their supporters, now recalled them. The rich merchants held up their goods in foreign harbors or at towns over the frontier. In the first weeks after the October rising everybody was busy transferring his available wealth to foreign banks. In vain the new masters of the country stretched out their hands for help, in vain they implored for support in the organization of the new régime: everybody turned away and left them to deal unaided with the sovereignty they had seized. This situation was naturally exploited by ambiguous characters; they quickly cast off the "bourgeois" attire that they had worn overnight, put on workmen's blouses, refrained from shaving for several days, proceeded, with a proletarian genealogical tree in their pockets, to the competent authorities and reported: "I come of very poor people. Have always been a friend of the revolution. Prepared to serve the proletariat."

Then they were given a seat at a writing-table and began to rule.

The position grew worse from day to day. Odessa and the Ukraine stopped the supplies of grain, Kiev would supply no sugar, Baku no petroleum, Moscow no longer produced linen, and even the Volga ceased to provide the capital with fish and caviar. The shops were almost empty. Anything that was still to be had—a packet of needles or a shirt—was literally torn from the shopkeepers' hands. The rich piled up provisions in their houses. Speculators set out before the sun was up and cleared out the surrounding villages.

Little sledges could be seen driving through the streets with a few pounds of flour or a few bundles of firewood. Rich women began to appear at the old clothes markets, carrying lace-frilled chemises under their arms, which they exchanged for potatoes. A heavy peasant sledge drove all through Petersburg with a sack of barley meal, and stopped at the Winter Palace. There the driver asked for the new Czar. Hearing that Russia's new Czar was starving, he had brought him a sack of meal. He was sent to the Smolny Institute, the seat of the new government. Next morning the papers had whole columns featuring this touching story, and drawing from it the inevitable moral: "The new régime is establishing itself among the people."

The darker elements who clustered in Petersburg exploited the menace of famine. Demonstrations were held in the outskirts of the city. Disturbances were feared. The new government sent out patrols with commissars at their heads to search all the hotels and restaurants. Their first measure was to destroy all supplies of alcohol. Enormous quantities of wines and spirits of all kinds had been accumulated in "the city of the Czar and his officials"; for from time immemorial drunkenness and corruption had raged there in countless open and secret resorts. From innumerable cellar windows thick red streams of wine and spirits ran over pavements and into drains. Champagne flowed, foaming and bubbling, over the cobbles. Boozers and beggars flung themselves on the ground and held their open mouths to the gutters; women greedily licked the wine from the wet stones.

Hunger drove the prostitutes out of the brothels to walk the streets. Dressed in all their finery, in silks and laces dating from the good old times, heavily powdered and scented in accordance with their profession, they offered themselves to any vagabond who reeled past. But they found no buyers, for any decent woman could be had for a loaf of bread or a pound of rice. Love had become cheap. . . . So the splendor and finery of the Czarist Babylon wandered hungry through the streets, and nobody stopped to look at it. . . .

Like an inundation, want swept first of all over the poor quarters of the city. Although the October uprising had succeeded, the poor were the first to starve. The cry for bread and clothing rose more loudly day by day. Deputations marched to the Smolny Institute: "Where are the cakes and ale that the Octoberists promised us?"

And the man with the Mongol eyes said to them: "Why do you come to us? Everything belongs to you: the factories, the shops, the houses, the palaces. Take what is yours!"

Madame's boudoir was as friendly and comfortable as ever. And there still stood in it the Louis Seize sofas and chairs and the glass cabinets filled with Petersburg and foreign porcelain that "The Englishman" had been collecting for years from the "antique" shops and had presented as silent pledges of love to the lady of the house. Olga Michailovna's room was the only one in the great house that was heated. The whole staff had deserted, and only Misha's old nurse remained. She was on good terms with the house steward (the title given to the porter now) and a friendly handshake now and then secured her firewood enough to keep the room warm. This tiny corner of the house had been occupied, since their return from Moscow, by Halperin and his son-in-law....

An experienced business man, old Mirkin foresaw that he would not enjoy much longer the possession of his own villa near the Finland Railway Station. Consequently he vacated voluntarily the comfortable house with its antique furnishings, amid which the youngest shoot of the Mirkin family was to have spent its childhood, kept only the few articles that were valuable in his own and his wife's eyes, and emigrated to his father-in-law's. The two men were cut off from their wives, who were in the Caucasus. Communication with them was hardly possible if their husbands wished to avoid the suspicion of conspiring with the counter-revolutionary forces which were then concentrating in the south under the leadership of General Kornilov, who had succeeded in making his way there from the front. So old Mirkin had to leave his young wife and his little son to their fate. His father-in-law did the same as far as his wife was concerned; and indeed every man who found himself in similar circumstances did the same: they all waited for better times to come, which they still expected with full confidence.

Misha, the lawyer's young son, was away at the front with his air squadron; he had taken part in Kerensky's offensive in Galicia. But military operations had already ceased. The peace negotiations were proceeding slowly at Brest-Litovsk. So father-in-law and son-in-law were alone in the great house.

In spite of all difficulties old Mirkin proceeded with his business, went every day to his office, and every hour expected to be expelled from it. But he would remain at his post as long as it was possible. For the time being everything was taking its course undisturbed. Although upset by the recent happenings and oppressed with cares for the future, old Mirkin kept his head up and tried to adapt himself to the new conditions.

Quite differently did the celebrated advocate comport himself. He had never recovered from his experience in the streets of Moscow during the siege of the hotel, and fell deeper and deeper into hopeless resignation and apathy. Not even the cheerful exhortations and confident optimism of his son-in-law could rouse him. He sat in his wife's room in his dressing-gown, his hair unkempt, his beard disheveled, and gazed motionlessly into vacancy, as if he were looking into an abyss that had opened before himself and Russia.

More than one of the new men who were now in power owed their lives to the famous lawyer, whose acuteness and eloquence had saved them from the hands of the Czar's hangman. . . .

In the first days after their victory the Bolsheviks still dealt indulgently with all those who had helped to bring about the revolution; more, they sought for their collaboration. In view of the scarcity of intelligent men in their ranks, a scarcity made acute by the universal boycott against them, they were actually prepared to make concessions, not, of course, involving their principles, but of a personal character. But Halperin turned his back in contempt on the new rulers and regarded them all as traitors, who were working in conjunction with "the German agent-provocateurs" (as he stubbornly termed them, even in public), or at least supporting them. The fact that his son-in-law Mirkin and Goldstein, the petroleum king, were working in collaboration with the new régime caused violent differences of opinion more than once. For the advocate did not scruple to make known his views to all the world, and it actually looked as though he were trying to get arrested. Yet he was ignored; and that wounded and embittered him still more. Now, like all the rest of Russia, he set all his hopes on the approaching constituent assembly.

The whole world seemed to be trying to defy the new order; but worst of all was the business world. It not only stuck to its old ways; it became challenging and insolent.

The shares of the "New Russia" syndicate stood very high and they were bought and sold, though secretly, as in normal times. Indeed quite recently, when it became known that the power of the Bolsheviks was being gravely threatened, they had risen almost to dizzy heights. The faces of the shareholders became less careworn and unslept. Even their bellies, which had become visibly smaller during the siege of the Hotel Metropole, filled out again, if not with good eating, at least with favorable reports and joyful hopes. Rosamin, the tea magnate, had recovered his chubby well-groomed cheeks; he could also indulge once more in his affected little cough, spare himself and follow with scrupulous exactitude his doctor's orders.

In spite of the critical situation the gentlemen met regularly every evening, as in the good old times, in Halperin's wife's heated boudoir for a glass of "tea" without tea or sugar (though Russia's "Tea" and Russia's "Sugar" were present). At one of those gatherings Rosamin ventured to make an ironical remark at old Mirkin's expense, a very mild one, naturally, for he did not wish to agitate himself.

"All your hurry, Gabriel Haimovitch," he began half-seriously, half-jokingly, "to collaborate with these people has been labor lost. How long will they manage to hold together? Only until the constituent assembly!"

"And what will you do if they fling out the constituent assembly?" asked old Mirkin.

"How could they dare to do that?" cried the advocate in horror.

"Just as easily as they dared to drive out the Provisional Government and seize supreme power over Russia! Just as easily as they dared to depose the commander-in-chief and hand the command of the whole army over to a sailor, or treat for peace on their own initiative. Who will prevent them from 'daring' this as well? You, perhaps?"

"Then we'll shut up shop, close the banks, stop credit, delay our goods outside the frontier or in foreign harbors: bring the whole machine to a stop! Then the starving people will march against them and shake their fists under their noses. The only way of teaching them a lesson is sabotage."

Old Mirkin became sunk in thought and his face grew sad: "Sabotage? I would like to know against whom! Against the Bolsheviks or against Russia? You won't frighten the Bolsheviks by that. If you sabotage, they'll simply bring in other people, inexperienced and incapable people: there's plenty of them to be found. But the country will only suffer the worse. You propose to hold back your tea and your sugar and starve out the wretched people. But against whom, do you think, will they raise their fists? Not against these other people, but against you. It is Russia that will feel the weight of your action, and *we'll* have to pay for it."

"So that means, then, that you're ready to march in step with them, to work for them?"

"Not with them, but with Russia. We daren't forget that this is a matter involving not the Bolsheviks merely, but the Russian people. If we hold back the flour, sugar and tea we won't starve out a few hundred Bolsheviks, but the Russian people, and then God knows what will happen."

"Well, what are we to do? Sit still and let them bring everything to ruin?" exclaimed the advocate angrily. "Such arguments are a sad proof how far we've sunk!"

"You see yourself what we've brought Russia to! And it may be that now her time has actually come! Perhaps they will really lead Russia into a new path and with it the whole suffering world, which has been led astray by its masters and is wading in rivers of its own blood. Perhaps the Russian people are really destined to create a new and just social order and through that to redeem the world. In any case we mustn't disturb them in their task, simply because our wretched little store of copeks is at stake; on the contrary we must show them that we, who have helped to build up the country hitherto, will put no obstacle now in the way of their new attempt. If the world were already so perfect that there were no more just and unjust people, no more strong and weak people, no more want and suffering, then it would be a crime to make new experiments. But as it is the world is in a mess; well, let them try to better it! And I fear nothing for Russia: the Khans and the Romanovs could not destroy it, and the Bolsheviks won't be able to destroy it either. Russia is a strong, healthy peasant woman with an iron constitution that can digest anything, even the Bolsheviks, and feel the better afterwards. I want to help, not because I believe in the Bolsheviks, but because I believe in Russia——"

Before old Mirkin could finish what he had to say he was interrupted by sounds of hasty movements in the adjacent rooms. The thud of soldiers' heavy feet rang on the parquet flooring. Pale as death the old nurse entered and reported that the house steward had come up along with a commissar and several soldiers; the commissar wished to see the gentlemen.

Before the gentlemen had time to grow pale, there appeared in the doorway of Madame Halperin's boudoir Misha's former school friend, Ossip Markovitch.

In astonishment the advocate contemplated the change that had taken place in his son's friend. Instead of the carefully ironed and faultlessly cut suit and the beige vest and the carefully harmonized tie and socks, Ossip Markovitch now wore a short sports jacket of military cut, and a black shirt fastened up to his neck and where his tie had been the red strap of his revolver holster was now tied in a loop.

Thinking there was some mistake and that Ossip Markovitch had simply come to ask after Misha, the advocate had already opened his mouth to reprove the young man for his rudeness in opening doors without knocking first. But the youth's defiant and insolent glance surprised him and his guests so much that they lost all power of speech.

"What is this? A meeting? Against whom are you conspiring here? Against the revolution?" began Markovitch without any sign of recognition. Only his white nostrils quivered, as if he were sniffing something.

"Ossip Markovitch, what's taken you?" asked the advocate in astonishment, making a movement towards him.

"Please don't address me as Ossip Markovitch!" said the young man, repulsing Halperin with an insolent gesture. "I want to know what's been going on here."

The company grew rigid with terror. Rosamin's plump cheeks sagged, and all life seemed to have faded from them. Goldstein's face wore a smile of strained indifference as ever. The only one who did not lose his composure was old Mirkin. He divined the situation at once, stepped in front of the advocate, and answered in his stead: "This is no conspirators' meeting. You can see for yourself we're simply a few old friends having a cup of tea."

"A cup of tea?" The young man drawled the words ironically. "We know already what to think of your cups of tea."

"Young man, don't be impertinent! If you have a warrant, do your duty, but let us have none of your impertinence!"

"I only wish I had a warrant to arrest you! But I have only powers to appropriate this house for the use of the proletariat. How many rooms has it got?"

"Twelve, I think—isn't that so, Solomon?" said old Mirkin, turning to his father-in-law.

"And how many occupants?"

"Only us two at present, but we're expecting our families."

"You see, comrades, how the bourgeois live! Two persons in twelve rooms! That's how they've lived in luxury at the cost of the proletariat!" Ossip Markovitch harangued the soldiers. "Gentlemen, from now on you will have to content yourselves with two rooms; the remaining ten are requisitioned herewith for the proletariat. House steward, kindly take a note of that! Gentlemen"—he turned now to the visitors—"I'm very sorry to disturb you, but you'll have to go now."

"May I see your warrant, comrade?" asked old Mirkin, instead of replying.

It was the young man who now grew pale. He drew a sheet of paper out of his breast pocket and handed it to old Mirkin. That gentleman, without any sign of haste, as if he were in his counting-house, put on his glasses and unhurriedly read the document.

"I don't see anything here that empowers you to drive peaceable visitors from the house of their host. I shall have to inform your superiors, comrade, that you've overstepped your powers," said old Mirkin, handing the paper back to Markovitch.

"Do what you like! You're attending a conspiratorial gathering! I know you all and I know what you've been hatching—sabotage against the Soviet Government! I order you to disperse at once; otherwise I'll have you arrested!"

Old Mirkin grew purple in the face. Great sweat drops started out on his forehead and his breath came in gasps. He seemed no longer able to control himself. But a sudden outburst from Halperin brought him to his senses. His eyes glittering like daggers, Halperin rushed up to the young man and shouted: "Get out, you scoundrel! Shoot us, but get out!"

Old Mirkin at once became cool again. He pushed his father-in-law aside, stepped forward and said to Markovitch, who was now chalk-white and shivering with terror: "We submit to your instructions. We shall reserve this room here for ourselves. Do your duty, comrade. But if you have no warrant to arrest us, you must leave this room immediately. You are disturbing the peace of peaceful and faithful Soviet citizens. We are working hand in hand with the Soviet Government."

Markovitch's inflated braggadocio immediately collapsed, as it does with all cowards at such crises. The young man slunk cravenly from the room.

"This is the result of your sabotage," whispered old Mirkin to the pale tea magnate. "When respectable people stand aside, every villain is given a chance to take their place. . . ."

Along with the house steward Markovitch went through all the rooms in Halperin's huge house. When he came to the long bright drawing-room which was familiar to him from his former visits to Misha, and where he had so loved to sit, he could no longer repress his desires and sat down in one of the large, softly cushioned armchairs. He remembered how much he had envied Misha for being able to sit in this bright drawing-room. And just as of old, he began to inhale through his nose the pictures, the chairs and the carpets, as though he wished to absorb the odor of riches. A smile appeared on his lips and he cried to the house steward: "Comrade, I shall take this room for myself. One must keep one's eyes open and find out what conspiracies against the Soviet are being hatched in this house."

CHAPTER XVI

PORCELAIN FIGURES

THE CAPACITY of human beings to adapt themselves to their environment is boundless. In Halperin's huge house all sign of individual life had disappeared—and yet one went on living. All the confiscated rooms were quickly filled with strangers, a different married couple in each. In the passages the advocate encountered faces whose appearance made him shrink apprehensively against the wall. Everything individual and personal with which the hands of Olga Michailovna and her art-loving daughter had embellished every nook and corner of their home was destroyed. The rooms became like barracks or railway waiting-rooms. Everywhere, even in the most hidden corners, the rude and boorish strangers made their presence felt. The lavatories were polluted with filth, the baths filled with filthy sheets and all manner of things. There was perpetual trouble in the kitchen, and the swearing and screaming of women quarreling for room on the great stove to set down their petrol cookers could be heard all over the house. The dense, evil-smelling stench of stale food hung over everything. Through walls, doors and cracks there penetrated, along with the sweaty smell of strange bodies, the sound of familiar colloquies leading up to intimate situations. Often one was the involuntary witness of happenings that usually take place only behind closed doors.... One was robbed of one's personal life—and yet one went on living.

Olga Michailovna's boudoir and the adjoining bedroom were the only rooms in which Halperin still knew himself, and for them he fought with all his strength as for the honor of his house. Here, as a cat carries her kittens, he carried all the little souvenirs reminding him of his personal life, his career or his family. But it was impossible to house his library there, too, much as he desired it; with a heavy heart he had to resign himself and be content with collecting the numberless addresses that had been presented to him during the long course of his public life by Jewish communes, village peasants and various sects in gratitude for their deliverance from the injustice of the Czar's officials. But he gathered together with particular love everything belonging to his wife and his daughter, such as dresses, lingerie and toilet requisites; he snatched up every trifle he saw, as if the sacred shrine of his family life would be desecrated if he left these things in the open street that his house had become.

And now a strange thing happened. Suddenly the advocate conceived an almost extravagant affection for everything, no matter how trifling, that his wife's old admirer, "The Englishman," had given her during the long course of his dumb worship. Formerly Halperin had always laughed at these knick-knacks and seized every chance of expressing his contempt for them (since he knew well enough their secret significance). But now in his loneliness he found himself attached to them in a curious way, as if they belonged to the inviolable secrets of his private life and would be sullied by the touch of a vulgar hand and the glance of a stranger's eye. He wandered about the whole house with an unsteady gait, his gray hair sticking up wildly, his beard disheveled, and with feverishly glittering eyes searched tables and sideboards, collecting every coffee-cup, every piece of Saxon porcelain, every Sèvres plate, every old Viennese, Dresden or Russian china figure that his wife's admirer had brought into the house; and whenever he found one he pressed it tenderly to his breast and bore it carefully to his room.

The old nurse Katayeva, who during the last few years had been a pensioner of the family, remained true to her master. She fought stoutly with the new tenants for a place at the kitchen fireside, prepared the scanty meals consisting of a few potatoes or a little rice mixed with starch-flour and margarine (the only foods that could now be got at any price in the shops), and served them up to the advocate in his wife's boudoir. Thick tomes of high court verdicts from Halperin's library were already being used as fuel. True, he fought against this crime with all his might, and tried to shield his juristic classics, his legal encyclopædias, his Roman and Napoleonic codices from destruction; but what was the use? As it was, his neighbors were flinging his books wholesale into their stoves, for in their eyes the books only occupied unnecessary space; and so Halperin soon became indifferent what legal classics wandered into the gleaming, beautifully rounded, white-tiled stove in his wife's boudoir, so long as the room was warm.

He hardly ever left the house. He lined the walls and blocked the doors of his two rooms with massive chests and sideboards and hung all cracks and rents with rugs so that he might not hear what was happening in the other rooms. For hours he would sit by the warm stove, staring into the fire. Now and then he would rescue a document that fell out of the stove door, absorb himself in it and remember his old glory. But mostly he spent his time shifting about the porcelain figures, the Meissen dolls, the Old Viennese rococo cups, looking at them and playing with them like a child with its toys. As he looked at each piece he tried to remember the occasion when "The Englishman" had brought it, the parties in the boudoir, the dinners in the great dining-room, the talk round the table, the faces of his friends and acquaintances. While doing so he always fell into a sentimental mood and felt that he had been unjust to his wife's silent admirer. . . .

And against his will he began to acquire in his loneliness an affection for "The Englishman," found him an understandable, more, an interesting figure. And for Olga Michailovna herself he was filled now with a boundless love and longed intensely for her. All day he kept thinking of her and would say to himself: "Thank God, she's spared all this! What a good thing that she has Naum Grigorovitch by her side to shield her! Perhaps a miracle will happen after all and they will manage to escape. This war can't go on for ever; it must come to an end some time! Perhaps the allies will send a warship to some port in the Crimea—then Olga, Nina and the child will be saved! They'll be able to live somewhere abroad. . . . And I—what will happen to me? Oh, I don't care what my fate is, so long as they're safe! . . .

"They're beautiful little toys, these porcelain figures," his thoughts wandered on, while his eyes fell on the collection of knick-knacks. "A pity I've never appreciated them before! I hadn't an eye for them, it seems. Perhaps nothing remains with us of our whole life but a few happy moments, a few little fleeting pleasures that brush us like a spring wind and leave behind nothing but a very faint fragrance that brings them to mind again in days of trouble. Queer! I've never noticed until now how much grace and purity a little piece of porcelain like this can have," and his eyes rested in delight on one of the figures. "There's infinite feminine charm in the lines of that little thing."

And suddenly it broke upon him that he had never really lived. His career and his fame had so occupied him that he had had no time left either for himself or for loving his wife or enjoying the company of his children: it seemed to him now that his own life had run out drop by drop unobserved while he was busy with his career and his fame. . . . And all that lay in the dust now like cast-off rags, and nothing was left but those trifles, every one of which bore it in some feeling, some longing, some intimacy. They stood there now like dumb witnesses, and from their noble forms, their soft hues, their delicate smiling lines, their tender frail loveliness, radiated the warmth of for ever vanished desires. This was all that was left—a few withered leaves from the opulence of summer. . . .

Halperin did not notice that he was holding a Dresden china figure in his hand and cooling his forehead with the porcelain, smooth as a child's hand. "A pity that I knew nothing of all this before," he muttered dreamily.

Ashamed of his thoughts, he put the figure back in its place again and wandered up and down the room. His eyes fell on a few half-burnt sheets that had fallen out of the stove. He lifted them up and began to read. They were excerpts from the celebrated process against the revolutionaries in the Transbaikalian silver mines which at one time had set all Russia in wild excitement. His speech for the defense had gone from hand to hand for months afterwards, as if it were a new evangel. The censorship had forbidden the newspapers to publish it, so it had been hectographed and circulated privately from friend to friend. The advocate remembered his famous peroration that had been in everybody's mouth: "Give our youth an ideal for which they can live and fight, and they will bring all their youthful faith and enthusiasm to the altar of the fatherland instead of to the altar of revolution." And then the words with which the judge had interrupted (and which were later passed from mouth to mouth): "The freedom that they saw waiting behind the portals of revolution worked like a magical spell on these youths. Open these portals, allow freedom to enter, and there will be no revolutionists any more, but only patriots!" As once before the court of justice, Halperin now raised aloft impressively the two fingers of his right hand, his thick mane of hair settled like a crown on his head and fell like a river over the back of his neck; his brow and eyes shone, his face took on again the ecstatic Christlike look, his bent back straightened, his uplifted arms grew longer. It was the old Solomon Halperin whom people had called the soldier of freedom, the fighter for a bright new dawn. Once more a phrase was trembling on his lips, once more words of deliverance were shaping that would give utterance to all that was happening in Russia now. . . . But the cloud of dejection settled on his face again, his cheeks fell in, his eyes grew dead and retreated into their sockets, a bitter smile appeared on his pale dry lips, and instead of words winged with hope he exhaled a strangled sigh: "Freedom, freedom! Who knows what face you really wear?"

And all his regret for his wasted life was in the hopeless gesture with which he added: "How wearisome the whole business is!"

He sat down again by the stove and stared into the fire. Before his eyes documents, law-books, high court verdicts went up in flames and dwindled to black, wrinkled leaves; but he could still distinctly read the words on them, white on black now instead of black on white: "The Supreme Court decides. . . ." "In the name of his Majesty the Czar . . ." A breath—and everything was reduced to gray ashes.

"The law books are going up in flames, the laws are vanishing, justice is falling from its throne!"

Halperin felt that the foundations of the world were collapsing.

"The world is going under!" he muttered to himself. "We must try to live in the world that is coming to life: otherwise there is nothing left but death."

He felt it much easier to picture the second possibility; it did not alarm him.

It did not escape old Mirkin that the advocate was growing more childish day by day. He tried to shake him out of his apathy and exhorted him to be brave and hopeful. But the advocate did not wish to be dragged out of his childish memories, where he felt warm and comfortable. He felt so well there: why return again to the cold, naked and pitiless world of reality?

Ossip Markovitch was already absolute master in Halperin's huge house. He himself had taken possession of the drawing-room, where all the best furniture was gathered, including the precious, high-backed, gilded armchairs, and the pictures by Levitan, Eivasofsky and Rerich. Nothing was allowed to be removed from that room.

"That doesn't belong to you!" he screamed at the advocate, when, with the childish simplicity that had gradually grown on him, Halperin attempted to confiscate this or that thing he fancied. "Everything here belongs to the proletariat!"

Markovitch had housed his family in one of the other rooms. His father, the former stock-jobber, a wizened little man with a dried-up acidulous appearance, and the mother, a good-natured old woman, lived next door to the son in the great dining-room adjoining the kitchen. Mother Markovitch loved to bake and cook and so was occupied all day in preparing from the stores that he brought in lavishly favorite dishes for her son, who in her eyes and his father's had risen so high in the world.

The two old folk still had a deep respect for the famous advocate, but a still deeper one for that once so powerful figure, Gabriel Mirkin. When either of these celebrities passed through the room Markovitch's parents would rise hastily from the comfortable and luxurious armchairs in which they usually sat. The old jobber, who so often had stood in Mirkin's waiting-room to snap up some trifling commission, was still filled from head to foot with the reverence mingled with envy and flattery for the rich that he had always had, and he shrank back in alarm with a pale face whenever he encountered the advocate or old Mirkin. He tried to make himself still more inconspicuous and smiled a sympathetic and apologetic smile as if to say: "I am innocent of this." And the old woman would obsequiously scrub with her apron the chairs which they had quitted on the appearance of these erstwhile wealthy men, and murmur with her toothless mouth, smiling in awkward apology: "Gospodin Halperin, we're being careful of your property."

A cutting glance from the son sent the old people back to their chairs again: "What are you getting up for? What are you apologizing for? They've sat long enough on comfortable chairs—it's your turn now!"

"But, Ossip, my child—don't you see it's the famous lawyer Halperin!"

"Sit down, mother!" her son said severely.

And the old woman sat down apprehensively, as if the chair were filled with needles. The old jobber, who could not be brought by any arguments to sit in the presence of such great people, shrank with a pale face against the wall.

Mother Markovitch—needless to say, without her son's knowledge—actually brought the advocate from time to time a plateful of the food she had cooked for her darling. Her heart beat loudly when she knocked at the door of Halperin's room. Timidly she would step in and hold out the plate towards him with a confidential and inviting smile: "Gospodin Halperin, please eat it quickly before my son comes!"

The lawyer felt insulted and inclined to order the woman out roughly; but he did not do so; instead he took the plate, meanwhile throwing the old woman an eloquent glance in which gratitude and disdain were equally mingled. Yet he ate, for he was hungry. And while the sauce was still dripping on his beard, since he had been gobbling, the old Jewish woman would say: "Believe me, Gospodin Halperin, it's a good thing after all that we're quartered on you! We know at least who the Halperins were once. . . ."

But Halperin did not always submit quietly to the insults of his neighbors. All the raging furies would break out in him on occasion; then he would rush like a storm demon into the great dining-room, where Ossip Markovitch sat eating with his parents at the long table, lolling comfortably in an English club chair, and rolling on his tongue the food prepared by his mother. Once Halperin shook his clenched fists at him and shouted in a voice that did not sound human: "You swine! What have you done to Russia? You've turned it into nothing better than a brothel! Swine, the whole lot of you are swine!"

Old Markovitch trembled in all his body and scurried about in terror. His little wizened figure fluttered like the last leaf of autumn. The gray-haired Jewish woman bent her shoulders as if beneath the lash, left her dinner uneaten and crept into a corner. Both were terrified by the advocate's looks, by his gray hair wildly standing on end and his glittering eyes starting from their sockets.

"Sit down! Why do you get up?" the son thundered at his parents. Like whipped dogs the two old people crept back to the table.

"Citizen Halperin, I demand that you leave this room immediately! You have insulted the Soviet Government."

"You're a fine government! Robbers, that's what you are! A band of robbers, that's what you are! There—shoot me, bludgeon me, murder me if you like!" And Halperin pointed to his breast.

"Citizen Halperin, you'll have to answer for the words you have just spoken. I shall charge you before the Revolutionary Tribunal!"

"Charge me, set me against the wall, you bandits, you thieves! Leave my table! Everything here belongs to me! These are my chairs, my plates, my spoons!" The advocate rushed at the table and made to seize the plates.

"That doesn't belong to you but to the proletariat! I warn you not to touch anything. You'll have to answer for it, Citizen Halperin!"

"It belongs to me, it's mine!" screamed the advocate, and he emptied the food on the floor, tore the cover from the table, snatched a plate, a knife and a fork, pressed them to his bosom, and fled to his room. . . .

That same evening Ossip Markovitch, accompanied by Red Guards, hammered on the door of Olga Michailovna's boudoir and without waiting for an answer forced his way in.

"What's wrong, why are you disturbing us, comrades?" asked old Mirkin coolly, who had just come in.

"We require you to hand over the rifles which you have stored in your room for the use of the enemies of the revolution. You'd better obey before it is too late!" cried young Markovitch, pale with fury.

"Rifles?" old Mirkin smiled in astonishment. "What would two old people like us be doing with rifles?"

"You aren't too old to fling insults at the Soviet Government!"

"Insults? But, comrade, you must take into account that he's an embittered old man—can't you understand that?" said old Mirkin, trying to set right the damage that had been done.

"We understand, we understand very well—what the heart thinks the tongue speaks! In any case, to make quite certain, comrades, we must search the house thoroughly. We have every ground to suspect that it is a nest of counter-revolution." And Markovitch turned to his Red Guards. "Begin at once. Leave no stone unturned. There is our search-warrant!"

And now began a more than scrupulous search, in which every nook and cranny of the house was turned up and rifled. The doors of the wardrobes were torn open, the drawers of the dressing-tables pulled out and the most intimate requisites of Halperin's wife and daughter relentlessly exposed. The soldiers held ladies' chemises, stockings and night-gowns up to the light and contemplated them with lustful eyes and obscene gestures, winking broadly at each other. . . .

Father-in-law and son-in-law stood rigidly watching. They avoided each other's eyes. The search proceeded. The blankets were flung on the floor and every mattress thoroughly punched and felt. During this process the men were not sparing in their remarks on the softness and comfort of the mattresses. . . .

No rifle was found. On the other hand the comrades discovered countless figures, vases, cups and plates of white and painted porcelain. There were so many of those that the room soon resembled a nursery full of little dolls. Comrade Markovitch seized the white porcelain statuette of a woman which the advocate had been contemplating a few days previously and showed it to the soldiers: "You see, comrades, what toys the bourgeoisie were wasting their time on while we had to hunger and freeze!"

The soldiers gazed at the delicate lines of the naked porcelain figure and made rude remarks. Comrade Markovitch raised it up and crashed it to the floor.

That was a signal for the soldiers; one porcelain figure after another flew with accurate aim against the iron door of the stove.

The Dresden coffee cups, old Viennese plates, Sèvres vases, Russian faience pottery smashed against the walls, and the little male and female figures that a moment before had curtseyed with coquettish grace towards each other with their porcelain bodies lay now armless and headless on the floor and covered it with splinters.

"What are you doing? What are you doing?" screamed the advocate, pale in the face and quite beyond himself. He moaned like a sick animal and madness stared out of his eyes.

Old Mirkin burst out laughing, turned calmly to his father-in-law and said in a careless voice: "Oh, if it were only a matter of porcelain puppets! But it's Russia that we must think about, Solomon Ossipovitch."

"What is Russia to me? It's my life that they're smashing!" Halperin panted in a sobbing voice and put his hands to his face.

"You see, comrades; that's what a bourgeois is like! He cares more for these dolls than for Russia! Just go on smashing, comrades, go on smashing!" said Markovitch encouragingly to the soldiers.

"Just go on smashing, comrades, go on smashing!" old Mirkin took him up, smiling encouragingly, and he himself snatched a piece and flung it to the floor. . . .

Comrade Ossip Markovitch and the soldiers gazed at old Mirkin in the highest astonishment. They did not know what to make of him. . . . But his attitude robbed them of all pleasure in smashing the porcelain figures, and they did not finish their work of destruction.

CHAPTER XVII

MISHA "MOLODYETZ" ON TOP AGAIN

Old Mirkin was like an aged oak. Without even rocking he held his ground against all the storms that swept over him. More—in these days of threatening ruin new resources of energy awakened in him which he seemed to have saved up for bad times. Every organism does this, but with Gabriel Mirkin it was the characteristic expression of his whole mode of life. His experience, his penetration and knowledge of mankind also came to his help; they prescribed for him with infallible certainty the tempo that he had to observe in every single situation he encountered. So he was able quickly to adapt himself to the new position in Russia and act in accordance with it.

It was his devotion to his business that gave him such energy.

For him the organization which he himself had created for supplying Russia with railroad sleepers was not a mere business, but the highest and the ideal aim of his life. He knew himself; he knew that his energy was tireless, his talent for organization brilliant, his will firm—and he was proud of it. Not of the riches and power that his abilities had brought him: these results of his activities he regarded as irrelevant and secondary. The organization itself was the chief thing to him. For him all his undertakings meant much the same as statues do to a sculptor while his hand gives life to the clay.

The firm which his father had founded and he had taken over, to which he had devoted all his powers, his love, his whole life, until he finally raised it to a position in which it controlled all the railways in the Russian Empire—the firm that he had raised from the very ground by using every means at his disposal, including bribery in the highest quarters and banquets to the most powerful personages in the country, and had maintained and developed by overcoming all the obstacles that

Russian neglect, incapacity, laziness and drunken malice could put in his way—the firm that he had preserved from destruction in the darkest days of reaction by exploiting every legitimate and illegitimate means he could think of—that firm must now be preserved, safeguarded and, if it must be, handed over to the new government as an efficient economic organization. That firm, his life-work, was dearer to him, meant more to him than his personal fate, more even than the new domestic happiness that he had dared to find in the late evening of his life. For his firm he was prepared to sacrifice everything, as a great artist sacrifices everything for his art.

Immediately after his return from Moscow he called together all his lieutenants, engineers who had grown gray in the service of the firm, directors, heads of departments whose duty it was to correlate the activities of the various railway lines—in short, everybody down to the junior clerks. To this assembly he explained: "Gentlemen, I do not know what decision the new government will come to about our firm and about us. But I know one thing; that Russia must be kept going: whatever happens. Our organization is the controlling nerve in the body of Russia. Without it the railways are bound to break down within the next few weeks. Therefore we must maintain our organization at all costs and be able to hand it over as a living, efficient organism to the new masters of the country. Accordingly I move, gentlemen, that each of us shall remain at his post until the new government decides what is to be done with us. I am convinced that all Russia, including our new rulers, will be grateful to us later for preserving the most essential organ of the Russian railways, our firm, from ruin in these difficult times."

Most of the directors and officials of the firm were old friends of their chief, and had shared his ups and downs with him through the long years they had worked together. They silently pressed his hand. But there were others who distrusted him and moved that a supervisory committee should be appointed to prevent any possibility of sabotage against the new government; this committee was to be chosen from the employees by themselves and was to remain in office until the future fate of the firm was more clearly known.

The old engineers fought violently against this proposal. Old

Mirkin himself put an end to the discussion: "I'm prepared to serve the firm in any form and in any way whatever, whether it is carried on by us or independently of us. The organization must be maintained. Carry out your suggestions if you wish! I am prepared to accept any terms!"

These words won him the sympathy of the younger men as well, and it was decided to let the present functionaries keep their posts until their fate should be decided by the competent authorities.

Now hard and evil days began for old Mirkin. In the Ministry of Railways, which was being reorganized, chaos reigned. The old experienced officials had left their posts so as to make the boycott of the government more effectual. The most important and responsible positions were thus filled by young inexperienced men without any expert knowledge; their only qualification for the work was their readiness to collaborate with the new rulers. The whole administration of the railways threatened to collapse. Nobody knew what to do. The few old officials who remained were distrusted and their words were not listened to, for they were suspected of trying to commit sabotage on the sly; the new officials were ignorant of the whole mechanism.

When old Mirkin appeared before the People's Commission for the Railways and declared himself ready to collaborate with the new government, he was received with instant suspicion. The commission were resolved to get at what was hidden behind this offer. Mirkin, a helper of the old Czarist régime, who had kept his place of power even in the worst times of reaction during the reign of the Black Hundred, more, had not even been required to abjure his Jewish religion—Mirkin, the boon-companion of Grand-Dukes, the friend of reactionary bureaucrats, offered his collaboration to the Soviet Government! All his friends and acquaintances in the financial and business world were practicing sabotage—and this sly old fox wanted to maintain the firm founded by him and put it unconditionally at the disposition of the new government? Didn't that smack of secret collusion with the Whites, the Czarist generals who were organizing a revolt of the Cossacks? It was for them that the old boy wanted to keep the railways running at full strength, so that it might be easier for them to fling their troops against Petersburg!

They began to watch old Mirkin, made sudden and unexpected examinations of his books and went through all his papers. But for the moment they could find nothing against him; and they would have to stick to him until fresh arrangements could be made. But the sly old fox agreed to everything: he did not have any objection even to work under a commissar, whereas the banks had replied to a similar suggestion by closing their doors!

So for the time being they left him in peace, for they needed the "old rascal." As he had declared himself ready to work under a commissar, they did not even appoint one. They simply had not the time to do so and entrusted the supervision of the firm to a few young clerks in Mirkin's office, who obviously were in close connection with "official circles." His oldest and most experienced engineers were taken from him, and as his closest collaborators he was given quite young people who were trusted in high quarters.

The position of the firm grew worse and worse. Difficulties mounted from hour to hour. Presently all connection with the central timber depot was cut off. The firm no longer had any communication with its more remote depots and branches, for transport in whole regions of the country had come to a stop. Soon the most essential source of all failed; there was difficulty in getting credit, the banks having decided, as a protest against the appointment of supervisory commissars, to shut their doors.

Old Mirkin did all he could to tide his firm over these confused and chaotic times until a minimum of order should return. He exerted his enormous powers of work to the utmost and set his genius for organization moving to fling surplus material and money from one point to another. But like a captive wild beast he felt the fetters on his limbs whenever he made a movement. The new collaborators that he had been given enclosed him as in a cage. He had to expend more energy in convincing his helpers of the efficacy of his decisions than in executing them. They vigorously opposed every plan he thought out (in which they invariably divined a concealed purpose), simply and solely because it was the "old fox" who had suggested it.

But old Mirkin endured it all. He paid no attention to the suspicious smiles and the ironical remarks, ignored even the casual, impertinent insults directed at him; all for the sake of piloting the organization across the storm-tossed waters. He almost broke down beneath the dreadful strain of his labors. The sacks under his eyes swelled and swelled, until his eyes almost disappeared behind them. The neck muscles behind his white pointed beard grew daily slacker, his cheeks thinner. He completely forgot his family and his own personal fate. He did not trouble about food or drink. When one of his old assistants brought a meal from the workers' canteen (which had been set up here as in all other businesses) into his office he would eat it. If nothing was brought he would munch a slice of black bread that one of his faithful subordinates had laid on his desk, working on while he did so. In the evening he would return in a packed tram or on foot to his quarters with Halperin. There he fell exhausted on his bed. It took a long time before he could pump out of his lungs the heavy, overheated air that he had breathed in through his long and feverish day, and sink into a leaden, restless sleep. . . .

One of the first measures of the new government was to confiscate the private property of the bourgeoisie. To secure this they set Red Guards on all the safes and steel vaults of the big banks. The owners of the deposits were presently summoned to the banks and compelled to open their safes. Gold, jewelry and papers of any value were confiscated; private letters and documents of no importance were returned to their owners.

Gross abuses arose in the execution of this order. By paying over a bribe to the people in control one was allowed to remove all one's belongings. Any one who had no ready cash to pay this "tax" simply handed a share of what was in the safe to the soldiers who were present when it was opened; he seized a handful of gold and jewelry and stuck it in his pocket, and left the rest to the military. This compromise was generally arranged through the bank attendants, who again had a separate arrangement of their own with the soldiers. So most people were able to rescue a part of their property.

As old Mirkin was sitting one day with a worried face buried in work, his office door opened and a visitor entered who seemed familiar and yet strange to him. Several moments passed before he recognized the youngish man with the fairly recently shaven chin, the cap with the communist badge planted on a rough shock of hair, and the commissar's portfolio under one arm. It was Misha "Molodyetz."

Old Mirkin could not keep from bursting out laughing at the sight of this completely transfigured Misha.

Misha smiled good-naturedly. "What is one to do, Gabriel Haimovitch? One must go with the times," he said apologetically.

"What can I do for you?" Old Mirkin became grave again.

"Gabriel Haimovitch, I have offered you my help in good times and in bad; and you've always thrown it back at me. I really don't know what you have against me. So I've had to wait for a time when you would be forced to accept my help, so as to convince you once and for all that I'm your true friend. And I think that time has come. I hope that you won't reject my help now."

"Your help? How? In what connection?"

"In saving your property—as Rosamin and many other people have done. Gabriel Haimovitch, I can get your bonds for you and your wife's jewelry that are lying in your safe in the bank. There's no danger for you; I'll take all the risk."

Old Mirkin remained quietly sitting and began, as was a habit of his when he had to make an important decision, to play with the heavy paper-knife that lay on his writing-table: "How do you propose to do that?"

"That's my business. I'll take it on myself; I'll arrange everything."

Old Mirkin fixed his sly eyes on his visitor and said, looking him steadily in the face: "And what would you do, 'Molodyetz,' if I divulged this proposal to the gentleman you serve?"

"They wouldn't believe you," replied Misha coolly, contemplating his nails, an old habit of his; they were much longer than formerly and had black rims. "I've provided for that."

"So there's no way of getting at you?" asked old Mirkin gravely.

"I'm afraid not," replied Misha just as gravely.

"If that is so, then I'll just have to get on as best I can without these things," sighed old Mirkin, and he got up from his low armchair as a sign that the interview was ended. Pointing with his paper-knife at Misha he said: "I've already told you that I would never, under any circumstances, accept your help—and I stick to that."

"Never, under any circumstances—one shouldn't say that! There may come a moment yet when you'll be forced to accept my help—we're living in strange times, Gabriel Haimovitch! All I'm afraid of is that it will be too late then!"

"We'll see! For the moment, thank God, that time has not come. But your being here may bring suspicion on us both. Be so good as to leave my room before I call someone to make you do so."

"One more word, Gabriel Haimovitch! I can't understand you! Do you really intend to hand over everything to these people and keep nothing to yourself in these uncertain times?"

"Not to these people, but to Russia! Do you understand? Get out, you scoundrel!" Old Mirkin's cheeks were purple.

"I'm going, I'm going!" Misha hastily left the room.

Old Mirkin went to the bank, opened his safe, and did not even cast a glance into it.

"I don't want to take any of it," he said to the soldiers.

They looked at him in amazement and thought he was off his head. And before he had left the safe deposit vault they had already begun to stuff his valuables into their pockets. . . .

Then came edicts, one after another. An edict setting up an economic commission, then one nationalizing the banks.

One clear cold winter morning old Mirkin found the door of his private office forced and open when he reached his counting-house. When he entered he saw a strange young man sitting in his chair at his writing-table and looking through a pile of papers along with Misha "Molodyetz." On the table between them lay a large revolver. This time, too, old Mirkin recognized Misha with difficulty; for he wore now a black Russian shirt with many buttons and—wonder of wonders—had suddenly taken to wearing eye-glasses!

Neither paid any attention to old Mirkin's entrance, nor did they notice the look of astonishment on his face. At last the old banker drew their attention to him.

"What has occasioned me the pleasure of this visit, gentlemen?" he began with a smile.

The strange young man looked up in surprise and flung a furious glance at this intruder who had dared to disturb him. Then he inquired coolly: "Oh, you're Citizen Mirkin, I take it, the former head of this firm?"

"Himself in person," replied old Mirkin.

"By order of the Supreme Economic Council we have taken over for the proletariat the organization for supplying railway sleepers which you have brought to the verge of ruin by your sabotage. I have been sent as commissar to keep an eye on the firm. Comrade Binstock-Papalov," he pointed towards Misha, "will direct the affairs of the firm. We shall continue to employ your experience, Citizen Mirkin, as long as we find it necessary," said the stranger tersely without lifting his eyes from the papers and documents that he was examining, so that he did not see the ironical smile with which the old banker greeted this speech.

"Nevertheless we expect you to make peace with the new régime and recognize the present position, also to give up your sabotage and apply yourself actively to the reorganization of the railways for the good of the proletariat," Misha added, employing a gesture he had aped from the old man himself, and pointing at him with his own heavy paper-knife.

"If you don't, we'll find other means of persuading you." The strange young man now lifted his eyes to old Mirkin.

"And your warrant?" asked old Mirkin coolly.

"There's the warrant, if you insist on seeing it!" The young man pushed a sheet of paper over to him without looking up.

Old Mirkin picked up the sheet, slowly put on his glasses, and carefully read the warrant.

"It's correct," he said half to himself. "What do you want of me, gentlemen?"

"At the moment the code for opening your safe," Misha hastened to reply.

"22, B, 7, A, 33—and the door is open!" Old Mirkin flung open the heavy steel door.

"Thanks." Misha nodded and softly repeated the code to himself.

"One moment!" cried Mirkin, snatching a document from the safe.

"That isn't allowed! It isn't allowed!" screamed the strange young man excitedly, and he rushed, revolver in hand, towards the safe.

"Don't excite yourself, comrade! This is only my will. It has no point and no value now in any case." And he tore it in two. "Everything else is at your disposal. Allow me!"

CHAPTER XVIII

THE CONSTITUENT ASSEMBLY

THE HOPES of all Russia were fixed on the Constituent Assembly.

It had been the dream of generations of Russian revolutionists, the last cry uttered by all the martyrs.

For months, ever since the fall of the Czar, Russia had been preparing for its Constituent Assembly. As it was to be fashioned according to the most inviolable and sacred laws of democracy, its inauguration was postponed from month to month until the last peasant woman in the most remote village of the huge empire should express her will by putting a cross on a ballot paper. Would the Bolsheviks dare to oppose the will of the people? Would they dare to trample underfoot the hopes that generations had set on this great day?

Presently the delegates began to appear in the capital. A gay confusion of peoples and costumes: top-boots, short fur jackets, high fur caps; many of the men wore the native costumes of their districts. A Babel of races clothed in all manner of colors. The Bolshevik delegates were quartered near the "Smolny," those of the other parties wandered about the great city for days, roofless, hungry and jeered at, until they were lodged finally in an old empty hospital where the stench of carbolic and medicaments still clung to the rooms. There they were allowed to remain by permission of the city commissar Uritzky, and were even fed; but they were surrounded everywhere by spies who watched their every step.

By permission of Commissar Uritzky the representatives of the people were also allowed on the great opening day to pass through the strong cordon of soldiers and Red Guards who surrounded the Taurian

Palace, where the Assembly was to be held. So thickly, indeed, were the Red Guards posted round the Holy of Holies of new Russia that the people's chosen representatives might have thought that they were being conducted, not to the supreme, sovereign national assembly which had been fought for so long and painfully, but to a prison from which they would never return. Besides, they were greeted by every new group of soldiers with shouts of "Pals of France and England" and "Lick-spittles of the bourgeoisie," and threats such as "Lenin will soon show you what an assembly is!" or "To the wall with them!" were flung at them along all the way.

The delegates were expecting the worst and had made their preparations. It was said that the electric light was to be cut off in the middle of the solemn proceedings; so all the delegates had come with tallow candles in their pockets. The rumor also was going about that they were to be starved out, so each one had brought a few dozen sandwiches and was resolved rather to die of hunger than forsake the first legislative assembly of a free Russia. There was only one thing for which the delegates were not prepared: bayonets. "Oh no, they won't dare to rouse the people's fury by driving out their chosen representatives. The people have chosen us and they will shield us with all their might."

But very soon they were made to hear the voice of the people. The processions in honor of the Constituent Assembly—they were composed mostly of students, officials, burghers and intellectuals, with only an occasional soldier or workman—were held up, in spite of their red banners with the most unexceptional inscriptions that the revolution had been able to invent, on the outskirts of the town by the military patrols and refused permission to march to the Taurian Palace.

On the other hand long processions of workmen, soldiers and sailors bearing red flags with provocative legends marched ceaselessly past the Taurian Palace. The window panes trembled with their menacing shouts: "Drive the traitors out!" "Down with the bourgeois democrats!" "To the wall with the war patriots!" "All power to the Soviets!"

From the windows rose opposing shouts: "Long live the people's assembly!" "All power to the people's parliament!" Outside the Internationale was struck up. The delegates standing at the windows joined in. Friend and enemy united in a mighty choir.

The hostile demonstrations before the Taurian Palace seemed never to approach an end; the threatening shouts and the singing lasted without a break all day.

The White Hall, in which the solemn opening session was to take place, slowly filled. The Russian people had sent its best: young heads grown prematurely gray in the prison camps of Siberia; pallid faces from which the prisons of the Czar had bleached all color; thin, boyishly lean bodies which had lost all their fat in working for the revolution; bowed backs weighed down with the troubles of the people. Old comrades met again who had bled in the fight for freedom, had stood side by side before the judge, shared the same prison cell, lived in the same prison encampment in Siberia, wandered through its forests, escaped together over its frontier, taken part in the same attempts on the lives of Grand-Dukes.

Many of them who had been hiding from the Bolsheviks since the October uprising now laid aside their beards and disguises and made themselves known to their friends and comrades. These reunions were celebrated with genuine Russian ardor. Men kissed and embraced each other. The eyes of the older men were wet with tears. Dead comrades were called to mind, their holy devotion to the revolution, their martyrdom for the cause; and the last words were repeated that Sassanov, who had freed the world from that monster Plehve, had written from his prison cell: "Hail to the rising sun!" The air was filled with hope and the fiery halo of the revolution seemed to surround the heads of the delegates. Manes of hair waved with leonine pride; eyes shone; they all seemed on the verge of words that would be worthy of the great moment—yet it was something beyond all utterance.

The internecine fight in which they were engaged was forgotten; the October rising was forgotten: in spite of everything the Bolsheviks, too, must be for the Constituent Assembly! It was the Bolsheviks themselves who had given the signal for it; they themselves had fought for a National parliament, they themselves had helped to bring about this day. And could one suppose that they would fail to acknowledge the solemn moment of fulfillment? Would not they, too, feel the presence of the martyrs that hovered over the heads of the people's chosen? Would they not hear the cry of vanished generations who had died in the fight; would they not thrill to the last hopes of countless men who had ended their lives on the gallows of the Czar? They, too, were revolutionists, were a part of the revolution. It was we, we, all of us, who flung ourselves against the foundations of Czardom until the whole structure came crashing down at last! Together we wove the garment of freedom, together we plowed with bleeding hands the fields that were choked with stones and weeds, together took upon us imprisonment, Siberia's snows, and the gallows, until at last it was granted us to see the harvest appear!

That day seemed designed to drain off all accumulations of partisan bitterness and unite all parties into one homogeneous stream of force. People firmly believed that the Constituent Assembly alone was capable of reawakening the lofty ideals of Russian revolution. It would tear away the dark veil that had suddenly obscured the eyes of the revolutionists, and in a trice everybody would behold the long road of heroism which they had trodden together. Brother would recognize brother and fall in each other's arms. . . .

The delegates were firmly resolved to avoid any recrimination prompted by party passion that might lessen the greatness and solemnity of the first opening of this assembly, so painfully achieved and so eagerly awaited. They wished rather, by recalling the memory of the heroic martyrs of Russian freedom, to awaken a mighty enthusiasm whose power would unite all warring groups. This, if any, was the chosen moment for consummating that great miracle. And the delegates' tongues grew eloquent, they spurred each other on to higher flights by reminding each other constantly of the greatness of the occasion.

Meanwhile, however, the Bolsheviks and their new allies, the left-wing Social Revolutionaries, set themselves to deflate the enthusiasm of their opponents, to fritter away and belittle the whole proceedings, so that the solemn character which the other parties wished to give the opening session might become out of the question. To this end they postponed the opening of the assembly from hour to hour and held interminable sectional conferences in separate rooms. Half the day had gone, and the Bolshevik minority had not yet appeared in the hall of assembly. The majority became impatient and weary of waiting. They sent a message to the Bolsheviks declaring that the assembly would begin without them. They received the terse reply: "If Lenin allows you!"

The delegates had to acquiesce.

Meanwhile the galleries and boxes had been gradually filling with the audience which the commissar of Petersburg Uritzky had selected to be sole witnesses of the great moment.

Provided with entrance tickets by Uritzky, the "armed might" of the Bolsheviks was admitted to the hall: Red Guards who did not scruple even before the meeting was opened to point their bayonets and aim their revolvers from the gallery at the chosen representatives of the people.

Every delegate who belonged to the opposing party was greeted with insults and jeers by the gallery. Abuse that would have brought blushes to the cheek of a street-walker was poured on heads grown gray in fighting for Russian freedom, and the abuse was hailed with rude laughter. A lad with a snub nose and guttersnipe eyes that showed he had no sense of shame kept yelling down at the people's representatives: "Heh, you bourgeois swine! If Lenin took my advice he would stick you all up against the wall!"

At last the handful of Bolsheviks appeared, accompanied by the left-wing Social Revolutionaries, and took their places amid enthusiastic shouts and continued applause from the galleries and the boxes. The delegates hurried to their seats.

In the Taurian Palace on that day all Russia's Babel of races was represented—each in its national costume. Here and there could be seen a touch of the Orient: Bokhara silk robes in rich hues, bright gold-embroidered caps planted on Asiatic skulls shaved in the Tartar fashion. Most of the representatives tried to emphasize by their clothes the fact that they came from Russian villages; they wore peasant shirts in gay colors, long peasant smocks and top-boots—but many pale, intelligent faces betrayed their urban origin. The meeting gave the impression more of a revolutionary gathering than of a legislative body; here and there, it was true, men in ordinary city clothes and with finely cut aristocratic features could be seen, but there were so few of them that they actually looked conspicuous.

The man with the Kalmuck eyes and the gleaming bony skull appeared in one of the boxes. With a bored air he leaned his great head on his hands and shut his small eyes; one could not have said whether he was asleep or awake. He gave the impression of suffering almost physically from the proceedings. But from time to time he flung a sarcastic glance from between his half-shut lids at the delegate who happened to be speaking. Then he hastily turned his eyes away, gazed round the hall with a bored air, coughed, leaned his head on his hands and shut his eyes again. His thoughts—at least so it seemed—were far removed from the proceedings in the hall.

Much time was spent on the election of a chairman, in which the gallery, too, had its say. At last a huge man with a waving grayish mane of hair and a short pointed beard took his place in the seat of honor. With a triumphant smile he glanced round the lofty white hall. He continued smiling while his supporters applauded tempestuously, rising from their seats, and his smile broadened when the opposite side, and the gallery in particular, greeted him with loud protests:

"Traitor! Kornilov's boot-licker! Blood-sucker!"

"Down with him!"

"War hero! Butcher!"

"His dial needs to be peppered with bullets!" cried the youth with the snub nose from the gallery.

Several rifles were pointed at the man on the platform.

"So this is what your Constituent Assembly's like? To the devil with it!" yelled the gallery. . . .

The man with the waving hair waited, smiling patiently, until the tumult subsided. Then he cleared his throat, as if he were trying to find the right pitch, and began at last to speak.

He soon warmed to enthusiasm when he came to speak of the martyrs of the revolution. One by one he recited the names of these dead heroes. But almost at every sentence he was interrupted by shouts from the Bolsheviks in the hall and the gallery:

"What's all this drivel? We aren't interested in it."

"Tell us how your friends Kornilov and Kerensky are!"

"Listen, have you come from Saratov? What's the news from Saratov?"

The speaker's fiery words were lost in the torrent of insults and insinuations that was poured on him from the hall and the gallery. Beneath it his noble enthusiasm soon vanished, too, and he began to speak of more immediate things, above all of the differences between the parties. This increased the disorder. The spectators in the gallery suddenly appeared in the body of the hall and mingled with the delegates. The din grew more deafening. At last the speaker sat down. Another jumped to his feet. The same din greeted him. So it went on for hours, until at last a soldier in the gallery shouted down into the hall in a stentorian voice: "This is boring, boring! Devil take the lot of you!"

This was the signal for a fresh uproar. From all sides came wild shouts:

"What are you out for? Do you want us to starve here? Are we to spend the whole night here? We want to go to sleep. Go to sleep, the lot of you. . . ."

And from the hall, too, there came answering shouts: "End it! End it! It's high time this madhouse was shut up!"

All the time that the din was going on the man with the Kalmuck eyes sat in his box, his head resting on his hands. His angular gleaming bald head shone in the harsh light that fell on it. The whole hall felt distinctly his oppressive presence. All eyes were turned towards him and watched with anxious curiosity all his movements, every turn of his head, every gesture of his hand, as if there, in the narrow space of the box, were concentrated the meaning, the will and the moving force of all that was happening. Tense eyes returned persistently to that box to read, as from a barometer, what the real state of things was. . . .

But the man with the bald head remained silent. His eyes were tightly shut. Providence seemed to be slumbering. And yet one felt that it was awake, that it was there. The gleaming skull shone like a supernatural sun. All eyes were fixed on it as if they wanted to pierce into it, into the mysterious world that moved behind that barrier of bone—as though there the mechanism of Russia were at work, deciding the destiny of all the men in the hall. But the man with the bald head remained stubbornly silent.

At last he made a movement, raised his head, and opened his mouth in a mighty yawn. A quiver ran through the hall.

"High time to end this stupid game!" he said, turning to a man who was sitting with him in the box.

"Shall I go down and disperse them?" asked a black-headed youth whose curly hair betrayed his Jewish origin.

"Why should you go? Better send Comrade Shlesniak up to the platform; he'll express himself clearly enough," replied the man with the Kalmuck eyes.

"At once?"

"Better wait until I go." Another yawn made his broad Mongolian cheek-bones look broader than ever.

The man with the bald head left the box along with his whole escort. The hall breathed more freely. The voices of the delegates grew louder and more confident. Everybody became less constrained; they felt almost elated, like school-children when the teacher is absent.

Suddenly a sailor appeared on the platform. It was Comrade Shlesniak. He strode up to the chairman, interrupted him in the middle of a sentence, and said in a low but firm voice: "Comrade Chairman, it's time to clear the hall."

The chairman stared at the sailor in indignant astonishment. Then, raising his voice and gesticulating violently, he began to read him a lecture on respect to authority, to let him know his place. The representatives of the people left their seats and gathered round their chairman. But the sailor cut short all their explanations:

"Heigh, get out, granddads, get out before we fling you out!"

The delegates tried to protest. One of them shouted belligerently: "We won't go without making a fight for it! We've been sent here by the people!"

Then through every door armed sailors poured into the hall and drove out with the butts of their rifles the heroes of the Russian revolution, grown gray in its service, and the people's delegates of the first Russian Constituent Assembly.

From the gallery Zachary Mirkin had seen all this happening. As head of one of the reconstruction commissions for the stabilization of the Soviet régime which were set up shortly after the events of October, he was always journeying between Moscow and Petersburg. He was also drawn into the "Economic Commission" not so much because of his abilities or his inclinations in that direction as of the scarcity of men of intelligence. In one of his frequent official journeys to Petersburg, where he was always receiving instructions, he found himself at the opening session of the Constituent Assembly more out of curiosity than anything else.

There he had to look on while the chosen representatives of the people, these men with prematurely gray hair and pallid faces, among whom he recognized more than one famous revolutionist and popular leader, were insulted and shouted down by the rabble. He felt that the hopes of generations were being trampled down by hired ruffians, who were acting not on their own impulses but at the bidding of their leaders.

While still in Moscow just after the Bolshevist rising he had been alarmed by the new autocracy that, in the name of the "anonymous Czar," the self-ruling revolutionary masses, was gaining power. He saw it stretching out its mighty arms and seizing the leaders and the "prophets." It swallowed everything. Even in his work of reconstruction, into which he had flung himself at the very beginning, he came up against this power; he saw that day by day the leaders were becoming captives of this power which they themselves had evoked. This alarmed him, but, following the line of least resistance, he continued on the road on which he had started.

"It must be." With this argument he dispersed the shadows of doubt and mistrust that had gradually settled on his virgin faith.

From his place in the gallery Zachary, like everybody else in the hall, stared across at the man with the bald head gleaming in the shine of the electric light. "Behind that brow," it flashed through his mind, "is the meaning of all this. There lies the sense and the purpose of all that is being done. . . ."

"The whole power," his thoughts went on, "must be concentrated where justice is, so that the pinions of justice may bear the world unhindered to a radiant future. Therefore the whole power must be put in the hands of that man with the bony skull—for he must be capable of carrying out what his mind gives shape to. Yes—all power to the Soviets! Away with those who cannot rise to it, who are not equal to the flight!"

But when he saw sailors and soldiers driving before them with the butts of their rifles these pale gray-haired men in their peasant fur coats, a keen pain shot through him from head to foot. He shut his eyes and put his hands before them as one does when one does not wish to see some disgusting or unnatural sight.

"Stop! Stop! It's enough, enough!" he screamed all at once.

"What's gone wrong with you, comrade?" a Moscow acquaintance who was sitting next to him asked in surprise. "Are you anxious to join them, by any chance?"

"They're going anyway! Why beat them and push them?"

"To make them hurry up!" retorted someone with a laugh.

As Mirkin walked away from the Taurian Palace the snow crunched beneath his feet and sparkled in the darkness. Zachary walked with his back bowed as under a heavy burden. He felt that he had not been a witness merely, but an accomplice in a revolting crime. To himself he tried to justify the necessity of what had happened by the burning arguments that had set his heart and brain on fire that afternoon; but in vain, he did not succeed. The fire was quenched, and he could no longer remember even the logical line his ideas had followed. His heart was empty.

As he walked on, sunk in his thoughts, he heard someone running after him and crying: "Mirkin!"

It was snowing. In the yellowish light the figure behind Mirkin looked as if he were seen through a sieve:

"Comrade Anatol—isn't it?"

"Don't you recognize me?"

"Of course! I was simply wondering—were you in there?"

"No, they wouldn't let me in. I waited outside with lots of others."

"The whole thing is done for," said Mirkin.

"Well, what do you say to that? You approve, no doubt? After all you belong to the Bolshevik party."

"What can I say? It's a pity, certainly, that you ever let things come to this stage."

"Excuse me, I forgot about that. So you approve of these proceedings I suppose?"

A defiant feeling awoke in Mirkin. He was resolved not to reveal to a stranger the doubts that gnawed him; more, he wanted to show that he accepted full and complete responsibility for what had happened. To justify himself he used the argument that was universal among the Bolsheviks at that time: "Do you really call that a democratic assembly? It was a mere voting machine constructed by the Provisional Government. They employed all the pressure in their power to force the population to return the candidates they wished to the assembly. We know how these elections are carried on."

"And you'll mold the assembly now on better democratic principles?" Comrade Anatol's lips smiled beneath his sparse mustache.

"Do you believe in democracy?" replied Mirkin violently. "What has democracy effected up to now? Half the world is ruled democratically more or less—America, England, France, and even Germany to a certain extent. Hasn't the worst and most ruthless war in history broken out under the rule of democracy? Aren't the working-classes downtrodden under democracy? Don't people starve under democracy? Democracy has become a sort of legal and permitted prostitution; its time is past, my dear friend! Its heir is dictatorship—either the dictatorship of the proletariat or the dictatorship of capital. The only thing is to know where you belong and choose accordingly."

Anatol looked at Zachary in amazement: "It almost seems to me as if we had exchanged rôles. Only I'm surprised that you in particular should talk like that. I admit it frankly, you're the last one I would have expected it of. I still remember a time when you disputed with me about absolute freedom. You were afraid of the 'anonymous Czar' that one might awaken in the people."

"Oh, that's what you're getting at! My only reply to that is that freedom is too small a blanket to cover every one. Therefore I've made common cause with those who need it most, those who have been stark naked until now. It may be that we leave other people out in the cold. But they didn't do any better when they had their say. Perhaps a time will come when the blanket will be big enough to cover everybody. But until then we'll wrap in it the people who stand nearest to us. . . . But why do you keep out of it? Come in with us and help to make the blanket broader and longer! What or who has suddenly offended you? Are you angry at yourself? At your hopes? Forgive the comparison—but you remind me of a lover who has tried for years to get a girl to marry him and used every resource he could think of to make her his wife. And when at last he's successful he gets scared and takes to his heels on the wedding-day. Don't you like this bride of yours? It's the only one you can have, Comrade Anatol! The social revolution—that is the bride you are pledged to. And a man who runs away on the wedding-day is a coward—forgive me for being so frank!"

Comrade Anatol let Zachary finish what he was saying and listened, not without some of his former sympathy, to his companion's rhapsodies. Yet Mirkin could not get away from the ironical smile which he could see on Anatol's lips in spite of the darkness.

"Oh, if it was only a matter of a wedding-day!" Anatol laughed. "At a wedding one can dance and make merry. But we, my young friend, have to be responsible for the women we marry. We feel we have to take upon us, the very day after the wedding, the cares of married life, the cares of supporting a house and a family. But enough of comparisons! It's no wonder," Anatol's voice suddenly grew bitter, "that men who had no roots in the workers' movement before the Bolshevik rising—and I mean by that you, Comrade Mirkin, and people like you—men for whom socialism and revolution were not bound up with their very existence, but were a luxury, perhaps a spiritual luxury, in any case not a matter involving their bellies—just try and remember the talks we used to have in Warsaw, Mirkin! I say it's no wonder if these people should be able to make the final leap so easily and suddenly become burning revolutionists. For it costs you nothing, nothing! You, Mirkin, call revolution a wedding. But for us revolution is not a wedding, but a life of strict responsibility, don't you see? We, who have plowed the field step by step, watered it drop by drop—we can't take a sudden leap like this. We're married to revolution for good, comrade! Revolution is wife and child to us. We have dragged the cart forward step by step until it is where it is, but we can't take a leap, Mirkin, when we see an abyss in front of us, for we bear on our shoulders the responsibility for the revolution. We are married, you see, married to the workers' movement, and no obstacle, whether it comes from the right wing or the left, can hold up our slow but sure road to our goal—for we aren't going to any wedding."

Mirkin was alarmed by the fire that burned in Anatol's eyes. He hardly recognized him: the pale bowed Anatol had suddenly grown bigger and stood erect, his head high.

"Perhaps it *was* simply because we were not so deeply involved that it was easier for us to make a spurt than for those who had fallen into a jog-trot. It's said that newly settled peasants adapt themselves much more quickly to modern agricultural methods than old ones who think that a wooden plow drawn by a cow is the only way of plowing a field properly. Tradition, Comrade Anatol, is often an obstacle to progress. Our whole civilization is under the yoke of tradition. . . ."

"That's all words!" Comrade Anatol interrupted him. "I would like to ask you a simple question, quite apart from your present views, which I don't doubt are sincere. Tell me frankly: doesn't your heart protest at all, in the name of simple human justice, against all these things that are being done and that you yourself must see every day in the course of your work? Didn't your heart bleed when you had to look on while those soldiers and hooligans, who may have changed their coats by tomorrow, drove out and dispersed the people's chosen representatives?"

"Certainly, certainly—it's painful to have to witness such things. But these are the birth-pangs of the new life that's coming to being. We must accept them with the rest and transcend them."

"Transcend them? Accept them with the rest?" Anatol cut him short. "I want to tell you something: you came to me once and asked me to explain the deeper meaning of our policy. Forget all that I said to you then! Forget too all the bitter reproaches I have made against you tonight! Keep only one thing in mind and nurse it like the apple of your eye, like the greatest treasure there is—the original feeling for justice and truth that exists in all of us! It is the deepest meaning of socialism. Everything rests on it; it is the foundation of our humanity, it is the divine in us. Many of your comrades are now tearing that original feeling out of their hearts with burning pincers, and trying to put dead dogmas in its stead. The world has seen already to what lengths men can go when they exchange their natural feelings of justice for inquisitorial dogmas."

"Comrade Anatol, *you* to speak of a natural feeling for justice! What can that be to you?"

"It's a new truth that the revolution has taught me! Good night."

Mirkin watched Anatol's long, thin, almost transparent shadow flitting across the snow-covered Neva bridge.

CHAPTER XIX

ZACHARY'S MEETING WITH HIS FATHER

WHEN ZACHARY MIRKIN called at the offices of the Economic Commission next morning to settle the official business that had brought him to Petersburg he caught sight of a figure he seemed to know in the crowds that filled the passages, stairs and waiting-rooms of the great building. On looking more closely he recognized in the man sitting with bowed head on one of the many benches—his father.

His father's appearance, as he sat there, sent a pang to Zachary's heart. He had never known his father as a bowed old man. In his memory he held the image of a tall arrogant figure who, in bad times as in good, knew how to maintain a certain distance even with his family. This old gray-haired man, sitting there with his bowed head supported on his hands, was so unfamiliar to Zachary, so strange, that the son suddenly forgot the deep gulf that divided the two of them, and only felt a feeling of boundless pity and distress.

He crossed the waiting-room hastily so as not to be noticed by his father. It was impossible now to settle the business that had brought him here. He mingled with the crowd and from a corner of the room attentively scrutinized his father's face. Although he could not see it clearly, for the forehead and cheeks were partly covered by the old man's hands, he could see that his father had become infirm and aged. The reddish blonde beard that Zachary could remember not so long ago had turned white, the two points had grown together and fell in a tangled mass on the old man's breast, the sacks beneath his eyes hung down flaccidly.

Zachary resolved not to lose sight of his father, to follow him when he left and ask him what was the nature of his trouble. Since the day when he had recognized his father among the guests in the Hôtel Métropole he had been continually in his thoughts. But his new environment, his life as an active communist, was not calculated to make him over-anxious about the fate of his father, who was a bourgeois and therefore an enemy of the revolution. Yet now that he saw him face to face, all the distinctions, all the gulfs that divided the two of them were suddenly forgotten: in a trice all the accumulated bitterness of the past was gone. That face suddenly became to Zachary the nearest, the most intimate in the whole world. His former fear of his father vanished. And truly there was no cause to tremble before the helpless old man sitting over there. All the feelings that had once constrained him were cast off like a garment, and all that remained was the intimate bond of filial love.

Zachary longed to go up to his father and speak to him. But the place was not suitable. So he decided to wait until his father left.

He had to wait for a long time. He saw that his father, who seemed to be very angry over something, was fighting with difficulty his humiliation at having to sit there in the waiting-room until he should be called. He rose impatiently several times as if to go, but turned back again. When he turned the last time his seat had been taken.

The atmosphere in the crowded waiting-room was unendurable. It was stale, stifling, a dense barracks atmosphere that filled all the passages of the building. It was made worse by the painful tension and uncertainty that could be read in the eyes of the people who were waiting. This indeterminate fear was contagious: it spread from one to another. Everybody was afflicted by a racking nervous headache: this could be seen from their quivering, almost distorted faces. Zachary could not make out why they should be so disturbed and afraid. "The last goal to be achieved has been achieved: the revolution is victorious. So why all this alarm? What is the cause of it? Perhaps there's some misunderstanding?" he asked himself in astonishment.

At last he saw that his father's turn had come. An insolent youth gripped old Mirkin roughly. Zachary was seized by boundless rage; he had to keep himself in check or he would have assaulted the youth with his fists. He was himself amazed at his extraordinary outburst of passion. Then he saw his father disappearing behind a door with the youth. Five minutes, ten minutes passed—and his father had not yet returned. Zachary became uneasy and made for the room which his father had entered. But then he reflected that it might only make things worse. And he resolved to count up to five hundred: "If he hasn't come out by then I'll go in."

Just as he was thinking this he saw his father returning. The old man's face was working, and red spots burned on his cheeks. The two points of his beard stuck out and were stiffer than before. Erect, with his head high, Gabriel Mirkin made with rapid steps for the door. Zachary followed him.

Over the streets hung a sad twilight, although it was almost midday. The day had started with that faint half-darkness, for ever since early morning a comfortless gray veil of snow had hung over the city. The snow was falling thick now. Large snowflakes like fragments of cotton-wool fluttered down and whirled in a confused dance through the air. Space seemed to have shrunk and the big snowflakes seemed to fill it more and more completely. Zachary was afraid to let his father out of sight and kept close behind him. The tramway stop that old Mirkin made for was crowded, so he continued on his way. Zachary expected that his father would hire a sledge. But the old man didn't—for a reason that his son was ignorant of; besides, no vehicle could be seen. Gabriel Mirkin continued on foot, the collar of his fur coat turned up. The white flakes settled on his shoulders and his back and soon completely covered him. But he kept on. His back no longer seemed bowed merely by age; rather it gave Zachary the feeling that his father was carrying a sack of snow beneath whose weight he was growing smaller and smaller and more and more bent—soon the snow must cover him up completely.

Although Zachary had already followed him for a long while he could not find the courage to go up to him. He kept on whispering to himself: "Father! Father! Father!" but softly, so that he himself could hardly hear it or know that he was saying it. At last his pity and love gave him the needed courage; he took heart and went right up to his father.

"Father!" he cried, and a helpless smile appeared on his lips.

"What is it?" Old Mirkin turned round quickly. And as by a magical spell his bearing and appearance had suddenly changed. He was taller all at once. His back was no longer bent, the sack had vanished from his shoulders. His face, flushed by wind and excitement, looked healthy, and it seemed to Zachary that even his two-pointed beard had grown auburn again, as it once had been.

It was only the old man's eyes that gazed out a little uncertainly beneath his eyebrows, which were clotted with snow. With a sharp movement of his hand he brushed the snowflakes from his face. When he recognized his son he shrugged his shoulders grimly and without a word, without even casting a second glance at Zachary, he went on with firm, decided steps.

But Zachary caught him up again and gazed insistently into his face, whispering the one word: "Father!"

"What do you want? Go to your own people! It will only damage you with them if you have anything to do with me!" said old Mirkin between his teeth, walking on.

It took Zachary all his time to keep up with his father.

"I am not afraid of that. I want to know how things are going with you."

The old man gave no reply and continued his firm, rapid walk.

"Father!" cried Zachary again, quickening his step.

As his father still refused to reply Zachary tried to grasp his hand: "Please don't run away from me!"

The old man seemed to be touched by his son's helplessness; he slowed up a little and said, less angrily than before: "I don't understand you! If one pledges oneself to any cause one must stick to it. I am a bourgeois. You mustn't inquire into my fortunes: that can only bring you harm!"

"Father!" Zachary repeated, looking beseechingly into his father's eyes.

Old Mirkin stopped irresolutely. Clearly he was struggling to come to a decision. Then he asked crossly: "What do you want to know?"

"How are things with you? How is your health?"

"I'm all right. Everything is as it should be and will go its destined course. But they've arrested Solomon Ossipovitch."

"Solomon Ossipovitch Halperin, the advocate? But why?"

"He expressed his opinions too openly."

"Arrested him for his opinions?" Zachary asked in surprise. "But we don't punish people for their opinions, but only for their actions. Who had him arrested?"

"As for whether you punish people for their opinions or not, I don't know about that; it's not my business, anyway. It was Ossip Markovitch that arrested him."

"Who is he?"

"An old school friend of Halperin's son, at present a commissar. He has confiscated the Halperins' house."

"He couldn't have done that on his own responsibility. Someone must have given him orders to do it!"

"I know nothing about that. Can you do anything about the matter? I'm very upset about Halperin." Old Mirkin's tone had changed.

"I'll go at once to the commissar of justice. But first I'll take you home."

"Take me home? Why?"

"You're not looking too well and it's snowing."

"You needn't concern yourself about me! I can look after myself. See what you can do about Solomon Ossipovitch instead."

"I'll go at once. I'll just get a sledge first—it would be best for you to drive home."

"I tell you again, you needn't concern yourself about me! I can take care of myself. If you can do anything for Solomon Ossipovitch it will be a godsend."

"I'll go at once. Where can I find you?"

"In Solomon Ossipovitch's house—no, in Ossip Markovitch's house, for it no longer belongs to us."

"Do take a sledge, father, and drive home."

"That's enough!" the old man burst out and his cheeks swelled angrily. "Go!" And he added softly: "He's taken part in a revolution and yet he's still only a silly boy."

In the offices of the Commissariat of Justice, which were in the former Ministry of Justice whence all the unjust regulations in Russia had once gone out, Zachary found a great throng of clients just as in the good old times. But now they belonged to the higher circles of Russian society, and consisted mainly of the wives of high officials, capitalists and generals, who were being persecuted by the new régime; most of them had come to beg for the release of their husbands and sons.

These women, still wearing the stylishly-cut black gowns that had been fashionable in better-class circles before the revolution, behaved exactly as the unlettered petitioners of the lower classes had done before them. Grief looked out of their reddened eyes, painful apprehension out of their drawn faces. They were just as little ashamed of showing their sorrowful tear-stained faces to the whole world as their humbler sisters had once been. Now and then a deep groan would come from them, and, just as among the common women who had sat there once, it worked contagiously and soon sounds of stifled sobbing and weeping filled the whole room, their minds totally filled with their misery.

The commissar of justice, still a young man, was resolved in spite of his communist views not to renounce the ideals that he had absorbed in the well-to-do house of his parents. So he constituted a sort of line of communication between religion and communism—a feat easily achieved by a mind schooled in the Talmud. He had attained his high post simply because his party had been the first to join the Bolsheviks and he as its representative had become a member of the government. Naturally nobody ever thought of consulting him, and the most horrible crimes against justice happened behind his back.

This made him suffer deeply from scruples of conscience, and so he was in a perpetual state of nerves.

When he heard of Halperin's arrest he jumped up from his chair: "Who has dared to do such a thing? I empowered nobody to do it. The city commissar and his crew in Gorochovaia Street must be behind this!"

With the gesture of a dictator he seized the telephone and called up the city commissar:

"Who is commissar of justice, you or me? I won't tolerate such things being done behind my back!"

The authority of the Commissar of Justice did not seem to be greeted with much respect at the other end; for the answer made the young man quite furious. He turned hopelessly to Mirkin: "Tell me yourself: What can I do? I am Commissar of Justice, it's true, but the revolution is too strong for me. I'm powerless! But things can't go on like this! I'll let my party know about it; we'll just have to leave the coalition; I'll hand in my resignation!" His threats became more and more violent.

Mirkin was no longer listening to them. He was on his way to Gorochovaia Street.

In the offices of the city commissar he found a still greater crowd of waiting people. The place seemed designed for nothing but petitioners. As in the time of the old governors, the stairs, passages and waiting-rooms were crammed with unhappy figures. Every class was represented, the rich, well-to-do middle classes no less than the poorest of the poor. Again the great majority were women. Some were in black, others in lower middle class attire, and many also appeared in the shawls which only poor women wore. And Mirkin was struck here, too, with the dreadful fear in the women's eyes and their unhappy countenances.

Zachary simply could not understand why this should be so: "Why this terrible fear of the mechanism of the revolution? After all it is their own government, it's what they've always wanted! Who has filled these people with this incomprehensible fear? Can it be that the people who stand before my door in Moscow have the same terror in their eyes? It must surely be power itself that fills them with such fear. But if that's so, what's the good of power? All power must be exterminated!" something cried in him.

The city commissar was also a young man, a Jew. Like many of his kind he had only joined the Bolsheviks after their October triumph. As he was a party novice, so to speak, he was resolved to shine in the eyes of his comrades; and as a new broom sweeps clean, according to the old saw, he was perpetually busy in proving his efficiency and his value. Before the Bolshevist era he had had a weakness for pure idealism: so that to convince himself and others that he had broken with his whole past he now gave himself up heart and soul to the party, as a dipsomaniac takes to drink, and did its most difficult and filthy donkey-work for it, which he carried out with the coldest brutality, as if to prove his own firmness of character.

He crawled before his superiors and cold-shouldered his inferiors, like all cowards.

"Ah, Comrade Mirkin! Very pleased to meet you! Take a seat." The young man sitting behind the broad, massive mahogany writing-table pointed towards an easy-chair standing beside it. "What can I do for you, Comrade Mirkin?" he asked in as easy and self-assured a tone as if he had sat all his life behind the massive mahogany table in the Governor's huge and uncomfortable work-room, which had once struck fear into all Petersburg. No muscle of his face moved; it seemed to have hardened into a cardboard mask. His lips were firmly closed; his whole posture registered attention.

"Since when have you begun to arrest people for expressing their opinions? Can the remarks of an hysterical old man whom the revolution has ousted from his place be really so dangerous that you have to employ such means against him? It seems to me rather that the arrest of an old man because he has said a few stupid words will only compromise us, for it will be construed as a mark of weakness and fear."

The young man listened to Mirkin with friendly sympathy. A cool smile played round his firmly-shut lips and seemed to be saying: "We've heard all this already and know all about it. We're listening to it simply out of politeness."

"No doubt your words refer to the case of Halperin, the advocate? If I'm not mistaken you are related to him by marriage or in some way?" he added casually, as if he wished to infer nothing by it.

"Whether I'm related to him or not has nothing to do with the matter! I know that Halperin has defended revolutionists all his life. I was myself his assistant at one time and know what he did for the revolution in the Czar's time."

"Of course, of course—we all know that. But just because of that he constitutes a greater danger for the revolution than anybody else. When someone with no revolutionary reputation makes unseemly remarks about the Soviet Government in public it has no significance—we can afford to ignore such remarks. But when a man like the advocate Halperin, a man who, as you put it, comrade, was a defender of revolutionary ideas in the Czar's time—when a man like him with a certain reputation, if I may so express myself, openly and persistently denounces the revolution and its institutions, then he is dangerous to us. The words of a man such as Halperin impress the people; he has influence, his opinions are received with respect. We can't let that pass in silence. We must inculcate respect among the population for the revolution and its institutions. Aren't you of the same opinion, comrade?" He turned languidly and politely to Mirkin with an amicable smile.

"Where did he pick up this style of his?" Zachary asked himself in astonishment and said aloud: "As far as I know Halperin did not publicly insult the Soviet Government, but only let fly a few violent expressions while he was in a state of great excitement because a man called Ossip Markovitch appeared one day to confiscate his house, a man whom he had once known in very different circumstances. Surely one must take all that into account!"

"But, comrade," the commissar completely forgot his affected calm and hastily interrupted Mirkin, "this man called Ossip Markovitch is one of my most trusted colleagues! He has already done much service for the revolution; what he was before does not concern us. We know that already, we know all about him; nor do we ask other people, either, what they were doing before the October revolution. We need people and any one who is prepared to work for the revolution is welcome to us."

"Well, can you help me at all in the case of the advocate Halperin, comrade? I notice that there are a great number of people waiting outside to see you, and I have no desire to waste your precious time."

"I'm sorry—I can do nothing. The matter is no longer in our hands, but has already been given over to the Committee for the Defense of the Revolution. Comrade Marek is engaged on it."

Mirkin grew pale when he heard that name. He bit his lip and said between his clenched teeth: "In that case nothing remains for me but to appeal to the Smolny. In the Smolny there's more than one man who owes his head to Halperin, more than one who has been saved from the Czar's gallows by Halperin's abilities as a lawyer and orator. And comrade T. is one. No one forgets a thing like that so easily."

At the words "Smolny" and "Comrade T." the commissar became very grave and his face grew white as marble. He compressed his lips still more tightly and knitted his brow.

"But why bother the Smolny at this stage?" the commissar began. "Particularly as it's only an individual case! You know yourself, comrade, that the Smolny has all it can handle in dealing with the peace negotiations in Brest-Litovsk. So why trouble these gentlemen with an individual case? Let me think for a moment, comrade."

The commissar knitted his brow still more fiercely and seemed to be reflecting. As Mirkin saw a gleam of hope he refrained from replying to the man's last observations.

"I'll be back in a minute. Wait for a minute, comrade."

Thereupon the commissar went into the next room, where he remained for about five minutes. While Mirkin, alone now, was looking round the room he suddenly saw two gleaming eyes in a corner following all his movements. He realized then that the commissar and he had not been alone: a third man had been overhearing all they had said. Mirkin could not make out the appearance of the third man, for he sat concealed in a dark corner.

Presently the commissar returned with a radiant face and said, smiling: "You're in luck; I've just discussed the matter with the comrades. The whole business is very disagreeable to us, too, you must see that—a man with such a reputation, who has defended revolutionists—

really very, very painful. If you, comrade, will vouch for the advocate, we'll release him with pleasure."

"The best plan would be to furnish him with a passport and let him leave the country," Mirkin replied.

"We'll see about that. The best thing of all would be if you, comrade, could persuade him to join us. . . ."

"We'll see about that too!" Mirkin interrupted him cheerfully. "I'll try to, at any rate."

"Yes, do try, comrade." The commissar also was now highly pleased.

"Where is he?" asked Mirkin after a pause.

"You can take him with you straight away. I've already given instructions to release him."

The terror had not yet begun at that time. . . .

It was no easy task to get the advocate out of the city jail where he had been ever since Comrade Markovitch had arrested him in the name of the city commissar. He was unwilling to leave his cell at any price and had to be forcibly ejected by the soldiers. While this was happening he never stopped cursing the Soviet régime and flinging the deadliest insults at it.

"Come! Shoot me! Shoot! Put me against the wall!" he kept shouting, pointing at his breast.

Mirkin was seriously alarmed by Halperin's state, which showed definite signs of a deranged mind, and still more alarmed by his insulting words, which would be bound to anger the soldiers. So he tried to belittle the advocate's agitation and turn it to ridicule by nods and winks to the soldiers, putting his finger to his forehead as if to indicate that the man was not quite sound in the head.

When Halperin caught sight of Mirkin he refused to give him his hand and called him a villain and a scoundrel before everybody. Zachary smiled coolly, and taking hold of the advocate firmly pushed him into a sledge that was waiting and took him home.

It was night by the time they reached the advocate's house. There they found old Mirkin sitting in lonely thought in the room he shared with Halperin. Naturally enough he was surprised and delighted by his friend's release, and in his elation he even addressed a few words to his son: "The wisest thing now would be for you to get him a pass, if you can manage it."

"And what will happen to you? What plans have you, father?" asked Zachary.

The old man's pride woke again. He measured his son from head to foot and retorted: "I'm not accustomed to have boys troubling about my affairs, particularly if they've shown damned little interest in me till now. Go to your own chosen associates! I can look after myself, even in spite of your friends."

"I won't leave you to yourself," cried Zachary, looking his father defiantly in the face.

"You are a revolutionary—I am a bourgeois. You've no business to trouble your head about me." Old Mirkin smiled ironically and looked away.

"That's got nothing to do with it. I'm your son, after all!"

"Are such family ties recognized by your friends? I thought these things didn't exist for them!"

"That depends," replied Zachary, smiling calmly.

Old Mirkin seemed to reflect.

"Well, we'll see about that. But now go to your friends! When you do a thing you must do it whole-heartedly." And for the first time in years Zachary felt his father's fleshy hand in his own. It was flaccid and cold. . . .

When Zachary stepped out into the passage he knocked into Ossip Markovitch, who as usual had been spying through the key-hole and listening to what was being said. Mirkin had only a faint memory of the young man and scarcely recognized him now, for Markovitch had changed greatly.

"What are you doing here?" Mirkin flung at him violently.

"I'm here on my own business," retorted the young man coolly and superciliously, looking Mirkin brazenly in the face.

"You're too zealous, comrade!"

"Not zealous enough by half, where the revolution is in question," Markovitch replied impudently.

"What were you before October?"

"What does it matter what I was? *This* is what I *am!*" Thereupon the young man drew his red party ticket from his breast pocket. "And you, comrade?" he said, turning to Zachary.

Mirkin could say nothing, for he had no party ticket. Without deigning to reply, he left the young man standing and went....

Next morning he returned to Moscow. There was a great emptiness in his heart, a whirling chaos in his mind.

CHAPTER XX

THE GREAT ILLUSION

IN HIS large room in the Smolny, which was patroled by soldiers and Red Guards, the man with the mighty bald skull sat at his work-table. His tired head rested on one hand and with the other he kept breaking off without noticing it fragments of bread from a little loaf someone had laid on the table, which he chewed absently while following the train of thought that absorbed him.

The room was still electric with the exuberant energy and the flaming temperament of Comrade T., who had just left it. Employing all his prodigious powers of persuasion, he had been advocating the view that their acceptance of the peace conditions laid down by Germany must absolutely be postponed until Germany was forced to launch another attack against the Russian army; this would make plain to the whole world that the Soviet Government had been forced only at the point of the sword to accept the crushing peace terms dictated by the enemy.

But the Germans had broken off the armistice too soon, had declared that they were once more in a state of war with Russia, had flung troops into Finland, and were slaughtering wholesale and filling the prisons with Finnish workmen. Their appetite was apparently sharpening from hour to hour, their terms grew harsher and harsher. It almost looked as if they did not want peace at all. Could it be that they had actually come to an understanding with the Allies and now intended to conclude a general peace at the cost of the Russian proletariat and sacrifice the Russian revolution on the altar of world imperialism? A lust for war had suddenly awakened among the members of the Central Committee: they were resolved to continue the war without arms and ammunition, even at the price of having to accept aid from the imperialistic *entente.* But from the front deputations of soldiers were arriving every day, and they threatened that if peace was not concluded at once the whole army would march on Petersburg and force the government at the point of the bayonet to accept the German conditions. . . .

Suddenly the man with the Kalmuck eyes tore himself from his thoughts and shook from him all the melancholy forebodings that had been weighing him down. It looked as though his marvelously effective brain, accustomed to run exclusively in the grooves of logical reality, was seeking the peace and coolness of bodiless abstraction. Perhaps, too, the snowy winter evening, whose incomprehensible sadness and beauty looked in through the window, subduing his chaotic thoughts to its noble melancholy, contributed to his state of mind.

The flight into the infinite began by the man's asking himself: Why don't the comrades in the Central Committee see the position as clearly as I do? Why can't they understand the situation and see that what has happened among us must happen tomorrow or the next day in the enemy countries? What does it matter for the course of the world revolution whether we give up to the Germans a larger or smaller slice of the Ukraine, Finland or Estonia? How long, after all, would they be able to hold it? This that has happened among us is not a transient and fortuitous event, but the beginning of a world revolution. True, it was the war that brought the revolution. But the whole course of events, the whole chain of circumstances, the capitalist system, all these had necessarily to lead to a world catastrophe. Entangled in its predestined fate the capitalist order has plunged into the pit dug by itself, so that it may be destroyed and clear the ground for the social order of the future. What has happened is no trick of chance, but a predestined step forward on the endless path of world development. Why, then, should further blood be shed? What is the sense of diverting the course of this world process into side issues, using it for national ends? For the sake of a strip of land in the Ukraine or in Estonia, which will be lost only for a short time in any case? Who will ask after it is all over whether we acted patriotically or not? These are ideas of yesterday! What consequence have they in relation to the world revolution? The proletariat of tomorrow will soon come to terms about such trifles. They won't divide up the world into territories. One day of actual socialism will do more to undermine the foundations of the capitalist world than years of victorious war. That is as clear as that two times two make four. Why can't they see it?

These questions and the beauty of the winter evening that filled the room led him on to a new train of thought: "What is logic actually? That two and two make four is the result of a logical assumption. Good—but why do two times two make four and only four? What confines the result within these precise limits?"

His mind which was trained to grind like a mill the thoughts that poured through it into food for the social revolution soon drew in this abstract thought, too, like a grain that had got there by mistake, and proceeded to grind it into the standard article.

Whence comes the intellectual diversity of mankind? he asked himself. From the same causes as physical diversity? Is intellectual backwardness caused by lack of education, just as physical degeneration is caused by undernourishment continued through many generations? Or is there a deeper power independent of such external causes, which endows the individual with greater or lesser intellectual capacities according to its whim, as it were? That's a dangerous assumption!

As a pious Jew flees from the sight of a beautiful woman for fear that she might—God forbid!—lead him into temptation, so the man with the huge skull turned away from this perilous idea.

Intellectual abilities, he went on, just like physical ones, are the product of circumstances. The poor are just as shut off from culture and knowledge as from the luxuries on the tables of the rich. They are kept in the darkness of ignorance that their masters may find it easier to rule them. That is the reason for the intellectual inequality of mankind. It will be necessary to level up that inequality: a generation of high-school boys and girls drawn from the working and the peasant classes, a generation of darkness for the effeminate heirs of the bourgeoisie—and the disparity will be corrected.

It must have been the magic of the soft twilight in the room that influenced the "seer"; in any case, for the first time his conclusions seemed fallible.

Like the maddening beauty of a woman gleaming through mysterious veils there flitted through the world of his materialistic thought the alien intuition that one could never succeed in turning out human beings by machinery, like buttons; for somewhere in the mysterious depths of the human spirit an unknowable power was at work, which could never be mastered. And for the first time the doubt rose in him whether it would be possible to bind humanity with one single cord and reduce all men to one measure by regulating their external circumstances and their education.

Won't there always be the strong and the weak, the clever and the stupid, the quick-witted and the slow? he thought. But if that is so, who can guarantee that certain men will not attempt to exploit their natural gifts to their personal advantage? True—the social order will be a kind of balance maintaining equilibrium and preventing the individual from employing his gifts to the detriment of the community instead of in its interests. Obviously it will be possible for us to control men's physical powers, for what they are worth. We shall allot work to people according to their strength. And their intellectual powers can be controlled too, wherever they manifest themselves, and be turned in any direction likely to benefit the community. But what about the motive force, the inner incentive to make people exert their powers to the utmost, as personal interest and egoism have done under capitalism? What incentive can we hold out to make men use their intellectual powers for more than the gratification of their personal ambitions? What reward and what punishment have we to offer similar to those religion found by inventing the next world? . . . The enjoyment of the universal happiness that communism will bring. But that is such an exalted enjoyment that only the chosen few would be able to feel it. Can it be an incentive for the many?

True, our idea, by concentrating honestly on the real needs of humanity, has put an end to the vague, shadowy mysticism and ambiguous idealism of a few rare spirits and left nothing but a genuine faith in the moral force in man which will free him from all the changing forms of age-long slavery and lead him to the dawn of communism.

But what are these moral powers? Whence do they come? Are they instincts innate in everybody which have been diverted by false prophets to erroneous ends, to idols such as Czar, fatherland, religion? And even if the goal were clear as day—would these moral powers flame up and become a dynamic force strong enough to redeem the whole world? Or in the last resort do they amount simply to a matter of habitude created by man's upbringing, and are there in actual fact no real moral powers at all? . . .

We grope about in the darkness with empty hearts, mere dead machines furnished with a few physical powers that function so long as they are provided with fuel—that is, food. The only true instinct is selfishness and it is the motive force of our world! All the rest is imagination. Mankind is boundless in cunning and inventiveness when it comes to a question of procuring food for itself. One of these forms of cunning mankind has cleverly disguised as "the moral force," so as to feed its lust for power. But there is nothing behind it in reality: the phrase is a superficial deception. As soon as the rod of correction that the priesthood has been holding for centuries over men's heads, or our own rod, the revolution, grows a little feebler, man will fall back again on his animal instincts, and everything will be as it was before.

"At bottom we're doing exactly the same as the old priests!" the man exclaimed in his despair. "They fed the human animal for a while on a pabulum of punishment and reward in the next world, until their ideas collapsed and they with them. We are trying to feed the human animal on the idea of the moral power of communism—until another idea will arise and wrest mankind from us, to keep it in subjection by means of another illusive and transient value. . . . Then what is the good of it all? Why not let everything plunge into the abyss if there is no enduring inner force that enshrines its own value? Let them destroy themselves in their egoism like wild beasts; let everything plunge to destruction once and for all!"

His broad, salient, bony face was ashen gray. His eyes were clouded, as though a misty veil lay over them. He felt tired and sleepy.

Suddenly he felt a draught blowing on his back. The door had opened softly. Noiselessly as a cat a sailor had slipped into the room. The fair young lad gently set a cup of tea before his leader.

"You're sitting in the dark, comrade. Shall I put on the light?" he asked in a solicitous voice full of respectful devotion.

"It isn't necessary. I've been resting a little."

"They're waiting outside for you to sign some papers."

"Tell the comrades I don't want to be disturbed before the meeting of the Central Committee."

"Very good." The young sailor made to retire, leaving the room backwards on the tips of his toes.

"Stay for a minute, comrade!" the man with the bald head cried suddenly.

The sailor drew himself up and stood at attention as before an admiral.

The man got up, went over to the sailor and put his hands on his shoulders. Then he half shut his eyes and stared long and deeply into the young lad's blue eyes.

The sailor, who had been devoted heart and soul to him from the first encounter, following him everywhere and carefully looking after him, stood as motionless as a pillar and gazed at him frankly from his blue-gray eyes. They shone happily in his simple open face, which was as candid as the day.

For a long time the man's piercing glance scanned these two blue pools as if trying to reach the bottom of them.

"Well, comrade, do you really believe we'll overcome all our difficulties?" he suddenly asked.

"As I believe in God!" the sailor cried. He was at once aware what a dreadful word had escaped him. But he could not take it back now. He blushed.

His leader had not noticed.

"They're simply throttling us, these imperialistic German generals: we're in a terribly difficult position."

"The devil fly away with them; never mind them—*nitchevo!* Only let us get over this and we'll reach our goal, comrade! There is no doubt about it."

"When will that be?" the man asked dreamily.

"I don't know; *you* know. But we'll do our best to break down all the walls, the devil take them!"

"Thank you, comrade!" The man pressed the sailor's hand warmly.

"Shall I put on the light?"

"Yes. And tell the secretary that she can bring in the papers for signature."

The sole moment of irresolution that he had felt before agreeing to the peace of Brest-Litovsk was overcome. From the eyes of the sailor he had drawn new power and faith.

His broad bony face lit up and became irradiated by an almost celestial joy and trust. It was ecstatically beautiful, like the face of a rapt musician. His eyes were open and frank and smiled with a dark fire. His lofty brow shone. Winged with fresh enthusiasm he sat down at his writing-table and buried himself in the papers lying before him. And behind the black letters his eyes saw—worlds. . . .

The long path lay clear before him, from its first beginning to its radiant end. All that had happened till now was not a confusing process leading nowhere: the road was marked off by great milestones set there by an inexorable hand, one after the other. Proud and strong, man marched on from milestone to milestone, driven by the holy and everlasting spirit of truth that burned within him. Now he could see the whole history of man. Like a savage beast he emerged from dark mist-wrapped forests and wastes. With iron claws and teeth he fought a way for himself through the jungle; savage and bleeding, he strode out of the thick darkness into the faint dawn, out of the dawn into the dewy morning, lured on in spite of himself, driven on by the moral force that burned within him. He tried to resist it, true, but it always drove him back to his true road again. No obstacle, no image of terror, human or divine, could stop the onward march of the giant. The way was predestined from the beginning. It was long. It began in darkness, it went on through thick and thin, it made men destroy one another in bloody fights—until at last it reached the gate of the morning. And the Russian people with their blue childlike eyes and unshakable faith—to them it had been given to knock first at that gate, to fling it open, to step over the threshold. To them, the naked and destitute—with nothing to lose—it had been given to break the fetters for the first time. "Break them, brothers! Those that feel the agonies of the new birth can weep and howl if they like! The agony of parting won't cause you much pain. You aren't firmly grown into the old world; you are naked and destitute. Tear open the door! Step over the threshold and draw all the world after you!"

Certainly, the paths that lie beyond the portal are unknown! the man went on in thought. Who knows what circuitous ways we may be forced to take? But we want to be able to choose them at least! If it's necessary to take roundabout roads we want to decide them ourselves. With our faces turned towards the radiant morning, we'll take a step back when necessary—to go forward a mile. Undeterred by the shrieks of farewell, regardless of the sufferings of those who fall by the way, we shall blaze a path for ourselves and for those who will follow us. And if it is necessary to help on man's forward march with a whip, we shall use it. With rods we shall knock into him the joys of communism and teach him our "reward and punishment." Then he'll begin to feel them himself!

And sitting at his writing-table he heard the song of a redeemed world that the misty snowbound twilight bore to him. On his broad Mongolian face was a smile of bliss as he signed the new edicts.

At the meeting of the Central Committee to decide whether the harsh peace terms of Brest-Litovsk were to be accepted or refused he replied to all the reproaches and objections of his comrades, to their warnings concerning his "responsibility in the eyes of history" and his disregard for the "national honor" and such like things, by saying in an almost beseeching voice: "Comrades, why all this hesitation? Look at the thing as a whole. It's only the first step that we're taking. The others must follow us. They're already starting on the road we've cleared for them. They must and will follow us because of an iron law, because their circumstances are the same as ours. And you talk about Finland and the Ukraine, about national honor and responsibility in the eyes of history! These are ideas of a dying world. What importance have they in the light of the new world that is coming to life? The German generals are robbing us—but how long will they be able to keep what they've robbed? We'll presently come to an understanding with the German proletariat and then we'll band together and rap the robbers over the knuckles!"

The peace treaty of Brest-Litovsk was signed.

CHAPTER XXI

FLIGHT

EVERYBODY made preparations to leave Russia, and took advantage of the loophole opened by the peace of Brest-Litovsk to flee the country.

The Ukraine became the vessel of the hopes that Russia had disappointed; for it had now a democratic government with toleration for minorities and other amenities of liberty. If one wanted a pass on any pretext for the Ukraine, now a "foreign" country, the Soviet Government put no obstacles—for the time being—in one's way. Those who did not succeed in securing a pass tried to get across the frontier by other means, to wait in the rich Ukraine for the madness to end that had seized Russia and by all signs could not last very much longer.

Among the many people who were preparing to leave Russia were Goldstein the petroleum king, and Rosamin the tea magnate.

For various reasons it was almost impossible now for these men and their friends to meet regularly. Halperin's house had become "trefe." Comrade Markovitch ruled there unchecked and now listened quite openly and brazenly to the talks in the little boudoir, where the lawyer and his son-in-law were still living.

In old Mirkin's business Misha Molodyetz and the young commissar were in control. Old Mirkin, however, was invited to the business conferences. His advice was listened to attentively and also followed. So, even now, he still remained in a sense "the chief."

He, too, was ordered to remove to Moscow, where his firm, now a branch of the whole nationalized railway administration, had been transferred when the Bolsheviks changed their seat of government. Yet as he could find nobody to look after his father-in-law, who was growing more and more childish and irrational: He took a short holiday from his work and remained for the time being in the sick and empty capital of the Czars.

A few days after the government left Petersburg old Mirkin met his friend Goldstein in the street. The captain of industry, though one of the richest men in Russia, had never been distinguished for the elegance of his attire. He perpetually trained his body, so to speak, for the time when it might have to live in poverty. Consequently he lived in a style that was more than modest, almost always traveled by train, scarcely ever using a droshky or a sledge, and invariably appeared in shabby old suits. But this time he was dressed like a veritable workman. He wore a short fur coat of an extraordinary cut and had a black scarf wrapped round his neck. Over the low shoes which he wore like a Tartar, instead of top-boots, he was now wearing a pair of battered galoshes.

Old Mirkin, who in his outward appearance had made no concessions to the new order, wore as usual his ample gray Kamchatka beaver-fur coat. With his pointed gray beard he looked like a rich land-proprietor of the old days.

When Goldstein caught sight of the elegant Mirkin he tried to avoid him lest any one should see that he had such fine acquaintances. Old Mirkin could read in his friend's eyes that the beaver-fur alarmed him and turned discreetly away. But meanwhile Goldstein had thought again and walked up to old Mirkin, assuming deliberately as he did so an obsequious air such as a servant might use.

"Good heavens! Wearing a beaver-fur in times like these!" he whispered.

"All my life, whatever I've done I've done openly. I've no intention of disguising myself now in my old age."

This rather blunt hint put the petroleum king somewhat out of countenance: "I wasn't asking you to disguise yourself. But a coat like that attracts people's attention."

"How are things going with you?" asked old Mirkin to change the painful subject.

"I'm trying to get a passport to the Ukraine and have hopes of getting it. What plans have you?"

"The same as before. I'll have to shift to Moscow. The business has been transferred there already. But I don't know what I'm to do with Solomon Ossipovitch. . . ."

"You're working under Misha Molodyetz, I'm told?"

"I would work even under the devil!"

"I've something important I want to discuss with you," began Goldstein after a short pause, "but not here. Good heavens, to think of wearing that coat! All the people are staring at us! Come and see me this evening; your house is 'trefe.' We won't be disturbed."

In the evening old Mirkin went along to the little hotel in which Goldstein had lived since time immemorial (this fact had also saved him from being forcibly ejected). After a brief greeting Goldstein began:

"Listen to me, Gabriel Haimovitch! You know that from the start I've trained myself to be able to live in any circumstances whatsoever. In fact the present way of life suits my character better than the old did. I could never look on quietly and see people throwing away their money on pleasure and personal ease. The world thinks it's greed and miserliness that makes me live as I do. But you know that that isn't true. The value of gold consists in the fact that it is a means of satisfying human needs, so that if I waste money I not only squander my own property but the savings of other men which have been intrusted to me. I have never allowed myself to live any better than any of my workmen, and I've never felt any need either to live differently. Now I decided lately, as you know, to work with the new government—whether I acted rightly or not we'll leave aside—and was prepared to devote everything I had to it, my abilities and the wealth I've gathered together, and serve the community. Perhaps you were right when you said recently: 'We have sinned, and the best proof of it is that things have come to such a pass.' I was never ambitious and I'm not one of those people who lay much store on externals. I've silently borne the insults and sarcasms of inexperienced lads. But I can't go on any longer, Gabriel Haimovitch, I can't go on! Not because I feel insulted in my dignity—but I can't stand their methods. Who are more strictly bound than these people to preserve and maintain the people's property? They took it over from us: well and good. But surely it has some value? And they're completely destroying it. Not only by their inexperience and incapacity: that could be gradually mended. No, the destruction has inner causes, not merely external ones. I can see no real sign of a belief in anything in what they're doing. They're simply squandering everything barefacedly. None of them thinks of the morrow, every one tries to push the blame on to someone else so as to make some show of efficiency. And I'm afraid the rest are just impossible. Perhaps it's different with the greater people, the men at the head—but the people who actually carry things out are just a set of Misha Molodyetzes. No, there's no working with any of them!"

Old Mirkin listened attentively with knitted brows, and the points of his beard moved up and down as he nodded every now and then. When Goldstein had finished he began: "That's just why we must stick to our posts. We old fellows who built all this up must be at hand when anything goes wrong. Not for our own sakes—God forbid!—but for the sake of the whole business, for Russia. We can't leave a living thing to its own devices that we have created ourselves. We must protect and nurse it until better times come."

"What do you mean by better times? The better times are dead forever."

"The old times are dead, but life isn't. And life will need the businesses that we created. If our new rulers are destroying so many things at present, that's simply because they didn't create them themselves. When they begin to build they'll learn the happiness that there is to be found in work instead of mere destruction. Then perhaps they'll be able to appreciate our services at their true value. But until then we must stick determinedly to our posts and save what can be saved."

"If things go on any longer as they're going everything will be ruined, and that will cost nobody his head—except us."

"What do you mean by talking in that wild way?" asked old Mirkin a little apprehensively. "I've long ago renounced all personal profit from the firm."

"I'm not speaking of personal profit, I'm speaking quite soberly and literally. The experiment will not only undermine Russia's very existence; it will cost us our heads as well. Why, do you think, are they keeping us on, asking our advice, taking us to Moscow with them? Do you know why? They're keeping us as scapegoats for the people's fury. When there's a shortage of petroleum or railway sleepers they won't say: 'The system is bad'; no, they'll say: 'The bourgeois are to blame.' Then they'll declare we have been practicing sabotage and fling us to the fury of the mob. We're simply being held as scapegoats."

Old Mirkin fell into deep thought: "I've smelt something like that in the air, but I'm not certain of it."

"But I know it's so, I've had it from reliable sources. The blow may fall at any moment. Follow my example: you won't have much to pack! Time presses. At present one can still get a passport."

The petroleum king lowered his voice to a whisper and looked about apprehensively to see if there was anybody listening: "The frontiers aren't very well guarded just now either, for everything is in confusion: one can always find a gap where one can slip through into the Ukraine. But even that isn't necessary, for you can get a genuine and valid passport for a few roubles."

"For a few roubles?" old Mirkin repeated. His eyes were dead and his cheeks hung down flaccidly like two empty purses.

"Yes, but with your beaver-fur it will naturally cost you more," Goldstein smiled bitterly.

"Do you know, Goldstein, it's always gone against my grain to bribe petty officials? If I had to bribe I always preferred to go to the people at the top."

"Let me tell you, this isn't a time for joking! Soon it will be too late, I'm afraid."

Once more old Mirkin sank into thought: "And how do you think of employing yourself as an exile in a foreign land? Are you going to rest from your labors? It's too early for that. I can't see you lying on the beach at Nice cooking yourself in the sun for the rest of your days. . . ."

"Why not make a new start?" Goldstein interrupted.

"A new start? At our age?" Old Mirkin shook his head incredulously.

"If one only has something to work for age doesn't matter. As for me, I've made up my mind to start on something quite new. Up to now I've worked for strangers: now I'm going to try to do something for my own people."

"What do you mean by that?"

"Well, you know my old affection for Palestine. Up till now it's been a kind of Platonic friendship. Now I'm going to try actually to work for it."

"In Palestine?" asked old Mirkin in astonishment.

"Of course you've heard about the Balfour Declaration—it's been the main subject of discussion in Jewish circles for weeks. The English ambassador has expressly assured the Zionists that the Balfour Declaration means nothing less than a Jewish nation with its own government. In other words the age-old dream of the Jews will be realized when 'the Messiah comes,' that is when the allies have won the war. But whether that's so or not—Palestine is a country, and a beautiful country too. And Jews will live there. So why not employ what abilities I have there, and do some work fit for Jewish hands and Jewish brains? And in any case we're connected by some bond, however slight, with the land. We remember it in our prayers. Generation after generation has passed into eternity with this hope on their lips. And after all everybody has something to live for, something that is wife and child to him. God hasn't granted me that happiness, I've remained an old bachelor—so Palestine will be my wife and child."

Old Mirkin glanced at his friend and suddenly noticed that Goldstein's eyes were glittering with tears. This dried up man for whom sentiment did not exist, who, so his friends said, had refrained from marrying because he grudged sharing his wealth with any one, even those who were most intimately related to him: this man was talking now of settling down in a strange and savage land and devoting his life to it, and as he spoke his eyes gleamed as though he were speaking of a beloved woman!

Goldstein caught Mirkin's glance and went on somewhat shamefacedly: "Besides, it isn't idealism or sentimentality that makes me want to go: I'm thinking chiefly of my own comfort. I fancy that the Orient will suit me very well. My tastes are really those of an Arab. All that I want is a white sheet to wrap round me. I'll live on a few dates or pieces of sugar cane and gaze at the stars all night."

Old Mirkin remained silent and seemed to be thinking deeply. As was his custom when he reflected, he slowly stroked the long points of his beard with his fingers. Then he said half to himself: "It's a very good thing to have an ideal. It keeps us right, it gives us new energy. You needn't be ashamed of it. I envy you."

"You have no need to do that! You can do the same thing as I'm doing. You have just as much interest in it—for, after all, you're a Jew too. Come, Gabried Haimovitch, what do you say to the two of us starting to build for our people in Palestine as we once built here in our young days, built things that these devils have taken from us now without as much as a 'Thank you'? Come, Gabriel Haimovitch, what have you to say to it?"

"My dear friend, such things are no longer for me. I've never been able to take leaps in the dark. I've been rooted here for generations. I've had good times here—and am I to run away when bad times come? That wouldn't be right. No, Goldstein, go with God's blessing, but I'll stay here, I'm too much of a slow-poke to move."

"Gabriel Haimovitch, what I told you is no joke! It's serious, quite serious!"

"Ah, you mean about losing one's head?" old Mirkin laughed. "Well, heaven knows this head of mine has run into danger often enough in its day and nobody ever wanted it. Who can want it now when it's old?"

"Gabriel Haimovitch, I ask you to think it over again. You're risking your life! You have duties, you have a wife and child!"

A sudden flush swept over Mirkin's cheeks; he flung back his head and the points of his beard pointed almost horizontally at Goldstein. Grim as a turkey-cock he glared at his friend: "That's my business! Soldiers, too, have wives and children, but they march to war all the same."

"It's easy to say that."

"Some say it; others do it!"

"Then do as you think best."

"I shall. Go with God's blessing. I hope with all my heart you'll succeed in your new work. But I can't go with you. Here is an undertaking that gives a livelihood to over twenty thousand people. A captain does not forsake his ship. But I understand you, I wish you . . ."

"Thanks!" Goldstein seized the hand that old Mirkin held out to him.

"And as for my wife and child that you've reminded me of, probably you'll have a chance of seeing them both before I can. You'll be passing through the Caucasus on your way. When you see them give them my greetings and tell them they needn't worry about me—I've got used to dodging danger. And I'll send Nina her father soon too. I'm only waiting for Misha, who is expected back from the front in the next few days. Wait, that's right—there's something else I want you to do for me—our last transaction," old Mirkin laughed. "Will you transfer both our 'New Russia' shares to Nina's account, and take her petroleum shares in exchange for your 'New Russia' ones, which are easier to sell? I don't want my family to starve for a bit yet."

"I'll see to that. We needn't write it down in black and white. No use encumbering oneself with needless baggage."

"Good. Thanks! Go with God's blessing! It's time I was getting home. The streets aren't too safe."

The two men kissed each other after the Russian custom....

When old Mirkin got back he found the advocate engaged in the new favorite occupation which he had taken up after the loss of his porcelain figures: he was drawing up an inventory of all the objects in his house. On this he worked with pedantic exactitude, observing all the usual legal formalities as if he were executing a work of the utmost importance.

"I've a piece of news for you: petroleum Goldstein has decided to go to Palestine! He says that the English have promised to give the land to the Jews to set up a Jewish state. A very interesting idea! Wouldn't that be an opportunity for you, Solomon Ossipovitch?" old Mirkin said, turning to his father-in-law.

The famous advocate ceased writing up his inventory and listened as though he had heard a long forgotten but familiar song.

"Palestine—Palestine—Palestine," he muttered. "It's a pity one hadn't thought of that before..."

Father-in-law and son-in-law sat for a long time in silence opposite each other. Then old Mirkin got up, went to the door, opened it to make sure that nobody was listening, and whispered to his father-in-law: "But first of all you must get to the Caucasus. I've heard that it can be done by going through Charkov. In any case one can get through by paying. Misha is bound to be here in a day or two now."

"And you?" asked the advocate.

"Me—oh yes—me. . . . Why, what do you think? Somebody must remain here; otherwise the whole plan would fail!"

A few days later Misha returned from the front, where he had been serving in a flying squad. He had already been informed by letter of the events at home and it was arranged that he should not show himself in his father's house in case it should excite the suspicion of his former school friend Markovitch. Old Mirkin met him at an address that had been fixed beforehand.

Misha had changed to his advantage during the last few years. The war, the latest phases of the revolution and the sad fate of his father had made him more serious. He looked manlier. In his army coat with the tattered epaulettes and his unkempt young beard he looked like hundreds of thousands of other returned soldiers who in the brief interval between the demobilization of the front army and the formation of the Red Army had quickly overflowed all Russia.

Besides the desire to act as escort to his father, Misha had another reason for wishing to reach the south of Russia. He wished to get to the Don, where General Krassnov was gathering Cossacks and other Whites to his banner with the object of joining forces with other White generals who were preparing to wage war on the Bolsheviks.

Residence in Petersburg was risky both for Misha as a counter-revolutionary and his father. So old Mirkin urged them to leave the city without delay. The journey to the Caucasus over the Moscow-Charkov route was very uncertain, but certainly preferable to staying on in Petersburg.

It was no easy task for old Mirkin to persuade the advocate to set out. Halperin was firmly resolved to take with him all the china cups that still remained, as well as all sorts of lace knick-knacks for his wife and his daughter. But the journey would have to be made with as little baggage as possible, and the travelers' coat linings and bootsoles would have to serve as places of concealment for more valuable objects than china and lace. At last the advocate allowed himself to be dissuaded from his intention; but in return he insisted that the house inventory, which was now completed, should be stitched into the lining of his coat collar.

Old Mirkin sewed all the jewels and papers of value that he still possessed into the two men's clothes and the lining of their traveling bags. At last they set out.

"We'll soon see each other again!" he said to his father-in-law. "But if we don't, see that my son down there in the south isn't brought up to hate Russia." And half to himself he added: "We've always had bitterness and to spare in Russia, and these are the sorts of things that bitterness brings forth."

After Halperin and his son had left, old Mirkin packed up the most essential of his own and his wife's belongings and also everything that had any personal value for them both; for he, too, like the advocate, could not bear to leave anything personally connected with his wife to the mercy of strange hands. Then he removed to Moscow, where his firm, in which he now served as an "expert," had been transferred for a long time.

Therewith Halperin's establishment and Mirkin's establishment, like so many others in the former city of the Czars, vanished once and for all.

CHAPTER XXII

THE HUNTED QUARRY

Vassily Andreyevitch, the lord of Sapianka, whom we left last in the Hôtel Métropole in Moscow, flew, when those tempestuous October days were past, to his illegitimate wife, Natalia Stepanovna, also called Natasha.

Like everybody else in Moscow Vassily Andreyevitch was confident that "the Bolshevist adventure" would soon come to an end; the Cossacks would sweep back from the front and scatter the Reds. He waited in Natasha's flat for this to happen. Meantime he wrote every now and then to his wife Maria Arkadievna in Sapianka, asking her to send him provisions. But he received no reply.

In the beginning of winter Akim, a peasant who was friendly to him, arrived from the village in a cart bringing Vassily a few sacks of potatoes, some wheaten flour, several pounds of butter, and five dozen eggs. He related that Maria Arkadievna had become "a big bug" among the peasants; she had herself summoned a meeting of the younger people and set up a committee to run the village in the new spirit. Up to the present the peasants in the neighborhood seemed to be contented, living in peace with their masters. But they were angry at him, Vassily Andreyevitch, and spoke very badly of him. Maria Arkadievna had confidentially asked him, Akim, to tell the master to stay in town for a while yet, and not to return until she sent him word.

Since then no more carts with provisions had come from Sapianka, nor had Vassily Andreyevitch received any word from it.

Meanwhile in Natalia Stepanovna's house food grew more and more scarce. The small store of provisions came to an end. There was nothing in the little flat that could be sold, for it had always been simply furnished. Natasha began to grumble rebelliously, showed not the slightest respect for her former master and present husband, and more than once told him he was a bird of misfortune and of no use to anybody. And when that had no effect and Vassily still would do nothing, she herself girded up her loins, to use the Biblical phrase. She had always been energetic; now she became a veritable demon. She took half the potatoes that were left, and half a sack of flour, piled them in a little sledge, and ordered Vassily to drag them to the Sucharevsky Market. In the afternoon she returned laden with silk wraps, table linen, bed linen and a pocket book filled with twenty-rouble notes of the Kerensky variety.

"Tomorrow morning early you take a sack and a train to the nearest village you can find and bring back food with you! I'll sell it at the Sucharevsky Market or exchange it for valuables as all the respectable people are doing now."

Vassily had long since exchanged his ample fur jacket with the gray Persian collar, which looked quite stylish, for a peasant sheepskin coat which fastened with a string, his elegant patent leather boots for a pair of low shoes, and his tall Persian fur cap for a peasant's fur cap with ear flaps.

Every evening Natasha filled a sack for him with useful objects such as underclothes, silk shawls, elegant footwear, fur collars and lace, and put a pocketbook of Kerensky roubles in his hand. Early in the morning Vassily had to forsake his couch and fare by the Nijni-Novgorod, Brest or Kirsk line into the country, at the beginning to the nearest villages only, but later farther and farther until he reached the remotest ones. He had strong arms, broad shoulders and the looks of a brigand. These made him feared. Carrying his sacks and bundles he pushed his way unceremoniously into the packed carriages, butting with his shoulders and belly until he secured a place, and using his strong arms when necessary; when a curse or a threat was required he drew upon his rich arsenal of vituperation; he clung to strangers' shoulders and flung his sacks and bundles down on strange feet and bellies. So, covered with curses and blows, he returned with sore ribs and trampled feet, drenched in sweat and half-dead, to Moscow once more.

At the station the "bagmen" were awaited by the "Soviet horses" (as the tattered and neglected street boys were called who waited at the stations with the sledges they themselves drew and quarreled for the custom of the "bagmen"). These lads conveyed the provisions Vassily had collected to the house.

Every morning Natasha, assisted by her two children, dragged sledges laden with potatoes, rye flour, butter and a few bunches of onions to the Sucharevsky Market, and there the food was exchanged for the valuable articles that the aristocracy were now glad to get rid of. When the militia appeared one flung the sack over one's shoulder and took to one's heels. And what could the militia do after all? They couldn't close the whole Sucharevsky Market, for all Moscow went there to pick up the little food it could get. And besides, bribery could still do a great deal, just as in the good old days; for a little piece of butter or a few onions were worth a fortune.

So trade flourished in the Sucharevsky Market and Natasha was soon the owner of silk lingerie, precious furs, Persian carpets and silver table services. But what the dealers coveted most of all were the Czarist thousand-rouble notes, which were still quite new and crackled reassuringly. All the Armenians and Tartars were convinced that the Czar would return again, and in all Moscow—apart from the Kremlin—Czarist bank notes were eagerly accepted. The damaged ones were less highly prized. The most current and eagerly sought-after notes were the comparatively new thousand-rouble ones which looked as if they had just left the press. So as not to crease them they were not folded, but rolled up in a wad, as the Armenian and Tartar dealers were in the habit of doing with their paper money. Accordingly Natasha paid for the goods she bought with Kerensky notes; but she kept the roubles of the Czar and filled a cushion with them which she carried all day in her bosom and hid under the mattress at night. So she waited and hoped, like everybody else, that the Czar would soon return and drive out the Bolsheviks, so that the world might be a real world again, one's life a real life, and money—real money.

At night Vassily reposed beside his mistress. The windows were thickly curtained, the doors securely barred, and by the faint light of a candle the cushion was emptied of its contents. The notes were counted: a hundred thousand—two hundred thousand, three—four hundred thousand—half a million—almost a million roubles! They were millionaires!

"Just think what you could buy with that in the good old days! Whole stretches of land, forests, houses, people—you could get anything you liked for it!"

Vassily looked at his Natasha. He could hardly recognize her. Her hardy peasant face had become a fleshy mass. Her gray eyes were buried behind layers of fat and sparkled malignantly. Her hair, now quite gray, stuck out round her head as stiffly as wire. Suddenly Vassily thought: she's just like a witch. Her thick fingers stroked the crackling thousand-rouble notes which she held close to her fat body as if to protect them from being touched by anybody else. She ran her fingers over every one of them, listening critically to hear them crackle, and smacked her lips: "Thousand-rouble notes, thousand-rouble notes —real thousand-roubles notes!"

Vassily flung a glance at the smooth, glistening notes. No, they hadn't changed! The same yellowish color, the strong paper, a little rough to the touch. With the Czar's eagle on it and the portrait of Nicholas II in waterprint. Genuine! They evoked the same confidence as they had once done; it made one's heart beat faster to look at them. One felt sure of oneself, carefree and content with the world. But the world had changed. And the very fact that there were so many of them and that they were lying there on the bed beside Natasha's fat bosom made them lose prestige in Vassily's eyes, and he saw them suddenly as things that had fallen from their greatness.

"They seem to be the same notes that one used to be handed across the bank counter—and yet not the same," he said half to himself.

Natasha flung him an angry glance. Vassily felt for a moment that her eyes had turned quite around in her head, presenting their backs to him.

"Not the same!" she said, aping him. "Once the Czar returns, people will cringe before these notes just as they did in the old days. They're real money!" she shouted and hastily covered the notes with the blankets as if to shield them from the evil eye.

"Yes, they're real money and yet they aren't," Vassily sighed.

"Why, are you going over to the Reds next?" Natasha flung at him.

"I shan't go over to the Reds, but the whole business of these notes seems childish make-believe to me."

Giving her husband a black look Natasha turned on her other side. . . .

Vassily had long since tired of his new way of life. Yet all winter he bore with it, trudging from village to village, haggling and cheating. But when spring approached, when the ice on the Moskva melted and through the vanishing snow round patches of earth like kind brown faces appeared, a painful longing for the soil overcame him and he had only one wish—to return to his village and his fields.

His idle life—for so he called in his heart his bargaining and haggling with the villagers—became loathsome to him and he longed with all his heart for real activity, real work.

And for Vassily that meant work in the fields. And it was high time it was started. In former years he had been up to his neck in work at this season, had tramped in his great top-boots through the melting snow with his steward ten times if not more, and discussed which fields should be sown with wheat and which with corn and which should be left as pastureland for the sheep. "This year there will be a great need for green fodder in any case." At the words "green fodder" he could smell the fragrance of milk fresh from the cows, and his longing became still more painful.

"In other years," he thought, "the sparks would be flying in the village smithy long before this. About this time the peasants always have to give the smith a hand, there's so much to be done. Every day carts will be going to town to fetch implements that are needed, axes, spades, scythes and ropes. They'll be hauling logs from the woods and leaving them at the joiners'. There will be a fine hammering, sawing, planing and what not. And thick smoke will be rising from all the chimneys, for the peasants' wives will be burning up the waste wood. The dogs will be barking happily, the children splashing in the puddles. There will be bigger patches of the ground to be seen every day, as if they were impatient of the snow covering them. The horses will be getting restive and hammering with their hoofs on the stable floors. The earth and everything on it will be out and about."

And, like the earth and the cattle, Vassily, too, longed to be out and about. In the city he felt constricted. Just as an animal feels in spring that it has a new hide, so Vassily felt with all his senses that he had slipped out of the skin of the city, the bargaining and haggling, and got a country and woodland skin. His legs longed to tramp through muddy roads and sink up to the knees in the new miry soil. His lungs thirsted for the scents of spring that breathed from every moist and blackened fence, every dripping thatched roof.

Again he would wade through the watery swamps, his great fisherman's boots on his feet. His dog Lightning would look at him every morning, his tail rigid and his jaws wide open and seem to be asking: "Aren't you going to shoot any wild duck today? Is there going to be no spring this year?" And Vassily himself continued his dog's question: "Or will they till the ground at all this year at Sapianka now that the master's away?"

He knew that the village had become a dangerous place for him, that he dared not show his face there. But no—that must be nonsense! He felt with all his being that he belonged to the place and that everything would be right again as soon as he set foot on his land.

Like a child who believes that all its wicked exploits have been forgiven and forgotten because it has forgiven them itself, so Vassily, the strong and mature man, had long since forgotten what he once was. In his own eyes he was no longer the landlord, no longer the owner of Sapianka. He forgot that he had treated the peasants badly, that he had knocked their hats from their heads and, when nobody was looking, even knocked them down or gave them a drubbing with his fists. He forgot that he, Vassily Andreyevitch, was master of Sapianka and that these people were *his* peasants, the children of serfs, who lived on his land in his houses and tilled his fields in return for wages in kind. In his own eyes he had long since become one of them, an ordinary dweller at Sapianka: the only difference being that he as steward, as head man, would occupy one or two rooms in the big house and eat a little better in recognition of the superior value of his work. But in everything else there would be equality, as the spirit of the age demanded. And as the wish was father to the thought, it seemed to him self-evident that the peasants must agree with him.

When the first spring days came nothing could keep him in Moscow: he set out for his village.

In the middle of the night he tapped at the window of the friendly peasant who had brought him the cartload of food at the beginning of the winter. Akim's hut was outside the village, a good distance from the other houses and close to the edge of a wood.

"Akim, in Christ's name let me in! It's me, Vassily Andreyevitch."

At first nothing stirred inside the hut; then the sound of subdued bickering could be heard, and at last the door was opened a very little, and a small sack of bread fell at Vassily's feet. Through the door the old peasant whispered: "For God's sake, master, fly from here! If they notice you've been visiting me they'll burn the hut over my head. Think of yourself and my family."

"Akim, open in God's name! I only want to warm myself for a little. I'll go as soon as the first sign of light—I've always treated you well!"

"That's true and I can't deny it. But different times have come. It's a bad look-out for one if one goes against the commune."

"Let me in just to take a breath! You're a Christian, after all, Akim, aren't you?"

The peasant shut the door. For a long time he seemed to be taking counsel with someone in the hut. Then he opened the door a little wider and let Vassily in.

"May Christ reward you!"

"Just lie down where you are. It isn't advisable to light the lamp. Nobody in the village must know you're here!"

"Where is Maria Arkadievna, Akim? They've burned down the big house, I've noticed. Where is she now?"

"I can't tell you, master. At first they let her stay. None of us were communistic—so she explained to us what communism meant. And she ran the commune herself. Then some young lads came from Stara Gniasda, the next village. 'What?' they said. 'The landlord's wife is running your show for you?' And they set fire to the big house. And then, as far as I can remember, they put her in a sledge and drove away with her. It's bad times for you great people! Yes, bad times have come for you. You must fly as soon as the last star fades."

Vassily was lying on something wet, whose stench took his breath away. A sheep sniffed at him with its moist nose and began to lick him. He put the beast's nose to his mouth and kissed it: "You talk to them, Akim! So help me God, I only want to be the same as you, one of the commune! All I ask is a corner of a hut and a slice of bread. I'll work for two—you know me yourself, no work was ever too hard for me. And you need a steward—and it's better to have somebody belonging to Sapianka. Speak to them, for God's sake—I can't stand town life any longer!"

"It would be wiser for you to fly before the peasants find you! I've often listened to them talking about you. There's one of them in particular, he's a soldier back from the army—Ivan, Vavierucha's husband—that's furious at you, because you gave his wife a touch of the rod once in the barn. And Ivan is one of the leaders in the commune now."

"It's hard to live away from Sapianka, Akim!"

Before the last star had disappeared from the sky Akim roused his master from the dung heap that he shared with two new born lambs. Akim's wife offered him a bowl of milk; Akim handed him the little sack of bread. Vassily bowed deeply before the holy ikons in the

"God's corner," crossed himself thrice, and once more said imploringly: "I'll work for two. I'll go on my knees before the commune if they'll only forgive me and let me breathe the air of Sapianka. Where else have I to go? I'm a stranger everywhere else! Talk to them, for God's sake! I'll hide in the woods all day and come back here when it's dark for an answer."

The peasants learned that there was an exciting new quarry roaming the woods—the landlord of Sapianka. They immediately told the returned soldier Ivan, who ran the commune along with the pock-marked village teacher. The two leaders hastily summoned together the young people of the village without telling the older ones, for they were afraid some of these old men might send word to their former master. Some three dozen men and women set out, armed with rifles, axes and pitchforks, some of them on horseback, some on foot, and surrounded the wood on three sides. They took their landlord's dogs with them, too, which they had divided among themselves, and as their master had once hunted wild game, so now they hunted their master.

The fourth side of the wood, along which ran the Sadsavka River, they left open. For it was impossible to ford or swim the stream at that time of the year; anyone who tried to reach it would remain stuck in the perilous swamps that adjoined it, and these were still more dangerous than usual now because they were covered with a sheet of water left by the melting snow, which reached to the neighboring low-lying pastures.

When the peasants reached the wood they posted their best shots at the outskirts, while the others, taking the dogs with them, began to beat the wood with their axes and spades. Then they set the dogs loose that they might pick up their master's scent and drive him out of the wood.

Vassily knew all the nooks and corners of his wood, for he had hunted there every spring and autumn for years. As a place of concealment during the day he had chosen a little shelter of twigs whose corners were formed by four tree trunks, which he had once used as a place for drying the oak bark that he sold to the tanners. The branches were still almost bare, so he could have a clear view of all that happened in the wood and at its edges. His mind was filled with evil premonitions and he feared that the peasants might set out to hunt him if they decided not to take him as one of themselves into the commune. So all day he kept a vigilant watch on every side.

He knew, when he saw gray shadows stealing between the moss-covered oaks, that the peasants were after him. He was resolved not to surrender without a fight; he would wrest a rifle or an ax from the first peasant that came near him, kill the man and then fight to the death with the others. So he hastily barricaded the shelter with some logs that the peasants had sawed from the trees they had felled: and when he caught the thud of the axes and spades he put his ear to the ground to discover from what side the peasants were coming, and prepared himself for battle.

The first creature to find Vassily in his place of hiding was his hunting dog Lightning, which a neighboring land-proprietor had given him in exchange for a horse. Fleeter than all the others, Lightning had flown over everything, deep holes, soaking heaps of withered leaves and piles of snow, and made straight for Vassily.

When the dog recognized his master he leapt on him joyfully, licked his hands, and then, eager and tense, looked up into his face waiting for an order. Vassily hastily put his hand over the dog's mouth to keep him from barking; then he looked gravely into his eyes and said: "Lightning, you must save me! I'm in danger."

The dog gazed at Vassily with dumb and melancholy devotion. He seemed to be wanting to tell his master something that he could not express. Vassily put his face close to Lightning's. Gazing into each other's eyes, man and dog understood each other.

"You must save me," said Vassily again.

Lightning remained silent, gazed tensely at his master, wagged his tail impatiently, and asked with his eyes what he must do.

Vassily pointed with his hand towards the opposite border of the wood, where Akim's hut stood, and said: "Over there! Bark for all you're worth, Lightning! Bark, Lightning!"

The dog cast a reproachful glance at his master and sighed deeply as if someone had just snatched a bone from him; then he flew away in the direction he had been ordered to take, barking with all his might.

Vassily laid his ear to the ground and could hear that the peasants were following the dog. Now he ventured to leave his shelter and crept away on all fours between the trees, his belly to the ground, towards the river. He knew that that was his only way of escape. Now or never!

He heard Lightning's barking becoming fainter and fainter. The other dogs were joining in. So they must be following the faithful Lightning! And the peasants were running behind the dogs and encouraging them with loud shouts: "Holla! Holla!"

Vassily had to force his way through thorny thickets. The dry twigs broke beneath the weight of his heavy body. His face and hands were bleeding. The thorns held him up again and again, and his clothes were in tatters. At length he came to the Sadsavka.

It was not in vain that Vassily had hunted for so many years in his wood; he knew it inside out. He knew quite well that nobody could get through the swamp covered with melted snow. More than once he had sunk almost to the neck in these bogs and had had to shout to his peasants to come and pull him out. But once he had driven a deer to this end of the wood, feeling certain, just as the peasants did now, that the beast would never get across the Sadsavka. But the deer knew a secret way. Long ago, it seemed, someone must have made a path across the bog by laying a few oak trunks over it; or perhaps the trees had fallen in just such a position. The half sunken, green and rotting trunks could hardly be distinguished now from their surroundings, and so this path across the swamp had remained unknown until the flying deer discovered it to Vassily. Light-footed, it had leapt from trunk to trunk and got across. Vassily had watched the animal's escape with deep interest. One false leap would have cost it its life. Thrilled by the sight he had not fired, though the deer was well within range. "You've found a dangerous way of escape, so good luck to you!" he shouted after it. But he kept the secret of the hidden path to himself.

And now that he was being hunted himself he stole towards the path that the deer had shown him. He had time to look for and find it, for Lightning was still luring the peasants towards the other end of the wood with his barking. And now, like the deer, Vassily leapt in fear of his life from trunk to trunk across the swamp. But he found it harder, for Nature had not given him the agility and skill of the deer. Centuries of lasting security had blunted in him the instinctive skill in escaping from peril that is innate in all wild creatures: now and then he slipped, fell into the water, and was within a hair's breadth of disappearing for ever into the swamp. But the deadly fear that lowered behind him worked miracles: he overcame all obstacles and in spite of his weight even managed to swim across the Sadsavka.

For three days he wandered through fields and woods in his soaking sheepskin coat, his face and hands torn and bleeding; he avoided the villages and towns, although nobody would have recognized him now as the former master of Sapianka. He looked more like a wild man of the woods. And that was what he actually was now: he slept on heaps of damp leaves and lived on milk that he stole; he sucked it from the udders of cows that he chanced upon in the fields.

In the neighboring woods he came across a band of men who looked much like himself, but had rifles. Among them he recognized some of his former rich neighbors, whose lot resembled his more or less. It was a robber band consisting of land-proprietors that had gathered in the woods. Vassily joined them and was given a rifle. And as their numbers increased daily they decided to leave the woods and march on the towns.

CHAPTER XXIII

DIALOGUES IN THE NIGHT

After the October revolution Comrade Sofia got lodgings for Zachary Mirkin and herself in a private house in the Chistoprudny Boulevard. The house was an old-fashioned one and had large white rooms with vaulted ceilings. It was furnished in the Biedermeyer style, with glittering showy sideboards, chests and tables of ash, embroidered chair covers and hand-worked tapestries on the walls depicting romantic scenes.

Despite her revolutionary views Comrade Sofia regarded herself as an intellectual aristocrat: and that was the reason why she had chosen the house. It also went with her whole character; for from her earliest days she had always longed for elegant surroundings, and once in a school essay describing her parents' house her imagination had transfigured Rachel-Leah's humble dwelling into a veritable palace. . . . The pleasant old house in the Chistoprudny Boulevard was entirely to her taste. She had set all the wires moving to get hold of it and had succeeded, too, although the rooms had been intended for some of the "head people." When the government moved to Moscow, Comrade Ryshkov also took up his quarters in the house. Comrade Sofia had suggested this to him, hoping in that way to keep out a too great influx of lodgers.

Apart from the revolution, in which Comrade Sofia was involved up to the eyes, she had also her personal life.

In the first place she simply had to expend on someone the energy she had inherited from Rachel-Leah. Her imperious nature needed a victim, and she found one in Zachary Mirkin. She almost terrorized over him. Regardless of whether he wanted it or not, she forced her maternal affection on him and took upon her the task of making a "man" of her sister's intended. In doing this she reduced him to the position of a child in the nursery. As his future sister-in-law she considered herself justified in ordering him about. He had to obey her in everything, give account of every action, submit to an inquisition when he returned late, and eat what she thought good for him. She decreed that when fat was scarce white of egg was a perfectly good substitute, and made Zachary take the proportion of white of egg into account whenever the food was bought. She forced him to wash every day. The old-fashioned house had only one bathroom, which adjoined the kitchen. Accordingly she carried hot water into it from the kitchen and—quite in the style of her mother—compelled Mirkin to wash himself from head to foot. She also made shirts for him from linen sheets and bedspreads that she found in the house. Till late in the night she sat at the table and sewed shirts and drawers for Mirkin. While doing so she scolded him thoroughly just as if she were his wife—because he did not attend to his appearance and look after his clothes.

One could see that the maternal rôle she had assumed gave her pleasure, though it had little in common with the spirit of the revolution. But Sosha's whole nature demanded it. The most modern woman, even if she has overcome all her feminine weaknesses, will never renounce her maternal rights, and if she has no children or husband of her own over whom she can rule, she will choose the next best object that comes to hand and exercise her maternal powers on him. And Sosha had loved to rule ever since her childhood. Always she had had to have someone under her thumb. Formerly it had been her sister Helene; now that Helene was not there it was Helene's fiancé. Besides, the docile Zachary was a splendid subject. She could make him feel the full weight of her will. And by all appearances Mirkin did not find his rôle in the least irksome. He was not only content with it; he derived an inner comfort—as he had done in childhood—from being ruled by a strong woman's hand as if he were a child....

There are men over whom women love particularly to pour out all their maternal affection. Zachary was one of these; he was, so to speak, a sort of well at which women quenched their thirst, not for a lover, but for a child....

And for Mirkin all the women to whom his repressed smoldering desires attracted him were incarnated in Sosha. To begin with she had a great deal of Rachel-Leah in her nature, above all the same energy and resolution. Outwardly, too, she reminded one very strongly of her mother. Her vigorous body, whose smooth gleaming skin was of a dazzling whiteness, seemed always on the point of bursting from her tightly fitting blouse with the low neck and the short sleeves. A newly released stream of immemorial, long suppressed feminine passion seemed to go out from her body.

All day there was silence in the lonely great house in the Chistoprudny Boulevard. The former owners, two ladies, one elderly and the other young, confined themselves all the time to the rooms that they still had. They were attended by an ancient serving woman who alone, apparently, had stayed faithful to them, and they seemed afraid even to show themselves, although there was nobody except them in the house all day (all the other lodgers being busy in their offices). But the two ladies remained invisible except when they were forced to go with some of their possessions to the market to get food in exchange.

But as soon as Comrade Sofia returned in the evening she soon made her presence felt in the whole house. She immediately took command in the kitchen, contended for a place with the other lodgers, and always came out on top. When she had cooked the supper she bore it with a firm, vigorous step to her room. The floors, old and shaky, trembled beneath her tread. Mirkin loved to listen to her footsteps that made the whole room quiver; it seemed to him as though the old world of which this house was a symbol were reeling beneath the strong tread of the new race.

Comrade Sofia had taken an active part in the October events, and had driven in the armored car, revolver in hand, from the Governor's palace to the various Bolshevist supports. With her effervescent energy she did the work of ten people: one hour she would be making some commission for education accept the most mad new methods, the most fantastic experiments, without even the oldest and most experienced educationists daring to raise the slightest objection; the next she would be forcing upon a commission for regulating the relations between husband and wife her views on marriage and divorce in the teeth of all the legal authorities present; and between the two commissions she would have spoken at a propaganda meeting in some factory yard or some barrack where the returned soldiers were being urged to enlist in the Red Army. Comrade Sofia was not daunted even by "the big bugs" and laid down the law trenchantly to them when it was necessary. Comrade Sofia was a personality to be feared, for she was in close touch with Comrade Marek. And this same Comrade Sofia was madly bent on fondling you, caressing and pampering you—and remaining as cold as a block of ice at the same time. Without any pretext she would suddenly slip into Mirkin's room during the night and lie down beside him in bed.

Completely clothed—as if she were resolved to deny herself any unrestrained expression of tenderness—she would lie beside Zachary, throw her bare arm round his head, press it to her voluptuous breast, and speak of the great plans ahead, the new kingdom of light that was approaching: "There are signs that the German army is breaking up, the soldiers' sympathy for the revolution is growing. German imperialism is making a last bid to maintain itself, but it won't succeed. . . ."

But when Mirkin, intoxicated with the warmth of her body, buried his face in her neck and tried to draw her to him, she repulsed him with a vigorous push; then she immediately pressed his head still more firmly to her with her strong arms. To her was allowed what she refused him. "Hush! Be quiet! And it's still better in the French army. A whole regiment mutinied the other day and refused to fire—did you see it in the papers? The world revolution is knocking at the door!..."

Mirkin's soft caressing hands had roused her. Her blood flowed faster and flew through her gleaming white body. Her neck lost its tautness, grew soft and yielding and snuggled against his head, almost begging to be caressed, kissed, embraced. Her loosened hair flowed out as if blown by a wind. Her eyes shone, her face glowed. Her whole body breathed youth and sweetness. At such unguarded moments Comrade Sofia became sentimental. For unbelievable as it may sound, she could become almost maudlinly sentimental, when, for instance, she thought of the sufferings of the workers.

"Do you realize, Zachary, what a time we're living in?" she cried ecstatically, not forgetting, however, to press Mirkin's face, eyes and mouth still more tightly to her tempestuously heaving breast. "Countless generations have lived and died in misery on this earth. No ray of light cheered their life, no hope sweetened their death. Oh, if one could only waken them to life now! Why don't we believe in the resurrection, like the religious people? Oh, if we could only raise them from their graves now and cry to them: 'Get up, children, and receive the reward for all your misery!' Do you realize, Zachary, what a great thing we have achieved? We have flung open the door; we have reached the goal! All life is in our hands, everything—we can do everything! Zachary! Do listen, Zachary!" she awoke him from his trance of passion. "We'll do everything we've set our hearts on. We'll create a society in which there are no strong and weak, no oppressors and oppressed! Do you realize it, the dream, the desire of generations and generations? Millennial times! Of course, we'll make science serve us too, harness it to our car. We shan't let it increase want and suffering as it did under capitalism, where it cast tens of thousands into the street every day, destroyed homes, ruined families and left children to die of hunger, while the whole profit flowed into the pockets of the bosses. We'll change invention from a curse into a blessing. Man will watch over the machine like a higher being and see that it does his will. We'll make the machine into the slave instead of man. A five-hour working day and a five-day working week! We'll remove all want, and everybody will be able to devote his time to his inner emancipation. Can you picture to yourself what the world will be like then? I think of it as a singing world. When man is happy he'll sing like a lark. You should just see our young men! I was at a foundry yesterday—there they stood, covered with sweat at the furnaces, and they sang! Can you understand that? They sang! Isn't it a fine thing to be a little link in the chain that binds us together in a magical ring? How could we be good to one another when everything round us was unkind and evil? And that's what the whole system was like: whether he wanted to or not every one had to be against every one else. Everybody was the slave of someone over him, the oppressor of someone beneath him. But once the system is changed, once a different type of life rules, it will have an effect on the character of every single human being and they won't be able to help themselves! I don't think it will be necessary even to go out into the world and preach our gospel to it. Our life will become an example to other peoples. We won't need to convert the world to communism with fire and sword, for the world will come to us and beg us, as the barbaric peoples did at the beginning of Christianity, to send out apostles to set up the new religion. . . . Are you listening to me, Zachary?"

"Yes, I'm listening, Sosha . . . to set up the new religion. And you, Sosha, do you firmly believe that all this will really happen?"

"Why? Don't you?" she asked in a shocked voice, starting up and sitting on the edge of the bed.

"I must confess that sometimes a sort of cloud falls on my mind and I lose faith. When I see the misery and suffering which—with or against our will—we spread around us, I often ask myself the question: Have we the right to demand so much sacrifice, to shed so much blood for the sake of this paradise of ours? And don't forget this—the misery is only beginning. We've done everything we could to put an end to the war, and now we ourselves are trying to get the workers to join the Red Army. The others did the same thing in the name of the fatherland and the revolution—we're doing it in the name of 'October.' It won't be long before we too shall be driving the people to the front at the point of the bayonet."

"What can we do when civil war is at the door? Kornilov is mobilizing Cossacks at the front. Are we to let ourselves be slaughtered like sheep?"

"Yes, yes—of course a reason can be found for it! When was that ever difficult? Reasons can always be found to justify any policy of violence. It seems that every idea is born with dialectical prickles, so to speak, so that it might be able to fight for its life. But God knows, all the same, that when they're in their embryonic stage, safely wrapped in their mother's womb, they peep out from there as inoffensively and innocently as calves whose only object in life is to provide milk later on; but no sooner are they well born than they grow sharp horns and begin to use them before they've begun to give milk at all."

"What do you mean by that?" asked Sosha.

"Well, take our attitude towards the bourgeoisie. In all their actions they were, like every one of us, the product, or if I may put it that way, the victims of time and circumstance. But we think of nothing but revenge. Surely they're a part of humanity too, the humanity for which we have liberated the world!"

"Not to me! To me they're nothing better than rats that should be caught, thrown into a locked room and given poison!"

"Sosha!" Mirkin shrank from the blaze of hatred in her eyes. It was a wild beast with a gleaming girlish body that sat on his bed. "I must tell you—when I hear you talking like that I tremble before you. I almost think you capable of doing such things with your own hands!"

"What things?" Sosha laughed in his face.

"Killing human beings."

"If it was necessary for the revolution—why not? I would kill off a certain species—and with pleasure!"

"With pleasure?" A shudder ran through Mirkin.

"But *they* could do it with us? As long as we were of use to them, as long as they needed our wretched lives, they let us live. But how?

Chained to their cellars and kitchens, their factories, their coal mines, their ship furnaces. If we had become superfluous in their eyes, they would have killed us off by deliberately spreading a pestilence among us. Just remember how they treated the human beings that looked after their bodily comfort, that cooked for them and served them and cleared away their filth from under them. They did the most hideous and humiliating things to these people, things which a mother would be ashamed of before her own child. Did they look upon their servants as human beings like themselves? They had more respect for dogs and cats than for their own fellow-creatures! And that's been going on for centuries. And now—we'll treat them as they treated us! I cry like a silly old woman when I see a horse falling under its load in the street—and I've often been called a weeping Jenny because of it. Whenever I find a stray dog or cat I bring it home with me. But I can have no pity for *them*. You know, it's all lies, what people say about different races and bloods. The bourgeoisie are quite cosmopolitan. But there are class races. When I see a worker or a proletarian I feel at once that I belong to the same race as he does, though I've never done any physical labor in my whole life. But that makes no difference: the hunger and want, the proletarian surroundings in which one has grown up, produce that feeling of belonging to the same race. I've got nothing in common with the people of other classes. They don't exist to me as beings like ourselves, who have blood in their veins and feel pain just as we do if one sticks a pin into them. For me they are a completely different species. I have neither the time nor the inclination to whip up any human interest in them. I don't look on their existence as necessary. If they're in the way, then they just must be swept out of it like withered leaves."

As Sosha was speaking she got up from the bed. The thin low-cut dress that she always wore in the house had slipped over one round shoulder, which glowed warmly in the rosy light of the lamp. The curly strands of her short hair fluttered confusedly round her head. Her face, strangely composed and serene, was really beautiful at that moment. There was an almost dreamlike look on it. And from her eyes shot a cold pitiless fire which was made only more provocative by the fact that she was smiling as she spoke.

Mirkin contemplated her with longing and delight, yet at the same time could not fight down a painful sense of uneasiness. He shrank from her words because he knew they were true. He himself had recently begun to feel the power of the thing called "race"; ever since that day when he had met his father in Petersburg, and still more strongly since his father had come to live in Moscow, where he visited him secretly now and then, Zachary felt a deep pity for his father and his father's whole class, which was suffering so grievously now. But this pity arose—or so he feared—not from mere family feeling, but from a far stronger cause, perhaps the very one of which Sosha had just been speaking.

"What are you thinking?" asked Sosha.

"I was thinking that if what you say is true, then I belong by birth to that very class that you are so anxious to wipe out in cold blood."

"You have betrayed it," Sosha laughed in his face, "and deserted to us."

"That's just the question: whether one *can* betray it. Can one rid oneself completely of one's race feeling? Doesn't it influence us, even against our will and our convictions? People's strongest impressions are those they receive in childhood. Their early years are their real fatherland, and they remain bound to them for all the rest of their lives. I have never witnessed the sufferings of the class you have just been talking of. Nor have I ever starved or been without a roof over my head. And I must confess frankly, Sosha, that I could never regard the rich classes with the same eyes as you and the other comrades. On the contrary, I feel very, very painfully the injustice with which you are treating them now. All my sympathies have always been for the side that is suffering, and as it's the others that are suffering now my sympathy belongs to them. Can that be because of the race feeling you speak of?"

"Well, I'm afraid, my dear Zachary, there's no help for you now. You've made the plunge. Whether you like it or not you're committed to us a hundred times over! No matter how your class feeling may rack and torment you—you'll stick to your post on our front all right!"

"I don't know about that," retorted Mirkin half-playfully and half in earnest. "I shan't do anything that goes against my conscience, anyway—I can say that with certainty."

"Not even if it was necessary for our cause, for the good of the proletariat?"

Mirkin reflected for a few moments: "I wouldn't call a thing necessary if it was essential only for this or that 'race' or 'class'; it must be essential for the whole community."

"Community? Which community? Ours or theirs? There are lots of communities."

"Sosha, I would like to say something to you. The sentiments I hear you and the comrades uttering so frequently nowadays give me very sad food for thought. It seems to me that the hatred that speaks out of you isn't merely a hatred of evil in itself. You have forgotten all that, and you aren't concerned with putting an end to evil, but with taking revenge on human beings. Hatred of that kind is not creative, but destructive. You yourselves are becoming the bearers of evil now, as the other side were once."

"Poor little Zachary! You're a child in spite of your beard! You and your morality! The old morality is dead along with the old world. It's a new morality that exists now—the morality of the revolution."

"That's been said a hundred times before, Sosha. Every dogma, every church has created its own morality, and that is just the great danger. But I believe that there is only one morality for all humanity and all ages—to speak the truth and love your fellow-men. There is no other morality."

"Splendid, splendid, dearest Zachary!" She drew his face to her panting breast and pressed it firmly there. "Can't you lie still for a minute? Be quiet now! I want to tell you something—about Helene. Do you know what we promised each other when we were small children lying in the same bed? Just listen . . . ! Do listen . . . !"

And Comrade Sofia became sentimental.

CHAPTER XXIV

REVENGE FOR PAST GENERATIONS

It had been discovered that the younger of the two ladies in the house in Chistoprudny Boulevard was a Countess S., the wealthy heiress of a Boyar family known throughout Russia, while the elder was her French governess. The Revolution had trapped them in Moscow, and they had to stay where they were since it was impossible for them to get out of the city. They were looked after by a devoted maid, who also procured food for them by selling in the market whatever they could dispense with among their belongings. The ladies themselves were hardly ever visible, remaining secluded, stricken with terror, in their own room. Every now and then the outline of an attractive girlish figure would be seen gliding swiftly along the corridor, only to vanish behind the mysterious door like a startled fawn if anybody else appeared. But the other occupants of the house paid no more attention to the two women than if they had been ghosts haunting their ancestral home. The one person who took an interest in them was Comrade Ryshkov.

He had taken up his quarters in the great Directoire drawing-room, which communicated by a door—which was always locked, of course—with the apartments in which the former owners sheltered. The tall, wooden-shuttered windows with their scented muslin curtains gave on the courtyard, once a lovely garden but now deep in snow. Last year's magnolias and rhododendrons were still standing there in their wooden tubs, exposed to the winter frost and cowering like shivering children, for no one troubled to cover them up. The caretaker who had been appointed by the new occupants and lived in the small lodge by the gate had, of course, cleared away all the old bourgeois prettifications, but by mere chance these delicate bushes had escaped being chopped up for firewood like the other trees in the garden.

The salon occupied by Ryshkov was old-fashioned in its lofty spaciousness; the walls, like those of all the other rooms, were white, with romantic scenes painted on them. Glass-fronted cabinets of light ash lined with green displayed a wealth of Russian porcelain. The chairs and sofas were covered with hand-made Gobelin tapestries in the bad Louis-Philippe style of two generations before. There was, besides, a heavy bronze-overlaid Empire bed which had been lugged in from another room for Comrade Ryshkov to sleep on.

The house was governed by his own "house-committee," which had appointed the caretaker to see to the heating of the building and to keep it clean and in order.

Comrade Ryshkov, now an organizer of the Red Army, was one of the busiest men in Russia. And yet he found time to spend his evenings at home, hardly ever going out, and receiving no visitors, sitting all alone at the great carved table on which, as on every other piece of furniture in the room, a hand-worked cover was spread. On this table sprawled his leather case of papers and the revolver he had taken from his pocket. His close-shorn head gleamed in the soft light of the great Venetian chandelier which had been fitted with electric lights, and a reflected glow from the broad white-tiled stove lit up his figure as he sat staring fixedly at the white-lacquered door leading into the rooms of the two ladies; he was listening intently, pricking up his ears for a single sound, a word, a rustle, from behind that locked door. In vain; all was as hushed in there as if the occupants were dead. . . .

Comrade Ryshkov had his reasons for becoming so unusually domestic in his habits.

From time to time in the corridor, late in the evening or early in the morning, he would start his quarry—the girlish shape whose features he could never discern in the prevailing half-light; and it was not without satisfaction that he sometimes heard a faint scream of terror uttered in sudden dismay before the slim silhouette fled swiftly out of sight again. The rustle of silken underclothing, which sounded like the tearing of tissue paper, and the swirl of a lightly flowing dressing-gown came gently and pleasantly to Ryshkov's ear, reminding him of the low purling of some spring hidden in a forest. On these unexpected encounters he usually murmured: "Excuse me for alarming you," but in the corridor, which was crammed with odds and ends and sparingly lit by a single small paraffin lamp, these words echoed unheard, for the apparition had long since vanished behind the door. . . .

Although Ryshkov had never really seen the girl's face he was enchanted by the charm of her lightly-flitting, shadowy form with its silken rustling and delicate fragrance of some elusive flower-scent, like a breath of spring, which he could just perceive, together with a hint of light gleaming on fine, loose-flying hair. Comrade Ryshkov had never had any dealings with women so ethereal in their movements, women who uttered faint cries of terror and started so nervously when they were suddenly surprised, women who left behind them a delicate, elusive fragrance of spring blossoms. All the women he had known had been hard-working and stodgy, women for whom the surrender of their bodies meant little more than eating and drinking. He had never seen fine silk on their bodies; they wore countless petticoats, one over the other, and the chill of the streets and the discomfort of the snow-flurries was all that their thick stockings and shoes had ever suggested to him. Their odor was anything but pleasant—a mingling of cooking-smells, kitchen steam and strong soap, variegated sometimes by the objectionable reek of a heavy cheap scent, while their faces, so thickly powdered that the skin could not be seen, were coarse and cynical. After a night with a woman like that Ryshkov always felt as if he wanted to get into a vapor-bath to scrub himself clean.

Recently he had taken to discussing these matters among his friends and comrades:

"Devil take them, they had plenty of time to pamper their women!"—he referred to the former privileged classes—"Sheltered them and wrapped them in cotton-wool to keep their bodies smooth—not like our women who climb into bed beside their men with hard rough hands and dirty feet."

He indulged in remarks of that kind, although less strongly couched, even before Comrade Sofia and Mirkin whenever he looked in to drink a glass of tea with them:

"I gave our aristocrat a fine fright today! She didn't half scream! And fluttered away like a bird. But I must admit that the trail of scent she leaves behind her smells sweet enough."

Comrade Sofia disliked the tone of Ryshkov's comments on his neighbors:

"They've always had people to work for them. They smell sweet because others stink for them. But I prefer the stink of our people to the sweet smell of those others!"—a verdict which must not blind us to the fact that Comrade Sofia delighted in perfuming herself with "the sweet smell of those others."

"Oh yes, that's true," assented Comrade Ryshkov with a smile, and he returned to his own room, whither the fragrance of his aristocrat drew him.

But Comrade Sofia disliked Ryshkov's whole attitude to the former owners of the house. It had become obvious that he was taking their part.

For instance, every time they carried out some of their belongings for sale in the market, they were examined by the caretaker at the gate to see that they were not removing goods confiscated for the benefit of the proletariat. As soon as Comrade Ryshkov became aware of this he gave the caretaker a secret hint to let the ladies pass unchecked.

One day in the House Committee, Comrade Sofia proposed that the ladies' rooms should be searched to make sure that they were not implicated in any conspiracy against the Soviet Government. When this came to Comrade Ryshkov's ears, he issued a strict injunction that the ladies were not to be molested: "What's the use? A couple of women! Why rake up more resentment?"

And recently he had even taken to bringing home parcels of food, not for his own consumption. On a chair in his room he carefully laid out some white bread (the rarest luxury, issued only to children and invalids), a tin of pressed caviar, a lump of butter and various other eatables, set the chair gently before his neighbors' door in the corridor, and ordered the caretaker to keep an eye on it and prevent anybody but the lawful recipients from making off with the food. On top of the pile he laid a small note: "For Citizeness S. from the Soviet Government."

In the evening Comrade Ryshkov came home and found the food still intact upon the chair. The caretaker reported: "She came out, gave it a hasty glance, read the note, looked angry and left it all lying."

Comrade Ryshkov smiled.

Comrade Sofia heard about his action. She twitched her shoulders impatiently, flushed to the roots of her hair, and did not forget to tell Comrade Ryshkov to his face what she thought:

"If you feel bound to present bourgeois women, enemies of the proletariat, with white bread that is supposed to go to children and invalids, that's your own affair, comrade. But what do you mean by calling it a gift from the Soviet Government? What has the Soviet Government to do with your private concerns?"

Comrade Ryshkov put on a grave air. Only his eyes smiled, and little tongues of cold flame darted from them. With an energetic gesture he retorted:

"That's my business, Comrade Sofia!"

"It's not your business, Comrade Ryshkov!"

"It was only a joke," he remarked, half to himself. "Besides, it's my private concern and I must beg you not to interfere. I don't interfere with your private concerns."

Comrade Sofia flushed again to the roots of her hair, and replied:

"I have no private concerns. . . ."

Comrade Ryshkov, however, was not to be daunted. Once more he set a chair with eatables on it in front of the door. This time there was sugar and tea in the parcel. But in the accompanying note there was no mention of the Soviet Government, merely the words: "A present from Comrade R. . . ."

Comrade Sofia had no further excuse for interfering. This was a private matter which concerned nobody.

In the evening Comrade Ryshkov found the parcel again intact. With a smile he muttered: "A hard nut to crack."

Then he let some time elapse. Behind the locked door not a sound was audible. The caretaker reported: "It's some days now since they went out with stuff to sell—probably they've nothing left." And Comrade Ryshkov realized that the right moment had come.

Again he brought food home and set it on the chair before the door. This time the parcel contained barley and rice, caviar, butter, bread, and a considerable quantity of the most precious substance in Russia—salt. The salt lay on the very top so that it jumped to the eye. There was no accompanying note.

When Ryshkov came home that evening he found everything still there but the salt. He laughed all over his shining face: "Hurrah! The salt has done the trick!" And he left the other things lying.

Next morning the chair was empty.

And the next time he encountered the delicate girlish figure in the dim corridor there was no more whisking away, no outcry. A pair of large gray smoothly lidded Russian eyes, above which faintly traced brows rose in a delicate arch, regarded him with detached seriousness and yet with a spark of fearful longing. Ryshkov's eyes too, which were ungraced by eyebrows, were detached, serious and sparkled with fearful longing. Two pairs of typically Russian eyes met and held each other for a second that seemed to last an hour, and each pair tried to master the other. Then the girl's eyes dropped. Ryshkov saw her smooth head humbly bend before him like the head of a strayed filly.

"Why did you do it?" asked the girl. And before he had time to utter a word she had fled away and vanished behind the door.

Ryshkov regarded himself in the great mirror in his room and saw that his face was white. He knew why. His heart was pounding as wildly as if he had just killed somebody. He could not control his agitation.

He spat suddenly, picked up his case of papers, and hurried away to his office. . . . He worked feverishly all day on various commissions, settled a dozen affairs at the same time, spoke simultaneously into the telephone and to the people standing by his desk and raced in his car, as if possessed, from one office to another. He was on fire with energy and his work soon made him forget everything else; even the fact that the charming bourgeois had spoken to him that morning.

But when he heard that Comrade Sofia had caused a cupboard in the wall to be broken open and all the linen in it to be handed over to the occupants of the house for making underwear, he flared up in a passion and forced the caretaker to reclaim the linen and send it back to the ladies.

"The House Committee has decided to confiscate that linen!" stormed Comrade Sofia, blenching with rage and foaming at the mouth. "Not one of us has a decent garment to wear, or a towel, and there's a whole pile of linen simply rotting away in the cupboard. Nobody's getting any good of it except the mice—and the leaders of the proletariat haven't a shirt to their backs!"

Comrade Ryshkov, too, flew into a rage and the quiet, cool smile faded from his thick lips:

"That's just what makes us proletarians! For all I care the aristocrats can smother in their linen! When we need to we'll put them against the wall and shoot them. But to steal things for our own benefit—that's for anarchists, not Bolsheviks! I'll have you up before the Party."

"It's a decree of the House Committee. . . ."

"I won't listen to another word about it. We're not a band of robbers—do you hear?"

He knew that he was in the wrong and was angry with himself for having been carried away by a rush of sentimentality. Spitting on the floor with disgust he determined to bother no more about his neighbors.

Yet that evening he whispered to the quartermaster in the Military Commissariat that he wanted an extra ration order for a private visitor to his room. The quartermaster understood the hint. . . .

Behind the locked communicating door, however, there was just as much loss of equanimity. If Comrade Ryshkov had been thrown into agitation by the blood of the old Russian Boyars that flowed in the sensitive boyish figure of the girl, she, the last survivor of an ancient family, had been no less agitated by her encounter with this new portent, the product of the Russian revolution: Who could this monster be, risen from some deep dark cavern to hurl the Czar from his throne—a monster who had conquered the capital city and was now ruthlessly deciding on matters of life and death in the Kremlin itself, the Little Father's stronghold? Who was this Ryshkov, before whose very name all the potentates whom she had seen at Court were now trembling? They had been so strong and mighty that it seemed unthinkable any power on earth could ever overthrow them. Who was this strange wild beast whose teeth and claws had torn down the magnificence of Russia and shattered its glory? This dreadful Ryshkov was living cheek by jowl with her, sitting in Papa's room, sleeping in Mamma's marriage bed. And the strange thing was that Ryshkov was not so very dreadful after all! He had an open Russian face with blue Russian eyes and an enormous angular skull: why on earth did he shave his skull? "I'd like to see him with his hair long—no, he's more interesting as he is. With that smooth-shorn angular head he looks extraordinarily strange and forceful, just as the terrible Ryshkov who has conquered Moscow ought to look. And that same Ryshkov is friendly to me. . . ."

In the beginning she had despised him for daring to set food outside her door. But now she understood his actions: "Ryshkov is protecting me from the frightful Jewesses who are running the house. It it weren't for him, they'd have murdered us long ago. He saved the linen for me. No, no—he wants nothing from me, he has no evil intentions in his friendliness to me; it's only his Russian soul that speaks—one Russian soul takes pity on another. And who knows, perhaps it's these men of the people, whom we have neglected, who will save Russia! The Russian peasants saved our Mother Russia once before from Polish invaders, and set the first Romanov, the Czar Michail Fedorovitch, on the Russian throne. Why shouldn't it happen again? The men of the people have not yet played their rôle in the life of Russia: they're only beginning now, and our salvation may well come from them."

She discovered a burning desire to get to know this Russian man, to speak face to face with him—even at the risk of falling into his power; perhaps, indeed, because of that risk. . . . The next time she met Comrade Ryshkov in the dark corridor she did not drop her eyes but looked full at him:

"I thank you." She stretched out a soft, cool, schoolgirl hand.

"What for?"

"If it weren't for you the Jews would have murdered me long ago."

Comrade Ryshkov frowned. He scorned her for saying that, but he scorned himself still more for having to listen to such heresies because of his foolish sentimentality. He wanted to let her understand that his interest in her had quite another motive. And to make his meaning clear and unambiguous he grasped her brutally by the hand, stared boldly into her face, and said with unmistakable emphasis:

"If you want to thank me this is hardly the place to do it. Come to my room this evening, I shall be alone."

A rush of blood shot into her face. Comrade Ryshkov could see the flush invading her very scalp and her girlish neck, for these were presented to his view now as she bowed her head in shame. Yet she did not scream or flee from him with her light, airy step. She merely dropped her head lower, like an animal led to the slaughter, and was dumb.

"Well—will you come? Shall I expect you?" whispered Ryshkov, his cheek already close to hers, and clasped her hand more tightly.

She nodded in silence—a victim.

"But not for conversation!" added Ryshkov with a brutal laugh.

Suddenly her whole body began to tremble as if in fever. A touching pallor covered her face; her tightly-closed lips opened slightly with a pathetic quiver, showing the gleaming pearls of her teeth, as she vainly sought to find words. Finally, with a lightning flash from her eyes that struck deep into Ryshkov's, she gasped in a low voice while her heart beat loudly:

"If you want me—I'll come," and vanished swiftly behind her door.

Ryshkov waited that night, and then a second night—but she did not come.

She wanted to please him, to bring herself down to his level, to become one with the people. And behind the locked door she had a hard struggle with all her past traditions. Finally her breeding triumphed: she would keep her word, even at the price of being roughly treated by him.

Her devoted maid was ordered to bring out a peasant costume that was still hanging in the wardrobe beside a few ball-dresses. The costume suited her. She turned herself into a simple peasant girl, her hair in two long plaits, a golden cap with a gauze veil on her head. The bodice was embroidered with shining tinsel, and the long skirt, falling in broad folds, was of flowered cotton. She wanted to be one of the people, to be handled like a peasant girl going in to her master in the stable. . . .

Comrade Ryshkov was sitting in his shirtsleeves at the gorgeously carved table, his revolver before him, bathed in sweat as he sipped tea and worked at his papers. There was a knock at the door and a trembling girlish voice asked: "May I come in?"

Ryshkov stared in astonishment at the aristocratic face crowning the peasant dress, and laughed scornfully. Then he said, with a cool smile:

"I've had all I want of that kind of girl. Come to me in your Countess rig, in the dress you wear at a Court ball."

There was a choked and tearful cry. The figure disappeared.

Comrade Ryshkov absorbed himself once more in his papers.

Long generations of stalwart Boyars were incarnated in this one frail girl and fought in her blood like demons to preserve her pride and her honor. But this last drop of Boyar blood wanted to lose itself in the common sea. This delicate girlish body was burning to feel the touch of a rough, strong hand: the fine limbs were longing to be overborne by a powerful and violent will, to be violated by a man, to pass like a sigh utterly, completely surrendered to a forceful and ineluctable necessity. For one night, for two nights, for a whole week the girl struggled in torment with the shades of her fathers and forefathers, but finally her resolution abruptly burst the bonds which joined her to the dead and she yielded herself to a stronger power.

She did what Ryshkov demanded.

In her Court dress of lace over golden-amber satin cut low both back and front, fragrant with the last drops of her delicate perfume, a silken black lace scarf over her bare shoulders and a fan in her hand, she entered Ryshkov's room and stood before him awaiting his commands.

He took her by the hand and made her sit down beside him.

"Lovely lace you have!" he touched her scarf.—"An heirloom, I suppose?"

"Family lace."

"Of course! Your serfs made it in the winter nights, just as they knotted the carpets in this room. There was no lack of hands and they didn't cost anything." Ryshkov laughed.

She would rather have turned the conversation to other matters, but he stuck to his theme obstinately:

"Did you have a lot of peasants in your village?"

"In which village?"

"In the big village you lived in."

"All our villages were big. But we lived in none of them; we spent the winter in Moscow and the summer abroad," she answered with an ingratiating smile.

"But what was the name of your family estate?"

"I suppose you mean our titular estate, where the castle is? Samietchko, in the district of Kursk."

"Kursk?" asked Ryshkov in amazement. "But I know Kursk. I came from that district myself. So I'm a kind of countryman of yours." He laughed again, showing his beautiful teeth, on which the girl's eyes were fixed as if spellbound.

"Were there any of your peasants who had bright red beards, quite short, pointed beards, with sly little eyes and open, honest faces, men who always laughed and said: 'Thank you very much'?" he asked merrily.

"Oh yes, there were men like that," she replied gayly.

"Do you know that that's what my father was like? He was the son of a serf, and I believe he was actually in the big house himself as a small boy. He came from the district of Kursk. And for all I know from your village. That would make us more closely related than ever!" and with these words he took her soft little hand between his thick fingers and pressed it hard. Her sudden start betrayed how much she was thrilled by the painful pressure.

"Perhaps even blood-relations, who knows? For our peasants have been settled for generations on the land, and we treated them like members of the family." She laughed.

"Well, since we come from the same part of the country, let us see if we suit each other!..."

He picked her up in his strong arms and carried her like a kitten to her mother's marriage bed. There was only a feeble cheep, as if a small bird were being crushed on Ryshkov's breast.

"Let me take off my dress; you'll tear it."

"That dress won't tear, it was made by hand in the big house."

At the same time it flashed through Ryshkov's mind:

"A pity my old father's not alive still. This would have warmed the cockles of his heart, too."

CHAPTER XXV

GNAWING DOUBT

In Zachary's heart a worm was gnawing—the worm of doubt.

So far as he could, he struggled to go on believing, tried to generate the same heat of enthusiasm as Sosha and all his other acquaintances, reproached himself with faintness of heart and that weakness of character which was solely responsible for his vacillations. In this way he kept his doubts under and did his work as punctually as ever, attending the sessions of all the committees to which he belonged, doing what was required of him in the Trade Committee, the Commission for Folk-Culture, and the various other offices that chance had assigned him.

"Suffering is unavoidable," he kept saying to himself. "These are the birth-pangs of a new age. The Revolution is pushing its way forward and breaking all the barriers that oppose it. The question is simply to find out how we can adjust ourselves as quickly as possible to our new and great potentialities . . ." But these were only words, and the worm went on gnawing.

Zachary had first been bitten in Petersburg when the Constituent Assembly was dispersed. He was not himself quite aware how deep an impression that incident had made on him. But he had come back from Petersburg much like a wild animal who has just escaped the hunters, saved, indeed, by the skin of its teeth, but carrying a bullet in its body that bores deeper and deeper into the flesh.

"What right have I to take on myself the responsibility for such an action?" he confided to Sosha, his future sister-in-law. "In spite of everything that can be argued in its favor, it was horrifying merely to see. To do a thing like that a man must have great courage . . . courage and faith," he added. "I don't know where our leaders get theirs from. Perhaps from the desperate situation that provoked the revolution?"

"From the darkness of the past and the brightness of the future!" asserted Sosha.

Mirkin thought it over:

"But will it ever come, that bright future, to make all these sufferings worth while?"

Like every Russian intellectual Mirkin had seen the revolution as the liberation of humanity from all constricting fetters. Much as pious Jews firmly believe that when the Messiah comes it will be possible to walk unharmed across bridges of paper, the Russian intellectuals believed unshakably that in the dawn after the revolution the world would be redeemed from all its cares, for bread would simply grow on the trees.

Immediately after the October overthrow Mirkin tried to spread his wings, so long pinioned. He had great projects and thought that they could be realized on the spot. The chief of them concerned the problem with which he had been preoccupied in Warsaw (without any practical result, to be sure): the problem of diverting the mass of the Jews from their speculative huckstering, to which their own indifference and the hatred of their neighbors confined them, and of initiating them into productive, creative labor. Zachary thought that this could be achieved simply by a decree, by ordering all Jewish shops to be closed and transferring their occupants to factories or farmwork; a mere stroke of the pen was to change overnight the structure of the whole Jewish community. "Who can prevent us?" he asked himself.

The Jewish shops were indeed closed down. But it proved impossible to get the Jews into factories or to allot land to them. For the actual round of daily life did not cease simply because the Revolution had happened; it went on its inexorable, monotonous, crawling course. It remained immovable, like a blank wall.

Like all the other great plans, the great project of regenerating the Jews had to be postponed to an indefinite future date when the times should have become more settled. Meanwhile the easiest thing to do, something that presented no obstacles and could quite well be enforced by law, was indeed accomplished: millions of people were deprived by an edict of their usual, straightforward means of livelihood. The old mechanism for distributing goods and services broke down and no new mechanism was supplied in its place.

But life persisted in asserting its rights and like a roaring stream burst through the barriers of the law. In one night a populace of loyal, industrious citizens, asking no more than that the Revolution should satisfy the hopes suppressed by the old régime, were turned by this edict into a throng of counter-revolutionaries and criminals, so that the prisons grew fuller and fuller. And all over Russia the same thing was happening.

Wherever Zachary looked he saw ruin and destruction, sorrow and tears, evoked by the October *coup*. Problems that were bound in any case to grow worse because of the country's desperate situation, were made a thousand times more difficult and complicated still by the daily promulgation of "decrees" which subserved neither the needs of life, nor those of the moment, nor even the personal interest of the men in power, but merely a dead dogma.

Mirkin observed not only, however, that dogma was exalted above the needs of living humanity, but that the whole Russian populace, just as in their most unenlightened days, had become a mass of slaves in the service of a fetish, and this fetish was called "the October Revolution."

But what chiefly exasperated him was the injustice dealt out on all sides to living human beings whose only crime consisted in belonging to another class. As a Jew he knew all the ruthlessness of racial hatred, having encountered it in person, and now it was being mercilessly directed against "an alien class."

"What's the end to be? Is there anything you would stop short of?" he once asked Sosha.

"Nothing whatever, if only the goal of the Revolution can be reached."

"Would you advance even over the bodies of your nearest and dearest?"

"Even over the bodies of my nearest and dearest!"

"But that's dreadful! The Revolution is killing your human feelings and turning you into an animal."

"No—it's only that the Revolution awakens nothing in you but racial feeling!" retorted Sosha with a cold smile.

Zachary asked himself:

"What is race? A common blood, flowing in the veins of a tribe, just as sap is drawn from a common root to flow through the trunk of a tree and through all its branches and twigs to the last leaf. Race means the same soil, the same rainfall, the same clouds, the same atmospheric conditions, the same sunshine, the same bit of sky. The root of the tree sucks all the life-energy from one plot of ground, using it for its own ends and destroying the roots of any other plants that may try to usurp its place. That is for the common good, for the advantage of every part of the tree. In the beginning race connoted all the members of one tribe, of one people, and it did not matter whether they were rich or poor. But now there's a different kind of demarcation; the racial blood is supposed to flow only in one *class*. The class is everything: nation, creed, heaven, and worldly goods."

But however strenuously Mirkin tried to discover in himself this new racial instinct for one particular class, he could not find a trace of it. To his disgrace and horror he had to admit that all his love and sensibility still came down on the side of those who had the greatest injustice to suffer, all the weary, poor and heavy-laden, only now these were the new poor, the one-time rich. "Of course," he said to himself, "the deformity of the world had to be changed, the social inequality of centuries that has crippled our backs had to be flung off. But what guilt attaches to these men? They were simply yoked like horses to their age, led in the harness of existing conditions along the traditional path, urged on by the lash of environment, training and custom. Of course they had to be unyoked from the crazy contraption, of course humanity must strike out in a new direction. But what is happening now is merely a purposeless, aimless flogging of these poor horses, out of sheer revengefulness. A new racial hatred is springing up."

Another thing that bewildered Mirkin was the attitude of his comrades to the former owners of the house in which he was living, for whom in his own heart there stirred a strong, warm feeling of sympathy. Every time that he traversed the corridor he was literally terrified that he might meet them, and he used to steal into his room like a thief. He shrank, too, from touching anything belonging to the house, and could not understand the unembarrassed self-assurance with which Sosha handled the furnishings of a strange house as if she had always owned them. More than once there was friction between the two of them because of this, rising even to open quarrels.

"That's just common theft!" shouted Mirkin on one such occasion.

"It was theft up till now. But now these things have fallen into the rightful hands," countered Sosha.

Yet after all he could make some allowances for Sosha's behavior. But Comrade Ryshkov's doings (like all the occupants of the house Mirkin was aware of the relations between Ryshkov and the Countess) appeared criminal to Zachary, and roused his deepest indignation.

Sosha met all his reproaches with the jeering comment:

"That's 'the race' speaking!"

And indeed Zachary felt that "the race" was beginning to stir within him, the race to which he belonged—the other side. Stronger and more intense than ever, his racial feeling was driving him to stand by his neighbor, to stand by his father. . . .

His relationship to his father had changed fundamentally. In face of the straits to which the old man was now reduced Zachary lost all the resentment that he had ever cherished towards him: there was nothing left but respect and an admiration, tinged actually with envy, for his father's dignified bearing. That in itself set Gabriel Mirkin on an unattainable pinnacle, and his son was proud of such magnificence. Louder and louder, ever more clear and unmistakable, there spoke in him now the feelings that any child has towards his father: hidden sources of love and reverence awoke in Zachary. Openly he now devoted his free time in the evening to visiting his father in the bare room of the "National Hotel" where he had been quartered since arriving in Moscow.

Old Mirkin was living like an anchorite. This aged man on the brink of the grave was as carefree as any youth, advancing serenely through the darkness and danger of these days as if he had his whole life before him and the future were still going to be full of surprises. From the rations he was allowed he cooked himself a meal in the evening on a paraffin stove. He had brought from Petersburg a sufficiency of underlinen, shoes, and suits, so that he was always clean and carefully dressed, a point on which he had always laid stress. Indeed, in his insistent respectability he reminded one somehow of a rubber doll carried off by a flood; the waters might overwhelm him and for a moment he might be lost to sight, but he would always bob up again. . . .

He treated Zachary, whenever he appeared, like a child; a naughty, ill-behaved child, but still his own child. He often drove him from the door:

"What's the use of coming here? Don't you know what kind of times we are living in? Your comrades will only look askance at you, and you're not doing me any good. I'm in earnest about this—stop coming to see me, since your visits don't benefit either of us."

When Sosha heard about Zachary's visits to his father she said reproachfully:

"The wolf's always drawn back to the forest. . . ."

This finding again of his father reawoke in Zachary the image of another figure that seemed to belong to a different, long-vanished life which could never return. The uproar and violent urgency of the daily struggle had utterly obliterated that figure, but now it appeared fleetingly, like a ray of sunshine athwart a heavy cloud; only, however, when he was alone. It never obtruded itself during working hours. But on days when he was quite forlorn and listened to the beating of his own heart that apparition often visited him. He saw her standing beside a great tub washing the faces of little children. She never appeared alone, but always surrounded by children's eyes and children's arms beside the old tree in the Warsaw courtyard. And, strangely, he felt as if in the heart of that throng of small boys and girls, all decked out in the big tattered garments cast off by their parents, his soul stood waiting, too, until its turn should come. . . . And all at once he realized that while he was being swept away in Moscow by the deafening roar of events, his soul had remained beside her, so that he was fleeing naked and defenseless through the world.

Yet precisely for that reason, because his soul was with her, under her protection, Zachary felt secure. It was as if she held in her hands the end of a rope that could rescue him at any moment.

One day when Zachary arrived at the hotel to see his father he found him in a state of violent agitation. Old Mirkin had never mentioned to his son the annoyances he had to suffer in his office, and his lips had never framed the words "Misha Molodyetz." But now he was actually foaming with rage. Zachary had never seen his father in such a state. The old man's eyes were red, as if he had spent several sleepless nights.

"Father, what's happened?" asked Zachary in alarm.

"It's the very devil!"—old Mirkin could no longer restrain himself. "They've stuck a traitor into my business, a criminal, that Misha Molodyetz—and now they want to make me responsible for him."

"Misha Molodyetz? Who on earth's he?"

"One of your precious comrades!" shouted the old man. "Before the Revolution no decent man would have anything to do with him. He was always coming to me then with dirty suggestions, and now he's at it again . . ." Old Mirkin broke off abruptly.

"Keep cool, father! I'll see what I can do. What's his name—Misha Molodyetz?"

"Yes, Misha Molodyetz—known through the whole of Russia as a speculating ruffian, and today he's in charge of my business, and I, Gabriel Mirkin, have to take my orders from him!"

"Keep cool, father, do keep cool! I'll see what can be done."

The Commissar for Trade and Commerce, a man whom Mirkin knew well and to whom he went at once about this affair of his father's, gave him the answer:

"We are quite well informed, and we know who the man is. We appointed him intentionally to this position, so that he could keep an eye on someone who is a bigger and more dangerous scoundrel than himself—I mean your father."

Mirkin grew pale with anger.

"I must beg you, comrade, not to insult my father in my presence."

"I had no idea that you would take it like that. We all thought that you, considering your share in the October revolution, must have long since severed your connection with your father, who was, of course, one of the main pillars of the old order. What does your father's honor matter to you? Most extraordinary."

"I regret that I seem to be of a different disposition. The honor of my father matters a great deal to me. And, although I'm a revolutionary and took part in the October action, I'm not afraid to admit that I respect my father, not only because he is my father, but because in his own way he is an extremely honorable and genuinely productive man—even an idealist."

"Comrade, I must insist that you do not adopt that tone!"

"I won't allow my father to be insulted. The Revolution can't hinder me from honoring and loving my own father. That's a matter of personal feeling."

"A revolutionary has no personal feelings! Besides, comrade, are you a party member?"

"No."

"Oh, that's understandable, then."

"I'm not aware that even if I were my attitude towards my father would change."

"No, citizen"—this sudden appellation disquieted Mirkin remarkably—"with your old-fashioned views on the family, with your devotion to your father, who is a counter-revolutionary, you couldn't possibly be a party member. Excuse me, I'm rather busy at the present time."

Mirkin decided to visit Comrade Ryshkov in his room (he knew that Ryshkov spent his evenings at home) and lay the matter before him. It hardly came within Ryshkov's province, but Mirkin built hopes on the great influence of his neighbor. He was convinced that Ryshkov would be highly incensed at the way such scoundrels were seeking sanctuary in the bosom of the revolution, and would take action accordingly. Moreover, Ryshkov was his last resource. . . .

That evening he knocked at Ryshkov's door. There was a fairly long pause before the door was opened. Obviously annoyed, Ryshkov came out in his shirt-sleeves, and greeted his visitor with these words:

"My evenings are my own, and I don't want my privacy disturbed!"

Mirkin apologized and turned to go.

"If it's an army matter come to my office about it—there's something else I want to talk to you about," cried Ryshkov after him.

"No, it's not about the army, it's a matter for the Trade Committee. Excuse me for disturbing you, I'll come in some other time."

"Oh, well, since you're here, comrade, you might as well tell me what it is," Ryshkov suddenly changed his tone and regarded Mirkin with a friendly eye. "You understand, comrade, don't you?—nothing but work all day until a man's head goes round. If I didn't have a bit of distraction in the evening I would go crazy. But make it brief—you know, one can't keep a lady waiting too long!" said Ryshkov with a wink, leading his visitor to the table, on which stood a half-empty cup of tea, and making him sit down in a soft armchair, which was still warm from the presence of somebody else.

"In any other place I wouldn't expect to be understood, but I'm sure that you'll see immediately how important it is"—and Mirkin embarked on an account of Misha Molodyetz's character and the part he was playing in the Mirkin firm.

"And is that all? And because of that you've interrupted a pleasant *rendezvous?* Oh you——" Comrade Ryshkov used a word that made Mirkin grow as red as a beetroot.

"What did you say? Used to be a traitor and now he's in our service? To the devil with him! When we've no more use for him, when he becomes dangerous, we'll soon polish him off; we'll simply put him against a wall and shoot him. But so long as he's helping us and we need him—he'll be looked after."

"But I know ever so many of these people who are admitted to the Party. I know, for instance, of another detrimental in Petersburg. And when they get their red cards these riff-raff are set in authority over others, over decent and honest people. We ought not to forget that it's the most honest people who don't trim their sails at once to every wind, because their honesty makes them scrupulous. And a man who has neither doubts nor scruples is a traitor. And it is most important that we should have moral and honest people to work for us. The only thing we have to oppose to the old order of things is the character of our men——"

"But, comrade, what is a man? A sausage-skin that can be stuffed with anything. The essential point is, whom does the man serve, what idea does he serve? The man himself is nothing—yesterday he was one thing, today he's another. The main question is simply, whom does he serve?"

"No, a man isn't just a sausage-skin! A man represents an absolute value in himself. He is sacred, he is an end in himself!" cried Mirkin.

"What? Are you an anarchist?"

"I'm not an anarchist. I believe in discipline. But in my opinion all that we do and create is done for the sake of humanity. Humanity is the most important thing. It was to serve mankind, to benefit mankind, that principles were evolved, not the other way about!"

"That's all theory, and we haven't time for theories, comrade. I don't see what there is to argue about. There are two divisions of men —ourselves and the others; that's to say, the Octoberists and those who are against them. And we ourselves divide mankind into two groups: those who help on the revolution and those who hinder it. If your man has joined the Octoberists he belongs to us, let him be the devil himself in person. If he's an Octoberist he's whitewashed, for the principle elevates the man. If he's disloyal to the idea we'll soon deal with him. But meanwhile, comrade, don't come interrupting my personal affairs —you understand me? Come to my office tomorrow. I've been thinking about you for some time. We've got to set to work again—they give us no peace, the damned swine!"—Comrade Ryshkov held out his hand.

"Forgive me for disturbing you, comrade."

"Doesn't matter. I'm always ready to help an Octoberist." Ryshkov clapped him benevolently on the shoulder, adding, as he escorted him to the door: "But come and see me tomorrow for certain, comrade; do you hear?"

Mirkin recounted this conversation to Comrade Sofia, expressing his surprise at Ryshkov's division of people into two categories, those for and those against the Octoberists, and at his conclusion that Octoberist sympathies could cleanse a man from all iniquities. She retorted:

"Oh, indeed—I really can't see why you should be surprised at that!"

"But can't you understand that you're simply setting up a new fetish, the October action? For untold years priests have been sacrificing mankind on fetish-altars. In the infancy of our race children were sacrificed to Moloch, and it's been going on like that for thousands of years. Over and over again men are sacrificed, not for higher human ideals but for petrified dogmas, for Moloch, for religion, for the Czar, for the Fatherland—and now for the October revolution. You're following the beaten path of all idol-worshipers! Do you imagine that Moloch in the beginning was anything else but an October revolutionary? In the beginning every idea comes charged with the mission to liberate mankind, to serve it, to help it in its predicament. But once the idea hardens into dogma it becomes an altar on which men are sacrificed. And so it was with Moloch. He made a revolution against the idols that preceded him. The priests persuaded the people that only Moloch could help them against evil spirits and destructive storms, that he alone was the true redeemer of mankind. But when he became the prevailing god men were offered upon his altars. That's the path trodden by all fetishes. And I fear that the October revolution is following suit."

Sosha grew pale:

"And *you* can say that, you, a revolutionary, a man who took an active part in the October movement?"

"That's just why I have a right to say it; that's just why it's my duty."

"Zachary, what's the matter with you?"

"I don't know, Sosha, I don't know! But I feel—that all this is anything but good."

Late that night he stole out and hurried to his father at the National Hotel.

"Father—pack and go! If you value your life, pack and go! You mustn't stay here! Pull all the strings you can and get clear away!"

Old Mirkin blenched. But in a moment he had recovered his composure, and there was now no trace of his former agitation and despair.

"I think, Zachary, that it's you who need to pack and go. It's high time," he said, wrinkling his forehead anxiously.

CHAPTER XXVI

FALLEN BY THE WAYSIDE

ONE WAR was at an end: another was beginning.

At all four corners of the gigantic empire wolfish eyes were gleaming, and in the capital the stink of corpses could already be smelt in the wind—it was the new war.

The German eagles had penetrated as far as Pskov and Orsha and were heavily oppressing the country. The Ukraine had separated itself and become a foreign land. The Germans were hastening to take the capital before any one else should anticipate them. In the north the French and English had besieged Murmansk and Archangel. In Jaroslavl the White Guards were assembled, supported by the Social Revolutionaries. On the Volga the Czech prisoners of war were concentrating. On the Don and in the Caucasus the refugee General Krassnov was again busy gathering his Cossacks. All of them were creeping nearer and nearer, stretching out hands to each other, attempting to join forces, and more grimly than ever was the serpent of war coiling itself round the promised fruits of the October revolution. Hardly had the first regiments been disbanded from the front (that was the price of Volhynia and White Russia) when in all the barracks, factories and empty school-buildings cadres were at once re-formed. Once more men with unshaven cheeks, dirty shirts and voices hoarse with speaking, exhorted the soldiers to "oppose their breasts as a wall of defense," and this time the fetish to be defended was no longer "the Czar" or "the Fatherland" or even "the Revolution"; the new Moloch was called simply "October."

When Mirkin returned he found Sosha rapidly packing a trunk and her large red-brown attaché case. Her brown leather jacket, for a long time laid aside, had been brought out again, nor was the red revolver-strap lacking round her neck.

"What's up?" he asked.

"Kornilov's turned up again among the Cossacks at Rostov. Troops from the Turkish front under Sorokin's command have already reached Novo-Tcherkask. We'll pulverize them! And if need be we'll turn Russia into a sea of blood! Oh, we'll give them the push all right! They won't get in! They'll have to cut and run!"—Sosha was feverishly excited—"I'm being sent out to the provinces as an agitator—to recruit for the Red Army. And where have you been? Comrade Ryshkov's sent two couriers to look for you already. Go to see him at once! They want to make you a commissar and give you a commando. Perhaps we might both be on the same front."

Mirkin paled and said nothing.

"Why are you so silent? You're not afraid, are you?" she laughed at him.

"And if I were afraid—would that be so surprising? I don't see why I shouldn't be afraid. There's something good in fear! It was perhaps fear that made us grow into human beings and killed the animal in us. To know fear, to be afraid, that's the right thing to do!" Mirkin almost screamed.

"Timid revolutionaries!" Sosha laughed mockingly. "If we had been timid we should never have begun the revolution."

"If I had a firm belief that whatever we do is inspired by a higher power, a faith such as the Crusaders had or the followers of Mohammed, I would be able to shift all responsibility for bloodshed on to some myth or some destiny that compels me to be a murderer in its service. But we don't believe in a higher power and have no destiny. So we have to answer for everything ourselves, according to our own consciences. And I admit it frankly: whatever others may steel themselves to, I haven't the strength for it."

Sosha glanced contemptuously at him and said with a compassionate shake of the head:

"What's all this nonsense about myths and destinies? It's the Revolution that concerns us, the October, the Proletariat! Everything's at stake!"

"I don't believe in war," returned Mirkin curtly.

"Anyhow, I advise you to find Comrade Ryshkov as quickly as possible!" And with that she turned her back on him and went on packing her trunk. . . .

In Comrade Ryshkov's bureau there was a bewildering, nervous and yet energetic bustle. The great building was crammed with people from top to bottom. Unceasing coming and going; excitement and expectation on every face. It was with difficulty that Mirkin made his way to Comrade Ryshkov. Surrounded by a dozen people, the man with the shaven head was sitting before a pile of papers telephoning continuously, issuing orders to someone beside him and at the same time perusing a document handed to him. Comrade Ryshkov could do ten men's work at once.

"Comrade Mirkin, if my eyes don't mistake me," he said rapidly, busying himself at the same time with the most varied things. He signed papers, gave instructions to people both going and coming, listened to reports, made notes, and turned round to Mirkin:

"Comrade Mirkin," he said, energetically scoring a name off a list. "You proved yourself very valuable to us in the October days. Where have you been tucking yourself away? In some Trade Office chaffering over sugar and salt? There are others who can do that! We need you here, we need you urgently!" Again he switched his attention to something else, without so much as a look at Mirkin. "We need men like you on whom we can depend. The Revolution has hosts of enemies. The counter-revolutionary forces are gathering. But we'll soon show them what's what! The forests are thick with their robber-bands; we'll comb them out! We're organizing the Red Army. We need you. I want you to give up your chaffering and come to us. We need politically mature people for the Army. In the October days you were of great help to us—very great help. Now—what do you say to my proposal, Comrade Mirkin?"

"I'm afraid, Comrade Ryshkov—it's not the job for me. An army? I've never been a soldier."

"Oh, that's what's bothering you? Don't worry, you'll learn quick enough. In the Revolution one learns everything—even how to nurse children." Ryshkov laughed to himself, but still found no time to lift his head. "None of us has ever been to a Military Academy. But if the Revolution requires it—isn't that so, Comrade Mirkin?"

"Still, Comrade Ryshkov, I'm not convinced that what we're doing now is right," began Mirkin hesitatingly.

"What?" With a violent start Ryshkov jerked up his gleaming, angular head from his papers and stared at Mirkin. "What did you say, comrade?" he asked, in a quieter voice as if he had not heard Mirkin aright. "What do you mean by 'what we're doing now'?"

"I mean the civil war we're entering on."

Ryshkov regarded him with a scornful smile and said:

"What are you thinking of? According to you we should look on quietly while the counter-revolutionaries snatch from us all we've gained, and smash the Revolution?"

"I don't know what we *should* do," answered Mirkin, "but I know that what we're doing now isn't right. The evil that we do must have a limit set to it that we may begin to do good. The evil shouldn't preponderate over the good. I think that in our zeal to save the world and liberate mankind we ourselves are sinking in the rivers of blood we are shedding, that we ourselves are drowning in the cesspool of evil created by ourselves. I've seen war with my own eyes—I know what war is: it turns men into beasts. Even the most righteous war turns men into beasts."

Ryshkov got up and stared at the white-faced Mirkin.

"Tell me, young man—what brought you over to our side in October? Did you fall into it by chance?"

"No, I did not come in by chance—I came in deliberately; yes, with a full consciousness of what I was doing. Existing circumstances and events drove me into the October action as with iron rods—the abominable war and Nikolai Nikolayevitch's pogroms. I came in because I believed the October Revolution was going to liberate and transform the world."

"What world?" shouted Ryshkov. "Which world? Yours, the rotten bourgeois world, or ours, the world of the proletariat? For us, young man, the 'October' was no attempt to 'liberate' the world—no attempt merely to drive out Kerensky and end the war and leave everything in the same old state, as you seem to imagine! For us the 'October' was an execution—yes, the execution of the old bourgeois world and the birth of a new proletarian world! Our proletarian blood must rule that world, not a bourgeois hotch-potch or a patched-up community of all the elements in Russia. And for that proletarian blood we are ready to sacrifice everything else, to flay the whole world if need be and let it run round screaming! . . . Ha, ha, ha! Come here, comrades, just listen to this! Out of pure humanity we're to refuse to organize the Red Army, we're to let the White Guards slit our throats! Out of pure humanity we're to dissolve the October Revolution! Come here, just listen!"

In a twinkling Mirkin was surrounded by a crowd of youngsters in military-looking leather jackets and top-boots; there were among them a few gray-bearded men with intelligent faces who looked rather queer in that rig.

For some time Ryshkov's heated discussion with the unknown young man had attracted the attention of everybody present. It seemed to them incredible that Ryshkov, who usually had no time to spare for two words with a comrade, should suddenly, among such a press of work, initiate an argument. But the riddle was quickly solved.

"And this man was with us in October and climbed for us on to the roof of the theater!" cried Ryshkov.

Most of them stared at Mirkin as if he were some queer new animal. Some, who were in a great hurry, merely glanced at him contemptuously and muttered. One girl in a military cloak, with cropped hair and a short turned-up nose which looked as if it had been too strongly filliped when she was born, voiced the feelings of all:

"I can't understand why we should bother with the creature at all. He should be chucked into the cellar for Comrade Marek to deal with!"

Then she advanced on Zachary and said, screwing up her nose still further:

"But this is Mirkin, the son of the timber merchant! His father was a great friend of all the Czar's officials, and a mighty big man. And now he's an expert on the Railways Committee. I really don't understand how such a responsible position should be given to a creature like him."

Comrade Ryshkov, already busy at something else, heard the laughter and saw Mirkin standing deathly white in the ring of comrades, who were regarding him with contemptuous looks. Involuntarily there welled up in Ryshkov, as happens in all strong, steadfast natures, a warm feeling of sympathy for the helpless, bewildered wretch at whom everybody was laughing:

"Comrade, the Revolution uses compulsion on nobody. In our

opinion to be a revolutionary is a privilege, an election—not a compulsion. Good-by! Go back to the job you have. Cowards are no good to us."

At first this epithet seared Mirkin like a red-hot iron. Then he thought it over: "Is what I did really cowardice?" And all at once he saw quite clearly; it might be precisely that kind of "cowardice" that men needed most if they were to remain men. In an excess of courage the holiest things of life are forgotten, and perhaps this so-called cowardice was the sole quality that could save humanity in an insane age.

On returning to his room he found no trace of Sosha except a note lying on the table, written in an energetic hand.

"I have heard of all that happened in Comrade Ryshkov's office. I'm ashamed of you. I won't have anything more to do with a coward, and, I hope, neither will my sister. It's all over between us."

Mirkin laughed aloud and crumpled the paper in his hand:

"They have made war against all Czars and tyrants except brute force. Even here brute force is the one acknowledged god. I'm the only person who dares to proclaim a revolution against the god of war; I'm a coward!"

He was filled with great pride.

He could not remain quietly in the house. Outside in the streets he wanted to shout to all passers-by:

"People, I'm a coward! Imitate me! Cowardice is the one thing that can save the world."

CHAPTER XXVII

MOSCOW

In Moscow spring advances timidly, with slow steps, like a child learning to walk. For weeks she hovers in the air before her touch can be felt on earth. Every day another winter-garment is shed until at last the earth's real shape is visible in all its nakedness.

This year the earth still showed no trace of spring but was covered with mud and slush. Yet, like everybody else, Mirkin knew that spring must be in the air because he suddenly felt his winter garments cumbersome, especially the short sheepskin jacket which he wore over his "brain-worker's" suit. All the same he could not take it off, for it was needed to cover his worn, disreputable suit.

He felt a longing to go into a bathhouse, to steam his body thoroughly and put on clean linen—a need which for a long time he had not known. At the very least he wanted a couple of dry linen foot-cloths to put on his feet, which were sticking out of his gaping shoes and rubbing against the wet stones. Most of all he would have liked to jump, just as he was, into the fresh cold waters of the Moskva, along whose banks he was now loitering aimlessly.

He came to a halt in an enormous, majestic square dominated by the huge Church of the Redeemer. Then he left the broad pavement and slithered down to the mud bank where he had noticed some half-naked derelict children playing by the water. He felt as homeless and outcast as they and had an impulse to sit down among them in his filthy garments.

By the waterside there were whole swarms of homeless children, mostly boys of ten to twelve years old, their tattered winter clothing held together with string, and their dirty street arab faces marked with all the signs of vice. There were girls, too, in the crowd, but their bold gestures, shameless bearing and boys' clothing made it almost impossible to distinguish them from their masculine playfellows. Only the long soft hair sticking out beneath the ragged boys' caps provided a clew to their sex, although here and there one saw a finely molded girlish face or a delicate childish body showing a budding femininity through the rents in its boyish garments.

A group of these youngsters were sitting on a pile of broken crockery and filthy straw, playing with dirty cards. Others, apparently still aware of their childhood, were sailing paper boats in the water. A few were right out in the river, having thrown off the draggled odds and ends of leather that were bound with string round their feet, and were splashing about with childlike abandon. Mirkin felt inclined to do likewise, to kick off his half-rotten shoes and cool his burning feet in the water—for after all it was spring!

Yet it was not for long that he was allowed to enjoy the feeling of spring. The beggar brats had observed him, and, quickly abandoning both playing cards and paper boats, turned all at once into cool and calculating adults. Their faces, whether hypocritical or brazen, assumed touching, doleful expressions and they came swarming round the stranger like bees around a honey-flower, thrusting against him dirty hands and bodies half sticking out of their rags. Their slyly downcast eyes sparkled impudently under the tangled hair plastered on their foreheads. Only their lips achieved the right begging droop and quivered pathetically.

"Comrade, give us something for a crust!"

A girl with a child's face detached herself from the crowd. Her terribly precocious and experienced eyes betrayed the fact that there was nothing in the world they had not seen, and her small, worn-down teeth looked as if they had already nibbled at every bitter fruit life had to offer. She squeezed her dirty child's body, whose most intimate parts showed with pathetic shamelessness through her filthy rags, close to Mirkin. Rubbing her soft hip against his leg she gave him a bold look of invitation:

"Comrade, come under the bridge with me!"

Vice is never more dreadful than when it looks out of the eyes of corrupted children. With silent glances and eloquent gestures the boys encouraged their small prostitute playfellow. Their urgency, however, was superfluous; she had her own instincts to help her. With awkward but knowing movements she caressed the stranger indecently and invited him to come on. . . .

Horror and disgust overcame Mirkin. But he felt also an unspeakable anger, and shouted wildly:

"October, is there anything you'll stop short of?"

He tossed to the children the piece of bread which, like everybody else, he always carried as his most precious possession, and fled.

Wishing to forget the abomination of child prostitution which he now perceived everywhere, Mirkin let his eye rest on the pure, deep black of the trees grouped on the opposite bank of the Moskva. The sight of these fresh, bare boughs, already shining with a bloom of spring, the sight of the gleaming mirrors of the Moskva and the soft contour of its banks, refreshed him.

Here and there in the melting snow there was already a hint of green. The trees gave off a reddish-purple mist. The world was as it had used to be: great, wide and beautiful. The sky—a sea of molten silver, in which blue strips were widening—stretched out mighty arms to enfold the whole universe. Its radiance, reflected on the earth-bound life beneath, made all the house-windows shine and lit up the golden domes and green-tiled roofs.

The same world as ever! Sky and earth were singing pæans while between them mankind lay suffering from open, festering wounds. . . .

Song descending from the shining sky! Song arising from the new-born earth! And on the stone bridge, too, there was a sound of singing, a cheerful, triumphant marching-song. But a deep sense of mourning lay over it, as if a wedding march were being sung at a funeral.

Mirkin looked up: these were recruits marching, countless ranks of workers, most of them still in civilian clothes, with a sprinkling of military cloaks. In that cloak of death the wearers looked quite different from the others; they belonged already to another world. The young men marched erect, with glowing, enthusiastic faces, filled with courage and force of will; the older men with their bearded faces were full of enthusiasm too, but marched with a more weary step, while in their eyes lurked fear. Yet they were all passionately singing the "Internationale," as if it were both creed and confession; the song fired their enthusiasm anew whenever it threatened to waver.

Mirkin gazed after them with envious self-reproach: Why was he not in their ranks? Why were his steps not ringing in time with theirs on the paving-stones? What right had he to detach himself and go his own way? A man who says A must be prepared to say B. What right had he to stray off in solitary freedom?

He could not justify himself; he felt guilty; and yet he could do nothing else. He knew what would happen: a minute ago he had been marching in imagination in those ranks and all at once he had felt weariness growing upon him and alarm as well. He would fall down and be left lying. He could almost feel his comrades trampling over him; hundreds of feet, thousands of feet, treading down his head and his backbone, marching on and leaving him behind, crushed and broken ike the homeless children by the water, like the child prostitute, like he whole of Russia. . . .

"Of course, it has to be like that. The Revolution has enemies nd must defend itself. What else can it do? Shall it let its opponents rush it? Shall it look on while the others destroy what it has so hardly von? Shall it dig its own grave? If the other side wins, then everyhing will be destroyed in any case. It is more honorable to save the Revolution and oneself as well, sword in hand. Of course they're in he right. That's the fate of every individual who attaches himself to n idea. The idea drags us behind it as if in chains. A man who says A must be prepared to say B. I have remained behind because I'm a oward—yes, a coward in the real sense of the word, for I'm afraid. t is only to justify myself that I invent theories to explain my attitude —it was only to evade the issue that I invented the theory of saving he world by cowardice. The truth is that my attitude comes from imple fear, plain cowardice, just as Sosha told me.

"Well, let me face the fact—I'm a coward, trembling for my own fe. But is fear merely a base emotion? Fear means uncertainty, oubt, an inclination to sympathize with the other side. Perhaps I'm ltogether wrong—perhaps the other side may be right: that's fear.

"But in that case is not fear a genuinely human, creative emotion?

"The human race, although thousands of years have developed it o a high pitch of creative power, although in its progress it has been efined and purified, is still bound to the great source of its blood, still as its secret affinities with the unknown from which it issued forth. And so its nature includes the incomprehensible attributes of its divine origin. One of these attributes is fear and cowardice. They have nly been repressed in the course of ages, quelled by mankind's assumption that it can exceed its own powers and become a kind of econd God. Primitive man knew fear—otherwise he would never have nade gods for himself. In his unceasing desperate struggle with the nimal world and Nature he knew himself for a weak and resourceless reature. Had this not been the case he would have taken himself to be he arbiter of his own destiny, he would have taken himself for God, nd would not have thought it needful to revere stronger powers like hunder, or weaker powers like cows and cats.

"So long as fear prevailed in our blood man was a genuinely human, religious being who created good for himself and knew love and humility. It was only in the course of time, when the divine element in him was suppressed by devilish fetishes, by myths devised for a slave mentality, that wars arose, usurpations, the piling up of material wealth and the inevitable sacrifice of the weak and helpless. And to restore the equilibrium of the world, to recover the supremacy of Love and Goodness, the first thing needful is to rouse again in humanity that divine spark—the feeling of cowardice and fear!

"Yet is that not merely playing a kind of hide-and-seek behind theoretical constructions? What have I done hitherto? Driven by circumstances, stung by injustice, I applied my feeble strength to help on a system which I believed would be capable, if it came to power, of establishing justice on the earth. I clambered up on roofs and killed men. My feeling of fear and cowardice was submerged by something higher, by faith. And my fear and cowardice have only reappeared because I have begun to lose my faith. So the fault lies not in me but in the system.

"Yet what was it I first began to doubt? The ideal? No—it is not ideals that are good or bad, but men. I began to doubt the methods of realizing the ideal.

"Life is not formed by ideals, but by daily actions. Ideals soar up, like souls, into heaven, but reality is wrought by deeds and actions. My mistake was merely that I began by believing in a system instead of in mankind. For a system always draws conclusions without taking its instrument, man, into account. It towers over man's head and becomes a rack for him, a dead dogma that brings subjection instead of freedom, sorrow and suffering instead of help and comfort.

"Man is the highest good, the only being in whom creative life pulses. He alone is capable of standing upright and perceiving the divine in himself. For man is of divine origin. Bound by blood to the unknown fount of all power from which he springs, he is as inviolable, as unassailable, as holy as the Godhead. And every ideal that does not allow for the unlimited wealth of the yet unexplained but existing Infinite, must weigh him down like a heavy chain. . . ."

As Zachary was plunged in these thoughts the Kremlin rose dazzling before him. That assembly of golden towers, green roofs and shining windows, surrounded by a thick wall with ten turrets, looked like a procession of beautiful women. In the far distance rose the small corner turrets, which, with their narrow, primitively ornamented windows, resembled children's paper lanterns. To Mirkin it seemed as if all the pitilessly Asiatic element in the soul of Russia, the rigid and tortuous greatness of its ancient past, lay in these childishly formed little window-arches on the Kremlin turrets, as if swarms of Russian souls had nested for centuries like birds under these lintels, cornices and roofs, hatching on these walls among the cobwebs of Russia's ancient history the mystical restlessness of the Russian character, with its eternal questing.

Now a window of the "Grand Palais" was lit up and sent a fiery ray over the shoulder of the Kremlin wall.

Deep in thought Zachary entered the Alexander Park. The snow was yet lying, trodden down and crumbling, but still white among the trees, as if it were asserting: "I will not give way so long as I have a single flake left."

Yet it had retreated perforce from some strips of ground, and in these patches there lay exposed not bare soil but dewy grass. The surrounding whiteness heightened the lovely green of the tender stalks, and they seemed to be imploring mercy and protection amid the snow. A young, soft spring breeze was ruffling them like the down on a chicken's breast; frail and trembling they swayed to and fro, exposing the mystery of their growth right down to the dark brown rootlets that held them in mother earth.

The mystery of the grass had attracted a crowd of spectators; on the green banks, caressed by the young spring airs, lay children of both sexes, like half-rotting decaying leaves, with sticky playing cards in their filthy hands. . . .

But in Vosnessenskaya Street Mirkin met a great troop of soldiers, not yet proper soldiers, rather the soldiers of tomorrow. A medley of garments of every description bedecked them; fur jackets, dirty lambskin coats, leather jerkins, and head-coverings of all kinds, among which here and there the neat uniform of an officer could be seen.

The marchers included many women, who stuck out their chests and put on brazen airs to make themselves look still more manly than the men. Yet they did not succeed; the longer their strides the more feminine and seductive they looked. Men and women alike were carrying rifles on their shoulders. This gave them a uniform appearance and distinguished them from the ordinary street crowd, turning them into a special kind of human beings—soldiers.

Following them, as if in a funeral procession, came the "Little Horses of the Soviet," those half-naked homeless children with small hand-sledges who helped "profiteers" to transport illicit stores of food from the railway stations. Childish curiosity made them forget for a while their profitable trade; disregarding the peremptory commands of their employers to take the road prescribed them they flocked after the soldiers with simple delight, hopping like merry foals in front of their sledges. Then they fell into step with the marchers and joined in singing the "Internationale."

Mirkin stopped and looked for a long time after them. The October Revolution suddenly seemed to him a voracious animal that swallowed human beings unceasingly—like any other beast of prey.

CHAPTER XXVIII

LINEN-HUNGER

But suddenly Mirkin observed something that made him forget everything else: he was walking almost barefoot; his naked soles were treading on worn-out, rotting foot-cloths, and through the holes in his shoes he could feel the damp asphalt of the pavement. And on his body he could feel the stale rags of his shirt. He was nauseated at himself. There surged up violently within him an irresistible longing for freshly-laundered, crackling linen.

It was the spectacle of some underwear that aroused this imperious longing, and the underwear consisted of women's shifts.

On the pavement at the entrance to the Red Square, just opposite St. Yeverskaya, whose countless devotional candles were quenched in the bright daylight, stood two thickly veiled ladies, one oldish and the other young, clad elegantly in black. They were offering for sale silken shifts which they held in their arms as carefully as infants. Both had a pious air, as if their whole lives had been spent among the fumes of church incense, as if their lips could murmur nothing but devotional prayers. And yet the soft wave of the hair that fell over their delicate foreheads, the fine arch of their strongly penciled brows and the shrinking fear visible under their black-fringed eyelids betrayed a former worldly and comfortable existence. From them as from the fresh pink silk chemises, trimmed with lace, that they were offering for sale, streamed a seductive fragrance, mingled with the strong household reek of camphor that hung in the clothes of the elder woman. The mere sight of that shimmering silk literally intoxicated Mirkin. More strongly than ever he yearned to take a bath and feel on his skin the crackling of freshly-laundered linen. He felt more keenly than ever that he was unclean, and he feared that his very glance might soil those delicate, carefully ironed garments which called to one's mind ardent bridal nights. In his mouth he felt a sweetish taste as if he had just bitten into a juicy plum. He stood a little way off and literally drank in that vision of spotless lingerie, as refreshing as spring blossoms; he thought he could almost hear the rustling of the silk. A childish longing overcame him to go near to it and at least touch it with his hand.

It is strange what varied trains of thought can be started by silken shifts! In Mirkin these garments awoke the purest and tenderest emotions, as if the mere sight of them had cleansed and purified him.

He observed a peasant woman in thick shoes and a warm shawl, who had just emerged from St. Yeverskaya's, walking up to the two ladies and pinching the fine silk with her coarse fingers; she said something—apparently she was bargaining. Mirkin felt somehow injured, wounded in his most sacred feelings. . . .

The thought of these silken garments clung to him as he sauntered farther along the street. He could not understand how people could bring themselves to sell their own shifts. Such a garment was the most intimate of personal possessions, a kind of second skin, worn close to the body, sharing in one's most private secrets, attending one's birth and one's death, the nearest witness of all one's experiences! How could any one permit a stranger to lay a finger upon it?

Mirkin became conscious of a tearing hunger for fresh linen. He had never known before that one could hunger for shirts as achingly as for bread. And as a thirsty man can think of nothing but water, so Zachary could not get away from the thought of fresh, crackling linen and clean cloths for his feet.

Crazy visions began to flit through his heated brain. He could see himself swimming naked in a river of flowing linen. . . .

The sight of any object can suggest countless associations, and so it often happens that an ordinary familiar thing can be as potent an intoxicant as a fiery wine. Mirkin was drunk with the sight of that delicate silk and soared as on wings through the streets of Moscow. Yearnings and desires awoke in him which the mad flights of events and the abrupt break with his past had seemed to have banished for ever. What was it that so suddenly brought the memory of Helene out of the night of forgetfulness?

He saw her bodily before him, yet at the same time the vision was unreal. The man's soft hat, the reddish-yellow fox collar on her indeterminate frieze coat now looked quite different; an unearthly purity, such as he had never noticed before, now radiated from her. The faint agitation which he had once felt when his hand caressed the smooth, cool curve of her slim rounded shoulders, now returned to him in the middle of the street; he could actually feel her touch on his lips and all at once the world grew bright before his eyes and he knew that he must see her.

The memory of Helene released him from the shame of his filthy garments and laved him as in cool crystal-clear mountain water. A shudder of awe thrilled him to the heart. Each cell in his body, each nerve, each thought was purified. As a child before it comes to the world is transmitted through countless bodies and must die and be born again in each, so Zachary now was reborn from the countless secret husks that had previously covered him; he stood there naked and defenseless, belonging only to himself. Not a single mask, not a single shift now veiled his visible self, not a single thought stirred in his inmost mind. . . .

This state lasted for barely a second; then the vision vanished, leaving only the damp filth of the street, the rags on his body, the wet feet squelching through puddles in their torn shoes, and the feeling that he was overgrown with marsh-weed and fungus. Like leaden weights the sorrows of the world dragged Zachary down into the depths again. . . .

But as a white wedding veil can make one long for the bride who wears it, Zachary's vision evoked, too, a yearning for the girl who had inspired it. And the vision and the longing raised him again above all his troubles, lending him wings to soar high enough to follow with his eyes the vanishing memory.

Suddenly he knew that a bright purity was throned in his very heart.

A magical hand spun gossamer threads that drew him out of the green mire in which life had bogged him, drew him back to his childhood: he felt strong warm arms bearing him up, comforting warm veils of water flowing over his back and breast; he was wrapped in clean linen and borne into another world. Old longings and desires began to stir, for Helene's slim girlish body now incarnated all the mother-women of his childhood. His physical exaltation aroused faintly exciting images of beautiful girlish shoulders, as sweet to the imagination as honey in the comb, yet other wishes and dreams emerged more and more clearly. A mingled odor of perfume and camphor which had always hung about his mother's scarves. Glances of sinful invitation from eyes long dead; a long dead face that haunted Mirkin's mind like a legendary adventure. Broken recollections of attempts at suicide. Long suppressed but still vivid lusts for robust bosoms that looked as if they were filled with milk, for ripe full bodies defined by elegant black silk gowns. . . . The after-taste of these painful desires was still perceptible on the outer fringe of his consciousness. . . . And all these unresolved lusts, which he had struggled against while they were still inchoate, were now purified and liberated, detached from their guilty passion, stripped of their serpentine carnality, freed from their veils of darkness, and purged in the fire of that dazzling whiteness which now reigned in Zachary's breast. The closely-knit web of association brought up his sins and changed them into good deeds.

Together with him they were bathed in the clear warm waters of childhood and were now, like him, arrayed in clean white linen. . . .

"What's up with me today? I must be feverish! Is it the spring, or have I caught a chill?"

Yet his self-reproaches, his shamed excuses, his forced struggles, availed nothing.

He suffered no longer from the burning of his naked foot-soles, the chafing of his worn shoes on the hard pavements. The ache in his feet was stimulating. He no longer found his hot sheepskin coat a burden, nor winced when his bare throat was chafed by the matted tufts of wool; he was no longer nauseated when the worn seams of his trousers excoriated his most sensitive parts. Streams of warm water ran down over his back, and motherly hands caressed his naked body. . . .

Beads of sweat started out on his hot forehead and ran down in chilly trickles.

"I must be ill! I must have caught a chill! I ought to go home. But where am I to go?"

Zachary hastily emerged from his dreams and found himself again on the earth. Only now did he remember that he had no home to go to, for he could not again enter the house on the Chistoprudny Boulevard. After that encounter with Comrade Ryshkov he felt he had no further right to be lodged there, and he had not yet found a new room.

For a couple of nights he had slept in a hostel for traveling Soviet officials, and last night he had spent in the street among the homeless. . . .

"Go to my father, perhaps? No, not in this state. I must certainly try to get a lodging somewhere. Whatever happens, I must go back to my work. I must make myself useful. After all, the Trade Committee is important enough. One must make oneself useful as far as one can. Yes—I'll go back to my work. I'll tell the comrades that I had to give up my room and I'll ask them to find me another."

Once more he repeated the words that since his break with Sosha had been constantly in his mind. "One must make oneself useful as far as one can." But they were only words, devised merely as a spur to himself. His whole body was sinking into a kind of tranced lethargy;

he felt drunken with sleep and dragged himself with difficulty across the Red Square, staring vacantly at the coiled turbans of St. Basil's Cathedral. Without noticing what he was doing he traversed streets and squares and he was very nearly run over by a heavy-laden wagon that came out of a courtyard. On the pavement he collided with hurried foot-passengers, all with shaven heads, new stubble on their chins and portfolios under their arms. Zachary staggered to the other side of the street, and the stink of rancid fat and fish met him full in the face. Shops with stale caviar. The stench of meat, the sharp, pungent reek of salted calf-hides. Noise and commotion. He bumped into a Russian with a red face and a huge patriarchal beard who was running along the street with a heavy box: the blow made Zachary reel so that he nearly fell.

"Accursed dog! What do you come creeping between people's legs for? Can't you see when somebody's carrying a box? Are you blind?"

Zachary found himself in Barbara Square. Innumerable booths and stalls; goods of every description piled on the dirty pavement. Whole suites of furniture and household utensils stood out in the street as if there had been a fire; plush covers and old boots lay cheek by jowl with crockery and cutlery. It looked as if the whole world had decided to eat with its fingers and thrown all its table furnishings out on the street. And again the sight of clean linen held Zachary spellbound. This time it was the real thing, men's underwear. An old man in a general's uniform without the epaulettes was standing stiffly at attention as if on parade; the wind was playing with the gray strands of his well-groomed beard and reddening his large, full face. He was holding linen pants on his outstretched palms with as much dignity and gravity as if they were a cushion covered with orders at the funeral of a fallen comrade. Beside him, with a similarly fixed look, stood several old ladies of the aristocracy wrapped in chinchilla cloaks and wearing small coquettish hats, who held in their hands beautifully laundered napery, pillowslips and underwear. Others were offering old silver and coats of Persian lamb, or marvelous Venetian and Brussels lace, but most of the goods on sale were of Russian handiwork, made by serfs on the family estates. A few had brought their ball-dresses to the market, and the white satin and beaver fur of Boyar costumes gleamed in the sun, the rich colors of old French brocade glowed golden.

None of the sellers uttered a word. Not a look did they condescend to cast on the people who fingered their wares and asked the price. The women's eyes, skilfully shaded by veils, stared over their clients' heads. They stood rigid as wooden puppets, offering for sale the objects they held in their black-gloved hands.

One lady who was wearing an elegant black spring costume with a silver fox fur round her neck as if she were paying a call on a friend was accompanied by a faithful maid carrying a magnificent Sèvres dinner-service. She languidly waved her aristocratic black-gloved hand in the direction of the blue and golden plates which the maid, still very respectably clad, was holding out carefully, and with a quiet, faintly provocative smile repeated from time to time with a strong French accent, as if mentioning the fact to herself: "Sèvres porcelain!"

A pale young dandy was trying to sell his frock-coat. A farm-laborer with dreadfully filthy boots was putting out all his strength to pull the garment over his wadded jacket. The spectators were roaring with laughter and giving him advice about what to do. The top-hat to match the coat was already stuck on the head of a ragged porter, who was in the thick of the merry crowd. . . .

A warning shout: "The militia!" and in a twinkling the market was empty. The aristocrats abandoned their pose of sad elegance and vanished in all directions. Through the fleeing throng the frightened general pushed his way with asthmatic gasps and wheezings, the linen pants tucked out of sight beneath his tunic.

Again Mirkin felt his imperious hunger for linen. But his visions were gone; he could think only of the ragged shirt on his own back which made him feel as if a toad were clinging to his body. His chafed foot-soles were again burning like fire. And he would have given the world for a pair of pants to shield him from the rough discomfort of his frayed and ragged trouser seams.

Suddenly he came to a halt and opened his eyes in amazement. Like a thirsty man staring at a brimming fountain he stood regarding mountains of garments which had risen around him all at once. His feet shuffled against men's underwear, new and second hand, women's shifts, stockings, socks, silk handkerchiefs, plush coverlets, trousers, corsets, boots, galoshes and the usual plethora of knives and forks and spoons.

Behind a stall in the background sat a fat, broad old woman with a red face, wrapped in a man's large beaver coat with a magnificent Kamchatka collar round her thick neck. On her enormous head she wore a still more enormous hat covered with unusually long, colored ostrich feathers. At one fleshy ear dangled a pearl pendant; the other ear was still waiting until its ornament could be picked up as a bargain.

Herself resembling a gigantic samovar, she was sitting among a medley of variegated samovars of brass and other metals, and without moving from the spot was directing a troop of assistants, young men in top-boots who obviously feared her fat face and red potato-nose as they feared the devil. They were all busy with innumerable clients, hauling in booty and selling it or exchanging it for food. The fat old woman conveyed her orders by a mere flicker of the eye.

Higher and higher towered the bales and piles of domestic articles. One had the impression that all the houses in Moscow had been sacked, that the entire contents of all their chests and cupboards, every bit of wearing apparel, household furniture and cutlery, had been cleared out, that all the carpets and curtains had been stripped from the rooms and flung in a great heap before this old woman.

With greedy eyes Mirkin surveyed the pile of loot and tried to fish out suitable garments to cover his nakedness. He noticed a pair of hand-knitted woolen stockings lying unregarded on the ground, and they looked familiar and homely, as if some dear hand had knitted them for himself. And although he had no money to buy them with he could not refrain from at least touching them and asking their price.

"Drop them! Drop them! They're not for the likes of you!" shouted the old woman.

"Why not?" asked Mirkin.

"Your dial gives you away, you're one of that crowd!" And she nodded at the aristocrats near by who were offering their wares to the assistants. "You're not one of us, you're a bourgeois."

"What do *you* call yourself?"

The fat old woman turned her head away as if Mirkin were not worth talking to.

"I'll tell you who she is, she's no less than Lenin's aunt!" cried another vagabond who was rather like Mirkin.

"Another word from you and I'll call the militia!" screamed the old woman. "Move on out of that!"

"Take my advice and leave her alone. She's got a big pull somewhere. She's a pet among the commissars. Everybody's goods are confiscated except hers." A neighboring dealer indicated the old woman with a significant wink.

"What's all this? Is this kind of thing allowed in the very heart of Moscow? Where's the militia?" Mirkin suddenly began to shout. "Militia! Here!"

"All my sons are Communists. I'm only collecting these things for my boys. My oldest son was in the 'October'! And what are you? A scoundrel, a damned bourgeois, a counter-revolutionary! Get out of this or I'll have you up before my son in the Commissariat!" the old woman shouted at Mirkin.

"That's true—she's one of our new rulers. You can't try conclusions with her," said the ragged onlooker, restraining Mirkin.

"Her son is a commissar, is he, and took part in the October Revolution? What does that matter? This kind of trafficking is forbidden! Away with it!" and in wild rage Mirkin rushed at the piles of garments and began tearing them asunder. "You cancers of the Revolution! You October-bourgeois!"

While he was blindly attacking the heaps of clothes a bundle of stockings unrolled and fell at his feet. Mirkin immediately forgot everything else, plunged his hand into the bundle and yelled like a madman:

"I was in the 'October' too, I was! Up on the roof of the Great Theater over yonder! And I'm going to have at least a pair of socks out of it!"

With that he took to his heels.

The old woman's assistants started to chase him. But their mistress, anxious to avoid an uproar, summoned them back with a wave of the hand:

"He's probably had all his money confiscated. Let the poor devil go."

Pushing his way like a madman through the crowds, Mirkin came to stop at length, exhausted and bathed in sweat, and drew out the prize he had captured in the fray. But instead of good socks he had only a woman's half-torn stocking in his hand. Shamed and repentant he flung it far from him.

"It seems I'm really ill," he said to himself, and bent his steps instinctively towards the one person left to him in the world, his father in his little hotel bedroom.

CHAPTER XXIX

THE GRACE OF PATERNAL LOVE

THE SIGHT of his son gave old Mirkin a deadly fright. Zachary was trembling from head to foot. A horrible pallor overspread his face, making his features, with their fixed smile, like an inanimate mask. On his dead-white forehead stood beads of anguished sweat.

"What's the matter with you? Aren't you well?" asked his father anxiously.

"There's nothing the matter with me!" shrieked Zachary.

"But you look awful! You're ill. Go home and go to bed!"

"I'm not ill! I'm not ill! I feel better than I've ever felt!"

Yet before Zachary had concluded his words his knees gave way, as if someone had suddenly pulled a chair from under him, and like a helpless animal he rolled his head sideways on his shoulder.

"What's the matter with you?" cried his father. As swiftly as a youth he leapt behind Zachary, caught him in his arms, lifted him up, led him to the bed and set him down on it. He took off his son's soaking sheepskin and with an effort removed the rotting shoes that were literally sticking to his feet. When he saw the rags on Zachary's body he was horrified:

"What kind of a state is this you're in? What *have* you got on?"

He brought out a last bottle of Eau de Cologne which he was

keeping for an emergency, wetted a towel with it and began energetically to rub down Zachary's body, which was as slim as a boy's.

"Why didn't you tell me you hadn't a shirt to your back? I've still some linen left."

Zachary made no reply. He was dreadfully drowsy and shut his eyes.

His father hunted out a clean shirt, put it on his son and laid him down in the bed.

"Don't fall asleep, don't sleep—I'm going to make you some tea. You've caught a chill. A little feverish—that's all."

Zachary managed to open his eyes. He repeated:

"A little feverish—that's all," and immediately his eyes began to close again.

Old Mirkin lit the small petrol-cooker, set the tea-kettle on it and hastily returned to Zachary whose eyes had meanwhile shut.

"Don't sleep! That's bad for you at the moment. You must have a hot drink to make you sweat, and then you'll be all right tomorrow."

"Yes, yes—sweat and I'll be all right tomorrow"—once more Zachary's heavy eyes closed.

"My God, what's to be done? I'll have to get a doctor," cried the old man in despair.

"No, no—I'm not going to sleep—it'll soon be better," muttered Zachary thickly, trying with all his might to overcome his drowsiness.

His father attended to the tea-kettle. But when he advanced to the bed holding a glass of hot tea that spilt on his shaking hand he found his son lying rigid, with tightly-shut eyes. Zachary was not asleep. His labored breathing betrayed that. He seemed rather to be suffering from a nightmare.

His father hastily set the tea on the table, lifted the bed clothes, opened the shirt, and attentively inspected Zachary's body.

"Anything but that! My God, anything but that!" he muttered.

But he could see no signs of a red rash.

"God be thanked, it isn't typhus," he whispered joyfully. "He's probably just caught a little chill. In any case I'd better watch beside him for tonight."

Only now did old Mirkin see how emaciated Zachary's slim, boyish body had become. It was mere skin and bone. The ribs stuck out like girders, the stomach was an empty hollow, the legs were like sticks, the hands strengthless. The whole body lay as if it had been flogged and tortured; it was animal-like in its helplessness, begging for pity.

"My God, what have they done to him? Have they been torturing him? He hasn't an ounce of flesh on his body. Zachary, my poor boy, what has been happening to you?" The father's gray head bent over the naked body of his son.

With a father's tenderness he rubbed Zachary's chest again with the wetted towel, wrapped him carefully in the blanket and in his own fur coat, sat down on the edge of the bed and touched him gently to make him waken.

"Zachary, can you hear me?"

Zachary had heard all that his father said and wanted to answer him but could not. He managed to move his lips but no sound would issue from them; he tried to open his eyes but there seemed to be leaden weights on his eyelids. All that was happening round him was as if veiled in a mist, and his father's voice came as if from behind a thick curtain. The room receded from him, farther and farther, until everything grew so small as to be almost indiscernible.

The father held in his own the hot hand of his sick son and gazed tenderly into his face. Suddenly he felt that Zachary was slipping away from him: he was resisting, but had not the strength to hold on; with seven-league boots he was receding from his father into an unknown world which he saw in his dreams.

With all his force the old man tried to hold his son back.

"Zachary, dear Zachary, can you hear me? Tell me that you can hear my voice. Don't sleep, don't fall asleep! Tell me that you can hear me!"

"Yes, father; yes, I can hear you," Zachary wanted to say; but the words were swallowed up in the mist that was spreading round him.

All the love that old Mirkin had in his heart for this child of his was now unsealed and flowed freely. He had never known that the face of a son could awaken such compassion in any father.... Zachary became the sole interest of his life; he suddenly saw in him its whole aim and purpose. The pitifully white and rigid face of his boy moved him to tears. The heaving of the laboring chest under the blanket roused a profound compassion in him; Zachary's body became more and more the body of his child. The limbs grew soft again and rounded with childish grace, filled with love and tenderness. Old Mirkin reverted to the days of Ekaterinburg: "I have really lived no other life, all that has happened since has been a mistake! And I have deserted my own son and paid no attention to him; I have taken my own solitary way through the world and associated with strangers! Why, oh why?"

He had the feeling that he was already quite alone again, as if Zachary had receded to some place where he could neither be seen nor heard. And as if he were sitting by a corpse the old man communed with himself:

"This is my fault, and my fault only. For what is he but a boy? And I expected him to be a full-grown man, and cast him out and left him to his fate. Yes, it is my fault. In my old age I founded a new family, and took his bride from him to do it, old sinner that I am! And he has been walking the streets in broken shoes without a shirt to his back, like the most wretched vagabond! And on top of all that I've been pretending to be the injured party—old egoist that I am!"

Old Mirkin felt his eyes growing wet. He no longer tried to repress his tears and lamented aloud like the veriest beggar, regardless of the heavy drops that rolled down his old cheeks and on to his beard. He threw himself down beside the bed; sought with his shaking hands the hands of his son and laid his bearded cheek upon them.

"O Zachary, my dear and only son, don't die, don't die! I love you! I never really had a life apart from you; it was only you I loved! My dear, sick boy—forgive me, forgive me!"—his tears ran over Zachary's hands—"Do you hear me, my boy? Speak to me, give me a sign, give me only a nod of your head to show that you can hear me! Zachary, my dearest Zachary!"

The son heard all his father's words, but they came to him as from behind a curtain. He felt more deeply comforted than ever before in his life. He had become a child again, as a little child, and it was as if all the loving kindness of all the mothers in the world streamed into him from the living flesh and blood that caressed him with such watchful anxiety. And the hand now fondling him was all the dearer for being the unhoped-for hand of his father. He felt as if it were wiping away every sin into which life had plunged him—it was absolving him from all injustice and hardship; everything had a meaning and was justified of itself; the evil that had weighed on his spirit was banished and blotted out. This hand was supporting him, leading him to clear streams where wave after wave broke over him; soft airs were breathing round him, thrilling through him like rays of light, enfolding and lapping him as in cool, soothing linen; all the wrinkled garments of age and wickedness had slipped from him and he was lulled again in childhood, cleansed, absolved and blessed.

"Father, I'm so happy," he kept saying—but his lips remained motionless.

All night Zachary's face and whole body burned in fever. His eyes were still shut. Sweat ran in streams from his damp hair over his brows and cheeks. His flat, hard breast heaved more and more painfully. His father turned down the blanket and saw, with anguish, through the shirt how strenuously the ribs were laboring in that meager body.

Zachary babbled incomprehensible words in his sleep. He dreamt he was in a cemetery. He was scrambling with difficulty up a steep slope, and at every step there yawned an open grave in which lay corpses shaped like sausage-skins. They stretched sausage-like limbs towards him to drag him down among them. Hand in hand with Helene he climbed through the cemetery looking for a path among the open graves. They both wanted to reach the top of the hill as quickly as possible, for up there was the sanctuary, and only there would they be safe. But more and more graves kept opening and blocking their way. The whole world was shrouded in a smoldering haze. Blue and yellow tulips rose in their footsteps, glowing like the Temple candles on the Day of Atonement. At last the hill-top came in sight—and there, too, was the path leading up to it! But their feet had suddenly grown heavy, as if weighted with lead. They floundered among bog-holes and could not go on. Zachary was standing before an open grave. "Thus far and no farther," he knew all at once with dreadful clearness. But

Helene let go his hand and went on, leaving him rooted to the spot. Out of the grave a sausage-like hand came stretching to grab him.

"Stop! Wait for me! I'm coming! I'm coming!" shouted Zachary, struggling to jump out of the bed.

"What is it, Zachary? I'm here beside you!" Old Mirkin anxiously embraced the dripping body of his son, who tried with all his strength to fling him off and get up.

Not for a single moment did the old man quit his son's bedside that night. He rubbed him continuously with Eau de Cologne and laid wet towels on his burning brow. In his fever Zachary called on many people by name; then he quarreled with somebody and immediately begged for forgiveness and began to reproach himself.

"Oh, if you'll only get better, Zachary, only get better! I'll never desert you again, never! Can you hear me, Zachary? Tell me, can you hear me?" cried his father desperately.

"I'm not to blame! I'm not to blame! Tell me that you believe me—I'm not to blame!" Zachary kept imploring somebody.

His father thought that he had come to his senses again and was speaking to him. With tears in his eyes he caressed his son:

"My dear Zachary, my own boy! You meant it for the best."

"But we'll soon show them! On the Red Square we'll set up a Holy of Holies for humanity!"

Next morning old Mirkin went to the hotel porter, who was friendly to him, and bartered a white linen shirt for a Russian peasant blouse; then he donned Zachary's old sheepskin coat. His once well-tended beard was tangled now, his sunken eyes had purple rings round them, and he looked like a poor broken man. In this guise he made a pilgrimage from one hospital to the next, begging: "Comrades, a bed for a sick Soviet-man who took part in the 'October'!" . . .

Zachary, it was discovered, had pneumonia.

Old Mirkin neglected his work completely. The welfare of the firm meant nothing to him now. He had only one task in life: to nurse his sick child.

CHAPTER XXX

ON THE STEPPE

After the rain a pungent fragrance rose from the meadow-grass on the steppe. The sky was still ashen-gray and covered with dark clouds, yet these had lost their power, having discharged their rich burden, and like torn sacks were shredding away into trails of vapor. In the rifts gleamed the serene, authentic silvery-blue of heaven, while on the horizon a glowing eye of fire opened that soon mastered the whole sky.

The soil of the steppe, leavened by the rain, swelled and burgeoned. A thousand mouths seemed to have opened, drinking in the fertile showers. Cows were just going home, guarded by the herd-boy's whip, from the soaking pastures; they were dripping wet like the herd-boy himself, who had a sack slung over his shoulders. Yet they lowed contentedly, chewing the cud as they shambled on, their strong legs plodding unconcernedly through the mud of the village street and their damp red skins giving off an effluvium of milk and cow-dung. From behind the rain-blackened fences of the village barefooted peasant women emerged to drive their beasts into the byres.

A country cart, lined with fresh straw and drawn by two small gray Cossack horses, drew up in front of a hut, and a peasant issued from the low door bearing baskets and traveling cases, followed by two townsmen wrapped in hairy black Caucasian capes. They sat down in the cart and the peasant turned his horses towards the steppe.

These two passengers were Halperin the advocate and his son Misha.

Their journey had already lasted many weeks. From Petersburg they had taken the train to Moscow, then to Kursk, then from Kursk to Charkov. With the help of forged Soviet papers, which had cost them much money, they had pushed on from there through the steppe until they had at last reached the village of Michailovka near the railway junction of Ivanovka. During the whole of their wanderings in the steppe they had been in constant danger of falling into the Bolsheviks' hands. From Charkov onwards the steppe was alternately "Red" and "White"; the railway line was torn up in places, and marauding bands of soldiers and ruffians made the whole region unsafe. The political color of the country was always changing; one district would be governed by "Reds" and the next by "Whites," so that the travelers never knew which of their papers to produce, whether to appear as "Bolshevik delegates" or register under their own names. Michailovka, however, was unquestionably "White," and two railway lines ran from the neighboring town of Ivanovka, one to Zaryzin on the Volga and the other to Rostov in the south. That made Ivanovka the goal of all escaping officers, aristocrats and others pursued and plundered by the Bolsheviks; landed proprietors driven from their estates and officials dismissed from their posts, who were all flocking south to organize warfare against the Reds. But the largest stream of reinforcements consisted of disbanded soldiers whose profession had vanished with the abandonment of the Front and who were looking for fresh opportunities to loot and murder.

In Michailovka the advocate was clear at last of his Bolshevist pursuers and rested there three days: in the fertile steppe-village there was plenty of food, and Halperin could at last breathe freely after all the experiences of the past month and the panic which had ravaged him ever since the Bolshevik *coup*. He felt as if re-born. The interlude in the village had banished his depression; his old faith sprang up again and gave him the strength and courage to renew his hopes.

Halperin and Misha ought to have started early in the morning, but rain had hindered their departure until the first hours of the afternoon. They hoped, however, to make the railway station at Ivanovka by that evening, and it was with the cheerful conviction that they would soon be sitting in a train again that they set off on their way.

When they emerged from the village into the open plain the hot sun was already at work drying up the soft wet soil. The surface of the steppe here swelled into low hills, as if pregnant, and after the rain the small ears of corn, luxuriant in their soft green, were exhaling an odor that distinctly reminded one of fresh bread. The stalks of young wheat, oats and hay, beaten down by the rain, were straightening again under the comforting rays of the sun and quivering with dewy freshness. A light breeze sent waves rippling across the sensitive pale-green levels of the fields as over a lake.... At last the advocate had time to enjoy without preoccupation the fragrance and beauty of the steppe in springtime. With delight he cried to Misha:

"How lovely Russia is! It's worth while suffering anything for her sake!"

These last years had brought Misha to maturity. During the war he had shed his effeminate softness. He was still as handsome as ever —he still had the smooth, heavy eyelids, the finely-penciled brows, and the soulful almond-shaped eyes which he had inherited from his mother; but his face and his character had grown manly.

"In this part of the steppe they've sown the fields again and there aren't so many ruined farmhouses, either," he said to his father. "Russia hasn't gone entirely mad. It almost looks as if the Revolution hadn't touched this district."

"No, Russia hasn't gone entirely mad. I'm beginning to believe in the plain, honest man, and I'm losing faith in the intellectuals. The intelligentsia have perhaps been Russia's ruin. We took all our opinions from abroad; we never understood the Russian soul, and tried to force upon it attitudes that might do quite well for Germans but not for Russians. The intellectuals have betrayed and undermined Russia. But the remedy lies with the Russian peasant, with the simple man of the people. More than once the Russian peasants have proved the salvation of Russia—at the time of the Polish invasion, under Czar Michail, and at the overthrow of Napoleon in 1812—and they'll save Russia from the Bolsheviks, too. The peasants won't let themselves be enslaved. See how they're flocking in from all sides! Ivanovka is their rallying point, and they're pouring in from every direction. The Czechs are near Kazan already, marching on Nijni-Novgorod; General Krassnov has mobilized the Don Cossacks; the army from the Turkish front is coming nearer every day. No—everything's not lost yet. Sometimes I think there's no point in our running off to the Caucasus. The women can wait awhile. I should really be doing my bit, too, if not at the front then in some other capacity."

"But, father, it's not necessary in the least; you've done your bit already. Your first duty is to see to the women's safety."

"No sacrifice is too great for this wonderful country!"—the advocate waved a hand at the blossoming steppe. "The worst thing about us Jews is that we have always let ourselves be driven far too easily from our homes. Whenever we were beaten up in one country we simply picked up our traps and went off to another where we were tolerated. But Russia is our home-land; here we have survived pogroms and persecutions, here we have helped to rid the country of the Czar's yoke and will help to rid it of the Bolshevik oppression too. We must not abandon it, we must stand shoulder to shoulder with Russia's noblest sons and give our blood a second time for freedom! Then nobody will be able to cast it up to us later that we only came back when everything was over. We Jews must buy our freedom dearly—more dearly than others. No, no—don't let us stir a step from here! Let us share the fate of all our fellow-countrymen, be it good or bad! I'm very proud of you, my son, very proud because you've joined the army ..."

The advocate looked up and fell silent. One of Russia's "noblest sons" was galloping straight towards them. He wore a tall Cossack cap, a torn sheepskin coat, and carried a rifle whose barrel was pointing belligerently at the occupants of the cart:

"Halt! Who are you?" With a voluptuous eye the Cossack gloated over his victims.

The advocate blazed with indignation:

"How dare you attempt to stop us? We are officers traveling to join General Krassnov's army to fight the Bolsheviks. This is my son—he's an airman."

"We'll see about that. Show me your papers!" The Cossack bent down to search the advocate.

"These are our papers!" As quick as lightning Misha set a revolver against the Cossack's temple. "Do you want to find out what's in them, you dog?"

The Cossack displayed two rows of shining teeth in his pale face, blew out his nostrils and laughed:

"Excuse me—I thought you were Jews running away from the Bolsheviks. All kinds of queer people are sneaking across the steppe. I beg your pardon!" With that he spurred his horse and rode off.

After this adventure the patriotic discussion between father and son was never rightly resumed. They were both sunk too deeply in their own thoughts. The sleepy peasant on the box and the small horses in the harness instinctively turned away from the wide levels of the steppe and directed their course towards Ivanovka.

The railway junction of Ivanovka was a tiny township set down in the middle of the steppe, and consisted of a few newly-erected shingle-roofed houses and a large railway-station not yet quite completed. It was crammed with officers, soldiers, and other people more or less military in appearance who had obviously hustled on odds and ends of uniform to secure the privilege of robbing instead of being robbed.

In Ivanovka, Halperin had opportunity enough to examine the elements which were now offering to liberate Russia from the Bolshevik yoke. "Russia's noblest sons," as the advocate had called them, were a medley of highly suspicious and sinister figures. Their appearance, behavior and speech betrayed the real motives which had brought them here. There was a Babylonian chaos of nations, races and tribes, officers and soldiers of the most diverse regiments, partly in uniform, partly in civilian garb—in Cossack caps, Caucasian fur cloaks and peasant sheepskin bonnets; some in broken boots, some in sandals or even city shoes of patent leather. They all wore Caucasian cartridge-belts or officers' sashes. Their weapons were as variegated as their garments: Turkish rifles of doubtful efficiency, revolvers, scimitars, lances or simple knives. All in all, they looked much more like an assembly of bandits than an army. And every one of them was waiting in feverish impatience for trains that did not come. The floor of the dirty narrow waiting-room was covered with heaps of living bodies which exhaled the stuffy smell of meat gone stale. The human species seemed to have disintegrated into a chaos of irrelevant limbs and anatomical portions; heads lay on shoulders, legs and arms across bellies. It looked as if countless truncated limbs and bodies had been thrown promiscuously into a heap. Besides the soldiers and other dubious militarists, there were also refugees in no small number, who sat on their trunks and bundles like brooding hens, as if they feared that their wretched belongings, which they had saved from rape by the Bolsheviks, might be stolen from under them. Women and children were wedged among grown men, civilians among soldiers. One lay across the other, and each would have stolen his neighbor's last button without the slightest qualm.

Here and there quarrels and brawls arose among the various groups in the corners; men tore crusts from each other's mouths, sidled up to each other's wives and smacked each other's children. Some defended themselves by abusive language, others with blows, but most of them lay motionless like bales of cotton or pressed herrings and slept indifferently through everything.

Whenever a train came in the whole mass heaved asunder and scattered like a flock of birds at the sound of a shot. They all threw themselves at the train, regardless of its destination—anywhere to get out of this hell. They hurled their trunks, their bundles, their children, into the carriages, clung, at the risk of their lives, to the doors and the foot-boards, and fought their way into the crowded compartments. The soldiers standing inside the train thrust the intruders back, barred their way and refused to let them enter. For admittance to the train one bartered the whole of one's possessions. Women indicated by gestures that they were ready to pay for a place with their bodies.

Since Halperin and his son reached the station several trains had arrived and departed, but they had not succeeded in securing a place. Over and over again they were edged away, and so had to spend two days and two nights in the hell of Ivanovka.

During this period the advocate had more than enough time to become acquainted with the alleged saviors of Russia. Without shame or scruple they proclaimed their hopes, and like bandits decided beforehand on the division of the spoils. They promised each other the most glorious chances from the war. But the main theme of all these discussions were the Jews. As if they were the prizes that had been offered to all without exception who joined the White Army, the wealth, the wives and the daughters of the Jews were freely and openly apportioned by the soldiers among themselves:

"We'll get our share of the loot!"

"I've made up my mind: the first ten Jewesses I'll rape, but all the rest I'll do in to keep me from losing my appetite. . . ."

More than once the advocate was on the point of blazing up when he heard such comments. His son had difficulty in restraining him:

"Keep quiet! We have to get out of here as quickly as possible!" he whispered.

From a hidden pocket Misha brought out the officer's badge of the air squadron to which he had been attached at the front, and fastened it in his cap. (During the journey he had hidden it from the Bolsheviks.)

This distinction had its effect. The badge and Misha's revolver between them guarded the two men from annoyance and worse.

The advocate, newly escaped from the Bolshevist oppression, found himself still more exasperatingly and vilely oppressed by the riff-raff around him. Often he turned yellow and green with rage and darted fiery glances on all sides. He whispered angrily to his son:

"This is what's going to save Russia! What are they relying on? Bandit forces!"

Father and son nursed the same thought:

"On the other side there is at least some moral force."

But, of course, neither of them said so.

Finally, with the help of Misha's officer's badge, they succeeded in getting on a train bound for Novo-Tcherkask.

The carriage was packed with soldiers. At the end of the corridor flushed, disheveled heads and greedy hands were clustering round a woman who was prostituting herself for a place. Suppressed shrieks, laughter and grunts of lust could be heard. White as a sheet the advocate jumped from his seat, and Misha had to hold him back:

"For Heaven's sake, father, keep still! These people are just wild beasts."

"Misha, I'm afraid—Russia's done for! No, no—these aren't the men to save her."

"I know, father, I know."

Above their heads dirty bare feet dangled from the upper sleeping-berths. One of the groups squatting below conducted with the owners of the dangling legs a conversation which the advocate had to listen to, whether he would or no. A fellow with a red flap of skin in place of his right eye was relating to his neighbors:

"I was discharged from the hospital. That was in Charkov. I

hadn't had a woman for six months.... And so I got hold of the first likely wench I saw. At first she was willing enough, but when she spotted my eye she called off—gave her the creeps, she said. And that was the eye I lost for my country—but did she care? An enemy bullet had tickled me up there—but did she care? Not she. The devil take her, and her mother, too!"

"You'll soon get what you're hankering for, brother. The Jewesses'll make up to you for your six months' fast."

"Oh, they'll make it up to me all right! I'll cut their bubs off, I'll hack them off like apples!" shouted the one-eyed man, and his mouth was obviously watering.

"That's right. All the Jewesses are ours and we can do what we like with them. Krassnov has promised us that."

The advocate started with indignation:

"What . . . ?"

Misha restrained him:

"Quiet, father, for God's sake!"

"Misha, don't have anything to do with them—the other side have at least an ideal!"

Misha said nothing....

The train halted at a station. Two Cossacks with whips in their hands climbed in and asked in a loud voice:

"Are there any Jews among you, little brothers?"

"Jews?" repeated the soldiers, staring round at the civilian passengers. Their eyes rested on the pale advocate:

"Jews? To the devil with them!"

The advocate suddenly freed himself with all his strength from Misha's powerful arms and rising to his full height shrieked:

"I am a Jew! You dogs! I'm a Jew!"—with that he beat his fists upon his breast. "Here you have me, I'm a Jew."

Before Misha had time to snatch the revolver from his pocket the soldiers' hands were on his father, flinging him to the Cossacks.

Misha jumped forward to save him, but the soldiers held him, too, as in a vice:

"Give up that one, too!"

"No, he doesn't look like a Jew! This one's no Jew!"

"Father! Father!" screamed Misha.

The soldiers held him fast.

"This one'll be useful to us when the fighting comes. He's an airman."

At long last Misha tore himself free and rushed to the window. He saw his father on the platform, hatless and shoeless, his hair flying wild.

"Father!" Through the broken window the son stretched out his hands towards his father.

The train began to move. Laughing grimly the soldiers held Misha in an iron grip so that he could not stir a finger.

But from that moment Misha was haunted by the vision of his father standing on the platform with disheveled gray hair and bare feet, surrounded by Cossacks. And yet he did not feel the full horror of the situation, for what he saw seemed to him unreal: the figure of his father had such an uncanny resemblance to the Man whose image Misha had so often seen, the Christ led to his death by Roman soldiers. And that was how Misha saw his father for the rest of his life. . . .

At the next station he succeeded in getting out of the carriage. Breathless he ran back along the line in the dark for sixteen versts, and looked for his father.

He found no trace of him.

For several days Misha hunted through the neighborhood, but all his searching was in vain. All he could learn was that the Cossacks had dragged his father into the forest.

Misha turned back to the steppe and wandered about for many days and nights until he hit on a division of the Red Army marching against General Krassnov. He joined them. . . .

CHAPTER XXXI

TWO SWALLOWS

An illness is like a journey into a far country; it sifts all one's experience and removes it to a point so remote that it appears like a vision. . . .

During the weeks when Zachary was battling with death and overcoming it, he had really suffered death. And now he was lying new-born in the middle of a forest near Moscow on the veranda of what had been a country manor and was now a convalescent home for Soviet officials.

Not only Zachary, however, but his father, too, had died and been born again. These six weeks which old Mirkin had spent at the door of the hospital, waiting daily with red, swollen eyes to be admitted, exactly like all the other fathers, mothers, wives, children who were waiting to see their sick, had borne in upon him the fact that he had hitherto been walking the world in disguise, under a mask; that the dearest thing in life to him was his son, now sick to death and bathed in cold sweat, wrestling with an invisible foe as Jacob once wrestled with the angel. But precisely because he had to watch this struggle from a distance, his love and compassion for his son welled up more strongly than ever. Like hidden springs dammed up for years within him his feelings now broke out with overwhelming force and filled his heart. He cared less than nothing for the organization of his business, the future of Russia, his wife and young child: his whole interests were bounded by the ailing body of the young man lying there in fever, as if that body, apparently drained of blood, were the one thing that remained to him of his past life, like a dried flower; as if Zachary held his soul in his feeble hands like a flickering candle. The old man abandoned his business completely to Misha Molodyetz to do with it as he pleased. His wife and her child he left to their own fate. For here, under these blankets that rose and fell with the sick man's labored breathing, lay everything he now valued. And through his love for his son, which had awakened so suddenly within him, old Mirkin found himself again. As if a blessing had descended upon him he felt himself uplifted by his love, cleansed and restored to grace.

Next to Zachary's bed lay a sick boy, and every time that old Mirkin was allowed to visit his son a poor white-faced working man came to see the boy. This soon created a bond of friendship between Gabriel Mirkin and the boy's father. Day after day they met outside the hospital, and the illness of their sons brought them as near to each other as if they had been friends for years and had sprung from the same class. They consoled each other and gave each other encouragement. Their similar fate made old Mirkin feel as if the man and his boy were really in some way related to him. He himself used to sit by Zachary's bed in the shadow of his son's illness, holding his son's damp, weak hand in his own, and, a helpless spectator of that struggle with death going on behind the curtain of fevered dreaming. used to wipe the sweat from his son's brow in anxious silence. And the father of the boy in the next bed did exactly the same. On leaving the hospital the two fathers waited for each other, made mutual inquiries about their patients, shook each other by the hand and parted with a word of sympathy. Old Mirkin always looked for a long time after the poor workman miserably bowed down by his load of sorrow, and thought to himself: "There's an inexhaustible mine of wealth—paternal love—which is open to every man, even the poorest, and which no one can steal from us. But how long I have taken to discover it!" And it seemed to him as if his whole life had been spent in devious side-paths, and that only now, at the very end of his journey, had he caught sight of the true way which led to his happiness. In his heart a prayer took shape: "I thank Thee, O God, that Thou hast not let me die before granting me Thy grace, the grace of knowing that paternal love which is freely given to all, even the poorest. . . ."

And, in spite of Zachary's grave condition, old Mirkin always returned from the hospital comforted and enriched. It was worth while living merely to experience that feeling. . . .

Zachary's frail bark had survived the storm and had reached the shore. He was still lying stranded, listless and motionless, but he could see the blue sky over his head and could look once more at God's world.

The house stood on the verge of a thick and scented fir wood beside a broad, free stretch of moorland blossoming with heather. From the veranda one could see both the forest and the moor. Zachary on his *chaise-longue* commanded two continents, for he called one side "America" and the other "Europe." When he took a journey to America (that is to say, when with the nurse's help he turned round to face the forest), he saw tall fir-trees standing on tip-toe, peering with childlike timidity into the world, as if they had strayed there by mistake and did not know whither the road led. From time to time a cool wind blew through the matted fir-tops and plucked at the youthfully straight trunks, and together with the rustling of the wind there rose a wordless lament, as if deep within the forest living creatures were being tortured. . . . But whenever Zachary traveled to Europe he saw a lofty sky with silvery clouds arching over a warm, soft moor starred by thousands and thousands of pinkish blossoms. Here and there blood-red poppies glowed among the heather—poppies which are the merriest of the field-flowers, for they seem to dance from spot to spot, flaming up and dying down again. High over all the others, a single field-lily lifted up its proud pale crown, and isolated ears of corn, sown by the wind, raised their bristling heads and as bread-winners thought more of themselves than of the useless field-flowers. Swarms of wild bees hummed above the rich blossoms, and among them on razor-sharp wings darted twittering swallows catching insects as they flew. . . . Later on Zachary made a new discovery—he found a "No Man's Land" where one could hover, so to speak, in the air, a land to which no one journeyed but himself. One got to "No Man's Land" by lying flat on one's back and gazing into the sky. There one could discover worlds at will, could be everywhere and nowhere at once, for one was at home with oneself. . . .

Recently, however, as his strength increased, these worlds and countries had become more contiguous and almost indistinguishable. So Zachary spent most of his time now in watching closely the five dirty-gray ugly little swallows that peeped like nut-kernels from their nest under the balcony of the veranda, and squawked deafeningly all day long.

From his chair Zachary had a clear view of the nest which the parent swallows had plastered against the supporting beams close beside him. With amazement he observed that the mother swallow flew unweariedly from dawn to dusk between the nest and the moor, bringing insects, grubs or other scraps in her beak to drop into the gaping maws of her brood. As often as the mother-bird appeared a jubilant cheeping arose and five little beaks rose wavering out of the nest. Each fledgling struggled to reach the mother's beak before its brothers and to secure the tiny morsel of food for itself.

Zachary resolved to discover if the mother-bird followed any method in feeding her youngsters, or if the swallow-nest, too, was governed by the law of the wild and of the world—that the stronger survives in the struggle, that is, secures the most food. The books about swallows which Zachary had read provided no information on this subject.

Soon he arrived at the conclusion that the mother-bird did not feed her brood systematically. So here, too, as everywhere in Nature, the ruthless laws of selection held good. Zachary observed that the weakest and smallest fledgling of all, which was pushed to the outer verge of the nest, had much less chance of reaching its mother's beak than the others who had usurped the "privileged" places in the middle and could therefore more easily establish contact with the mother-bird. For that reason he bestowed his own name on the weakling, and called it "little Zachary."

He was further able to observe the consequences of this law of selection, later on, when the young swallows learned to fly.

The mother-bird was a harassed and overworked housewife. To begin with she had to bring grubs and insects from the moor all day long. As her family grew older she taught them cleanliness; she seized the youngsters one after the other by the tail and turned them round so that their hinderparts stuck out over the nest and so preserved it from defilement. And then school-time arrived for the young brood—the swallows had to learn to fly.

Helped by her otherwise lazy mate, the mother-bird constructed a port of call for her youngsters against the wall opposite, pressing into her service some telegraph wires; she brought up straws and laid them together and plastered them with swallow-lime. A day or two later a comfortable platform was ready, a kind of "flying-ground." Then the mother-bird, encouraging her youngsters in her penetrating screeching language, began to fly to and fro between the nest and the platform, meanwhile never ceasing her exhortations. This flying lesson lasted for half a day. The first to venture from the nest in imitation of their mother were in truth the three fledglings who had sat in the middle and had had most chance of gorging themselves. Next day the fourth one followed. Only "little Zachary" stayed where he was, crouched in the cup of the nest, feebly cheeping as if he were afraid to move from the spot.

That went on for two days. But when Zachary was wheeled out on to the veranda on the third day, on a bright, sunny morning, he was amazed to see the swallows' nest empty save for "little Zachary," who was stretching out his awkward gray beak and cheeping mournfully without cease.

Zachary the man sat up in his chair to get a closer view of Zachary the swallow. He felt as if the small bird were not only his brother-weakling but actually a part of himself, as if his own "ego" had been transferred to a living creature of another species.

"Little Zachary" unceasingly advertised his presence. His crying was a lament, a plea for someone to take pity on him. Yet nobody could help him.

At long last Zachary saw the mother-swallow flying back from the moor. She circled a few times over the nest, dropped a few insects into the beak of "little Zachary" and screamed at him in her swallow-talk, probably telling him: "I have no time now but I'll be back soon." Then she darted off.

She repeated this performance at intervals during the day. "Little Zachary" had to put in hours of torturing expectation and pitiful crying until she came back again. Breathless, harassed by her task of teaching the rest of her brood how to catch insects on the wing, the mother-bird fed her forlorn weakling, hastily threw him a friendly word or two, obviously adding some maternal consolation in the swallow language which, unfortunately, we do not understand, and made off again at full speed.

A few days later "little Zachary" had grown stronger. His mother now gave him some flying lessons, but with more patience and gentleness than she had shown to the four lustier fledglings. At the first attempt little Zachary's head drooped out of sheer weakness and his tiny naked wings trembled and quivered so anxiously that every moment he seemed to be about to fall and be dashed to death on the ground. But finally he mastered the art of flying and soon he was fluttering to the moor with his brothers and could no longer be distinguished from them.

"So there is something in Nature," Zachary communed with himself, "which stands above the law of selection and not only corrects that law, not only redresses inequality, but like an armored knight with a divine mission defends the right from the consequences of natural law in all its ruthlessness. And that something—it is divine motherhood, and its driving force is love. Am I therefore saved from under the wheels of the law of selection? Am I sheltered by the law of mother-love? Indeed I am; I claim a place under its wings by the rights of the weak!"

In the minds of children and sick people everything concrete and objective wavers on a loose foundation, the hardened shapes of things are shaken and broken, everything takes on a flowing shapelessness in which the impossible can be vaguely embodied and by the force of imagination even brought to life.

For the sick man illness is a kind of mother enfolding him, and he gets a certain pleasure from it. Illness has a comforting feminine quality about it, and the sick man is to some extent a child. Therefore, like a child parting from its mother, he finds it difficult to part from his illness. So long as he is ill, he dreams easily and is borne up on light pinions. . . .

The Hurvitz family in Warsaw, Rachel-Leah's kitchen, Zachary's betrothed Helene, whom he had deserted, were now so close to him that it seemed he had only to stretch out a hand and touch them, for nothing had occurred since he saw them last. And in his fantasy his return to them was an easy and natural proceeding, exactly like a child's return home after a day's wandering. With these thoughts came a strong desire to see them.

But the more he emerged from the lulling arms of his illness, the more he came back to life, the more swiftly did his dream illusions fade. Reality once more took on fixed and definite contours. And these unshakable entities said to him: "Thus far and no farther!" and his fancied "return home" suddenly bristled with difficulties. What had appeared to him so easy to carry out was now weighted with moral objections: "What right have I to do such a thing? For so many years I have neglected all of them. I never wrote to them. I took up with strangers, and my incestuous desires drove me into the arms of another woman. And now that I am naked and defenseless, now that my heart is empty and has lost its faith—am I now to lay my feeble head on the bosom of a woman who has not seen me for years? I should be a beggar at her door—they would look on me as a beggar, an outcast fallen by the way who drags the bare life that is left to him into a stranger's house!"

And so, as once he did not want to leave his mother's lap, Zachary was now reluctant to part from his illness, for it lulled him with visions of tender arms stretched out to him beyond the barriers of reality, and that was a solace. Convalescence merely tore him out of his shadowy dreams and left him shivering on a wide bleak plain, hemmed in on every side by the walls of hard fact.

In his despair he sought to find some way out. And it was Zachary the swallow that brought help and encouragement to Zachary the man:

"I'll do as 'little Zachary' did, guided by the same power. Since I am not strong enough to assert myself according to the law of selection, I'll claim the right of the weaker."

His weakness now appeared to him as the highest strength. . . .

Next Sunday when Gabriel Mirkin visited Zachary in the forest manor-house, he remarked an unexpected improvement in his son's condition. Zachary was in a cheerful mood and his large clear eyes were shining in his pallid, sunken face. With childish delight he began at once to tell his father what had been happening in the swallows' nest:

"Just think of it, Papa! Little Zachary has flown away, too!"—and he pointed to the empty nest.

His father, who for some reason or other was looking remarkably serious, replied:

"Well, we'll hope that the other little Zachary will soon spread his wings as well."

"Oh yes, I can feel them growing," smiled Zachary.

"It's more than time"—the old man could not suppress a sigh.

"What's the matter, Father? Has something bad happened?" asked Zachary anxiously.

"Oh no, nothing out of the usual—but it's time you were well again, my boy."

"What has been happening?" Zachary grew more insistent.

"Nothing at all"—with a smile old Mirkin banished whatever it was. "I believe, if I'm not mistaken, that you left a sweetheart somewhere abroad, didn't you? It's high time you got married to her, my son!"

"I've been thinking that too." Zachary smiled at his father and blushed like a boy.

Then they both fell silent.

By the end of the summer Zachary was so far recovered that he could leave the convalescent home. He returned to Moscow with his father.

CHAPTER XXXII

COMRADE MAREK'S KINGDOM

SEVEN wounds gaped in the body of Russia and from each wound blood was flowing.

Rage and fury were accumulating, and since they could not break out openly they seethed below the surface, as in the days of the Czar. Their first victim was the commissar for the city of Petersburg, Comrade Uritsky. Then the German Ambassador was murdered as a challenge to Germany. And even against "Him," against Lenin himself, a Jewish girl raised her hand.

In Great-Lubianka Street there stood a new building erected by some insurance society. It had deep cellars cased with steel, burglar-proof and fireproof, which had been designed to hold the society's documents. Whatever happened in the subterranean chambers remained secret as the grave, for the steel walls permitted no sound to escape. That made the building peculiarly fitted for the function it had now to fulfill. Comrade Marek took up his quarters in it. And soon the very name of Great Lubianka Street became as terrible to the "liberated" citizens of Russia as that of the destroying angel, and made their hearts beat quickly with deadly fear.

Comrade Marek awoke in the mornings from his heavy sleep on a camp-bed in one of the rooms in the topmost story. He slept in a different room every night, doubtless to avoid the "evil eye," and was a permanent prisoner in the building since he did not dare to leave it. On a second camp-bed in the same room slept Comrade Burshanov, who was now Marek's chief assistant. For safety's sake (they distrusted even their own comrades, since one could never know who might have slipped through the party net) they slept in couples, their revolvers beneath their blankets.

When Comrade Marek opened his eyes one morning the Lettish soldier, still in the notorious military coat that he never seemed to discard, was already sitting on the edge of his bed drinking "Kipiatok," or hot water, from a small pan which he had routed out somewhere, and chewing a piece of wholemeal bread.

Comrade Marek, as usual, had awakened with the frightful nervous headache which had been bothering him for some time. His bristling hair, sprinkled with gray, stood upright like wire on his pear-shaped skull. His high forehead glistened, and his small bony nose stuck out sharply from his long and haggard face. Red patches always burned on his sunken cheeks, telling of the deadly disease he had contracted in Siberia. The small goatee on the very point of his chin was all disordered and stuck up almost vertically, so that it looked as if it had been glued on.

"How late is it?" he asked hastily of his Lettish comrade.

"Time," answered the latter curtly, without pausing in his breakfast.

Comrade Marek stretched his lean hairy legs out beneath the military blanket and then hastily, as he did everything, got into his trousers. Whenever one hand was free he combed and smoothed his beard with his fingers, and during all these operations he was assembling his thoughts and pouring out words in a rapid flood:

"Overslept, frightful headache. Today the cells must be emptied. No time for ceremony. The building's cram-full, and yet we've got nothing out of the wretches. Counter-revolutionaries thick as fleas everywhere; there isn't room for all of them to hide."

The Lettish soldier answered as usual by a silent nod and went on with his breakfast.

Comrade Marek soon forgot the terrible *migraine* that was like a searing iron band around his head. He plunged with fiery zeal into every task he undertook, with all his nerves, so to speak, and when he began on a job he could think and speak of nothing else. His temperament flared up like tinder but did not die down again so quickly. His brain worked even while he was eating and satisfying the most elementary physical needs—yes, even while he was sleeping. Like a wild animal in a net he was imprisoned within his own zeal and could not free himself for even a moment.

Hastily, as if the house were on fire, he flung on his clothes, speaking all the time:

"We have more important things to do than this kind of beastly work—we have to organize the Socialist State. But how can we build while these others are getting in our way? They're gnawing and riddling everything like mice. How can we build, with them destroying everything, attacking us with fire from an invisible front, trying to ring us round? How can we do our work when we don't know what instruments are in our hands, what kind of thoughts the man is thinking who stands before us? High time we made a good clearance here! We've left it too long, the ground's thickly cumbered already. Only yesterday I said to Comrade Ilyitch: 'It's not revenge we're taking; the Revolution's only doing what is absolutely needful.' "

He poured a jug of cold water over his head and washed himself in an iron basin in a corner of the room which stank like a latrine, dried his face and hands with a dirty towel and again smoothed his beard with his fingers:

"Granted that now and then we make a mistake; what does that matter? For the sake of certainty, for the sake of securing the ground beneath our feet, twenty-five per cent of error, yes, even fifty per cent, isn't too much to carry. The pettiest war run by the bourgeoisie costs the proletariat hundreds of thousands, millions of lives; and tens of thousands of workers lay down their lives daily for the sake of imperialistic exploiters. Like sheep they are driven to the slaughter, and nobody says a word about it because the victims are merely poor, tormented proletarians. Yet, because our victims belong to the privileged classes, a great cry is raised that we must be careful and make no mistakes. But the Revolution's in the middle of a bloody struggle. The capitalism of the world, in alliance with its wage-slaves and its volunteer helpers, with Mensheviks and Social Revolutionaries of every stamp, has declared war to the knife on the proletariat. And it isn't an open war, it's a secret, a treacherous war. They set traps for us at every step. Yes, it's *they* who have made the bloodiest war on the proletariat, and it's *we* who have become moral and sensitive weaklings! We have to fight the petty bourgeois mentality that still prevails in our own ranks. War is war. And we must drown our enemies in their own blood till they've had enough of it!"

The sinister Lettish soldier silently poured out a cup of tea for his comrade and pushed him a loaf of black bread:

"Eat, comrade!"

Absorbed in thought, Comrade Marek absent-mindedly broke off a piece, stuck it in his mouth and took a sip from the cup. Even while doing that he had something to say; since his mouth was full, however, the sounds he uttered were incomprehensible. But as soon as he had swallowed the first mouthful he pushed the cup away:

"Well, comrade, let's go down now. It's time to begin."

"Won't you eat something? It's a long time till noon and today there's a lot to do," the Lett reminded him.

"I'm not hungry—I feel a little sick. Come along, comrade!"

He put on his commissar's cap, took his loaded automatic in his hand, and with his beard sticking out like a pointer before him left the room. The Lettish soldier followed him, still chewing a piece of bread; his face was more melancholy than ever; his long coat trailed on the ground so that his footsteps were muffled.

On the stairs and in the passages they met prisoners being escorted by soldiers to the various rooms of the examining commissars. All shrank to one side, making way, with pale, submissive faces, for Comrade Marek and his companion. Both men strode through the building, their revolvers in their hands, and Comrade Marek vanished into his office, where the most important prisoners were brought for interrogation.

The first on the list was a tall aristocrat with a narrow, horse-like face. A reddish growth of stubble, the result of his imprisonment, covered his long upper lip, and his hanging chin trembled. With naive blue eyes he gazed in horror at the fidgety man with the bristling hair who could not, apparently, sit calmly in his chair behind the table, but had to spring up every few minutes and scurry about. The prisoner cast his bewildered gaze round the room and his eyes fell on the sinister deadly solemn countenance of the Lettish soldier, who sat holding a thick red pencil poised above a sheet of paper, apparently waiting for some order to be given.

"Recruiting officers for the White Army among the aristocracy—eh? Hiding weapons—eh? Pining for the Czar to come back—eh? No intention of putting up with the Soviet Government—eh?" Comrade Marek's words came tumbling out pell-mell, and he fingered at his beard all the time, while his long, lean, stooping body rocked backwards and forwards behind the table.

The nobleman, feeling somewhat like a cosseted lap-dog let loose for the first time in its life and finding itself among a pack of wolves, was so agitated that he could not bring out a single word. Big drops of sweat ran from his high forehead down his nose and cheeks. His eyes were fixed and staring in his long face like those of an animal in deadly fear. His hanging mouth fell farther open, showing two rows of excellent horse-teeth. He made an effort to speak, but could not utter a sound. Two tears suddenly trickled instead from his eyes.

"A cousin of the Czar's, are you? Who are your accomplices—why are you concealing their names? Why do you refuse to name them—eh? We don't want to be cruel; it's you who force our hands. Give me the names of your accomplices!"

The aristocrat began to stammer. Sheer terror blinded him, so that there was a white mist before his eyes. Sheer terror paralyzed his voice; and for all that his tongue went on moving not one word was comprehensible.

"You've named them already, you say—eh? Already confessed

. . ."—Comrade Marek peered at the document—"And no other names to be got out of him, Comrade Ivanov?"

Comrade Ivanov, a thick-set little man with ferrety eyes who had conducted the previous examination of the prisoner, jumped up from behind his desk, came hastily up to Marek and whispered something in his ear.

"He says you have confessed all the names. All of them—good, very good. You are free, citizen. He can go, comrade."

The aristocrat stood as if petrified. His eyes grew bigger, his mouth opened wider. His tall body remained helplessly where it was.

"You are free, citizen, you may go!" shouted Comrade Marek a second time.

But the paralyzed aristocrat still stood as if rooted to the spot, without making a single movement.

"You are free." Comrade Ivanov turned him round and pointed to the door. Still the man did not move. Only his eyes flashed and his face worked. He threw a confused glance at Marek as if to convince himself that he had heard aright, and then as if he were walking on stilts stalked stiffly to the door.

But before he reached it he heard a rattling noise. A short, loud crack—and a bullet from the automatic lodged in his back. He had only time to look round in surprise—as if someone had called to him, then he sat down suddenly on the floor and slowly keeled over. Two soldiers dragged him out of the room by the legs. . . .

The next to be led in was a Jewish girl, a brunette with short-cropped hair and a long, pale, hooked nose. The red and blue weals across her face and the crippled stoop of her body showed that the prisoner had been recently knocked about. Her legs supported her with difficulty. But as soon as she caught sight of Comrade Marek an obstinate light flashed in her eyes; she struggled to fight down her physical weakness and stood up, proud and challenging, a cool, contemptuous smile on her strained lips, before the man she hated.

Minutes of silence followed. Comrade Marek and the girl measured each other with their eyes like two fighting cocks. Marek was as white-faced as his victim. Foam gathered at the corners of his mouth, and it was some time before he could utter a word:

"Well, Terrorist—was there nothing better you could find to do?" he shrieked, springing from his chair and rushing about the room. "I suppose you think you're still living in the days of the Czar, when people went in for such romantic nonsense! Give us the names of your accomplices! We'll make you speak, we have means of our own for that!"

"I know that," answered the girl, looking Comrade Marek straight in the eyes.

At this brief answer Comrade Marek seemed to collapse, not so much because of the words themselves as of the tone and the manner in which they were hurled at him.

"And why do you force us to it? Do you think it's pleasant for us to dirty our hands with work of this kind? You've made common cause with the enemies of the Revolution, turned yourselves into lackeys of the capitalists, sold and betrayed the proletariat! Why? I ask you, why?"

The girl answered not a syllable. Not only her eyes, but even the angry weals on her face now seemed to burn with hatred for Comrade Marek.

"You refuse to name your accomplices?"

The girl remained obstinately silent.

"I repeat—we have means of our own for making you speak out."

"I know that," returned the girl once more.

Comrade Marek exchanged a look with Ivanov, who had turned round from his seat by the window to regard his chief inquiringly.

Comrade Marek's beard nodded in assent.

Ivanov waved an arm. The soldiers led the girl away.

The sinister Comrade Burshanov looked searchingly at Marek who had returned to his chair.

"Yes, yes—we haven't any time for ceremony."

Comrade Burshanov's red pencil energetically crossed out something on the paper lying in front of him.

The air in the room could have been cut with a knife and it was stifling hot. Comrade Marek's *migraine* was afflicting him with violent stabs of pain. The red patches on his yellow cheeks were brighter than ever. Nervously he fingered his beard and screeched:

"Open a ventilator, it's stifling in here!"

Someone carried out the order. A fresh waft of air came wandering into the room. . . .

The third prisoner on the list was Gabriel Mirkin.

"Why are you organizing sabotage against us? Why are you trying to starve out the proletariat? Why are you in alliance with our enemies? Why? Why?" lamented Comrade Marek in a voice that sounded tearful because he was suffering from an especially acute spasm of headache. Pale but firm, old Mirkin stood erect before him. The points of his gray beard seemed to be chiseled in stone. His eyes were greenish and protruded over the bags beneath them so that they looked as if at any minute they might fall out. Calmly he waited until Comrade Marek had finished speaking, and then answered in a steady voice, emphasizing his denial by a shake of the head:

"That is not true—I'm organizing no sabotage. I have done my duty by the Soviet Government."

Comrade Marek was amazed by this answer. The assured tone and quiet bearing of the man both astounded and convinced him; he raised his childlike eyes and looked at old Mirkin inquiringly:

"If that is so, then somebody else in your organization is a traitor. The whole railway system is in a state of collapse; there's a shortage of railway sleepers and of fire-wood for the locomotives—and that at a time of crisis like this! If you're not to blame for it then somebody else must be."

"I'm not so sure of that. A good deal of the blame must be assigned to the general situation. The sources of supply have been cut off and the depots are empty. My proposal to fell trees at once in the forests round Moscow and elsewhere was turned down. They told me there was a shortage of labor for wood-cutting. My best assistants have been taken from me and inexperienced and irresponsible people drafted in their stead. As for myself, I have been treated with continuous suspicion. So how could I mend matters?"

Old Mirkin's calm voice made Comrade Marek nervous; involuntarily he felt it as a personal insult that the fellow should "argue" with him. Yet at the same time the assured bearing of the old man made an impression on him. He broke in sullenly:

"If you're not guilty then somebody else must be—I tell you that again! Things can't go on like this!"—he jumped up and began to stride to and fro—"We must convince ourselves that you are really innocent, and set a trap to find the actual traitors!"—he repeated these words to himself once or twice and then rushed back to the table, sat down again, took the report of Mirkin's interrogation from Burshanov and turned over the pages:

"Your business was founded during the old régime. How did a Jew like you manage to establish such a confidential footing in Court circles?" he asked, fixing the old man with his eye.

It was only then that Mirkin noticed that the man behind the desk had no eyebrows, that his eyes were naked and unshaded. This alarmed him at the moment much more than the ordeal in front of him.

"I took some trouble to get on a confidential footing," he answered calmly.

"That is to say—you were on the best of terms with the officials, of course with the help of bribes? I suppose you drank with them, and worse—eh?"

"It wasn't possible to do things in Russia in any other way. These men had the power, and any one who wanted to get something done had to be on good terms with the governing classes."

Comrade Marek said nothing. He looked away to avoid meeting the old man's eyes. Thoughtfully he fingered his beard:

"Tell me, then—how did it happen that you didn't clear out when your friends did—Goldstein the old magnate, your own family, Halperin the advocate? What made you stay here and work for us?"

"I wanted to help in building up Russia."

"Which Russia?" burst out Comrade Marek. "Our Russia, the Russia of the Soviets, the Russia of the October Revolution, the Russia of the proletariat—or the Russia of the Czar's clique with whom you were on such good terms?"

"Which Russia? It's all one to me. I only know *one* Russia—our fatherland—and I want to serve anybody who will build it up."

"But it's not all one to us! Now I'll tell you, Citizen Mirkin, why you stayed behind! Because you were expecting us to collapse! You didn't want to leave your business in the lurch, and you kept the reins in your own hands because you were waiting for us to come a cropper. Tell me, citizen—isn't that true?" Comrade Marek's naked eyes looked deep into Mirkin's.

"That is not true," countered the old man, flushing.

"We'll have to make sure of that! Well—you plead not guilty?"

"I am not guilty of any offense against the Soviet Government so far as I know," returned Mirkin with dignity.

"Take the citizen away, Comrades. The interrogation is finished for the present."

When old Mirkin had left the room the Lettish soldier with his gloomy air looked inquiringly at Comrade Marek.

"The devil only knows whether the old man's guilty or not! But anyhow he must be eliminated, so that we can know for certain who the real traitors are."

Comrade Burshanov made a mark with his red pencil over the dossier of Mirkin.

Old Mirkin had been seized at night in his hotel and Zachary was up at dawn next morning trying to gain access to the man with the Mongolian eyes in the Kremlin. But all his efforts were unavailing. The comrades of his acquaintance to whom he applied for assistance in getting a pass roundly refused to do anything as soon as they heard that it was his father's arrest he was bothering about. They were amazed that any man could dare to think of troubling the Kremlin about the fate of a private individual, especially at a time when civil war was breaking out on all fronts and the Revolution was menaced by enemies at home and abroad.

To avoid losing time—he knew well enough that speedy action was necessary—Zachary decided to appeal personally to Comrade Marek. He had but little hope of such an appeal, but every hour that passed increased the danger. Zachary had an idea that the best course would be to appeal to Marek's human feelings.

With great difficulty he succeeded in getting a pass to the house in Great Lubianka Street. For old acquaintance' sake Comrade Marek admitted him, and received him, like everybody else, with a loaded revolver in his hand.

"I pledge my head for it, he is innocent! Save an innocent man!" pleaded Zachary, stretching out his hands.

"Innocent or guilty—the Revolution must be secured. We must have certainty. If he is not guilty, then others must be. So we must first eliminate him to find out who is actually organizing sabotage."

Pale with illness and anxiety Zachary imploringly seized Marek by the hand: "How can you do such a thing—simply to get information? There's a man's life at stake! You're playing with a human life!"

"What does one man matter compared with the Revolution? And the fact that thousands of our brothers are falling daily at the front, that because of the sabotage our children are dying of hunger, that the best men in the Soviets are being sent to certain death—that doesn't worry you at all? But you plead for the life of a bourgeois who was well in with the old régime and only stayed at his post because he was waiting for our downfall!"

"But he's my father, he's all I have!"

"I'm very sorry that he's your father. But in any case a revolutionary cuts his father off when his father is a hardened bourgeois and an old friend of the Czar's tyrants."

"Comrade Marek—he saved my life! Do you know what he did for me? He picked me out of the gutter. I have nothing in this life but him. I implore you, give him back to me!" Zachary fell on his knees.

"I'm ashamed for you, that I have to see you driveling like this. And you're supposed to be a revolutionary, a man who took an active part in the 'October,' who worked for us even before the Revolution! A genuine revolutionary would hand over a father like that of his own accord, or shoot him down with his own revolver, but he wouldn't come begging for his life like you!"

"I'm not a revolutionary, I'm a sick and feeble man. I'm . . ." Zachary broke off, for his voice was choked with tears.

"That's easy to see, Comrade Mirkin."

Zachary wavered and nearly fell; his legs were doubling up beneath him; he tried again to seize Marek's hands:

"Comrade Marek, I've risked my life many a time for the Revolution. In war-time—you know it well enough—and in October on the roof of the theater—*you* know that, Comrade Burshanov, better than anybody!" he turned to the melancholy Lett—"I've never so much as mentioned it. But in return for all that I beg you—let my father go! Don't shoot him! Deport him, if you like—I'll take him away myself! If you don't it'll be the same as if I had killed him with my own hands. I'll always have his death on my conscience."

"All that you say only confirms me in my belief that we're doing the right thing. Even if your father is not guilty of sabotage he's guilty of undermining the Revolution. He has infected you with his bourgeois mentality, since you're capable of abandoning your whole revolutionary career for the sake of a father who is a bourgeois. Tell me, by the way, Comrade Mirkin, why haven't you gone to the front like all the others, at this moment when the Revolution has most need of you?"

"I—I couldn't," stammered Mirkin.

"I'll tell you why: your father wouldn't let you. His bourgeois mentality has infected you already. We know that you're in constant communication with him."

"That isn't true! That isn't true!" Zachary began to scream as if he had suddenly seen the pit he had himself dug for his father.

"Your intervention on your father's behalf merely convinces us how harmful his influence over you has been. Comrade Burshanov, we have now an excellent proof of Citizen Mirkin's guilt."

"Citizen Mirkin, this interview is at an end. Next!"

Zachary was pushed out through the room.

When Comrade Marek entered his room after his day's hard work he fell exhausted on his camp-bed. The hectic patches on his cheeks glowed like red roses, and his cheekbones and temples were painfully prominent. He covered his eyes with his hand and his goatee trembled on the point of his chin. In his mind he saw the Polish village where he was born: it was autumn. Barefooted village children with osier switches were driving the ducks and geese to the brook.

Comrade Marek felt sentimental and turned spontaneously to Comrade Burshanov who was sitting, still in his cloak, on the second bed, staring thoughtfully into vacancy with gloomy eyes.

"Comrade Burshanov, are you fond of children?"

The Lettish soldier stared in dumb astonishment.

"I'm very fond of children. When we've polished off all this dirty work I'm going to do something for our homeless children. . . ."

At the onset of night armed soldiers led by Comrade Burshanov escorted all those who had been sentenced during the day into the deepest cellar of the building. They reached first a roomy antechamber which had no window-gratings and so was artificially ventilated. There were long wooden benches against the walls. The delinquents were admitted in groups. The group in which old Mirkin found himself consisted of nobles, revolutionaries and tradesmen.

"Citizens, take off your clothes!" commanded Comrade Burshanov in a melancholy voice.

"Why?—What for?" screamed hysterical voices.

"What difference does it make to you whether you have clothes on or not? They'll only be riddled with bullets, and they might be of use to somebody else," said the Lett, still in a melancholy tone.

The condemned prisoners sat as if petrified.

Old Mirkin was the first to take off his boots. . . .

"But we can't do that! It's impossible! We'll catch cold on this stone floor!" cried an aristocrat anxiously.

Nobody answered him.

Two Red Guards collected the clothes and footwear and entered the various articles in a book. The condemned men went into the steel vault—some in night-shirts, others mother-naked.

On leaving Comrade Marek's room Zachary reeled mechanically to the Kremlin bridge. He knew well enough that he could not get in without a pass, but he was resolved to make the attempt. Of course the Red Guard on duty thrust him back with his bayonet. So he wandered to and fro for hours between Lubianka Street and the Kremlin bridge.

Late in the evening he observed a large transport lorry drawing up in front of the building in Lubianka Street and coming to a stop exactly outside the cellar-gratings.

Suddenly the lorry's engine began to race, making a continuous clatter that overwhelmed all other noises. And Zachary knew that at that moment his father was being shot in a cellar.

He did not even put his hands over his ears, and wondered to himself why the dreadful deed seemed to make so little impression upon him. But his hands clung to the cold wall over which he leaned, and it was as if he were embracing the cold body of his father.

A few days later Zachary found a package sewed up inside his coat. It contained a considerable sum in securities and a letter from his father:

"I am expecting arrest daily and am ready for it. In any case, I have not much longer to live, and death, after all, is the best asylum for old age. Nobody is to blame for it; things had to happen like this. Every man is a victim of his own times and circumstances. Try to get out of the country as quickly as possible. Do your best to forget, and force yourself to make a new start. These papers are your share of your mother's dowry. I have made other provision for the rest of my family. Begin a new life; you have the whole of life in front of you. I thank God that He has granted me the blessing of being reconciled to you. I have always loved you; all the rest was a mistake."

These words of counsel from his father gave Zachary courage. He set out on his way.

CHAPTER XXXIII

PETERSBURG LADIES

Olga Michailovna and Nina Mirkin were living in the handsome Moorish villa which they rented every year from a rich Tartar in a fashionable summer resort in the Caucasus. Some time previously old Mirkin had bought a piece of ground on which to put up a villa of his own, but the building had never been begun, partly because of the unsettled times and partly because Nina could never make up her mind which style of summer residence to have. As usual, the ladies had the pleasure of "The Englishman's" society, for Naum Grigorovitch Rosamin had accompanied Olga Michailovna on her summer holiday for the last twenty years to any country and any place that she saw fit to select. Since Nina had "played her mother such a trick" as to make her a grandmother (that was the victim's own phrase, although she should have been accustomed by now to her daughter's tricks) Olga Michailovna had become "resigned," and described herself to all and sundry as "an old woman who has nothing more to expect from life." And, being such an elderly lady, she could not be looked at askance for indulging in an innocent and rather "romantic" flirtation which harmed nobody, so she now openly spent all her time in the company of "The Englishman," who attended her like a shadow. He helped her to collect oriental plants for her garden, which had recently become her great hobby. Nina did not interfere; she was not particularly interested in either her mother or "The Englishman" and saw but little of them; for, against the expectations and prophecies of all the friends of the family, Nina had turned out to be a loyal wife and a tender, assiduous mother. She devoted herself entirely to her infant son and even insisted on nursing him herself, much to the annoyance of her mother, who pointed out to her in horror that she would ruin her figure. Nina had not even a smile to spare for the gallantries of the young gentlemen from her own Petersburg circle who were holidaying in the elegant resort and hoped for a chance of consoling a young wife "deserted by her old husband." Her mother announced that she simply did not understand how Nina could have settled down so early to be "a matron."

Here, too, as all over the rest of Russia, the Bolshevik thundercloud was hardly noticed at first. Bolshevism was regarded as another of those unpleasant "episodes" with which the new Russia was constantly surprising its citizens, and people were merely waiting for its overthrow before hastening back as quickly as possible to Petersburg. Meanwhile life continued in the grand manner. The banks went on cheerfully paying out money, and there were few signs of revolution in the Caucasus. The servants, indeed, were a little difficult and put on surprising airs; but people were growing accustomed to that kind of thing and made allowance for it. At most Olga Michailovna wondered privately whether it had been really worth while to make a Revolution at all (as if she had been the sole responsible instigator) and whether it mightn't have been better to stick to the old way of living. She did not, of course, air these opinions in public, for they would not have conformed to the tone that prevailed in all fashionable circles, and especially in her own circle, that of the rich Jews and Russian liberals.

Soon, however, the effects of the Bolshevik *coup* began to be felt even in that quiet, remote resort. The banks suspended payment, suspicious characters prowled about the streets, there were riots in the poor quarter of the town, and disquieting rumors flew from mouth to mouth. The little summer resort proclaimed its adherence to the new order, and the elegant world, finding things too hot for it, lost its last hopes.

But that stage was now long past.

It took the ladies a full year to get from the Caucasus to Paris, and more than once their lives and honor were in jeopardy. Often by a sheer miracle, and many a time by Nina's cleverness, the two women extricated themselves from one danger after another, employing a thousand feints and ruses, and managed finally to board a French ship bound from Batum to Constantinople. The jewels they had with them paid for the journey. As it was, they had to deny their Jewish origin and exploit their acquaintance with members of the Black Hundred to escape death.

They arrived in Paris immediately after the conclusion of the Treaty of Versailles. The humming life of the great world surrounded them. At every step they encountered refugees of their acquaintance. The whole of Petersburg, the whole of Moscow, the whole of Russia was in exile. Everybody was optimistic, waiting for a happy ending to the civil war which Russia's "noblest sons" were now waging under the "White" Generals with the help of the Entente—heroes fighting to free their country from the Bolshevik yoke.

In Paris the two ladies were informed of their bereavement. Mirkin and Halperin were dead, Misha in the Red Army.

Olga Michailovna went into elegant mourning. From somewhere or other she hunted up a mysterious "badge" which she proudly wore on her breast. She also joined a fairly dubious association of emigrés. And although it was really the Whites who had murdered her husband, and Misha was fighting in the Bolshevik ranks, Olga Michailovna refused to admit these facts; she attributed all her troubles to the Reds, formed close connections with the exiles in sympathy with the Black Hundred, and even took an active part in a secret society of that affiliation. She wore her elegant black mourning with the air of a woman who had sacrificed "everything" on the altar of her country.

Meanwhile the ladies' sorrow for their husbands did not prevent them from living in style. The Bolshevik régime, of course, was expected to collapse at any moment. Besides, they had received the small subsidy which old Mirkin had entrusted for them to Goldstein the oil magnate. In vain that prudent business man hinted discreetly that the hopes which the ladies were setting on the "White" generals were extremely questionable; in vain he expended himself in tactful circumlocutions about the "dark future." His suggestion that they should begin at once to make some arrangements for securing a livelihood was regarded by the ladies as a piece of shameless impertinence, to which they were exposed only because the cruelty of fate had stranded them alone and helpless in Paris. Was not everybody waiting with serene assurance for the inevitable moment when the "heroes," with the help of the Entente, would put an end to the domination of the "robbers" and restore the splendor of Russia? And then, of course, the two ladies would recover the gigantic fortunes which their husbands had bequeathed to them.

So they persisted in living in first-class hotels, as they had always been accustomed to do; they were open-handed to needy exiles and associated with the Russian aristocracy, now somewhat of a drain on their friends' purses—but only, of course, out of sheer humanity, since "in the hour of need we are all one family." And that went on until their last franc was spent.

Only then did Nina begin to look round for some means of earning a living.

There are people who never come to their senses and discover themselves until they have had a crack over the head. Not until her credit was exhausted and her last jewel sold, not until Goldstein the oil magnate, who had moved meanwhile to London, ceased answering her requests for a loan, did Nina transfer herself and her infant to a cheap *pension* on the left bank of the Seine. There she encountered a few elderly ladies of title whom she had known in Petersburg. Acting on their advice, she opened a small workshop for the production of fine lingerie, which she sold to the large shops. Nina's good taste and the organizing ability which to her own surprise she discovered in herself proved excellent assets: she soon enlarged her business with Goldstein's help, for he showed himself ready enough to advance money on a business proposition, and engaged as workers a number of her Petersburg acquaintances. Today Nina owns a very presentable establishment on the right bank. Thanks to her energy, her refined and exquisite taste and her clear head, she has built up a good business and is the employer and benefactor of countless Russian aristocrats. Some years ago she married her managing director and partner, a former Russian banker, and has two children besides her son by Mirkin; she is bringing them all up to be French.

Olga Michailovna is very unhappy because her daughter has "sunk so low," and even today cannot forgive Nina her "plebeian adaptability." "That's the new generation for you," she adds contemptuously, "the post-war generation." Her disapproval, however, does not prevent her from sending begging letters to the "establishment" demanding money.

Olga Michailovna cannot find her bearings in the new age. Like a child she is incapable of understanding that everything has been altered, and cannot adjust herself to her changed circumstances. Money runs through her fingers. And that is a continual cause of friction between the mother and the daughter. Olga Michailovna has had to betake herself to Nice to escape the horrors of the post-war attitude. Nina sends her a sum of money every month—enough to live on. But of course it is all spent in the first few days, and Olga Michailovna bombards her daughter with furious letters in which she threatens eventually "to find some other way of escape from the wretched existence of a Mater dolorosa," since God is so cruel as to linger out her natural end. At first these letters genuinely alarmed Nina; but their frequent recurrence has diminished their effect, and now Nina contents herself with sending punctually on the first of each month a modest remittance. The begging letters she leaves unanswered.

Today Olga Michailovna is living quite alone in Nice, lost in memories of the romantic past. In the mornings she makes her appearance on the Promenade des Anglais, clad in elegant black (generally a very shabby black lace dress) as a sign of her grief for her husband and her country, and she still has a coquettish way of carrying her black lace parasol in a delicately gloved hand. She lays out her last francs on an *aperitif* in the *Pavillon bleu,* watching with some contempt and not a little envy the new generation that parades itself in "shameless" bathing costumes and dances to the sound of the gramophone those "indecent" modern dances.

On her way home she enters one of the Russian delicatessen shops in the Rue de la France to buy something for her lunch, which she prepares with her own hands on a small spirit stove in her more than modest lodging. . . .

One day as she was returning from her morning promenade by way of the Rue de la France, Olga Michailovna remarked a newly opened delicatessen shop which she had not seen before. Her credit in most of the other shops being exhausted, she went in to strike up an acquaintance with the owner and open a new account. The face behind the counter seemed familiar, but it was some time before she remembered where she had seen that elegant bald brow and those cunning blue eyes. It was Akimov, the once all-powerful Akimov, now busily occupied with a Russian counting-board, showing a child what the sum total of its purchases amounted to, and his reckoning on this occasion was much more conscientious than his former operations as President of the Chamber for the Russian State Forests. At first Olga Michailovna's conversations with him contained frequent references to the old days in Petersburg, but later on the only topics that came up for discussion were sour gherkins, herrings and unpaid debts. . . .

CHAPTER XXXIV

ACROSS THE BORDER

A LOW, DARK ROOM, so low and dark that the people moving about in it were barely discernible. The roof almost touched their heads, and beneath it both parties were kneaded in an indistinguishable mass—murderers and victims together. In a human rabble near the door Zachary was lying; his eyes were absently fixed on an obviously crazy old Jew who never ceased groaning and speaking to himself. The old man with the long beard reminded Zachary of someone he had seen before, but he could not recollect when or where. . . . The anguish of death was in the room, shrieks of terror, a babel of laughter, lewd screeching, and the stupefying reek of samogon, a home-made spirit, mingled with the smell of stinking sausage. Beside the stove soldiers were crowded round a half-naked farm girl. From his point of vantage Zachary could see a soldier offering her a pair of boots which he had just drawn from the feet of one of the prisoners. Amid the dark rays of death and night that burned in Zachary's head a flicker of living energy made its way into his half-inanimate body, roused by the sight of the girl's rosy flesh. Her naked gleaming back banished all his fear of what was before him, made him forget his concentration on the great moment of death, roused desire in all his limbs and tried to summon him back from the uttermost verge of life on which he was poised.

But he had to go on to the final boundary between life and death. Zachary was surprised to find it all so natural and simple. There was nothing extraordinary about it. He was aware that he was leaning against a wooden wall. He knew that his head was touching a roof of rotten straw that was letting the last rain-drops fall upon his face. He was standing among other human bodies. He was barefoot, but he did not mind that; on the contrary, he liked to feel the damp earth on his naked foot-soles—it was like the touch of a soft, caressing body. Oh, it was good to feel contact with living earth when one was about to die! In front of him, bordered by freshly-turned clay, yawned the cavernous mouths of the graves which he and the others had dug at dawn. He simply did not realize that in a minute or two he would be lying under that wet and slippery mass. He was too preoccupied with the miracle that had just happened—his eyes had failed him! There was no better proof of their failure than the fact that he could see nothing. He could not even distinguish whether it was day or night; he had the feeling that it was day and night together. He could not see five paces ahead of him. The graves, too, had vanished. He had no idea now of what was going on around him. Instead of eyes incredibly fine lenses must have been slipped into his head, for the soldiers with their rifles appeared so remote—far, far away. Many miles away, many days' journey away, for they looked minute as if the enormous distance to which they had receded had reduced them to infinitesimal proportions. Now they were moving even farther away, and yet he could see them quite sharply and distinctly, thanks to the crystal lenses in his eye-sockets. No, they weren't going to shoot just yet, they were quarreling over something. The old peasant woman from the hut in which he and the others had been packed was railing at the soldiers and haggling with them, backed up by the girl with the rosy body peeping through her tattered blouse. They were both shouting. He could hear their voices from a far distance, as if they were speaking through the telephone. Yes, yes—whatever it was that was happening between the two women and the soldiers on the other side of these graves must be miles and miles away! Only a miracle such as one might expect to meet on the borderline between life and death could enable him to perceive it and hear it so clearly. The old woman was offering the soldiers four quarts of her home-made samogon if they would let their prisoners escape across the Polish frontier. The soldiers were arguing that they dared not do it, for it was contrary to "orders," but that if "something else" was thrown in they would take the risk. What the "something else" might be Zachary neither knew nor cared, for he was as good as dead already, and all that he was seeing was merely a delusion of his anguish. The young farm-girl had agreed to spend a whole night with the soldiers if they would let the prisoners go. The soldiers were undecided—something was still lacking, but Zachary did not know what.

Now the old woman was shrieking with rage; she shook her fist at the soldiers, she even threw a stone at them as if they were snarling dogs.

"You call yourselves Christians? Tartars is what you are, gypsies, damned Turks, mad beasts! You fling men's lives away like blackberries! What do you want to take a mortal sin on your souls for? These folks have a God, too, and He'll revenge them! He'll see to it that bullets don't miss you and that wolves will eat your dead bodies! Let the poor devils go, and come inside. I'll stand you four quarts of samogon—that's surely enough for you—and the girl into the bargain! Come and enjoy yourselves instead of brazenly murdering God's creatures."

The soldiers had yielded. The old woman and the girl tore the bonds from the prisoners' hands and the whole rabble poured into the house. It flashed through Zachary's mind: "What a pity, so near ... only one little step and I should have crossed the border. . . ."

In the hovel there was a stink of raw spirits and stale sausage. Once more the girl's rosy body gleamed among the soldiers' top-boots. The sight of their lust was an intoxicating drug that made one forget all else. . . . The crazed Jew babbled unceasingly a verse from the Lamentations:

"Our end is near, our days are fulfilled, for our end is come."

A Jewish woman was struggling with a soldier; her hair was loosened, her breasts bare. The old woman tried to comfort her: "Better than death, anyhow!" The soldier snatched off the woman's skirt and weighed it in his hand: all the others crowded round him and flung themselves on the skirt as if it were a prize. In a twinkling it was rent asunder and gold coins fell scattering on the floor. The Jewish woman went into hysterics. An enormous pock-marked fellow in army trousers with his coat thrown round his shoulders was beginning to get drunk and banged his fist on the table:

"I've been a soldier in three countries and I don't know where I belong! The Ukrainians come and tell me I'm a Ukrainian—the Poles come and say I'm a Pole—the Bolsheviks tell me I must be a Bolshevik! . . . It's a damned, accursed age—the devil's let loose among mankind! Everybody sticks a rifle in your hand and tells you to shoot —and I'm sick of this eternal murdering!"

The peasant woman was going round with an enormous jar of samogon, holding it to each one's mouth in turn. The floor was covered with soldiers and Jews, murderers and victims, amicably huddled in drunken embraces. Fired by the same intoxication they embraced amid all the filth. Beside the stove a babel of voices. Lewd screechings peppered with oaths, drowned in women's shrieks of laughter. Naked female bodies gleamed seductively among the soldiers' booted legs. The crazed Jew in the cap with the torn peak was still babbling portions from the Lamentations. The old woman rounded on the soldiers in a tone of maternal reproach:

"Well, you sons of dogs, isn't it better to do a bit of whoring than to take mortal sin on your souls? Here's samogon for you, and a girl—and yet all you had in your minds was to murder these poor creatures!"

A man in a sheepskin cap which never quitted his head was sitting half-undressed, heated with raw spirit, by the table, patiently unripping all the garments which he was stripping one by one from the prisoners. The others might drink and enjoy their women—he was doing his duty. He slit open all the seams and, holding his knees together, laid out on them all that he found, so that everybody might see he was stealing nothing. Without pausing in his labors he answered the old woman:

"You've had your own way this time—you'd better see that you get them out of the house before the others come along! Turn them out into the forest. . . ."

Then came the maddest night of all, with evil spirits and demons lurking in every corner,—the night in which Zachary smuggled himself across the frontier. Do you know what night is? Night frees us from the close confinement of the ego in which we are condemned to languish all our wretched lives: night lets us stream out into the eternal non-Being from which we come and into which we go. Night is the infinite, bottomless pit into which we fall unceasingly. All life, all form is constantly thrown back into the formless void of chaos from which it emerged, and becomes what it was once—a ray of energy vibrating through the ether. The forms that limit Being by day are dissolved, and the power of night releases life into the greater Being of the illimitable. Men and things become once more what they were in their primal beginnings. A dripping tree takes on man's shape, a man appears as a tree—he is aware of the past from which he is descended. The twin creations of the organic and the inorganic acknowledge their affinity after long division, and return to their sole matrix—the wide-spread night. . . .

Who can define boundaries on such a night, ranging through black and dripping forests? You hear the wailing of invisible beings. Looming shapes bar your way. You come to places where you have walked of old, places that you recognize, for they are carried deep in your unconscious mind. Who are the fellow-humans flitting beside you? Who are you yourself on such a night? . . . But when the cold gray dawn glimmers on the dew-laden grass your ranging spirit returns to its certainties, to its prison and its curse, the ego.

"Are we across the frontier yet?" someone asked.

"Across the frontier? Who can tell what frontiers one crosses in such a night of darkness!"

The spell of silence that all night long had lain heavily on men and things was suddenly broken. As soon as the first pale gleam of dawn came stealing through the forest trees the fugitives felt assured—they had reached certainty. From the vague fluidity of the night they had crystallized again into solid form, into individuals.

The crazed Jew with the torn cap staggered heavily through the deep sand, stooping under the load of the heavy bundle on his back. Dust—or was it something else?—lay so thick on his clothes and on his face that his white beard had grown dark overnight. He was still muttering continuously to himself snatches of verse from the Lamentations, portions of the psalms, texts from other parts of the Bible; it sounded as if he were praying unceasingly.

And strangely enough Zachary was now quite certain that he had met the man before. In the first red rays of the spring sunlight, now glowing through the tall fir-trunks, the man's face was extraordinarily familiar. Yet Zachary could not tell whether it was in the course of his real life that he had met him, or in one of the many, many lives he had recently experienced. . . .

It was not long before they came upon the first Polish frontier guards.

All these things are now fragmentary recollections, vague clouds drifting in the dark, unfathomed depths of Zachary's mind. From time to time they drift a little nearer, floating up like threads of gossamer only to vanish again. . . .

But his arrival in the house of Hurvitz the teacher happened like this:

Instead of Rachel-Leah, a Polish serving-maid was standing by the stove in the kitchen, and she asked Zachary what his business was. Without making any answer he walked into the adjoining room. Everything was exactly as he had left it—the sofa, the chairs, the pictures on the walls, the lamp on the table. And yet it was not the same, something had changed. But Zachary could not make out what it was. He had a feeling that his eyes were out of focus. The walls were shabby, with wallpaper peeling off in patches; it was as if Time had drawn its claws along them. Zachary returned to the kitchen and at that moment heard children's voices coming through the corridor from the school. "So the school's still there," he decided. Hesitatingly, feebly, he opened the door.

And there she stood, exactly as he had so often seen her in his dreams, surrounded by poorly-clad children. She was listening to them and talking to them.

She was the same; it was the same figure, only the dress was not the same, it was not the old black and white check. ("I wish it had been," thought Zachary.) And yet her face was different. At first Zachary could not identify the change, but he suddenly realized what it was—she looked much older; it might have been an elder sister of hers standing there.

"Teacher, there's a man at the door," cried one of the children, pointing to Zachary.

Helene looked round in surprise and suddenly went white. Her mouth opened as if to scream, but she kept control of herself:

"Keep quiet, children, I'll be back in a minute." And she advanced towards Zachary. Without a word she took him by the hand and led him out of the schoolroom.

In the corridor she kissed him and for a moment leaned her head gently on his breast, then quickly pushed him away, smoothed her hair, and smiled through her tears:

"When did you arrive?"

"Early this morning."

Without letting go his hand she led him into the kitchen and shut the door. Then she fell upon his neck and wept for a long time.

"I thought I was never going to see you again," she sobbed, and her tears ran down his neck.

Zachary stood as if turned to stone.

"Where is your mother?" he asked at last.

"Mother's gone. She died during the German occupation."

Zachary gazed into her face. Round her eyes and mouth Rachel-Leah's wrinkles were deeply engraved; her chin and her throat were beginning to lose their tautness. Yet suddenly he saw her spirit, her very self, rising towards him from that aging face, like a boat floating across a still lake. He knew her again. . . .

Not until then did he approach her and touch with his eyes and his mouth the woman who was his. . . .

Hurvitz the teacher came home later. He had changed but little during all these years; he only seemed to have grown taller, for he was thinner than before and quite gray. Zachary's sudden appearance did not seem to surprise him at all, and he welcomed him as if he had only been away for a day. He thrust his bony hand into Zachary's, took off his glasses, inspected him closely with reddened, lashless eyes, and said not a word. Then with youthful elasticity he flung himself down in a chair, crossed one leg over the other, and began with a shake of the head:

"We thought it would all turn out very differently."

"What? The Russian Revolution?" asked Zachary.

"Not only the Russian Revolution—everything!" And, half to himself, he added with a sigh:

"The liberation of Poland—don't you understand?"

"But it's better than before," remarked Zachary.

"Yes, it's better. But I thought it would all be quite different," murmured the teacher, with a deep sigh for the fine dreams that had been so brutally liquidated by reality. Then he turned to Zachary:

"Now tell me—what are you thinking of doing? Your beard has gray hairs in it already."

"I'm going to begin all over again," returned Zachary firmly.

Silently the teacher stretched out his bony hand to him.

As Zachary watched Helene at her daily task the thought flashed through his mind: "While I've been jumping over the tops of houses *she* has been spending herself here day after day, drop by drop. . . ."

THE END